W9-BGU-925

SelectEditions

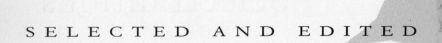

SELECTED AND EDITED

SelectEditions

BY READER'S DIGEST

THE READER'S DIGEST ASSOCIATION, INC.
MONTREAL • PLEASANTVILLE, NEW YORK

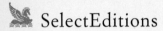 SelectEditions

Vice President, Books & Home Entertainment: Deirdre Gilbert

INTERNATIONAL EDITIONS
Executive Editor: Gary Q. Arpin
Senior Editor: Bonnie Grande

The condensations in this volume have been created by The Reader's Digest Association, Inc., by special arrangement with the publishers, authors, or holders of copyrights.

With the exception of actual personages identified as such, the characters and incidents in the selections in this volume are entirely the products of the authors' imaginations and have no relation to any person or event in real life.

The credits that appear on page 576 are hereby made part of this copyright page.
© 2001 by The Reader's Digest Association, Inc.
Copyright © 2001 by The Reader's Digest Association (Canada) Ltd.

FIRST EDITION

All rights reserved. Unauthorized reproduction, in any manner, is prohibited.
ISBN 0-88850-935-9
Printed in the U.S.A.

Reader's Digest and the Pegasus logo are registered trademarks of
The Reader's Digest Association, Inc.

254-271-0701

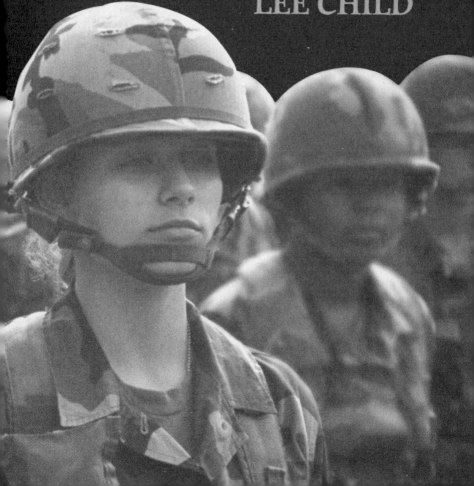

RUNNING
BLIND

LEE CHILD

THEY LOOK LIKE PERFECT CRIMES.

NO EVIDENCE IS EVER LEFT BEHIND:

NO SIGNS OF FORCED ENTRY,

NO WOUNDS ON THE BODIES,

NOT EVEN A HINT OF HOW THE WOMEN DIED.

PERFECT CRIMES?

NO ONE IS PERFECT.

CHAPTER 1

PEOPLE *say that knowledge is power. The more knowledge, the more power. Suppose you knew the winning numbers for the lottery? Not guessed them, not dreamed them, but really knew them. What would you do? You would run to the store. You would mark those numbers on the play card. And you would win.*

Same for the stock market. Suppose you knew what was going to go way up? You're not talking about a hunch or a trend or a tip. You're talking about real, hard knowledge. Suppose you had it? What would you do? You would call your broker. You would buy. Then later you'd sell, and you'd be rich.

Same for killing people.

Suppose you wanted to kill people. You would need to know ahead of time how to do it. Some ways are better than others. Most of them have drawbacks. So you use what knowledge you've got, and you invent a new way. You come up with the perfect method.

You pay a lot of attention to the setup. Preparation is very important. But that stuff is meat and potatoes to you, after all your training. The big problems will come afterward. How do you make sure you get away with it? You use your knowledge. You know what the cops look for, so you do not leave anything for them to find. You go through it all in your head, very precisely and very carefully.

JACK REACHER WAS SITTING alone at a restaurant table in Tribeca, in New York City, gazing at the backs of two guys twenty feet away and wondering if it would be enough just to warn them off or if he would have to go the extra mile and break their arms.

It was a question of dynamics. The dynamics of the city meant that a brand-new Italian place like this was going to stay pretty empty until the food guy from *The New York Times* wrote it up or some celebrity was spotted in there two nights in a row. But neither thing had happened yet, and the place was still uncrowded, which made it the perfect choice for a guy looking to eat dinner near his girlfriend's apartment while she worked late. The dynamics of the city also meant any bright new commercial venture would sooner or later get a visit from guys like the two he was watching, on behalf of somebody wanting a steady three hundred bucks a week in exchange for not sending his boys in to smash it up with baseball bats.

The two guys were standing close to the bar, talking quietly to the owner, a small nervous guy who had backed away until his backside was jammed against the cash drawer. His arms were folded tight across his chest, defensively. Reacher could see his eyes. They showed disbelief and panic.

It was a large high-ceilinged room, easily sixty feet by sixty, which had probably started out as a factory. Now it was the type of Italian restaurant that has three hundred thousand dollars invested up front in bleached avant-garde decor and that gives you seven or eight handmade ravioli parcels on a large plate and calls them a meal. The place was named Mostro's, which as far as he understood Italian translated as Monster's. He wasn't sure what the name referred to. Certainly not the size of the portions. But the quality of the food was good, and the place was attractive. In Reacher's inexpert opinion he was watching the start of a big reputation.

But the big reputation was obviously slow to spread. Tonight there was just one other couple eating, five tables away. The guy was medium-sized, short sandy hair, fair mustache, light brown suit. The woman was thin and dark, in a skirt and a jacket. They were both maybe in their thirties. They weren't talking much.

The two guys at the bar were talking, that was for sure. They were leaning over, talking fast and persuading hard. They were dressed in identical dark wool coats. Reacher could see their faces in the mirrors behind the liquor bottles. Olive skin, dark eyes. Syrian or Lebanese maybe. The guy on the right was making a sweeping gesture with his hand. It was easy to see it represented a bat ploughing through the bottles. The owner was going pale.

The guy on the left tapped his watch and turned to leave. His partner straightened up and followed him. He trailed his hand over the nearest table and knocked a plate to the floor. It shattered on the tiles. The sandy guy and the dark woman looked away. The two guys walked to the door, heads up, confident. Reacher watched them go. Then the owner came out from behind the bar, knelt down, and raked through the fragments of broken plate with his fingertips.

Reacher walked over to him. "You okay?"

The guy shrugged and pushed the shards into a pile.

Reacher squared his napkin on the tile next to him and collected the debris into it. "When are they coming back?" he asked.

"An hour," the guy said.

"How much do they want?"

The guy smiled a bitter smile. "I get a start-up discount," he said. "Two hundred a week, goes to four when the place picks up."

"Who were they?" Reacher asked quietly.

"Not Italians," the guy said. "Just some punks."

"Can I use your phone?"

The guy nodded.

"You know an office-supply store open late?" Reacher asked.

"Broadway, two blocks over," the guy said.

Reacher stood up and slid around behind the bar. He picked up the phone and dialed a number and waited until it was answered a mile away and forty floors up.

"Hello?" she said.

"Hey, Jodie."

"Hey, Reacher, what's new?"

"You going to be finished anytime soon?"

He heard her sigh. "No. This is an all-nighter," she said. "Complex law, and they need an opinion like yesterday. I'm real sorry."

"Don't worry about it," he said. "I've got something to do. Then I guess I'll head back on up to Garrison."

"Okay, take care of yourself," she said. "I love you."

He hung up, came out from behind the bar, and stepped back to his table. He left forty dollars under his espresso saucer, shrugged into his coat, and headed for the door. "Good luck," he called.

The owner nodded vaguely, and the couple at the distant table watched him go. He turned his collar up and stepped out into the dark. He walked east to Broadway and found the office store. He bought a small labeling machine and a tube of superglue. Then he headed north to Jodie's apartment.

His four-wheel drive was parked in the garage under her building. He drove it up the ramp and turned south on Broadway and west back to the restaurant. He slowed on the street and glanced in through the big windows. Every table was empty, and the owner was sitting on a stool behind the bar. Reacher came around the block and parked illegally at the mouth of the alley that led to the kitchen doors. He killed the motor and settled down to wait.

The dynamics of the city. The strong terrorize the weak. They keep at it until they come up against somebody stronger. Somebody like Reacher. He had no real reason to help a guy he hardly knew, but he couldn't just walk away. He never had.

He fumbled the label machine out of his pocket. Scaring the two guys away was only half the job. What mattered was who they thought was doing the scaring. Nobody is afraid of a lone individual, because a lone individual can always be overwhelmed by sheer numbers. What makes a big impression is an organization. He smiled and started to print letters in white on blue plastic ribbons. When he finished, he laid the ribbons on the seat next to him. Then he unscrewed the cap off the tube of superglue and pierced the metal foil with the plastic spike, ready for action. He put the cap back on and dropped the tube and the labels into his pocket. Then he got out of the car and stood in the shadows, waiting.

The dynamics of the city. His mother had been scared of cities. She had told him cities are dangerous places. They're full of scary guys. As a teenager, he became convinced the scary guys were always right behind him. Then he realized, no, I'm the scary guy. It was a revelation. He saw himself reflected in store windows and understood. He had stopped growing at fifteen, when he was already six feet five and two hundred and twenty pounds. A giant. They're scared of me. From that point on he knew that for every city person he needed to be scared of there were nine hundred and ninety-nine others a lot more scared of him. He used the knowledge like a tactic, and the confidence it put in his walk redoubled the effect he had on people. The dynamics of the city.

The two guys came back right on time in a black Mercedes sedan. It parked a block away, and they stepped out of the car with their long coats flowing, opened the rear doors, and pulled baseball bats off the seat. They slipped the bats under their coats, slammed the doors, and strode confidently along the sidewalk.

Reacher stepped out of the shadows. "In the alley, guys," he said.

Up close they were young, some way short of thirty. Wide necks, silk ties, suits that didn't come out of a catalogue. The men were gripping the bats with their left hands through their pocket linings.

"Who the hell are you?" the right-hand guy said.

Reacher glanced at him. The first guy to speak is the dominant half of any partnership, the one you put down first. Reacher stepped to his left and turned a fraction, blocking the sidewalk, channeling them toward the alley. "Business manager," he said. "You want to get paid, I'm the guy who can do it for you."

The guy paused. "Okay, but screw the alley. We'll do it inside."

Reacher shook his head. "Not logical, my friend. We're paying you to stay out of the restaurant starting from now, right?"

They looked at him and looked at each other and stepped into the alley. They were happy enough. Big confident guys, bats under their coats, two against one. Reacher stepped back like he wanted them to precede him. Like a courtesy. They shuffled forward.

He hit the right-hand guy on the side of the head with his elbow.

The guy went down like a trapdoor had opened up under his feet.

The second guy got the bat clear of his coat and swung it ready, but he swung it way too far back and way too low.

Reacher caught the bat in both hands, jacked the handle up, and hurled the guy off-balance. Kicked out at his ankles, tore the bat free, and jabbed him with it. The guy went down on his knees and butted his head into the wall. Reacher kicked him over onto his back, squatted down, and jammed the bat across his throat. He used his left hand to go into each pocket in turn. He came out with an automatic handgun, a thick wallet, and a mobile phone.

"Who are you from?" Reacher asked.

"Mr. Petrosian," the guy gasped.

The name meant nothing to Reacher, but he smiled incredulously. "Petrosian? You have got to be kidding."

He put a lot of sneer in his voice, like out of all the whole spectrum of worrisome rivals his bosses could possibly think of, Petrosian was so far down the list he was just about totally invisible.

"We've got a message for Petrosian," Reacher said softly.

"What's the message?"

Reacher smiled again. "You are," he said. "Now lie real still."

He went into his pocket for the labels and the glue. Then he eased glue onto one of the labels and pressed it onto the guy's forehead. The label read MOSTRO'S HAS GOT PROTECTION ALREADY.

"Lie still," he said again.

He took the bat and turned the other guy faceup. Used plenty of glue and smoothed the other label into place on his brow. This one read DON'T START A TURF WAR WITH US. He checked the pockets and came out with an automatic handgun, a wallet, and a cell phone, plus a key for the Benz. He emptied the tube of glue into the first guy's palms and crushed them together. Chemical handcuffs. He hauled him upright, then tossed the car key to the second guy.

"I guess you're the designated driver," he said. "Now go give our regards to Mr. Petrosian. Beat it." They staggered out of the alley.

The handguns were Beretta 9-mm M-9s, military issue. Reacher had carried an identical gun for thirteen years. The serial numbers on both guns had been filed off. Reacher stripped them in the dark and pitched the barrels, slides, and bullets into the Dumpster outside the kitchen doors. He scooped a handful of grit into the firing mechanisms and worked the triggers in and out until the grit jammed them. He pitched them into the Dumpster. Then he smashed the phones with the bat and left the pieces where they lay.

The wallets held cards and licenses and cash. Maybe three hundred bucks in total. He rolled the cash into his pocket and kicked the wallets away into a corner. Then he straightened and walked back into the deserted restaurant. The owner was behind the bar, lost in thought. He looked up as Reacher peeled a ten from the stolen wad and dropped it on the bar.

"For the broken plate," he said. "They had a change of heart."

Reacher turned and walked back out. Across the street he saw the couple from the restaurant standing on the opposite sidewalk, watching him. He climbed into his four-wheel drive and pulled out into the traffic. A block away he used the mirror and saw the dark woman stepping out to the curb, watching him go.

GARRISON is on the east bank of the Hudson River, about fifty-eight miles north of Tribeca. Late on a fall evening, traffic is not a problem. With empty parkways, average speed can be as high as you dare to make it. But Reacher was anxious to stay out of trouble. So he drove slow enough not to be noticed.

One hour and seventeen minutes later Reacher turned into his driveway, and the headlight beams swung toward the garage door and washed over two cars waiting nose out in front of it. He jammed to a stop, and their lights came on and blinded him just as his mirror filled with bright light from behind. He ducked away from the glare and saw people running at him with guns.

A figure stepped close to his car. A hand came up and rapped on the glass next to his head. It was a woman's hand. A flashlight beam turned on it and showed it was cupping a bright gold badge in the shape of a shield with an eagle perched on the top. Reacher stared at it. It said FEDERAL BUREAU OF INVESTIGATION. The woman pressed the shield against the window and shouted, "Turn off the engine and place both hands on the wheel."

He did so. The door opened, and the light clicked on and spilled out over the dark woman from the restaurant. The sandy guy with the fair mustache was at her shoulder. She had the FBI badge in one hand and a gun in the other. The gun was pointed at his head.

"Out of the vehicle," she said. "Nice and slow."

She stepped back, the gun tracking his head. He swung his legs out of the footwell and slid his feet to the ground.

"Turn around," she said. "Place your hands on the vehicle."

He did as he was told. He felt hands on every inch of his body. They took his wallet and the stolen cash from his pants pocket. Somebody leaned into the car and took his keys from the ignition.

"Now walk to the car," the woman called.

She pointed to one of the sedans near the garage. He walked toward it. A guy in a dark blue bulletproof vest opened the rear door and stepped back. As Reacher folded himself inside, the opposite door opened up and the woman slid in alongside him, the gun, a SIG Sauer, still pointing at his head. The front door opened, and the sandy guy knelt in on the seat and stretched back for the woman's briefcase, which was upright on the rear seat. The guy flipped the case open and pulled out a sheaf of papers.

"Search warrant," the woman said to him. "For your house."

The sandy guy ducked back out and slammed the door. Reacher heard footsteps growing fainter through the fog.

"You're not asking what this is about," the woman said.

It's not about what happened an hour and seventeen minutes ago, he said to himself. No way was this all organized in an hour and seventeen minutes. He kept quiet and absolutely still. He was worried about the whiteness in the woman's knuckle where it wrapped around the SIG Sauer's trigger. Accidents can happen.

The woman shrugged at him. Have it your own way, she was saying. Her face settled into a frown. Not a pretty face, but interesting. Some character there. She was about thirty-five, and there were lines in her skin. Her hair was jet-black but thin. He could see her white scalp. It gave her a sickly look. But her eyes were bright. She glanced through the car window into the darkness, out to where her men were searching his house. She smiled. Her front teeth were crossed. The right one was canted sideways, and it overlaid the left one by a fraction. An interesting mouth. It made her face distinctive. She was slim under her bulky coat and wore a black skirt and jacket and cream blouse loose over her small breasts. The skirt was short, and her legs were thin and hard under black nylon.

"Would you stop doing that, please?" she said.

"Doing what?" Reacher asked.

"Looking at my legs."

He switched his gaze up to her face. "Somebody points a gun at me, I'm entitled to check them out head to toe, wouldn't you say?"

The gun moved. "I don't like the way you're looking at me."

He stared at her. "What way am I looking at you?" he asked.

"Like you're making advances," she said. "You're disgusting."

He stared at her thin hair, her frown, her crooked tooth.

"You think I'm making advances to you?"

"Aren't you? Wouldn't you like to?"

He shook his head.

AFTER twenty minutes the sandy guy with the mustache came back to the car and slid into the front passenger seat. The driver's door opened, and a second man got in. He fired up the motor, and in hostile silence they headed back to Manhattan.

They parked underground someplace south of midtown and forced him out of the car into a brightly lit garage. The woman pointed toward a black elevator door located in a distant corner. There were two more guys waiting there, like they were hosts. Reacher suddenly understood that the woman and the sandy guy were not New York agents. They were from somewhere else.

They put Reacher in the center of the elevator car and crowded in around him. One of the local boys touched a button, the door rolled shut, and the elevator traveled upward. It stopped hard with twenty-one showing on the floor indicator. The door thumped back, and the local boys led the way out into a blank gray corridor.

The guy who had driven the sedan down from Garrison paused in front of the third door and opened it up. Reacher was maneuvered into a bare space, maybe twelve by sixteen, concrete floor, cinder-block walls, all covered in thick gray paint like the side of a battleship. There was a single plastic garden chair in the corner.

"Sit down," the woman said.

Reacher walked to the corner opposite the chair and sat on the floor. Everybody backed out into the corridor and closed the door on him. There was no sound of a lock turning, but there didn't need to be, because there was no handle on the inside.

He sat like that for an hour. Then the door opened and a gray-haired guy with thick spectacles stepped into the room. Two junior agents took up station behind him.

"Time to talk," the guy said.

Reacher jacked himself upright and stepped away from his corner. "I want to make a call," he said.

The guy shook his head. "Calling comes later," he said. "Talking first, okay?"

Reacher shrugged. The problem with getting your rights abused was that somebody had to witness it for it to mean anything. And the two young agents were seeing nothing.

Reacher was ushered out into the gray corridor and into a big knot of people. The woman was there, and the sandy guy with the mustache, and there was an older guy with a big red face puffy with blood pressure, and a younger guy with a lean face, in shirtsleeves. They were all pumped up with excitement. There were two clear teams, and there was tension between them. The woman stuck close to his left shoulder, and the sandy guy and the blood-pressure guy stuck close to her. That was one team. At his right shoulder was the guy with the lean face. He was the second team, alone and outnumbered and unhappy about it.

They walked down a narrow gray corridor and into a gray room with a long, shiny mahogany table filling most of the floor space. On one side, backs to the door, were seven plastic chairs. A single identical chair was placed in the exact center of the opposite side.

Reacher paused in the doorway. Not too difficult to work out which chair was his. He sat down on it.

The two junior agents took up position against the walls at opposite ends of the table. Their jackets were open, and their shoulder holsters were visible. Opposite Reacher, the gray-haired guy took the center chair. Next to him on his right-hand side was the guy with the blood pressure, next to him was the woman, and next to her was the sandy guy. The guy with the lean face and the shirtsleeves was alone in the middle chair of the left-hand three.

The gray-haired guy leaned forward, claiming authority. "We've been squabbling over you," he said.

"Am I in custody?" Reacher asked.

"No, not yet."

"So I'm free to go?"

The guy looked over the top of his spectacles. "We'd rather you stayed here so we can keep this whole thing civilized for a spell."

"So make it civilized," Reacher said. "Let's have some introductions. That's what civilized people do, right? They introduce themselves. I'm Jack Reacher. Who the hell are you?"

The guy nodded. "I'm Alan Deerfield," he said. "Assistant director, FBI. I run the New York field office."

"Special Agent Tony Poulton," the sandy guy said.

"Special Agent Julia Lamarr," the woman said.

"Agent in Charge Nelson Blake," the guy with the blood pressure said. "The three of us are from Quantico. I run the Serial Crimes Unit, and Special Agents Lamarr and Poulton work for me."

"Agent in Charge James Cozo," the guy in the shirtsleeves said. "Organized crime, here in New York City, working on the protection rackets."

Reacher nodded. "Okay," he said. "Pleased to meet you all. But you can't talk to me until you read me my rights. Whereupon you can't talk to me anyway, because my lawyer could take some time to get here, and even then she won't let me talk to you."

"Your lawyer is Jodie Jacob, right?" Deerfield asked. "Your girlfriend. She's at Spencer Gutman. Big reputation as an associate. They're talking about a partnership for her. But Spencer Gutman is a financial firm. Not much expertise in the field of criminal law. You sure you want her for your attorney? Situation like this?"

"What situation am I in?"

"Reacher, I already wasted an hour stopping these guys fighting over you. So now you owe me. Answer their questions, and I'll tell you when and if you need a damn lawyer."

"What are the questions about?"

Deerfield smiled. "Stuff we need to know, is what. To find out if we're interested in you."

"Okay," Reacher said. "What are the questions?"

Lamarr leaned forward. "You knew Amy Callan pretty well, didn't you?" she asked.

Reacher stared at her. Then a woman called Amy Callan came back at him from the past and slowed him just enough to allow a contented smile to settle on Lamarr's bony face.

"You didn't like her much, did you?" she said.

There was silence. It built around him.

"Okay, my turn," Cozo said. "Who are you working for?"

Reacher looked at Cozo. "I'm not working for anybody."

" 'Don't start a turf war with us,' " Cozo quoted. "Us is a plural word. More than one person. Who is us, Reacher?"

"There is no us."

"Bull, Reacher. Who sent you to that restaurant?"

Reacher said nothing.

"What about Caroline Cooke?" Lamarr said. "You knew her, too, but you didn't like her either, did you?"

"Give us the whole story, Reacher," Blake said.

Reacher looked at him. "What story?"

"Who sent you to the restaurant?" Cozo asked again.

Reacher turned to him. "Nobody sent me anywhere."

Cozo shook his head. "Bull, Reacher. You live in a half-million-dollar house on the river in Garrison, and as far as the IRS knows, you haven't earned a cent in nearly three years. And when somebody wanted Petrosian's best boys in the hospital, they sent you to do it. I want to know who the hell it is."

"I'm not working for anybody," Reacher said again.

"You're a loner, right?" Blake asked.

Reacher nodded. "I guess."

"I thought so. When did you come out of the army?"

Reacher shrugged. "About three years ago."

"Military policeman, right?"

"Right. I was a major."

"So why did you muster out?"

"That's my business. You wouldn't understand."

"So, three years. What have you been doing?"

"Nothing much. Having fun, I guess."

"Working?"

"Not often."

"Doing what for money?"

"Savings."

"They ran out three months ago. We checked. So now you're living off Ms. Jacob, right? How do you feel about that?"

Reacher glanced at the wedding band on Blake's fat finger. "No worse than your wife does living off you, I expect," he said.

Blake grunted. "So you came out of the army, and since then you've been mostly on your own."

"Mostly."

"Bull. He's working for somebody," Cozo said.

"The man says he's a loner, damn it," Blake snarled.

Deerfield fixed Reacher with a quiet gaze. "Tell me about Amy Callan and Caroline Cooke," he said.

"What's to tell? Callan was small and dark; Cooke was tall and blond; Callan was a sergeant; Cooke was a lieutenant. Callan was a clerk in Ordnance at Fort Withe, near Chicago; Cooke was in War Plans at NATO HQ in Belgium."

"Did you have sex with either of them?" Lamarr asked.

Reacher turned to stare at her. "What kind of a question is that?"

"A straightforward one."

"Well, no, I didn't."

"They were both pretty, right?"

Reacher nodded. "Prettier than you, that's for damn sure."

Lamarr looked away.

"Did they know each other?" Blake asked.

"I doubt it. There's a million people in the army, and they were serving four thousand miles apart at different times."

"Do you approve of women in the military?" Deerfield asked.

Reacher's eyes moved across to him. "What?"

"Do you approve of women in the military? Do you think they make good fighters?"

Reacher shrugged. "Women can do it the same as anybody else. You ever been to Israel? Women fight in the front line there."

"How did you meet Amy Callan?" Deerfield asked.

"She came to me with a problem she was having in her unit."

"What problem?"

"Sexual harassment."

"And what did you do?"

"I arrested the officer she was accusing."

"And what did you do then?"

"Nothing. It was in the hands of the prosecutor. The officer won the case. Amy Callan left the service."

"But the officer's career was ruined anyway."

Reacher nodded. "Yes, it was."

"How did you feel about that?"

Reacher shrugged. "Confused, I guess. My opinion was he was guilty, so I guess I was happy he was gone. But it shouldn't work that way, ideally. A not-guilty verdict shouldn't ruin a career."

"So you felt sorry for him?"

"No. I felt sorry for Callan. But the whole thing was a mess. Two careers were ruined, where only one should have been."

"What about Caroline Cooke?"

"Cooke was different. It was overseas. She was having sex with some colonel. Had been for a year. It looked consensual to me. She only called it harassment when she didn't get promoted."

"So you did nothing?"

"No. I arrested the colonel, because by then there were rules. Sex between people of different rank was effectively outlawed."

"And?"

"And he was dishonorably discharged and his wife dumped him and he killed himself. And Cooke quit anyway."

"And what happened to you?"

"I transferred out of NATO HQ. I was a good investigator. I was wasted in Belgium. Nothing much happens in Belgium."

"You see much sexual harassment after that?"

"Sure. It became a very big thing."

"Lots of good men getting their careers ruined?" Lamarr asked.

Reacher turned to face her. "Some. It became a witch-hunt. Most of the cases were genuine, in my opinion, but some innocent people were caught up in it. The rules had suddenly changed."

"Did you see Callan and Cooke after you had handed their cases over to the prosecutor?" Blake asked.

"Once or twice, I guess, in passing."

"Did they trust you?"

Reacher shrugged. "I guess so. It was my job to make them trust me. I had to get all kinds of intimate details from them."

"You had to do that kind of thing with many women?"

"There were hundreds of cases. I handled a couple dozen."

"Would those women remember you as a nice guy?"

Reacher nodded. "It's a hell of an ordeal, so the investigator has to build up a bond. He has to be a friend and a supporter."

Blake nodded, and the three agents from Quantico sat back as if to say, Okay, we're interested. Cozo stared at Deerfield in alarm. Deerfield leaned forward, staring through his glasses at Reacher.

"Exactly what happened at the restaurant?" he asked.

"Nothing happened," Reacher said.

Deerfield shook his head. "You were under surveillance. My people have been following you for a week. Special Agents Poulton and Lamarr joined them tonight. They saw the whole thing."

"You've been following me for a week? Why?"

"We'll get to that later."

Lamarr reached down to her briefcase. She pulled out a file, opened it, and took out a sheaf of papers covered in dense type. She smiled icily at Reacher and slid the sheets across the table to him.

They were a list of everything he had done in the previous week. Reacher glanced at Lamarr's smiling face.

"Well, FBI tails are pretty good," he said. "I never noticed."

"So what happened in the restaurant?" Deerfield asked again.

"I committed a small crime to stop a bigger one happening."

"You were acting alone?" Cozo asked.

Reacher nodded. "Yes, I was."

"So what was 'Don't start a turf war with us' all about?"

"I wanted Petrosian to take it seriously, whoever he is. Like he was dealing with another organization."

Deerfield leaned over the table and retrieved Lamarr's surveillance log. He riffled through it. "This shows no contact with anybody except Ms. Jodie Jacob, and she's not running protection rackets." He looked up at Reacher. "Phone log is clear. You spoke to nobody except Ms. Jacob. No contact with gangsters." He turned to Cozo. "You comfortable with that?"

Cozo shrugged. "I'll have to be, I guess."

"A concerned citizen, right, Reacher?" Deerfield said. "You saw an injustice, you wanted to set it straight."

Reacher nodded.

"So why did you steal their money?"

"Spoils of battle, I guess. Like a trophy."

"You wouldn't mug an old lady, but it was okay to take money off a couple of hard men."

"I guess."

"Know anything about criminal profiling?" Deerfield asked.

Reacher paused. "Only what I read in the newspaper."

"It's a science," Blake explained. "Special Agent Lamarr here is our leading exponent. Special Agent Poulton is her assistant."

"We look at crime scenes," Lamarr said. "We look at the underlying psychological indicators, and we work out the type of personality that could have committed the crime."

"What crimes?" Reacher asked. "What scenes?"

"Callan and Cooke," Blake said. "Homicide victims."

Reacher stared at him.

"Callan was first," Blake said. "Very distinctive MO, but one homicide is just one homicide, right? Then Cooke was hit. With the exact same MO. That made it a serial situation."

"We looked for a link," Poulton said. "Between the victims. Army harassment complainants who subsequently quit."

"Extreme organization at the crime scene," Lamarr said. "Indicative of military precision. A bizarre, coded MO. No clues of any kind left behind. The perpetrator was clearly familiar with investigative procedures. Possibly an investigator himself."

"No forced entry at either abode," Poulton said. "The killer was admitted to the house in both cases by the victim."

"So the killer was somebody they both knew," Blake said.

"Somebody they trusted," Poulton said. "A friendly visitor."

"We explored the psychology of the crime," Lamarr said. "We looked for an army guy with a score to settle. Maybe somebody outraged by the idea of pesky women ruining good soldiers' careers and then quitting anyway."

"Somebody with a clear sense of right and wrong," Poulton added. "Somebody confident enough in his own code to set these injustices right by his own hand. Somebody happy to act without the proper authorities getting in the way, you know?"

"Somebody they knew," Blake went on, "well enough to let right in the house, no questions asked, like an old friend or something."

"They never knew each other," Lamarr said. "They had very few mutual acquaintances. Very few. But you were one of them."

"Profiling," Blake said, "is an exact science. It's good enough evidence to get an arrest warrant in most states of the Union."

"It never fails," Lamarr said with a satisfied smile.

"So?" Reacher said.

"So somebody killed two women," Deerfield said. He nodded to his right, toward Blake, Lamarr, and Poulton. "And these agents think it was somebody exactly like you. Maybe it was you."

"Why a guy like me?" Reacher asked. "That's just a guess. That's what this profiling crap comes down to. You've no evidence."

"The guy didn't leave any behind," Lamarr said. "The perpetrator was a smart guy, a loner, a brutal vigilante. That narrowed it down from millions to thousands, maybe all the way down to you."

"Me?" Reacher said to her. "You're crazy."

Deerfield shrugged. "Well, if you didn't do it, the Bureau's experts think it was somebody exactly like you."

"Dates," Reacher said. "Give me dates, and places."

"Callan was seven weeks ago," Blake said. "Cooke was four."

Reacher scanned back in time. Four weeks was the start of fall, seven took him into late summer. Late summer he had been battling three months of unchecked growth in the yard in Garrison. He had gone days at a time without seeing Jodie. She had been tied up in the city with legal cases.

The start of fall he'd transferred his energies to doing things inside the house. But he'd done them alone. Jodie had stayed in the city, working her way up the greasy pole. There were random nights together, but no trips, no ticket stubs, no hotel registers. No alibis.

"I want my lawyer now," he said.

THE two sentries took him back to the small room. His status had changed. This time they stayed inside with him, one standing on each side of the closed door. Reacher sat on the plastic chair and ignored them. He waited almost two hours.

Then suddenly the door opened and the sentries stepped out and Jodie walked in. She was wearing a peach dress with a wool coat over it, a couple of shades darker. She was a blaze of color against the gray walls. Her hair was still lightened from the summer sun, her eyes were bright blue, and her skin was the color of honey. Every time he saw her, she looked more beautiful.

"Hey, Reacher," she said. She bent down and kissed him.

He could see worry in her face. "You talk to them?" he asked.

"I'm not the right person to deal with this," she said. "Financial law, yes, but criminal law, I've got no idea."

He stood up and stretched wearily. "There's nothing to deal with," he said. "I didn't kill any women."

"I know that. And they know that, or they'd have taken you straight down to Quantico. This must be about the other thing. They saw you do that. You put two guys in the hospital."

"It's not about that. They reacted too fast. This was set up before I even did the other thing. And they don't care about the other thing. I'm not working the rackets. That's all Cozo's interested in—organized crime."

She nodded. "Cozo's happy. He's got two punks off the street, no cost to himself. But it's turned into a catch-22, don't you see that? To convince Cozo, you had to make yourself out as a vigilante loner, and the more you made yourself out as a vigilante loner, the more you fitted this profile from Quantico."

"The profile is bull."

"They don't think so. You're in big trouble, Reacher. Whatever else, they saw you beat on those guys. I'm not the right person for this," she said again. "I don't do criminal law."

"I don't need any lawyer," he said.

"Yes, Reacher, you need a lawyer. This is for real." She stepped into his arms, stretched up, and kissed him, hard. "I love you, Reacher, I really do. But you need a better lawyer."

There was a long silence.

"They gave me a copy of the surveillance report," she said.

He nodded. "I thought they would."

"Why?"

"Because it eliminates me from the investigation. Because this is not about two women, it's about three. Whoever's killing these women is working to a timetable. He's on a three-week cycle—seven weeks ago, four weeks ago. The next one's probably already happened this past week while they've had me under surveillance."

"So why did they haul you in if you're eliminated?"

"I don't know," he said.

The door opened, and Deerfield stepped into the room. "Your client conference is over, Ms. Jacob," he said.

Deerfield led them back to the room with the long table. The two local agents followed him. A second chair had been placed on the far side. Jodie moved around the end of the table and sat down with Reacher. He squeezed her hand under the shiny mahogany.

The same lineup was ranged against Reacher: Poulton, Lamarr, Blake, Deerfield, and then Cozo. Now there was a squat black audio recorder on the table. Deerfield pressed a red button. He announced the date and identified the nine occupants of the room.

"This is Alan Deerfield speaking to the suspect Jack Reacher," he said. "You are now under arrest on the following two counts. One, for aggravated assault and robbery against two persons yet to be identified."

Cozo leaned forward. "Two, for aiding and abetting a criminal organization engaged in the practice of extortion."

Deerfield smiled. "You are not obliged to say anything. If you do say anything, it will be recorded and may be used as evidence against you in a court of law. You are entitled to be represented by an attorney. If you cannot afford an attorney, one will be provided for you by the state of New York. Do you understand your rights?"

"Yes," Reacher said.

"Do you have anything to say at this point?"

"No."

Deerfield reached forward and clicked the machine to OFF.

"I want a bail hearing," Jodie said.

Deerfield shook his head. "No need," he said. "We'll release him on his own recognizance. Your client is free to go."

REACHER was out of there at just after three in the morning. Jodie had to get back to the office to finish her all-nighter, so one of the local guys drove her down to Wall Street. The other drove Reacher back to Garrison and took off again as soon as the passenger door slammed shut. Reacher watched the car disappear into the mist and walked down to his house.

He had inherited the house from Leon Garber, Jodie's father and his old commanding officer, back at the start of the summer. It had been a week of big surprises, both good and bad. Running into Jodie again, finding out she'd been married and divorced, finding out old Leon was dead, finding out the house was his. He had been in love with Jodie for fifteen years, since he first met her on a base in the Philippines. She had been fifteen herself then, right on the cusp of womanhood, and she was his CO's daughter. He had crushed his feelings. He felt they would have been a betrayal of her and of Leon, and betraying Leon was the last thing he would have ever done, because he loved him like a father.

After Leon's funeral he and Jodie had sparred uneasily for a couple of days before she admitted she felt the exact same things.

So meeting Jodie again was the good surprise and Leon dying was the bad one, but inheriting the house was both good and bad. It was a half-million-dollar slice of prime real estate standing on the Hudson opposite West Point, but it represented a big problem. It anchored him in a way that made him profoundly uncomfortable. He had moved around so often it confused him to spend time in any one place. And the idea of property worried him. His whole life he had never owned more than would fit into his pockets. After mustering out, he added a few clothes, a wristwatch, a toothbrush that folded in half and clipped into his pocket like a pen. And that was it. Now he had a house. And a house is a complicated thing. There was insurance to consider. Taxes.

The only thing he had bought for the house was a gold-colored filter cone for Leon's old coffee machine. He figured it was easier than always running to the store to buy the paper kind. At ten past four that morning he filled it with coffee, added water, and set the machine going. Before it had finished, he heard the crunch of tires on his asphalt drive. Then a flashing red beam swept over his kitchen window. Doors opened, and feet touched the ground. Two people. Doors slammed shut. The doorbell rang.

There were two light switches in the hallway. He pressed the one that operated the porch light and opened the door. Nelson Blake and Julia Lamarr were caught in the yellow spotlight. Blake's face was showing nothing except strain. Lamarr's was full of hostility.

"Come on in," Reacher said. "I just made coffee."

He walked back to the kitchen. "Black is all I got," he called.

"Black is fine," Blake said. He was standing in the kitchen doorway, staying close to the hallway, unwilling to trespass.

Lamarr was alongside him. "Nothing for me," she said.

"Drink some coffee, Julia. It's been a long night." The way Blake said it was halfway between an order and paternalistic concern.

Reacher glanced at him and filled three mugs. "Who was the third woman?" he asked.

"Lorraine Stanley. A quartermaster sergeant, serving in Utah someplace. They found her dead in California this morning."

"Same MO?"

"Identical in every respect."

"Same history?"

Blake nodded. "Harassment complainant, won her case but quit anyway, a year ago. So that's three out of three. So the army thing is not a coincidence, believe me."

Reacher sipped his coffee. "I never heard of her," he said. "I never served in Utah."

Blake nodded. "Somewhere we can talk?"

Reacher led the way into the living room. There were three sofas in a rectangle around a cold fireplace. Blake sat facing the window. Reacher sat opposite, and Lamarr sat down facing the hearth.

"We stand by our profile," she said.

"Well, good for you."

"You were a plausible suspect," Blake said. "As far as the first two went. Hence the surveillance."

"Is that an apology?" Reacher asked.

"I guess so."

"You got anybody who knew all three?" Reacher asked.

"Not yet," Lamarr said.

"We're thinking maybe previous personal contact isn't too significant," Blake said.

"You thought it was, couple of hours ago. You were telling me how I was this friend of theirs, I knock on the door, they let me in."

"Not you," Blake said. "Somebody like you. This guy is killing by category, right? Female harassment complainants who quit afterward? So maybe he's not personally known to them. Maybe he's just in a category known to them. Like the military police."

Reacher smiled. "So now you think it was me again?"

Blake shook his head. "No. You weren't in California."

"Wrong answer, Blake. It wasn't me, because I'm not a killer."

"You never killed anybody?" Lamarr said.

"Only those who needed it."

She smiled in turn. "Like I said, we stand by our profile. Some self-righteous son of a bitch just like you."

Reacher saw Blake glance at her half disapprovingly. Blake sat forward, forcing Reacher's attention his way. "What we're saying is, it's possible this guy is or was a military policeman."

"Anything's possible," Reacher said.

"There's an agenda here," Blake went on. "And the way we read it, there's army involvement. The victim category is way too narrow for this to be random."

"So?"

"As a rule, the Bureau and the military don't get along too well."

"Big surprise. Who the hell do you guys get along with?"

Blake looked uncomfortable. "Nobody gets on with anybody," he said. "Military hates the Bureau, the Bureau hates CIA. Everybody hates everybody else. So we need a go-between."

"Me?"

"Yes, you. You were a hell of an investigator in the service."

"That's history."

"Maybe you still got friends there, people who remember you. Maybe people who still owe you favors."

"Maybe, maybe not." He leaned back into the sofa.

"Don't you feel anything?" Blake asked. "For these women getting killed? You knew Callan and Cooke. You liked them."

"I liked Callan."

"So help us catch her killer. Without somebody like you we're just running blind."

"No."

"You son of a bitch," Lamarr said.

Reacher looked at Blake. "You seriously think I would want to work with her? Can't she think of anything else to call me except son of a bitch?"

"What about an advisory role?" Blake asked. "Consultative?"

Reacher shook his head again. "No, not interested."

"Would you agree to be hypnotized?" Blake asked.

"Hypnotized? Why?"

"Maybe you could recall something buried. You know, some guy making threats, adverse comments. Something you didn't pay too much attention to at the time. Might come back to you."

"You still do hypnotism?"

"Sometimes," Blake said. "Julia's an expert. She'd do it."

"No thanks. She might make me walk down Fifth Avenue naked."

Blake looked away; then he turned back. "Last time, Reacher," he said. "The Bureau is asking for your help as an adviser. You'd get paid and everything. Yes or no?"

"This is what hauling me in was all about, right?"

Blake nodded. "Sometimes it works. You know, make them feel they're the prime suspect, then tell them they're not. Make them feel gratitude toward us. Makes them want to help us."

"Kind of cruel, don't you think?"

"The Bureau does what it has to do. So, yes or no?"

"Take Ms. Lamarr off the case and I might consider it."

Lamarr glowered, and Blake said, "I won't do that."

"Then my answer is no."

Blake turned the corners of his mouth down. "We talked with Deerfield before we came up here," he said. "You can understand we'd do that, right? As a courtesy? He authorized us to tell you Cozo will drop the racketeering charge if you play ball."

"I'm not worried about the racketeering charge. I'll beat it. I'll look like Robin Hood to a jury of Tribeca merchants."

Blake wiped his lips with his fingers. "Problem is, it could be more than a racketeering charge. One of those guys is critical. Broken skull. If he dies, it's a homicide charge."

Reacher laughed. "Good try, Blake. But nobody got a broken skull tonight. Believe me, I want to break somebody's skull, I know how to do it. So let's hear the rest of the big threats."

Blake looked at the floor. "Cozo's got guys on the street, undercover. Petrosian's going to be asking who did his boys last night. Cozo's guys could let your name slip. Petrosian's a hard guy."

"I'll take my chances."

Blake nodded. "We thought you'd say that. We're good judges of character. So we asked ourselves how you'd react to something else. Suppose it's not your name and address Cozo leaks to Petrosian? What if it's your girlfriend's name and address?"

"I CAN'T believe they're acting like this," Jodie said.

They were in her kitchen, four floors above lower Broadway. Blake and Lamarr had left Reacher in Garrison, and twenty minutes later he had driven to Manhattan. Jodie came home at six in the morning and found him waiting in her living room.

"They're desperate," he said. "And they're arrogant. And they like to win. They'll do what it takes. I have to call them by eight."

She was pacing nervously back and forth. She had been awake and alert for twenty-three straight hours, but there was nothing to prove it except a faint blue tinge at the inside corners of her eyes.

"Maybe they're not serious," she said.

"Safest strategy is assume they might be."

"Why are they so desperate? Why the threats? And why you?"

"Lots of reasons. I was involved with a couple of the cases; they could find me; I was senior enough that the current generation probably still owes me a few favors."

She nodded. "So what are we going to do?"

"I could go take Petrosian out."

She stared at him, shook her head, then said, "We have a thing at the firm. We call it the so-what-else rule. Suppose we've got some bankrupt guy we're looking after. Sometimes we dig around and find he's got some funds stashed away that he's not telling us about. He's cheating. First thing we do, we say, 'So what else?' What else is he doing? What else has he got?"

"So?"

"So what are they really doing here? Maybe this is not about the women at all. Maybe this is about Petrosian. He's presumably a smart, slippery guy. Maybe there's nothing to pin on him. So maybe Cozo is using Blake and Lamarr to get you to get Petrosian. They know if they use Petrosian to threaten me, your very first thought will be to go get Petrosian. Then he's off the street without a trial, which they probably couldn't win anyway. And nothing is traceable back to the Bureau. Maybe they're using you as an assassin. They wind you up, and off you go."

"Then why didn't they just ask me straight?"

"They can't just ask you. It would be a hundred percent illegal. And you mustn't do it anyway, Reacher. A vigilante homicide, with their knowledge? Right under their noses? The Bureau would own you the whole rest of your life."

He leaned on the window frame and stared at the street below.

"You're in a hell of a spot," she said. "We both are. So what are you going to do?"

"I'm going to think," he said. "I've got until eight o'clock. All I know is I can't go base myself at Quantico, Virginia, and leave you here alone in the same city as Petrosian. I just can't do that."

JODIE went back to work. Before she left the apartment, they kissed, long and hard, like the feeling was going to have to last them long into the foreseeable future. Reacher sat and thought for thirty minutes. Then he was on the phone for twenty. At five minutes to eight he called Lamarr's number. She answered first ring.

"I'm in," he said. "I'm not happy about it, but I'll do it."

There was a brief pause. "Go home and pack a bag," she said. "We're going to Virginia. I'll pick you up in two hours exactly."

"No need. I'll meet you at the airport."

"We're not going by plane."

"We're not?"

"No. I never fly. We're driving."

LAMARR arrived exactly on time in a shiny new Buick.

"Where's your bag?" she asked as Reacher opened the passenger door and slid in beside her.

"I don't have a bag," he said. His folding toothbrush was clipped into his inside pocket.

She looked away from him like she was dealing with a social difficulty and eased out into the traffic. She drove in silence. I-84 took them across the Hudson River and through Newburgh. Then she turned south on the Thruway.

"You never fly?" he asked.

"I used to, years ago," she said. "But I can't now."

"Why not?"

"Phobia," she said simply. "I'm terrified, is all."

"Driving a car is a million times more likely to kill you."

She nodded. "I guess I understand that, statistically."

"So your fear is irrational. The Bureau got many irrational agents?"

She made no reply, just reddened slightly under the pallor.

"We need to talk," Lamarr said.

"So talk. Tell me about college."

"We're not going to talk about college. We need to discuss the cases."

He smiled. "You did go to college, right?"

She nodded. "Indiana State."

"Psychology major?"

She shook her head. "Landscape gardening, if you must know. My professional training is from the FBI academy at Quantico."

"Landscape gardening? No wonder the FBI snapped you up."

"It teaches you to see the big picture, and to be patient."

"So are there many irrational phobic landscape gardeners at Quantico? Any bonsai enthusiasts scared of spiders?"

"I hope you're real proud of yourself, Reacher, making jokes while women are dying. The Defense Department says there are ninety-one women who fit the same category as the murder victims. My stepsister is one of the eighty-eight who are left."

He went quiet and looked out the window. She was driving fast. "I'm sorry," he said. "You must be worried about her."

Soon they entered New Jersey. The road was wet, and there were gray clouds ahead. They were chasing a rainstorm south.

She gripped the wheel. "So let's discuss the cases," she said again. "Locations are obviously random, but the victim group is very specific, right? He's chasing particular victims and goes where he has to. Crime scenes have all been the victim's residence. Single-family housing in all cases, but with varying degrees of isolation."

"What about husbands and families?" Reacher asked.

"Callan was separated, no kids. Cooke had boyfriends, no kids. Stanley was a loner, no attachments."

"You look at Callan's husband?"

"Obviously. Any married woman, we look at the husband. But he was alibied, nothing suspicious. And then with Cooke the pattern became clear, so we knew it wasn't a husband or a boyfriend."

"No, I guess it wasn't."

"First problem is how he gets in. No forced entry. He just walks in the door."

"You think there was surveillance first? Any evidence of a stakeout? Cigarette butts and soda cans piled up under a nearby tree?"

"This guy is leaving no evidence of anything."

"Neighbors see anything?"

She shook her head. "Not so far."

"And all three were done during the day?"

"Different times, but all during daylight hours."

"None of the women worked?"

"Like you don't. Very few of you ex-army people seem to work. Why is that?" she asked.

"In my case because I can't find anything I want to do. I thought about landscape gardening, but I wanted a challenge, not something that would take me two seconds to master."

She fell silent, and the car hissed into a wall of rain. She set the wipers going, switched on the headlights, and backed off the speed a little.

"Are you going to insult me all the time?" she asked.

"Making a little fun of you is a pretty small insult compared to how you're threatening my girlfriend. And how you're so ready and willing to believe I'm the type of guy could kill two women."

"So was that a yes or a no?"

"It was a maybe. An apology would help turn it into a no."

"An apology? Forget about it, Reacher. I stand by my profile. If it wasn't you, it was some scumbag just like you."

The sky was turning black, and the rain was intense. Up ahead, brake lights were shining red through the deluge on the windshield. Traffic was slowing to a crawl. Lamarr braked sharply.

"Fun, right? And right now your risk of death is ten thousand times higher than if you were flying, conditions like these."

She made no reply. She was concentrating, riding the brake, crawling forward. "Where were we?" she said after a while.

"He's staked them out sufficiently to know they're alone. It's daylight; somehow he walks right in. Then what?"

"Then he kills them."

"In the house?"

"We think so."

"You think so? Can't you tell?"

"He leaves no evidence," she said. "Absolutely nothing. No fibers, no blood, no saliva, no hair, no prints, no DNA—nothing."

"So maybe he's not killing them in the house."

"He leaves the bodies in there. In the tub."

"In the tub?" he repeated. "All three of them?"

"Right," she said. "Naked. And their clothes are missing."

"He takes their clothes with him?" he asked. "Why?"

"Probably as a trophy. Taking trophies is a very common phenomenon in serial crimes like these."

"He take anything else?"

She shook her head. "Not as far as we can tell."

"So he takes their clothes and leaves nothing behind."

"He does leave something behind," she said. "He leaves paint."

"Paint?"

"Army camouflage green. In the tub. He puts the body in there, naked, and then he fills the tub with paint."

Reacher stared out at the rain. "He drowns them? In paint?"

"He doesn't drown them. They're already dead."

"Tell me about the paint," he said quietly.

She looked at him oddly. "It's army camouflage base coat. Flat green. Manufactured in Illinois by the hundred thousand gallons."

He nodded vaguely. He had never used it, but he had seen a million square yards of stuff daubed with it. "Messy," he said.

"But the crime scenes are immaculate. He doesn't spill a drop."

"The women were already dead. Nobody was fighting. No reason to spill any. But it means he must carry twenty to thirty gallons into the house to fill a tub. That's a lot of paint. It must mean a hell of a lot to him. You figured out any significance to it?"

"Not really, beyond the obvious military significance. Maybe covering the body with army paint is some kind of reclamation, putting them back where he thinks they belong, in the military, where they should have stayed. It traps them. Couple of hours, the surface is skinning over. It goes hard, and the stuff underneath jellifies. Leave it long enough, I guess the whole tub might dry solid."

Reacher stared ahead through the windshield. The horizon was bright. They were leaving the weather behind.

"Twenty or thirty gallons of paint is a major load to haul around. It implies a big vehicle. Very visible. Nobody saw anything?"

"We canvassed door to door. Nobody reported anything."

He nodded. "The paint is the key. Where's it come from?"

"We have no idea. The army is not being especially helpful."

"I'm not surprised. It's embarrassing. Makes it likely it's a serving soldier. Who else could get that much camouflage paint?"

She made no reply. She just drove south. The rain was gone, and she switched the wipers off. He fell to thinking about a soldier somewhere, loading cans of paint. Ninety-one women on his list, some skewed mental process reserving twenty or thirty gallons for each one of them. Truckloads of it. Maybe he was a quartermaster.

"How is he killing them?" he asked.

She swallowed hard. "We don't know."

"You don't know?" he repeated.

"We can't figure out how."

CHAPTER 2

THERE *are ninety-one altogether, and you need to do six of them in total, which is three more, so what do you do now? You keep on thinking and planning is what. Because you need to outwit them all. The victims and the investigators. More investigators all the time. New angles, new approaches. They're looking for you. They'll find you if they can.*

The investigators are tough, but the women are easy. You planned long and hard, and the planning was perfect. They answer the door; they let you in; they fall for it. They're so stupid they deserve it. And it's not difficult. It's like everything else. If you plan it properly, it's easy. Three more. Then you're home free.

"WHY don't you know how they died?" Reacher asked.

"There are no wounds, injuries. The crime-scene guys take the bodies out of the tubs; the pathologists clean them and don't find anything. No water or paint in the lungs, so they didn't drown."

"No hypodermic marks? Bruising?"

Lamarr shook her head. "Nothing. But remember, they've been coated in paint. That military stuff is full of chemicals, and fairly corrosive. It's conceivable the paint damage might be obscuring some marks on the skin. But whatever killed them was very subtle."

"What about internal damage?"

She shook her head again. "Nothing. No subcutaneous bruising, no organ damage. Toxicology was clear. No sexual interference."

"It's a very unsoldierly way to kill somebody. Soldiers shoot or stab or hit or strangle. They don't do subtle things."

"We don't know exactly what he did."

"But there's no anger there, right? If this guy is into retribution, where's the anger? It sounds too clinical."

Lamarr yawned. "That troubles me, too. But look at the victim category. What else can the motive be? And if we agree on the motive, what else can the perpetrator be except an angry soldier?"

They lapsed into silence. The miles rolled by. Lamarr yawned again, and Reacher glanced sharply at her. "You okay?"

"I'm a little weary, I guess. You worrying about me now?"

He shook his head. "No. I'm worrying about myself. You could fall asleep, run us off the road."

She yawned again. "Never happened before."

He looked at her long and hard. "I'm going to sleep for an hour," he said. "Try not to kill me."

WHEN he woke up, he could see that Lamarr was rigid with exhaustion, staring down the road with red unblinking eyes.

"We should stop for lunch," he said.

She yawned again. "Okay," she said. "So let's stop."

She drove on for a mile and coasted into a rest area. The place was the same as a hundred others Reacher had seen—low-profile '50s architecture colonized by fast-food operations.

They got out, and Reacher stretched his cramped frame in the cold, damp air before strolling inside to line up for a sandwich.

The line shuffled forward, and he changed his selection from cheese to crabmeat, because he figured it was more expensive and assumed she was paying. He added a large cup of black coffee and a doughnut, then found a table while she fiddled with her bag.

She joined him, and he raised his coffee in an ironic toast. "Here's to a few fun days together," he said.

"More than a few days," she said. "It'll be as long as it takes."

He sipped his coffee and thought about time. "What's the significance of the three-week cycle?"

"We're not sure. Maybe he's on a three-week work pattern—two weeks on, one week off. He spends the week off staking them out, organizing it, and then doing it."

Reacher saw his chance. Nodded. "Possible," he said.

"So what kind of soldier works that kind of pattern?"

"That regular?" He swallowed. "Special Forces maybe." Then he waited to see if she'd take the bait.

"Special Forces would know subtle ways to kill, right?"

He started on his sandwich. "Silent ways, unarmed ways, improvised ways, I guess. But I don't know about subtle ways."

"So what are you saying?"

"I'm saying I don't have a clue who's doing what, or why, or how. You're the big expert here."

She paused. "We need more from you than this, Reacher. And you know what we'll do if we don't get it."

"She gets hurt, you know what I'll do to you, right?"

She smiled. "Threatening me, Reacher? Threatening a federal agent? Now you're really stacking up the charges against yourself."

He drained his cup and made no reply.

"Stay on the ball, and everything will be okay," she said.

"I'll be a go-between, but you need to tell me what you want."

She nodded. "First thing, check out Special Forces."

He clenched his teeth to stop himself from smiling.

THEY walked back to the Buick in silence. She fired it up and eased it out onto the highway.

"Tell me about your sister," Reacher said.

"My stepsister."

"Whatever. Tell me about her."

"She's a rich girl who wanted adventure."

"So she joined the army?"

"She believed the advertisements. You seen those, in magazines? They make it look tough and glamorous. She thought it was going to be all rappelling down cliffs with a knife between your teeth."

"And it wasn't?"

"They put her in a transport battalion, made her drive a truck."

"Why didn't she quit, if she's rich?"

"She's not a quitter; she pushed for something better. She saw some jerk of a colonel five times, trying to make progress. He suggested if she was naked for the sixth interview, that might help."

"And?"

"She busted him. Whereupon they gave her the transfer she wanted. Infantry close-support unit. But you know how it works, right? No smoke without fire? The assumption was she had screwed the guy even though she had busted him, and he was canned. In the end, she couldn't stand the whispers, and she quit."

"So what's she doing now?"

"Nothing. She's feeling a little sorry for herself."

"You close to her?"

"Not very," she said. "Not as close as I'd maybe want to be."

"You like her?"

Lamarr made a face. "She's a great person, actually. But I handled it all wrong. I was young, my dad was dead, we were real poor, this rich guy fell in love with my mother and adopted me. I was full of resentment that I was being rescued, I guess. I figured it didn't mean I had to love her. She's only my stepsister, I said to myself. Then when my mother died, I was left feeling isolated and awkward. So now my stepsister is just a nice woman I know. Like a close acquaintance. I guess we both feel that way. But we get along okay."

"If they're rich, are you rich, too?"

"I'm richer than you'd think. My stepfather is very fair with us, even though I'm not really his daughter and she is."

"Lucky you."

She paused. "And we're going to be a lot richer soon. Unfortunately, he's real sick. He's been fighting cancer for two years, but now he's going to die. So there's a big inheritance coming our way."

"I'm sorry he's sick," Reacher said.

She nodded. "Yes, so am I. It's sad."

There was silence, just the hum of the miles passing under the wheels. "Did you warn your sister?" Reacher asked.

"My stepsister."

"Why do you emphasize she's your stepsister?" he asked.

"Because Blake will pull me off if he thinks I'm too involved. And I don't want that to happen. I want to take care of this myself." She was quiet for a moment. "The family thing is awkward for me," she went on. "When my mother died, they could have cut me off, but they didn't. They have always been generous, very fair, and I feel guilty for calling myself a Cinderella at the beginning."

"Did you warn her?" Reacher asked again.

She glanced sideways at him. "Of course I warned her. I've told her not to let anybody through the door, no matter who they are."

"She pay attention?"

"I made sure she did."

He nodded. "Okay. Only eighty-seven others to worry about."

AFTER New Jersey came eighty miles of Maryland; then they skirted the District of Columbia and entered Virginia for the final forty miles of I-95 down to Quantico.

When Lamarr turned off the highway onto an unmarked road that wound through forest, Reacher sat forward and paid attention. He had never been to Quantico. The car rounded a bend, came clear of the trees, and stopped at a sentry's hutch made from bulletproof glass. An armed guard stepped forward. Over his shoulder, in the distance, was a long, low huddle of honey-colored stone buildings, a couple of high-rises standing among them surrounded by immaculate lawns. Except for the razor-wire perimeter and the armed guard, it looked like a college campus.

Lamarr had the window down and was rooting in her bag for I.D. The guy clearly knew who she was, but rules are rules and he needed to see her plastic. He nodded as soon as her hand came clear of the bag. Then he switched his gaze to Reacher.

"You should have paperwork on him," Lamarr said.

The guy nodded again. "Yeah, Mr. Blake took care of it."

He ducked back into his hutch and came out with a laminated plastic tag on a chain. He handed it through the window, and

Lamarr passed it on. It had Reacher's name and his old service photograph on it. The whole thing was overprinted with a pale red V.

"V for visitor," Lamarr said. "You wear it at all times, or you get shot. And I'm not kidding."

The guard was raising the barrier. Lamarr buzzed her window up and accelerated through to a parking lot in front of the largest building. She eased into a slot and shut down.

"So now what?" Reacher asked.

"Now we get to work."

He slipped the I.D. chain around his neck, opened his door, and slid out. The plate-glass door at the front of the building opened up, and Poulton, the sandy-haired guy, walked out.

"I'll show you to your room," he said. "You can stow your stuff."

"I don't have any stuff," Reacher said to him.

Poulton hesitated. "I'll show you anyway," he said.

Lamarr walked away with her bag, and Poulton led Reacher to an elevator. They rode together to the third floor and came out on a quiet corridor. Poulton walked to a plain door and unlocked it. Inside was a standard-issue motel-style room. Bathroom on the right, closet on the left, bed, table and two chairs, bland decor.

Poulton stayed out in the corridor. "Be ready in ten."

The door sucked shut. There was no handle on the inside. There was a view of the woods from the window, but the window frame was welded shut. There was a telephone on the nightstand. He picked it up, hit nine, and heard the dial tone. He dialed Jodie's office, let it ring eighteen times before trying her apartment. Her machine cut in. He tried her mobile. It was switched off.

He put his coat in the closet, unclipped his toothbrush from his pocket, and propped it in a glass on the bathroom shelf. Rinsed his face at the sink. Then he sat on the edge of the bed and waited.

EIGHT minutes later he heard a key in the lock and looked up expecting to see Poulton at the door, but it was a woman. She looked about sixteen. She had long, fair hair in a loose ponytail, white teeth in an open, tanned face. Bright blue eyes. She was wearing a man's suit, extensively tailored to fit; a white shirt; and a tie. She was over six feet tall, long-limbed, and completely spectacular.

"Hi," she said, smiling at him.

Reacher made no reply. Her face clouded, and her smile turned a little embarrassed. "So you want to do the FAQs right away?"

"The what?"

"The FAQs. Frequently asked questions."

"What are the frequently asked questions?" he said.

"Oh, you know, the stuff most new guys around here ask me. It's really really tedious." She made a face, resigned. "I'm Lisa Harper. I'm twenty-nine—yes, really; I'm from Aspen, Colorado; I'm six feet one—yes, really; I've been at Quantico two years; yes, I date guys; no, I dress like this just because I like it; no, I don't currently have a boyfriend; and no, I don't want to have dinner with you tonight." She finished with another smile, and he smiled back.

"Well, how about tomorrow night?" he said.

She sighed. "All you need to know is I'm an FBI agent, on duty."

"Doing what?"

"Watching you," she said. "You're classified status unknown, maybe friendly, maybe hostile. Usually that means an organized-crime plea bargain, you know, some guy ratting on his bosses."

"I'm not organized crime."

"Our file says you might be."

"Then the file is bull."

She nodded. "I looked Petrosian up. He's Syrian. Therefore his rivals are Chinese. And they never employ anybody except other Chinese. Implausible they'd use an American WASP like you."

"You point that out to anybody?"

"I'm sure they already know. They're just trying to get you to take the threat seriously."

"Should I take it seriously?"

"Yes, you should. You should think very carefully about Jodie."

"Jodie's in the file?"

"Everything's in the file."

She held the door open. It closed softly behind him as they

walked to a different elevator. Inside, this one had buttons for five basement floors. She pressed the bottom button. The elevator settled with a bump, and the door slid back to reveal a gray corridor.

"We call this the bunker," Harper said. "It used to be our nuclear shelter. Now it's BS. That stands for behavioral science."

She led him to a door in the left-hand wall, stopped, and knocked.

"I'll be right outside," she said, opening up the door for him.

He went in and saw Nelson Blake behind a crowded desk in a small untidy office. There were piles of paper everywhere.

"Case conference in two minutes," Blake said. "So listen up for the rules. Harper stays with you, all the time. Everything you do, everywhere you go, you're supervised by her. But don't get the wrong idea. You're still Lamarr's boy, only she stays here because she won't fly. And you'll need to get around some. And don't get ideas about Harper. Thing with her is, she looks nice, but you start messing with her, she's the bitch from hell, okay?"

"Okay."

Blake scrabbled in the pile of paper on his desk and came up with a large brown envelope. Held it out.

"With Cozo's compliments," he said.

Reacher took the envelope. It contained photographs—eight of them. Crime-scene photographs. Mutilated corpses. Pieces missing.

"Petrosian's handiwork," Blake said. "Wives and sisters and daughters of people who pissed him off."

Reacher nodded. "So where's Jodie?"

"How should I know?" Blake said. "We're not tailing her. Petrosian can find her himself if it comes to that. We're not going to deliver her to him. That would be illegal, right?"

"So would breaking your neck."

Blake shook his head. "Stop with the threats, okay? I'm not worried about you, Reacher. Deep down you're a good person. You'll help me, and then you'll forget all about me."

Reacher smiled. "I thought you profilers were supposed to be real insightful."

THE CASE CONFERENCE WAS held in a long, low room a floor above Blake's office. There was a long table surrounded by cheap chairs set at forty-five-degree angles so they faced the head of the table, where a large empty blackboard was set against the end wall.

Harper led Reacher to a seat at the end furthest from the blackboard. She sat one place nearer the action. Poulton and Lamarr came in together, carrying files. Blake waited until the door closed behind them, then flipped the blackboard over.

The top right quarter was occupied by a map of the United States, dotted with a forest of flags. Ninety-one of them, Reacher guessed. Most of them were red, but three of them were black. Opposite the map, on the left, was an eight-by-ten color photograph of a woman squinting against the sun and smiling. She was in her twenties, pretty, a plump, happy face framed by curly brown hair.

"Lorraine Stanley, ladies and gentlemen," Blake said. "Recently deceased in San Diego, California."

Underneath the smiling face were more eight-by-tens pinned up in a careful sequence. The crime scene. There was a long shot of a small Spanish-style bungalow. Wide shots of a hallway, a living room, the master bedroom. The master bathroom. There was a shower stall on the right and a tub on the left. Full of green paint.

"She was alive three days ago," Blake said. "Neighbor saw her wheeling her garbage to the curb in the morning. Nobody saw anything after that. She was discovered yesterday, by her cleaner."

"We got a time of death?" Lamarr asked.

"Approximate," Blake said. "Sometime during the second day. MO identical to the first two."

"Evidence?"

"Not a damn thing, so far."

Reacher was focusing on the picture of the hallway. It was a long, narrow space leading past the mouth of the living room, back to the bedrooms. On the left was a narrow shelf at waist height, crowded with tiny cactus plants. On the right were more shelves, at random heights, packed with small china ornaments.

"Okay," Reacher said. "She answers the door, this guy wrestles her through the hallway, into the bathroom, and then carries thirty gallons of paint through after her and doesn't knock anything off those shelves. Where's the violence? Where's the anger?"

Blake shook his head. "He doesn't do any wrestling. Medical reports show the women aren't touched at all. There is no violence."

"You happy with that? Profile-wise? An angry soldier looking for retribution, but there's no uproar?"

"He kills them, Reacher. The way I see it, that's anger enough."

"And what about the paint? How does he bring it to the house?" Reacher continued. "We should go to the store and check out what thirty gallons looks like. He must have a car or a truck parked outside for twenty, thirty minutes at least. How does nobody see it?"

"We don't know," Blake said.

"How does he kill them without leaving any marks?"

"We don't know."

"That's a lot you don't know, right?"

Blake grimaced. "Yes, it is, smart guy. But we're working on it. We've got eighteen days till the next killing's due, and with a genius like you helping us, I'm sure that's all we're going to need."

"Suppose he doesn't stick to his interval," Reacher said.

Blake looked at Lamarr. "Julia?"

"I stand by my profile," she said. "Right now I'm interested in Special Forces. They're stood down one week in three. I'm sending Reacher to poke around."

Blake nodded, reassured. "Okay, where?"

Lamarr glanced at Reacher, looking at the three black flags on the map. "Geography is all over the place," he said. "This guy could be stationed anywhere in the United States. So Fort Dix would be the best place to start. I know a guy there. A colonel called John Trent. If anybody's going to help me, he might."

"Okay," Blake said. "We'll call this Colonel Trent, get it set up."

"Make sure you mention my name loud and often. He won't be very interested unless you do," Reacher said.

"That's exactly why we brought you on board. You'll leave with Harper first thing in the morning."

MAYBE IT'S TIME TO THROW them a curve. Maybe tighten the interval. Maybe cancel it altogether. That would unsettle them.

Or maybe let a little of the anger show, too. Because anger is what this is about, right? Anger, and justice. Maybe it's time to make that a little more obvious. Maybe it's time to take the gloves off. A little violence could make the next one more interesting, too.

So what's it to be? A shorter interval? Or more drama at the scene? Or both? How about both? Think, think, think.

HARPER took Reacher up to ground level and outside into the chill air just after six in the evening. She led him down a walkway toward the next building. "Cafeteria's in here," she said, pulling open a glass door.

There was a long corridor with the clattering sound and the vegetable smell of a communal dining room at the end of it.

"Okay, help yourself," she said. "Bureau's paying."

At the service counter Reacher joined a line of personnel waiting with trays in their hands, Harper at his side.

The line shuffled up, and he was served a filet mignon by a cheerful Spanish guy. He got vegetables from the next server, filled a cup with coffee from an urn, then looked for a table.

Harper led him to an empty table, put her tray down, took her jacket off, and draped it on the back of her chair. Her shirt was fine cotton, and she wore nothing underneath it. She rolled her sleeves to the elbow. Her forearms were smooth and brown.

"Nice tan," Reacher said.

She sighed. "Yes, it's all over, and no, I don't want to prove it."

He smiled. "Just making conversation," he said.

"I'll talk about the case. If you want conversation."

"I don't know much about the case. Do you?"

"I know I want this guy caught. Those women were pretty brave, making a stand like that."

"Sounds like the voice of experience," he said.

"It's the voice of cowardice. I haven't made a stand. Not yet."

"You getting harassed?"

She smiled. "Are you kidding?" Then she blushed. "I mean, can I say that without sounding bigheaded or anything?"

He grinned back. "Yes, in your case I think you can."

"It's just talk, you know, loaded questions and innuendo. Nobody's said I should sleep with them to get a promotion or anything. But it still gets to me. That's why I dress like this now. I'm trying to make the point, you know, I'm just the same as them, really."

He made no reply, just smiled again.

"Is there a camera in my room?" he asked. "Video surveillance?"

"Why?"

"I'm just wondering if this is a backup plan. In case Petrosian doesn't pan out. Blake assigned you to look after me so you could get real close to me. So he's got something else to twist my arm with, like a nice intimate little scene, you and me in my room, on a nice little videocassette he can send to Jodie."

She blushed. "I wouldn't do a thing like that."

"But he asked you to, right?"

She was quiet for a long time. Reacher drank his coffee. "He practically challenged me to try," he said. "Told me you're the bitch from hell if anybody puts the moves on. But I wouldn't fall for it. I'm not stupid. I'm not about to give them more ammunition."

She looked at him and smiled. "So can we relax? Get past it?"

He nodded. "Sure. What do people do here in the evenings?"

"Mostly they go home," Harper said. "But not you. You go back to your room. Blake's orders."

"We're following Blake's orders now?"

She laughed. "Some of them."

HE SLEPT badly and woke before six. Dialed Jodie's apartment. Got the machine. Her office. No reply. Her mobile. Switched off.

He showered, dressed, and sat down to wait.

He waited forty-five minutes. There was a polite knock at the door; then it opened and Lisa Harper was standing there, smiling. "Good morning," she said.

He raised his hand in reply. She was in a different suit. This one was fitted, charcoal gray, with a white shirt and a dark red tie. An exact parody of the unofficial Bureau uniform. Her hair was loose, hanging front and back of her shoulders, very long.

"We've got to go," she said. "Breakfast meeting."

They rode down to the lobby together and paused at the doors. It was raining hard outside. She sprinted down the walkway, and he followed behind, watching her run. She looked pretty good.

Lamarr, Blake, and Poulton were waiting for them in the cafeteria, in three of five chairs crowded around a table by the window. There was a coffee jug in the center, surrounded by mugs. Harper took a chair, and Reacher squeezed in next to her.

"We called Fort Dix last night," Blake said. "Spoke with Colonel Trent. He seems to like you. Said he'll give you all day today."

"That should do it."

Lamarr nodded. "Good. You know what you're looking for, right? Concentrate on the dates. Find somebody whose stand-down weeks match. My guess is he's doing it late in the week because he's got to get back to base and calm down afterward."

Reacher shrugged. "We do it by dates alone, we're going to come up with maybe a thousand names."

"So narrow it down some. Get Trent to cross-reference against the women. Find somebody who served with one of them."

Reacher smiled. "Awesome brainpower around this table."

"You got better ideas, smart guy?" Blake asked.

"I know what I'm going to do."

"Well, just remember what's riding on it, okay? Lots of women in danger, one of them yours."

A MOTOR-POOL guy brought a car to the doors and left it there with the motor running. Harper watched Reacher get in and then slid into the driver's seat. They drove out through the rain, past the checkpoint, out onto I-95. She blasted north and fifty minutes later made a right into the north gate of Andrews Air Force Base.

"They assigned us the company plane," she said.

Two security checks later they were at the foot of an unmarked Learjet's cabin steps. They left the car on the tarmac and climbed inside. It was taxiing before they had their seat belts fastened.

"Should be a half hour to Dix," Harper said.

"McGuire," Reacher corrected. "Dix is a marine corps base. We'll land at McGuire Air Force Base."

She looked worried. "They told me we're going straight there."

"We are. It's the same place. Different names, is all."

She made a face. "Weird. I don't understand the military."

"Well, don't feel bad about it. We don't understand you either."

Thirty minutes later the Learjet touched down and taxied to a distant corner of tarmac. A green Chevy was racing through the rain to meet it. By the time the cabin steps were down, the driver, a marine lieutenant, was waiting at the bottom.

"Major Reacher?" he asked.

Reacher nodded. "And this is Agent Harper, from the FBI."

The lieutenant ignored her. "The colonel is waiting, sir," he said.

"So let's go. Can't keep the colonel waiting, right?"

They drove out of McGuire into Dix and stopped at a huddle of brick offices a mile from the runway.

"Door on the left, sir," the lieutenant said.

Reacher got out, and Harper followed him into a spacious anteroom full of metal desks and filing cabinets. Three sergeants worked at separate desks. One of them hit a button on his telephone.

"Major Reacher is here, sir," he said into it.

There was a moment's pause, and then the inner office door opened and a tall man stepped out, short black hair silvering at the temples. "Hello, Reacher," John Trent said.

Reacher nodded. Trent owed the second half of his career to a paragraph Reacher had omitted from an official report ten years before. Trent had assumed the paragraph was written and ready to go. He had come to see Reacher, not to plead for its deletion, not to bribe, but to explain how he'd made the mistake and that it was not malice or dishonesty. He had left without asking for a thing and then sat and waited for the axe. It never came. The report was published, and the paragraph wasn't in it. What Trent didn't know was that Reacher had never even written it. Ten years had passed, and the two men hadn't spoken until Reacher had called him from Jodie's apartment the previous morning.

"Hello, Colonel," Reacher said. "This is Agent Harper, FBI."

Trent smiled and shook hands with the agent.

"Pleased to meet you, Colonel," Harper said. "And thanks in advance for your cooperation."

Trent smiled. "I'll do what I can, but the cooperation will be limited. We're going to be examining personnel records and deployment listings that I'm just not prepared to share with you. Reacher and I will do it on our own. There are issues of national and military security at stake. You're going to have to wait out here."

"All day?" she said.

Trent nodded. "As long as it takes. You comfortable with that?"

It was clear she wasn't. "I'm supposed to watch over him."

"I understand that. But you'll be right here, outside my office. There's only one door. The sergeant will give you a desk."

A sergeant showed her to an empty desk with a clear view of the inner office door. She sat down slowly, unsure.

"You'll be okay there," Trent said. "This could take us some time. It's a complicated business. I'm sure you know how paperwork can be."

Then he led Reacher into the large inner office and closed the door. It had windows on two walls, a big wooden desk, leather chairs.

Reacher sat down in front of the desk and leaned back. "Give it two minutes, okay?" he said.

Trent nodded. "Read this. Look busy."

He handed over a faded green folder, one of a tall stack of files. Reacher opened it, and Trent walked to the door. Opened it wide.

"Ms. Harper?" he called. "Can I get you a cup of coffee?"

Reacher glanced over his shoulder and saw her staring in at him, taking in the leather chairs, the desk, the stack of files.

"I'm all set, right now," she called back.

"Okay," Trent said. "You want anything, just tell the sergeant."

He closed the door again, walked to the window. Reacher took off his I.D. tag and stood up. Trent unlatched the window and opened it.

"You didn't give us much time," he whispered, "but we're in business."

"They fell for it right away," Reacher whispered back.

Trent stuck his head out the window and checked both directions. "Okay, go for it," he said. "Good luck, my friend."

"I need a gun," Reacher whispered.

Trent shook his head firmly. "No," he said. "That I can't do."

"You have to. I need one."

Trent paused. "Okay, a gun," he said. "But no ammunition."

He opened a drawer and took out a Beretta M-9. Same weapon as Petrosian's boys had carried, except Reacher could see this one still had its serial number intact. Trent took the clip out and thumbed the bullets back into the drawer one by one. Then he clicked the empty clip back into the gun and handed it to Reacher.

"Take care," he whispered as Reacher sat on the window ledge, swiveled his legs outside, and dropped to the ground.

He was in a narrow alley. The lieutenant was still waiting in the Chevy, ten yards away, motor running. Reacher sprinted for the car, and it was rolling before his door was closed. The mile back to McGuire took a little over a minute. The car raced out onto the tarmac and headed straight for a marine corps helicopter. Its belly door was standing open, and the rotor blade was turning.

"Thanks, kid," Reacher said, stepping out of the car. He ran up into the darkness, and the door whirred shut behind him. The machine came off the ground, and two pairs of hands grabbed him and pushed him into his seat. He buckled his harness, and a headset was thrust at him. The intercom crackled.

"We're going to the coast guard heliport in Brooklyn," the pilot called. "Close as we can get without filing a flight plan, and filing a flight plan ain't exactly on the agenda today, okay?"

Reacher thumbed his mike. "Suits me, guys. And thanks."

"Colonel must owe you big," the pilot said.

"No, he just likes me."

CHAPTER 3

THE coast guard heliport in Brooklyn is sixty air miles northeast of McGuire. The marine pilot made the trip in thirty-seven minutes. "You've got four hours," he said when they had touched down. "Any longer than that, we're out of here, okay?"

"Okay," Reacher said. He unstrapped himself, slipped the headset off, and followed the ramp down as it opened. There was a dark blue sedan with navy markings waiting on the tarmac.

Reacher slid in alongside the driver.

The guy stamped on the gas. "I'm navy reserve," he said. "We're helping the colonel out. A little interservice cooperation."

"I appreciate it," said Reacher.

"So where we headed?" the guy asked.

"Manhattan. Aim for Chinatown."

Traffic was light, but it was thirty minutes before Reacher was where he wanted to be. The guy stopped short on a hydrant.

"I'll be waiting right here," he said. "Facing the other direction, exactly three hours from now. So don't be late, okay?"

"I won't," Reacher said. He slid out of the car and headed south. It was late morning, and he started worrying he was too early.

After five minutes he stopped walking. If any street was going to do it for him, this was the one. It was lined on both sides with Chinese restaurants. The sidewalks were crowded, delivery trucks double-parked tight against cars. He walked the length of the street twice, inspecting the terrain, looking for his targets.

He glanced at his watch and saw his time ticking away. He looked into doorways. Nothing. He watched the alleys. Nothing. He walked a block south and tried another street. Nothing. He walked back to his starting point, leaned on a wall, and watched the lunch crowd build. Then he watched it ebb away. He had been waiting two hours. He had an hour left.

The lunch crowd died away to nothing. He walked east and south. Came back again and walked up one side of the street and down the other. Checked his watch. He had thirty minutes left.

Then he saw them. Two guys. Chinese, of course. Young, shiny black hair worn long on their collars. They wore dark pants and light windbreakers, with scarves at their necks, like a uniform.

One carried a satchel, and the other carried a notebook. They strolled into each restaurant in turn, strolled out again, with one guy zipping the satchel and the other guy noting something in his book. Reacher crossed the street and watched them go into a restaurant and approach an old guy at the register. The old guy reached into the cash drawer and took out a wad of folded bills. The guy with the book took it and handed it to his partner. Wrote something in the book as the money disappeared into the satchel.

Reacher stepped ahead, up to where a narrow alley separated two buildings. He waited with his back to the wall. Then he stepped out of the alley and met them head-on. He seized a bunch of windbreaker in each hand and swung them through an explosive half circle back first into the alley wall. The guy with the satchel followed a wider arc and therefore hit harder. Reacher caught him solidly with his elbow as he bounced off the wall, and he went down on the ground. Didn't come back up again.

The other guy dropped the book and went for his pocket, but Reacher had Trent's Beretta out first. He stood close and held it down toward the guy's kneecap. "Be smart, okay?" he said.

He reached down and racked the slide. The sound was muffled by the cloth of his coat, but to his practiced ear it sounded empty.

The Chinese guy didn't notice. Too shocked. He just pressed himself to the wall like he was trying to back right through it. "You're making a mistake, pal," he whispered.

Reacher shook his head. "No, we're making a move."

"Who's we?"

"Petrosian," Reacher said.

"Petrosian? You're kidding me."

"No way," Reacher said. "I'm serious. This street is Petrosian's.

As of today." He slammed him left-handed in the stomach. The guy folded forward, and Reacher tapped him above the ear with the butt of the gun and dropped him on top of his partner. He put the gun back in his pocket, picked up the satchel, and tucked it under his arm. Walked out of the alley and turned north.

He was late, but he didn't run. Running in the city was too conspicuous. He walked away as fast as he could, threading his way along the sidewalks. He saw the blue car, USNR painted on its flank, moving away from the curb. Now he ran.

He got to where it had been parked four seconds after it had left. Now it was three cars ahead. The light changed to red. The car braked to a neat stop. Reacher ran to the intersection and pulled open the passenger door. Dumped himself into the seat, panting. The driver nodded to him. Didn't offer an apology for not waiting. When the navy says three hours, it means three hours.

REACHER spent the flight back to Trent's office at Dix counting the money in the satchel. There was a total of twelve hundred dollars in there, six folded wads of two hundred dollars. He gave the money to the pilot for the next unit party, then tore the satchel along its seams and dropped the pieces through the flare hatch, above Lakewood, New Jersey.

It had stopped raining. The lieutenant drove him back to the alley. Reacher walked to Trent's window and rapped softly on the glass. Trent opened it up, and Reacher climbed back inside the office.

"We okay?" he asked.

Trent nodded. "She's just been sitting out there, quiet as a mouse, all day. Must be real impressed with our dedication. We worked right through lunch."

Reacher handed back the empty gun, slipped his I.D. around his neck, and picked up a file.

"Success?" Trent asked.

"I think so. Time will tell, right?"

"Don't forget your notes," Trent said.

He handed over a sheet of paper with a list of maybe thirty

names printed on it. Probably Trent's high school football team. Reacher put it in his pocket and shook Trent's hand. Walked back into the anteroom where Harper was waiting.

"SO, YOU found our guy yet?" Blake asked.

He, Poulton, and Lamarr were sitting at the same table in the Quantico cafeteria.

"Maybe. I've got thirty names," Reacher said. "He could be one of them."

"So let's see them."

"Not yet. I need more."

Blake stared at him. "Bull. We need to get tails on these guys."

Reacher shook his head. "Can't be done. These guys are in places where you can't go. You even want a warrant on these guys, you're going to have to go to the Secretary of Defense, right after you've been to the judge. Defense is going to go straight to the Commander in Chief, who was the President last time I looked, so you're going to need more than I can give you right now."

"So what are you saying?"

"I'm saying let me boil it down. I want to see Lamarr's sister."

"My stepsister," Lamarr said.

"Why?" Blake asked.

Reacher wanted to say, "Because I'm just killing time and I'd rather do it on the road than stuck in here," but he composed his face into a serious look. "Because we need to think laterally," he said. "If this guy is killing by category, we need to know why. He can't be mad at the whole category. One of these women must have sparked him off, first time around. Then he must have transferred his rage from the personal to the general. So who was it? Lamarr's sister could be a good place to start. She got a transfer between two very different units. That doubles her potential contacts."

"Okay," Blake said. "We'll set it up. You'll go tomorrow."

"Where does she live?"

"Washington State," Lamarr said. "Outside of Spokane."

Reacher turned to Blake. "You should be guarding these women."

Blake sighed heavily. "Do the arithmetic, for God's sake. Eighty-eight women, and we don't know which one is next. Seventeen days to go, if he sticks to his cycle. That's more than a hundred thousand man-hours. We can't do it. We don't have the agents."

"Have you warned the women?"

Blake looked embarrassed. "We can't. If we can't guard them, we can't warn them. Because what would we be saying? You're in danger, but sorry, girls, you're on your own? Can't be done."

"We need to catch this guy," Poulton said. "That's the only sure way to help these women."

Lamarr nodded. "He's out there. We need to bring him in."

"So eat and get to bed," Blake said. "It's a long way to Spokane. Early start tomorrow. Harper will go with you, of course."

"To bed?"

Blake was embarrassed again. "To Spokane, you ass."

THE *decision was made. About the interval. The interval was history. Three weeks was way too long to wait now. This sort of thing, you let the idea creep up on you, you look at it, consider it, see its value. You see its appeal, and the decision is really made for you, isn't it? You can't get the genie back in the bottle, not once it's out. And this genie is out. All the way out. Up and running. So you run with it.*

THERE was no breakfast meeting the next morning. The day started too early. Harper opened the door before Reacher was even dressed. He had his pants on and was smoothing the wrinkles out of his shirt with his palm against the mattress.

"Love those scars," she said.

She took a step closer, looking at his stomach with undisguised curiosity. "What's that one from?" She pointed to his right side.

He glanced down at a violent tracery of stitches in the shape of a twisted star. They bulged out above the muscle wall.

"My mother did it," he said.

"Your mother?"

"I was raised by grizzly bears. In Alaska."

She rolled her eyes, then moved her gaze to the left side of his chest. There was a bullet hole punched into the pectoral muscle.

"Exploratory surgery," he said. "Checking if I had a heart."

"Where are they really from?" she asked. "The scars?"

He buttoned his shirt. "The gut is from bomb shrapnel," he said. "The chest, somebody shot me."

"Dramatic life."

He took his coat from the closet. "No, not really. Pretty normal. A soldier figuring on avoiding physical violence is like a C.P.A. figuring on avoiding numbers."

"Is that why you don't care about these women?"

He looked at her. "Who says I don't care?"

"I thought you'd be more agitated about it."

"Getting agitated won't achieve anything."

She paused. "So what will?"

"Working the clues, same as always."

"There aren't any clues. He doesn't leave any."

He smiled. "That's a clue in itself, wouldn't you say?"

THE same motor-pool guy brought the same car to the doors. This time he stayed in the driver's seat and drove them to National Airport. It was still before dawn when they arrived at the terminal. Harper collected two economy-class tickets from the United desk and carried them over to the check-in counter.

"We could use some legroom," she said to the guy behind the counter, and snapped her FBI pass down. The guy hit a few keys and came up with an upgrade. Harper smiled.

First class was half empty. Harper took an aisle seat, trapping Reacher against the window like a prisoner. She stretched out. She was in a third different suit, this one a fine check in a muted gray.

When they had taken off, Reacher pulled the in-flight magazine out and started leafing through it.

Harper had her tray unfolded, ready for breakfast. "What did you mean?" she asked. "When you said it's a clue in itself?"

"Just thinking aloud, I guess," he said. "Lamarr said you've got forensic tests I wouldn't believe. I bet they can find a rug fiber, tell you where and when somebody bought it, what kind of flea sat on it, what kind of dog the flea came off."

"So?"

"This guy killed Amy Callan and beat all of those tests, right?"

"Right."

"So what do you call that type of a guy?"

"What?"

"A very clever guy is what."

She made a face. "Among other things."

"Sure, a lot of other things, but whatever else, a very clever guy. Because then he did it again, with Cooke. And again, with Stanley."

"So?"

"So that's the clue. We're looking for a very very very clever guy."

"I think we know that already."

Reacher shook his head. "I don't think you do. You're not factoring it in."

"In what sense?"

"You think about it. I'm only the errand boy. You Bureau people can do all the hard work."

The stewardess came out of the galley with the breakfast trolley. It was first class, so the food was reasonable. Reacher smelled bacon and egg and sausage. Strong coffee. He flipped his tray open.

"How aren't we factoring it in?" Harper asked.

"Figure it out for yourself," Reacher said.

"Is it that he's not a soldier?"

He turned to stare at her. "That's great. We agree he's a really smart guy, and so you say, well then, he's obviously not a soldier. Thanks a bunch, Harper."

She looked away, embarrassed. "I'm sorry. I didn't mean it like that. I just can't see how we're not factoring it in."

He didn't reply, just drained his coffee and climbed over her legs to get to the bathroom. When he got back, she was still contrite.

"Tell me," she said.

"No."

They didn't speak again, all the way to Seattle. Five hours without a word. Reacher was comfortable enough with that. He just sat there like he was making the journey on his own.

Harper was having more trouble with it. She was like most people. Put her alongside somebody she was acquainted with, she felt she had to be conversing. But he didn't relent.

Those five hours were reduced to two by the West Coast clocks. It was still about breakfast time when they landed. The arrivals hall had the usual array of drivers holding placards. There was one guy in a dark suit, striped tie, short hair. He might as well have had FBI tattooed across his forehead.

"Lisa Harper?" the guy said. "I'm from the Seattle field office." They shook hands.

"This is Reacher," she said.

The Seattle agent ignored him completely. "We're flying to Spokane," he said. "Air-taxi company owes us a few favors."

He had a Bureau car parked in the tow lane. He used it to drive a mile around the perimeter road to General Aviation, which was acres of fenced tarmac filled with parked planes, all of them tiny. A pilot led them toward a white six-seat Cessna.

The interior of the plane was about the same size Lamarr's Buick had been. It taxied out to the runway and lined up behind a 747 bound for Tokyo the way a mouse lines up behind an elephant. Then it wound itself up and was off the ground in seconds.

At Spokane airfield, a Bureau car was waiting on the tarmac, a clean dark sedan with a man in a suit leaning on the fender.

"From the Spokane satellite office," the Seattle guy said.

The car rolled over to where the plane parked, and they were on the road within twenty seconds of the pilot's shutting down. The local guy drove east toward the Idaho panhandle, then turned north on a narrow road into the hills. There were giant mountains in the middle distance, snow on the peaks. The road had a building every mile or so, separated by thick forest and broad meadow.

The address itself might have been the main house of an old cattle ranch. It was boxed into a small lot by new ranch fencing.

Beyond the fencing was grazing land; inside it the grass had been mowed into a fine lawn. There was a small barn with garage doors punched into the side and a path veering off from the driveway to the front door. The whole structure stood close to the road and to its own fencing, which gave it a suburban feel, but the nearest man-made object was at least a mile away.

The local guy stayed in the car, and Harper and Reacher got out and walked together along the shale driveway toward the front door. The silence of the empty country fell on them like a weight. There was a big iron knocker in the shape of a lion's head with a heavy ring held in its teeth. There was a fish-eye peephole above it. Harper grasped the iron ring and knocked twice on the door.

There was no response. Harper knocked again. They waited. There was a creak of floorboards inside the house. Footsteps.

"Who is it?" a voice called. A woman's voice, apprehensive.

Harper held up her badge in front of the peephole. "FBI, ma'am," she announced. "We called you yesterday, made an appointment."

The door opened to reveal an entrance hall and a woman smiling with relief. "Julia's got me so damn nervous," she said.

Harper smiled back and introduced herself and Reacher. The woman shook hands with both of them.

"Alison Lamarr," she said. "Really pleased to meet you."

She led the way inside. The hall was square and floored in old pine, which had been stripped and waxed to a dark gold shade.

"Can I get you coffee?" Alison Lamarr asked.

"I'm all set right now," Harper said.

"Yes, please," said Reacher.

She led them through to the kitchen, which occupied the whole rear quarter of the ground floor. It was an attractive space, waxed pine floor polished to a shine, big country range, new cabinets in unostentatious timber, a line of gleaming machines for washing clothes and dishes, yellow gingham at the windows.

Alison Lamarr was medium height, dark, and she moved with the bounce of a fit, muscular woman. Her face was open and friendly, tanned like she lived outdoors. She smelled of lemon scent and was dressed in clean, carefully pressed denim and cowboy boots.

She poured coffee from a machine into a mug, handed it to Reacher, and smiled in a way that proved there was no blood relationship with her stepsister. It was a pleasant smile, interested, friendly—the kind that Julia Lamarr had no idea existed.

"Can I look around?" Reacher asked. "Security check."

"Be my guest."

He took his coffee with him. The two women stayed in the kitchen. The first floor had four rooms—entrance, kitchen, parlor, living room. The house was solidly built out of good timber, with excellent renovations. All the windows were new storm units in stout wood frames, and each had a key. The front door was original, old pine two inches thick. A city-style lock. The back door, similar vintage and thickness. Same lock.

Outside, there was a steel cellar door with a big padlock latched through the handles. The garage was a well-maintained barn, with a new Jeep Cherokee inside and a stack of cartons proving the renovations had been recent. There was a new washing machine, still boxed up and sealed, a workbench with power saws and drills stored neatly on a shelf above it.

He went back into the house and up the stairs. Same windows as elsewhere. Four bedrooms. There was a new master bathroom. It held a toilet, a sink, and a shower. And a tub.

He went back down to the kitchen. Harper was standing by the window, looking out at the view. Alison Lamarr was sitting at the table. "Okay?" she said.

"Looks good to me. This guy isn't into breaking doors down, so if you don't open up to anybody, nothing can go wrong."

"That's how I figure it. You need to ask me some questions?"

"That's why they sent me, I guess."

He sat down opposite her. Tried to think of something intelligent to say. "How's your father doing?" he asked.

"That's what you want to know?"

He shrugged. "Julia mentioned he was sick."

"He's been sick two years. Cancer. Now he's just hanging on day by day. He's in the hospital in Spokane. I go there every afternoon."

"I'm very sorry."

"Julia should come out. But she's all hung up on this stepfamily thing, as if it really matters. Far as I'm concerned, she's my sister, pure and simple. And sisters take care of each other, right? Anyway, right now that's not too important. What can I help you with?"

"You got any feeling for who this guy could be?"

"It's some guy who thinks it's okay to harass women. Or maybe not okay, exactly. Could be some guy who thinks the fallout should be kept behind closed doors."

"Is that an option?" Harper asked. She sat next to Reacher.

Alison glanced at her. "I don't really know. I'm not sure there is any middle ground. Either you swallow it or it goes public in a big way. I just went ballistic."

"Who was your guy?" Reacher asked.

"A colonel called Gascoigne. He was always saying come to him if anything was bothering me. So I went to him about getting reassigned. I wanted something more interesting to do."

"So what happened?"

Alison sighed. "At first I thought he was just kidding around." She paused. Looked away. "He said I should try next time without my uniform on," she said. "I thought he was asking for a date, you know, meet him in town, some bar, off duty, plain clothes. But then he made it clear he meant right there in his office, stripped off."

"Not a very nice suggestion."

Alison made a face. "He was pretty jokey about it at first. It was like he was flirting. But clearly he figured I wasn't getting the message, so all of a sudden he got obscene. He described what I'd have to do, you know? Like a porno movie. Then it hit me, the rage, all in a split second, and I just went nuclear and busted him."

"How did he react?" Reacher asked.

She smiled. "He was puzzled more than anything. I'm sure he'd done it lots of times before and got away with it."

"Could he be the guy?"

She shook her head. "No. This guy is deadly, right? Gascoigne is a sad, tired old man. I don't see him having that kind of initiative."

Reacher nodded. "If your sister's profile is correct, this is probably a guy from the background, a distant observer turned avenger."

"Right," Alison agreed. "But at the end of the day the target group is so specific it has to be a soldier. Who else could even identify us? But it's a weird soldier. Not like any I ever met."

"Nobody?" Harper said. "No threats while it was happening?"

"Nothing significant. Nothing that I recall. I even flew out to Quantico and let Julia hypnotize me, in case there was something buried there, but she said I came up with nothing."

Silence again. Harper nodded. "Okay. Wasted trip, right?"

"Sorry, guys," Alison said.

"Nothing's ever wasted," Reacher said. "Negatives can be useful, too. And the coffee was great."

Alison followed them out of her kitchen, crossed the hall, and opened her front door.

"Don't let anybody in," Reacher said.

Alison smiled. "I don't plan to."

"I mean it," Reacher said. "It looks like there's no force involved. This guy is just walking in. So you might know him. Or he's some kind of a con artist with a plausible excuse. Don't fall for it."

He followed Harper out onto the shale path. They heard the door close behind them and then the sound of the lock turning.

THE local Bureau guy saved them two hours' flying time by pointing out they could hop from Spokane to Chicago and change there for D.C. Harper did the business with the tickets, and they boarded a Boeing for Chicago. This time there was no upgrade. The economy seats put them close together, thighs touching.

"So what do you think?" Harper asked.

"I'm not paid to think," Reacher said. "So far I'm not getting paid. I'm a consultant. So you ask questions and I'll answer them."

"I did ask you a question. I asked you what you think."

He shrugged. "I think it's a big target group, but if the other eighty-seven do what Alison Lamarr is doing, they should be okay."

"That's it?" Harper said. "You think we should just tell the women to lock their doors?"

He nodded. "I think you should be warning them, yes."

"That doesn't catch the guy."

"You can't catch him."

"Why not?"

"You're not factoring in how smart he is."

"Yes, we are. The profile says he's real smart. And profiling works. Those people have had some spectacular successes."

"Among how many failures? It's not an exact science."

"So you think the profile is worthless?"

"I know it is. It's flawed. It makes two incompatible statements."

"What statements?"

He shook his head. "No deal, Harper. Not until Blake apologizes for threatening Jodie and pulls Julia Lamarr off the case."

"Why would he do that? She's his best profiler."

"Exactly."

THE motor-pool guy was at National Airport in D.C. to pick them up. It was late when they arrived back at Quantico. Julia Lamarr met them, alone. Blake was in a budget meeting, and Poulton had signed out and gone home.

"How was she?" Lamarr asked.

"She was okay," Reacher said.

"What's her house like? Is it very isolated?"

"Isolated," he said, "but secure. Locked up tight as Fort Knox." She nodded. He waited.

"She wants you to visit," he said eventually.

"I can't. It would take me a week to get there."

"Your father is dying."

"My stepfather."

"Whatever. She thinks you should go out there."

"I can't," she said again. "She still the same? Dressed like a cowboy, tanned and pretty and sporty?"

"You got it."

She nodded again, vaguely. "Different from me."

He looked her over. Her cheap black city suit was dusty and creased, and she was pale and thin and hard. Her eyes were blank.

"Yes, different from you," he said.

"I'm the ugly sister," she said, and walked away.

CHAPTER 4

NEXT morning Reacher was awake and waiting thirty minutes before Harper showed up. She unlocked his door and breezed in, looking elegant and refreshed, wearing the same suit as the first day. Clearly she had three suits and wore them in strict rotation.

They walked to the cafeteria. It was Sunday, and the whole campus was quiet. The weather was better. No warmer, but the sun was out. He hoped for a moment, as they walked between the buildings, that it was a sign that this was his day. But it wasn't. He knew that as soon as he saw Blake at the table by the window, alone. There was a jug of coffee, doughnuts, a pile of Sunday newspapers, opened and scattered, with *The New York Times* sitting on top, which meant there was no news from New York. Which meant it hadn't worked yet, which meant he was going to have to keep on waiting.

Harper and Reacher sat down opposite Blake. He looked old and tired and very strained, but Reacher felt no sympathy for him.

"Today you work the files," Blake said.

"Whatever," Reacher replied.

"They're updated with the Lorraine Stanley material. So you need to spend today reviewing them and you can give us your conclusions at the breakfast meeting tomorrow. Clear?"

Reacher nodded. "Crystal."

"Any preliminary conclusions I should know about?"

"Let me read the files. Too early to say anything right now."

Blake nodded. "But we need to start making progress soon."

"I get the message," Reacher murmured.

AFTER BREAKFAST HARPER took him to a quiet room filled with light oak tables and comfortable leather chairs. There was a stack of files about a foot high on one of the tables.

The stack was split into three bundles, each one secured with a thick rubber band. He laid them out on the table side by side. Amy Callan, Caroline Cooke, Lorraine Stanley. Three victims, three bundles. He checked his watch. Ten twenty-five. A late start.

"Did you try Jodie?" Harper asked.

"No point. She's obviously not there."

"Worried?"

"I can't worry about something I can't change."

There was silence. He pulled the Callan file toward him, took the rubber band off, and opened up the folder. Harper took her jacket off and sat down opposite. The sun was directly behind her, and it made her shirt transparent. He could see the curve of her breast swelling gently past the strap of her shoulder holster.

"Get to work, Reacher," she said.

THIS is the tense time. You park at the curb, leaving the car facing the right direction. You switch the engine off. You take the keys out and put them in your pocket. You put your gloves on.

You get out of the car. You stand still for a second, listening hard, and then you turn a complete circle, slowly, looking again. This is the tense time, when you must decide to abort or proceed. Think. Keep it dispassionate. It's just an operational judgment.

You decide to proceed. You close the car door quietly. You walk into the driveway. You walk to the door. You knock. The door opens. She lets you in. She's glad to see you. A little confused at first, then delighted. You talk for a moment. You keep on talking until the time is right. You'll know the moment when it comes. You keep on talking.

The moment comes. You stand still for a second, testing it. You make your move. You explain she has to do exactly what you tell her. She agrees, of course, because she has no choice.

You make her show you the master bathroom. She stands there like a real estate agent, showing it off. The tub is fine. You tell her to bring the paint inside. You supervise her all the way. It takes her five trips, in and out of the house, up and down the stairs. She's huffing and puffing, starting to sweat. You tell her to smile.

You tell her to find something to lever the lids off with. She nods happily and gets a screwdriver from the kitchen drawer. You tell her to take the lids off one by one. She kneels next to the first can. She works the tip of the screwdriver under the metal flange of the lid and eases it upward. She works around it in a circle. The lid sucks off. She moves on to the next can. Then the next.

You pull the folded garbage bag from your pocket. You tell her to place her clothes in it. She nods and smiles. Tugs off all her clothes. Drops them in the bag. She's naked. You tell her to smile.

You make her carry the bag and prop it against the front door. Then you take her back to the bathroom and make her empty the cans into the bathtub, slowly, carefully, one by one. She concentrates hard. The cans are heavy and awkward. The paint is thick. It runs slowly into the tub. The level creeps up, green and oily.

You tell her she's done well. She smiles, delighted at the praise. Then you tell her she has to take the empty cans back where she got them. But now she's naked, so she has to make sure nobody can see. She nods again. She carries the cans downstairs. You ease the door open and send her out. She runs all the way there and all the way back.

You take her back up to the bathroom. The screwdriver is still on the floor. You ask her to pick it up. You tell her to make marks on her face with it. She's confused. You explain. Deep scratches will do, you tell her. Three or four of them. She smiles and nods. Scrapes the screwdriver down the left side of her face. A livid red line appears, five inches long. Make the next one harder, you say. She nods. The next line bleeds. Good, you say. Do three more. She nods and smiles. Good girl, you say.

She's still holding the screwdriver. You tell her to get into the tub, slowly and carefully. She puts her right foot in, then her left. She sits. The paint is touching the underside of her breasts. You tell her to lie back, slowly and carefully. She slides down into the paint.

You tell her what to do. She doesn't understand at first, so you ex-plain again. She nods. Her hair is thick with paint. She slides down. Now only her face is showing. She tilts her head back. She uses her fingers to help her. She does exactly what she's been told. Her eyes jam open with panic, and then she dies.

You wait five minutes. Then you do the only thing she can't do for herself. It gets paint on your right glove. Then you press down on her forehead with a fingertip and she slips under the surface. You peel your right glove off inside out, and carrying it in your left hand, you walk downstairs, your right hand in your pocket for safety. This is the only time your prints are exposed. Slip the glove into the garbage bag with her clothes. Open the door. Listen and watch. Carry the bag out-side. Turn around and close the door behind you. Walk down the driveway to the road. Pop the trunk lid and place the bag inside. Open the door and slide in behind the wheel. Drive away.

THE Callan file started with a summary of her four-year military career. She had passed out of basic training and gone straight to the ordnance storerooms. She was a sergeant within twenty months, working at Fort Withe, near Chicago, in a warehouse full of the stink of gun oil and the noise of clattering forklifts. She shuffled pa-pers and sent consignments around the world. She had been con-tent at first. Then the rough banter got too much and her captain and her major had started stepping over the line and getting physi-cal. The dirty talk and pawing and the leering eventually brought her to Reacher's office.

After she quit, she went to Florida. Lived there a year, got mar-ried and separated—then died there. The crime-scene photographs showed no damage to any doors or windows of her house and no disruption inside, just a white-tiled bathroom with a tub full of green paint and a slick indeterminate shape floating in it.

The paint had a molecular structure that penetrated anything it was slapped onto. Removing it removed the skin. There was no evidence of bruising or trauma. The toxicology was clear. No air embolisms. There are many clever ways to kill a person, but the

Florida pathologists couldn't find any evidence of any of them.

"Well?" Harper said.

"She had freckles. I remember that," Reacher said.

"You liked her."

He nodded. "She was okay."

The final third of the file was some of the most exhaustive crime-scene forensics he had ever heard of. Every particle of dust or fiber in Callan's house had been vacuumed up and analyzed, but there was no evidence of any intruder.

"A very clever guy," Reacher said. He pushed Callan's folder to one side and opened Cooke's. It followed the same format.

Cooke had joined as an officer, starting out a second lieutenant. She had gone straight to War Plans, where she had been promoted to first lieutenant and posted to NATO in Brussels, where she started a relationship with her colonel. When she didn't get promoted to captain early enough, she complained about him.

Reacher remembered it well. There was no harassment involved, certainly not in the sense that Callan had endured. But the rules had changed: Sleeping with somebody you commanded was no longer allowed, so Cooke's colonel went down and then ate his pistol. She quit and flew home to a cottage in New Hampshire, where she was eventually found dead in a tub full of setting paint.

The New Hampshire pathologists and forensic scientists told the same story their Florida counterparts had. A gray cedar house crowded by trees, an undamaged door, an undisturbed interior, a bathroom decor dominated by the dense green contents of the tub.

"What do you think?" Harper asked.

"I think the paint is weird," Reacher said, closing the file. "It's so circular, isn't it? It eliminates evidence on the bodies, which reduces risk, but getting it and transporting it creates risk."

"And it's like a deliberate clue," Harper said. "It underlines the motive. It's definite confirmation it's an army guy. It's like a taunt."

"Lamarr says it has psychological significance. She says he's reclaiming them for the military. But if he hates them enough to kill them, why would he want to reclaim them?"

"I don't know. A guy like this, who knows how he thinks?"

"Lamarr thinks she knows how he thinks," Reacher said.

Lorraine Stanley's file was the last of the three. Her history was similar to Callan's, but more recent. She was younger. She had been a sergeant in a giant quartermaster facility in Utah, the only woman in the place. She had been pestered from day one, and her competence had been questioned. One night her barracks was broken into and all her uniform trousers were stolen. She reported for duty the next morning wearing her regulation skirt. The next night all her underwear was stolen. The next morning she was wearing the skirt and nothing underneath when her lieutenant called her into his office. Made her stand easy in the middle of the room, one foot either side of a large mirror laid on the floor. The lieutenant ended up in prison, and Stanley ended up serving out another year and then living alone and dying alone in San Diego.

Reacher closed the file. "Caroline Cooke was killed in New Hampshire, and Lorraine Stanley was killed three weeks later in San Diego. That's about as far apart as you can get, right? Maybe thirty-five hundred miles. And he's hauling hundreds of gallons of paint around."

"Maybe he's got a stockpile stashed away someplace."

"That makes it worse. Unless his stash just happened to be on a direct line between where he's based and New Hampshire and California, he'd have to detour to get it. It would add distance."

"So?"

"So he's got a three-, four-thousand-mile road trip . . ."

Harper frowned. "Say seventy hours at fifty-five miles an hour."

"Which he couldn't average. He'd pass through towns and road construction. And he wouldn't risk breaking the speed limit."

"So call it a hundred hours on the road."

"At least. Plus a day or two surveillance when he gets there. That's more than a week, in practical terms. It's ten or eleven days."

"So? This is not some guy working two weeks on, one week off."

"No, it's not."

AT LUNCHTIME THEY WALKED over to the cafeteria again. They met Blake, who was on the way to the library. He looked agitated. There was worry in his face. "Lamarr's father died," he said.

"Stepfather," Reacher said.

"Whatever. He died early this morning. The hospital in Spokane called for her. Now I've got to call Julia at home."

"Give her our condolences," Harper said.

Blake nodded vaguely and walked away.

"He should take her off the case," Reacher said.

Harper nodded. "Maybe he should, but he won't. And she wouldn't agree anyway. Her job is all she's got."

AFTER lunch they went back to the folders. Reacher arranged them on the table and stared at them, musing about the geography again. He leaned back and closed his eyes, thinking hard.

"Making any progress?" Harper asked after a while.

"I need a list of the ninety-one women," he said.

"Okay," she said. She left the room.

He waited with his eyes closed, enjoying the silence. Then she was back with another thick blue file.

He opened the new file and started reading. First item was a Defense Department printout, four pages stapled together, ninety-one names in alphabetical order. Then there was a matching list with addresses and a thick sheaf of background information. Reacher flipped back and forth between pages, went to work with a pencil, and twenty minutes later did a count.

"It was eleven women," he said. "Not ninety-one."

"It was?" Harper said.

"Eleven," he said again. "Eight left, not eighty-eight."

"Why?"

"Lots of reasons. Ninety-one was always absurd. A guy this smart would limit himself to what's feasible. A subcategory. What else did Callan and Cooke and Stanley have in common?"

"What?"

"Unmarried or separated, single-family houses in the suburbs or the countryside. He needs somewhere isolated. No interruptions. No witnesses. He wants women who live alone."

Harper shook her head. "There are more than eleven of those. We did the research. I think it's more than thirty. About a third."

"But you had to check. I'm talking about women who are obviously living alone and isolated. We have to assume the guy hasn't got anybody doing research for him. All he's got is this list."

"But that's our list."

"Not exclusively. All this information came straight from the military, right? He had this list before you did."

FORTY-THREE miles away the exact same list was lying open on a polished desk in a small windowless office in the darkness of the Pentagon's interior. It was two Xerox generations newer than Reacher's version but otherwise identical. And it had eleven marks on it, against eleven names. Not hasty check marks in pencil, like Reacher had made, but neat underlinings with a pen and a ruler.

Three of the eleven names had second lines struck through them.

The list was framed on the desk by the uniformed forearms of the office's occupant, and the wrists were cocked upward to keep the hands clear of the surface. The right hand held a pen, which slowly scored a thick line straight through a fourth name.

"SO WHAT do we do about it?" Harper asked.

Reacher leaned back. "I think you should gamble. I think you should stake out the surviving eight around the clock because the guy will walk into your arms within sixteen days."

"Suppose you're wrong?" she said uncertainly.

"As opposed to what? The progress you're making?"

She still sounded uncertain. "Okay, talk to Lamarr tomorrow."

"Will she be here? Won't there be a funeral for her father?"

"She won't go. She'd miss her own funeral for a case like this."

"Okay, but you do the talking, and talk to Blake instead. Keep it away from Lamarr."

"Why?"

"Because her sister lives alone, remember? So her odds just went down to eight to one. Blake will have to pull her off now."

"He won't pull her off."

Reacher shrugged. "Then don't bother telling him anything. I'm just wasting my time here. The guy's an idiot."

"Don't say that. You need to cooperate. Think about Jodie."

He closed his eyes and thought about Jodie. She seemed a long way away. He thought about her for a long time.

"Let's go eat," Harper said. "Then I'll go talk to Blake."

FORTY-THREE miles away the uniformed man stared at the paper, motionless. There was a look on his face appropriate to a man making slow progress through a complicated undertaking. Then there was a knock at his door.

"Wait," he called.

He capped his pen and clipped it into his pocket. Folded the list, slipped it inside a drawer in his desk, and weighted it down with a book. It was a Bible, King James Version. Slid the drawer closed and locked it. "Come," he called, putting the keys in his pocket.

The door opened, and a corporal stepped inside and saluted. "Your car is here, Colonel."

BEFORE daybreak the next day Reacher stood at the window, staring out into the darkness. It was cold again. He shaved and showered, dressed, put his coat on, and clipped his toothbrush into the inside pocket. Just in case today was the day.

He sat on the bed and waited for Harper. But when the key went into the lock and the door opened, it wasn't Harper standing there. It was Poulton. Reacher felt the first stirrings of triumph.

"Where's Harper?" he asked.

"Off the case," Poulton said.

"Did she talk to Blake?"

"Last night."

"And?"

Poulton shrugged. "And nothing."

"You're ignoring my input?"

"You're not here for input."

Reacher nodded. "Okay. Ready for breakfast?"

"Sure."

The sun was coming up in the east and sending color into the sky. It was a pleasant walk through the early gloom.

Blake was at the usual table in the cafeteria. Lamarr was with him, wearing a black blouse in place of her customary cream. There was coffee on the table, and doughnuts. But no newspapers.

"I was sorry to hear the news from Spokane," Reacher said.

Lamarr nodded silently.

"You're not going to the funeral?"

"Alison hasn't called me," she said. "I don't know what the arrangements are going to be."

"You didn't call her?"

She shrugged. "I'd feel like I was intruding."

There was silence. Reacher poured coffee into a mug.

"You didn't like my theory?" he asked Blake.

"It's a guess, not a theory," Blake said. "We can't turn our backs on eighty women just because we enjoy guessing."

"Well, the next woman to die will be one of the eleven I marked, and it'll be on your head."

Blake said nothing, and Reacher pushed his chair back. "I want pancakes," he said. "I don't like the look of those doughnuts."

He stood up before they could object and stepped away toward the center of the room. Stopped at the first table with a *New York Times* on it. It belonged to a guy on his own who was reading the sports pages. The main section was discarded to his left. The story Reacher was waiting for was right there, front page, below the fold.

"Can I borrow this?" he asked, picking up the paper.

The guy nodded without looking.

Reacher tucked the paper under his arm and walked to the serving counter. He helped himself to a stack of pancakes and added syrup. Then he came back to the table and propped the paper in front of his plate and started to eat. He pretended to be surprised by the headline. "Well, look at that," he said with his mouth full.

The headline read GANG WARFARE EXPLODES IN LOWER MAN-HATTAN, LEAVES SIX DEAD. The story recounted a brief and deadly turf war between two rival protection rackets, one of them allegedly Chinese, the other Syrian. The body count ran four to two in favor of the Chinese. Among the four dead on the Syrian side was the alleged gang leader, a suspected felon named Almar Petrosian.

"Well, look at that," Reacher said again.

They had already looked at it. That was clear.

"Cozo call you to confirm it?" Reacher asked.

Nobody said a thing, which was the same as a yes.

Reacher smiled. "Life's a bitch, right? You get a hook into me, and suddenly the hook isn't there anymore. Harper wouldn't play ball with the femme fatale thing, and now old Petrosian's dead, so you got no more cards to play. And since you're not listening to a word I say, is there a reason why I shouldn't walk out of here?"

"Lots of reasons," Blake said.

"None of them good enough," Reacher said, and stood up and stepped away from the table again. Nobody tried to stop him. He went out through the glass doors and started walking.

AT THE guardhouse on the perimeter he ducked under the barrier, dropped his visitors pass on the road, and walked on. He heard the car behind him five minutes later, stopped and waited for it. It was Harper, which was what he had expected. She drew level with him and buzzed her window down. "Want a ride?" she asked.

"I-95 will do it. Going north."

"Hitchhiking?"

He nodded. "I've got no money for a plane."

He slid in next to her, and she accelerated away.

"They tell you to bring me back?" he asked.

She shook her head. "They decided you're useless. 'Nothing to contribute' is what they said."

He smiled. "So now I'm supposed to get all boiled up with indignation and storm back in there and prove them wrong?"

She smiled back. "Something like that. Lamarr decided they should appeal to your ego."

"That's what happens when you're a psychologist who studied landscape gardening in school. But she's right. I've got nothing to contribute. This guy's too smart for me, that's for damn sure."

She smiled again. "A little psychology of your own? Trying to leave with a clear conscience?"

"My conscience is always clear."

"Even about Petrosian? Hell of a coincidence, don't you think? They threaten you with Petrosian, and he's dead within three days."

"Just dumb luck."

"I don't like coincidences. Nobody in the Bureau does. They could dig around. Might make it hard for you later."

He grinned. "This is phase two of the approach, right?"

Her smile exploded into a laugh. "Yeah, phase two. There are about a dozen still to go. You want to hear them all?"

"Not really. I'm not going back. They're not listening."

She drove on. "Jodie's home," she said after a while. "I called Cozo's office. Apparently they had a little surveillance going. She's been away. Got back this morning, in a taxi. Looked like she'd come from the airport. She's working from home today."

"Okay, so now I'm definitely out of here."

"We need your input, you know."

"They're not listening. And they're wasting their time with this profiling crap. They need to work the clues."

"There aren't any clues."

"Yes, there are. How smart the guy is. And the paint, and the geography. They're all clues. They should work them. Starting with the motive is starting at the wrong end."

"I'll pass that on."

She pulled over at the junction with the interstate.

"You going to get into trouble?" he asked.

"For failing to bring you back? Probably. That was phase ten," she said. "I'll be perfectly okay."

"I hope so," he said, and got out of the car. He walked north to the ramp and stood watching her car turn back toward Quantico.

A MALE hitchhiker standing six feet five and weighing two hundred and thirty pounds is on the cusp of acceptability. But Reacher was showered and shaved, and dressed quietly. That shortened the odds, and there were enough trucks on the road with big, confident owner-drivers so that he was back in New York City in seven hours.

He was quiet for most of the seven hours, partly because the trucks were too noisy for conversation and partly because he wasn't in the mood for talking. The old hobo demon was whispering to him again. Where are you going? Back to Jodie, of course. Okay, smart guy, but what else? Yard work behind your house? Painting the damn walls? His final ride was on a vegetable truck delivering to Greenwich Village. He got out and walked the last mile to Jodie's apartment, concentrating on his desire to see her.

He had his own key to her lobby, and went up in the elevator and knocked on her door. The peephole went dark and light again and the door opened and she was standing there, in jeans and a shirt, slim and beautiful. But she wasn't smiling at him.

"Hey, Jodie," he said.

"There's an FBI agent in my kitchen," she replied.

He followed her into the apartment, through to the kitchen. The Bureau guy was a young man in a blue suit, white shirt, striped tie. He was holding a cell phone up to his face, reporting Reacher's arrival to somebody else.

"Wait here, please, sir," he said after he'd made the call. "About ten minutes."

"What's this about?"

"You'll find out, sir. Ten minutes, is all."

Jodie sat down. There was something in her face. Something halfway between concern and annoyance. *The New York Times* was open on the countertop. Reacher glanced at it. "Okay," he said.

He sat down, too. They waited in silence. Then the buzzer sounded from the street and the Bureau guy went into the hallway.

They heard the apartment door open, footsteps on the maple floor.

Alan Deerfield walked into the kitchen. "I got six people dead in my city," he said. "So I came to ask Ms. Jacob here a couple questions."

Jodie didn't look up. "What questions?" she said.

"Where have you been the last few days?"

"Out of town," she said. "On business."

"Where out of town?"

"London. Client conference."

"Reacher knew you were there, right?" Deerfield said.

"No. I didn't tell him. It was a last-minute trip."

"So he was a worried man. Right after he got to Quantico, he was trying to get you on the phone. Office, home, mobile. That night, same thing again. Couldn't get you. A worried man."

Jodie glanced at Reacher. "I should have told him, I guess."

"Hey, that's up to you. But the interesting thing is, then he stops calling you. Suddenly he's not calling you anymore. Now why is that? Did he find out you were safe over there in London?"

She started to reply, and then she stopped.

"I'll take that for a no," Deerfield said. "So as far as Reacher knew, you were still right here in town. But he's suddenly not worried anymore. Maybe because he knows Petrosian isn't going to be around for much longer."

Jodie's eyes were focused on the floor.

"He's a smart guy," Deerfield said. "My guess is he whistled up some pal of his to set the cat among the pigeons up here in China-town, and then he sat back and waited for the Tongs to do what they always do when somebody starts messing with them. And he figures he's safe. Because while Petrosian is getting the good news with the machete, he's locked into a room down in Quantico."

Deerfield turned to Reacher. "So am I on the money?" he asked.

Reacher shrugged. "Why should anybody have been worrying about Petrosian?"

Deerfield smiled. "Oh, sure, we can't talk about that. We'll never admit Blake said a word to you on that subject. I just want to be sure what I'm dealing with here. If you stirred it up, just tell me, and maybe I'll pat you on the back for a job well done. But if by some chance it was a genuine dispute, we need to know about it."

"I don't know what you're talking about," Reacher said.

"So why did you stop calling Ms. Jacob?"

"That's my business."

"No, it's everybody's business," Deerfield said. "So tell me about it, Reacher. Petrosian was a piece of crap for sure, but he's still a homicide, and we can crank up a pretty good motive for you. We could call it a conspiracy with persons unknown. Careful preparation of the case, you could be inside waiting for the trial."

Jodie stood up. "You should leave now, Mr. Deerfield. I'm still his lawyer, and this is an inappropriate forum for this discussion."

Deerfield nodded slowly and looked around the kitchen. "Yes, it sure is, Ms. Jacob," he said. "So maybe we'll have to continue this discussion someplace more appropriate. Maybe tomorrow, maybe next week, maybe next year."

He turned on the spot, walked out of the apartment.

"So you took Petrosian out," Jodie said after they heard the door slam shut.

"I never went near him," Reacher replied.

She shook her head. "Save that stuff for the FBI, okay? You engineered it. You took him out as surely as if you were standing right next to him with a gun. And Deerfield knows."

"He can't prove it."

"That doesn't matter," she said. "Don't you see that? He can try to prove it. And he's not kidding about jail. A suspicion of gang warfare? The courts will back him up all the way. It's not an empty threat. He owns you now. Like I told you he would."

Reacher said nothing.

"Why did you do it?"

He shrugged. "Lots of reasons. It needed doing."

There was a long silence.

"So why did you stop calling me?" she asked eventually.

He looked down at his rough hands. "I figured you were safe," he said. "I figured you were hiding out someplace. I was taking care of Petrosian; I assumed you were taking care of yourself. We know each other well enough to trust assumptions like that."

"Like we were comrades," she said softly. "In the same unit, a major and a captain maybe, in the middle of some dangerous mission, relying on each other to do our separate jobs properly."

He nodded. "Exactly."

"But I'm not a captain. I'm not in some unit. I grew up in the army, just like you did, and I could have joined up if I'd wanted to, just like you did. But I didn't want to. I wanted to go to college and law school. I wanted to live in a world with rules. And now I'm caught up in something I don't want to be caught up in."

"I'm sorry."

"And you're not a major anymore. You're a civilian."

He nodded, said nothing.

"And that's the big problem," she said. "You're getting me caught up in something I don't want to be caught up in, and I'm getting you caught up in something you don't want to be caught up in. The civilized world. The house, the car, living somewhere, doing ordinary things. My fault, probably," she went on. "I want those things. It is hard for me to accept that maybe you don't want them."

"I want you," he said.

She nodded. "I know that. And I want you. You know that, too. But do we want each other's lives?"

The hobo demon erupted in his head, cheering and screaming. She said it! Now it's right there, out in the open! So go for it!

"I don't know," he said.

"We need to talk about it," she said.

But there was no more talking to be done, not then, because the buzzer from the lobby started up an insistent squawk. Jodie stood up and hit the door release and moved into the living room to wait. Reacher stayed where he was. He felt the elevator arrive and heard the apartment door open. He heard urgent conversation and fast, light footsteps through the living room, and then Jodie was back in the kitchen, with Lisa Harper at her side.

CHAPTER 5

"It's all gone crazy," Harper said. "Alison Lamarr."

"When?" he whispered.

"Yesterday. He's speeding up. He didn't stick to the interval."

"How?"

"Same as all the others. The hospital was calling her because her father died, and there was no reply, so they called the cops, and the cops found her. Dead in the tub, in the paint, like all the others."

"But how the hell did he get in?"

Harper shook her head. "Just walked right in the door."

"I don't believe it."

Harper glanced around Jodie's kitchen nervously. "Blake wants you back on board," she said. "He's signed up for your theory in a big way. Eleven women, not ninety-one."

"So what am I supposed to say to that? Better late than never?"

"He wants you back," Harper said again. "This is getting out of control. We need to start cutting some corners with the army. He figures you've demonstrated a talent for cutting corners."

"You should go," Jodie said. "Go do what you're good at."

He went. Harper had a car waiting at the curb on Broadway. It was a Bureau car, borrowed from the New York office, and it took them straight to Newark Airport for a flight to Seattle. Blake wanted them to go direct to the crime scene.

They were the last passengers to board. "How's Lamarr taking it?" Reacher asked when they were in their seats.

Harper shrugged. "She's not falling apart, but she's real tense. She wants to take complete control of everything. But she won't join us out there. Still won't fly."

"A country this size, it's kind of limiting, isn't it? Especially for a federal agent. I'm surprised they let her get away with it."

"It's a known quantity. They work around it."

The plane lifted off the ground, and the earth tilted below them.

"Did you think about the geography?" Reacher asked. "Spokane is the fourth corner, right?"

She nodded. "Eleven potential locations now, all random, and he takes the four farthest apart for his first four hits."

"But why?"

She made a face. "Demonstrating his reach?"

"And his speed, I guess. Maybe that's why he abandoned the interval. To demonstrate his efficiency. He's a cool, cool customer. I wonder who the hell he is."

Harper smiled grimly. "The trick is to find out."

You're a genius, an absolute genius. Four down! And the fourth was the best of all. Alison Lamarr! The look on her face as she opened the door! The dawning recognition, the surprise, the welcome!

There were no mistakes. Not a single one. You replay your actions in your head. You touched nothing, left nothing behind. You brought nothing to her house except your still presence and your quiet voice. The terrain helped, of course; nobody for miles around. It made it a real safe operation. Maybe you should have had more fun with her. You could have made her sing. Or dance!

But you didn't, because patterns are important. Stick to the pattern, that's the key. And keep on thinking. Plan ahead. You've done number four, and sure, you're entitled to savor it for a spell, but then you have to just put it away and prepare for number five.

THE food on the plane was appropriate for a flight that left halfway between lunch and dinner and was crossing all the time zones. Reacher fueled up on coffee and thought about Jodie.

He recalled the day in June he had walked back into her life, the exact second he had laid eyes on her and understood who she was. He had felt a flood of feeling as powerful as an electric shock. He had felt the same thing on random days since he left the army. He remembered stepping off buses in towns he had never heard of in states he had never visited. He remembered the feel of the sun on his back and long roads stretching out straight and endless in front of him. The drifter's life. Its charm was a big part of him, and he missed it when he was stuck in Garrison or holed up in the city with Jodie. He missed it bad. About as bad as he was missing her now.

THE Bureau's Learjet flew Blake and his team to Spokane, and then he sent it to Sea-Tac to collect Harper and Reacher. The road outside the Lamarr place was blocked by a gaggle of cars. There was a local police black-and-white with its roof lights flashing, a pair of plain dark sedans, a black Suburban, and a coroner's wagon. The vehicles were all beaded with raindrops.

Harper and Reacher stepped out of the Bureau car and walked over to the Suburban. Nelson Blake slid out of the passenger seat to meet them. His face was nearer gray than red, like shock had knocked his blood pressure down. He was all business.

"Not much more than an hour of daylight left up here," he said. "I want you to walk me through what you did the day before yesterday, tell me what's different."

Reacher nodded. He suddenly wanted to find something. Something important. Not for Blake. For Alison.

"Who's been in there already?" he asked.

"Just the local uniformed guy," Blake said. "The one that found her. Nobody else has been in. I wanted your input first."

"So she's still in there?"

"Yes, I'm afraid she is."

"Okay," Reacher said. "Front door was unlocked?"

"Closed, but unlocked."

"Okay." He walked past the parked vehicles, past the mouth of the driveway, and twenty yards up the narrow road.

"Where does this go?" he called.

Blake was ten yards behind him. "Back of beyond, probably."

Reacher strolled back to join him. "You should check the mud on the shoulders, maybe up around the next bend. Our guy came in from the Spokane road most likely. Cruised the house, kept on going, turned around, came back. He'd want his car facing the right direction for the getaway."

Blake nodded. "Okay, I'll put somebody on it. Meantime, take me through the house."

He called instructions to his team, then joined Reacher and Harper at the front door. "Put these on your feet," he said. He pulled a roll of large food bags from his coat pocket. They put a bag over each shoe and tucked the edges down inside the leather.

"I knocked on the door. She opened up second knock," Harper said. "I showed her my badge in the peephole."

"She was pretty uptight," Reacher said. "Told us Julia had been warning her."

Blake nodded sourly and nudged the door with his bagged foot.

"We all went through to the kitchen," Harper said.

They filed into the kitchen. The range was cold, but there were dishes in the sink and one of the drawers was open an inch.

"Anything different in here?" Blake asked.

"Dishes in the sink," Reacher said. "And that drawer was closed."

They crowded the sink. There was a plate, a water glass, a mug, a knife, and a fork. Smears of egg and toast crumbs on the plate.

"Breakfast?" Blake said.

"Or dinner," Harper answered. "An egg on toast—that could be dinner for a single woman."

Blake pulled the drawer with the tip of his finger. There was an assortment of household tools in there.

"Okay, then what?" he asked.

"I stayed here with her," Harper said. "Reacher looked around."

"Show me," Blake said.

He followed Reacher back to the hallway, leaving Harper alone.

"I checked the parlor and the living room," Reacher said. "Looked at the windows. I figured they were secure, so I went outside, checked the grounds and the barn."

"We'll do the upstairs first," Blake said.

"Okay." Reacher led the way. "I checked the bedrooms. Went into the master suite last."

They walked the length of the master bedroom, paused at the bathroom door. "Let's do it," Blake said.

They looked inside. The place was immaculate. No sign that anything had ever happened there, except for the tub. It was seven eighths full of green paint, with the shape of a small muscular woman floating just below the surface, which had skinned over into a slick plastic layer, delineating her body. The head was tilted backward, the mouth slightly open, the lips drawn back in a grimace.

Reacher stood there and tried to read the signs, but the bathroom was exactly the same as it had been before.

"Anything?" Blake asked.

He shook his head. "No."

"Okay, we'll do the outside."

They trooped down the stairs, silent. Harper was waiting in the hallway. Blake just shook his head, like he was saying, Don't go up there. Reacher led him out into the yard.

"I checked the windows from outside," he said.

"Guy didn't come in the damn window," Blake said. "He came in the door."

"But how the hell?" Reacher said. "When we were here, you'd called her ahead on the phone, Harper was flashing her badge, and Lamarr still practically hid out in there."

Blake shrugged. "Like I told you right at the beginning, these women know this character. They trust him. He knocks on the door, they check him out in the peephole, and they open right up."

The cellar door was undisturbed. The garage door in the side of the barn was closed but not locked. Reacher led Blake inside. The new Jeep was there, and the cartons. The big washing-machine carton was there, flaps slightly open, sealing tape trailing. The workbench was there, with the power tools on the shelf above it.

"Something's different," Reacher said. "Let me think."

He stood there, opening and closing his eyes, comparing the scene in front of him with the memory in his head.

"The car has moved," he said.

"It would have. She drove to the hospital after you left."

Reacher nodded. "Something else. Let me think."

Then he saw it. "That washing-machine carton. She already had a washing machine. Looked brand-new. It's in the kitchen."

"So? It must have come out of that carton when it was installed."

Reacher shook his head. "No. Two days ago that carton was new and sealed up. Now it's been opened. Okay. Now we know how he transports the paint. He delivers it ahead of time disguised in washing-machine cartons."

THE *problem with rerunning it like a video over and over again is that little doubts start to creep in. You go over it, and you can't remember if you really did all the things you should have done.*

You sit there cold and sweating for an hour, and at the end of it you know you made a mistake. You forgot to reseal the carton. You know how investigators work. A just-delivered appliance carton in the garage or the basement was going to attract no interest at all. Your best guess was that the primary investigators would never open it at all. You were proved right three times in a row. Maybe much later when the heirs came to clear out the houses, they'd open them up and find all the empty cans, but by then it would be way too late.

But this time it would be different. They'd do a walk-through in the garage, and the flaps on the box would be up. They'd glance in, and they wouldn't see Styrofoam packaging and white enamel.

THEY brought in portable arc lights from the Suburban and arrayed them around the brown carton. The manufacturer's name was screen-printed with black ink on all sides, along with the model number. Inside the box were ten empty three-gallon paint cans. No manufacturer's name. Just a small printed label stenciled with CAMO/GREEN. Standard-issue field supply.

"Okay, so how did it get here?" Blake said.

Reacher frowned. "Like I said, it was delivered ahead of time by a shipping company. FedEx or UPS or somebody."

Blake sighed, like the world had gone mad. Stared at the box. Walked all around it. One side showed damage where the surface of the cardboard had been torn away. "Shipping label," he said.

"Maybe one of those little plastic envelopes," Reacher suggested. "You know, Documents Enclosed. The guy must have torn it off afterward so it can't be traced."

"But how can the delivery happen?" Blake asked. "You're Alison Lamarr, and UPS or FedEx shows up with a washing machine you never ordered? You wouldn't accept the delivery, right?"

"Maybe it came when she was out," Reacher said.

"Wouldn't the driver need a signature?"

"The guy probably specified no signature required."

"Why didn't she unpack it?"

Reacher made a face. "She figures it's not really hers, why would she unpack it? She just calls UPS or FedEx. Tells them to come pick it up. Maybe she tore off the envelope herself. Carried it into the house, to the phone, to give them the details."

"Well, if the details are in the house, we'll find them. Crime-scene people are going in soon as the coroner is through."

"Coroner won't find anything," Reacher said.

Blake looked grim. "This time he'll have to."

"So you're going to have to do it differently. You should take the whole tub out. Maybe fly it back to Quantico."

"How the hell can we take the whole tub out?"

"Tear the wall out. Tear the roof off. Use a crane."

Blake thought about it. "I guess we could. We'd need permission. But all this must be Julia's now. She's next of kin, I guess."

Reacher nodded. "So call her. Get her permission. And get her to check the field reports from the other three places. This delivery thing might be a one-shot, but if it isn't, it changes everything. It means the guy isn't driving truckloads of paint all over the place. He could be using the airlines, in and out quick as you like."

BLAKE went back to the Suburban to make his calls, and Harper found Reacher and walked him up the road to where agents from the Spokane office had spotted tire marks in the mud where a car had turned. It had gone dark, and they were using flashlights.

"Probably a midsize sedan," one of the Spokane guys said, looking at the tire marks. "Fairly new radial tires. We'll get the exact tire from the tread pattern. And we'll measure the width between the marks, maybe get the model of the car."

They left the Spokane guys and walked back toward the house. Blake was waiting. "We've got appliance cartons listed at all three scenes," he said. "No information about contents. Nobody thought to look. We're sending local agents back to check. And Julia says we should go ahead and rip the tub out."

Reacher paused, immobilized by a new line of thought, then said, "You should check on something else. You should get the list of the eleven women, call the seven he hasn't got to yet. Ask them if they've had any deliveries they weren't expecting. Because if this guy is speeding up, maybe the next one is all ready and set to go."

EVENTUALLY you relax. You've got a lot of talent. Everything was backed up, double safe, triple safe. You know the investigators won't find where the paint came from. Or who obtained it. Or who delivered it. You're too smart for them. So you relax.

But you're disappointed. You made a mistake. And now you probably can't use the paint anymore. Maybe you can think of something even better. But one thing is for sure. You can't stop now.

THEY waited an hour and a half, crowded inside the Suburban. The evening crept toward night, and it got cold. Dense night dew misted the windshield. A sudden electronic blast broke the silence. Blake fumbled the phone out of the cradle and listened hard, his eyes focused nowhere. Then he hung up and stared at the windshield.

"What?" Harper asked.

"Local guys went and checked the appliance cartons," Blake said. "They were all sealed up tight, but they opened them anyway. Ten paint cans in each of them. Used cans, exactly like we found."

"But the boxes were sealed?" Reacher said.

"Resealed," Blake said. "They could tell, when they looked closely. The guy resealed the boxes afterward."

"Smart guy," Harper said. "He knew a sealed carton wouldn't attract much attention."

"But not totally smart anymore," Reacher said. "Or he wouldn't have forgotten to reseal this one, right? His first mistake."

"And you haven't heard the really good news yet," Blake said.

"One of the other women got a delivery, right?" Reacher said.

Blake shook his head. "Wrong. All seven of them got a delivery."

"YOU'RE going to Portland, Oregon," Blake said. "You and Harper. So you can visit with an old friend of yours, Rita Scimeca. I believe you handled her case some years back. A lady lieutenant who got raped down in Georgia. She lives east of Portland. She's one of the eleven on your list. The closest to where we are now. You can get down there and check out her basement. She says there's a brand-new washing machine in there. In a box."

"Did she open it?" Reacher asked.

Blake shook his head. "No. A couple of Portland agents are on the way over there right now. They told her not to touch it."

"If the guy's still in the area, Portland could be his next call."

"That's why there's somebody on the way over."

Reacher nodded. "So now you're guarding them?"

Blake shrugged. "Hey, only seven left alive. Makes the manpower much more feasible."

It was a cop's sick humor in a car full of cops, but it still fell flat. Blake colored slightly and looked away. "Losing Alison gets to me much as anybody," he said. "Like family, right?"

"Especially to her sister, I guess," Reacher said.

"Tell me about it," Blake said. "She was burned as hell when the news came in. Never seen her so agitated."

"You should take her off the case."

Blake shook his head. "I need her."

SPOKANE to the village east of Portland measured about three hundred and sixty miles on the map Blake showed them. They took the Buick the local agent had used to bring them in from the airport.

"Six hours," Harper said. "You drive three, and I'll drive three."

The road ran southwest through hilly terrain. Reacher put the headlights on bright and eased the speed upward. Harper reclined her seat, her head tilted toward him. Her hair glowed red and gold in the lights from the dash. Reacher accelerated toward eighty miles an hour, but minutes later a long, low sedan blasted past them.

"Maybe that's the guy," Harper said sleepily. "Maybe he's heading down to Portland, too. Maybe we'll get him tonight."

"I've changed my mind," Reacher said. "I think the guy flies."

"Then what?" Harper said. "He rents a car at the airport?"

Reacher nodded in the dark. "That's my guess."

"Risky," Harper said. "Renting cars leaves a paper trail."

"So does buying airplane tickets. But this guy is real organized. I'm sure he's got cast-iron false I.D."

Harper stretched. Reacher caught a breath of her perfume as she moved. "So he gets off the plane, picks up the car, drives a half hour to Alison's place, spends a half hour there, drives a half hour back, and gets the hell out. He wouldn't hang around, right?"

"Not near the scene, I guess," Reacher said.

"The rental car could be returned in about two hours. We should check short rentals from the airports local to the scenes."

Reacher nodded, and they said nothing for a spell.

"Tell me about Rita Scimeca," Harper said.

"She was a little like Alison Lamarr, I guess. She had the same feel about her. Tough, sporty, capable. She was a second lieutenant. Great record. She blitzed officer training." He fell silent, picturing Rita Scimeca in his mind, as fine a woman as the army would ever get.

"So here's another puzzle," he said. "How is the guy controlling them? Think about it. He gets into their houses, and thirty minutes later they're dead in the tub, naked, not a mark on them. No disturbance, no mess. How is he doing that?"

"Points a gun, I guess."

Reacher shook his head. "If he's coming in by plane, he doesn't have a gun. You can't bring a gun on a plane."

"If he's coming in by plane. That's only a guess right now."

"Okay, but I was just thinking about Alison Lamarr. She had infantry training. Either she'd have got mad and started a fight or she'd have bided her time and tried to nail the guy somewhere along the way. But she didn't, apparently. Why not?"

"I don't know," Harper said.

"And you're never going to find out, because you're all so blinded by this profiling crap that you're wrong about the motive."

Harper stared out the window at the blackness speeding past. "You want to amplify that?"

"Not until I get Blake and Lamarr sitting still and paying attention. I'm only going to say it once."

THEY stopped for gas just after they crossed the Columbia River. Reacher filled the tank, and Harper went inside to the bathroom. Then she came out and got into the car on the driver's side, ready for her three hours at the wheel, twisted the key, and took off again south. Reacher dozed.

It was nearly three in the morning when they got to Scimeca's village. There was a gas station and a general store on the through road, both closed up tight. There was a cross street running north into the lower slope of the mountain. Harper nosed up it.

Scimeca's house was easy to spot. It was the only one with lights on. And the only one with a Bureau sedan parked outside. Harper stopped and turned off her lights, and the motor died. The sedan door opened, and a young man in a dark suit stepped out. Reacher and Harper slid out into the chill air.

"She's in there," the local guy said. "She's waiting for you."

Harper nodded. The house in front of them was a big square clapboard structure, built side-on to the street so it faced the view to the west. There was a generous front porch with railings, and the slope of the street made room for a garage under the house at the front. The garage door faced sideways, under the end of the porch.

Harper skipped up the steps in the center of the porch, but Reacher's weight made them creak in the night's silence. The front door was open, and Rita Scimeca was standing there.

"Hello, Reacher," she said.

"Scimeca," he said back. "How are you?"

"Reasonable, considering it's three o'clock in the morning and the FBI has only just got around to telling me I'm on some kind of hit list with ten of my sisters, four of whom are already dead."

"Your tax dollars at work," Reacher said.

"So why the hell are you hanging out with them?"

"Circumstances didn't leave me a whole lot of choice."

"Well, whatever, it's kind of good to see you."

"Good to see you, too."

She was a tall woman, muscular, not in the compact way Alison Lamarr had been, but in the lean, marathon-runner kind of way. She was dressed in jeans and a sweater and had medium-length brown hair, worn in a fringe above bright brown eyes. She had heavy lines all around her mouth. It had been nearly four years since he had last seen her, and she looked the whole four years older.

"This is Special Agent Lisa Harper," he said.

Scimeca nodded. "Well, come on in, I guess," she said.

Harper stepped inside, and Reacher filed after her. The door closed behind them. They were in the hallway of a nicely furnished little house. Warm and cozy. There were wool rugs on the floor. Polished mahogany furniture. Vases of flowers everywhere.

"Chrysanthemums," Scimeca said. "I grow them myself. Gardening's my new hobby."

Then she pointed toward a front parlor. "And music," she said. "Come see." The room had a grand piano in the back corner.

"Nice instrument," Reacher said. "So, you're doing okay?"

She looked him in the eye. "You mean have I recovered from being gang-raped by three guys I was supposed to trust with my life?"

"Something like that, I guess."

"I thought I'd recovered. As well as I ever expected to. But now I hear some maniac is fixing to kill me for complaining about it. That's taken the edge off it a little bit, you know?"

"We'll get him," Harper said in the silence.

Scimeca just looked at her.

"Can we see the new washing machine?" Reacher asked.

"It's not a washing machine, though, is it?" Scimeca asked.

"It's probably paint," Reacher said. "Camouflage green, army issue. The guy kills you, dumps you in the tub, and pours it over you."

"Why?"

Reacher shrugged. "Good question. There's a whole bunch of pointy heads working on that right now."

Scimeca led the way to the garage. A new car filled the space, a Chrysler sedan. They walked single file along its flank, and Scimeca opened a door in the garage wall that led to the basement. Scimeca pulled a cord, and a light came on. "There you are," she said.

There was a carton standing in the middle of the floor. Same size, same brown cardboard, same black printing, same manufacturer's name. It was taped shut with shiny brown tape.

"Got a knife?" Reacher asked.

Scimeca nodded toward a work area. There was Peg-Board screwed to the wall, and it was filled with tools. Reacher took a linoleum knife off a peg, slit the tape, and eased the flaps upward. He saw ten paint-can lids. He lifted one of the cans up. Rotated it. The label was printed with the words CAMO/GREEN.

"When did this come?" he asked Scimeca.

"I don't remember," she said. "Maybe a couple of months ago."

"A couple of *months?*" Harper said.

Scimeca nodded. "I guess. I don't really remember."

"You didn't order it, right?" Reacher said.

Scimeca shook her head. "I already got one. I assumed it's for my roommate," she said. "She moved out a couple of weeks ago."

"But you didn't ask her?"

"Why should I? Who else could it be for? I figured she left it because it's heavy. Maybe she's getting help to move it."

They stood in silence, three jagged shadows in the yellow light.

"I'm tired," Scimeca said. "Are we through?"

"One last thing," Reacher said. "Tell Agent Harper what you did in the service."

"I was in armaments proving. We tested new weapons incoming from the manufacturer."

Harper glanced at Reacher, puzzled.

"Okay," he said. "Now we're out of here."

Scimeca led the way through the garage and up into the foyer.

"Good-bye, Reacher," she said, opening the front door. "It was nice to see you again." She turned to Harper. "You should trust him. I still do, you know. Which is one hell of a recommendation."

"She had a roommate," Harper said as they walked down the path. "So your theory is wrong. Looked like she lived alone, but she didn't. We're back to square one."

"Square two, maybe. It's still a subcategory. Nobody targets ninety-one women." They got into the car. "So now what?" he said.

"Back to Quantico."

IT TOOK nearly nine hours of plane-hopping. When they reached D.C., a Bureau driver met them and drove them south into Virginia.

Harper led the way into the building, and they took the elevator four floors underground to the seminar room where Blake, Poulton, and Lamarr were at a table with drifts of paper in front of them. Blake and Poulton looked busy and harassed. Lamarr was as white as the paper in front of her, her eyes jumping with strain.

"Let me guess," Blake said. "Scimeca's box came a couple of months ago, and she was vague about why. No paperwork on it."

"She figured it was for her roommate," Harper said. "She didn't live alone. So the list of eleven doesn't mean anything."

But Blake shook his head. "No, it means what it always meant. Eleven women who look like they live alone to somebody studying the paperwork. We checked with all the others. Eighty calls. None of them knew anything about unexpected cartons. So Reacher's theory that there are eleven women in the loop still holds."

Reacher glanced at him, gratified. And a little surprised.

"I'm sorry for your loss," Reacher said to Lamarr.

"Maybe it could have been avoided," she said. "You know, if you'd cooperated like this from the start."

"So we've got seven out of seven," Blake said after a long silence. "No paperwork on any of the cartons."

"You chasing the delivery companies?" Reacher asked.

"We don't know who they were," Poulton said.

"There aren't many possibilities," Reacher said. "Try them all."

Poulton shrugged. "And ask them what? Out of all the ten zillion packages you delivered in the last two months, can you remember the one we're interested in?"

"You have to try," Reacher said. "Start with Spokane. Remote address like that, middle of nowhere, the driver might recall it."

Blake nodded. "Okay, we'll try it up there. But only there."

"We need to catch this guy," Lamarr said.

"Not going to be easy now," Blake said. "Obviously, we'll keep round-the-clock security on the seven who got the packages, but he'll spot that from a mile away, so we won't catch him at a scene."

"How long are we keeping the security on?" Harper asked.

"Three weeks," Blake said. "Any longer than that it gets crazy."

"So we've got three weeks to find the guy," Poulton said.

Blake laid his hands on the table. "Plan is we spell each other twenty-four hours a day. One of us sleeps while the others work. Julia, you get the first rest period, twelve hours, starting now."

"I don't want it. I need to be involved right now."

Blake looked awkward. "Well, want it or not, you got it. They just flew your sister's body in for the autopsy. And you can't be involved in that. I can't let you."

CHAPTER 6

THE pathology lab at Quantico was no different from others Reacher had seen. It was a large low space, brightly lit, its walls and floor lined with white tiles. In the middle of the room was a large examination table sculpted from gleaming steel and surrounded by a cluster of wheeled carts loaded with tools.

"Gowns, gloves, and overshoes," said Dr. Stavely, Quantico's senior pathologist. He pointed to a steel cupboard filled with folded nylon gowns and boxes of disposable gloves and footwear.

Harper handed them out to Reacher, Blake, and Poulton.

They smelled the paint as soon as the technician pushed the gurney in through the door. The body bag lay on it, bloated and slick and smeared with green.

"Take her to X ray first," Stavely said.

The technician steered the gurney toward a closed room off the side of the lab. He was gone for a moment, and then he stepped back into the lab and eased the lead-lined door closed behind him. There was a distant powerful hum that lasted a second and then stopped. He went back in and came out pushing the gurney again.

"Roll her off," Stavely said. "I want her facedown."

The technician stepped beside him, grasped the nearer edge of the bag with both hands, and lifted it half off the gurney, half onto the table. Then he walked around to the other side, took the other edge, and flipped the bag up and over. It flopped zipper-side down.

"Get the film," Stavely said.

The technician ducked back to the X-ray room and came out with large gray squares of film that mapped Alison Lamarr's body. He handed them to Stavely. Stavely shuffled them like a dealer and held one up to a light box.

"Look at that," he said.

It was a photograph of the midsection. Reacher saw the outlines of ghostly gray bones: ribs, spine, pelvis, with a forearm and a hand lying across them at an angle. And another shape, so bright it shone pure white. Metal. Slim and pointed, about as long as the hand.

"A tool of some sort," Stavely said.

"The others didn't have anything like that," Poulton said.

Stavely clipped the gray photographs in sequence on the light box and studied them. "Her skeleton is relatively undamaged. There are no fresh injuries, so she wasn't killed by blunt trauma."

He hit the switch, and the light behind the X rays went out. He turned back to the examination table. "Okay, let's go to work."

He pulled a hose from a reel mounted on the ceiling and turned a small faucet built into its nozzle. A stream of clear liquid started running. "Acetone," Stavely said. "Got to clear this damn paint."

He used the acetone sluice on the body bag and on the steel table. The chemical stink was overpowering as green liquid eddied sluggishly to the drain below.

Stavely handed the hose to the technician and used a scalpel to slit the bag lengthwise from end to end. He made sideways cuts top and bottom and peeled the rubber back in two long flaps. Alison Lamarr's body was revealed, facedown, slimy with paint. The skin turned greenish white as the paint was washed off. Stavely used his gloved fingertips to peel the crust away from her body, and the acetone ran continuously, rinsing the green stream into the drain.

"Roll her over," Stavely said.

She slid faceup and lay there, her skin greenish white and puckered. Her eyes were open, the lids rimmed with green. A piece of the body bag stuck to her skin from her breasts to her thighs, like an old-fashioned bathing suit, protecting her modesty.

Stavely probed with his hand and found the metal implement under the rubber. "A screwdriver," he said, pulling the object out.

"Matches the others," Reacher said. "In her kitchen drawer."

"She's got scratches on her face," Stavely said, using the hose to wash her face. Her left cheek had five parallel incisions running from the eye to the jaw. "I think they're self-inflicted."

"He made her do it," Reacher said.

"How?" Blake asked.

"I don't know how. But the scratches were probably an afterthought. I think he makes them put the paint in the tub themselves, and the screwdriver is to get the lids off with. If he'd been thinking about the scratches, he'd have made her get a knife from the kitchen as well as the screwdriver."

"But why?" Blake said. "Why make her scratch herself?"

"Anger?" Reacher said. "Punishment? Humiliation? I always wondered why he wasn't more violent."

"But how did he kill her?" Blake asked.

Stavely had the final section of the body bag peeled back and was washing paint away from her midsection with the acetone jet.

"Is it possible you can kill somebody and a pathologist can't tell how?" Reacher asked.

Stavely shook his head. "Not this pathologist," he said. He shut off the acetone stream and let the hose retract into its reel on the ceiling. "Fundamentally, there are two ways to kill a person. Either you stop the heart or you stop the flow of oxygen to the brain. But to do either thing without leaving a mark is a hell of a trick."

"How would you stop the heart?" Blake asked.

"Short of firing a bullet through it?" Stavely said. "Embolism would be the best way. A big bubble of air, injected into the bloodstream, hits the inside of the heart like a stone. It's usually fatal."

"You'd see the hypodermic hole, right?"

"Not on this corpse. The skin is ruined by the paint. But you'd see the damage to the heart. I'll check when I open her up, but I'm not optimistic. They didn't find anything like that on the others."

"What about oxygen to the brain?" Blake asked.

"Suffocation, in layman's terms," Stavely said. "It can be done without leaving much evidence. Classic thing would be a pillow held over the face. Pretty much impossible to prove. But this is a young and strong person. She would have fought like crazy."

Reacher looked away. The room was silent and cold.

"I think she was alive," he said, "when she went in the tub."

"Reasoning?" Stavely asked.

"There was no mess. None at all. What was she, one twenty? One twenty-five? Hell of a dead weight to heave into the tub without making some kind of a mess."

"Maybe he put the paint in afterward," Blake said.

Reacher shook his head. "It would have floated her up, surely."

"We'd need to experiment," Stavely said. "But I agree she died in the tub. The first three, there was no evidence they were touched at all. No bruising, no abrasions, no nothing. My guess is they did whatever they did strictly under their own power."

"Except kill themselves," Harper said.

Stavely nodded. "Obviously, this isn't suicide."

"And they weren't drowned," Blake said.

Stavely nodded again. "The first three weren't. No fluid in the lungs. We'll know about this one soon, but I would bet against it."

"So how the hell did he do it?" Blake muttered.

Stavely stared down at the body. "Right now I have no idea," he said. "Give me a couple of hours, I might find something."

THEY left their gowns, gloves, and overshoes in a tangle by the door and exited the pathology building. They took the long way back to the main building, as if the chill air would rid them of the stink of paint and death. In the seminar room, Julia Lamarr was sitting alone at the table.

"You're supposed to be out of here," Blake said to her.

"Any conclusions?" she asked quietly. "From Stavely?"

Blake shook his head. "Later. You should have gone home."

"I can't go home. I need to be on top of this. We need to work. We've only got three weeks to catch this guy."

"That's plenty of time," Reacher put in. "If we talk about his motive right now."

Lamarr stiffened in her seat, turned to Blake, appealing. "We can't start arguing this all over again."

"We have to," Reacher said.

"Relax, people," Blake called. "Just relax. We've got three weeks, and we're not going to waste any of it arguing."

"You're going to waste all of it if you keep on like this," Reacher said. "You're wrong about his motive, and it's keeping you from looking in the right places."

"His motive is clear," Lamarr said icily. "Do we need this?"

Blake nodded. "Reacher, give us what you've got."

Reacher took a breath. "This is a very smart guy, right? He's committed four homicides—bizarre, elaborate scenarios—and he hasn't left a shred of evidence behind. He's made one mistake, and that was a fairly trivial one because it's not getting us anywhere."

"So?" Blake said. "What's your point?"

"His intelligence is of a specific type. It's practical, efficient, intensely rational. He's a planner. He deals with reality."

"So?" Blake said again.

"So think about it. Any guy who gets in a big tantrum about this harassment issue is a guy who's irrational. And any guy who goes around looking for revenge against victims has got a screw loose. He's not rational. He's not dealing with reality. He's an idiot. Our guy is not motivated by anger at these women. It's not possible. You can't be rational and irrational all at the same time."

"We know what his motive is," Lamarr said. "What else could it be? The target group is too exact for it to be anything else."

"A deranged guy couldn't commit these crimes," Reacher said.

"So what's his real motive, smart guy?" she asked.

Reacher shook his head. "I don't know."

"You question my expertise, and you don't know?"

"It'll be something simple. It always is, right? Something simple and obvious. And lucrative enough to be worth protecting."

"He's protecting something?" Poulton asked.

Reacher nodded. "I think maybe he's eliminating witnesses."

"Witnesses to what?"

"Some kind of a racket, I suppose. Something big."

"Inside the army?" Lamarr asked.

"Obviously," Reacher said.

Blake nodded. "Okay, so what is it?"

There was silence. Then Lamarr buried her face in her hands and started sobbing like her heart was breaking.

"Julia?" Blake called. "You okay?"

She took her hands away from her face. It was contorted and anguished. "I'm sorry," she gasped. "I've made a terrible mistake. Because I think Reacher's right. I screwed up. I missed it. I should have seen it before."

"Don't be sorry," Blake said. "It's the stress."

She stared at him. "My sister died because I wasted all this time. It's my fault. I killed her. Because I was wrong."

"You need to take time out," Blake said.

Reacher watched her. She was collapsed in her chair like she had taken a savage beating. "Maybe later I'll rest," she said. "But first we all work. We've got to think. What racket is he protecting?"

"Give us what you've got, Reacher," Blake said. "You didn't go this far without something on your mind."

"Okay, what was Amy Callan's job?"

"Ordnance clerk," Poulton said.

"Lorraine Stanley's?" Reacher asked.

"Quartermaster sergeant."

Reacher paused. "Alison's?" he asked.

"Infantry close support."

"No, before that."

"Transport battalion," Lamarr said.

Reacher nodded. "Rita Scimeca's job?"

"Weapons proving," Harper put in.

"What's the potential link between them?" Reacher asked.

"You tell me," Blake said.

"What did I take from those guys at the restaurant?"

Blake shrugged. "I don't know. That's Cozo's business, in New York. I know you stole their money."

"They had handguns," Reacher said. "Beretta M-9s, with the serial numbers filed off. What does that mean?"

"They were illegally obtained."

Reacher nodded. "From the army. Beretta M-9s are military issue. Now, if this is some army guy protecting a racket, the racket most likely involves weapons theft, because that's where the money is. And these women were all in a position where they could have witnessed weapons theft. They were transporting and testing and warehousing weapons all day long."

Blake shook his head. "It's too coincidental," he said. "What are the chances all these witnesses would also be harassment victims?"

Lamarr leaned forward. "Think about it laterally. They weren't harassment victims *and* witnesses. They were harassment victims *because* they were witnesses. If you're some army racketeer and you've got a woman in your unit who's not turning a blind eye to what you need her to be turning a blind eye to, what do you do about it? You get rid of her is what. And what's the quickest way to do that? You make her uncomfortable sexually."

There was silence. Then Blake shook his head again. "No, Julia," he said. "It's way too coincidental. On the other hand, what are the chances Reacher just happened to stumble across the back end of the same racket that's killing our women? A million to one."

Lamarr stared at him. "Think, for heaven's sake," she said. "He's not saying he saw the same racket that's killing our women. There must be hundreds of rackets in the army. Right, Reacher?"

Reacher nodded. "Right," he said. "The restaurant thing set me thinking along those lines, is all, in general terms."

There was silence again. Blake colored red. "There are hundreds of rackets?" he said. "So how does that help us? How are we going to find the right one? Needle in a damn haystack."

"And what about the paint?" Poulton asked. "If he's eliminating witnesses, he'd walk up and shoot them in the head with a silenced twenty-two. He wouldn't mess with all this other stuff."

"Exactly," Reacher said. "Your perception of the motive is defined by the manner of the killings. Think about it. If they had all got a silenced twenty-two in the head, you'd have been more open-minded about the motive. Sure, you'd have considered the harassment angle, but you'd have considered other things, too. You'd be all over the army looking for scams. But the guy deflected you by dressing it up with all this bizarre bull. He hid his true motive. He manipulated you because he's smart."

"Julia?" Blake said.

Lamarr said slowly, "It's possible he could be right. I think we should check it out. Maximum effort."

"But he's wrong," Poulton said, riffling through paper. "Caroline Cooke makes him wrong. She was in War Plans at NATO. Never anywhere near weapons or warehouses."

Reacher smiled. "Cooke was an officer candidate. People like that, they send them all over the place first, getting an overview."

The room went quiet again. Then the silence was broken by

Stavely hurrying into the room. He was dressed in a white lab coat, and his wrists were smeared green where the paint had lapped up above his gloves. Lamarr stared at the marks, then closed her eyes and swayed like she was about to faint.

"I want to go home now," she said, standing up.

She walked unsteadily to the door, her eyes fixed on the remnants of her sister's last moments of life daubed across Stavely's stained wrists. Then she wrenched her gaze away and walked out.

"I know how he kills them," the pathologist announced. "Except there's a problem."

"What problem?" Blake asked.

"It's impossible."

"LIKE I told you," Stavely said when he was seated, "you stop the heart or you deny oxygen to the brain. So first I looked at her heart. Completely undamaged. Same as the other three. So the only remaining possibility is that he denied them oxygen."

"But you said there are no signs of strangulation," Blake put in.

Stavely nodded. "There aren't. That's what got me interested." He turned to Reacher. "Did she have a cold when you met her?"

"No," Reacher said. "She seemed pretty healthy to me."

Stavely looked pleased. "There was some very very slight swelling inside the throat. It's what you'd get recovering from a head cold. Normally I'd ignore it completely. But the other three had it, too. That's a little coincidental."

"So what does it mean?" Blake asked.

"It means he pushed something down their throats," Stavely said. "Something soft, which would slip down and then expand a little. Maybe a sponge. Were there sponges in the bathrooms?"

"I didn't see one in Spokane," Reacher said. "Before or after."

Blake looked back to Stavely. "So that's how he's doing it? Sponges down their throats?"

Stavely stared at his big red hands resting on the tabletop. "Sponges, or something similar. Something soft enough not to cause trauma internally but dense enough to block the airway."

Blake nodded slowly. "Okay, so now we know."

Stavely shook his head miserably. "No, we don't, because it's impossible. There's no way you can force something into somebody's mouth against their will without leaving bruises on their cheeks, their jaws. Their lips would be bruised and cut. They'd be biting and scratching and kicking. Traces under their nails. It would be a fight to the death. And there's no evidence of fighting."

"Maybe he drugged them," Blake said. "Made them passive."

Stavely shook his head again. "Nobody was drugged," he said. "Toxicology is absolutely clear, all four cases."

"I told you, this is a smart guy," Reacher said to Blake.

"So what's the answer?"

"I don't know," Reacher said. "But I intend to find out."

"Yeah, like how?"

"Easy. I'll go find the guy, and I'll ask him."

"So what do you need to find the guy?" Blake said.

"Remuneration," Reacher said.

"You find the guy, I'll speak to Deerfield up in New York, get the Petrosian thing forgotten about."

"Plus a fee."

Blake nodded. "I'll think about it. And Harper goes with you, because right now the Petrosian thing ain't forgotten about."

"I can live with that," he said. "I'll need you to set me up with Cozo. I'll start in New York, and I'll need information from him."

"I'll call him. You can see him tonight."

Reacher shook his head. "Tomorrow morning. Tonight I'm going to see Jodie."

FORTY-ONE miles away the colonel was two miles from his office after a ten-mile journey. He had taken the shuttle bus from the Pentagon's parking lot and got off near the Capitol. Then he had hailed a cab and headed back over the river to National Airport's main terminal. His uniform was in a leather one-suiter slung on his shoulder, and he was cruising the ticket counters at the busiest time of day, anonymous in a teeming crush of people.

"I want Portland, Oregon," he said. "Open round-trip, coach."

A clerk entered the code for Portland, and his computer told him he had plenty of availability on the next nonstop.

"Leaves in two hours," he said.

REACHER and Harper got a ride in a Bureau Chevrolet and were at the airport in D.C. before dark. They lined up for the shuttle with the lawyers and the lobbyists. Harper chose seats at the back.

"We can talk back here," she said. "I don't like people listening."

"Talk about what?"

"The scratches on her face," she said. "I need to understand what that's about."

The engines screamed as the plane rolled onto the runway.

"I think it proves my point," Reacher said. "I think it's the single most valuable piece of evidence we've got so far."

"Why?"

He shrugged. "I think it proves the guy is hiding behind appearances. It proves he's pretending. Somewhere he is reviewing his progress and he's thinking, wait, I'm not showing any anger, and so on the next one he tries to show some, but he's not really feeling any, so it comes across as really nothing much at all."

"Why Alison, though? Why did he wait until number four?"

"He's thinking and refining all the time, I suppose."

"Does it make her special in some way? Significant?"

"That's pointy-head stuff. Don't stray into their territory."

Harper nodded. "The motive is probably money."

"Has to be," Reacher said. "Always love or money. And it can't be love, because love makes you crazy, and this guy isn't crazy."

The plane paused for a second, accelerated, and lifted into the air.

"Why did he change the interval?" Harper asked.

Reacher shrugged. "Maybe he just did it for fun. Nothing more disruptive for you guys than a pattern that changes."

"Will it change again?"

"It's over," Reacher said. "The women are guarded, and you'll be making the arrest pretty soon."

"You really want this guy, right?"

"Yes, now I do."

"For Amy Callan? You liked her, didn't you?"

"She was okay. I liked Alison Lamarr better, what I saw of her. But I want this guy for Rita Scimeca."

"She likes you, too," she said. "Did you have an affair?"

He shook his head. "I only met her after she was raped. Because she was raped. She wasn't in any kind of a state to be having affairs. Still isn't, by the look of it. We got very friendly, but it was like a big brother and little sister, always completely platonic."

"And now this guy is setting her back, and it's making you mad."

Reacher nodded. "I feel responsible for Rita. He's messing with her, so he's messing with me."

"And people shouldn't mess with you."

"No, they shouldn't."

"You are kind of arrogant, you know?" she said. "Prosecutor, judge, jury, executioner, all in one? What about the rules?"

He smiled. "Those are the rules," he said. "People mess with me, they find that out pretty damn quick."

Harper shook her head. "We're going to do this according to my rules, okay? We find the guy and arrest him."

"I already agreed to that." He yawned and closed his eyes. "Wake me when we get there."

THIS time there will be guards, so this time will be very difficult. But not impossible. Putting guards into the equation will elevate the whole thing up a little nearer to interesting. A challenge to beat.

So who are the guards? Out here in the sticks, first impression is you're dealing with dumb-ass local cops. But out here in the sticks there aren't enough cops to keep up a twenty-four-hour watch. So they'll be looking for help, and you know for sure that help will come from the FBI. The way you predict it, the locals will take the day, and the Bureau will take the night.

Given the choice, you aren't going to tangle with the Bureau. So you'll take the day, when all that stands between you and her is some *local fat boy in a car full of cheeseburger wrappers and cold coffee. The day is a more elegant solution. Broad daylight. You love the phrase. "The crime was committed in broad daylight," you whisper to yourself.*

Getting past the locals in broad daylight won't be too hard. But you're going to have to invest some time in careful, patient observation. And it won't be hard to do. The place is mountainous, so you just get yourself concealed high up on some peak or knoll. Then you settle in and watch. And you wait.

A BUREAU car met Reacher and Harper at La Guardia, and after the driver had dropped Harper at her uptown hotel, he drove Reacher to Jodie's place.

Reacher let himself into the apartment. Nobody home yet. He lay down on the living-room sofa and closed his eyes. When he woke up, he found her bending over him, kissing his cheek.

"Hey, Reacher," she said softly.

He pulled her down on top of him. She struggled out of her coat and let it fall. The silk lining whispered and sighed. She was in a wool dress with a zipper all the way down her spine. He unzipped it slowly and felt the warmth of her body underneath. Her hands scrabbled at his shirt. He pushed the dress off her shoulders.

She stood up, and her dress fell to the floor. She held out her hand and he took it and she led him to the bedroom. They stumbled out of their clothes as they walked.

She pushed him down onto the bed, with her hands on his shoulders. She was strong, like a gymnast. Urgent and energetic and lithe on top of him. He was lost. They finished filmed in sweat in a tangle of sheets. Her face was tucked into his shoulder, and he could feel the smile against his skin. The shape of her mouth. She was beautiful in a way he couldn't describe. Somehow shot through with energy and passion. Crackling with restless intelligence.

"How was your day?" he asked.

She put her hand flat on his chest and pushed herself up onto her elbow. "Great. They're going to make a partnership offer."

He smiled. "Who to?"

She smiled back. "Guess."

He pretended to think about it. "They'd go for somebody special, right? The smartest, hardest-working associate they got?"

"That's usually what they do."

He nodded. "Congratulations, babe. You deserve it."

She smiled happily and threaded her arms around his neck. "A partner at thirty," she said. "What I always wanted."

"You deserve it," he said again.

"There'll be a party. Will you come?"

"If you want me to. If I won't ruin your image."

"You could buy a suit. Wear your medals."

He was quiet for a spell, thinking about buying a suit. If he did, it would be the first suit he'd ever worn.

"Have you got what you want?" she asked.

He wrapped his arms around her. "Right now?"

"Overall?"

"I want to sell the house," he said. "I can't handle it."

She lay still for a moment. "Okay. Not that you need my permission, but you should think carefully. It's the only asset you've got."

"Not to me. The house is a burden. And I could live the rest of my life on the money I get for it."

She was silent.

"I'm going to sell my car, too," he said.

"I thought you liked it," she said.

"It's okay. For a car. I just don't like owning things."

"How will you get around?"

"Same as I always did—hitch rides, take the bus."

"Okay, sell the car," she said. "But maybe keep the house."

He shook his head, next to hers. "It drives me crazy."

He felt her smile. "You're the only person I know who wants to be homeless," she said. "Most people try real hard to avoid it."

"There's nothing I want more," he said. "Like you want to make partner, I want to be free."

"Free of me, too?" she asked quietly.

"Free of the house," he said. "It's a burden. You're not. The house makes me feel bad. You make me feel good."

"So you'd sell the house, but you'd stick around New York?"

He was quiet for a moment. "I'd maybe move around a little. You're busy a lot of the time. We could make it work."

"We'd drift apart."

He shook his head. "I don't think so."

She was silent.

"It won't change anything," he said.

"So why do it?"

"Because I have to."

THEY fell asleep in each other's arms with a strand of melancholy laced through the afterglow. Morning came, and there was no time for more talk. Jodie left without asking him what he was doing or when he'd be back. He showered and dressed, locked up the apartment, and rode down to the street, where he found Harper waiting for him, leaning on the fender of the Bureau car.

"You okay?" she asked.

"I guess."

"So let's go."

The driver fought traffic twenty blocks uptown and went underground into the same crowded garage Lamarr had brought him to. They used the same elevator in the corner. Rode up to the twenty-first floor. Stepped into the same gray corridor. The driver preceded them like a host and pointed to a door on his left.

"The return of the vigilante," James Cozo said when they entered the room. He closed a file and pushed back from his desk. "So what do you want?"

"Addresses," Reacher said. "For Petrosian's boys."

"The two you put in the hospital? They won't be pleased to see you. You going to hurt them again?"

"Probably."

Cozo nodded. "Suits me, pal."

He pulled a file from a stack and rooted through it. Reversed the open file on the desk and tossed paper and pencil on top of it. "They live together. They're brothers. You copy it down. Don't want my handwriting anywhere near this, literally or metaphorically."

The address was near Fifth, on Sixty-sixth Street.

"Nice neighborhood," Reacher said. "Expensive."

"Lucrative operation." Cozo smiled. "Or it was until you got busy down in Chinatown. Take a taxi," he said to Harper. "And you stay out of the way. No overt Bureau involvement here, okay?"

THEY caught a cab uptown and got out at Sixtieth Street.

"We'll walk the rest of the way," Reacher said.

"We?" Harper said. "Good. I want to stay involved."

"You have to stay involved. I won't get in without you."

The address led them six blocks north to a plain, medium-height apartment building. Air conditioners built through the walls under the windows. No doorman, but clean and well kept.

The lobby was narrow, with a single elevator at the back. They stepped in. Reacher pressed eight.

"You knock on their door," Reacher said. "Get them to open up. They won't if they see me in the peephole."

She nodded, and the elevator stopped on eight. They stepped out on a dull landing and found the apartment they were looking for.

Reacher stood flat against the wall, and Harper knocked on the door. A chain rattled inside, and the door opened a crack.

"Building management," Harper said. "I need to check the air conditioners."

Wrong season, Reacher thought. But Harper was more than six feet tall, had blond hair more than a yard long. The chain rattled again, and the door swung back. Harper stepped inside.

Reacher peeled off the wall and followed her in before the door closed again. The living room held a sofa and two armchairs, and the guys Reacher had last seen leaving the alley behind Mostro's.

"Hey, guys," he said.

They both had broad strips of hospital gauze taped to their foreheads, a little longer and broader than the labels Reacher had stuck there. One of them had bandages on his hands. They were dressed identically in sweaters and golf pants. Without their bulky overcoats they looked smaller. They watched him with fearful eyes.

Reacher felt his aggression drain away. "Sit down," he said.

They sat on the sofa. "Petrosian's dead," the first guy said.

"We know that already," Reacher said back.

The second brother with the bandaged hands was older. The spokesman. "What do you want?" he asked.

"Information. In exchange for not sending you back to the hospital."

"Okay," the guy said.

Harper smiled. "That was easy."

"Things change," the guy said. "Petrosian's dead."

"Where did you get those guns you had?" Reacher said.

"Petrosian gave them to us," the younger brother said.

"Where did he get them from?"

"We don't know," the older brother said.

Reacher smiled. "Well, they came from the army."

"He bought them and gave them to us," the guy said.

Reacher shook his head. "No, he didn't. He sent you to pick them up someplace. Probably in that Mercedes you were using."

The brothers stared at the wall, thinking, like there was a decision to be made. "Who are you?" the older one asked eventually.

"I'm nobody," Reacher said. "Not a cop, not FBI, not anybody. There's an upside and a downside here. You tell me stuff, it stays with me. I'm interested in the army, not you. The downside is, if you don't tell me, I'm not concerned with sending you to court with all kinds of civil rights. I'm concerned with breaking arms and legs."

There was silence.

"New Jersey," the older brother said. "Through the Lincoln Tunnel, there's a roadhouse set back where Route 3 meets the turnpike. Somebody's Bar. Mac something. Like Irish."

"Who did you see in there?"

"Guy called Bob."

"How does it go down?"

"You go in the bar, you find him, you give him the cash, he takes you in the parking lot and gives you the stuff out of his car."

"A Cadillac," the other guy said. "Old DeVille, dark color."

"What stuff?"

"Berettas."

"What time of day?"

"He's always there by evening time, eight o'clock," the younger brother said. "That's what Petrosian told us."

Reacher nodded. "So what does Bob look like?"

"Like you," the older brother said. "Big and mean."

CHAPTER 7

"OKAY, what now?" Harper said as she headed south on Fifth.

In order to preserve some distance between the FBI and Reacher's activities, Cozo had withdrawn the Bureau's sedan and its driver and given Harper the keys to a black Nissan Maxima.

"Bob's not around until eight," Reacher said. "We've got the whole afternoon to kill."

"So what do we do?"

"First we eat," Reacher said. "I missed breakfast."

She drove the Nissan into a parking garage on West Ninth, and they found a bistro with a view of Washington Square Park.

"I told Jodie I'm selling the house," Reacher said.

She looked across at him. "She okay with that?"

He shrugged. "She's worried. I don't see why. It makes me a happier person. How can that worry her?"

"Because it makes you footloose. You need to convince her you're going to stick around even though you're selling the house."

"I told her I might travel a little, too," he said.

She stared at him. "That's not very reassuring, Reacher."

"She travels. She's been to London twice this year. I didn't make a big fuss about it."

"Do you figure you'll be in and out?"

"In and out a little, I guess."

"You'll drift apart."

"That's what she said."

"Well, I'm not surprised."

He said nothing, just drank his coffee and ate his Danish.

"It's make-your-mind-up time," Harper said as she picked up the bill. "On the road or off the road. You can't do both together."

THE *way you predict it, it's going to be a straight half-each split between the local police department and the Bureau, with change-overs at eight in the evening and eight in the morning. You saw it happen at eight in the evening yesterday, so now you're back bright and early to see it happen again at eight this morning.*

You're not dumb enough to rent a room anywhere close by, so you wind your way through the mountains and leave your car on a gravel turnout half a mile from your spot.

You climb up a small hill maybe a hundred feet high. There are scrawny trees all over the place. They have no leaves, but the terrain keeps you concealed. You drop to your knees and shuffle forward to where two giant rocks rest on each other, giving a wonderful view of Lieutenant Rita Scimeca's house through the triangular gap between them. The Bureau car is parked outside. A Buick, dark blue. One agent in it. You use your field glasses. The guy is still awake. He's not looking around much. Just staring forward, bored out of his skull.

The house has a wire fence around the perimeter of the yard. There's an opening onto a short driveway. A single garage door stands at the end of it, under the end of the front porch. The Bureau car is parked at the sidewalk right across the driveway opening, facing down the rise. That puts the driver's line of vision directly in line with the mouth of the path. Intelligent positioning. If you walk up the hill to the house, he sees you coming all the way. You come on him from behind, he maybe spots you in his mirror, and he sees you for certain as soon as you walk up the looping path.

A black-and-white Crown Victoria enters the road, stops flank to flank with the Buick. You don't see it, but you know greetings are being exchanged. Information is being passed on.

The black-and-white moves up the hill and turns in the road. The Buick moves away down the hill. The black-and-white rolls forward and stops. Exactly where the Buick was, inch for inch. The cop turns his head to the right and gets exactly the same view of the path the Bureau guy had. Maybe not such a dumb-ass after all.

HARPER wanted to see the city. Reacher walked her south through Washington Square Park and down to the World Trade Center. It was about a mile and three quarters. They sauntered slowly. The sky was bright, and the city was teeming.

"We could go up to the restaurant," Reacher said. "Bureau could buy me lunch."

"I just bought you lunch," Harper said.

"No, that was a late breakfast."

They checked their coats in the lobby and rode up to the top of the building. Harper showed her badge, and they got a table for two right at a window facing directly back up West Broadway.

The view was awesome. Far below them the city was khaki in the fall light. Packed, intricate, infinitely busy.

"Bob's out there someplace," she said. "He's not our guy, right?"

"He's small-time," Reacher said. "Selling out of the trunk of his car? Not enough at stake to make it worth killing people."

"So how can he help us?"

"He can name names. He's got suppliers, and he knows who the other players are. He'll point us in a new direction."

YOU wait and you watch her house. You keep the field glasses tight to your eyes and you watch. By now you're sure the cop in the black-and-white is a permanent fixture. He eats in his car, he uses her bathroom from time to time, and that's it.

Either he has to be moved or you have to go in right past him. What would it take to get him out of there? A major automobile accident at the crossroads. But that would be hard to stage.

Maybe a bomb threat. But where? At the station house? That would be no good. The cop would be told to stay where he was until it was checked out. And a bomb threat would mean a phone call. Where from? Calls can be traced. And there are no pay phones near where you're crouched. You can't use your mobile, because eventually the call would appear on your bill.

But the more you think about it, the more your strategy centers around the phone. There's one person you can safely let hear your voice. But it's a geometric problem. Four-dimensional. Time and space. You have to call from right here, in the open, within sight of the house, but you can't use your mobile. Impasse.

REACHER drove out of the city that evening. Harper preferred not to in the dark and the rush hour. And rush hour was bad. Traffic was slow up the spine of Manhattan and jammed at the entrance to the tunnel. They inched forward deep under the Hudson River.

Eventually they were on Route 3, angling north toward the New Jersey Turnpike. There were billboards and neon signs left and right.

The roadhouse they were looking for was labeled with a beer company's neon sign that said MACSTIOPHAN'S, which Reacher understood in Gaelic meant Stevenson's. He parked the Nissan near the door, slid out, and looked around.

"No Cadillac DeVille," he said. "He's not here yet."

"We're a little early," Harper said. "I guess we'll wait."

"You can wait out here," he said. "If you prefer."

She shook her head. "I've been in worse places."

It was hard for Reacher to imagine where and when. The outer door led to a lobby with a sisal mat worn smooth with use. The inner door led to a dark space full of the stink of beer and smoke.

There were eight customers in the room, with glasses of beer in front of them. All of them were men; none of them was a soldier.

Reacher stepped up to the bar and rolled a stool out for Harper.

"What's on draft?" he asked the bartender.

The guy was maybe fifty, gray-faced, paunchy.

"Haven't seen you in here before," he said.

Harper smiled. "No. We're new customers."

"What do you want?" the guy said.

"Two beers," Reacher said.

"Apart from that. People like you don't come in a place like mine without wanting something."

"We're waiting for Bob," Harper said.

"Bob who?"

"Bob with the old Cadillac DeVille," Reacher explained. "Bob from the army, comes in here eight o'clock every night."

The guy smiled. Yellow teeth, some of them missing. "Well, you've got a long wait, then," he said. He placed two beers on the bar.

Harper pulled out her wallet and dropped a ten-dollar bill between the glasses. "Keep the change. So why the long wait for Bob?"

The guy slid the ten into his pocket. "Because Bob's in jail."

"What for?"

"Some army thing. I don't know the details. The Military Police came in and grabbed him right here. Couple of months ago."

THEY left the beer untouched on the bar and headed back to the parking lot, unlocked the Nissan, and slid inside.

"Couple of months is no good," Harper said. "Puts him right outside the picture."

"He was never in the picture, but we'll go talk to him anyway."

"How can we do that? He's in the army system somewhere."

He looked at her. "I was a military policeman for thirteen years. If I can't find him, who can? Regional MP HQ for this region is Fort Armstrong, outside of Trenton, less than two hours away."

"Check it first." She opened her bag, came out with a cellular phone the size of a cigarette pack. "Use my mobile," she said.

YOU'RE sitting in the airport food court watching a woman of about twenty-three or twenty-four. She's dressed comfortably, like she's got a long flight ahead, and she's leaning back in her chair with her head tilted left and her phone trapped between her shoulder and chin. She's smiling as she talks. This is a lazy chat with a friend.

*On the floor near her feet is her carry-on bag, a backpack, all cov-
ered in little loops and catches and zippers. It's clearly so complicated
to close that she's left it gaping open. She wraps up the chat, flips her
phone closed, and drops it in her backpack. Picks up her handbag and
goes off to get coffee.*

*You're on your feet instantly, car keys in your hand. You hustle
straight across the court, swinging the keys, looking busy. She's in
line, about to be served. You drop your keys. As you bend to retrieve
them, your hand skims her backpack. You come back up with the keys
and the phone together. The keys go back in your pocket. The phone
stays in your hand. Nothing more ordinary than somebody walking
through an airport lounge holding a mobile. You smile. Now the crucial call is going to end up on someone else's bill.*

THE phone call to the Fort Armstrong duty officer revealed nothing, but the guy's evasions were voiced in such a way that Reacher
took them to be confirmation.

"He's there," he said to Harper. "I guarantee it."

They pulled off into the next service area to get gas and a map.

"We're on the wrong road," Reacher said, looking at the unfolded map. "Route 1 would be better."

"Okay, next exit," Harper said, craning over.

She used her finger to trace down Route 1, found Fort Armstrong. "Close to Fort Dix," she said. "Where we were before."

Less than two hours later they drew up at a vehicle barrier outside a two-story guardhouse. A sentry peered through the window
and came out to the car. Reacher buzzed his window down.

"You the guy who called the captain?" the sentry asked.

Reacher nodded. The sentry grinned.

"He figured you might show up," he said. "Go ahead in."

He stepped back into the guardhouse, and the barrier came up.
Reacher drove toward a low symmetrical building with white-
washed steps leading up to double doors in the center.

"Duty office," Reacher said.

The doors opened, and a man in uniform stepped out.

"That was me, about a million years ago," Reacher muttered.

The captain waited at the top of the steps, sheltered from the drizzle. He was a head shorter than Reacher, but he was broad and looked fit. His uniform jacket was buttoned, but his face looked open enough. Reacher slid out of the Nissan and walked around the hood. Harper joined him at the foot of the steps.

"Come in out of the rain," the captain called. His accent was East Coast urban. Reacher went up the steps first. Harper followed.

"This is Lisa Harper," Reacher said. "She's with the FBI."

"Pleased to meet you," the captain said. "I'm John Leighton."

The three of them shook hands, and Leighton led them along a corridor to his office. Every surface was overloaded with paper.

"We'll try not to take up too much of your time," Reacher began.

"Don't worry. I called around after you called me, naturally. Friend of a friend said I should push the boat out. So how can I help?" Leighton said, gesturing for them to sit down.

Harper ran through it all from the beginning. Leighton listened attentively, interrupting here and there.

"I know about the women," he said. "We heard."

She finished with Reacher's smoke-screen theory, the possible army thefts, and the trail that led from Petrosian's boys in New York to Bob in New Jersey.

"His name is Bob McGuire," Leighton said. "Quartermaster sergeant. But he's not your guy. He's too dumb."

"We figured that," Harper said. "Feeling was he could name names, maybe lead us to a bigger fish. Somebody doing enough business to make it worth killing witnesses."

Leighton nodded. "Theoretically, there might be such a person."

"You got a name?"

Leighton shook his head. "Now we're computerized, we can keep track of everything better than we used to. For instance, we know how many Beretta M-9s have been delivered, we know how many have been legitimately issued, and we know how many we got in store. If those numbers didn't add up, we'd be worrying."

"So do the numbers add up?"

"They do now. That's for damn sure. Nobody's stolen an army Beretta M-9 in the last year and a half."

"What was McGuire doing two months ago?" Reacher asked.

"Selling out the last of his stockpile. He'd been thieving ten years, at least. Computer analysis made it obvious. Him, and a couple dozen others in different locations. We were leaking weapons like crazy. We put procedures in place to dry up the stealing, and we arrested a couple dozen guys. The leakage stopped."

"You got them all?" Harper asked.

Leighton nodded. "All of them. Big push, worldwide. There weren't that many. Computers did the trick."

"Well, there goes that theory," Harper said.

"Maybe not," Leighton replied. "We've got a theory of our own. Like I told you, we've got a couple dozen guys waiting for trial. But the way we picked them up was, we sent undercover guys in to buy the stuff. Entrapment. McGuire, for instance, he sold a couple of Berettas to a couple of lieutenants in a New Jersey bar."

"We were just there," Harper said. "MacStiophan's."

"Right," Leighton said. "Our guys bought two M-9s out of the trunk of his car, two hundred bucks apiece. So we haul McGuire in and start looking for the money. We find about a half of it, either in bank accounts or in the form of stuff he's bought."

"So?" Reacher said.

"So nothing, not right then. But we're pooling information, and the story is pretty much the same everywhere. All these guy have got about a half of their money missing."

"Enter the theoretical big fish," Reacher muttered.

Leighton nodded. "Exactly. How else to explain it? We started to figure some big guy in the shadows, maybe organizing everything, offering protection in exchange for half the profit."

"Or half the guns," Reacher said.

"Right," Leighton said. "A scam inside a scam."

"Looks good from our point of view," Harper said. "Guy like that, he's smart and capable. He has to take care of problems in various locations. Could explain why he's interested in so many different women. Not because all the women knew him, but because maybe each one of them knew one of his clients. Who is he?"

Leighton rubbed his eyes. "We have no idea. We've got two dozen guys, all of them with their mouths shut tight. We figure the big guy's really put the frighteners on."

There was silence in Leighton's office.

"Well, we need his name, I guess," Reacher said. "I should go talk to McGuire for you."

Leighton smiled. "I figured you'd say that. I was all set to say no, it's improper. But you know what? I changed my mind."

THE cellblock was underground, like it always is in a regional HQ. Leighton used an old-fashioned bellpull outside the iron door, and it opened after a second to reveal a bright hallway with a huge master sergeant standing in it. Leighton led them in out of the rain.

There was a cubbyhole office on the right, with a big desk piled high with video recorders taping flickering images from twelve cells, eleven of which were empty. In the twelfth there was a humped shape under a blanket on the bed.

"Quiet night at the Hilton," Reacher said.

Leighton nodded. "Right now McGuire's our only guest."

"The video recording is a problem," Reacher said.

"Always breaking down, though," Leighton said. He bent over the desk, touched a switch. The recorders stopped humming. "See? Very unreliable system."

"It'll take a couple hours to fix," the sergeant said. "At least."

The sergeant took a hoop of keys off a wooden board and moved to the inside door, unlocked it, and swung it back. Reacher stepped through, and the sergeant locked the door again behind him. Pointed to a staircase. "After you."

The staircase led to another locked door at the bottom. Then a lobby with three locked doors to three blocks of cells. The sergeant unlocked the middle door, flipped a switch, and fluorescent light flooded a bright white area forty feet by twenty. There was an access zone the length of the block and about a third of its depth. The rest of the space was divided into four cells. Three of the cells were empty. In the fourth McGuire sat up, surprised by the light.

"Visitor for you," the sergeant called. There were two tall wooden stools in the corner of the access zone. The sergeant carried the nearer one over and placed it in front of McGuire's cell, walked back, and sat on the other. Reacher ignored the stool and stood gazing silently through the bars. McGuire was pushing his blanket aside and swinging his feet to the floor. He was wearing an olive undershirt and olive shorts. He was more than six feet tall, more than two hundred pounds. Heavily muscled, a thick neck, big arms, big legs. Thinning hair cropped close, small eyes, a couple of tattoos.

"Hell are you?" McGuire said. His deep voice matched his bulk. Reacher made no reply. He walked over to the master sergeant and whispered in his ear. The guy nodded, stood up, handed Reacher the hoop of keys, went out through the door, and closed it behind him. Reacher walked back to McGuire's cell.

"What do you want?" McGuire said.

"I want proof of exactly how dumb you really are."

McGuire's eyes narrowed. "Easy for you to talk like that," he said. "Standing on the other side of these bars."

Reacher took a pace forward. "Want me to open the cell gate? Even things up a little? Keys are right here."

McGuire's eyes narrowed more. "Yeah, open the gate."

Reacher unlocked the gate, swung it open. McGuire stood still. Reacher walked away, hung the hoop of keys on the doorknob.

"Sit down," he said, gesturing. "I left the stool there for you."

McGuire came out of the cell. "What do you want?" he said.

"It's complicated," Reacher replied. "You're going to have to juggle a number of factors."

"What factors?" McGuire asked blankly.

"First factor is, I'm unofficial, okay?" Reacher said. "It means I'm not an army cop, I'm not a civilian cop. In fact I'm not anything at all. So if I leave you walking on crutches, there's nothing anybody can do to me. And we got no witnesses in here. Second factor is, whatever the big guy says he'll do to you, I can do worse."

"What big guy?"

Reacher smiled. "Now it gets sophisticated. Third factor is, if you give me the guy's name, he goes away somewhere else, forever. You give me his name, he can't get to you. Not ever, understand?"

"What name? What guy?"

"The guy you were paying off with half your take."

"No such guy."

Reacher shook his head. "We're past that stage now, okay? We know there's such a guy. So don't make me smack you around before we even get to the important part."

McGuire tensed up, breathed hard, then quieted down.

"So concentrate," Reacher said. "What you need to understand is, if you rat him out, it actually makes you safe, the rest of your life, because people are looking at him for a bunch of things a whole lot worse than ripping off the army."

"What's he done?" McGuire asked.

Reacher smiled. So the guy exists.

"He killed four women. You give me his name, they'll put him away forever. Nobody will ask him about anything else."

McGuire was silent. Thinking about it. It wasn't the speediest process Reacher had ever seen.

"Last factor," Reacher said gently. "You need to understand sooner or later you'll tell me. You can tell me now, or you can tell me in a half hour, right after I've broken your arms and legs."

"You ain't going to do nothing," McGuire said.

Reacher turned and picked up the wooden stool, flipped it upside down, and held it chest-high with his hands around two of the legs. Took a firm backhand grip and snapped his elbows back. The legs tore away from the rungs. The rungs clattered to the floor. He reversed the stool, held the seat in his left hand, splintered a leg free with his right, dropped the wreckage, and retained the leg. It was about the size and weight of a baseball bat.

"Now you do the same," he said.

McGuire turned over his stool and grasped the legs. His muscles bunched and the tattoos swelled, but he got nowhere.

"Too bad," Reacher said. "I tried to make it fair."

"He was Special Forces," McGuire said. "He's real tough."

"Doesn't matter," Reacher said. "He resists, the FBI will shoot him down. End of problem."

McGuire said nothing.

Reacher swung the leg of the stool. "Left or right?" he asked. "Which arm you want me to break first?"

"LaSalle Kruger," McGuire said. "Supply battalion CO. He's a colonel."

STEALING *the phone was candy from a baby, but the reconnaissance is a bitch. Timing it right is the first priority. You need to wait for full dark, the daytime cop's final hour. Because somebody's last hour is always better than somebody else's first hour. Attention will have waned. Boredom will have set in.*

So your window extends to about forty minutes, say seven to seven forty. You drive back from the airport and you approach on the through road. You drive through the junction three streets from her house. You stop at a hiker's parking area two hundred yards farther north. You get out of your car and work your way west and north through lightly wooded terrain. You're about level with your first position, but on the other side of her house, behind it, not in front.

You ease through the brush and come out at her fence. Stand motionless in the dark and observe. Drapes are drawn. You can hear a piano playing, very faintly. The house is built into the hillside, at right angles to the street. Facing you is the side wall, dotted with windows. No doors. You ease along the fence and check the back of the house. No doors there either. The only way in is the front door on the porch or the garage door facing the street. Not ideal, but you've planned for it. You've planned for every contingency.

"OKAY, Colonel Kruger," Leighton said. "We're onto you now."

They were back in the duty office. Leighton was scrolling through a menu on his computer screen, and Reacher and Harper were sitting side by side in front of his desk.

"Okay, he's in the personnel listings," Leighton said.

"Has he been in trouble?" Reacher asked.

"Can't tell yet. You think he'll have an MP record?"

"Something happened," Reacher said. "Ex–Special Forces, and now he's working supply? What's that about?"

"It needs explaining. Could be disciplinary, I guess. But I'm afraid I can't let you look at our computer stuff. You know how it is, don't you? Anyway, this could take all night."

"Could you trace some missing camouflage paint?" Harper said.

"Maybe," Leighton said. "Theoretically, I guess."

"Eleven women on his list, so look for about three hundred gallons. Put Kruger together with the paint, that would do it for me. And dates," she said. "Find out if he was off-duty when the women were killed. And match the locations. Confirm there were thefts where the women served. Prove they saw something."

Leighton exited the personnel listings and clicked on another menu. Then he paused. "The army is going to just love me, right? Kruger's our guy, and I'm busting my butt all night so we can give him away to the Bureau."

"I'm sorry," she said. "But the jurisdiction issue is clear, isn't it? Homicide beats theft."

Leighton nodded, suddenly somber. "Like scissors beats paper."

ONCE you've seen enough of the house, you step away from the fence and duck into the brush. You work your way back to the car in the dark, slide in, and head back down through the crossroads. You've got about twenty minutes to complete part two of your task. Two miles west of the junction there's an old-fashioned one-story shopping mall, shaped like a squared-off letter C. A supermarket in the middle like a keystone, small single-unit stores spreading either side of it. You pull into the parking lot at the far end and you nose along, looking. But you don't like it. Every storefront has a direct view of the lot. So you drive around behind the arm of the C, and you smile. There's a single row of overspill parking back there, facing plain painted delivery doors in the back walls of the stores. It's perfect.

You drive back into the main lot and you park up alongside a small group of other vehicles. You wait and watch for ten minutes, and then you see the Bureau Buick heading by, reporting for duty.

"Have a nice night," you whisper.

LEIGHTON recommended a motel a mile down Route 1 toward Trenton. It was cheap, clean, and the only place for miles around. Harper drove, and they found it easily enough.

"Number twelve is a nice double," the desk clerk said.

Harper nodded. "Okay, we'll take it," she said.

"We will?" Reacher said. "A double?"

"Talk about it later," she said.

She paid cash, and the desk guy handed over a key.

"What?" she said as they walked to the room. "It's not like we're going to sleep, is it? We're just waiting for Leighton to call. May as well do that in here as in the car."

He just shrugged. She unlocked the door, and they went inside.

It was a standard motel room. There were two chairs and a table at the far end by a window. Reacher sat in the right-hand chair, put his elbows on the table and his head in his hands. Kept very still.

"What is it?" Harper asked. "Something's on your mind."

He looked straight at her. "Truth is, I don't especially want to be alone in a room with you and a bed."

She smiled happily, mischievously. "Tempted?"

"I'm only human."

"So am I," she said. "If I can control myself, I'm sure you can."

He said nothing.

"I'm going to take a shower."

"Great," he muttered.

IT'S a standard motel room, like a thousand you've seen coast to coast. You hang your coat in the closet, but you keep your gloves on. No need to leave fingerprints all over the place.

You walk through the room and sit in one of the two chairs. You lean back, close your eyes, and think. It has to be tomorrow. You plan the timing by working backward. You need dark before you can get out. But you want the daytime cop to find her. You accept that's just a whim, but hey, if you can't brighten things up with a little whimsy, what kind of life is that? So you need to be out after dark, but before the cop's last bathroom break. Somewhere around five thirty.

Okay, five thirty. Twilight, but it's acceptable. You're going to allow a half hour for this one. So you need to be inside and started by five. You think it through from her point of view, and it's clear you need to make the phone call at about two o'clock.

HARPER came out of the bathroom wearing nothing but a towel. Her face was scrubbed, and her hair was wet. Cornflower-blue eyes, white teeth. Without makeup she looked about fourteen, except she was more than six feet tall. And that kind of height made a standard-issue motel towel seriously deficient in terms of length.

"I'd better call Blake," she said. "I should really check in."

"Keep it vague, okay? Quantico gets involved at this point, they'll pull Leighton off. He's only a captain. They'll haul in some two-star ass, and then we'll never get near the facts for the bull. Just say we're seeing some guy tomorrow who might have something."

"I'll be careful," she said. She got her phone out of her bag.

"I guess I'll shower, too," he said.

She smiled. "Enjoy. I won't come in, I promise."

He went into the bathroom and closed the door. Harper's clothes were hanging from the hook on the back. The underwear was white and lacy. He thought about setting the shower icy cold, but decided to rely on willpower. So he set it hot and stripped off his clothes. He stood under the shower for a long time, trying to relax. Then he gave up and turned the handle to cold. He held it there, gasping. One minute. Two. He shut it off and groped for a towel.

She knocked on the door. "Are you done? I need my clothes."

He lifted them off the hook, opened the door a crack, and passed them through. He toweled himself dry and dressed, then rattled the door handle and came out. She was standing by the bed, wearing some of her clothes. The rest of them were folded over the back of the dresser chair. Her hair was combed back. Her phone was closed, lying next to the ice bucket.

"What did you tell him?"

"That we're meeting some guy in the morning, nothing specific."

She was wearing the shirt, but the bra and tie were draped over the chair. So were the suit pants. Her legs were lean and long.

"He have anything to say?"

"Poulton's in Spokane," she said. "Hertz did come up with a real short rental, Spokane Airport, the exact day Alison died, in and out inside about two hours. But it just turned out to be some woman on business. The UPS guy is coming through with stuff, though. He's pulling the records."

"Won't say LaSalle Kruger on the paperwork, that's for sure."

She sat down on the edge of the bed, her back to him. "Probably not, but that doesn't matter anymore, does it? We found him. We should celebrate," she said.

Reacher propped the pillows on the far side of the bed, sat down, and leaned back against them, looking up at the ceiling.

She turned to face him. The first two buttons on her shirt were undone. "It's Jodie, isn't it?" she said.

He nodded. "Of course it is."

"Wasn't for her, you'd want to, right?"

"I do want to," he said. "But I won't, because of her."

She smiled. "I like that in a guy, I guess. Steadfastness."

He said nothing. She sighed, just a tiny sound. She moved away, just an inch. But enough to ease the crisis.

"So you're going to stick around New York," she said.

He nodded again. "That's the plan."

"She'll be angry about the house. Her father willed it to you."

"She might be," he said. "But she'll have to deal with it. The way I see it, he left me a choice. The house, or the money I'd get for it. He knew what I was like. He wouldn't be surprised or upset."

The room went quiet. "I still feel like celebrating. Celebration kiss," she whispered. "Nothing more, I promise."

He looked at her, reached around with his left arm, and pulled her close. Kissed her on the lips. She tilted her head and opened her mouth. He felt her tongue deep in his mouth, urgent. It felt good. He opened his eyes and saw hers, too close to focus on. They were shut tight. He let her go and pulled away, full of guilt.

"Something I need to tell you," he said.

She was breathless. "What?"

"I'm not being straight with you," he said.

"How not?"

"I don't think Kruger's our guy. He's Leighton's guy," Reacher said. "But I don't think he's ours. I really never did."

"What? You always did. This was your theory, Reacher."

He shrugged. "I made it up. I just wanted some kind of a plausible excuse to get me out of Quantico. To give myself time to think. And I wanted to see who would support it and who would oppose it. I wanted to see who really wants this thing solved."

"I don't believe this," she said. "We all want it solved."

There was pounding at the door. Loud, insistent. He stood up and walked toward the door. "Okay," he called. "I'm coming."

The pounding stopped. He opened the door. Leighton was standing on the stoop, his jacket open, raindrops on the shoulders.

"Kruger's our guy," he said, pushing past into the room. Saw Harper buttoning her shirt. "Excuse me," he said, surprised.

"It's hot in here," she said, looking away.

"He's our guy," he went on. "Everything fits like a glove."

Harper's mobile started ringing. Leighton paused, gestured I can wait. Harper flipped the phone open and listened. Reacher watched the color drain out of her face. She closed the phone.

"We're recalled to Quantico," she said. "They got Caroline Cooke's full record. You were right. She was all over the place, but she was never anywhere near weapons. Not ever, not for a minute."

"That's what I'm here to tell you," Leighton said. "Kruger's our guy, but he isn't yours."

Leighton sat down at the table. "First thing, there was no list," he said, looking at Harper. "You asked me to check thefts of paint where the women worked, so I needed a list of the women to do that, so I tried to find one, but I couldn't. So I made some calls, and what happened was when your people came to us a month ago, we had to generate a list from scratch. It was a pain, trawling through all the records. So some guy had a bright idea, took a shortcut, called one of the women herself on some fake pretext. We think it was actually Alison Lamarr, and she supplied the list. Seems they'd set up a big support group among themselves."

"Scimeca called them her sisters," Reacher said. "Remember that? She said four of her sisters are dead."

"Then Kruger's records started coming in, and the dates and places didn't match. Not even close." Leighton paused for breath. "So I checked out why he went from Special Forces to supply battalion. He was a top boy in the Gulf. Big star, a major. They were out in the desert, behind the lines, looking for mobile Scud launchers; small unit, bad radio. And when they start the artillery barrage, Kruger's unit gets all chewed up under friendly fire. Kruger was seriously hurt. So they gave him the promotion all the way up to colonel and stuck him somewhere his injuries wouldn't disqualify him, hence the desk job in supply. My guess is he started running the rackets as a kind of revenge or something. You know, against the army. The guy lost both his legs. He's in a wheelchair. No way he's running up and down any stairs to any bathrooms."

Harper stared at the wall. "Okay," she said. "Bad idea."

"I'm afraid so. And you need to hear about the paint, too. I started a search for reports about missing camo green, and the only definitive thing was hidden in a closed-access file. A theft of a hundred and ten three-gallon cans. They fingered a supply sergeant in Utah."

"Who was he?"

"She," Leighton said. "She was Sergeant Lorraine Stanley."

Total silence.

"That's impossible," Harper said. "She was one of the victims."

Leighton shook his head. "I called Utah. Spoke to the investigating officer. He says it was Stanley, no doubt about it. They didn't proceed against her, because she'd just come off the harassment thing not long before. They just watched her until she quit."

"One victim stole the paint?" Reacher said. "And another provided the list of names?"

"That's how it was, I promise you."

REACHER drove fast, and it took a fraction under three hours from the outskirts of Trenton all the way back to Quantico.

Reacher killed the motor and the lights and looked at Harper. They slid out of the car. Inside the building it was quiet. They went down in the elevator to Blake's underground office, found him sitting at his desk, staring at a sheet of paper, his face totally blank.

"Fax in from UPS," he said gently. He looked beaten, confused. "Guess who sent the paint to Alison Lamarr and all the others?"

"Lorraine Stanley," Reacher said.

Blake nodded. "Correct. From an address in Utah that turned out to be a self-storage facility. And guess what else? She sent one of the cartons to herself, but she didn't even have her own place when she put the paint in the storage facility. She waited until she was settled, then went back up to Utah and dispatched it all. What do you make of that?"

"I don't know," Reacher said.

"And Poulton just called from Spokane. He just got through interviewing the UPS driver. The guy remembers the delivery pretty well. Alison was there when he called. She was listening to the ball game, radio on in the kitchen. She asked him inside, gave him coffee; they heard the grand slam together. A little hollering, another coffee, he tells her he's got a big heavy box for her."

"And?"

"And she says 'oh good,' and clears a space for it in the garage. He brings it in, dumps it, and she's all smiles about it."

"Like she was expecting it?"

Blake nodded. "That was the guy's impression. Then she tears off the Documents Enclosed thing and carries it back to the kitchen. He follows, to finish up his coffee. She pulls the delivery note out of the plastic, shreds it up into small pieces, and dumps them in the trash, along with the plastic."

"So what's your take?"

Blake shook his head. "I have no idea."

"I apologize," Reacher said. "My theory led us nowhere."

Blake made a face. "It was worth a try."

"Is Lamarr around? I should apologize to her, too."

Blake shook his head. "She's at home. Hasn't been back. Says she's a wreck, and she's right. Can't blame her."

"A lot of stress. She should get away."

"Where to?" Blake sighed. "She won't get on a damn plane. And I don't want her driving anyplace, the state she's in." Then his eyes hardened. "I'm going to look for another consultant. When I find one, you're out of here. You're getting nowhere. You'll have to take your chances with the New York people."

"Okay," Reacher said.

Harper took her cue and led Reacher out of the office, into the elevator, up to the third floor. They walked to the familiar door.

"Why was she expecting it?" Harper said. "Why was Alison expecting the box of paint, when all the others weren't?"

He shrugged. "I don't know."

Harper opened his door. "Okay, good night," she said.

"You mad at me?"

"You wasted thirty-six hours."

"No, I invested thirty-six hours."

"In what?"

"I don't know yet."

"You're a weird guy."

"So people say." He kissed her on the cheek and stepped into his room. She locked the door and walked back to the elevator.

He walked to the bed and lay down, still in his coat. It was three in the morning, too late to call Jodie. He stared up at the ceiling. Tried to see Jodie up there, but all he saw instead were Lisa Harper and Rita Scimeca. He thought about Scimeca's face, the hurt in her eyes. Her rebuilt life out there in Oregon—the flowers, the piano, the buttoned-up defensive domesticity. He closed his eyes and then opened them and stared hard at the white paint above him. He thought about Harper's body, the way she moved, the guileless smile, her frank engaging stare. Rolled onto his elbow and picked up the phone. Dialed Harper's cell-phone number.

When she answered, he said, "I want to see you now."

HARPER didn't knock, just used her key and walked right in. She was in shirtsleeves. "What did you want?"

"I want to ask you a question," he said. "What would have happened if we'd already known about the paint delivery and we'd asked Alison Lamarr about it? What would she have said?"

"The same as the UPS guy, presumably."

"No," Reacher said. "She would have lied to us."

"She would? Why?"

"Because they're all lying to us, Harper. We've spoken to seven women, and they all lied to us. Vague stories about roommates and mistakes? All crap. If we'd got to Alison before, she'd have given us the same kind of a story."

"How do you know?"

"Because Rita Scimeca was lying to us. I just figured that out. She didn't have any roommate. It doesn't fit. You saw how she lives. Everything so neat and clean and polished. Obsessive. Living like that, she couldn't stand anybody else in her house. And she didn't need a roommate for money. You saw her big car. And that piano. You know how much a grand piano costs?"

"So what are you saying?"

"I'm saying she was expecting the delivery, just like Alison was. Just like they all were. The cartons came, they all said 'Oh good,' just like Alison did. Then they stored the cartons."

"It's not possible. Why would they?"

"Because the guy has got some kind of a hold over them," Reacher said. "He forced Alison to give him their own list of names; he forced Lorraine Stanley to steal the paint and send it out at the right time; he forced each one of them to accept the delivery and to destroy the delivery notes immediately. And he's forcing them to be happy about it, too."

Harper stared at him. "But how? How would he do all that?"

"I don't know," Reacher said.

"Blackmail?" she said. "Threats? Fear?"

"I don't know. They weren't an especially fearful bunch."

"So what do you want me to do?" Harper asked.

"Just keep on thinking, I guess. Blake won't listen to me anymore. I've exhausted my credibility with him."

She sat down on the bed next to him. He was looking at her.

"What?" she said.

"Is the camera on?"

She shook her head. "They gave up on that. Why?"

"Because I want to kiss you again."

She blushed. "Just a kiss?"

He nodded.

"Well, okay, I guess," she said.

She turned to him, and he took her in his arms and kissed her. She moved her head like she had before, pressed harder, and put her tongue into his mouth. He moved his hand down to her waist. She kissed harder. Then she put her hand on his chest and pushed herself away. "We should stop now," she said.

"I guess."

She stood up, tossed her hair behind her shoulders.

"I'm out of here," she said. "I'll see you tomorrow."

When she had gone, he lay back on the bed. Didn't sleep, just thought about obedience and acquiescence, means, motives, and opportunities. And truth and lies.

SHE came back at eight in the morning, showered and glowing and wearing a different suit. She looked full of energy. He was tired and crumpled, but he was standing inside the door with his coat buttoned, waiting for her, his heart hammering with urgency.

"Let's go," he said. "Right now."

Blake was in his office, at his desk, same as he had been before.

"Today you work the files again, Reacher," Blake said.

"No. I need to get to Portland. Will you lend me the plane?"

"The plane?" Blake repeated. "Are you crazy? Not in a million years."

"Okay," Reacher said. He moved to the door, took a last look at the office, and stepped into the corridor.

Harper crowded past him. "Why Portland?" she asked.

He looked at her. "Truth, and lies."

"What does that mean? What the hell's going on?"

"No. Right now it's just a house of cards. You'd blow it down. Anybody would blow it down. You need to see it for yourself. Hell, I need to see it for myself. But I want you there for the arrest."

"What arrest? Just tell me."

He shook his head again. "Where's your car?"

"In the lot."

"So let's go."

CHAPTER 8

REVEILLE had been 0600 the whole of Rita Scimeca's service career, and she stuck to the habit in her new civilian life. She slept six hours out of twenty-four, midnight until six in the morning, a quarter of her life. Then she got up to face the other three quarters.

Today she was scheduled to work on Bach. She was trying to perfect the three-part inventions. She loved the way they moved forward, on and on, inescapably logical, until they ended up back where they started. But they were very difficult pieces to play.

The fifth was one of the hardest in the canon, but it was her favorite. She played the piece all the way through twice and was reasonably pleased with what she heard. She decided to play for three hours, then stop and have some lunch.

YOU take up your position early. Early enough to be settled before the eight-o'clock changeover. It's the same as yesterday. The Bureau guy still awake but no longer very attentive. The arrival of the local cop. *The flank-to-flank pleasantries. The Buick rolls away down the hill; the local cop car crawls forward and settles into its space. The engine dies, and the guy's head turns. He sinks low in his seat, and his last shift as a cop begins. After today they won't trust him to direct traffic around the Arctic Circle.*

"SO HOW do we get there?" Harper asked as she climbed into her own little yellow two-seater. Reacher realized he had never seen it before. He folded himself into the passenger seat, and she dumped her bag in his lap. Shoulder room was tight.

"We'll have to go commercial," he said. "Head for National, I guess. You got credit cards?"

She was shaking her head. "They're all maxed out," she said. "They'll get refused. What about you?"

"I'm always broke," he said, thinking fast.

He opened her bag and took out her phone. Closed his eyes and tried to recall sitting in Jodie's kitchen, dialing the number. Tried to remember the sequence of digits. He entered them slowly, heard the ring tone for a long moment. Then the call was answered.

"Colonel John Trent," a deep voice said.

"Trent, this is Reacher. You still love me?"

"What?"

"I need a ride, two people, Andrews to Portland, Oregon."

"Like when?"

"Like right now. Immediately."

"You're kidding, right?"

"No. We're on our way there. We're a half hour out."

Silence for a second. "Okay," Trent said. Then the line went dead.

"So is he doing it?" Harper asked.

Reacher nodded. "He owes me," he said. "So let's go."

She let out the clutch, drove out of the Bureau lot, and blasted along the approach road and onto I-95.

"So what is the key?" she asked.

"Means, motive, opportunity. The holy trinity of law enforcement. We know everything we need to know. Some of it we've known for days. But we screwed up everywhere, Harper. Big mistakes and wrong assumptions."

"What mistakes?" she said. "What assumptions?"

"Very very ironic ones, under the circumstances," he said. "But it's not entirely our fault. I think we swallowed a few big lies, too. So big and so obvious nobody saw them for what they were."

WHEN they reached Andrews, a captain showed them to a preflight waiting room. It was a utilitarian space, lit by fluorescent tubes.

"Talk to me," Harper said when the guy had gone. "What is it?"

"Start with the motive," he said. "Who's got a motive?"

"I don't know."

"Go back to Amy Callan. Suppose she'd been the only victim. Who would you be looking at for a motive?"

"Her husband. Dead wife, you always look at the husband," she said. "Because motives are often personal."

Reacher nodded. "Okay, so suppose it is Amy Callan's husband. How does he avoid suspicion?"

"He can't avoid it."

"Yes, he can. He can avoid it by finding a bunch of women with some kind of a similarity with his wife and killing them, too. He can take the spotlight off himself by burying the personal connection in a crowd. Like where's the best place to hide a grain of sand?"

"On the beach."

"Right," he said.

"So you're saying all but one are decoys. Sand on the beach."

"Camouflage," he said. "Background noise."

"So which one? Which one is the real target?"

Reacher said nothing.

The captain came back and led them out to a waiting staff car. The car drove to a brand-new Boeing standing alone on the apron. The captain had explained that it was a transport plane, undergoing a flight test that was being rerouted to Portland. There was a wheeled ladder at the forward cabin door, flight crew in uniform clustered at the top, with clipboards thick with paper.

"Welcome aboard," the copilot said. "You should be able to find an empty seat." There were two hundred and sixty of them.

Reacher took three seats for himself and sat sideways, propped up against a window. Harper sat down behind him, buckled her belt.

"So which one is the real target?" Harper asked again.

"You can figure it out," Reacher said.

The plane headed for the runway. A minute later it was in the air, smooth, quiet, and powerful. Then it climbed hard over D.C.

IT's two o'clock, and the local cop is still right there in front of her house. Time for the call. You open the stolen mobile, dial her number. You hear the connection go through. You hear the ring tone. You crouch low in the lee of your rock, ready to speak.

She picks up. "Hello?" she says.

"Hello, Rita," you say.

She hears your voice. You feel her relax. "Yes?" she says.

You tell her what you want her to do.

"THE first one," Harper said, "would be random. Leading us away from the scent. And the second establishes the pattern."

"I agree," Reacher said. "Callan and Cooke were background noise. They started the smoke screen."

"But he wouldn't leave it too late," Harper said. "He's got a target, he'd want to hit it before anything unraveled, right?"

"I agree," Reacher said again.

"So it's the third or the fourth."

Reacher nodded, said nothing.

"But which one?" Harper asked. "What's the key?"

"Everything," Reacher said. "Same as it always was. The clues. The geography, the paint, the lack of violence."

"Lorraine Stanley stole the paint," Harper said. "The lack of violence proves the guy is faking it. The geography demonstrates scope."

"And speed. And mobility," he added. "Don't forget mobility."

"Why is a demonstration of mobility important?" Harper asked.

"That's one of the lies," Reacher said. "We swallowed it whole."

LUNCH WAS A COLD WRINKLED apple and a square of Swiss cheese, which was about all Rita Scimeca's refrigerator had to offer.

Afterward, as she washed the plate, there was a ring on the bell. It was the cop wanting to use the bathroom again. She waited in the hallway until he came back out of the bathroom, watched him all the way back to the car, locked the door again, and stepped into the parlor. Sat at the piano and played for another hour and a half.

Her touch improved until it was better than it had ever been. Her mind locked onto the notes, and she brought the speed to a point just a little slower than the tempo was marked. But it sounded magnificent. She was pleased.

She pushed back on the stool, knitted her fingers, and flexed them above her head. Then she went to the coat closet and took out her jacket. She unlocked the door to the basement stairs and went down to the garage, used the key-chain remote to open her car, and switched on the garage-door opener. Slid into the car and started the engine while the door rumbled upward.

She backed onto the driveway and hit the button to close the door again. Twisted in her seat and saw the police cruiser parked in her way. She got out and walked toward it.

"I'm going to the store," she said. "I'll be about an hour."

"Okay, but I wait here," he said. "We're watching the house, not you personally. Domicile-based crimes, that's what we do."

"Fine. Nobody's going to grab me at the store."

YOU see the garage door open; you see the car come out; you see the door close again. You see her stop on her driveway, and you see her get out. You watch the conversation with the local cop. You see the cop back up, and you see her reverse out onto the roadway and take off down the hill. You smile to yourself and stand up. You go to work.

SHE made the left at the bottom of her hill and then the right onto the road toward Portland. After two miles she turned left into the shopping center, parked up alone in the lot behind the stores, got out, and walked toward the supermarket.

Inside, she took a cart and walked every aisle, selecting things she figured she was out of. She ended up with little enough in the cart to get her into the express line at the checkout.

The girl put it all into one paper sack. She paid cash for it and walked out with the sack cradled in her arms. Turned right on the narrow sidewalk and headed for the hardware store.

She juggled the grocery sack into one arm and pulled the door. There was an old guy in a brown coat at the register. She walked past the tools and the nails and found the paint section. She put her groceries on the floor and took a color chart from a rack.

"Help you, miss?" the old guy said.

"Does this stuff mix with water?" she asked.

He nodded. "They call it latex, but that just means water-based."

"I think I'll take the olive. I want it to look kind of military."

"Okay," the old guy said. "How much?"

"One can," she said. "A gallon."

He carried it back to the register for her and rang up the sale. She paid cash, and he put it in a bag with a wooden stirring stick.

"Thank you." She carried the grocery sack in one hand and the hardware bag in the other, walked along the row of stores, then looped around behind the last one to the overspill parking lot out back. Hurried to her car. Dumped her bags on the back seat, climbed in, slammed her door, and started the engine.

THE cop saw the approaching figure when it was still about a hundred yards away down the hill. The guy was tall, and he had thick gray hair neatly trimmed and brushed. He was dressed in army uniform. Eagles on the shoulder boards, eagles through the lapels: a colonel. A clerical collar where the shirt and tie should be. A padre, a military chaplain, approaching fast up the sidewalk.

The guy stopped a yard from the cop's right headlight. Just stood on the sidewalk, looking up at Scimeca's house. The cop buzzed the passenger window down. He called, "Can I help you?"

The colonel ducked his head in through the open window. "I'm here to visit with the lady of the house," the padre said.

"She's not home temporarily," the cop said. "And we've got a situation here."

"A situation?"

"She's under guard. Can't tell you why. But I'm going to have to ask you to step inside the car and show me some I.D."

The colonel hesitated for a second; then he opened the passenger door and folded himself into the seat. He put his hand inside his jacket and came out with a wallet. Flipped it open and pulled out a worn military I.D. The cop checked it over, nodded. "Okay, Colonel," he said. "You can wait in here with me if you like."

RITA Scimeca made the left off the main road and the right into her street. The cop was parked across her drive again. Somebody was in the front seat next to him. She stopped on the crown of the road, ready to turn in, hoping he'd take the hint and move, but the cop just opened his door and got out, like he needed to talk to her. She opened her window, and he walked across to her.

"There's a guy here to see you. An army padre. His I.D. is okay."

"Get rid of him," she said.

The cop was startled. "He's all the way from D.C."

"I don't care. I don't want to see him."

The cop said nothing, just glanced back over his shoulder. The colonel was getting out of the car, easing up to his full height on the sidewalk, walking over. Scimeca slid out of her car.

"Rita Scimeca?" the padre asked when he was close enough.

"What do you want?"

"I'm here to see if you're okay," he said. "After your problems."

"My problems?"

"After the assault."

"And if I'm not okay?"

"Then maybe I can help you."

His voice was warm and low and rich. A church voice.

"The army send you?" she asked. "Is this official?"

"I'm afraid not," he said. "I've argued it with them many times."

"If they offer counseling, they're admitting liability."

"That's their view," the colonel said. "So this is a private mission, against orders. But it's a matter of conscience, isn't it?"

Scimeca glanced away, pulled her jacket tight around her.

"Why me in particular?" she asked. "There were a lot of us."

"You're my fifth," he said. "I started with the ones who are obviously living alone, who might need my help most. I've been all over the place. Some fruitful trips, some wasted trips. I try not to force myself on people. But I feel I have to try."

"Well, you've wasted another trip, I'm afraid," she said coldly. "I decline your offer. I don't want your help."

"Are you sure? Please think about it. I came a long way."

She didn't answer, just glanced at the cop impatiently. He shuffled his feet, calling the colonel's attention his way. "I'm going to have to ask you to leave now, sir," he said.

"The offer is always open," the colonel said. "I could come back, anytime." He turned and walked back down the hill.

Scimeca watched him for a while and slid back into her car. The cop walked back to his cruiser, reversed it up the hill. She turned into her driveway, pushed the button on the remote, and the garage door rumbled upward. She drove inside and pushed the button again. Saw the cop moving back into position before the door came down and left her in darkness.

She opened her door, and the dome light clicked on. She pulled the little lever and popped the trunk, got out of the car, took her bags from the back seat, and carried them upstairs. Placed them on the kitchen countertop and sat down on a stool to wait.

IT's a low-slung car, so although the trunk is long enough and wide enough, it's not very tall. So you're lying on your side, cramped. Getting in was no problem. She left the car unlocked, just like you told her to. You watched her walk away to the store, and then you just stepped over and opened the driver's door and found the lever and popped the trunk. Closed the door again and walked around and lifted the lid. Nobody was watching. You rolled inside and pulled the lid closed on top of you. It was easy.

It's a long wait in there. But you feel her get back in, and you hear the engine start. You follow the turns in your mind, so you know when she arrives back at her place. You hear the cop talking. There's a problem. Then you hear some idiot padre, pleading. You tense up. What if she asks him in? But she gets rid of him. You smile in the dark when you feel the car move off again. Then the engine shuts down, and it goes very quiet. She remembers to pop the trunk. You knew she would, because you told her not to forget. Then you hear her footsteps moving away and you hear the basement door open and close. You ease the trunk lid upward, and you climb out. You pull your gloves on tight.

"HELLO, Rita," the visitor said.

Rita looked up and saw the visitor she was expecting standing at the head of the stairs from the garage. "Hello," she said back.

The visitor gazed at her from the doorway, eyes inquiring. "Did you buy the paint?"

"Yes, I did," she said.

"So, are you ready?"

"I don't know," she said.

The visitor smiled. "I think you're ready. What do you think?"

She nodded slowly. "I'm ready," she said.

The visitor was silent for a long moment, just watching carefully. "You did good with the padre."

"He wanted to help me."

"Nobody can help you."

"I guess not," Scimeca said.

The visitor stepped into her kitchen. "Show me the paint."

Scimeca took the can out of the bag and held it up by the wire handle. "It's olive-green," she said. "Closest they had."

The visitor nodded. "Good. You did very well. Now you need to concentrate, because I'm going to tell you what I want you to do."

"Okay," Scimeca said.

"First thing, you have to smile for me. That's very important."

Scimeca came up with a shy, weak smile. She held it, desperately.

"That's nice," the visitor said. "Got to be happy in our work. We need something to open the can. Have you got a screwdriver?"

"Of course," Scimeca said. "I've got eight or nine."

"Go get a big one for me. And don't forget the smile."

AFTER landing at Portland International, Reacher and Harper stood waiting for a taxi. Head of the line was a battered Caprice with a checkerboard stripe down the side. The driver headed east toward the tiny village on the slopes of Mount Hood. As the gradient steepened, the old car dug deep and rumbled upward.

"Who is it?" Harper asked.

"The key is in Poulton's report from Spokane."

"It is?"

Reacher nodded. "Big and obvious. But it took me some time to spot it."

"The UPS thing? We went through all of that."

He shook his head. "No, before that. The Hertz rental car."

SCIMECA came back with a large screwdriver in her hand. "I think this is the best one," she said. "For the purpose."

The visitor looked at it. "It's fine. So where's your bathroom?"

"Upstairs."

"Bring the paint," the visitor said. "And the screwdriver."

Scimeca picked up the can.

"Do we need the stirring stick, too?" she called.

The visitor hesitated. New procedure, needs a new technique.

"Yes. Bring the stirring stick."

Scimeca picked up the items and led the way up the stairs, across her bedroom, and into the bathroom. "This is it," she said.

The visitor pulled out a black plastic garbage bag from a coat pocket. "Okay, put the stuff down on the floor. I need you to put the clothes you're wearing in here."

Scimeca nodded vaguely. "Okay."

"I'm not happy with the smile, Rita," the visitor said. "You want to make me happy, right? So put your clothes in the bag. And smile."

Scimeca hauled off her heavy knit sweater, leaned over, and dropped it in the bag. She unbuttoned the jeans, pushed them down her legs, kicked off her shoes, and stepped out of the jeans. Rolled the shoes and the jeans together and put them in the bag. Pulled off her socks and underwear and tossed them in the bag. She stood there, naked, waiting.

"Run the bath," the visitor said.

Scimeca bent down and put the stopper in the drain. Then she opened the faucets, three quarters hot and one quarter cold.

"Open the paint," the visitor said, "then pour it in the tub. Be careful. I don't want any mess."

Scimeca levered off the lid, then picked up the can, clamped it between her palms, and carried it to the tub. Twisted from the waist and tipped it over. The paint was thick. It smelled of ammonia. The swirl from the faucets caught it. It eddied into a spiral pattern and sank like a weight. She held the can upside down until the thick stream thinned and then stopped. She turned the can the right way up and placed it gently on the tile next to the lid.

"Now get the stirring stick. Mix it up."

Scimeca picked up the stick, knelt at the edge of the tub, worked the stick into the thick sunken mass, and stirred. The color changed as the paint dissolved, from dark olive to the color of grass growing in a damp grove.

"Okay, that'll do. Put the stick and the screwdriver in the can."

Scimeca pulled the stick out of the water and shook it carefully. Stood it upright in the can. Stood the screwdriver next to it.

"Put the lid back on."

She picked the lid up by its edge and laid it across the top of the can. It canted up at a shallow angle because the stirring stick was too tall to let it go all the way down.

"You can turn the faucets off now."

She shut off the water, which was within six inches of the rim.

"Now I want you to put the can down in the basement," the visitor said. "Right where the carton was. Can you do that?"

Scimeca nodded. "Yes, I can do that," she said.

She raised the metal hoop, eased it up alongside the unsteady lid. Carried the can out in front of her, down the stairs and through the hallway, down to the garage and through to the basement.

When she returned to the bathroom, slightly out of breath, the visitor said, "Now you have to get into the tub."

Scimeca stepped to the side of the tub, raised her foot, pointed her toe, and put it in the water. She put her weight on the foot in the water, then brought the other in after it. Stood there in the tub with the paint up to her calves.

"Now sit down. Carefully."

She put her hands on the rim and lowered herself down.

"Arms in."

She let go of the rim and put her hands down beside her thighs.

"Good," the visitor said. "Slide down, slowly and carefully."

She shuffled forward in the water and lay back, felt the warmth moving up her body. She felt it lap over her shoulders.

"Head back."

She tilted her head toward the ceiling. She felt her hair floating.

"Have you ever eaten oysters?" the visitor asked.

She nodded. "Once or twice," she said.

"You remember how it feels? They're in your mouth, and you just suddenly swallow them whole? Just gulp them down?"

She nodded again. "I liked them," she said.

"Pretend your tongue is an oyster," the visitor said.

She glanced sideways, puzzled. "I don't understand."

"I want you to swallow your tongue. I want you to just gulp it down, real sudden, like it was an oyster."

"I don't know if I can do that."

"Push it back with your finger. It worked for the others."

"Okay." She raised her hand, opened her mouth.

"Put your middle finger right under your tongue," the visitor said, "and push back hard."

She opened her mouth wider and pushed back hard.

"Now swallow."

She swallowed. Then her eyes jammed open in panic.

CHAPTER 9

THE cab pulled up nose to nose with the police cruiser. Reacher was the first one out, partly because he was tense and partly because he needed Harper to pay the driver.

"Everything okay?" he asked the cop.

"Who are you?" the cop said.

"FBI," Reacher said. "Is everything okay here?"

"Can I see a badge?"

"Harper, show this guy your badge," Reacher called.

The taxi backed off and pulled a wide curb-to-curb turn in the road. Harper reached into her bag and came out with her gold-on-gold badge. The cop glanced across at it and relaxed.

"It's all quiet here," the cop said through his window.

"She in there?" Reacher asked him.

"Just got back from the store," he said, pointing at the garage.

"She went out?"

"I can't stop her from going out," the cop said.

"You check her car?"

"Just her and two shopping bags. A padre came calling for her. From the army, some counseling thing. She sent him away."

Reacher nodded. "She would. She's not religious." He turned to Harper. "Okay," he said. "We're going inside."

They walked up the path, up the steps to the door. Harper pressed the bell, waited ten seconds, and pressed again. Noise, echoes, silence. "Where is she?" she said.

Reacher looked at the big heavy lock on the pine door. He stepped back to the edge of the porch, sprang forward, and smashed the sole of his foot against the lock. Felt the timbers yield.

"What the hell are you doing?" Harper said.

He hit the door again—once, twice, three times. The frame splintered, and part of it followed the door into the hallway.

"Upstairs," he gasped.

He raced up, with Harper at his back. He ducked into a bedroom. A made bed, dimpled pillows, a telephone, and a water glass on the nightstand. A connecting door, ajar. He stepped across the room and shoved it open. He saw a bathroom.

A tub full of hideous green water.

Scimeca in the water.

And Julia Lamarr.

Julia Lamarr, turning and rising and twisting off her perch on the rim of the tub, whirling around to face him. She was wearing a sweater and pants and black leather gloves. Her face was white with hate and fear. He seized her by the front of the sweater and spun her around and hit her once in the head, a savage blow. It caught her solidly on the side of the jaw, and her head snapped back. She went down like she had been hit by a truck. He turned back to the tub. Scimeca was arched up out of the slime, naked, rigid, eyes bulging, head back, mouth open in agony.

Not moving. Not breathing.

He put a hand under her neck and held her head up, then straightened the fingers on his other hand and stabbed them into her mouth. He scrabbled in her throat, hooked a finger around her tongue, and eased it back up out of her throat. He bent down to blow air into her lungs, but as his face got near hers, he felt a convulsive exhalation from her and a desperate cough, and then her chest started heaving. Giant ragged breaths sucked in and out. He cradled her head. She was wheezing. Tortured sounds in her throat.

"Get the shower running," Reacher shouted.

Harper ran to the stall and turned on the water. He lifted Scimeca under the shoulders and knees, stood up, and stepped back and held her in the middle of the bathroom, dripping green slime everywhere.

"Got to get this stuff off her," he said helplessly.

"I'll take her," Harper said gently.

She caught her under the arms and backed into the shower. Jammed herself into a corner of the stall and held the limp body upright, like a drunk. The shower turned the paint light green, and then reddened skin showed through as it rinsed away. Two minutes, three, four. Harper was soaked to the skin, and her clothes were smeared with green. She was tiring.

"Get towels," she gasped. "Find a bathrobe."

They were on a row of hooks directly above where Lamarr was lying inert. Reacher took two towels, and as Harper staggered forward out of the stall, he held one in front of him and caught Scimeca through the thickness of the towel. He wrapped her in it, carried her out of the bathroom into the bedroom. Laid her down on the bed, leaned over, and wiped the wet hair off her face. She was still wheezing hard. Her eyes were open, but they were blank.

He caught her wrist and felt for the pulse. It was there, strong and fast. "She's okay," he said. "Pulse is good."

"We should get her to the hospital," Harper called. "She'll need sedation. This will have blown her mind."

"She'll be better here," Reacher said. "She'll wake up, and she won't remember a thing."

Harper brought out a bathrobe. "Are you kidding?"

He looked up at her. "She was hypnotized. That's how Lamarr did it all," he said. "Everything, every damn step of the way. She was the Bureau's biggest expert."

"When did you know?" Harper asked.

"For sure?" he said. "Last night."

"But how?" she said.

Reacher took the bathrobe from her and laid it over Scimeca's passive form. Her breathing was still strong, and it was slowing. She looked like a person in a deep sleep.

"I just went around and around it all," he said. "Right from the beginning, for days and days. Thinking, thinking, thinking, driving myself crazy. I knew they were wrong about the motive. I knew it all along, but I couldn't understand it. They're smart people, right? But they were so wrong. I was asking myself why. Why?"

"And you knew Lamarr was driving the motive," Harper said. "Because it was her case, really. So you suspected her."

He nodded. "Exactly. Soon as Alison died, I had to think about Lamarr doing it, because there was a close connection, and like you said, close family connections are always significant. So then I asked myself, What if she did them all? What if she's camouflaging a personal motive behind the randomness of the first three? But I couldn't see how. Or why. There were no family issues. No unfairness about the inheritance, for instance. No jealousy there. And she couldn't fly, so how could it be her?"

"But?"

"But then the dam broke. Something Alison said. I remembered it much later. She said her father was dying but 'sisters take care of each other, right?' I thought she was talking about emotional support or something. But then I thought, What if she meant it another way? Like she'd take care of Julia financially? Like she knew the inheritance was all coming her way and Julia was getting nothing and was all uptight about it? But Julia had told me everything was equal, and she was already rich, anyway, because the old man was generous and fair. So I suddenly asked myself, What if she's lying about that? What if the old guy wasn't generous and fair? What if she's not rich? She certainly doesn't look rich."

"And then I thought, What if everything is a lie? What if she's lying about not flying? What if that's a big lie, too, so big and obvious nobody thinks twice about it? I even asked you how she gets away with it. You said everybody just works around it. Well, we all did. We just worked around it. Like she intended."

"But it's an impossible lie. Either a person flies or she doesn't."

"She used to, years ago," Reacher said. "She told me that. Then presumably she grew to hate it, so she stopped. So it was convincing. Nobody who knows her now ever saw her fly. So everybody believed her. But when it came to it, she could put herself on a plane. If it was worth it to her. And this was worth it to her. Biggest motive you ever saw. Alison was going to get everything, and she wanted it for herself."

"Well, she fooled me," Harper said. "That's for sure."

"She fooled everybody. That's why she did the far corners first.

To make everybody think about the geography, the range, the reach, the distance. To move herself right outside the picture."

Harper was quiet for a second. "But she was so upset. She cried, remember? In front of us all?"

Reacher shook his head. "She wasn't upset. She was frightened. It was her time of maximum danger. Remember how she refused to take her rest period. Because she knew she needed to be around, to control any fallout from the postmortem. And then I started questioning the motive, and she got tense as hell because I might be heading in the right direction. But then I said it was weapons theft, and she cried, but not because she was upset. She cried with relief."

"She backed you up on the weapons theft thing."

"Exactly," Reacher said. "She jumped on the bandwagon because she saw the bandwagon was heading in the wrong direction. She was thinking hard, improvising like crazy, but she wasn't thinking hard enough, because that bandwagon was always bull. There was a flaw in it a mile wide."

"What flaw?"

"It was an impossible coincidence that the eleven witnesses should all be living alone. It was partly an experiment. I wanted to see who wouldn't support it. Only Poulton wouldn't. Blake was out of it, upset because Lamarr was upset. But Lamarr backed it all the way. And then she went home, with everybody's sympathy. But she didn't go home. She came straight here and went to work."

Harper went pale. "She actually confessed to killing her sister. Right then and there, before she left. Remember that? Because of wasting time, she said. But it was true. It was a sick joke."

"She's sick as hell. She killed four women for her stepfather's money. And she enjoyed it. Very smart, too. Can you imagine the planning? She must have started two years ago. Her stepfather fell ill about the same time her sister came out of the army. She started putting it all together then, meticulously. She got the support-group list direct from her sister, picked out the ones who obviously lived alone; then she visited all eleven of them. Walked in everywhere she needed to because she was a woman with an FBI shield, just like you walked past that cop just now. Then she maybe gave them some story about how the Bureau was trying to finally nail the military. Said she was starting a big investigation. Sat them down and asked if she could hypnotize them for background information on the issue. She even got Alison to come to Quantico for it. Remember that? Alison said she'd flown out to Quantico so Julia could hypnotize her for deep background. But there were no questions about deep background, just instructions for the future. What to do, just like she told all of them what to do. Lorraine Stanley was still serving then, so she told her to steal the paint and hide it. She told the others to expect a carton sometime in the future and store it. She told them all to expect another visit from her, and in the meantime to deny everything if they were ever asked about anything."

Harper closed her eyes. "She was off-duty the day Alison died. It was Sunday. Quantico was quiet. I never even thought about it."

"She's very smart," Reacher said.

Harper opened her eyes. "And I guess it explains the lack of evidence everywhere. She knows what we look for at the scene."

"And she's a woman," Reacher said. "The investigators were looking for a man because she told them to. Same with the rental cars. She knew if anybody checked, they would come back with a woman's name, which would be ignored. Which is what happened."

"But what name?" Harper asked. "She'd need I.D. for the rental."

"For the airlines, too," Reacher said. "But I'm sure she's got a drawerful of I.D. From women the Bureau has sent to prison."

Harper looked rueful. "I passed that message on, remember? From Hertz? It was nothing, I said. Just some woman on business."

Reacher nodded. "She's very smart. I think she even dressed the same as the victims while she was in their houses. Like she's in here now wearing an old sweater like Scimeca's. So any fibers she leaves behind will be discounted. She asked us what Alison was wearing, remember? Is she still all sporty and tanned and dressed like a cowboy? she asked. We said yes, she is, so no doubt she went in there wearing denim jeans and boots."

"And she scratched her face because she hated her."

"No, I'm afraid that was my fault," Reacher said. "I kept on questioning the lack of violence, so she supplied some the next time around. I should have kept my big mouth shut."

Harper glanced at the bathroom door, shuddered, glanced away. "How did you figure the hypnotism thing?"

"Like everything else," Reacher said. "I thought I knew who and why, but the how part looked impossible. It took me a long time. But eventually it was the only possibility. It explained everything. The passivity, the obedience, the acquiescence. She just reestablished the spell and told them what to do, step-by-step. They did everything themselves. Right down to swallowing their own tongues. The only thing she did herself was what I did, pull their tongues back up afterward so the pathologists wouldn't catch on."

"But how did you know about the tongues?"

He was quiet for a beat. "From kissing you," he said.

"Kissing me?"

He smiled. "You've got a great tongue, Harper. It set me thinking. Tongues were the only things that fitted Stavely's autopsy findings. But I figured there was no way to make somebody swallow their own tongue, until I remembered Lamarr was a hypnotist, and then the whole thing fell together."

Harper shivered. "Where would she have stopped?"

"Maybe one more. Six would have done it. Sand on the beach." Reacher turned toward Lamarr. "Go wake her up," he said. "Make the arrest, start the questioning. You've got a big case ahead of you."

Harper stepped out to the bathroom. The bedroom went quiet. No sound anywhere, just Scimeca's breathing. Then Harper came back in, white in the face. "She won't talk to me," she said.

"How do you know? You didn't ask her anything."

"Because she's dead."

Silence.

"You broke her neck."

Then there were loud footsteps in the hallway below them, coming up the stairs, in the corridor outside.

The cop stepped into the room. "Hell's going on?" he said.

SEVEN HOURS LATER REACHER was locked up in a holding pen inside the FBI's Portland field office. It was hot in the cell. His clothes dried within an hour, stiff as boards and stained olive with paint. Apart from that, nothing happened. He guessed it was taking time for people to assemble.

After midnight things started happening. He heard sounds in the building. Arrivals, urgent conversations. First person he saw was Nelson Blake. He must have flown in on the Learjet.

Blake walked past the bars and glanced into the cell, something in his face. You really screwed up now, he was saying.

Past one o'clock in the morning Alan Deerfield arrived from New York. He walked in, silent and morose, the same contemplative look he'd used all those nights ago. Then a local agent came in and unlocked the door. "Time to talk," he said.

He led Reacher out of the cellblock and into a conference room. Deerfield and Blake were sitting on one side of a big table. There was a chair opposite. He sat down in it. Blake sat forward. "I've got a dead agent," he said. "And I don't like that."

Reacher looked at him. "You've got four dead women," he said. "Could have been five."

"We had the situation under control. Julia Lamarr was right there rescuing the fifth when you killed her."

The room went silent again. Reacher nodded slowly. "That's your position?" he asked.

Deerfield looked up. "It's a viable proposition. She makes some kind of breakthrough in her own time, she overcomes her fear of flying, she gets herself out here in the nick of time, she's about to start emergency medical procedures when you burst in and hit her. She's a hero, and you go to trial for the murder of a federal agent."

"The cop see her get in the house?"

Deerfield shrugged. "We figure he fell asleep. You know what these country boys are like."

"He saw a padre come calling. He was awake then."

Deerfield shook his head. "Army will say they never sent a padre. He must have dreamed it."

"How did she get in?"

"Knocked on the door, interrupted the guy. He bolted out past her. She didn't chase him, because she wanted to check on Scimeca, because she's a humanitarian."

"The cop see the guy running out?"

"Still asleep."

"And she took the time to lock the door behind her, even though she was rushing upstairs because she's a humanitarian."

"Evidently."

The room went quiet.

"Scimeca come around yet?" Reacher asked.

Deerfield nodded. "We called the hospital. She's fine. But we won't pursue her for a description of her attacker. That would be grossly insensitive, given her circumstances."

"Where's Harper?" Reacher said.

"On suspension," Blake said.

"For not following the party line?"

"She's unduly affected by a romantic illusion," Blake said. "She told us some fantastic story."

"You see your problem, right?" Deerfield said. "You hated Lamarr from the start. So you killed her for personal reasons and invented a story to cover yourself. But it's not a very good story, is it? You can't put Lamarr anywhere near any of the scenes."

"Where's her car?" Reacher asked. "She drove up to Scimeca's place from the airport. Where's her car?"

"The perpetrator stole it," Blake said. "She surprised him; he took off in her car."

"You going to find a rental in her real name?"

Blake nodded. "Probably. We can usually find what we need to."

"You see your problem, right?" Deerfield said again.

Reacher nodded. "I guess this means I'm not going to get paid."

"This is not a joke, Reacher," Deerfield said. "Let's be clear about that. You're in big trouble. You can say you had suspicions. But nobody will listen. And it won't matter anyway, because our counsel will say that even if you had mistaken but sincere suspicions, you should have gone straight for Scimeca in the tub and let Harper deal with Lamarr. It was two against one. It would have saved you time if you were so concerned about your old buddy."

"It might have saved me half a second."

"Half a second could have been critical," Deerfield said. "Our counsel will make a big point out of it. He'll say spending precious time hitting somebody proves something, like personal animosity."

"And you can't claim it was accidental," Blake put in. "You once told me you know all about how to break someone's skull; no way would it happen by accident. That guy in the alley, remember? Petrosian's boy? And what goes for skulls goes for necks, right? So it wasn't an accident. It was deliberate homicide."

"Okay," Reacher said. "What's the deal?"

"You're going to jail," Deerfield said. "There's no deal."

"There's always a deal," Reacher said.

"Well, we could compromise," Blake said. "We could call Lamarr a suicide, tormented that she couldn't save her sister."

"And you could keep your big mouth shut," Deerfield said.

"Why should I?" Reacher said.

"Because you're a smart guy. Don't forget, there's absolutely nothing on Lamarr. You could come up with a little meaningless circumstantial stuff, but what's a jury going to do with that? A big man hates a small woman? He's a bum, she's a federal agent? He breaks her neck, and then he blames her for it? Some fantastic story about hypnosis? Forget about it."

"So face it, okay?" Blake said. "You're ours now."

Reacher shook his head. "No, thanks."

"Then you go to jail."

"One question," Reacher said. "Did I kill Lorraine Stanley?"

Blake shook his head. "No, you didn't."

"How do you know?"

"You know how we know. We had you tailed all that week."

"And you gave a copy of the surveillance report to my lawyer, right?"

"Right."

Reacher smiled. "So maybe you can lock me up for Lamarr, but you can't ever claim I'm also the guy who killed the women, because my lawyer has got your own report proving that I'm not."

"So what?" Blake said. "You're locked up anyway."

"Think about the future," Reacher said. "You've told the world it's not me, and you're swearing blind it's not Lamarr, so you've got to be seen to keep on looking, right? Think about the negative headlines. ELITE FBI UNIT GETS NOWHERE, TENTH YEAR OF SEARCH. You'd just have to swallow them. And you'd have to keep the guards in place, you'd have to spend more and more budget, year after year, searching for the guy. Are you going to do that?"

Silence in the room.

"No, you're not going to do that. And not doing that is the same thing as admitting you know the truth. Lamarr is dead, the search has stopped, it wasn't me. Therefore Lamarr was the killer."

More silence. Reacher smiled. "So now what?"

They recovered. "We're the Bureau," Deerfield said. "We can make your life very difficult."

"My life's already very difficult," he said. "Nothing you guys can do to make it any harder. But you can forget the threats, anyway. Because I'll keep your secret."

"You will?"

Reacher nodded. "I'll have to, won't I? Because if I don't, it'll all just come back on Rita Scimeca. She's the only living witness. She'll get pestered to death—prosecutors, police, newspapers, television. I don't want that to happen. So your secret is safe with me."

Blake stared at the tabletop. "Okay," he said. "I'll buy that."

"But we'll be watching you," Deerfield said. "Always."

"Well, don't let me catch you at it. Because you guys should never forget what happened to Petrosian. Okay?"

IT FINISHED like that, as a tie, as a wary stalemate. Reacher stood up and left the room. He found an elevator and made it to street level. Nobody came after him. He pushed open the main oak doors and stepped out into the chill of the night.

"Hey, Reacher," Harper called.

She was behind him in the shadow of a pillar flanking the entrance. He turned and saw the gleam of her hair and a stripe of white where her shirt showed at the front of her jacket.

"Hey, yourself," he said. "You okay?"

She stepped across to him. "I will be," she said. "I'm going to ask for a transfer. Maybe over here to Oregon. I like it."

"Will they let you?"

She nodded. "Sure they will. This is going to be the quietest thing that ever happened."

"It never happened at all," he said. "That's how we left it."

"So you're okay with them?"

"As okay as I ever was."

"I'd have stood up for you," she said. "Whatever it took."

"I know you would. There should be more like you."

"Take this," she said.

She held out a slip of flimsy paper. It was a travel voucher, issued by the desk back at Quantico. "It'll get you to New York."

"What about you?" he asked.

"I'll say I lost it. They'll wire me another one."

She stepped close and kissed his cheek, stepped away, and started walking. "Good luck," she called.

"To you, too," he called back.

HE SLEPT through four hours in the air and touched down at La Guardia at one o'clock in the afternoon.

He used the last of his cash on a bus to the subway and the subway into Manhattan, got out at Canal Street, and walked south to Wall Street. He was in the lobby of Jodie's office building a few minutes after two o'clock. Her firm's reception area was deserted. He stepped through an open door and wandered down a corridor lined with law books. Left and right of him were empty offices.

He came to a set of double doors and heard the heavy buzz of conversation on the other side. He pulled the right-hand door, and the noise burst out at him. He saw a conference room jammed full of people in dark suits, snowy white shirts, and quiet ties. There was a long table under a heavy white cloth loaded with ranks of sparkling glasses and bottles of champagne. Two bartenders were pouring the foamy golden wine as fast as they could. People were drinking it and toasting with it and looking at Jodie.

She was rippling through the crowd like a magnet. She turned left and right, smiling, clinking glasses. She saw Reacher at the door at the same moment he saw himself reflected in the glass over a Renoir drawing on the wall. He was unshaven and dressed in a crumpled, stiff khaki shirt covered in green stains. She was in a thousand-dollar dress. A hundred faces turned with hers, and the room fell silent. She hesitated for a second. Then she fought her way through the crowd and flung her arms around his neck.

"The partnership party," he said. "Congratulations, babe. And I'm sorry I'm late."

She drew him into the crowd, and people closed around them. He shook hands with a hundred lawyers the way he used to with generals from foreign armies. Don't mess with me, and I won't mess with you. The top boy was an old red-and-gray-faced man of about sixty-five. His suit must have cost more than all the clothes Reacher had ever worn in his life, but the mood of the party meant there was no edge in the old guy's attitude.

"She's a big star," he said. "I'm gratified she accepted our offer."

"Smartest lawyer I ever met," Reacher said over the noise.

"Will you go with her?"

"Go with her where?"

"To London," the old guy said. "Didn't she explain? First tour of duty for a new partner is running the European operation for a couple of years."

Then she was back at his side, smiling, drawing him away. The crowd was settling into small groups, and conversation was turning to work matters. She led him to a space by the window.

"I called the FBI uptown," she said. "I was worried about you, and technically I'm still your lawyer. I spoke with Alan Deerfield's office, but they wouldn't tell me anything."

"Nothing to tell. They're straight with me, I'm straight with them."

"So you delivered." She paused. "Is there going to be a trial?"

He shook his head. "No trial."

"Just a funeral, right?"

He shrugged. "There are no relatives left. That was the point."

She paused again, like there was something important coming up. "I have to go to work in London," she said. "Two years."

"I know," he said. "The old guy told me. When do you go?"

"End of the month."

"You don't want me to come with you."

"It'll be very busy. It's a small staff with a big workload."

"And it's a civilized city."

She nodded. "Yes, it is. Would you want to come?"

"Two straight years?" he said. "No. But maybe I could visit."

She smiled vaguely. "That would be good."

He said nothing.

"This is awful," she said. "Fifteen years I couldn't live without you, and now I find I can't live with you."

"I know," he said. "Totally my fault."

"We've got until the end of the month."

He nodded. "More than most people get. Can you take the afternoon off?"

"Sure I can. I'm a partner now. I can do what I want."

"So let's go."

They left their empty glasses on the window ledge and threaded their way through the knots of people. Everybody watched them and then turned back to their quiet speculations.

LEE CHILD

© RUTH GRANT

Born in England, Lee Child spent eighteen years working as a production technician in British television. Then, caught in a downsizing drive, he found himself out of work. It turned out to be a golden opportunity for him to do what he had long been yearning to do: write novels. Four months later he finished *Killing Floor,* his first Jack Reacher thriller. Published in 1997, it won awards and rave reviews. Two other hit novels followed, establishing Child as a top-rank author—a dream he had cherished since childhood.

In 1998 Child realized another long-held dream: He moved to America. With his American-born wife he now lives north of New York City, not far from the home of his fictional hero, Jack Reacher.

To learn more about Lee Child and *Running Blind,* visit the Select Editions website:

ReadersOnly.com
Password: *gift*

Dream
COUNTRY

Luanne Rice

*I*t was a glorious place of mountains . . .
and grasslands . . . and wide-open skies.

Once, it was a place where a family's dreams
came true.

Could it be that way again?

Chapter ONE

DAISY Tucker paused at the foot of the stairs to smell the laundry she held in her arms. She had gotten up an hour early to wash her daughter's clothes, throwing an extra sheet of fabric softener into the dryer the way Sage liked it.

Mounting the stairs, Daisy wondered why her heart was pounding. She felt nervous, as if she were applying for a new job instead of waking up her sixteen-year-old with a pile of clean clothes. The house was quiet, flooded with thin morning light. While waiting for the laundry to finish, Daisy had gone to her spare-room jewelry studio to work on a bracelet that she hoped to finish that afternoon. But she had been too upset to concentrate.

Daisy and Sage lived alone. There had been no witness last night to hear Daisy screaming like a banshee. There had been no one present to watch Sage sitting back in her inflatable chair, messy hair falling across her face, observing her frustrated mother with cool detachment in her wide green eyes. No one to watch that composure crumble under Daisy's words.

Sage had been wearing the clothes Daisy now held in her arms, and they had been mud-stained and sopping wet. Sage had been out with Ben Davis, her boyfriend, until midnight, even though she had promised to be home by nine. They had gone canoeing and capsized.

It was late October, frosty and cold, and all Daisy had been able to think about was how they might have drowned in the dark.

The phone rang. Still holding the clothes, Daisy walked to her bedroom and picked up the receiver. "Hello?"

"How's my wayward niece?"

"Sleeping," Daisy said, relaxing at the sound of her sister's voice. "But last night I wanted to kill her."

"Kill?" Hathaway asked. "That seems like a strong word. Perhaps you mean maim."

"Oh, Hath," Daisy said, almost laughing. Talking to her sister could break the tension like nothing else. "She was bad, but I was worse. I told her only stupid girls go out canoeing with boys until midnight on school nights." Daisy cringed as she remembered her words. "Stupid, slutty girls. I hate that I called her slutty."

"No, you just *compared* her to slutty girls. That's different."

"I feel awful." Daisy was an overprotective mother, and she knew it. Sage's twin brother, Jake, had disappeared when he was three, and that fact informed every decision Daisy had made ever since regarding Sage. "I don't want her to get hurt," Daisy said.

"I know," Hathaway said gently.

"I have to go wake her up now."

"And tell her you love her."

"And everyone makes mistakes."

"But you'll ground her for life if she ever does it again."

"Right," Daisy said, laughing.

Hanging up, she felt better. Talking to Hathaway had helped her put the situation into perspective. Generations of daughters had been staying out too late, falling into lazy rivers. That didn't make them bad children, and it didn't mean they had bad mothers.

Sunlight streamed through the bedroom windows, into the upstairs hall. Walking toward Sage's room, Daisy thought about what a nice house they lived in. It was a small saltbox, with a sliver of view down the cove. Daisy had paid for it herself, selling the jewelry she made and saving her money. She reassured herself that she was doing a good job as a single mother.

Taking a deep breath, Daisy took hold of the doorknob to Sage's room. She said a prayer that she could stay calm no matter what. Forcing herself to smile, she entered.

The room was empty.

Sage's bed had not been slept in. It was neatly made, the Indian blanket drawn up over the pillows. A drawer was partly open, and Daisy saw that clothes were missing.

Posters of Wyoming hung everywhere. Purple peaks—the Wind River Range, the Medicine Bows, the Bighorns—filled the walls, along with blowups of galloping mustangs. Her father had sent her a rack of elk antlers, and she had turned them into a shrine: The single picture she had of him hung among turquoise beads, horse-shoes, and her brother's blue booties.

A note lay on Sage's desk. The second Daisy saw it a small sound escaped her. She dropped the neatly folded laundry and, hands shaking, picked it up.

Sage had been upset when she'd written it. Daisy could tell by the spidery handwriting, the terrible terseness of the message from a girl who loved to talk.

Daisy stared at the words. She looked for "Dear Mom" and "Love, Sage," but there were only four words: "I have to go." And in the time it took to read them, Daisy felt the world cave in around her.

DAISY called Hathaway. As she waited for her sister to arrive, she paced the house, concentrating on where Sage might have gone. It was Thursday, a school day. Could "I have to go" mean simply "I have to go to school"?

Just in case, she telephoned the office at Silver Bay High School. Sage was in eleventh grade. She had finished sophomore year with honors, gotten A's on her first junior-year tests, and had received two deficiencies last week—chemistry and history. Sage, her bright light, her brilliant girl, letting herself slip? "Hi, Mrs. Wickham," Daisy said to the school secretary. "It's Daisy Tucker. Um—"

"Hello, Ms. Tucker. I was just about to call you. If Sage is going to be absent, we really need to get a call from you."

"I'm sorry," Daisy said, covering her eyes and dropping the phone. Of course Sage had not gone to school. Hurrying now, she dialed Ben's house. No one was home. The same for Sage's friends Zoe, Amanda, and Robin.

Hathaway walked in, looking tall and tough. She smothered her younger sister in a hug.

And then Daisy was crying. "It was just a fight. It was bad, but still . . . it was just an *argument*. Why would she go?"

"Who have you called?" Hathaway asked.

"Ben, some of her friends, the school."

"What did Ben say?"

"I got the answering machine at his house," Daisy said. "I know his mother works at a bank, but I'm not sure which one. His parents are divorced, and his father lives in Boston."

"This note," Hathaway said, frowning at it. "She sounds serious." Hath was chic and no-nonsense. She ran a boutique where she sold western jackets, suede skirts, and Daisy's jewelry. For some reason people vacationing in their East Coast town loved items evocative of the Old West. Hathaway had gotten the idea back in the days when she would visit Daisy and James in Wyoming.

"She ran away," Daisy said, unable to keep the tremor out of her voice. Her thoughts were darting all over the place to avoid the fact that it was nine fifteen a.m. and Sage hadn't slept in her bed and she had no idea where her daughter was.

DAISY called four banks before she got the right one. Ben's mother, Paulina Davis, managed the wharf branch of Southern Connecticut Bank & Trust.

"Hello?" Paulina said.

"Hi, this is Daisy Tucker," Daisy began. Although the two women weren't friends, they had spoken on the phone several times since the previous summer, when Sage and Ben had started spending so much time together.

"Did Ben . . ." Daisy paused. How could she word this without offending the woman? Did Ben skip school today? Did he run away from home? Did he leave you a note that scares the hell out of you?

"Did Ben and Sage lose our canoe last night? Yes," Paulina Davis said. "Did I just get a call from school telling me he's absent without my permission? Also yes. I'm furious, Daisy."

"At Sage?" Daisy felt the heat in her face. Was this supposed to be Sage's fault?

"Ben's a senior," Paulina said. "He's always been a good student, and this year he's captain of the soccer team. It's been his dream, and yesterday he missed the game. He should be visiting colleges, planning—" She had to stop, her voice shaking with rage. "I've forbidden him to see Sage before, but this time I mean it."

"Listen, Sage is a good student, too. An honor student," Daisy said hotly. "I'm not wild about her spending every free minute with Ben. I trusted them all summer because they're good kids—"

"Look, I'm sorry." Paulina cut her off. "I'm upset. Seeing each other nonstop all summer was one thing, but now school has to come first. I'm sure you agree."

"Have you been home since the school called?" Daisy asked.

"No, of course not. I work until— Why?"

"I think they've run away. Sage has, anyway. She left a note."

"Did she mention Ben?"

"No."

"Ben wouldn't run away," Paulina said flatly. "Would not."

"I didn't think Sage would, either," Daisy said.

BEN hadn't left a note, but he had taken his backpack and tent. Paulina had left work immediately to go home, and she called the minute she checked his room.

"He doesn't have a car, she doesn't have a car," Paulina said.

"They're hitchhiking, probably," Daisy said.

"This is great," Paulina said. "This is wonderful."

"Should we . . ." Daisy didn't want to finish the question: "Should we call the police?"

"The police," Paulina said. "For one thing, they're teenagers old enough to play hooky, and your daughter left a *note*. So the police won't give this the time of day. For another, my son is seventeen, and I don't want them getting the idea that this is *his* plan."

"Maybe it is!" Daisy said harshly.

"No, Daisy, it is not. My son would not run away from home unless someone was coercing him."

"I want to call the police," Daisy said with her eyes closed. Jake's image flooded her mind. Her son, then only three years old, had been strong and solid. He had the same dark hair and green eyes as his twin sister, a brilliant smile, and an amazing laugh. Oh, God, she had never thought he could just disappear. Jake had been missing, presumed dead, for thirteen years. And now Sage was gone, too.

DAISY dialed 911. When the operator answered, Daisy had to concentrate on not losing it. "My daughter . . ." she began.

"Yes?" the operator asked.

"My daughter's missing. She left a note. We had a fight, and she was very upset."

The operator patched her through to a detective. He gave his name, but Daisy didn't even hear it. "You say you had a fight and she left a note?" the detective asked. "This isn't unusual. It's a gorgeous day out, and she's playing hooky maybe."

"But it's not like Sage."

"She's a teenager," he said calmly. "They like to go pumpkin picking at Halloween time. You're the third mother to call today."

Daisy almost felt lulled by the officer's tone. What he said made perfect sense. Daisy herself had played hooky at sixteen.

"She'll be home before dark," the officer said. "If she's not there by suppertime, call us back. Okay?"

Daisy's heart was skidding out of control, but she pulled herself together. "Okay." She had to tell herself she was overreacting because of what had happened to one child thirteen years ago. Sage would come home on her own.

DAISY spent the day hunched over her workbench in the darkened cubicle at the back of the spare room. Those customers who knew about it called it her magic cave. A gooseneck lamp cast a circle of light on the work surface where she made her jewelry. Stones, bones, silver, and gold covered the workbench. Gold dust stuck to Daisy's fingertips. She tried to concentrate on carving a disk of cow bone to look like the face of an Indian ghost.

Daisy made jewelry that brought people love. With sharp tools she etched fine designs in the bone, filling them with black ink, like tattoos. Drawing on myths and Indian lore, she used dot, circle-and-dot, and concentric circle designs to symbolize love, eternity, and spiritual vision.

When she set the carved bone faces in gold or sterling silver, strung them together with polished granite and tourmaline for a bracelet or necklace, they looked like parts of a totem pole.

"Bring her back," Daisy whispered to the bones. Sometimes customers wanted to heal broken relationships, win back husbands who had left, sweethearts who had walked away. Daisy would whisper their intentions as she carved the faces. People would write her to say that her jewelry had brought miracles to their lives—so many that Hathaway had once remarked, "You don't have customers. You have devotees."

The letters really got to her. There were so many different kinds of love in the world, and everyone wanted it. To fall in love, to heal broken hearts, to bring families back together.

DAISY and Hathaway waited all day, until the school bus passed by and Sage didn't get off. Daisy called all of Sage's friends to ask if they had seen her or Ben. No one had. They waited until suppertime. Hoping that hunger would bring Sage back home, Daisy made her favorite: tuna noodle casserole.

The October evening was still and cold. Opening the back door, Daisy gazed into the garden, through the pine trees to the bay. Trying not to think of that other waiting time, when the search parties had fanned out over the range and into the canyons, Daisy now imagined Sage hiding nearby, nursing her anger over the fight. Smelling her favorite supper, she would finally come home.

"Are you going to call the police or am I?" Hathaway asked.

"Should I give her a few more minutes?" Daisy asked, looking at her watch. "Sometimes we don't eat until a little later."

"It's getting dark," Hathaway said.

That did it.

"THIS isn't like her," Daisy told Detective Barbara LaRosa. They were standing in Daisy's kitchen. Daisy had called 911 again, and this time the officer had said someone would be right over.

"What's she like?" Detective LaRosa asked.

"Well," Daisy said, "she's incredible. She loves to write essays and stories. Poems. She wants to be a writer."

"What does she look like?"

"She's about five three. She weighs one hundred and fifteen pounds. She has reddish brown hair down to"—she touched her own shoulder—"here. Her eyes are green."

"She looks like her mother," Hathaway said, handing over Sage's school photo. "Very pretty."

"Yes, she is," said the detective. "May I see her room?"

"Of course." Daisy's throat ached as she led the way.

Detective LaRosa was about fifty, with handsome gray streaks in her dark hair. "Does she use drugs or alcohol?"

"She's very straight," Daisy replied. "She's totally against drinking and drugs. She tolerates other people doing whatever they want, but she knows what's for her and what's not. Her schoolwork has slipped since the beginning of the year, but—"

"That's often a sign of drugs. Even the best kids—"

"Not Sage," Daisy insisted, shaking her head.

"She likes the Wild West," Detective LaRosa commented, gazing at the mountain posters and the elk antlers.

"She loves it," Daisy said.

"Why is that?" The detective was staring at the photo of red mesas against a bright blue sky. "Did you take a trip there once?"

"She was born in Wyoming," Daisy said. "We lived there until she was four years old, and we haven't been back since."

"Her father lives there," Hathaway added.

"We're divorced," Daisy explained. "He lives on a ranch, and he sent her those antlers for her tenth birthday. She covers them with things like they're a Christmas tree." Stepping forward, she looked at the photo of James dangling from a blue ribbon. He was a stranger to her now, older, still lean and tan and unsmiling.

"They're in touch?"

"Not very much."

"He doesn't visit?"

"No."

Hathaway stepped forward, as if she sensed Daisy needed protection. Daisy felt tears coming. She had gone to Wyoming to find inspiration in the wilderness. Instead, she had met James Tucker, a man with the wilderness inside him.

"He hasn't seen his daughter since she was four?" LaRosa asked.

"He won't leave the ranch," Daisy answered. "And I wasn't going to send my daughter out to Wyoming alone."

"Blue booties?" The detective touched the tiny knitted shoes hanging from the antlers.

"My son," Daisy explained. "He was Sage's twin, and he died when he was three."

The detective's head snapped up. "How did he die?"

"We don't know," Daisy said quietly. "James—my husband—took him out riding. It was a roundup, lots of men. James often took Jake with him. He put Jake down for one minute, told him to sit still and watch . . ." At the detective's expression Daisy shook her head. "I know you think that was crazy, but we did it all the time. We thought the kids were so lucky—all those wide, open spaces. They loved the animals. Jake was such a good little boy. He'd do what he was told—"

"So your husband told him to sit still," the detective prodded. "What happened next?"

Daisy swallowed, the words hard to get out. "We don't know."

"Was there an investigation?"

"Yes," Daisy said. "Oh, yes."

The police had immediately focused their attention on James, treating him like a murder suspect, bombarding him with questions.

"They never found anything," Daisy said. "No sign of my son. We had search parties, helicopters, a Shoshone shaman. By the time they let my husband join the search, he was like a tornado. He promised me he wouldn't come home until he had Jake." Daisy swallowed. "And I didn't see him again for fifteen days, until long after the search party quit. He was sick and dehydrated—his father and the foreman had to go find him, bring him home."

"What about Sage? Where was she in all this?"

"With me," Daisy said, remembering how quiet the little girl had been, as if she'd sensed that her mother needed calm. Daisy had made a necklace for Sage that week, praying while she worked, sending all her love for Jake into the stones and bone. Sage wore it still. She never took it off.

"James will never leave Wyoming," Daisy said. "In case Jake comes back."

"Is there any reason to believe . . ." the detective started to ask.

Daisy shook her head. Hathaway's hand rested on her shoulder.

"There's animosity between the two of you?" the detective asked. "You and your ex-husband?"

"Maybe so. I'm not sure animosity's the right word," Daisy said.

Detective LaRosa nodded. Examining the things on Sage's desk, she flipped through a pile of notebooks, looked in drawers. Opening a plastic film canister, she looked inside and sniffed. Daisy bit her tongue. She knew the detective was searching for drugs.

The detective held up a bracelet Daisy had given Sage last Christmas. "This is beautiful. Very unusual."

"Daisy made it," Hathaway said.

"I know your work." The detective smiled. "My sister has a pair of your earrings. What does your daughter's necklace look like?"

"It's a circle of bone set in white gold, with four gold nuggets dangling below, on a long chain. I carved the bone on both sides, a two-sided face. The only one I've ever done. I called it The Twins," Daisy answered. She could picture Sage touching her necklace. She always kept the boy's face, her brother, turned toward her heart.

"Daisy often uses circles in her work," Hathaway said. "They're an ancient image of protection—the clan gathering around to keep out intruders, evil spirits, wild animals."

"Intriguing," LaRosa said, then, "Tell me about her boyfriend."

"His name is Ben Davis," Daisy told her. "They've been friends since Sage got to high school. He's a good kid."

Detective LaRosa was looking into Sage's jewelry box and pushing aside some rings and bracelets. Daisy felt like shouting at her. There were no drugs to be found in there. Frowning, the detective removed something that looked like a white plastic popsicle stick. At one end was a small square window, colored blue.

"Oh, no," Hathaway whispered. "She's pregnant."

Daisy's hand went to her mouth. She stared at the white stick. It was a home pregnancy test. She remembered using one herself, over sixteen years ago. Way out on that Tucker ranch, in the privacy of her bathroom, she had waited for the little window to turn blue. Blue as the big sky over the Wind River mountains, blue as the unknowable depths of James Tucker's eyes.

And as blue as the window of this other pregnancy test, the one Sage must have taken, the one that told Daisy Tucker the reason her sixteen-year-old daughter had run away.

Chapter
TWO

JAMES Tucker rode down the ridge, dust swirling up from beneath his horse's hooves. Wyoming's Wind River mountains rose around him, and he galloped through their purple shadows on his way home for supper. Thousand-foot cliffs rose to his left. He swung through the dark canyon, where it was cool and lonely. The setting sun turned the rock pinnacles bloodred, but down here in the shade the summer heat dissipated.

His mind was on cattle and water. All summer they'd had the

worst drought he'd ever seen. Here it was the middle of October, and the streambeds were as dry as they'd been in August.

The horse ran fast and steady. James knew he was close to home—the DR Ranch, named for his parents, Dalton and Rosalind. He felt his breathing change. His horse knew it, too. This was how it was to understand the land, to be as much a part of it as the red rocks and riverbeds. Newcomers never got that. Like the sheep owners who'd come in when his father was a child, ignoring prior claims of cattlemen, nearly ruining the basin land for cattle grazing.

In Tucker lore cattle were good and sheep were bad. James's father had told stories about his father driving those overgrazing sheep straight over rimrock precipices. True tales: The Tuckers had defended this land against the sheepherding Rydells. James's wife hadn't liked those stories much.

Daisy was a New Englander and didn't understand the measures people took to keep their land here. James would take her on rides, searching for bones and gems to use in her jewelry. He had given her sagebrush trails and ancient cave drawings. They'd given each other twins—Jake and Sage—and that had kept her out west a while.

But when the nightmare came, Daisy had to leave this country that took her son. James couldn't blame her. New England was her home, just like Wyoming was his. Sometimes he imagined following her and Sage back east to Connecticut, but that would be like trying to plant a cactus in an apple orchard. Wouldn't take. Besides, there were other reasons why James couldn't leave this land.

Jake was here. They had never found his body, so there wasn't a grave to visit. His spirit dwelled in the canyon. After all this time, James knew Jake wasn't coming back, but he wasn't going to abandon his son, no matter what.

The ranch buildings were visible now. James had a log cabin out back, but wanting to check on his father, he rode up the trail toward the big gabled stone house. Reining in his horse, he stepped down from the saddle and led him to the corral. James could smell Louisa's cooking. She wasn't quite his stepmother—she and Dalton had never seen fit to get married—but she'd lived with the old man for over twenty years. Louisa Rydell was as different from James's mother, Rosalind Tucker, as any woman could be. James had never been happy about the idea of seeing his mother replaced. But with his father losing ground, lately he'd been almost glad of Louisa's presence.

Slapping his hat across his chaps, he shook off the trail's dust. Bending over the water trough, he scooped up a careful handful of water and drank. Two squawking juncos flew out of the eaves of the ranch house onto a cottonwood branch. They chattered noisily.

"What the hell's that noise?" Dalton Tucker asked, walking out onto the porch. Small-framed, he had a pigeon-toed gait.

"Birds, Dad."

"Building nests in the eaves? In October? In the middle of a drought? We're in for a bad winter, a blizzard year. I'm telling you, son," the old man said, shaking his head, "the birds know."

Standing there, Dalton looked confused. His face was red and leathery, as dry as beef jerky. He coughed, and walked over to the rail to spit. Then he turned around. Seeing James, he jumped.

"Damn it, you scared me," Dalton said. "What are you doing home?" he asked, as if he were seeing James for the first time.

James just stood there. He was six inches taller than his father, with shoulders twice as wide. Dalton squinted, as if he was trying to remember something, attempting to weave together the facts of James riding home, the time of day, and the birds in the eaves. The more he thought, the more frustrated his expression became.

"Suppertime, Dad," James said. "Where's Louisa?"

"Louisa?" The old man's face registered confusion.

Inside the house something was burning. The odor was sharp and sweet, like sugar turning to caramel. James ran past his father and found the kitchen filled with smoke. A pan in the oven was on fire. James grabbed a mitt, reached inside, grabbed a flaming brick of corn bread, and threw it into the sink.

In the next room a child began to fret. Louisa sometimes babysat her daughter Ruthie's young girl, Emma. Dalton must have been minding the stove, watching the girl, and forgotten both in the commotion of the birds.

"What's this? Where's Dalton?" Louisa Rydell asked, running in with an armful of sunflowers.

"Corn bread caught fire, looks like to me," James said. "You left Dad in charge of cooking and Emma?"

"You lose that tone with me, James Tucker," Louisa said. "I just stepped out to pick some flowers."

"Yeah, well, you shouldn't let her out of your sight," James said sharply. "Not for a minute. The house could have burned down."

"You telling me how to be a grandmother?"

"My father can't take care of himself, much less a baby."

Dalton came to the door with Emma on his hip. "Forgot, that's what I did. Smelled the corn bread burning and forgot I had this little angel to look after."

James didn't say anything. His father had forgotten the sequence, but it hardly seemed important now. Emma held Dalton's ears, looking him straight in the eyes. That's how it used to be with Sage, James thought. She had loved her grandfather, and he'd adored her.

"Don't worry, darling," Louisa said. She was still a fantastic-looking woman, tan and tall. She wore a denim skirt, lavender blouse, and purple boots. Her thick black hair hung in a long braid down her back. She flashed a big smile to reassure Dalton Tucker. "We're all here. Emma's fine, you're fine, we're all fine."

James walked away. He had ten thousand head of cattle in need of water. Why wait till tomorrow? Tonight he was going to ride back, start burning the briers and sagebrush from irrigation ditches to clear the way and catch whatever rain might come.

Ranchers lived in a perpetual state of hope. They hoped for rain during dust season, dry spells after deluges. But James knew something most men never find out: Men who lost their sons didn't have much left in the way of hope. Hope to James was scarcer than this season's rain. But when the skies finally opened, he'd be prepared. Then he thought of what his father had said about blizzards coming, and he shook his head.

Maybe Daisy had known what she was doing, leaving. Wyoming was one damned hard place to try to live.

THE TRAIN JOLTED ALONG THE tracks, making Sage feel as if she was going to throw up again. It took all her concentration not to. Staring at Ben helped. She loved him so much.

He was asleep, lying in his bedroll on the hard wood floor. The boxcar was dark and cold. It wasn't heated, and last night the temperature had been so low they could see their breath.

"Oh!" A terrible wave of nausea went through her.

"Huh?" Ben woke. "What's wrong? You sick again?"

Sage nodded miserably. "If only the train wasn't so bouncy."

"It's weird without windows," he said. "Even I feel kind of sick."

"Bet you wish you were safe and warm at home," she said.

"Coming was my idea," he reminded her.

Ben amazed her. When she had tried to say good-bye to him, he had refused to let her go alone. Ben loved her, and they were going to be together forever. He had said so, and he kept saying so.

They were in the seventeenth car of a freight train, chugging west through New York State. Their car was carrying machine parts bound for Boise, Idaho. But Sage and Ben were heading for Wyoming to see Sage's father. They had to go somewhere. Even if her father didn't want any part of her, he could let her and Ben stay in one of the ranch cabins till the baby was born.

It had been her idea to jump this train. Six cars had been standing behind the old depot. With Ben hiding behind the station, Sage had watched men loading crates, and she'd asked straight out which cars were heading west.

"This one, little lady." One old codger had laughed, spitting tobacco juice. "Why, you want to make your way to Hollywood?"

"No. I'm just doing a report for social studies," Sage had replied.

"Good for you," the man had said. "What on?"

"Freight trains—where they go, how long it takes."

"Well, this car you asked about," he began, "heading out to Boise, Idaho, with a load of engine parts. Later today the old four fifty-two is gonna swing down from Worcester, and these cars are gonna hook aboard. It'll take around a week, going straight through Chicago and over the Great Plains, through the Rockies."

Later, while the men were taking a break, she and Ben had wheeled their bikes right up the loading ramp. They had knapsacks full of supplies, bedrolls, and Ben's tent. Stowing everything had been no problem. The boxes were stacked four high, creating instant hiding places. She and Ben had curled up in the dark, waiting until four fifty-two, feeling the ground shudder as the train started to move.

Now Ben checked his watch. "I missed history class. Good."

"We'll see more history than you can imagine," Sage said. She knew he liked school, but she was thinking of the tales about cowboy-and-Indian battles fought right on her family's land.

"Yeah?" Ben asked, kissing her lightly on the lips.

"Yeah." Sage tried to hide her tears. Six months pregnant. This seemed to be someone else's life. Just three years ago she'd gotten her first period, and here she was ruining two futures.

"Do you think our mothers got the letters yet?" she asked.

"They will today."

"I'm sorry I made you leave home," she said. "Leave school."

"I don't want you to go alone," he said.

He loves me, she told herself. She wished he'd say it again. He hadn't spoken the words enough that day. They had met during Sage's freshman year, but they had fallen in love thirteen months ago, when they had met again on a mountain hike. Ben had slipped away from his friends to follow her.

Way up on that mountaintop, that very day, they had kissed. Ben had taken her hand, and their fingers had interlocked. Their hands had been a perfect fit, and so had their hearts.

They had been virgins when they met on that hike. Sage had always wanted to save herself for marriage. Ben had felt the same way. They told each other that last Christmas, lying in each other's arms on an old mattress in the attic of Ben's house.

"But you're the love of my life," Ben had said, smoothing Sage's hair back from her eyes.

"And you're mine," she had whispered.

Even now, feeling him push the hair back from her face as he kissed her forehead, cheeks, and nose, she knew those words were true. Last Christmas, knowing they were years too young to get married, they had decided to make love. Their love was real. It was as if their bodies had been born to be together.

But now her body told her she was going to be sick. Tearing herself from Ben's arms, she stumbled across the car and threw up into a plastic bag she'd taken from her knapsack.

"You okay?" Ben asked from across the swaying car.

"I'm fine," Sage called back, leaning against a crate. There was a trapdoor in the middle of the car. She and Ben had opened it earlier, watching the tracks fly by underneath, needing to know they had an emergency escape hatch. She opened it now and pushed the plastic bag out onto the tracks, even though she felt bad about littering.

She didn't want to be running away from home, but she had to. The other night her mother had been so crazed, so furious, because she'd fallen into a river. She had called her slutty just for staying out late with Ben. How would she feel when she found out Sage was going to have a baby? Sage couldn't hide it much longer.

She wished she wasn't pregnant. It was going to change everything. It already had. Morning sickness was supposed to last only three months. For Sage it had been going on nearly the whole time.

She needed a lot of prayers. She said one now to her brother, Jake. With the train rattling west, with her boyfriend anxiously waiting across the dark boxcar, she touched her twin's carved face and prayed. "Let me have a boy," she said in the tiniest voice.

Her brother had been lost in a canyon, and her father had disappeared from Sage's world. For years Sage had prayed for Jake to return. If he did, maybe her father wouldn't stay a prisoner on his ranch, searching for the little boy he had lost.

"A boy," Sage prayed, touching her belly with one hand and her necklace with the other. "Let it be a boy."

Concentrating hard, she could feel the small bone face pressing hard into her palm. Her lips moved in prayer. Maybe if she brought a boy into her family, everyone could be happy again.

Chapter
THREE

THE morning after Sage left, Daisy stood on the back porch watching gold leaves shower down from the birch trees. Hathaway came to stand beside her sister. "It's cold out here. What are you doing without a sweater on?"

Hathaway gently put her arm around Daisy's shoulders and led her through the kitchen door.

"Where is she?" Daisy asked. "I can't stand not knowing, Hath."

"She's taking care of herself," Hathaway said. "That's what this is all about. She had to run away so she could figure out what she's going to do. When she's clearer, she'll come home."

"I wish she could have told me," Daisy said. "I wish she didn't think she had to go off on her own to figure it out."

"She's so independent," Hathaway said. "What she's doing is like Outward Bound. Testing her limits. And you paved the way for her."

"Me?"

"Going out west by yourself, finding new ideas for your work. She's your daughter, and she wants to live up to your adventurous life."

"But I wasn't adventurous. I was scared of everything."

Daisy and Hathaway had been raised by quiet parents. Their father had been a drama professor and their mother an English teacher who'd died at thirty-six. She had named her daughters after Anne Hathaway, Shakespeare's true love, and Daisy Buchanan of *The Great Gatsby*. There hadn't been much room for adventure in their scholarly household.

"Being scared of everything makes some people brave," Hathaway said. "You went out west because otherwise you might have been too afraid ever to leave home."

Just then the mail truck pulled up, and the letter carrier began stuffing envelopes into the box by the road. Hathaway walked down the drive to get the mail. Flipping through the letters and catalogues, she suddenly began to run back.

Daisy knew even before she saw Sage's handwriting. Hands shaking, she tore open the blue envelope.

Dear Mom,

I'm sorry I worried you so much. Ben and I didn't mean to upset you with staying out late and tipping over the canoe. I never want to upset you. But I love him. I know you say I'm too young to know, but I do anyway. When we capsized last night, Ben saved me. He swam over and pulled me out. He put me first. He always does, and I do the same with him. That's how love should be.

We're running away. This is the part that's hard to write. We're going to have a baby. I can almost see your face. You're mad. I know, and I'm sorry. I wish I could take it back, or I mean, turn back time. We are together, and that's what matters. I'll go crazy if I stay here. I will. In fact, I almost am already. I'm dying of love for Ben, Mom, and we have to be together. Don't worry. I'll call and write a lot.

Love,
Sage

"Oh, God," Daisy said.

"Where's it postmarked?" Hathaway asked, checking.

"Silver Bay. She must have mailed it before she left."

The phone rang, and Hathaway hurried to answer it. When she turned around, there were tears brimming in her eyes. "They have a clue," she said. "That was Detective LaRosa, and she said they questioned some men who work at the railroad depot. A girl who looks like Sage was asking questions about some freight cars, about which ones were going west."

"Going west—"

"She asked about the train's route, the man said."

"She wants her father," Daisy said. "She's going to James."

From his seat on a crate Ben watched Sage pacing around the boxcar, tidying up their sleeping area, plumping up their bedrolls, trying to make a nest from a bundle of rags she'd found. He wished she would stop.

"Sage, hey. Come over here."

"In a second. This floor's so hard. Maybe you'll sleep better if I pile up some of these old cloths under your bedroll."

"Don't worry about it." Ben yawned, wishing he hadn't told her he couldn't sleep. Whenever he mentioned any discomfort, any problem, Sage always tried to fix it. He'd been amazed at first that anyone would be so concerned about his comfort. But now it was making him crazy, watching her try to improve something that couldn't be fixed. That floor would never be comfortable. He was sore and hungry, a thousand miles from home and getting farther.

"Sage, will you stop?"

She turned to look at him. She'd been smiling, but at his sharp tone her face fell, and she began crying. Ben wrapped her in his arms.

"Let's go back," he whispered. "This is too much for us."

"I can't."

"Your mother won't be mad." Ben thought of his own mom. She'd been so disappointed in his last grades, the fact he'd been missing soccer games. They had an appointment with a college admissions office next week. "Not for long."

"But we're going to live on the ranch. You, me, and the baby."

Ben held her tight. When she'd come to his house in the middle of the night—just thirty-six hours ago—he had freaked when she'd said she was leaving. Being with Sage made him do things he'd never done before, got him into situations he couldn't believe were real.

But now, after a day and a half in a sour-smelling boxcar, sleepless all night, he knew he couldn't keep this up. Sage was sick constantly. She was trying hard to make everything seem fun and adventurous, but she couldn't disguise the fact that they were tossing away their lives. Ben loved her, loved her still. But he wasn't going to live with her on a ranch in Wyoming. He had made up his mind, he realized, sometime during the night before.

He'd get her as far as he could, then call his mother to send him the airfare home. It made him sick to know he'd hurt her, gotten her pregnant. Now he was going to hurt her worse. Her dream of them living on the ranch wasn't going to come true.

The thought sent a shiver through his body, and Sage felt it.

"Are you cold?" she asked, pulling her head back.

"No, I'm fine."

Ben looked around the freight car and realized that all he'd eaten for nearly two days was beef jerky and some raisins and peanuts. Holding the trembling girl in his arms, he still felt love, but in that moment Ben learned something terrible: Love wasn't always enough.

THE bar was dark and smoky. Elk horns hung from the walls, and old license plates dangled by wires. James stood alone, drinking a beer. He had come to the Stagecoach Tavern that night to get away from his own thoughts. Lately his mind had been a bad neighborhood, dangers lurking in every corner. Blame, guilt, resentment, and recriminations. Worrying about the herd not having enough water got him thinking about others he'd let down, failed to provide for.

He felt like talking, hearing some laughter, but now that he was here, he wasn't sure he wanted to stay. No one except Daisy had ever gotten the solitude out of him. But thinking of Daisy never did him any good anymore, so he twisted toward the pool tables and looked at a blonde.

Just then the door swung open. His father and Louisa walked in, dressed as if they were going to the rodeo—his father all in black, with a string tie, Louisa in a tight cream-colored top and full red skirt. Dalton looked bewildered. James hadn't seen his father at the Stagecoach in many months, and neither had anyone else.

"Dalton!" someone called.

"Hey, man, where've you been?"

"Where are we, Louisa?" Dalton asked. James heard the fright in his father's voice.

Louisa proudly marched him to the bar. She surveyed the room, and her eyes fell on Todd Rydell, her nephew, over at the dartboard.

Todd was lanky and fair, the kind of cowboy who rode with a Walk-man and used sunscreen. He was descended from the Rydells, who'd grazed their sheep on Tucker land and nearly started a range war. Louisa was a Rydell, too. But Dalton loved her, so James had to respect her. Todd was another story.

"Dalton, good to see you." Todd shook the old man's hand. He kissed his aunt's cheek, let her pull him against her in a big hug.

"It's Todd," Louisa explained to Dalton.

"Why are we here?" Dalton asked.

"For a good time, man." Todd laughed, slapping Dalton on the back. "'Cause it's Friday night and the music's cranking."

"Hi, Dad," James said, moving between his father and Todd.

His father's face softened. "Jamey," he said.

Louisa had been holding court here on Friday nights for over thirty years, singing country-and-western songs. That's how Dalton had met her—the winter after James's mother had died. Louisa had drifted to his table between sets, offered to buy him a drink, moved in before the spring thaw.

Daisy had loved to hear her. Once or twice a month they'd leave the twins with Betsy March, the wife of James's foreman. They'd come down to the Stagecoach and sit right in front of the stage. Louisa and Daisy's bond had been thick and strong.

"C'mon, Dalton." Todd handed him some darts. "Let's have a game. I'll beat you fair and square."

"Can't beat me." Dalton was laughing like his old self. "I can knock the tail off a swallow with my eyes closed."

"Show me, man."

While the two men headed down the bar, James felt something in his stomach tighten. He didn't like Todd, and not just because he was a lousy cowboy. Todd had worked for him years before, and he'd been there the day Jake had disappeared. James had ridden off to rope a steer, leaving Jake to sit on a big rock. Todd and a few others had been riding drag—picking up defectors who'd stop to graze on the sweet grass around Jake's rock—and James had trusted them to watch his son. Jake's disappearance wasn't Todd Rydell's fault, but James hated him anyway. He hated himself worse, but that was beside the point.

"What are you doing, Louisa?" James asked now.

"Doing?" Louisa's eyes widened.

"Yeah. What're you thinking, bringing my father here?"

"Well, I'm thinking of showing him a good time," Louisa said.

"He's sick, Louisa."

"A little confused, that's all."

"He's got Alzheimer's disease," James said. "The doctor told us."

"So what?" Louisa said, her golden eyes flashing.

"He gets confused. He's embarrassed when people come up to him and he can't remember their names. I feel sorry for him."

"I don't feel sorry for Dalton Tucker," Louisa snapped. "I feel sorry for this *disease.* I don't think Alzheimer's has ever come up against anyone like Dalton. And another thing, young man—"

"Whoa," James said, stepping back.

Louisa stepped forward. She grabbed his chin and shook it hard. "You ought to take a lesson from your father. He knows what's happening to him. You think he doesn't? But he's full of life, and he's not quitting. That's something *you* should try."

"What *I* should try—"

"Damn right. You're a walking zombie. You lost your son; we all lost him." Louisa was tearing up, drying her eyes with both index fingers to keep her mascara from running. "But you act like you were the only one. You chased Daisy and that baby girl away."

"Leave them out of this," James said.

"Don't you tell me who to leave out of anything. I've got love in my heart, James Tucker, but you wouldn't know that if it bit you. You don't give anyone the time of day. It's you and your boy's ghost."

"You done?" James handed her a handkerchief to dry her tears.

Nodding, she blew her nose noisily. Together they watched Dalton draw the dart back even with his ear, throw a perfect bull's-eye. The young men standing around went wild.

"Look at him," Louisa said.

"He's still got it," James admitted.

"Mean as a cougar, with the eye of an eagle," Louisa said.

"Dead aim," James said. "I remember seeing him shoot the head off a rattlesnake hanging out the beak of a flying hawk." As he spoke, his father scanned the crowd, looking for Louisa. At the sight of her he smiled and looked proud.

It was time to go. James grabbed his jacket, then heard Louisa call his name.

"What?"

"Same goes for you," she said, smiling.

"What's that?"

"What you said about your father. He's still got it."

James turned and walked out of the bar.

IT WAS a long ride home, Louisa's words ringing in his ears. Got it, he thought. Got the ability to ride a horse, birth a calf. To smile at a girl, buy her a beer, take her to bed when you both knew you'd be gone before sunup. His truck swirled up a storm of dust, and James thought about how there was more than one kind of drought.

Driving through the gates of the DR Ranch, he passed the big stone house where his father and Louisa lived. He pulled around back to the narrow drive that took him to his log cabin. He had built it himself sixteen years ago from cedar logged on the mountain.

As he walked into the cabin, the telephone rang. "Hello?"

"James?"

"That you, Daisy?"

"Yes."

He waited to get his breath back again. He heard from her once or twice a year, always telling him something about Sage—her good grades, the essay she'd had published in the town newspaper—and informing him in none-too-kindly tones that he should send his daughter a telegram, a letter, a bunch of flowers. That he should get on a plane and visit her. Every time it was as if he were hearing Daisy's soft voice for the first time.

"How is she?" he asked, knowing Daisy had to be calling about Sage. There wasn't ever any other reason.

"She's . . . I don't know how to tell you this. Sage is missing."

"Missing?"

"She ran away. She left a note. Two notes, actually. The police are looking for her. We think she's heading out to see you."

"So you know where she is?" he asked, feeling relieved.

"No, we don't know, but I'm pretty sure she's on her way west. She's with her boyfriend."

James didn't reply as he thought about his daughter's having a boyfriend, how the last time he'd seen her she'd been just ready to start kindergarten.

"She's always wanted to go to you," Daisy said. "I know you think I should have sent her. You probably think that if I'd let her spend summers with you this never would have happened."

"No, I—"

"But I didn't want her traveling alone, and I couldn't stand thinking of her going to the place where Jake—"

"I know, Daisy."

"You could have come here," Daisy said.

"No," he said, "I couldn't."

"He's not coming back, James." Daisy's voice was shaking. "We've known that since the third or fourth day. Our son is dead, but your daughter's needed you all this time."

"He might," James said. "And I'm staying here in case he does."

"You're crazy, James," Daisy snapped. "It's been thirteen years. And now our daughter's so starved for your love, she's on a freight train heading out to see you!"

"You know that for sure?"

"No! I said no already." Daisy sounded frantic. "But she was asking questions at the depot, and they identified her picture."

"Which picture?"

"What's the difference?" Daisy asked, her voice rising.

But it did matter. James was standing by the stone mantel staring at the gallery of Sage's photographs from birth onward.

"They've alerted police departments all along the train line," Daisy said. "People will be checking the train at the next stop."

"Good." James's eyes stung; his vision was blurry.

"If she calls you—"

"I'll call you right away," James said.

"Thank you." Daisy's voice was clipped, as if she'd said everything she needed to say. James held on to the receiver for a long time, wishing she'd think of something else. Instead, she just said good-bye, and so did he.

Chapter
FOUR

THE train stopped in a cornfield outside Lone Tree, Iowa. Sage was lying on her side, curled into Ben's body, dreaming of cantering across her father's ranch on a white horse, feeling so happy—until the train began to stop with a screech, metal grinding against the tracks.

"What's happening?" she asked, terrified.

"It's . . . We're crashing!" Ben said.

Ben held her tight for the thirty seconds it took the brakes to hold back several thousand tons of hurtling locomotive and freight cars. Sage closed her eyes, both arms instinctively clutching her middle, to hold the baby inside her.

When the train shuddered to a stop, the silence was deafening. Ben and Sage looked at each other, then got up and hurried to the sliding door. Through a narrow crack Sage could see a midnight-blue sky, luminous over the cornfields. Several police cars were parked along a road running parallel to the tracks, their strobe lights flickering.

"What are they doing?" Sage asked. "Are we at a station?"

"I don't think so," Ben said.

Sage knew he was right. They had been traveling aboard the train for four days, long enough to know the rhythm of station stops. The engineer would start putting on the brakes gradually, slowing the big train bit by bit instead of all at once.

"Start at the front and work back!" someone yelled outside.

"Two teams," a different voice called back. "One takes the rear, the other goes forward."

Sage pressed her face harder against the crack in the door, trying to see what was going on. Police officers with flashlights seemed to be everywhere. Sage tried to tell herself maybe the train had hit something—a cow or a deer or even a person. But deep down she knew: They were looking for her and Ben.

"What should we do?" she asked.

"I don't know." Ben took her place, peering out the crack.

The last two days he hadn't said much. She had a nervous feeling all the time, as if she was waiting for something to happen—that she already knew what it was, but she was afraid to tell herself.

"I love you," she whispered.

"They're checking the cars," Ben said as if he hadn't heard her. "They're looking for us."

Sage wanted Ben to tell her everything would be fine; he'd take care of them; they could hide among the crates and keep going.

"You think they'll arrest us?" he asked.

Sage hadn't thought of that. She tried to take his hand, but she couldn't pry it off the metal door. "Ben?" she asked. "Ben?"

"They're two cars back," he said. "Maybe three."

"We have to get to the ranch."

"Oh, Sage," he said without looking at her. "That's just a dream."

"No," she said, holding her stomach. "It's real. There's a cabin for us there. The sky is so big, the stars fall right down to the ground. We could fish in the streams."

"Our mothers called the police." Ben's voice was cracking.

"I know," Sage whispered. Sitting down, she pressed her face against her knees. Tears spilled over as she thought of her mother.

"I think we should go home," Ben said, crouching beside her.

"I *am* going home," Sage said. She meant Wyoming.

Outside, the searchers were closing in. Sage heard them sliding train doors open, clanging them closed. Two state policemen stopped outside their car to light cigarettes. Holding her breath so they wouldn't hear her, Sage crawled over to look out.

"Whose brainstorm was this?" one asked. "Five more miles, the damn train would've been in the station."

"Element of surprise," the older guy said. "Where're two kids gonna run to out here? Into a cornfield? We take 'em in town, they could slip off, hide anywhere."

"Engineer's mad as hell."

"Tough luck."

"What are they, teenagers?"

"Yeah, boy and girl."

"Romeo and Juliet," the younger policeman said.

"Yeah, well, Romeo's old enough to know better. We got him for kidnap, statutory rape. He's looking at real time."

"Probably just young love."

"The court doesn't give a damn about young love. You don't stop a freight train, get two police forces out in the middle of the night, and not pay for it. The kid's going to jail."

Sage snapped her head to look at Ben. His mouth was hanging open with shock.

The two men ground out their cigarettes, drifted away. Sage grabbed Ben. "We can't let them catch us."

"They think I did that." He sounded bewildered. "I'm going to jail. I can't go to jail. I'm supposed to go to college."

"No," Sage said firmly. "I won't let them. I'll tell them it's all my fault, that I love you so much that—"

"Let's turn ourselves in." Ben's voice was shaking.

"Let's sneak off," Sage said. She began to pry the door open.

"They'll believe us," Ben said. "I know they will."

"I don't want to go back," Sage said, panicked.

"Sage," Ben said, "I want to go home."

"Ben, please," she said, gulping down a sob. Their journey across country, a new family together, had come to an end. Ben was leaving her—had left her already. Staring at Ben's hands clutching hers, she blinked away tears. If only she could make it last forever, this moment with Ben. Oh, why did God give people love, then take it away?

"I love you," she whispered. She was sobbing quietly.

"I love you, too," he said, his eyes sharp.

"Will you do something for me?"

"Yes," he said gruffly, wiping tears from his eyes.

"Tell them you're alone. Tell them I got off in Chicago some-where. Give me a little time."

"A head start." He glanced at the door. The policemen were get-ting closer; he could hear their voices.

"Yes." Pulling her hands away from his, she moved over to the trapdoor. She knew she had to move fast.

The trapdoor was about a yard square, big enough to push her bike and backpack through. Ben helped her, and Sage was think-ing she'd slip out, lie on the tracks under the train, waiting for everyone to move away. Ben would distract them for her, and by the time the ruckus died down, she'd be hiding in the field.

"I think you should come with me," Ben said.

"Please," she said, tears rising again. "Don't try to talk me into it."

"I know how much you want this, but—"

"You'll be okay, won't you?" She couldn't believe they'd arrest him. "I'll tell them you didn't do anything. As soon as I get to my dad's—"

"I'll be fine. I promise."

"Will you do something else for me?" she whispered.

"Yes."

"Hold me." His arms came around her. His breath was warm in her hair, and she felt their hearts pounding together.

"We're too young," he said. "I didn't want this to happen."

But it's happening, Sage thought. She memorized the feeling of his arms, the smell of his sweater, the dampness of his tears.

"You have to leave."

"I know."

"Fool them," she said. "Don't let them see you near this car."

"I'll try." He backed toward the trapdoor. "Sage . . ." he said, as if maybe he was reconsidering.

"Go!" she said, sobbing.

She heard his side brushing against the opening, his feet hitting the ground. Then she heard him running away. Her heart squeezed smaller and smaller as she wondered whether she would ever see him again.

Cradling her belly, she told the baby everything would be fine. She made her voice brave to sound as convincing as she could. The strange thing was, the more she talked, the more she believed it.

She heard men starting to shout and hustle past her car. Heart pumping, she took one last look around, then dropped through the opening. Landing softly on her pack, she lay on her back and tried to get her bearings. She could hear the voices of the officers surrounding Ben but couldn't make out his voice. This was her chance.

Scooting out from beneath the train, she hauled her bicycle out behind her. The air felt dry and cold. Sage strapped her pack on her back and climbed aboard. The police cars were on the other side of the train, but she could see their strobe lights reflected in the low clouds. Dawn was breaking.

A line of red showed above the horizon. Sage pointed her bicycle away from the rising sun and began to pedal west, between rows of dry cornstalks.

THE night before, while James had been burning irrigation ditches in the red-rock mine canyon, he heard a wild snarl. When he looked up, he saw a bobcat drive a calf off a cliff.

He had found the calf with its back broken. The animal struggled, trying to stand, still thinking it could run away. James crouched and petted the calf's long neck, trying to calm the creature. The calf's eye was wide and dark, and it stared up at James with terror.

"I'm sorry," James said.

Kicking its front legs, the calf was paralyzed in its hindquarters. It squealed, and its mother called back from above.

"You're not alone," James had said, because he thought it was important for creatures to know that. More than anything, he hated to think of anyone or any animal suffering alone. Standing, he had drawn his gun and fired, killing the calf instantly.

Now, the next morning, while saddling up, James tried to think about anything but the look in that calf's eye. He wished he hadn't seen the fear, known that the calf wanted nothing more than its mother. He wished he didn't think of his own children with that same look. Several days had passed since Daisy's call, and he hadn't gotten much sleep since, waiting for the phone to ring.

"Rain's coming."

James turned and saw his father standing by the stalls. The old man stepped forward, dressed for work in chaps and boots.

"Morning, Dad," James said.

"Seen those thunderheads over the basin? We'll get rain for sure today. Where you heading?"

"To the east pasture. Thought I'd check on the herd there."

"Want some company?"

James hesitated. The last time his father had come with him, Dalton had gotten disoriented and upset. He'd thought James was his father instead of his son, spun back fifty years to a time when they had been driving the Rydells' sheep off their land. James had brought him back to reality, set him straight on the father-son relationship, reminded him that he was living with Louisa Rydell—granddaughter of his archenemies—and that peace had been made a generation ago.

"Sure," James said now. "I'd be glad to have you."

They finished saddling up, led their horses outside, mounted up, and started riding east. "Damnedest drought I ever saw," Dalton said, cantering alongside past a stand of cottonwoods. "Lasting clear into October."

James didn't need to be told. He'd been praying for rain all summer. He had cows so thirsty they were trying to drink dirt.

"Taught you how to irrigate," Dalton said. "The old way, the right way."

"The hard way."

"You complainin'?" Dalton asked testily.

"Wouldn't do that, Dad." Neighboring ranches had fancy irrigation systems with pumps and sprinklers on timers. Everything was automatic, computer-operated. But when the well ran dry, they also paid to have water trucked in.

The Tucker way suited James. It wasn't the easiest, but it felt real to him. He had to climb on his horse twice a day, ride out to the pastures to regulate the water. He had to walk the land, know every rock and crevice. It gave him comfort to know he was part of the land, closer to Jake. It was a small thing, but it gave him a little peace.

"Louisa said Daisy called."

"Yeah, she did." James had passed Daisy's message on to Louisa, just in case Sage tried to call the ranch and she happened to answer.

"Your girl's gone missing?"

"That's what Daisy says." James felt his stomach drop.

"She's a teenager. Teenagers hate staying home. You think I don't remember the time you decided to borrow my pickup, drive all the way to Lander? You were all of fifteen—no license, no nothing."

"I remember," James said. It was the year his mother had died and Dalton had started seeing Louisa. James had acted half-crazed, drinking till dawn, skipping class, taking his father's truck. When Louisa moved in, the half-crazed became full-blown.

"Well, there you go. Nothing's wrong with your daughter that growing up won't fix."

"Hey, Dad . . ." James didn't know exactly what he wanted to say, but he knew the subject had to do with his children and Daisy, the losses they'd suffered—things he never talked of to his father.

"Clouds are movin' in," Dalton said. "Hope Louisa remembers to take her wash in early, because the sky's gonna open up."

James didn't say anything. His father had sensed something coming and saved them both from James's saying something stupid. Tuckers didn't talk about love. They didn't cry about the past or speak of dreams for the future. They didn't express fears or doubts. They just got the job done.

FROM the ridge he could see so far. Canyons, pastures, ranch, and range. The mountains ringed the scene. Whenever he stood here, he felt as if he mattered, as if he had a home.

He also felt very alone. No one knew he was here, and no one cared. Sometimes he saw the ranchers tending to calves, and his eyes would burn with tears. That's what fathers were supposed to do: look after their own.

Mothers and fathers. Out on the range he saw so many parents and young: deer and fawns, cows and calves, coyotes and pups. The babies deserved a chance to grow up, but plenty didn't make it. The ranch was a brutal place to live—or die.

He didn't care anymore. He'd sit up here while the storms passed, wait forever if he had to. Thunder cracked, but to him it was a dream song. This was his mountain.

You're a good boy. The words came from far away, in another voice. Someone had told him that once, and he told himself now. Hoofbeats sounded below, and he shrank against the rock ledge. He wasn't ready to be seen. Yellow leaves were falling now. Maybe when the snows came, then he'd show himself. Maybe then he'd claim his mountain home. Another thunder crack, and he inched closer to the ledge. He'd always needed something to believe in, and he'd always found it here, on the ranch.

Growing sleepy, he curled up in a dry spot and let the dream songs come. *You're a good boy,* he heard. *You are a good boy.*

LOUISA Rydell stood on the wide porch, drinking coffee as she watched a line of antelope climb the side of the mountain. She watched the big purple clouds billow over the valley, and she thought about Sage. She hadn't seen the girl in years, but there had been a time she had considered her her own grandbaby. She had baby-sat the twins every chance she'd had, back when they'd all been one happy, crazy, extended western family—Rydells and Tuckers on the same ranch. Louisa's father would never have believed it.

Even James had come around. After a decade of despising Louisa for—as he'd probably put it—taking his mother's place in Dalton's heart, he had come to respect her. A woman good enough to be liked by Daisy was good enough to be tolerated by James. Louisa certainly missed that younger woman's presence.

Louisa sighed. One of the cow dogs had smelled her breakfast roll, and he came nosing up the porch steps.

"What do you want?" she asked, as if she didn't know.

The sheltie licked her hand, then rolled onto his back so she'd scratch his belly. Louisa thought of all the kids she'd sat with on this porch, all the cow dogs whose bellies she'd scratched. The more she tickled the dog's belly, the more he wanted. His left leg was kicking the air like a jackrabbit's. Louisa tried to laugh, but that just made the pain in her heart feel bigger.

"Damn it all," she said. There had been so much love on this ranch—back when this family wasn't falling apart, she thought.

She straightened up. She wore a flowing blue dress, the color of mountain gentians. Her eye makeup matched. Around her neck hung BEAR MOTHER, the necklace Daisy had made for her. It came from the bones of a female grizzly shot by James one summer night when it had attacked the tent where he, Daisy, and the kids were camping. After the attack James had found two cubs waiting down the hill. The mother had sensed her babies were in danger, and she had done what she had to do.

Daisy had understood. She had wept for the bear, and for weeks afterward she made James ride into those hills to search for the cubs, make sure they were surviving on their own. He'd spotted them twice, but after that he'd seen only one. The other had disappeared.

Louisa's necklace was meant to symbolize the mother bear's great spirit. She reigned over the ranch, the mountains and canyons, protecting the young of mothers everywhere.

Louisa held the necklace in her hands. The beads were polished jasper, turquoise, and bear bones. Teeth and claws hung around the medallion. When James had seen it, he'd said it looked too aggressive and wild, like nothing Daisy had ever done before. Louisa had understood that his words were directed at her, that no one else could have inspired the delicate Daisy to make such a violent piece, fanged and clawed. But Louisa hadn't cared. She and Daisy understood there wasn't a more aggressive creature in the world than a mother protecting her babies.

Having worn the necklace every day since Daisy gave it to her, Louisa had taken it off after they lost Jake. It had seemed futile to wear an amulet of protection that had failed to protect. But this morning, thinking of Sage, Louisa had put the necklace on again.

The first drops of rain fell, hitting the ground and raising dust. Shooing the dog away, Louisa knew what she had to do. She walked inside, ready to make a telephone call that wasn't going to be easy.

WRAPPED in a shawl, Daisy huddled in her workroom. Five days after Sage's disappearance it hurt to breathe. Detective LaRosa had just called and reported that Sage wasn't on the train. Ben had told them she'd gotten off in Chicago.

Although the police had not believed him, they hadn't found her yet. Sage hadn't been kidnapped, nor was she a criminal; therefore, the FBI had not been called in. The investigation depended on the efforts of many small jurisdictions, none of which rated a pregnant runaway their top priority.

The telephone rang. Daisy lunged for the receiver. "Sage!"

"No, darlin', it's me," came Louisa's low western voice. "Have the police called yet?"

"They can't find her." Daisy squeezed her eyes shut. Her intuitive sense that Sage was headed for the ranch had grown into a conviction. "I just know she's on her way to James."

"Daisy, ever since you called James with the news, I've been thinking," Louisa said. "We were close once, you and I . . ."

The older woman's voice was full of affection and something like nostalgia, but Daisy didn't have time to talk about old times. "I . . . I can't talk right now. I'm waiting for my daughter to call."

"I want you to hear me out," Louisa insisted, her voice stern.

Hathaway must have just arrived, because she came into the room still wearing her jacket.

"It's Louisa," Daisy told her.

"Is that your sister?" Louisa asked from half a country away. "I'm glad she's there. You shouldn't be alone right now, and when you hear what I'm about to say, you'll want to run it by her."

"What do you want to tell me?" Daisy asked hesitantly.

"It's this," Louisa said. "I want you to come to the ranch."

Daisy felt the blood pounding in her ears. "You're joking. I can't do that." The ranch was the site of her worst nightmare. She wouldn't be able to see those jagged rocks, smell that sage-scented air, without thinking of her little boy. Besides, what did this have to do with Sage? "I can't," she said. "I won't."

"Don't you want to help your daughter?" Louisa asked.

"How dare you!" Daisy's voice was shaking.

"Hang up, Daisy," Hathaway said, not understanding what was going on, just seeing her sister's distress.

"Settle down," Louisa said. "You're out of your mind, Daisy. I would be, too. But this is where you belong right now. Not forever, but for this waiting time."

"What good will my going there do?"

"It'll show Sage that you and her father can set your differences aside for now. Put her first. Be at the ranch waiting for her with open arms when she comes walking through the gate. She's a troubled little girl, and she needs her parents. Both of them."

"She's pregnant," Daisy said, the words spilling out.

"Well, I figured that might be the case," Louisa said. "Her running off so fast and dramatic. It's just what I did."

"What you did?"

"When I got pregnant. I was barely older than Sage—seventeen."

"I hadn't known."

"My father had died a few years back. I'm not saying that fact alone made me get pregnant, but it contributed. I missed him so, wanted his love so badly, I went running off with the first boy who came along. I just needed to be filled with love."

"But you were married when you had Ruthie," Daisy said, remembering the story about Louisa's husband Earl, how he had died right after the baby was born.

"That's just what I told people."

"But you said Earl died—"

"In my heart. I killed him off in my heart when it came clear he wasn't going to marry me and give our baby a name."

"But—"

"Daisy, my lying about Earl's neither here nor there. I just did it to protect Ruthie. The point is, all I wanted was to go home. My daddy was dead. My mother'd remarried, but her house wasn't a refuge to me. All I wanted was home. *My* home."

"The ranch," Daisy said. "Sage's first home."

"The only home where you all lived together as a family."

Confused and hurting, Daisy shook her head. Still, there was something in what Louisa was saying. When Daisy moved back east, she had ripped Sage away from everyone who loved her: father, grandfather, and Louisa. Daisy had been so busy trying to survive her own grief, she had made some selfish decisions. Needing to keep her only living child away from the ranch, she had kept her from her father.

"Thank you," she managed to say. "For being so honest with me. I'll think about it. I really will."

"That's all I'm asking you to do," Louisa said kindly.

"Louisa, will you keep this between us? I mean, don't tell James about Sage being pregnant."

"Never, Daisy."

Carefully Daisy hung up the phone. She turned to Hathaway. "Louisa thinks I should go to Wyoming."

Daisy waited for her sister to laugh, scoff, shake her head in disbelief. Instead, Hathaway said gently, "I agree with Louisa."

"But why? I don't understand."

"To be waiting at the ranch when Sage gets there. She has her reasons for going back there, and so do you."

"I don't want to go to the ranch," Daisy heard herself say, the words sounding like echoes in a deep canyon.

"But I think you're going to go anyway. It's meant to be."

"How do you know?"

"Because I'm the older sister," she said. "I know everything."

ELEVEN hours after leaving the train, Sage stopped to check her map. She was exhausted. Digging through her pack, she pulled out the travel kit she had made before leaving home: flashlight, matches, and a map of the United States.

She realized how near she had come to being caught and sent back home. One part of her wished she would be found. She kept thinking of Ben, wondering where he was, remembering that moment when he'd said he wanted to go back to Silver Bay. The memory made her feel alone in ways she had never felt before.

She got back on her bike and rode past empty cornfields, the stalks shorn to foot-high stubble. Sage's stomach rumbled. A few miles back she had found some unharvested ears, and she'd eaten the dry kernels, trying to pretend they were unpopped popcorn.

A pickup passed, going in her direction, and she saw the driver check his rearview mirror. Sage felt her stomach lurch. What if he came back? She was way out in the middle of nowhere, and she knew full well to be leery of strangers offering her rides. But the driver just kept going.

There were no twists in the road, no hills. She could see two houses up ahead, two red barns. The first house had a tricycle parked by a lamppost. A neatly trimmed hedge ran around the yard. There was a flagpole surrounded by chrysanthemums, the American flag standing out straight in the stiff wind. Sage thought about going right up to the front door, asking for a place to stay that night.

They'd call the police in two seconds flat.

Instead, Sage wheeled her bike around to the barn. She watched the house windows to see if anyone was looking. The sky was getting dark, and gentle shadows coated the yard. Pushing the heavy barn door half open, she slipped inside. She felt cold and alone, furtive as a criminal. Here she was in Iowa, hiding in a barn.

A horse whinnied. Small and shaggy, it tossed its head as she approached. She saw a pile of apples and carrots on a low shelf, and she ate some hungrily. The pony nickered, and she fed it an apple. Bone-tired, Sage climbed a ladder to the hayloft, crawled into the hay pile, and snuggled into a ball. She felt her belly. "We're safe now," she whispered. "We're not there yet, but we're safe for the night."

DAVID Crane loved the car because it took him away. He stepped on the gas and sped on. The car was ancient, with rust holes and missing trim, and it smelled of wet fur. Inside, animals huddled all through the car. Their eyes were wide open, alert in the night.

Driving east through Wyoming, he neared the Nebraska border. He hesitated, rolling down his window to listen to the wind. Here the ponderosa pines were dark and thick, and their boughs brushed against each other, telling him which way to go: *Turn left, take the highway, drive fast.* It was as specific as that.

He got his directions from nature: the sun, the moon, the wind—signals he couldn't explain—and he followed them without too many questions. The directions always led him to creatures who needed to be rescued.

One of the dogs barked, and he knew it was time to stop.

"Want to go out?" he asked.

Two of the dogs whimpered in response.

He pulled over, then opened the car's rear door to let the dogs out. They tromped into the trees, without any of the joy of normal dogs. Doing their business, they kept close watch on their driver. When they had finished, he whistled. They dutifully marched back to the car, one clenching an old stuffed toy in her teeth.

"Inside, Petal," he said, giving her a gentle pat. "That's a girl."

Petal was his first rescue. A white, black, and brown pit bull, she gripped her toy in her massive jaws, drool soaking it. He had given her the toy himself, something ancient from his own childhood, to help her feel secure.

With everyone safe in the old car, he opened the glove compartment. He had dropped out of school years ago. Nature taught him better than any teacher. And right now nature was pulling him hard.

His work—saving things—kept him mostly in Wyoming, where there were plenty of barns filled with stray cats, hundreds of puppy farms run by cruel owners. But right now he felt the tug toward Nebraska. He had never felt such a compulsion.

Something needed him. Rifling through the glove compartment, he found his kit. He took out a fine-tipped fountain pen and ink. Then he dipped the pen point into the bottle of ink and shook the loose drops onto the dirty floor of the old car.

Pen point nearly dry, he adjusted the rearview mirror. It was dark, but he could see by the moonlight slanting through the pine boughs. He drew a dot on his left cheek, another on his right. He enclosed each dot with a fine circle. The markings were significant, although he couldn't have explained where the idea to make them came from. They symbolized protection, things to be saved. He knew he had something big ahead of him. It might be a hurt dog, a litter of abandoned kittens, an owl with a broken wing. David didn't know; he'd have to wait till he got there.

That's how it felt to him, starting up the car, driving into Nebraska—as if he was heading into danger, as if whatever needed him was bigger than anything he had ever handled before.

DALTON Tucker's prediction came true: The rain came. And once it started, it fell in torrents. Sheets of silver rain blew down the mountains, filling the lakes and riverbeds. Bison, moose, elk, and antelope drank alongside cattle. Dust turned to mud.

On horseback James was moving cattle down from the summer range. He wore his hat, chaps, a boot-length green slicker, but he was still drenched. The brim of his hat acted as a spout, and rain trickled down his collar. At least it kept his mind off the worst of what might be happening—off the six days his daughter had been missing.

The calves scrabbled in the mud, trying to get closer to their mothers. The younger ones wailed and the mothers moaned.

"James," Paul March called. "Got a stuck one over there."

James turned to look. A calf had sunk up to its chest. It looked helpless and frightened. James galloped over, drew back his rope, and threw a loop around the calf's neck.

"She's stuck good," Paul said, riding over.

"We'll get her out," James said. With a half hitch around the saddle horn, he kicked his horse forward. The calf began to move. She popped out of the mud, found her legs, ran to her mother.

"Heard about Daisy coming out," Paul said. "That true?"

"That's what Louisa says." James had heard the news last night. Seems Louisa had taken it upon herself to stir the pot.

"Well—" Paul began.

James cleared his throat to cut Paul off. His eyes narrowed, watching his father. Across the pasture Dalton sat tall in the saddle, seeming oblivious to the rain.

"Been a long time since she was here," Paul said, not getting the message.

"Hmm. Yeah," James said, not wanting to think about Daisy. It was a thought that picked up emotion as it passed through his mind. Long time ago it might have been attached to hope. Now he found it was linked to dread. "Where'd you hear about her?"

"The Rydell boys," Paul said. "Talking at the bar last night."

Louisa's nephews, James thought. She must have told them, getting the word out. He wondered whether she'd included the part about Sage's running away from home. Paul March was his ranch foreman—a good man and a real friend. But James didn't want Todd Rydell talking about Daisy or Sage.

"Nothing's definite," James said. "She might come, might not."

"Look, I know about your daughter being missing," Paul said. "You've got to be worried sick. But she'll show up."

"Yeah." James wiped rain off his face with the back of his hand.

"James, talk to me. Okay? I was there, remember?"

"There?"

"When Jake went."

"Went . . ." James repeated, considering the word. A mild, gentle word for the whole world falling apart.

"You've got to be going crazy. Why haven't you said anything?"

James looked Paul straight in the eye. The foreman was big and stocky, going bald under his hat. He had pale brown eyes, the color of the land. The men had grown up together, right here on the DR Ranch. Paul's father had been foreman to Dalton, just as Paul's grandfather had been foreman to Dalton's father, Asa.

James had gone to school with the March kids—Paul, his sister June, and their brother Luke. He and Paul had their first beers together at a bar in Lander. They had attended each other's weddings. Paul and his wife had baby-sat for the twins. Paul was the closest

James had to a best friend. But in a million years James wouldn't have considered telling him about Sage's leaving home.

"Nothing to say," James replied after a long minute.

"I don't know." Paul shook his head. "Seems like there's a whole lot to get off your chest."

"My chest's fine," James said. "Mind your own business."

"Whatever you say." Paul, his jaw set, seemed about to add something more, but then he wheeled on his horse and rode away.

It was hard being James's friend. Daisy had told him that. He could sit and listen to another man's woes about money, wife, kids, but James couldn't take kindness. Expressions of love, friendship—whatever you wanted to call it—made him want to crawl out of his skin.

Now maybe Daisy was coming west.

Daisy Tucker. Those big eyes. She'd look at the mountains, the animals, the big blue sky and have it all come out of her hands in the jewelry she made. Daisy had love in her hands. The first time she'd held James, he had felt himself come alive. When she touched his skin, he believed in heaven. Heaven had been Daisy's gift. For their five years together James had lived with more peace and bliss than he'd ever dreamed possible.

Suddenly he heard his father cry out, then call, "I'm all wet!"

"Dalton, hey—"

Shaken from his thoughts, James looked across the field of cattle. Dalton had climbed off his horse. Trying to dry himself off with a red bandanna, he stood among the herd, getting jostled.

"It's raining, Dalton," Paul said. "We're all wet."

"Why am I all wet?" Dalton asked, as if he hadn't heard him.

Some of the young cowboys were laughing. James turned away from them. He didn't want to remember who to resent for making fun of his father. James shouldered through the herd. His father had no business being here. He had ridden out on his own after James and the other hands had left the barn that morning. Now Dalton was trying to get his sopping clothes off, stripping off his slicker, unbuttoning his shirt. James felt the pressure of so many worries: Sage, Daisy, now his father. He wanted to explode.

"All wet," Dalton said sorrowfully. "Soaking wet."

"You're okay," James said. Swinging down from his horse, he stood by his father in the middle of the swirling herd. Cattle stepped on their feet, bumped against their bodies. "Don't worry, Dad."

"I don't like it," Dalton said. His expression was childlike, panicked. He was naked, having pulled off all his clothes.

James picked up the old man's yellow slicker and wrapped it around him. He held his father, and he used the words Daisy had come up with at times to soothe their son: "It's only water," James said. "There's nothing to worry about. Nothing at all."

DAISY rang the Davis house twenty times before noon. Half the time it was busy; the other half she got the answering machine. When both kids had still been missing, Paulina had answered Daisy's calls screaming that she would like to kill Sage; she had known she was bad news from the minute Ben had brought her over. Daisy had hung up on her.

But Daisy had kept calling. The parents had to stay connected, to report any new developments. With Ben on his way home, Paulina was smug and cold. At least he was safe. Paulina had promised he would call, but still he hadn't.

Just about to dial again, Daisy heard a knock at the back door, and she pulled it open.

Ben stood on the porch. He wore a parka and looked scared. "My mother told me you called," he said. "It seemed better that I come over than call you."

"Come in." Then swallowing, she said, "Tell me, where is Sage?"

He stared at the floor. "I don't know. We were together until—"

"Don't lie to me!" she yelled. "You lied to the police, you lied to your mother. But damn it, you're going to tell me the truth." Choking on a sob, she stared into Ben's shocked eyes. "I'm sorry," she said. "I have to know. Tell me, Ben."

"She was in Iowa, Mrs. Tucker, just like I told the police—"

"After you said she'd gotten off the train in Chicago?"

"She told me to. She wanted time to get away from the train.

She didn't want to get found. I don't think she will be, until—"

"Until what?" Daisy asked, desperate to hear.

"She gets to Wyoming," he said.

Daisy tried to breathe. Wyoming. She broke down with the relief of finally knowing for sure. Her instinct had been right: Sage was going to James.

"Is she pregnant, Ben?" Daisy asked.

"Yeah."

Daisy heard herself moan. Ben had just confirmed what she'd already known. "Is she okay?"

"She's feeling sick."

"Then she's not very far along."

"Six months," Ben said, and Daisy's heart fell.

"Six—" How was it possible that she hadn't noticed?

Chapter FIVE

FLYING across the country, Daisy had watched the cities of the East give way to the flat Midwest. She had seen the Mississippi River glisten, the badlands darken.

Now, looking down, she saw the Rocky Mountains rise. She and Sage were on their way to the same place. Ben had returned home and confirmed that Sage was determined to reach her father. "Let her be safe," Daisy whispered, her forehead against the airplane window.

Louisa had offered to pick her up at the airport, but Daisy wanted to be as independent as possible, so she had decided to rent a car and drive to the ranch. As the plane circled the airport, the sky seemed hinged to mountaintops. The land was red, rust, and purple. Something inside her stirred, a part that had been asleep for a long time.

Daisy closed her eyes. She didn't want to be seduced by the land, by the big sky. Sage would show up soon, she told herself. They would be in and out of the state quickly.

After the plane landed, she went into the terminal to the Hertz counter. As the clerk processed her reservation, a pregnant woman passed by, pushing a stroller. That gave her two pictures to consider: Sage pregnant; Sage as a new mother.

Daisy got a midsize Ford, threw her bags in, and began to drive. She kept her eyes on the road. Anytime she raised her gaze, she saw the Wind River mountains: rugged and majestic against the blue sky. She kept the car windows open, and the perfume of the West blew in: sage, spice, fur, and dust.

She passed a rock formation spray-painted with the name "Sacagawea," a graffiti tribute to the Shoshone girl kidnapped in an Indian raid. Daisy jammed on the brakes and pulled over. She stared at the boulder, reading the name. From Daisy's first days in Wyoming, Sacagawea had intrigued her. Many of her first western necklaces had been inspired by the Shoshone girl: carvings depicting courage, mother love, living in nature, stepping into the unknown.

Kidnapped from her family, Sacagawea was sold as a wife to a fur trader. Daisy could think of nothing more disgusting than being forced to marry someone she didn't know or love, to have his baby.

But Sacagawea had loved and protected her child. She and her infant boy survived their harrowing journey with the Lewis and Clark expedition. People always thought Daisy had named her own daughter Sage after the beautiful sagebrush so common to Wyoming soil, and it was partly true. But Daisy had named her also after Sacagawea.

Strengthened by the sight of the name, Daisy pulled back onto the road. She found herself raising her eyes now, looking around. The mountains were already capped with snow, were filled with mystery and magic, wind and spirits.

By the time she reached the gates of the DR Ranch, it was starting to get dark. She drove through the tunnel of cottonwood trees. The main house was warmly lit, the stone and logs glowing like a jewel box, smoke curling from the enormous chimney.

Louisa was at the window. She stepped outside onto the porch, the wind blowing her red shawl. Parking the car, Daisy felt her heart beating in her throat. Looking around at the barns, the paddocks, and the house itself, she felt as if she'd gone back in time.

"Hello, stranger," Louisa called, coming down the porch steps.

"Hi, Louisa," Daisy said as Louisa swept her into her arms and held her tight. When Louisa finally stood back, Daisy saw that she was wearing the Bear Mother necklace.

"Has there been any word?" Daisy asked. "I've been out of touch since early afternoon, and I told Hathaway to call here if she heard from Sage. I also gave this number to Detective LaRosa."

"No word yet," Louisa said.

Daisy nodded, feeling dizzy. A burst of wind fluttered Louisa's shawl, and as she drew it closer around her body, her fingers jangled the bones and metal of her necklace. She met Daisy's eyes.

"I'm wearing it for Sage."

"Thank you," Daisy said.

A pack of cowboys rode in, and Daisy tensed. She looked for James among them, but he wasn't there. Recognizing Paul March, Victor Lansing, and some other ranch hands, she watched them ride around the barns to the back pasture.

"The Marches and Lansings are still here?" she asked.

"Yes, they are. James runs a good operation, just like his father did. I'll say that for him."

"How is Dalton?" Daisy asked.

"He's my mountain," Louisa said. "That's how he is."

Daisy nodded, wondering about the pain—fleeting, hardly apparent—in Louisa's eyes. Louisa hadn't changed a bit. Her hair was still dark and lustrous, her makeup dramatic.

"We'll have time to catch up later," Louisa said. "But right now you must be dog-tired. Let me take you to your cabin."

"Sounds good." Daisy wanted a hot bath, a chance to get used to the idea she was back here. The sensation of being in a time warp was intense: She would look up and see James loping down the trail, holding the twins on his saddle.

"I've put you down by the river. Remember that little white cottage? It's all ready for you. It's the closest thing we have to a seaside cottage."

Daisy knew that little house very well. Although she and James had lived in it together only briefly, some of their most important history had taken place there.

"Does James—"

"He knows you're coming." Louisa paused. "One of the hands said he had a crisis down on the range, so—"

"You don't have to apologize for him," Daisy said. "I didn't expect him to be here."

"I put you as far from James as possible," Louisa said confidentially, wrapping her right arm around Daisy's shoulders. "You know he lives at the way other end of the ranch."

"In our old house," Daisy heard herself say.

"Yep. He's still there. I picked the little house so you won't be running into each other every ten seconds. I know this reunion, under these circumstances, can't be easy for either of you."

MAKING headway, Sage had ridden her bike for twenty-five miles, through more cornfields than she could imagine. Iowa seemed endless. She'd slept in another barn the night before, eating grains and vegetables left for the animals. Twice she'd milked cows, filling her cup with warm milk.

She coasted into a small town with three stores, a post office, and a bowling alley. The parking lot was crowded. Sage hadn't eaten since dawn, and she was so hungry and weary.

She noticed a bread truck pulling into the parking lot: bright blue. Stenciled in yellow were the words CINDERELLA BAKED GOODS. SERVING WESTERN IOWA. Sage heard the driver call hello to the bowling alley's cook, say he was running late on his trip back to Nebraska. Her heart beat faster.

When the deliveryman went inside, he left the back of the truck open. A little silver ramp tilted up from the pavement. Sage pushed her bike straight in. Nebraska was one state closer to Wyoming.

The truck's bread shelves were wide and deep, and right away she saw a good hiding place: under the bottom shelf. It was low to the floor, and Sage had to take the front wheel off to shove her bike underneath. By twisting and pushing, she got it well hidden. Then taking a snowflake roll from a box on a shelf, she rolled under the low shelf opposite her bike.

A few minutes later the truck door clanged shut and the engine started up. Sage lay on her back, enclosed by metal shelves and the truck's wall and floor. Her heart ached with loneliness as she pictured her mother's face. She missed her with all her heart.

DAVID tried to stay warm. The night was so cold, his breath was white. As he drove, the dogs slept beside him, all crowded into the front seat. He knew he should stop to get some rest, but the terrible thing was pulling him onward.

Terrible—that was the word that kept filling his mind. A creature who needed him would be hurt, possibly killed, unless he got there. He had never felt this sense of urgency before.

Nebraska was much flatter than Wyoming. It seemed like a lot of farmland, a lot of barns and houses. He had a list of puppy farms he'd taken from his parents' office, and at certain times he thought maybe he should be heading to one of them. But nature seemed to be urging him to head southeast.

Petal stayed awake beside him. She gnawed her toy, feeling it in her mouth. He knew she needed something to bite on, to hold, to take the place of all the puppies she had lost.

He had been passing farm after farm, but suddenly his headlights caught a long flash of white along the road. White dots, one after the other, low to the ground: a speckled snake, a huge white caterpillar. He slammed on the brakes and steered onto the shoulder. Maybe this is it, he thought. Whatever it is I'm here to save.

Leaping out of the car, he ran after the slinky white creature into the field. Overhead he heard wings beating. He saw yellow eyes: an owl on the hunt. He watched it swooping down.

As his own eyes became accustomed to the darkness, he saw that the white dots were in fact paws. He was chasing a family of black cats. The mother had been leading a pack of six white-footed black kittens, trying to hide them from the owl.

"Yah!" he yelled to chase the bird away. "Yee-hah!"

He knew owls—he loved them for reasons he couldn't explain—but he knew they meant death to small animals.

"Get away!" David screamed, chasing the owl. He ran in a circle, keeping the cats safely inside. For a minute he thought he had been successful. But the owl came back, diving with feet extended. Grabbing the mother cat, it lifted her into the sky.

He remembered a cave. Owls had filled the dark space—scores of yellow eyes watching over him when he was all alone. They had called, low and wise, telling him that soon he would be found.

David sobbed. He cried so hard his tears washed off the last of the dots on his cheeks. He couldn't hate the owls for being owls, but his heart ached at seeing the mother ripped from her babies. It reminded him of himself: Right now, most of the time, he felt yanked in half.

Something scratched his leg through his jeans, and he felt claws on his skin. Then he felt fur on his face, and he realized the kittens had climbed up his pants and wanted to slide down the neck of his shirt. Fuzzy black balls, white paws.

"Okay," David said, wiping his eyes. "I'll find you guys a bottle somewhere." A drugstore, he thought. A doll's bottle and a can of baby formula. He'd keep the newborn kittens alive.

Maybe this was why he'd come to Nebraska.

These kittens had needed him, and he had been here to save them. Starting the car, he told himself that was it.

So why the hell did he keep driving east? If this was his big moment, why didn't the feeling of terror stop? He had it still—that awful pounding in his head, the slamming of his pulse, telling him to drive faster, get there or else.

THE afternoon of Daisy's arrival James had been checking water holes with Paul March when he came upon a dead calf. He dismounted and went over to it expecting to find teeth and claw marks. Instead, he found a bullet hole in the calf's back, the letter X carved on its side.

"What do you make of this?" Paul asked.

"I don't know." James stared down at the calf.

"Some sick jerk from off the highway?"

"Someone sick, that's for sure," James said. His ranch land lay in a notch of the Wind River mountains. A narrow pass led from it to the Indian reservation, and tourists used the route.

James hoped a stranger had done this, but he didn't know. Bad blood ran thick and deep around here. In past generations grandfathers and great-grandfathers had killed each other over grazing rights. Sheep ate faster than cows—they'd uncover a whole hillside in less than a year—and that had caused a near war long ago.

"This look like a warning to you?" James asked.

"That's what I was thinking myself," Paul replied.

"Killing a calf's one thing," James said. "Cutting it up's another."

"It was left here to be found, that's for sure. Different from the other times, though."

"Not different enough," James said grimly. He had hoped the bad things had stopped.

One morning nearly a year ago he had made a gruesome discovery: a cow head stuck on a fence pole. Three riders, Paul among them, found three more. All together four cows had been slaughtered.

Last July someone had poisoned the water tank. Twenty head of cattle had drunk from it, taken sick. Eleven had died before nightfall, and James had had to have the others put down.

Suspicions in both cases had ranged from anti-beef people to folks with grudges against the Tuckers. That made a long list. Their family dated back a hundred and fifty years here. People wanted their land for sheep, gold, cattle, and now subdivisions, and the Tuckers had always held on.

"Where's Todd Rydell?" James asked.

"Where is he?" Paul sounded confused. "Working, I guess."

"Still driving a truck?"

Paul nodded. "Think so. Last I heard he was delivering packages for one of those freight companies. Couldn't make it on a horse, had to get himself a truck. He was the sorriest cowboy I ever saw. But you're not figuring him for this, are you?"

"I don't know what I'm figuring." James didn't like coincidences, and it bothered him that someone would butcher a calf the day Daisy was due in. He knew Todd carried a resentment over the way he'd been questioned about Jake, that he held against all Tuckers the fact that they still had the ranch while his family had lost their land.

"Todd's not vicious," Paul said.

"He likes a grievance, though," James told him. "He sticks it in the bank, hoards it like the family fortune."

"That *is* his family fortune," Paul said. "The only Rydell living on a ranch these days is Louisa, and it's your ranch she's living on."

"Take a look at him next time you're downtown, that's all."

"I'll do that." Paul stood, looking down at the calf. Then he raised his eyes to James. "Seen Daisy yet?"

"Not yet. Don't see how I can avoid it, though, seeing as how she's staying on the ranch."

"Huh." Paul scuffed his boot in the dust.

"You seem mighty curious about me seeing Daisy."

Paul frowned. He squinted into the sun, which made him frown harder. "Could just be that I care," he said.

"About Daisy."

"About all of you."

Two weather-beaten cowboys standing over a dead cow, talking about caring. James wanted to treat it like a joke, but all he could do was nod his thanks.

James had that in mind a few hours later when he galloped through the notch toward the DR Ranch. Louisa had told him she was putting Daisy in the white cottage, a fact that had stopped James cold. He had thought about suggesting somewhere different, but he'd held his tongue. Daisy had probably done a better job of setting the past to rest than he had.

The lights of the ranch were coming on. James felt the evening chill in his bones. He rode toward the corral, then changed his mind and steered his horse down toward the narrow river. The harvest moon shimmered between two peaks, lighting his way.

Looking toward the white cottage, he saw her. James pulled on the reins, stopping in the shadows. The big bay lowered his head, and James let him drink from the river. Daisy came out the doorway. The little cottage was old, one of the original ranch buildings. It had served as a one-room schoolhouse, a potting shed, and James's mother's music studio. Now, standing on the porch, Daisy gazed up at the moon. Her brown hair looked coppery in the moonlight; her face and throat had the luster of a pearl. Her body looked full and beautiful under her pale robe.

Oh, that posture: James knew it well. As she reached out, she pointed her index finger, as if she could direct the moon to do what she wanted it to. And James knew her well enough to imagine what she was telling the moon right now: Light Sage's way. Wherever she is, however dark her path might be, bring her safely home. Along with her, James said the words he imagined Daisy saying.

Daisy's arm fell to her side, and he heard her crying. James wanted to jump down from his horse, go to her, and hold her. Of course, she wasn't his to hold. She hadn't been for a long time.

She gripped the porch railing and looked up at the moon again. Then she cupped her hands around her mouth. Right away James knew what was coming.

"Washakie!" she called, a cry like lightning in James's veins.

"Washakie," James said back, in a voice too low for her to hear.

When Daisy went inside, she closed the door behind her. She must have thrown dry branches on the fire, because suddenly sparks flew up the chimney. Then she closed the curtains and turned off the lights. James watched until the house was dark, and then he gave his horse a kick and headed for home.

HAPPY families home on the range.

He had pitched his tent near the ranch buildings. A lady had arrived: pretty and sexy. She had Tucker in a stir, the way he was snapping at everyone, riding home hours earlier than usual.

Mothers and fathers. Sheep and cows.

He felt drawn to this place. He marked his leather belt with another notch. The DR herd was a little smaller tonight. His knife had done its work—cutting cowhide. Now it was time for the whetstone.

Drawing out the stone, he wet it with spit. The blade flashed in the light from the kerosene stove, and he began to slice it back and forth across the stone. *Sssh, ssssh,* it went. A real cowboy lullaby.

His gun gleamed on the tent floor. He felt safe here. He was armed. If anyone attacked him, they'd get a big surprise.

Washakie. The name reminded him of something. Wasn't there a legend, some Shoshone chief? Didn't matter.

Her voice rang in his ears. He hated mournful women who coddled their own hurt feelings while everyone else suffered. Men were out trying to protect what was rightfully theirs—their family's— while the women cried at home.

Happy families home on the range.

DAISY woke up at first light the next morning. Her cabin was one small room, and as she lay in bed, she could see mountain peaks out the windows on all four sides. Very slowly she put her feet on the cold floor and looked around.

In daylight the room looked exactly as she remembered it. The walls were covered with old barn board. A bearskin rug lay on the floor in front of the stone fireplace, and bright Shoshone blankets covered the old sofa. Shivering, she opened her suitcase and pulled on clean clothes. She craved a cup of coffee.

Coffee and more. Daisy walked up the sage trail, around the corral, and through the kitchen door to find Louisa frying eggs and bacon. A fire crackled in the hearth; coffee perked on the back burner.

"Look who smelled breakfast cooking," Louisa said, smiling without turning from the stove. "She's up early, same as ever."

" 'Daisy, Daisy, give me your answer true,' " Dalton said. He sat at the big table, dressed in his chaps and wool jacket. Daisy felt a lump in her throat. He looked so old.

"Dalton," she began. She hadn't known what to expect, but looking at him in his usual spot at the head of the table, she realized she still considered him her father-in-law. The divorce was between her and James. Quickly crossing the room, she kissed his wrinkled cheek. "How are you—" she started to ask.

"What's keeping James?" he interrupted.

"James?" she asked, confused.

"Eat your eggs," Louisa said, pushing a plate in front of him. "What'll you have, Daisy?"

"Toast," Daisy said. "I'll get it myself."

"You'd better wait for James." Dalton reached for the huckleberry preserves. "You know how he likes to have his meals with you."

"That was a long time ago," Daisy said quickly, wondering why Dalton wanted to remind her of those old, happy days.

"Long time ago?" Dalton chuckled. "Yesterday, today, tomorrow. 'T'sall the same when it comes to you snow geese."

"Snow geese?" Daisy was pouring a cup of coffee, but Dalton's use of the old nickname made her spill it all over the counter. Was Dalton trying to be cruel?

"Madly in love and mated for life, just like snow geese," Dalton used to say about Daisy and James. Daisy had loved the comparison. Dalton's friend Louis Shoulderblade, a Shoshone shaman, had told her that geese build a nest with only one other.

"Where is he?" Dalton asked now, his mouth full of toast. "One of the kids sick?"

"The kids—" Daisy slammed down her cup.

Louisa had her face in her hands. Dalton held a half-bitten piece of toast, his blue eyes filmed with worry. Daisy's anger suddenly washed away, replaced by concern.

Age wrinkled the old man's face and clouded his eyes; it had obviously transported his heart back to a time when they were all together, when Daisy and James were the snow geese. Old age had stolen over him.

" 'Daisy, Daisy, give me your answer true,' " Dalton began again.

"WHEN did it start?" Daisy asked as they were cleaning up the breakfast dishes after Dalton had left.

"Started two years ago." Louisa swirled coffee mugs through the soapy water. "Thereabouts."

"He seemed to think . . ." Daisy began.

"Sometimes he's sharp as an eagle," Louisa went on. "He has a pair of eyes on him . . . sees everything. Recalls stories from the days when his daddy and mine were at each other's throats."

"But today . . ." Daisy said.

"Today he got a little mixed up," Louisa said. "I told him you were coming, and he understands about Sage running away, but seeing you . . ." She placed a dish in the drainer.

Daisy dried it. "Seeing him, too. It makes the years slip away."

"The years slip away for Dalton all the time," Louisa said. "It doesn't change who he is or how I feel about him."

"No, I know that," Daisy said, unsettled by Louisa's expression.

"His son questions my motives," Louisa said.

"Hmm." Daisy was careful not to say too much, thinking, He always has. James had lost his mother young, and he hadn't liked or trusted Louisa from the start.

"Snow geese," Louisa said, trying to laugh. "I used to be so jealous when Dalton'd call you that. As if you and James were the only lovers here—the only ones who belonged together."

Daisy felt hot tears. "We only *thought* we belonged together."

"Fate was cruel to you and James. But you know, I thought you belonged together anyway. I wish you had never left."

"I did what I thought was right. I didn't want to raise my daughter on the same ranch where my son—"

"I know that," Louisa said quickly. "I'm in no position to criticize, and I don't. But I've missed you, Daisy. I'm glad you're back."

THE DR barn was deep and cavernous, and as Daisy walked through, swallows flew in crisscross patterns through the darkness. The horses whinnied at her approach. There were Ranger, Chiquita, and Piccolo! It made her sad to see how they had aged, but grateful as she realized she hadn't expected to see any of the old horses at all. She greeted some new horses, ones she had never met before. Stopping by each stall, Daisy touched her head to theirs, said hello, caressed their velvety muzzles.

Her years back east had taken away her confidence as a rider, but right now she wanted to get up on a horse and gallop into the hills. Years ago James had kept some gentle horses for her and the children. Silver Star, she remembered, and . . .

"Scout!" she said out loud.

Could it be? The palomino stood in a stall midway down the row. Her coat looked matted, as if she hadn't been brushed in a long time. She faced into the corner, head down. How could James have let her get like this?

"Scout . . ." Daisy whispered. Scout had been her horse. She had held Daisy's children on her bare back and walked them through silvery fields. She had carried Daisy down steep mountain trails, across icy rivers, over narrow rock bridges.

"Scout," Daisy said, holding out her hand. "Remember me?"

The old mare stood where she was, frozen in place.

"Washakie," Daisy whispered.

Was it her imagination or had the old horse moved her head? Daisy kept talking, reminding the old horse of high trails and bright skies, wildflowers growing through the snow, blue ice on red rocks.

The horse moved. Her hooves shuffled through the hay as she lumbered across the stall. Daisy held her hand out and felt warm breath on her fingers.

"It's you," Daisy whispered, her throat thick.

The mare's eyes, dark brown pools, stared at Daisy with recognition. Daisy unlatched the stall door and reached her arms around the broad neck. The horse quivered, as if coming alive again. Daisy's tears were nothing new to her. Daisy had cried into her mane the first night Jake hadn't come home, and every night afterward. Scout knew her scent and voice, and she knew her tears. Daisy led her out of the barn and into the bright light of day. They stood by the corral, and Daisy used the split-rail fence to mount her and began to ride.

The old horse took it slow, moving like a riverboat, rocking back and forth. Daisy tangled her fingers in her long mane, letting her carry her past the barn and the bunkhouse, into the back pasture, toward the hills. Daisy nearly pulled back, but something made her let go inside, give up her tension and worry, just let the old horse carry her where she wanted to go.

"Good girl," Daisy said. She leaned down to hold her arms alongside the horse's neck and feel her warmth. Closing her eyes, she rode her horse. Her horse.

SAGE's bike had a flat tire. She was somewhere over the Nebraska state line, and storm clouds were gathering.

Last night, after hours on the road, the bakery truck had driven to a hospital. When the driver went inside to drop off his last load of rolls, Sage had wriggled out from under the bread trays. After stuffing a box of cupcakes into her backpack, she hauled her bicycle out from its hiding place and coasted down the ramp.

She had locked her bike to a rack and gone inside. The hospital had been bright and warm, and Sage had felt safe there.

The hospital seemed to have several types of rest rooms, including a shower room for disabled patients. She went inside, took off her clothes, and took a long shower.

Feeling a hundred times better, Sage had wandered the halls. In the hospital cafeteria she had counted out three dollars and dined sumptuously on beef stew, noodles, and Jell-O.

But now she was back on this lonely road. Somewhere between the hospital and here she must have ridden over a nail. She had dreaded this moment, but she had known it might come. To get to Wyoming, to reach her father, she was going to have to hitchhike.

Traffic was sparse. Sage laid her bike on the side of the road, hiding it under a juniper bush. She felt a lump in her throat: Her mother had given her half the money to buy the bicycle. The rest Sage had earned from baby-sitting and snow shoveling. She hated leaving it behind; her mother had held her hands over Sage's on the handlebars and blessed all her future rides. "Ride safely, my love," she had said. "Smooth roads, low hills, no bumps . . . and always come home."

"Always come home," Sage said out loud into the cold Nebraska air, her eyes bright with tears.

A car drove by, and Sage just watched it go. She reached under her jacket and touched the amulet her mother had made her. At least she had her necklace. Her fingers traced the boy's face, then the girl's.

Her baby kicked.

"We'll be there soon," Sage said out loud, seeing headlights in the distance. The road was flat, the car a long way away. Taking a deep breath, she stuck out her thumb. "Almost there."

Chapter SIX

NEARLY a full day now. That's how long Daisy had been on the ranch, and still James hadn't talked to her. He had set himself a slew of jobs far from the houses. With the temperature dropping and snow falling, he'd ridden north to survey his herd.

The range looked cold and bleak, a thousand shades of gray. Last week's rains had brought relief from the drought, and now it looked as if Dalton's prediction was going to come true. Winter would be early and hard. Cows huddled in clusters, grazing on brown grass. He'd be shipping five hundred head of cattle soon, and he and Paul would have to start driving them to the big sorting corrals. He tried to count the calves, but his mind couldn't stay focused enough. Daisy was here.

James could feel her presence. He could hear her voice, the way she'd yelled that word into the night—primal, yearning, full of rage. James knew, because he carried the same stuff inside himself.

He had told Paul he was riding the perimeter, searching for traces of whoever had killed that calf. So far they'd turned up a few things—beer cans, a stomped-out campfire, boot prints in the dirt along the sandstone ridge. James wanted to catch the bastard who'd done it and rip him apart. Most of the time he controlled his rage, but Daisy's presence had stirred him back up.

Now entering the red-rock canyon, James's heart was pounding. This was where it had happened, where his boy had disappeared.

James had to see, had to check, just in case. His gaze swept the area. Sagebrush grew from rock crevices. Ribbons of amber ran through the dark red canyon walls.

A pebble dislodged from the rim above, making him jump. It clattered off the eroded cliff, setting more pebbles loose.

"Who's up there?" James yelled.

He stared up the water-cut rock, watching for movement. The canyon was deep and silent, leading to a labyrinth of endless smaller canyons and crevices. The black shadows looked alive. Keeping to the canyon wall, he had the feeling of being watched. Another pebble fell, then more silence. Someone was walking up above.

"Show yourself!" he yelled. He felt crazed, the way he had in the first year after Jake's disappearance. He had come here constantly, searching every crevice.

Another stone fell, and a crow hopped to the edge of the rim. It cawed loudly, and James wondered whether that was what he had heard. The crow swooped down, flying into the next crevice. James nudged his horse with one knee, and the animal walked on.

Bones from a kill lay against a rock pile. Mouth dry, James rode closer. This was western life: finding dead rabbits, elk, cows. Crows eating the dead. But discovering it in this spot made him nervous. Bending down to check, he saw the bones bleached nearly white yet still connected by fur. Gray fur with brown glints. A wolf.

After slowly dismounting, he crouched by the dead thing. The stench was gone—more crows and buzzards had been here before him. Ordinarily he would have left the carcass alone. But something made him take out his knife and slice away a piece of the pelt. Then he cut off the animal's left front paw—the bones and claws nude of fur and gristle—and a section of its spine. He was glad it was an animal of prey. As he worked, he thought of the wolf's fierce spirit. The sensation of being watched from above was gone.

He sheathed his knife. He thought of a place down the Wind River, Crowhart Butte, where a century and a half ago the Shoshone and Crow chiefs had fought to the death in single-handed combat. Two fierce and brutal warriors ripping each other to shreds over land rights—the old Wyoming story. When Chief Washakie won, he'd honored the bravery of his dead enemy by cutting out his heart and eating it.

Daisy had loved the story of the chiefs, the myth of gaining strength from other creatures. It had given her courage many nights in the wild, including the time the grizzly had nearly attacked her and the twins in their tent. She had taught the word to their children, to say out loud whenever they were scared of the dark. James knew that Daisy's bone ghosts, her jewelry, came from the same deep belief that powerful spirits lived on.

And so James opened his saddlebag and stuck the wolf bones and fur inside. A peace offering.

KICK, kick. One pebble, then another. The Guardian stepped back from the cliff edge. That's how he thought of himself: the guardian of what should have belonged to him all along.

"Show yourself," the rancher had called.

Show this, the Guardian thought, giving him the finger. He stepped back from the edge, watched while the cowman busied himself cutting the foot off the dead wolf, then moved along.

The Guardian packed up his camera, knife, stove, and gun. Then he, too, moved on.

SAGE had gotten picked up by a woman driving home from work, a truck driver delivering chickens, and a life insurance salesman in a Ford. Ten cars passed by for every one that stopped.

Only the salesman had been weird. He wore a suit, for one thing, which struck Sage as a little pretentious, considering the only places around seemed populated by people in overalls. He also dyed his hair. Sage could tell by how the unusual shade of cordovan failed to blend with the stripes of white along his part and temples. It seemed so sad and vain, she didn't know whether to laugh or feel sorry for him.

But then all confusion was removed. He was driving with his hand over his crotch. The instant Sage saw that, she knew this was one of the perverts her mother had warned her about. Oh, God, she thought. Checking the door handle, she yanked so hard it flew open at full speed. The man had been more shocked than Sage, and she'd told him to let her out at the next mile marker—in the middle of nowhere—saying her father was meeting her there in ten minutes.

And there she'd been standing for the last ten minutes. Eight o'clock and no cars in sight. Sage's breath came out in white clouds. Her feet were cold and her hands numb. A car approached, and she tensed up badly, afraid it was the creep. The baby gave her a kick straight to the bladder. Oh, God, she had to pee.

Luckily the car passed by. Looking around for a bush or a tree, Sage spotted a row of poplars near a falling-down barn. There was a rusty old car there, too. Things to hide behind. But immediately she knew she wouldn't make it that far. She was glad of the dark. By the side of the road, so exposed she might as well be naked, she squatted in the dust.

After she'd finished, a car approached, slowed down, and even without streetlights Sage could tell it was the pervert.

"Couldn't leave you here all alone," he said, rolling down the window. He smiled, revealing perfect teeth. "I got to thinking, her father's not gonna find her *there*. Why don't you let me drop you off someplace proper?"

"Um, no, thank you," Sage said politely. "My father knows exactly where to find me."

The man opened his door and got out. Sage dropped her backpack. She turned to run, but he caught her arm, pulling her toward his car. Sage screamed. She tried to kick him. She felt him embracing her. She screamed again.

Just then a car started up. She looked wildly around, struggling. He was dragging her now, urgently, toward his idling Ford.

"My father," Sage sobbed, trying to tear away from the man. He yanked her hair. "Daddy!" she cried.

"Shut up," the man said, still holding her hair.

Out of the field a big black car appeared, no lights on. It was long and low, like some sort of highway maintenance vehicle. It clanked against ruts in the field. Sage saw the rust holes and realized it was the broken-looking vehicle she'd seen parked by the ramshackle barn. The front door opened even before the car had come to a complete stop, and the driver came tumbling out.

The driverless black car coasted slowly by, cruising down the road a few yards before coming to a gentle stop against a hump of grass, while the driver got to his feet. He came striding over to Sage and the salesman, who had released his grip on her.

"This is a family matter," the salesman said.

"No," Sage tried to say, but the stranger wasn't waiting to hear. He just wound up his arm and punched the pervert right in the mouth. Sage heard the breaking of teeth.

"Mmaaateeeffff," the creep said through fingers clamped over his now bleeding mouth.

"You're done with them," the stranger said.

"Mateeeffff," the salesman said again in disbelief as he scrambled into his Ford and roared away.

Sage turned to the stranger to thank him, but he had run a few yards down the road to where his car had stopped. She could see that he was about five six, just a few inches taller than she, and thin. He had brown hair, and he wore faded jeans. Sage heard dogs barking, and she realized the sounds were coming from inside the car. When her rescuer came walking back toward her, she could see that he was no older than she was—about sixteen, seventeen at the oldest.

Thank you, she wanted to say. But instead, she just stared.

"You okay?" he asked.

"I think so," she managed.

"That guy hurt you?"

"He tried." Sage's teeth were starting to chatter.

"I heard," the stranger said. He gestured toward the collapsing barn. "I was in there, and your scream scared every bird in the rafters. You see them fly out?"

"No. I was a little busy," Sage said. "Is that your barn?"

"Nah," he said, reaching into his breast pocket. He took out a pack of cigarettes. "Want one?"

Sage shook her head. Something about his voice made her want to hear him talk. In the match light Sage saw his eyes were pale green, and they looked hooded—as if he'd been hurt or hiding or both.

"Where you going?" he asked.

"Wyoming."

"Yeah?" he said. "I'm going that way. I'll give you a ride. My name's David."

"I'm Sage."

Calmed and steadied by his presence, Sage had no doubts. She knew she wanted to get into the warm car and hear the sound of David's voice again.

DALTON and Louisa had stopped at the Stagecoach to have supper and audition a new guitar player to replace Marty Hamlin, who'd gotten thrown in jail for a parole violation.

Sitting onstage, Louisa sang softly while the young man played. He had a beautiful style, and Louisa was relaxing into the thought that her show would go on even better than before—when she heard the crash.

Everyone surrounded Dalton. He lay on the floor, moaning in pain. Louisa burst through the crowd, crouched beside him. At first she thought he'd had a heart attack, but his eyes were wide open and he was breathing fine. "Think I've been shot," he said.

"Shot? My God!" Louisa actually looked for blood.

"He fell," the waitress said into Louisa's ear. "He was headed for the men's room, and his legs went right out from under him."

"Call the ambulance," Louisa said calmly. She gripped Dalton's hand, covered him with her shawl.

"They shot me," he said. "A gunfight, like when my daddy—"

"You're safe," Louisa said quietly. She heard the others talking behind them, laughing with discomfort at Dalton's confusion.

An hour later Dalton was having X rays at the medical center. Louisa called the ranch, and James answered. She knew from the way his voice fell he was disappointed it wasn't Sage. But he snapped to the moment Louisa told him about Dalton.

"What happened?"

"They don't know what's wrong," Louisa said. "He was healthy as all get-out this morning, and after supper he just collapsed. Fell down hard, James. He must've broken something."

"What are the doctors doing for him?" James asked.

"Tests. Trying to keep him comfortable." Louisa could hear his bootheels as James paced the floor.

"You just caught me," he said. "I just stopped in to check for news on Sage."

"The roundup, I know."

"Yeah, and I can't leave," James said.

"You don't have to. I'm here."

"I know, but he's my father."

"I'm here," Louisa repeated.

"Thanks. Tell him I'll get to the hospital as soon as I can. Okay?"

When Louisa hung up, her nephew Todd came walking in, dressed in his navy-blue package-express service uniform, as if he'd come to deliver something.

"Aunt Louisa," he said, a worried look in his eyes. "Mel at the Stagecoach told me you were here. I came straight over."

"Oh, Todd," she gasped, kissing his cheek. She felt so relieved to have family there. "Dalton fell. They're doing X rays right now."

"Man"—Todd shook his head—"a fall. Is he okay?"

"I don't know yet. They haven't told me anything."

Todd put his arms around her, and she was surprised by the deep, primal sense of family connection she felt.

"Mrs. Tucker?" a young man in a white lab coat asked. He introduced himself as Dr. Middleton.

"I'm Louisa Rydell," she began.

"She's Mrs. Tucker," Todd interrupted.

"Well," the doctor said, "your husband has suffered a fractured femur—the thighbone of his right leg. To put it simply, it just crumbled. Disintegrated, if you will."

"His thighbone *crumbled?*" Louisa asked, horrified.

"His convalescence will not be easy. He'll need round-the-clock care. Getting in and out of bed, to the bathroom—the most basic things will be impossible for him to do on his own. Coupled with the dementia . . ."

"Oh, God," Louisa cried, unable to control her distress.

"I'm going to send Mr. Tucker up to Dubois, get him admitted to the hospital until he's stabilized," the doctor said. "And then—"

"We'll talk about 'then' later," Todd said sharply.

"Thank you for being here. James has the roundup," she said to Todd when Dr. Middleton had walked away.

"I'm just glad to help," he said.

"Especially for saying that I'm Mrs. Tucker."

"That's how I see you," Todd said.

Louisa nodded. She hated getting upset in public places, and she couldn't stand having her makeup run.

"I just hope he's taken care of you," Todd went on. "Looking toward the future, I mean."

"You'd better not be talking about anything like a will," Louisa said, hardening her eyes. "I hear you mention Dalton and will in the same breath, you're gonna need one of your own."

"I just want to see you taken care of."

"Don't worry. Dalton's a man of integrity. He does what's right."

"I'm sure of that," Todd said. "Meantime, I'll help you handle anything needs handling. Tammy's sister's a nurse's aide. Does private duty, too. I'll give her a call."

"Thank you, dear." Louisa suddenly felt tired and old. Sitting, she stared at her feet. She was wearing red high heels. This morning she'd felt she could dance up a storm, and right now the love of her life was lying on a stretcher with his bones turning to dust.

Todd had gotten her thinking. She was just a visitor on the DR Ranch—the initials stood for Dalton and Rosalind, his first and only wife. Dalton loved Louisa—of that she had no doubt. But he had never changed the name of his ranch. He had never married her. James's dislike of her had carried too much weight.

Where would Louisa go when—if—Dalton were to . . . She shook her head hard, not even wanting to think the word. The ranch was her home. Dalton wouldn't leave her high and dry. Letting out a long, low breath, Louisa rose. She said good-bye to Todd, and then she walked, straight and tall in her red high heels, down the corridor to be with the man she loved.

AFTER climbing into David's rusty old four-wheel drive, Sage felt exhausted and relieved. His fist was bleeding from punching the man's teeth, and he'd wrapped it in gauze from his first-aid kit. In the wide-open Nebraska dark the moon threw silver light on endless frost-covered cornfields. David drove slowly, as if the car was too old to make it going fast.

Sage wanted to tell him how amazing his rescue had been, but she couldn't bring herself to talk about what had just happened. Her teeth were still chattering.

The old car rattled as he drove. It smelled of cigarette smoke, damp fur, and cat pee. The seats were torn, their stuffing coming out. The reason was obvious: The car was filled with animals. Sage saw a Scottish terrier curled in a ball, a brown-and-white spaniel with bandages over its head, a broad-faced dog with a shredded toy in its mouth, and at least six tiny kittens. The kittens were going wild, romping across the back seat.

"It's their busy time," David apologized.

He lit a cigarette and held it in his unbandaged hand. Sage saw tattoos on his forearm—a hawk, an owl, and three wavy lines that reminded her of how a little kid would draw a river.

Sage looked around the car, counting the animals. The tricolored dog cowered in the corner of the back seat.

"Don't hide," Sage said, holding out her hand.

"That's Petal," David said. "She's a pit bull."

Sage withdrew her hand. "Aren't they attack dogs?"

"Only ignorant people think that. Petal came off a puppy farm. You know what that is?"

"No, what?"

"A place where they stick dogs in crates and breed them until they die. The mothers spend their whole lives having puppies, one litter after another. The puppies get yanked away before they're finished nursing. The mothers get bred immediately, pregnant with another litter. They never get over missing their puppies."

"Petal lived there?"

"Yeah. She was one of the mothers before I took her away."

Sage looked at Petal. The dog had her small stuffed animal between her paws and was licking it tenderly. "She likes that little toy."

"She thinks it's one of her pups," David said.

"What's wrong with the other dogs? They're so quiet."

"Their spirits are gone. That's what happens to animals from those places."

"Why do you have them?" she asked after a long silence.

David just kept driving, staring at the moonlit road through the cigarette smoke. "I save things," he said. "It's what I do."

"You saved me," Sage said. "That guy would have—"

"Don't think about him," David said. "Think about anything else. Here." Reaching back, he picked up one of the kittens and handed it across to her. Sage held it on her lap, stroking it gently.

But the memory wouldn't go away. "I thought he was going to drag me into his car."

"He would have," David said.

"And you came zooming out of the field with your lights off, and I hoped . . . I prayed . . ." Sage gulped. It began to sweep over her, the terror of being attacked on an empty farm road. Tears ran down her face.

David didn't speak.

"All I could think of was my father," Sage said. "That he'd somehow know. That he'd save me."

"Parents aren't God. Sometimes they hurt more than they help."

David fell silent again. Sage stared at the tattoos on his right forearm. They were beautiful. The owl's yellow eyes, steady and alert, looked alive.

Sage had always considered tattoos scary and gross. But for some reason the pictures on David's skin brought tears to her eyes, and she didn't have a clue why.

"What were you doing in that old barn back there?" Sage asked.

"Bedding down," David said. "It's not good for the dogs to spend too much time cooped up in the car. Reminds them of their pens at the farms." David looked up at the sky. "It's going to snow."

"It's only October," Sage said. "Or November." What was the date, anyway? She'd been gone for a week now.

"November fourth. Lots of winters start around now."

"They don't at home, in Connecticut."

"I thought you said Wyoming was home."

"They both are," she said. "My mother's east, my father's west." Sage stifled a yawn. She hadn't really slept in days.

"What made you leave the place where your mother lives?"

"I don't know." Sage felt too shy to tell David she was pregnant. "Is this your car?" she asked, changing the subject.

"It was my uncle's. It has four-wheel drive, goes through mud, snow—anything. He gave it to my mother." He paused. "We should find a place to sleep tonight before it gets too much later."

Sage nodded, yawning. The kitten had fallen asleep on her lap.

David drove slowly into the dark night. The moon was gone, and snow had started to fall. Were those mountains in the distance or just low clouds? Sage snuggled deeper into her seat while David watched for a barn where they could spend the night.

DAISY'S third morning on the ranch, she pulled back the curtains to look outside. Snow had fallen during the night, and the ground was covered. Paul March, riding by, saw her and circled back to wave. Slowly she opened the door.

"Howdy, Daisy," he said. "Long time since . . ."

Daisy hugged herself, shivering in the cold. *Since she'd left the ranch, since Jake had been gone.*

"Good to see you, Paul."

"You, too. Any news on Sage?"

"Not yet." Her heart skipped, just saying the words. The ranch was still the same. News traveled fast.

"Don't worry too much. She'll be fine."

Paul sounded concerned, and for a minute she thought he might climb down off his horse to console her. She flashed back to the day after Jake's disappearance, when she had cried against his shoulder more than once. He had been a good friend then, and she appreciated his kindness now. She tried to smile.

"Hang in there, Daisy. If there's anything I can do . . ."

"Thanks, Paul."

Waving again, he kicked his horse and rode away, sending up clouds of snow. Daisy noticed a package on the front porch. She picked it up, stepped inside, and closed the door behind her.

Untying the parcel—a square of old red cloth—she found a bundle of bones. She sat at the oak table to examine them more closely: the paw of something—a coyote or wolf. Someone else might have felt alarmed, but not Daisy.

The bones calmed her. She knew James had left them for her, and although she couldn't have said why, she understood that they were his gift. She hadn't seen him yet; everyone seemed to be protecting them from each other. Eager suddenly to leave the little house, she pulled on boots and a jacket. Being cooped up inside couldn't be good. She'd visit Scout in the barn.

Sliding the barn door slightly open, Daisy slipped inside. She stamped her feet, closed the door behind her. The horses tossed their heads at her approach.

Music played in an alcove around the corner. Patsy Cline. Someone was working there. Daisy hung back, standing in the shadows.

Scout was clipped to the tie-offs, a long line holding each side of her halter to opposite walls. It hardly seemed possible that this was the same horse. She glistened yellow as butter. Her mane and tail flowed creamy white.

James stood with his back to her. He wore tight blue jeans under dusty chaps, and with a kerosene heater going, he'd worked up a serious sweat from vigorously brushing the horse. His plaid shirt was thrown on the floor, and his muscles strained under his faded black T-shirt. Daisy stared at his broad back and bare arms—arms that had held her, once upon a time.

James was grooming the horse he had given her. He was making right what he should have kept up all along.

"Pretty horse," Daisy said.

There was a moment of silence. "Palomino mare," James said finally, without turning around. "Registered quarter horse."

"She sure is strong," Daisy said, coming to stroke the horse's neck. She picked up a brush from the tack bucket.

James caught her wrist. "I can't believe I'm seeing you."

"I can't, either." Daisy gently pulled her arm away, petting the horse. "Scout's so old."

"She's going to be okay. She's going to make it out of this fine," James said, and Daisy knew he wasn't talking about Scout.

"Sage," Daisy said, her voice cracking. She kept brushing Scout, and then she stopped. They stood there, face to face. Daisy saw the lines in his tan face, the slashes of worry around his blue eyes. His hair was shot with gray. She looked for the brash young rancher she had once loved, but he wasn't there.

"Sage." He whispered the name.

"Oh, James." She shook her head.

He pulled her tight and close in an embrace so hard every bone in her body ached. She cried out, and he hugged her tighter. She knew he meant to comfort her, to give her solace, but all she could feel right now was hate for herself, for failing to forgive after all these years.

"I thought . . ." she tried to say. "I thought time softened things."

"Daisy," he whispered. "No, you didn't. You know time only makes things harder. Don't think I'm fooling myself. I know why you're here."

"Our daughter," Daisy said. "That's all."

"I know," James said.

JAMES rode across the range, shouting to the herd. He, Paul, and the others were driving them toward home. This was his money-making time of year, and usually the most fun.

With the weather they'd had, the ground was all mud and snow. Trying to dodge a straggler, James almost fell with his horse.

"You okay?" Paul asked.

"Fine," James said, putting the old what-are-you-talking-about look in his eyes.

"Daisy looks good."

"You saw her?" James snapped his head up. Then he caught himself and squinted back toward the cattle.

"Snow squalls up ahead," Paul said, pointing toward the mist-shrouded purple mountains.

"Makes this a little more fun," James said.

"Dalton's been saying 'early winter' for a month now," Paul said. "Looking out that hospital window, he's laughing because he knows we're gonna go snow-blind before this herd gets shipped."

A steer broke away from the herd. The stock dogs saw it before James. They took off barking, and James just rode away without another word to Paul. He thought of his father, lying in bed with shattered bones, and he kicked his horse into a gallop. Fall roundups had been Dalton's favorite time. He had taught James everything he knew about ranching, and James had never shipped a herd without him. He could feel his father with him now.

Pounding over wet ground, James chased the steer into canyon land. The animal veered around a corner like a truck on two wheels. James had his rope ready, arm back and prepared to throw. The canyon, wide at first, narrowed into a hundred skinny ravines. James had been here just yesterday, cutting the foot off a dead wolf. The steer was going to get caught, or it was going to get lost.

The canyon was empty.

The steer had disappeared. James stopped his horse, looking around. He felt the tenseness of muscle fiber flooded with adrenaline. The thrill of the roundup, he told himself. But he knew he was lying to himself—it was the canyon itself. Creatures disappeared here. The rock walls ate them up. Cattle, children . . .

Sitting stock-still in his saddle, James listened hard. Nothing but eerie, brooding silence. The steer must have found its way into the labyrinth of crevices. James scanned the ground for tracks. Plenty of them: deer, wolves, elk, the steer. A human.

This wasn't a place where people walked. There were no camp-sites or hiking trails. James bent over the saddle horn to see better. Size ten boots, from the look of them. The steer's tracks went straight into the deepest part of the canyon; the man's veered right.

James followed the footprints. They were fresh—hours, not days, old. And deep. The man had been carrying something heavy.

The tracks disappeared midstep, and James quickly saw why: Someone had clipped a low cedar branch to brush away footprints, hide his direction.

Someone was here. He sensed it again. Suddenly James felt a deep, terrible blackness, the empty part inside himself that was missing two children. He thought of how this canyon had eaten his son, and he thought of how his daughter was supposed to be on her way home—here to the ranch—right now.

Were those tracks deep enough to have been made by someone carrying a sixteen-year-old girl? James felt wild, his eyes burning. He jumped off his horse and started scrambling up the rimrock.

He skinned his wrist raw, climbing to the rock ledge. Thunder cracked down the valley, and from the top of the rim James could see the snow coming. Paul was driving the herd home, half of them obscured by driving snow. James saw the men on horseback doing the work he should be doing, but he turned away.

Unbelievably he found the tracks again. The cedar broom had missed a print. Panting, he started to run. The ledge narrowed, giving him a two-foot path. The cliff fell sharply to his left. James felt the altitude in his knees, and he touched his pistol as he ran.

James came to a bend in the trail, where he couldn't see what came next. He pulled his gun. He wasn't about to round a blind corner empty-handed. Edging around the protruding red rock, he entered the last crevice before the trail ended.

Someone had been here. James found a dead campfire built deep under a jutting boulder. The ashes were warm. From the pile, James pulled out three charred Polaroids, images of his grazing herd. James swore.

The camper had been furtive enough to brush his tracks away

and build a fire where the smoke wouldn't show. But he'd left other signs behind: an empty can of beans and a road map folded open to the land around the DR Ranch. James searched the ground for evidence that more than one person had been there. Frantic, he checked the three pictures again for hints of a sixteen-year-old girl.

Down below, the lost steer lowed. James had forgotten all about the roundup, and he didn't give a second thought to the steer. It might be frightened, dead-ended in one of the dark crevices. The storm had finally hit. Snow fell hard, coming down in white sheets. Thunder cracked—so loud it could split the rocks. Sticking the three Polaroids into his pocket, James fell to his knees and brushed the snow aside, wanting to keep the ground clear. The snow would blanket the canyon, the trail, this abandoned camp, and James would lose his chance.

Chapter **SEVEN**

DAISY hunched over her makeshift worktable, candles burning all around the room, her fingers hovering over the bones. Outside, the snow came down. The wind howled through the rafters of her small cottage. She had made a tape—many years ago, when she had lived here—of Shoshone chants. She had brought them from home, and they played now on the portable tape recorder.

She hadn't slept much, and staring at the bones had a hypnotic effect. Make something, she thought. Use your hands. Stop thinking.

She knew it was strange, but when she worked with bones, she tried to be gentle, as if to avoid further injuring the animal. From the size of these she guessed they'd come from a wolf. She conjured up its spirit and prayed for its release.

The region abounded with Coyote-Wolf stories. Wolf, considered good and benevolent, was believed to have created humans and stars. Coyote was a trickster, harming people and impeding Wolf's efforts. The shaman, Louis Shoulderblade, had once told her that wolves were born of the Long Snows Moon and were devoted to their young.

Now, hunched over her worktable, Daisy thought of the wolf spirit bounding across long distances to reach her young.

The candles flickered in the draft. Daisy pulled her sweater tighter. She wondered whether the men were back from their day, and she walked to the window. The snow was coming down so hard Louisa had decided to stay at the hospital with Dalton another night. Daisy thought of Sage out in that weather, then of James. She drifted back to her worktable, but the ability to make magic had left her.

Burying her head in her hands, she listened to the tapes of Indian chanting. She thought back to her first time here, searching for inspiration in the wilderness. Girls from other Eastern Establishment families might have tried backpacking through Europe or baby-sitting for families on the Vineyard or Nantucket, but something in her spirit had pulled her west. Every part of Wyoming had seemed huge, extreme, and magnificent.

The rocks had astonished her: black mica, green hornblade, crimson sandstone, rose quartz, chalky white feldspar. The Wind River mountains soared above the plains, and from the minute she saw them, she knew she had to go deeper into their land. She wanted to make jewelry like the Indians. She knew she had something primal inside that needed to be unleashed, and she knew that wasn't going to happen if she went home to Connecticut too soon.

She had decided instead to go panning for gold. She found a dude ranch near Lander, and they gave her riding lessons and a sense of how it felt to be a cowgirl. After two weeks Daisy felt confident enough to ride off on her own. She packed up for the day, picked a spot on the map, and rode out to Midsummer Creek.

She wore ranch clothes. The chaps and Stetson made her feel like part of the landscape. Riding through meadows of buckwheat and sorrel, she saw a sky so big and blue that she felt she was in heaven, and it was called Wyoming.

Panning for gold had been fun. Crouched by the cold stream, she had pulled her hat low over her eyes to keep the sun out.

She had heard the rattle just in time. Reaching into the water to scoop up a pan of pebbles, she had nearly put her dry hand down on a rattlesnake. The snake was huge and coiled. It had slithered out to sun itself on a nearby rock, and its camouflage was perfect. The gold-and-brown diamonds looked just like stones, and Daisy wondered how long it had been sitting beside her.

"Don't move," said a deep voice.

The snake rattled its tail. Daisy was frozen in place. This was happening in slow motion, as if another, braver girl were panning for gold and Daisy was just watching from afar.

"I won't," she said softly.

"This is gonna be loud," the voice said. The shot rang out, blasting Daisy's eardrums, and the snake's head disappeared.

Daisy clapped both her hands to her mouth. She jumped up, knocking over all the maybe-gold pebbles she'd panned.

A stranger walked out of the shadows across the narrow stream. Daisy smelled the gunsmoke and saw him sticking his pistol into a holster. They stared at each other.

"You didn't scream," he said.

"What were you doing, watching me?" she asked.

"Not for long," he said as he crossed the stream. "But yes."

Daisy tilted her head, gazing at him. He was tall and lean. He wore tight jeans and a dusty white T-shirt that said POWDER RIVER RODEO in red letters. His black hat was in his hands; the sun had bleached his brown hair, and although he wasn't much older than Daisy, he had lines around his mouth and eyes.

"Thank you for killing the snake," Daisy said.

"He was about to strike. I hope the shot didn't scare you."

Daisy nodded. She'd been having an out-of-body experience, blocking out the fact that she had nearly been bitten by a poisonous snake. Her hands began to shake.

"Oh, brother," she said, looking down at them.

"It happens that way sometimes," the young man said. "It hits you later, when you think what might have—"

Daisy nodded, and she put her face down so he wouldn't see her start to cry. She cried easily; her emotions always embarrassed her.

"Don't be scared," he said, putting his arm around her shoulders.

"I didn't see it," Daisy said, shaking. "I stared right at the rock, and I didn't see the snake."

"That happens all the time," he said. "It's happened to me."

"Really? And you're from around here?" she asked.

"Yeah. This is my land."

Daisy jumped back. She felt even more embarrassed now. "No," she said. "I'm staying on the dude ranch, and they sent me here. They gave me a map, showing good spots to pan for gold."

"They always do." He laughed. "They only own a few acres, and they figure we won't mind a few tourists taking our stones. They're not real gold, though. Hate to disappoint you."

"I'm sorry," Daisy said. "God, I can't believe they'd do that."

"It's okay. I'm James Tucker, and you're on the DR Ranch."

"I'll leave," Daisy said, backing away.

"No, stay," he said. "But tell me your name first."

"Daisy Lambert. From Silver Bay, Connecticut."

"Prospecting for gold?"

So Daisy had told him about going to art school, designing jewelry, being fascinated by western materials and designs. She asked if she could keep the pebbles she'd panned, and he said she could. But when she showed him, he picked one out of the bunch.

"It's real. I take back what I said. You found real gold."

"Honestly?"

Together they examined the small rock. It looked dull and dark, no different from any of the other stones she'd picked up. But James had seen the value, the sparkle under the river moss. Daisy knew she'd carry the small gold nugget home with her, use it in her first western-inspired necklace. The breeze blew, and she felt the first rush of wilderness inspiration—exactly what she'd been after on this trip.

"Oh!" she said, the force nearly knocking her over.

James had been holding his hat in one hand, and he took Daisy's right off her head, letting her coppery hair blow in the wind. Cupping the back of her head in his hand, he'd let the hats fall to the ground and kissed her till she saw stars. She gripped his forearm, dropping the gold.

James didn't stop kissing her for a long time. He made it slow and gentle, the way he tangled his fingers in her hair. The sun heated their bare heads and arms; every time Daisy felt a new muscle on his biceps or back, her knees went weak.

When they stopped, James crouched down, found the nugget, and handed her the gold, closing her hand in his fingers. His calluses were so rough they scraped her skin.

"Cowboy hands," she said softly.

"What?"

"Oh, nothing." She wanted to think of something else to say so he wouldn't go. "Just that I like being here. Riding. Everything."

"You can have cowboy hands, too," he said, grinning. "Just stay on the dude ranch for a while. Keep riding, panning for gold."

"I'm staying on a ranch that's not a ranch," she said. "It's just a bunkhouse with a barn and a map of someone else's land."

"Come stay on the DR," James said. "We have room."

"Thanks for offering, but I couldn't."

"Why not? You can make jewelry, ride when you want. It'd be nice to have you. You in a hurry to get back to Connecticut?"

"No."

"Then why not?"

Daisy shrugged, shaking her head. It seemed impossible, too much of an adventure to imagine. But then he kissed her again.

And she moved off the dude ranch and went to stay on the DR. James put her in the cottage where she was now. He kept a respectful distance for a good long time—at least twenty-four hours. Daisy had eaten her meals up at the main house with James, Dalton, and Louisa. She had made friends with Paul March and the others. Louisa's nephew Todd had been working here back then; Daisy remembered the time he'd brought her a bouquet of mountain daisies and looked in her window. James had nearly killed him.

Raising her head, Daisy looked around. She blinked at the window, almost expecting to see summer light instead of falling snow,

The little place hadn't changed at all. Thinking of James, of their first meeting, broke something deep inside. The candles flickered; the magic started again.

Picking up the wolf bones, Daisy went back to work, the inspiration delivering her from worry. Sage was coming. She was traveling west, just as Daisy had done herself so long ago.

TAKING shelter from the storm, David and Sage had found another old barn. Two nights on the road, and this was getting to be a habit. Outside, the snow picked up, three inches already.

"More in Wyoming, where we're heading," David said.

They were settled in a corner of the barn, the dogs and kittens sleeping on their laps. Petal chewed her stuffed toy, staring with devotion at David's face. Sage tried to arrange herself comfortably on the hay. Once, David had stared hard at her belly, as if trying to see whether she was pregnant. But he'd been too polite to say anything.

"Is it nice in Wyoming?" Sage asked.

"Same as anywhere. Nice some places, bad others."

Sage heard the cows mooing and rustling in the straw, and she felt a thrill of memory at the sound.

"We have cows," she said. "At my father's ranch."

David let out a scornful snort. "He's a *rancher?* I hate ranchers."

Sage felt shocked, as if he'd spit on her feet. "If you hate ranchers so much, why do you stay in their barns?"

"This is a dairy farm," he said, glowering, "not a ranch. There's a big difference."

"Cows," Sage said, holding out one hand and then the other. "And cows. Big difference."

"Milk," David said, turning his left palm up, then his right, "and hamburger. Ranchers get the cows to trust them, and then they slit their throats."

"My dad doesn't do that part himself," Sage said.

"It doesn't make any difference. It's cruelty to animals."

Sage watched his face twist up and turn bright red. She actually felt a little scared of him.

"Did you grow up on a ranch?" Sage asked, thinking it would be better if they got off this subject.

"No." There was a long pause. "On a puppy farm."

"You lived on a puppy farm?" she asked, shocked, remembering he had said he'd saved these dogs from puppy farms.

David nodded. His gaze was blank, as if he had long since decided it was better to feel nothing than to remember the details. "That's why I save things," he said. "Why I don't let them get hurt, no matter what. Okay? So don't worry anymore."

"I won't."

"You need to eat," he said.

Although he didn't mention her pregnancy, Sage realized then that he knew. She didn't care. She was kind of glad, because she felt close to David in some way she didn't quite understand.

"I know," she said, patting her belly. "I need to eat."

"Stay here," David said. "I'll be right back."

Sage let the animals gather around her. Their body heat warmed her, and their beating hearts comforted her. Closing her eyes, she felt almost peaceful.

She heard the sound of liquid hitting tin. At first she thought someone was spraying a hose at the roof, but then she saw David halfway down the barn. In the dim light she watched him crouching in the straw, milking a cow. It took him less than a minute to fill the small pail. When he handed it to her, his eyes were soft and eager.

"It's good," she said.

While she drank, David sat down to feed the kittens. A feeling of contentment started deep inside her, beneath the fear and anxiety that had been with her every day for months.

LOUISA sat in the hospital room by the bedside of her infirm beloved. It shocked her to see her Dalton looking so bad. He lay on his back, tubes running into his wiry arms, his mouth wide open. His color was worsening, and they hadn't shaved him that day. Due to the snowstorm, many nurses and aides had arrived late or not at all. She would give anything to hear him crabbing and yelling for the doctors to let her take him home. If Louisa had him at home, this wouldn't have happened.

Staring at Dalton's grizzled face, Louisa knew what she had to do. Rolling up her sleeves, she rummaged through the bedside cupboard and found a basin, soap, towels, and a razor. She ran the water in the bathroom till it was scalding hot, and she soaked the towels for a good while. Then, wringing them out, she rushed them to Dalton's bedside and wrapped them lovingly around his face.

"Relax, Dalton love," she whispered into his ear as he started to wake up. "I'll shave you better than any young nurse can."

She worked the cheap hospital soap into a rich lather and rubbed it into his beard.

"Feels good," Dalton said, still half asleep.

Louisa's heart leaped. "How are you feeling?"

"Can't feel much of anything," he said. "Just like I drank a tub of bourbon. Where's Jamey?"

"Fall roundup. He told me to tell you he's coming as soon as he gets the cattle shipped."

"Fall roundup." Dalton closed his eyes. "I should be there."

"Let the boys take care of it," Louisa said. "You rest up and let your sweetheart give you a nice shave."

"My sweetheart," he said. "Rosalind."

Louisa gasped. She jostled the water basin, spilling it over the side of Dalton's bed. He had made that mistake exactly twice at the beginning of their time together—Louisa had told him if he wanted her to stay, he had better never *never* call her by the name of his dead wife again. And he hadn't all these years.

"Damn it," he said. "I'm all wet, Louisa!"

"It's Louisa now, is it?" she asked, more sad than angry.

"What're you talking about?"

The doctor and nurse picked that exact moment to walk in. The nurse exclaimed over the mess, and the doctor began talking about a discharge date, how Dalton was stabilized now and how Louisa should make arrangements for his convalescence at home: physical therapy, a nurse's aide.

Louisa felt like crying. She and Dalton had never discussed their health-care desires with each other. She had once mentioned living wills to him—you'd think, with his high-risk life as a cattle rancher, he'd have thought once or twice about the possibility of falling off a cliff. But he'd about snapped her head off. The fact was, she wasn't his wife, and she didn't have his health-care proxy.

She thought of the name Rosalind, of how easily it had slid off Dalton's tongue. What did Louisa mean to him, after all? He had never asked her to marry him. The fact had stung her, but she had never realized before how it cut her to the core.

Rosalind of the DR Ranch.

What if Louisa wasn't in the will? James would kick her out in a second. She shook her head, unwilling to think such negative thoughts when Dalton was about to leave the hospital.

What had Todd said about a friend who worked in the nursing field? Something concerning home care—a cousin or an in-law? Louisa would give Todd a call.

THE snow fell deeper and faster than any early November storm on record. Exhausted from working through the storm, James and Paul had gathered the cattle, and now it was weaning time.

The semis were parked by the gate, ready to be loaded with calves. Two drivers sat waiting in one cab, smoking and telling stories.

Those Polaroids were burning up James's pocket. Who would want to take pictures of DR cattle? He kept looking at the photos.

"You seen anyone hiking the canyons?" he had asked Paul.

"Nope," Paul had answered. "Why?"

James had shown him the pictures, asked if he thought they might have something to do with the dead cows. Paul had suggested they show them to the sheriff, but thought it was probably some tourist from the dude ranch taking Wild West pictures.

James forced himself to concentrate on the task at hand. It was time to separate the calves from their mothers. Already the mothers were feeling it. They'd been nervous all morning. He hated this part of his job.

The cow dogs nipped at the calves' heels, urging them left, into the sorting corrals. The cows were sent to the right. Confusion reigned. At first the cows thought they'd just lost sight of the babies—nothing drastic, nothing permanent. They shifted uneasily from side to side. Then the truck drivers threw their cigarettes down, came around back. The doors opened wide, and suddenly the mood changed. Those trucks had carted many herds off to slaughter, and their walls held the stench of fear and death. The scent carried on the storm wind. The mothers knew.

James heard the bellowing start. Lining the fence of their sorting corral, the cows craned their necks toward the trucks where the calves were being loaded. They climbed on top of each other to reach their offspring, but the fence was in the way. The lowing turned to grief. The mothers crushed each other, bellowing with agony.

Thirty times. James had weaned and shipped cattle thirty times. It had never been easy, but he couldn't remember it ever being this hard. His stomach churned, reacting to the animals' noise. When Dalton was here, James stayed focused on being a good rancher, making his father proud. Today he felt sick. He didn't know why. Maybe it had to do with his father being gone, with Daisy being here. He didn't want to think of her hearing this.

With all the clamor, he almost didn't hear the woman's voice. Wearing a dark green jacket, Daisy blended with the stand of pines at the far end of the corral. She had climbed up one rung on the fence. With hundreds of calves being led away and four hundred cows bellowing to follow, Daisy had come to watch.

James felt his heart tighten, filled with inexpressible sorrow and rage. Daisy's cries came over the herd's noise, and he couldn't stand it anymore.

Galloping over, he pulled up in front of her. "Go inside, Daisy."

"Listen to them." She wept.

"It's weaning time," he said. "Happens every year."

"They're crying," she said. "Can't you hear them?"

"They always make a lot of noise. Go inside and close the door. It'll be over soon."

Daisy closed her eyes. Her face was pale. James had always thought her the most vulnerable creature alive, and it drove him crazy to think of the weight she'd had to withstand.

"For God's sake, Daisy, go inside!"

"I can't," she said. "I'm not going to leave them alone. I'm staying here till every calf is gone. Till—"

"Till they lose hope?" James asked, not knowing where the words came from. "That it?"

"I just want to be with them," Daisy said. "I can't explain it." She took a deep breath, and suddenly she wasn't crying anymore. She looked James straight in the eyes. "This has nothing to do with you. I'm fine. I mean it. Go back to work, James."

"Nothing to do with me." James furiously turned his horse and galloped away. He saw Paul watching him.

The calves stumbled up the ramps into the trucks, bleating like sheep, not knowing what was about to happen. Like life, James thought. Youngsters trusted their parents to take care of them.

"Damn it," James said, just before he got within earshot of Paul. He didn't feel like explaining anything, and he could see Paul wanting to ask questions.

Paul rode over. "Got fans watching the action?" he said.

"No fans here," James said.

"No? She looks pretty riveted."

"I didn't say she wasn't riveted. She's just not a fan."

"Ladies don't like this part," Paul said.

"She wouldn't like you saying 'ladies,' either," James said. "She's not very happy."

"We're almost done," Paul said. "The cows'll be quiet soon. They'll forget what just happened, and they'll settle down to a long winter's rest. Till we get 'em bred again, anyway."

"Hey, Paul?" James asked, trying to be heard above the cattle.

"Yeah?"

"Would you shut up," James said. Then he rode away to pull another drowned mother out of the mud.

D RIVING D ALTON'S TRUCK, Louisa pulled in midway through the weaning operation. She had gotten used to it over the years—the god-awful screaming of the cows—but today it hurt her ears. There were James and Paul, leading the cowboys as they separated the herd. And there was Daisy, watching the whole thing from the far end of the main corral.

Louisa shook her head. Daisy knew enough about loss without watching the damn cows bellow for their babies.

Once inside the house, she breathed a great sigh of relief. It felt good to be home instead of cooped up in that awful hospital. Louisa went to the sideboard and poured herself a whiskey. She didn't believe in drinking alone or before sunset, but today was a day to break the rules.

Flopping down on the living-room sofa, she looked around the room. Portraits of Tucker ancestors glared down from every wall. Louisa let her gaze travel to the silver tea service Dalton's wife had inherited from her grandmother.

Rosalind. She had been dead for many years—since James was fifteen. Louisa knew the story. They had been in the pony barn, mother and son, after a snowstorm just like this one. The snow had been heavy, and the weight had collapsed the roof, right on top of them.

James, hurt himself, had pulled his mother out. Oh, what that must have been like. Louisa had imagined it many times: the young boy with his broken leg, holding his dying mother.

Rosalind had been so many things Louisa was not: eastern, well-born, rich. Louisa was the girlfriend; Rosalind had been the wife.

Sighing, Louisa drifted across the living room and over to Dalton's desk. She began to casually tidy the papers on top, then realized what she was doing: looking for the will. She was nuts. Of course Dalton would take care of her. She knew the man, believed he loved her. Calling her Rosalind was nothing more than drug-and-pain talk. Thinking of her own family, she picked up the phone and called Todd's wife. Tammy was a nice girl, very loving and devoted to Todd.

"Well, hi, Mrs. Rydell," Louisa said into the mouthpiece.

"Hi, Aunt Louisa," Tammy said, laughing at the pretend formality. She asked about Dalton, and they talked for a while about his condition and prognosis.

"Listen, your big, handsome husband told me your sister does health care, and I'm thinking about hiring her."

"She's good," Tammy said, "and she needs the work."

"Which sister's this?" Louisa asked, trying to keep Tammy's family straight. "The one with kids or without kids?"

"They both have children," Tammy said, sounding confused.

Tammy gave Louisa her sister's name: Alma Jackson. A wayward husband and two boys to support. She had worked in hospitals and nursing homes, and she did private-duty work somewhere up north. Louisa thanked her niece-in-law and promptly dialed Alma's number. The voice on the answering machine sounded plain but nice, and Louisa left a message.

Hanging up, she looked around. The house felt strange without Dalton in it. Almost as if it still belonged to Rosalind.

KIDS run away all the time. That's what Detective LaRosa had told Daisy, and that's what the police said in every department she called. On a map Daisy had drawn a line from the town in Iowa where Sage had gotten off the train to the ranch. Choosing towns along the line, she'd called the local police departments. Some had received bulletins about Sage; most hadn't. None had seen her.

It was dark now; the night was silent. The semis had pulled out, taking the calves to their deaths. The cows huddled in the corrals, their noisy grief subsided. But Daisy couldn't get the sounds out of her head. She felt washed out, as if she'd been crying for days.

The howling started up again. Had she conjured it? Daisy felt powerful in her work: If she could bring love without intending to, perhaps she could call wolves down from the foothills.

When the knock came at the door, she nearly jumped out of her chair. Thinking it might be news of Sage, she flung open the door.

James stood there, scraping snow off his boots.

She gasped. "What are you doing here?"

"That's what I want to ask you," he said. "Can I come in?"

Daisy stood aside, her arms hugging herself.

"What the hell are you doing?" he asked.

"Right now? Calling police stations." She showed him her map.

"You can do that from back east," he said, interrupting her. "From your own house. Go home, Daisy. You don't belong here."

She looked up into his face. The lines were sharp and deep, his jaw set. "It's where I have to be."

"I heard you today. We all heard you."

"Crying? So what?"

"This is a ranch, Daisy. It's not a zoo. It's not a park, where you take the kids to pet a calf, play with the ducks. You always wanted it to be something it's not."

She shook her head. "You don't know what you're talking about."

James exhaled. He paced around the room. Seeing him in here, the first place they had made love, was almost too much for Daisy.

The fire sputtered, and James stared at it. He almost showed her the charred Polaroids to shake some sense into her and chase her away. Evil things were happening here.

"Sage is coming. I belong here."

"But stuff goes on here. What good does it do you, hearing the cows cry?"

"What good does it do *you?*" she asked quietly.

Surprised by the gentleness of her tone, he looked up. He wiped some imaginary dust from his cheek, the corner of his eye.

"It hurts you, James, sending those babies off to be killed. It's torn you up."

"I'm fine."

"No, you're not." Daisy wanted to touch his cheek. She wished she could take him to a healer, see if what was broken inside him could be fixed. For a long time, back when Jake had first disappeared, Daisy had wanted to be that healer herself. Now she knew she didn't have that much power.

He stared at her, but nothing about him softened. "You've got to get out of here. I'll get Sage home to you. Don't you believe me?"

"I believe you."

"You don't," he said. "You can't, after what went on with Jake. You think it's the same."

"It's not. Kids run away all the time." Daisy couldn't believe how easily the policeman's palliative words tripped off her tongue. But the fact suddenly seemed clear and comforting. At sixteen, pregnant and scared, Sage wanted her father, and she had run away to be with him. That's all. Nothing about this was James's fault.

"I don't blame you," she said quietly. "For any of it."

"I do," James said.

"I know." She wanted to take his hand, but she couldn't make herself do it. "You always have."

"I'm going to say it again," he said, his voice breaking. "Leave, Daisy. Go home. I know you believe Sage is safe, and so do I. I have to. But what happens when she gets to the ranch? This is where things happen, not out there."

"We're here," Daisy whispered. "Her parents."

"What good did we do before?" James asked like a man whose life was over, whose life had been over for a good long time.

"Our best," Daisy whispered back.

She turned to face James Tucker, and their eyes met and held. She watched his expression soften—his muscles were so taut it looked unbearable. He had to let go, she knew. She wanted to rub his tense shoulders and back, to whisper the things she said to the bones. Daisy felt herself wanting to love him again, and that scared her even more than the hardness in his eyes.

Louisa met Alma Jackson at the kitchen door and thanked her for driving all the way to the ranch in the snow.

"It was bad," Alma said woodenly.

Louisa didn't know quite how to respond to that.

"Well, I guess we could have postponed our meeting. Dalton's not even home!"

"Dalton?"

"Mr. Dalton Tucker. The man you'd be taking care of. Good care, from what your sister says."

"Well," Alma said, not corroborating the accolade one little bit. She licked her lips and looked around, seeming very nervous.

Could Alma have replied with one iota less enthusiasm? Was it possible that this little mouse could actually be related to Todd's Tammy—of the warm smile and twinkling eyes? Did she really want the position?

"Why don't you tell me a little about your résumé?" Louisa asked, getting down to business.

They sat at the kitchen table. Louisa gave Alma the once-over. She looked about forty, forty-one, with pasty-pale skin and a serviceable brown rinse to cover her gray hair. Alma mentioned working at hospitals in Laramie and Lander, rest homes in Cheyenne and Dubois. She listed six private homeowners she had cared for after strokes, heart attacks, and a broken hip, and frostbite.

"You sure sound qualified." Louisa was somewhat reassured.

They discussed working conditions and salary, and Alma's expression brightened when she heard the amount. Louisa said she'd want Alma to live in, at least until Dalton got on his feet.

"Tammy and Todd speak very highly of you," Louisa said. "You didn't mention any other names I recognize."

"I don't know many people around here," Alma said quickly. "I'm from the other side of Dubois. I've hardly even been here to visit."

"Except to see your sister?"

"That's right," Alma said. "Tammy and Todd have such a nice house. It's a showplace, compared to my old . . . oh, never mind. I don't want to get complaining about my sorry old life."

"So, assuming your references check out, you'll take the job?"

"I will," Alma said, flashing the closest thing to a real smile Louisa had seen. They shook hands, and Louisa told her what the doctors had said: that Dalton could return home in a few days.

Outside, Daisy came riding into view atop Scout. Her cheeks were rosy, and her coppery hair was streaming out in back.

Alma watched Daisy, too, a slight frown on the caregiver's face. "Does she live here?"

"She's visiting," Louisa said, not wanting to explain the relationships. It caused her embarrassment—pain—to have to say Daisy was Dalton's daughter-in-law but not her own. "Don't worry. Your duties won't involve anything but taking care of Dalton."

"It's just . . . she looks familiar," Alma said.

Louisa didn't reply. There had been so much publicity when Jake disappeared. Maybe Alma recognized Daisy from TV and newspapers. Thirteen years had passed, but Daisy looked almost the same.

Daisy waved at the house, then cantered toward the barn. Alma watched her disappear inside, then turned back to Louisa, her blank eyes flickering with something like worry. Louisa got the feeling that Alma was having second thoughts about working on the DR Ranch.

The strange thing, Louisa thought as she watched Alma drive away, was that seeing Daisy had had something to do with it.

Chapter
EIGHT

THE snowstorm was followed by several days of brilliant sunshine, and by the time the doctors had okayed Dalton to continue his recuperation at home, the snow was melting away. James went with Louisa to drive him back.

"You're sure Dad's ready to come home?" he asked.

"Of course I'm sure. You think I'd bring him home if it was the wrong thing to do?"

"No, Louisa, I don't," James said calmly. He couldn't help smiling. As much as she brought out the devil in him, he brought out the worst in her. They sped along the highway that traversed a quarter of DR ranchland. The mountains rose to their west, snow-covered peaks soaring into the blue sky. He hoped Sage, wherever she was, was seeing this sunny day. It was a hundred percent better than picturing her in the storm.

Three times on the way, Louisa told him he'd have to take care of Dalton's paperwork. "I'm not authorized, you know," she said. "Only a wife or a family member is able to sign."

"What about Dad?" James asked finally, wondering what she was getting at. "He can sign for himself, can't he?"

"They're going to have him sedated for the ride home."

That morning James and Paul had washed the big ranch wagon. They'd folded the back seats down, placed a thick bunk mattress in the cargo space. Daisy had brought out quilts and pillows. Making up the bed, her hand had brushed James's.

He'd wondered then if they were both thinking the same thing— about the time they'd driven the wagon to the rodeo in Cheyenne. James had competed in the team roping event. Driving home, James had held Daisy's hand while she'd kept his trophy on her lap. Halfway to the ranch James had stopped the car. He'd walked around the front, opened Daisy's door, lifted her in his arms. It was summertime, and a full moon painted the mountains and range with white light. He'd carried his wife through the sagebrush to a spot where they'd made love in the moonlight.

Back then the feeling for each other had been so wild and intense they'd stop everything to be together.

James tensed up, thinking about it now. For the rest of the drive home he'd held Daisy's hand and smelled the musk of their bodies mingled with the spicy scent of sage. All he'd been able to think about was loving her again the minute they got home.

"You sign your father out," Louisa directed now, as they pulled into the hospital lot, "and I'll make sure he's ready."

"Whatever you say." He heard Louisa's bitterness, her unspoken gripe about being Dalton's mistress and not his wife, but James had never considered that his problem. He'd let his feelings be known long ago, when he was just a boy missing his mother. Dalton was his own man; he'd had decades to propose if he wanted to.

Finally the papers were filled out and they were ready to go. Louisa held Dalton's hand while James pushed his wheelchair. He was shocked by his father's pallor, by the fact he'd lost so much weight. When Dalton talked, his voice sounded light and weak.

"What a good son," Dalton said. "Coming all this way to drive me home."

"I felt bad not visiting you," James said, "but—"

"I know, I know," his father said. "You had the roundup, and you wanted to keep an eye out for Sage."

Louisa let out a huge exhalation. She dropped Dalton's hand.

"Louisa," Dalton called, but she didn't turn around. "What's she mad about?" he asked James.

"I don't know," James said.

"Louisa . . ."

She just walked faster. James couldn't imagine what was eating her—getting temperamental at a time like this.

With the back cargo doors open, James bent down. He had never done this before—picked his father up. Slinging Dalton's arm around his neck, he slid his arms under the old man. Dalton rested his head against James's. Jake had done the same thing—touched his temple against James's when James would pick him up.

"Ready?" James asked. "I don't want to hurt you."

"Don't worry," Dalton said weakly.

Carefully James transferred his father from the chair to the mattress, covered him with the quilt. By the time they hit the highway, Dalton was asleep. Driving, James kept quiet as long as he could. He looked across the front seat and saw Louisa combing her hair.

"What was that about back there in the parking lot?"

"Nothing," Louisa said.

"Didn't look like nothing. What were you thinking of, getting him upset when he has this ride ahead of him?"

"Getting *him* upset," she began. "Do you ever think, James, that *I* might be upset?"

"He's the one coming home from the hospital—"

"He's the one, she's the one." Louisa tried to laugh, but her voice was full of tears. "That's how you think, isn't it? In families there is no 'he's the one.' When one person suffers, everyone does. Your father's pain is my pain."

"I never doubt that you care about him."

"No, you just doubt I'm good enough to be his wife. And now, with the Alzheimer's, he's started forgetting who I am. Forgets my name and thinks your mother's still alive. Think that doesn't hurt?"

"He does? He calls you by my mother's name?"

"Yes, he does. Once in a while. But you don't want to hear what I have to say, do you?"

"Tell me," James said. "I'll give it my best shot."

"He's the one coming home from the hospital," Louisa said, "but it affects me, too. I love him. I have to watch him learn to walk all over again. I have to open our home to a live-in aide, get used to a stranger at our breakfast table. When I sing at the Stagecoach"— she twisted her handkerchief into a tight ball—"I have to get used to him not being there."

"I'm sorry," James said, shocked by the force of emotion.

"Old age can go to hell!" Louisa shouted.

"Rrrrr . . ." Dalton mumbled in his sleep.

"You're not old," James said.

"I'm old enough to know more than you do," Louisa said. "So listen good. Get it out of your head, this business about 'my part and your part; I'm the one and you're the one.' "

"You mean with—"

"With Daisy! You're *both* the one. You both loved your babies, and you're both worried sick about Sage. For right now, till that girl gets herself home safe, you and Daisy are family. You're in this together."

James held the wheel. He wanted to tell Louisa to stay out of it, to tell her about the mutilated cattle and the pictures—he was trying to protect Daisy and Sage. But she just kept talking.

"You don't know the first thing about staying together. You blew your own world apart after Jake got lost."

"You don't know what you're talking about."

"You felt unworthy," Louisa said, suddenly sounding exhausted. "I saw it—we all did. You thought you lost your son, you might as well drive off your whole family. But there wasn't any talking to you then. You were determined to bear the whole weight yourself."

James just glared at the road.

"And the weight wasn't all yours to bear," Louisa finished.

She didn't say anything more. The land slid by. James looked up at the blue sky, saw a flock of geese coming down to land on a lake. A thin layer of ice had formed, but it held their weight.

"Rosalind," Dalton called from the back seat.

James glanced across at Louisa. An hour ago he might have felt happy to hear his father say his mother's name. But right now he felt sorry for the woman sitting beside him.

"Rosalind," his father said again, his frail voice plaintive.

Louisa half turned in her seat. Then, unbuckling her seat belt, she got up on her knees and reached back to take Dalton's hand.

"I'm right here, darling," she whispered. "Don't you fear. I'm with you all the way."

SAGE was feeling good. After being snowbound in a cow barn for ten hours straight, she and David were driving again. She felt free and light. But they had run out of money, so they stopped at a truck stop in the middle of nowhere and signed on to wash dishes for a few nights. In return they got minimum wage plus lodging. Sage was amazed that no one asked questions: They didn't have to give their names, addresses, or Social Security numbers. They were just shown the kitchen and told not to break anything.

A telephone hung on the kitchen wall, and every time Sage went near it to grab another stack of dirty dishes, she felt a pang in her heart. She hadn't called home once. Thinking of it hurt too much; she'd hear her mother's voice and go to pieces. Her mother would talk her into flying back east, and she'd never get to see her father.

"What's your dad like?" she asked David while he scrubbed roasting pans.

"He has a nice twinkle in his eye, and he spends his days petting the dogs and smoking a pipe," David said. "I love him a lot."

"You do?" Sage asked, beaming.

"No, I hate him."

Sage's heart fell. She never knew when David was kidding her.

"Let's just wash these dishes and get paid so we can feed the animals," David said. "I want to leave tonight."

"Tonight? I thought we told the manager tomorrow—"

"As soon as we're done with these. I'm on a mission."

Sage had saved some scraps of roast beef for the dogs. She wondered why David refused to talk about home, but she wasn't mad. She knew you couldn't make someone talk before they were ready, but you could be patient and keep listening. You never knew what you might hear.

And she wondered what the mission was he had planned.

HE HAD a list. He had things to do, items to buy. Still, he kept watch for the girl. Her family was ready for her, making everything nice. He watched her mother pace the small white house; he watched her father ride the range waiting for her to arrive.

It had never been like that for him.

Home. What a place.

There had never been people waiting, keeping the home fires burning. He had known yelling and silence—one or the other. And leaking roofs and empty cupboards and the heat getting turned off.

Cattle ranchers: They were the ones with happy families. They were the ones with new shingles and full pantries and hot water. Their children had new toys to play with and horses to ride.

The Guardian thought about how alone a person could be—a little boy, a grown man. It didn't matter. Being abandoned, being alone, felt bad no matter how old you were.

SUNLIGHT poured through the cottage windows. Finishing her latest round of calls to police departments, Daisy wondered what to do next. Suddenly she heard a whistle. Opening the door, she found James on his horse, leading Scout by the reins.

"Come on," he said. "Get your boots on."

Daisy hesitated, thinking of all the reasons why she shouldn't go. But James was smiling, a smile that made her think of the young cowboy who'd asked her to come stay in a cabin on his ranch.

"I'll be right there," she said, running back inside.

When she reemerged, wearing her boots and jacket and sunglasses against the glare on the snow, James climbed down to help her mount. First he put a white hat on her head: the old Stetson he'd bought her that first year on the ranch. She felt surprised—touched—that he'd kept it all this time.

"You'll need to keep the sun out of your eyes," was all he said, and he gave her a leg up.

Stroking Scout's neck, Daisy leaned over to whisper in her ear. Then James was atop his horse, and they headed out.

Daisy knew these trails by heart, and she concentrated on their beauty instead of questioning why James had come for her.

Riding along the stream, she saw water tumble over a small chute, spraying rainbows into the air. They passed beneath the Rydell Cliffs, so named because supposedly James's grandfather had driven an entire herd of the Rydells' sheep to their deaths here. Daisy had never liked imagining her husband's ancestors acting with such cruelty, and she nudged Scout now, urging him into a canter.

They rode through open meadows toward Daisy's favorite trail. With Scout beneath her, Daisy felt her worries slip away. They came to a clump of aspen, and James and his horse began to climb.

"That way?" Daisy asked, surprised. Their usual route took them farther along the trail, into the mountains through the red-rock canyons. James began to answer, but just as quickly Daisy realized what he was doing. He didn't want to take her past the place where Jake had disappeared. She just nodded and kept following. "I don't know this way," she said. "I don't think we ever rode here together."

"We've had some trespassers down back. I want to keep away from there. And anyway, I want to show you something new."

Daisy nodded. The mountain scenery was wild and romantic. James's knee brushed hers as the horses rode side by side, and she tried to block the electricity from passing through her body. She couldn't think; she was all emotion and instinct right now.

Riding Scout had always had a strange effect on Daisy. There was something about being borne by a big, warm creature up a craggy mountain trail, being filled with the smells of sage, pine, and wind, that stripped away one thousand years of civilization.

They scrambled up a particularly steep part of the trail. Daisy heard the rushing water before they rounded the bend. Gnarled cedars clung to the rocks, and through their sharp needles she saw the slender column of water. It plunged three hundred feet.

They dismounted, and Daisy stared down, inching toward the rock ledge. Her face was wet—from her own tears, not the spray.

"Washakie," she said. "Remember how we taught the kids to say his name?"

"I remember."

Daisy closed her eyes. She could see her children holding hands, trying to pronounce the Indian's name. "Washakie. Washakie."

"You're crying," he said, nearly touching her face. "I thought you'd think the falls were beautiful."

"I'm thinking of things I've lost," she said, her voice thick.

"Sage'll be here," he said. "Any day now she'll come—"

"I'm so worried," Daisy said, her words spilling over his.

"She's strong. She'll be—"

"She's pregnant!" Daisy said.

"Pregnant?" James asked, shocked. "She's only sixteen."

"Sixteen," Daisy said, "is old enough."

They stood there saying nothing, just listening to the falls.

"I was never there to protect her," he said.

"She needed you," Daisy said, swallowing hard. "Tell me why you never saw her, not once in all these years."

"I can't." His face turned hard again. Daisy could see how much he had invested in aloneness, in keeping it all inside.

"Tell me. I deserve an explanation!"

He grabbed her arms. "I stayed," he said through gritted teeth, "to kill whoever it was that took our son."

"Kill?"

"Kill, Daisy. Tear him apart."

"But we don't know—"

"I know," James said.

"You can't! The police never said anyone . . . There weren't any clues. He just disappeared, James. He must have died."

"We never found his body," James yelled. "We never found him to bury!" The look in his eyes was intense, borderline crazy. Suddenly he let go of her and bowed his head.

They stared together at the cascading water, and then Daisy let James spin her around and press her face against his shirt. When she glanced up, she could see that tears were pouring from his eyes.

"I'm sorry, Daisy," he said, the words cracking. "You should have both your children. There was nothing I could do."

"I never thought there was," Daisy cried, clutching him.

"They're gone," James said, wild with disbelief.

Grieving is a learned skill; she and James had not been taught it. They both knew the dark place where prayer couldn't enter or help. Clinging to each other at the water's edge, the parents of Sage and Jake Tucker did what they had never done before. They cried together for what they had lost, what had been taken from them: their chance to be a family.

PAUL March met James in the barn. He had a handful of papers in his hand, feed and maintenance bills, with checks to be signed. James had just finished putting the horses away and was filling the troughs with water.

"Have a good ride?" Paul asked.

James nodded, not really wanting to talk about it. His mind hadn't yet made sense of what had just happened between him and Daisy. He still felt the imprint of her head against his chest.

"What else do you want me to sign?" James asked.

Paul handed him the papers. This had been their way for years: Paul would catch James when he could—on the run, in the barn, by the corrals—and get him to take care of business. Paul was an efficient foreman. James hated paperwork, and neither man liked desks or offices. When James finished, he sensed Paul wanting to say more.

"What is it?" James asked. "What's going on?"

"Just—" Paul began. His eyes narrowed, like he was trying to figure James out. Maybe he wanted to be a friend; more likely he wanted to offer advice—something about him and Daisy.

"Leave it," James said. "Just leave it for tonight."

By NIGHTFALL DAVID AND Sage had left the truck stop. The old black car was bouncing along a rutted farm road, with Sage reading a map by flashlight. David had made an X on the map, and the closer they got to it, the angrier he became.

Without warning he stopped the car and went to the trunk. Sage turned in her seat, trying to see what he was doing. She heard a bag being unzipped, and she saw the glow of a light. When he got back in the car, fifteen minutes later, he kept his head averted.

"I'm not going to navigate if you won't talk to me," she said. "Is this the mission?"

She flashed the light in his face. What she saw made her gasp. He had drawn seven black dots across his cheeks, concentric circles and dots on his forehead and chin, four thin black lines down his neck. The markings looked like tattoos.

"David, what are you doing?" she asked.

"It's the tradition," he said. His voice sounded odd, as if it weren't his own. Sage's hair rose on the back of her neck.

"What tradition?" she whispered.

"Do you know about messengers between realms?" he asked.

She nodded. Her mother talked about such things. When she carved bones, she imagined calling forth spirits of the dead.

"These dots," he said, pointing to his cheeks. "They stand for savings. Each time I've been able to save things. One of the dots is you."

Reaching out, Sage touched David's face. This was bizarre, yet she somehow understood and wasn't afraid. Without being told, she knew what the other six represented.

"We're going to a puppy farm, aren't we?" she asked.

"Yes."

"Can I come in with you?"

David didn't answer.

They drove for half an hour more. Sage held all six kittens on her lap, curled into sleeping balls. The dogs lay still in the back seat.

A cluster of lights showed up ahead. David stopped, turned off the headlights, and slid a battered hacksaw from under the seat.

"You can come, but you have to wear something if you do."

"What?"

"The owl," he said.

Sage cocked her head. What was he talking about, wear an owl?

Opening the glove compartment, he pulled out a small leather case and extracted colored pens. He took hold of her right hand. He licked the tip of the brown pen and started to draw. The pen point tickled. He seemed to be drawing each individual feather.

"Why an owl?" she asked. "What does it mean?"

"It sees."

With a bright yellow pen he drew two piercing eyes. The finished owl was perfect, tiny, and fierce, exactly like the one on David's wrist.

Sage took a deep breath. She felt like saying a prayer or chanting a spell. She tried to remember the word her mother used to say, the Indian name that meant bravery. It was too elusive, like a feather in the wind, so she just crossed her fingers instead.

On the side of the dirt road a sign showed a hunting dog pointing at a dead pheasant: PUREBRED ENGLISH SETTERS, the writing said. Sage saw an old house, a truck, and several sheds. She could hear loud barking. The house was nearly all dark, except for a dim light in the kitchen and the blue glow of the TV.

From inside the house Sage heard a woman's voice raised in anger and a man's voice in response. Some kid was crying, and another joined in. She heard a smack, a door being slammed, then silence.

"They're sick," David whispered. "All the puppy-farm owners are the same. They beat their wives, and they both beat the kids. Come on."

They plodded through a muddy yard. David had stuck the hacksaw in his belt, and he removed it now to saw the flimsy lock off the shed door. Sage slipped in behind him. The space was pitch-black and very cold. The dogs were yelping. As her eyes grew accustomed to the darkness, she began to see.

The shed was about fifteen by thirty feet. Cages lined the long wall, two high. Each cage was about two feet square. David moved methodically along the wall. Training his flashlight on each cage, he opened all the doors.

Sage saw the dogs cowering against the back walls of the cages. Some were nursing puppies. The stench of excrement was strong, and Sage saw that some cages contained mother dogs and dead puppies. No one had bothered to remove them.

"Poor things," Sage said, reaching in to pet one trembling dog. The dog bared her teeth and snapped. Sage stepped back.

David was looking for something, going up and down the row. Some of the dogs had started to creep forward. The bravest ones stuck their noses out and jumped down.

David was going to set them all free.

"You can't," Sage said, grabbing his arm. "Where will they go? What will they eat?"

"They're hunters," David said. "They'll survive."

"They don't know how," Sage said. "They'll die!"

"You think that's as bad as this?" he asked, his voice as much a snarl as any animal's.

Sage looked around. Very slowly, one by one, the dogs had all hopped free of their cages. Many of them had dragged their puppies out, one at a time, holding them in their mouths.

Sage saw David wrap his jacket around one dog, lift her into his arms, and head for the door. He eased the shed door open, and the dogs slipped out. Some of them stopped to sniff the grass, but most of them limped for the hills. Their gaits were crooked and crippled, but their desire to escape was great.

"Come on," David said, carrying his bundle. She watched as he pulled his knife, went to the truck, and slashed all four tires.

With all the dogs free, the barking had stopped. By the time Sage and David got to the car, the farmer had noticed the silence. The porch lights blared on, and the screen door slammed. David didn't take time to place the dog—wrapped in his jacket—in the back seat. Starting up the engine, he kept her on his lap. Then he waited.

The farmer was yelling for his family to come outside and catch the dogs. His wife came running out, followed by two children. David thrust the dog onto Sage's lap and rolled down his window. Then he leaned on the horn.

"Hey, you bastard," he shouted. "You're gonna burn in hell."

"What? Did you steal my dogs?" the farmer screamed, running for his truck. "I'll kill you!" The farmer started his truck, but the tires just flapped around the axles. He jumped out again, pointing a shotgun as he started to run toward the car.

David did a long burnout. Sage's heart was racing as she heard the shotgun blast again and again, but they were out of range.

She expected David to drive back the way they'd come, but half a mile down the road he turned right and began traveling west. The road wasn't marked or paved. Pine trees grew right down to the edge, the low boughs brushing the car's roof.

"Do you know where we're going?" she asked.

"Of course I do."

"How do you know—"

"I've been to that farm before. My mother traded them a bitch for a sire one time, back when we used to have setters."

"Is this . . ." Sage asked, her heart in her throat, feeling the trembling dog on her lap. "Is this the same dog your mother traded?"

"No. She'd have died a long time ago," David said.

"Then why her?" Sage asked. "Of all the dogs, why take her?"

"Because she was the worst one." David's voice cracked. "She wouldn't have been able to get away. I always take the worst one."

During the night, while David drove and Sage slept with her head resting against the door, they crossed the border from Nebraska into Wyoming.

Chapter
NINE

DAISY walked up to the house to visit Dalton and came face to face with a stranger in the kitchen. The woman had tea and toast on a tray, but when she saw Daisy, she jumped and spilled it all over.

"Oh, I'm sorry," Daisy said, crouching down to help.

"Not your fault."

After they'd wiped up the mess, the woman set about making more toast and tea.

"I'm Daisy Tucker," Daisy said. "Have we met before?" The woman looked so familiar: a broad face, furtive dark eyes.

"I'm Alma Jackson. No. Louisa just hired me this week."

"I'm sure—at least I think—we've met before. Oh, never mind," Daisy said, smiling and shaking her hand. "It's nice to meet you."

"Thanks," the woman mumbled, turning back to her task.

Daisy walked into the living room, wondering about the bruises she'd noticed on Alma's arm. Dalton sat in his wheelchair by the window, watching a line of antelope cross the hillside. When he heard Daisy, he put down his binoculars and tilted his face up to kiss her.

"Daisy, you're a sight for sore eyes. Have you come to stay?"

"For now," she replied. She wasn't sure exactly what he meant— how much he remembered about where she'd been—but she didn't care. She felt content just to sit and hold his hand.

"Have you met the Hun?" he asked.

"The Hun?"

"Old what's-her-name, out in the kitchen. Louisa hired her from somewhere way down in the Rydell-family gene pool. A nasty one."

Daisy smiled. "You're probably working her too hard."

"She's here spying for Todd. Don't think I don't know it, either. How Rosalind got herself born into a clan like that—"

"I think you mean Louisa," Daisy said gently.

Dalton looked stricken. "Did I say Rosalind? Damn it. Hit me next time I do that. You're Daisy. I got that right, didn't I?"

"Yes, but it doesn't count as much." Daisy laughed. "Forget about my name and remember hers."

"Hard to forget yours, Daisy," Dalton said. "You're my only daughter-in-law."

"You're my only father-in-law," Daisy said.

"You gave James a run for his money. Never brought anyone around the ranch after you left."

"Never?" she asked. She knew it wasn't her business, but she couldn't help wanting to know.

"Nope. Never. You were it. Maybe still are. I don't know. He doesn't talk. Just rides and ropes and works. Maybe he talks to Paul. Go ask him."

Daisy's gaze moved to the pictures arranged on the stone mantel: she and James on their wedding; the twins' birth pictures; a picture of Sage wearing her red cowgirl hat; Jake smiling from up on Scout.

"My grandbabies," Dalton said, following Daisy's gaze. "I miss them. More every day. I gave them toy cows when they were born. Sage still have hers?"

"She does," Daisy said, looking at her children. They looked so happy, smiling into the camera, loving their life on the ranch, growing up with horses, cows, dogs, a grandfather in the next house. Life had been so perfect.

"Louisa's got a gig down the Stagecoach tonight," Dalton said. "Do me a favor and go for me. Take James and make him give her a big wolf whistle. She likes it when the young guys go wild."

"Don't you get jealous?" Daisy asked, smiling.

"I turn green, but it makes her so happy."

"Maybe I will."

Alma walked in at that moment, setting the tray down by Dalton's side. Dalton winked at Daisy, put a finger to his lips. He didn't want her talking Tucker business in front of a Rydell.

Lifting her eyes, Alma glanced at the pictures on the mantel. She did a double take, nearly spilling Dalton's tea a second time. Daisy watched her, unsure of why she looked so stricken. One thing Daisy was sure of: Those bruises on Alma's arm came from a man's hand.

"That's my grandson," Dalton said.

"I was looking at the girl," Alma said. "In the little red hat."

"My granddaughter," Dalton said.

"Oh," Alma said. "She's cute."

Dalton agreed, asking Alma if she had kids of her own. "Two boys," Alma answered. Dalton asked her their names, whether they liked to hunt and fish, and Alma answered. But Daisy hardly heard. It wasn't Sage's picture Alma had been staring at. It was Jake's.

Why had she lied? Daisy wondered.

TRY AS SHE MIGHT, DAISY told Louisa over the phone, she couldn't see herself going to the Stagecoach while Sage was still out there. Louisa listened to the younger woman, touched by the things she said—*and* by the fact that Dalton had put her up to calling.

"You should listen to Dalton," Louisa said, the phone wedged between her ear and the bar wall, "and get yourself down here." Behind her a couple of guys were making a beer delivery.

"I'm sure the place'll be full to the rafters without me."

"Well, it will." It wasn't immodest if it was true, and she knew for a fact the place would be packed tonight.

"Dalton was alert," Daisy said. "He's having a good day."

"He has them now and then," Louisa said. "Not as often as before, but we're grateful when they come."

"I wanted to ask you something about Alma."

"Oh, did Dalton put you up to that, too?" Louisa asked, frowning. "Honestly, just because her sister is married to Todd—"

"It's the way she looked at Jake's picture," Daisy said. "Do you know why she'd even notice him?"

"Well . . ." Louisa began, but she bit her tongue. Didn't Daisy know how everyone had talked back then? Jake's disappearance had caused so much communal worry and anguish—and a fair share of vicious talk. People always suspected the parents.

"Tell me, please," Daisy said urgently.

Louisa sighed. "From what Tammy told me, Alma's boys would be about the twins' age. I'm sure she remembered the news about Jake and she was just looking at his sweet face, thanking her lucky stars that it was him instead of them."

"Oh," Daisy said after a long silence.

"She's a simple soul." Louisa wished she could give Daisy a hug. "She doesn't mean you any harm. Her home life is ugly. They live in some squalid little place up north, too many animals and not enough money. Her husband drinks. She has a hard life."

"Thank you for telling me," Daisy said.

Louisa heard her guitar player start to tune up. "Tell Dalton this night's for him." Louisa choked up, wondering whether he'd ever sit in her audience again. "Dedicated to the one I love," Louisa said. "Tell him, will you?"

She saw Todd walk in, give her a big wave from the saloon doors. Louisa turned, pretending not to see him. He had really opened a Pandora's box, asking her about Dalton's will. Now she found herself cleaning drawers and boxes, straightening papers, doing everything to avoid the place she knew it had to be: Dalton's safe. She had thought their love would lead to marriage. Dalton had wanted to spare James thinking someone could take the place of his mother. But now Louisa wanted nothing more than a ring on her finger.

"Have a good show," Daisy said.

"You bet," Louisa said with all the false cheer she could muster.

JAMES stood outside in the dark for a long time, staring at Daisy's windows, where candlelight flickered. He had taken a shower and changed his clothes, combed his hair. Telling himself he'd just stay a minute, he moved toward the door.

There were a hundred excuses he could make about coming to see her. His father had told him she'd wanted to go see Louisa sing tonight; he could offer to loan her the truck or drive her himself. His mind raced with good enough reasons to knock on her door.

But when he actually did it, his head was empty. There wasn't a thought going on up there. His heart pounded in his chest.

"Hi," she said, opening the door. He was glad she didn't sound disappointed to see him. "Come on in."

James walked in. A lot like how it used to be, way back when. "This reminds me of that summer," he said. "When you were our lodger."

"Lodger," she said, smiling at the word. "That's what I was."

"Long time ago." He'd been less shy then, had known how to present himself: the brash young cowboy. What was he now?

"That was the summer all this started," she said. She'd walked over to her workbench and was looking down at the wolf bones he'd brought her.

"All this?" He wondered whether she meant them—him and her.

"My work. Making jewelry from things I found on the ranch."

James walked over and picked up the piece she was making. He looked at the faces she'd carved into the bone: a man and woman facing each other.

"Who are they?" he asked.

"I don't know. It's only the second two-faced piece I've made."

"What was the other? Who'd you make it for?"

"Sage," she said. "I did it of the twins."

He ran his thumb over the tiny faces. Their eyes were alive and full of longing, and he suddenly knew they were of him and Daisy.

"What do they want?" he asked.

"Each other."

"Why can't they have that?"

"I don't know," she said.

"It's us, isn't it?" James moved closer. He touched her hair.

She smiled. "Maybe that's why these things work. People see themselves."

James watched her gather a pile of stones in her hand, and he knew she was avoiding him. The candlelight flickered, throwing shadows around the room. Outside—close by—a wolf bayed. Louis Shoulderblade had said Daisy had power. James didn't know if he believed such things, but he couldn't deny he'd heard a lot of wolves recently, ever since he'd given her those bones.

She was still holding the stones. James said her name out loud, and she looked up. He took her in his arms, and he heard a pebble fall to the floor. Just as when he'd kissed her the first time, in the streambed, when she'd dropped the gold nugget. He kissed her.

"James, don't."

"Remember this place?" he asked, his mouth close to hers. "I don't think you could be staying here now if you didn't still think of us, if the memories weren't good."

"This place." Daisy shook her head. She pulled away, and she stared at the small bed. He wondered whether she was remembering the first time they'd made love, when they were young and full of passion and it had all been like a summer adventure.

"Remember?" he asked, kissing the back of her neck.

She resisted, but the memory unlocked something inside her. She turned and took his hand. He kissed her cheek. Arching her back, she let him kiss her neck, her shoulder, her collarbone.

Then she raised her lips to his. She tasted like spice, and he wanted more. Fumbling with her buttons, he started to undo her shirt.

"Tell me," he whispered. "Those faces are us, aren't they? Your carving—"

"They are," she whispered back.

James's heart pounded, knowing he would have died for Daisy anytime during the last thirteen years and before, that every mistake he had made—even the worst of them—had sprung from the fact that he loved her so much.

"I never stopped," he said, kissing her as they lay down on the small bed. "Never stopped loving you."

"It was you," she whispered, her breath hot against his ear, "in every single thing I did. All those necklaces I made, the necklaces that brought everyone else love. They have you in them. Nobody but you. I gave them our love because I couldn't have you. Because we lost what we had."

"Get it back, Daisy," he said, stroking the side of her face.

"It doesn't work that way."

"How does it work?"

She started to cry. "We would have to start over. Begin again."

He kissed her. "I think you're wrong. You put our love into your carvings. I think we can get it back right now."

They'd fallen into a river, and they were clinging to each other. The water swirled around them, carrying them downstream, down the mountain from the land of snow. The riverbed was ancient, and the flowing water made everything in its path smooth.

"Right now, Daisy," he whispered. "Get it back."

MOTHER *and Father. Mother and Father.*

They were in there together, in the nice warm house with candlelight bouncing off the walls, the fire keeping them toasty, while he was on the outside in the cold.

The Guardian adjusted the binoculars. She had drawn the curtains, but there was a spot where the fabric didn't quite meet, and through that gap he was able to see bodies, see them kissing.

A noise in the underbrush made him freeze. Someone was coming down the path. The Guardian darted into the chaparral and held his breath as the person came closer. He hoped his own tracks in the snow would be invisible in the darkness.

The boots came crunching through the snow, and then they stopped in the exact spot where the Guardian had been standing a moment ago, the perfect vantage point for peering through the woman's windows.

Peeping Tom, the Guardian thought derisively. He had his reasons for wanting to gather information, but this new watcher was just a voyeur.

After a brief interlude the watcher walked back the way he came—so focused on the curtained window, he hadn't noticed human tracks leading into the brush. Typical, the Guardian thought. He had left trails everywhere, evidence right out in the open, and they'd found only a fraction of it. In time they would find more.

Shivering in the cold, he knew it was time to go. He slept in the barn some nights, in the basement of the big house on others. But he had his main camp set up on the nearby cliff, his tent pitched and his stove ready to fire. Just thirty feet up a gently sloping mule track the Guardian had the best lookout a person could want. Oversee the ranch, the herd, the people—everything. His museum. From his lair he could see the whole display. And they all could see him if they'd just decide to look up.

Good night, Mother and Father. Good night, happy family.

Louisa had to give it to Alma. She was an expert when it came to caring for Dalton. She hefted him from bed to his wheelchair, his wheelchair to the living-room sofa. His cast was cumbersome, and moving him was no easy task.

Getting him ready for the day, Alma always wheeled him over to his closet so he could pick out whichever clothes he felt like wearing. Louisa admired Alma's patience, the way she treated Dalton with respect. On the other hand, Louisa wouldn't have let Alma stay if she was acting any other way.

While Dalton was sleeping in his chair, Louisa poured herself a mug of coffee and drifted over to the kitchen table, where Alma had settled down with a crossword puzzle.

"Mind if I sit down?" Louisa asked.

"No," Alma said, although her tone showed that she did.

Louisa pulled out a chair, acting oblivious. She had bought a book on nutrition and Alzheimer's, and she paged through it now. She read: "a progressive loss of function in the section of the brain responsible for memory and behavior." Her eyes focused on the word "progressive," and she closed the book.

"Tell me about you, Alma," she said.

"Me?" Alma asked, as if it were a foreign concept.

"How'd you get into this line of work?"

Alma shrugged. "Took care of my mother for a long time. I was good at it, doing it for free. So I figured, why not get paid?"

"That's smart of you."

"Tammy said—" Alma began, then stopped. "Never mind."

"What?" Louisa asked.

"I don't want to get too personal."

"Go ahead, Alma. We're practically family, your sister being married to my nephew and all."

"Well, she said it would just be you and the Tucker men here. She didn't mention nothing about the daughter-in-law."

"Daisy? What difference does Daisy being here make?"

"No difference." Alma looked at her crossword puzzle.

"Well, you must have mentioned her for a reason."

"Just . . . She seems to have trouble with her kids. The boy getting killed, and now the girl running away. A rich girl like her."

"Life's not easier for one mother than it is for another."

Alma thinned her lips and looked over with cynical eyes.

"Mothers have it rough," Louisa said. "You hear about the joys and the love, you think if you have enough money for bunny wallpaper and a nice white cradle, everything will turn out just fine. But you know the fairy tales? The queens in those magic castles are just as heartbroken as the rest of us."

"Bunny wallpaper," Alma said. "My kids didn't have none of that."

"But you love them anyway, right?" Louisa asked.

"Always did." Alma shook her head. "But my boys are sorely testing my patience these days. One in jail, one on thin ice. He knew I was working here, he'd come drag me out with a rope. Takes after his father and does things the mean way."

"What would he have against you working here?"

"He used to listen to his uncle Todd tell stories about the Tucker cows and how they ruined the Rydell sheep. Guess he thinks we'd be part of a big ranching fortune if the Tuckers hadn't been so high-handed about the land."

"That feud is long done," Louisa said.

"Some men like to fan the flames."

"Todd's one of them. Your sons and he are close?"

"Yep."

"Tammy must've known that when she recommended you to me," Louisa said. "I wonder why she suggested you work here if it would make your family uncomfortable."

"Tammy knew I needed the work," Alma said. "And no one else needs to know nothing about it."

"You didn't tell your sons you're working here?"

Alma shook her head. "How would I tell them? Like I said, one's serving time for damage he did in a bar fight, and the other never comes by. He dropped out of school. He drinks, just like his father and brother, and he lives in the hills."

"In the hills?"

"Somewhere in the Wind Rivers," Alma said. Two bright pink patches appeared on her cheeks. "He's a teen, but he thinks he's a mountain man. One of those survivalists, you know? I didn't do enough for him when he was young, so he's gonna pay me back by living like an animal now. Sometimes I wish I'd never—"

"I'm sorry," Louisa said. "What about your husband?"

"Never mind him." Alma shook her head hard, as if she was angry at herself for showing such strong feelings. When she looked up, her eyes were blank again. "I take care of myself."

Louisa stared at the salt and pepper shakers. Something was nagging at her from that morning's pool of memories. She had it— "I was wondering," Louisa began, almost as if she were going to say something about the weather, "why you said that about Daisy's son being killed. No one knows for sure. He's still considered missing."

"Missing? They still look for him?" Alma's cheeks reddened.

"Well, no. Certainly the police stopped long ago," Louisa said.

"Because I'm sure he was killed," Alma said quickly. "Todd was there that day. He's always told us there was no sign of any living boy, that the rescue party would have found him if he was there."

"I sometimes forget Todd was there," Louisa said. "Dalton had given him ranch work that year—to make me happy, I guess."

"Todd told us the whole thing," Alma said. "How the boy must've gotten dragged off by a wolf or a bear. Or how he might've crawled into the canyon and found a secret cave. Fallen into a crevice and not been able to get out. He's dead. Got to be."

"Tell that to James," Louisa said. "He's barely left the ranch in all these years, thinking his boy's gonna come walking out of the hills."

"He won't." Alma had spoken too fast, and her eyes widened as if she'd shocked herself. "Sometimes you just have to give up."

"I don't think this family believes that." Louisa wondered about Alma's vehemence.

"Being a parent's hard enough," Alma said bitterly, "without torturing yourself over the impossible."

Louisa didn't speak. She clasped her hands on the table, resting them on the Alzheimer's book. It couldn't be easy on Alma, she thought: one son in jail and another living somewhere in the mountains, "fanning the flames" of his resentments. Louisa could imagine that Alma had plenty to torture herself with.

Perhaps that's what her outburst had been all about. On the

other hand, Louisa thought, why had she seemed so adamant about Jake being dead?

WITH snow falling, James found it hard to leave Daisy's side in the morning. He had been spending nights at her cabin, and now he wanted to pull her close under the quilt and stay warm in bed all day. But he made himself get up, go to work.

He rode along the river, scanning the range with binoculars. He wanted to learn more about whoever had left those pictures behind. Spurring his horse, he took off through foot-deep snow toward the red-rock canyons. Paul and some of the others were mending fences, and James flew by them, galloping westward. High above, the cliff tops glowed gold with the strange mid-storm sunlight, but as he entered the canyon, it became almost dark.

Vultures had landed on something a hundred yards ahead. James yelled and waved his arms, scaring them off. His voice echoed. The birds circled up and around, their wings thundering with every flap.

James rode over to where they'd been feeding. He had found the missing steer. The animal lay ten yards from the closest canyon wall, obviously dead for a few days now. Predators had been at him. Chunks of flesh had been torn from his side; holes had been pecked in his skin. The steer had been shot. His head had been cut off.

Climbing off his horse, James crouched by the animal's shoulders. The snow was covered with bits of black fur and blood. James heard hoofbeats. He saw Paul galloping into the canyon. James waved him over.

"Did you see the birds?" James asked when Paul reined in beside him.

"Must have," Paul said, "but I didn't think anything of it. They're out here all the time." Paul stared at the bloody neck.

"Some bastard did this since the roundup. A butcher."

"The heads," Paul said, and James nodded, remembering the four cow heads stuck on fence posts.

"That's a big steer," Paul said. He was ranch foreman. It was his job to figure out how much money they had just lost at the market.

James was thinking about how long it would have taken someone to saw the head off a two-ton steer.

"Who did it?" Paul asked.

"I don't know." James looked around. Someone had taken pictures of his herd. Someone was killing his cattle, taunting him.

"Someone who hates animals," Paul said.

"Someone who hates me," James said.

THE will had to be in Dalton's safe. Louisa had been resisting the temptation to look there. Checking the desk and the bureau had been one thing, but now she was about to get serious.

Dalton was asleep in his wheelchair all the way down the hall in the study. Alma was downstairs, getting his dinner ready. Louisa pushed aside the painting of Rosalind that covered the safe.

Dalton had given her the combination years ago, after he'd gotten hurt during a roundup. In case anything ever happens to me, he had said. Now, taking a deep breath, Louisa turned the dial. The safe door opened.

Inside, Louisa saw many things: deeds, James's birth certificate, rodeo medals . . . and the last will and testament of Dalton Tucker.

Her fingers were shaking so hard she couldn't hold the paper still. Now she would set her mind to rest.

It won't change anything, she told herself. No matter what this says, I'll love Dalton just as much. I'll still go down to the Stagecoach on Friday night and sing love songs for Dalton Tucker—

"What's that you got there?" Dalton asked.

"Oh!" Louisa jumped. He had wheeled his chair down the hall, the Oriental rug muffling the sound. "You scared me."

"What's that in your hands, Louisa? That's my will, isn't it? Something got your curiosity going?"

"Well, with Daisy being here and all," Louisa began, "I got to thinking about family and the future."

"Damn it, woman!" Dalton shouted. He wheeled his chair painfully across the room and snatched the will out of her hands.

"Dalton—"

"You go there to that bar," he said, his voice ferocious, "every Friday night. They circle around you like buzzards, their tongues hanging out. They want to dance with you, to touch you. Don't think I don't see!"

"But I don't want them," she said.

"I trust you," he said, his eyes blazing. "I watch you go off to that bar, I think about those cowboys, but I trust you. And this"—he shook the document in his thin hand—"this is how you show your trust for me?"

"I have to see," she implored.

"Have to see with your two eyes what you can't see with your heart?" Dalton asked. "Is that it?"

"After you went to the hospital," Louisa said, desperately wanting to explain, "Todd asked me where I would live, if something ever happened—"

"Todd Rydell?" Dalton asked, his tone dangerous.

"He's my nephew. He cares about me."

"That s.o.b.," Dalton said. "You'd listen to him? Why didn't you just ask me? Aren't I worth talking to anymore?"

"Oh, Dalton. You're worth—"

"I'm worthless, that's what you think. I'm an old nothing. No-good legs, no-good brain, no-good love. That's it, isn't it?"

"I love you," Louisa said.

"This is how you show it." Dalton bowed his head. His shoulders shook, and Louisa knew he was crying.

"Look at me," Louisa said. "Dalton, please . . ."

"Rosalind," Dalton said.

Louisa's heart sank. This was it, the horrible disease that had started the whole thing. She couldn't trust his heart, because his brain was dying. Dalton looked up. His eyes were alert, stricken.

"I mean Louisa," he said.

"I know you meant that," she said, taking his hands.

"I said the wrong name." He dropped the will in his lap, holding Louisa's hands. His face was gaunt. "I'm sorry."

"Don't be sorry, love," she said. "Don't be sorry."

"Don't leave me, Louisa," he said, his voice cracking.

"Never," she whispered, laying her head on his lap. His legs were covered with a blanket, and the crumpled-up will had fallen to the floor. Louisa didn't pick it up; she couldn't even move. Dalton's hand felt so good on her hair. "Don't leave me, Dalton."

He didn't reply, but just kept stroking her hair.

THAT night, with the snowstorm covering the entire state of Wyoming, David, Sage, and the animals sought shelter in an abandoned wildlife observation station about fifty miles from the DR Ranch. The snow outside was so wet it stuck to the building, blocking all cracks in the wood, forming a sort of natural insulation.

Like an igloo, Sage thought, sticking her finger through a knothole in one board, feeling three inches of snow on the other side. The dogs and cats surrounded her. Sage sat quietly, watching David build a fire in the black potbellied stove.

"Dinnertime," she said.

"I know," he said. "Roast beef and mashed potatoes."

"Oh, I was thinking of lobster and french fries." She laughed. She watched him feed the animals, and she pulled out a package of cereal they'd brought from the truck stop. Arranging everything in front of the stove, they sat together munching dry wheat puffs.

When they had finished, David pulled a pen out of his backpack and began to trace tiny feathers on the back of his hand. Then he drew a series of dots and circles. As the time passed, they listened to the storm outside, and Sage leaned close while David drew designs on his skin. The fire glowed warm and red.

"The circle," he said quietly, drawing, "protects the dot." Then, drawing a larger circle around the smaller, he added, "And the circle protects the circle."

"You like protecting things," she said.

"Someone has to," he replied.

"Who's the first person you ever protected?"

"Wasn't a person," he said. "It was one of the dogs. Aunt Thelma—that was her name. I protected her from my father."

Something about the way he pronounced the word "father" made Sage turn her head. "Why do you say it that way? As if he's not your real father?"

"He's not," David said. "I'm adopted."

"Oh." Sage tried to imagine what that would be like. "But once people adopt you, they become your real family. Right?"

"That's what they say."

"It's not true?"

"If real families treat you like dirt."

Sage thought of what they had seen at the puppy farm. She had known then that all his rescuing and tattoos had to do with his own life, on a different puppy farm.

"What did they do to you?"

He shrugged, seeming to concentrate as he drew circle after circle. Finally he said, "Are you going to give your baby up for adoption?"

Sage slid her hands down to her belly. She was only sixteen, she had no job and no money of her own, but she knew there was no way on earth she would ever give her child to anyone, anywhere. "No," she said, "I'm not."

David frowned, but he nodded with approval. "I think . . ."

"What?"

David rolled back his left pant leg and pushed down his sock. He bent down and drew three wavy lines about an inch long, one on top of the other.

"A river," he said.

"Why?" she asked.

"A river ran by our house," he said. "I used to make boats from fallen logs and imagine I could float back to my real family."

"You mean, the people who gave you up?"

"I miss them," he said, not seeming to hear her. "I didn't even know them, but I miss them." He let out a crazy laugh, shaking his head. "You don't get it, do you? With your two good parents in two different places? If they're so fantastic, why don't they live together?"

"Because my brother disappeared," Sage said, "and they couldn't take it. It broke them up."

"Your brother disappeared?"

"Yes. My twin. We were three. His name was Jake. I know more about missing someone than *anyone*. My brother and I were in our mother's belly at the same time. We were made from the same blood."

"And you missed him when he left?"

"I felt half gone," Sage said.

"Half gone," David repeated.

"Where did your real family live? Wyoming?" Sage asked.

"Guess so. The people I grew up with—my family—hardly ever left the state, except to trade dogs in Nebraska." David stared into the stove. "Half gone . . . I know what you mean. Missing someone so bad you can't even live right. Like Petal and her toy. Missing her babies so much she went nuts."

"You think Petal's nuts?"

"Just half gone," David said. "Like me."

The other dogs and cats had settled in various parts of the room. The fire sputtered, and David threw more wood on.

"Where do you think your brother went?" he asked.

"I don't know." Sage felt prickles on her neck. "Into the earth."

"Into a cave?"

Sage tilted her head. "Why do you say that?"

David shrugged. "Those mountains are full of caves. Maybe he crawled into one. I got lost in one once. Fell down a crack headfirst and had to get pulled out by my foot. It's how I got this." Pushing back his brown hair, he showed Sage a thin white scar.

"How old were you?"

"Little. Four or five. Small enough to fit down the crack."

Sage closed her eyes. The image was so terrible: a little boy, curious and full of mischief, scuttling into a cave to investigate the mysteries inside, then tumbling in.

"Who saved you?" she asked quietly, stroking Petal.

"My uncle," he said. "My fake uncle, I mean. My adopted mother's brother. He hauled me out."

"That's good," Sage said, "that he was there."

"Yeah. He's pretty nice. Once when my dad was making me axe a litter of puppies, my uncle punched him out."

"Your father forced you to kill puppies?" Sage asked, horrified.

David nodded. "Yeah. That's my family. My uncle's different, though. I heard him yelling he was sorry he'd ever pulled me out of the cave if that was how they were gonna treat me."

"Couldn't you go live with him?" Sage asked.

David shrugged. "He stopped coming around. He and my parents quit speaking after that."

"Go find him," Sage said. "Move in with him."

Frowning, David began to draw on his skin again. Choosing a new spot on his right arm, he drew another owl. Dots, dashes, owls, and circles: the markings David seemed to like most. Sage watched, listening to the storm grow more ferocious outside.

"I saw owls in the cave," he said. "Yellow eyes watching me."

"Scary."

"No. I knew they were my friends."

"You're a good artist," Sage said, suddenly missing her mother. "You must have inherited that from someone in your real family."

"Yeah, maybe. My brother can't draw worth a damn."

"Your brother— Is he from your real family, too?"

"No," David said. "He's theirs. Their real son."

Sage nodded. Her baby kicked inside her, and suddenly she felt strange—as if she was going to be sick. Sage clutched Petal to her, feeling afraid.

David held her hand. "Don't worry. We're warm; we have food."

The wind howled outside; the glass rattled in the windows.

"The baby," Sage said. "What if something happens and we can't get out? The wind's scaring me."

"We could always call for help." David's face was perfectly serious. He began to draw circles and dots on her hand. "We could call the spirit."

"The messenger between realms?" she asked, trembling at the words. It was dark outside: David had told her he wouldn't talk about this during daylight, but night had long since fallen.

"Yes."

Sage felt excited by what David was saying. This reminded her of her mother: the studio filled with feathers, bones, rocks, and gold wire, and, hanging from the ceiling, the dream-catchers—netted hoops to catch the good dreams.

"What spirit?" Sage asked.

"The bravest one," David said. "It's a magic name that can keep you safe. If you say it, no one can harm you."

Again, swimming up from Sage's memory came that word—the Indian name her mother used to say. "What?" she whispered.

"Washakie." David said it once, then again, louder.

Sage's eyes clouded as a memory came out of nowhere. She could see trail dust and four small feet, hers and her brother's. She could hear their mother's and father's voices telling them about an Indian chief, how his very name meant bravery.

"Oh, my God. Jake."

David stared at her. "What?"

"Is it possible?" She fumbled for his hands as the salt tears poured down her cheeks. "I think you're my brother."

Chapter
TEN

JUST before dawn the ranch was frozen. White stars were brilliant in the blue-black sky. Last night the temperature had dropped hard and fast, freezing the wet snow solid. James knew the cattle wouldn't be able to break through the crust, so he went to the barn to saddle up and ride out to break the ice so they could graze.

He found Daisy brushing Scout at the tie-downs.

"You're up early," he said.

"I couldn't sleep."

"Did the storm bother you?"

She nodded, and he could see the tightness around her eyes. "Sage is all I can think about. Last night I sat up, praying."

"We could have done that together."

Daisy's face crumpled, as if she was in the most terrible pain. "I've just gotten so used to doing it alone."

"So have I." James took a step around Scout. He noticed that she had gotten Scout's bridle and saddle out of the tack room.

"You're not planning to ride, are you?"

"Yes," she said. "I can't stay inside today. I'll go crazy. Maybe if I head out toward the main road, I'll meet her coming in."

"There's ice on top of the snow," he said. "I don't think you should go. It might be dangerous."

"It's dangerous out there for Sage, too," Daisy said. "I'm going."

They saddled the horses. Daisy was wearing chaps over her jeans, a pale yellow sweater, and a dark green jacket. James gave her a blanket coat, took one for himself, and they rode out.

The sun was just starting to rise, turning the darkness to gray. Stars began to fade, leaving only the brightest constellations visible. Daisy seemed to relax as they rode. She wore her wool muffler pulled up over her mouth and nose to keep her face from freezing.

Snow covered everything. Crystal Lake spread off to the right, frozen and white. It should have been smooth, but as they got closer, James could see the surface was covered with bumps.

"Look," he said quietly, reaching over to grab Daisy's wrist.

"What?" she asked.

"There." He pointed at the lake. The horses stood still, their breath puffing into the frigid air. James saw Daisy's eyes narrow as she tried to make sense of the bumps.

"What are they?" she asked.

James kept the horses still, not wanting them to scare the wildlife before he was ready. His heart was beating fast, because he had seen this several times over the years, each time dreaming he could show it to Daisy.

"Do you believe in signs?" he asked.

"You know I do." She was smiling behind her scarf. He could tell by the way her eyes crinkled.

"What's the Indian totem for marriage?"

"Louis told me the Shoshones believed it was snow geese," Daisy said. "They mate for life."

"If I can make the snow geese appear," James asked, "will you marry me again?"

Daisy didn't answer, but she kept smiling. The sun was coming up fast, pouring pink light over the snow-covered land. He decided he'd better not wait another second.

Kicking his horse hard, he took off at a full gallop toward the lake, waving his arms and yelling wildly. "Yah! Yiii-ahhhhh!"

The bumps began to move. First the heads and necks appeared, then the first stirrings of wings as one goose rose in flight and then another. As James galloped to the edge of the lake, the entire flock of snow geese took off.

Turning to grin over his shoulder, he watched Daisy's delight and amazement. She held both hands to her scarf-covered mouth. The migrating snow geese had scattered on takeoff, but now they remembered their formation. Following their leader, they created a gigantic V and wheeled southward. Daisy rose in her stirrups, throwing her arms up as if she could catch what they had.

"Marry me!" he yelled across the dawn-pink snow.

Daisy didn't call back, but she began to ride toward him. When she pulled up beside him, he said again, "Marry me, Daisy."

"I love you, James."

The snow geese had disappeared from sight, but they could still hear the beating of a thousand wings, the loud honking that echoed off the mountain walls.

"Devoted for life," he said. "That's what I want to be to you."

"It's what I want, too."

"Say yes."

"When Sage comes home." Daisy's eyelashes were frosty with tears. "Ask me again then. I can't say yes until our daughter is safe."

FROM his bed Dalton had watched James and Daisy ride off, and now he sat by the window, withered hands folded on his lap, dreaming of being young. He'd had such strength then! He could ride all day, his muscles as strong as the horse's. He thought of how quickly life had passed by. In the blink of an eye.

"Good morning, darlin'," Louisa said as she walked in. "What're you doing up at the crack of dawn?" She bent down to embrace him, kiss the side of his neck. Oh, her lips still felt so good.

"Just watched James and Daisy head out for a ride," he said.

"Pretty early," Louisa said. "Maybe they're eloping."

"Now there's a thought."

"Nice, how they're getting along. I wasn't sure how that would go—her coming out here." Louisa rubbed her cheek against his.

Just then, in the midst of him getting all ardored up, he remembered: He was supposed to be mad at her. She had rifled through his vault, searching for his last will and testament.

"What's the matter?" she asked.

"Damn nasty business, you not trusting me."

She stepped back. "Do you have to start that up again?"

"I just remembered it."

"I apologized," she said. "Are you so ornery you've got to hold a grudge for the rest of your life?"

"Maybe," he snapped. "Maybe I will."

Louisa exhaled and strode away. As Dalton gazed across the snowy fields, he saw a formation of snow geese flying south. He knew if he were on horseback out there, they'd sound like thunder going over.

His old friend Shoulderblade had told him that snow geese were the luckiest creatures. They picked one mate, and that was that. Dalton had taken it to heart. Louisa thought he had never proposed because of James and his loyalty to his mother. But Dalton had another reason: He believed in snow geese, that you only got one real love in this world.

For Dalton it had been his first love—Rosalind. He had spent a lifetime telling himself that. He kept her portrait on the wall, her initial on the ranch's name: the DR Ranch. Dalton-Rosalind. For better for worse, for richer for poorer, through sickness and health.

Dalton blinked. Sickness and health. Would Rosalind have loved him the way Louisa did through this miserable decline?

Snow geese. As he watched, the great V circled around and landed in the field. He wondered about their ages, how many migrations they'd taken together. If he were a gander, he'd have passed twenty-eight winters with that goose in the next room. He and Louisa had had many more migrations together than he and Rosalind.

"Louisa!" he called.

She took her sweet time coming. Probably mad as hell at him, letting him cool his heels till she got good and ready.

Finally she showed up. "You called?" she asked frostily.

"C'mere, sweetheart," he said. "Hold my hand."

"Why should I?"

"Because you're the love of my life."

He prayed that he would remember to call Wayne Harding—his lawyer in Dubois—at the stroke of nine, the minute his office opened. Maybe he just hadn't wanted to consider his own death, hadn't wanted to imagine Louisa going on without him. But where had he thought she would live?

"Life is long," Dalton said, "but it's over in a lightning flash."

"Your life's not over," Louisa said.

"I'm a tired old rancher."

"And I'm a tired old saloon singer."

"You're my beautiful Louisa," he said.

She shook her head, but he could see he had pleased her. She was hiding a small smile. He thought of Daisy and James. Let *them* be the snow geese. Some people were given more than one love in their lifetime if they weren't too foolish to miss it.

As Louisa took his hand, Dalton was filled with peace. They were going to be okay. He knew it deep inside, as long as he remembered to call the lawyer.

TREACHEROUS driving lay ahead, but David had convinced Sage they should dig out of the wildlife station and try to get to a main road. They found shovels in a utility closet. Sage helped the best she could, but every time she lifted a shovelful, she felt a twinge in her belly. After a while she let David do the work. It was hard not to follow him around. Sage wanted to ask him a million questions, prove that he was actually Jake.

Once he had the car dug out, he loaded up the animals. Then he went back to help Sage. The car heater was on, blasting like a furnace. Sage let him get started—backing onto the logging road, getting stuck, engaging the four-wheel drive, puffing onto the flat surface. Then she took up her theory again.

"Everything fits," she said. "You have brown hair; I have brown hair. You have green eyes; I have green eyes."

"You have two legs; I have two legs," he said.

"See?" she asked, laughing. "That's exactly my humor!"

David lit a cigarette, scowling. "You're crazy."

"Start with the coincidence," she said. "What are the odds that two people the same age would meet on a dark road in Nebraska, one of them being attacked? And there you were to *rescue* me?"

"So that makes me your brother?"

"That fact, plus others."

He exhaled smoke, shaking his head as if he wished she'd just quit talking. But his curiosity got the best of him. "What others?"

"Your tattoos."

"Your family likes tattoos?"

"No. But they remind me of my mother's work. She likes Indian legends, and she uses circles and dots all the time. That owl on your wrist? She's drawn the same owl—the exact same bird!"

"She draws owls?"

"And dots and circles and hawks. She's magic. I know that sounds strange, but the women in our town say it's true. She can make love happen for people."

"Love?" he asked skeptically.

"Yes. For other people," Sage said, feeling momentarily sad. "Not for her and my dad. They ended back when you disappeared. Oh, God." She put her hands over her mouth. "Those tattoos you draw—they're how she stayed connected with you."

"What?"

"It's true!" Sage exclaimed, overcome by emotion. "Wherever

you were, she sent you those owls and hawks and circle dots!"

He grimaced in disbelief.

"Well, how did you learn to draw? Did you go to art school?"

"No. I just pick up a pen and it happens. No big deal."

"Why owls? Why circles around dots? I'll tell you. They're messengers from her to you."

"Messengers . . ." David said, the word striking a chord.

"Between realms," Sage said. "Her realm and your realm."

"You're crazy. I don't even know her."

"You do, you do."

He frowned, shaking his head. Holding the wheel, he pulled out of a bad skid, steering around the next patch of blue ice.

"How is it we both know about Washakie?" Sage demanded. "Is it one of your earliest memories, learning his name?"

"So what?" David glanced over.

"Our parents talked about Washakie." Sage rearranged the kittens to reach across and take his hand. "Jake, Jake."

"Stop calling me that."

"Jake," she said again. "Does that sound familiar? Do you remember hearing us call you that?"

"Stop."

Sage closed her eyes. She was positive she was right—about her mother magically sending him images and talent, about their parents teaching them about Washakie because they would need so much courage in their lives.

"You feel it, too, don't you?" she asked. "You know it's true."

He didn't reply, but she could see the flush starting in his neck. It rose into his face. Sage watched him recognizing what she knew by instinct: They had been together before birth.

Feeling for her necklace, she worked it free. She looked at the girl's face first, then the boy's. Now she glanced at the boy sitting beside her: same forehead, same nose, same chin.

"It's you," Sage said. "You're Jake."

"That's wishful thinking," he snapped.

"No—"

"It is." The blood in his face made him look angry. "You're a dreamer, Sage. Just a dreamer, hitchhiking across the country to a father who didn't want you that much in the first place."

"He did," Sage said, aghast.

"Give it up. Parents are only out for themselves. Did your wonderful, perfect father invite you to come out? Did he?"

"He loves me," Sage said.

"So much he never wanted to see you."

"He loves me," Sage screamed, pounding the seat. "He only stayed on the ranch to be there in case you—in case Jake—ever came back. That's the kind of wonderful father he is!"

"So wonderful he lost both his kids," he yelled back.

"Lost us? Never." Sage started to shake. "Someone kidnapped you. It's the only explanation."

"Don't say 'you,' " he warned.

"Kidnapped!" Sage yelled. "He would never lose us! He only let me go because my mother couldn't stand being there anymore." The emotion was so great she began to cry.

"Sage," he said, "calm down. The animals are getting upset. Petal's hiding under the seat."

"I'm sorry," Sage sobbed, trying to reach back and touch the dogs.

Outside, the road was dangerous. The topography had suddenly changed to rocky terrain, with big craggy bites taken from the road's shoulder.

"You okay?" he asked.

"Yes, Jake," she said defiantly.

"Call me David. Okay?" he asked. "I gotta concentrate on my driving right now, and you calling me that screws me up."

They didn't talk. He gripped the steering wheel with both hands. There didn't seem to be any sign of a main road anywhere. The logging trail just kept winding along. Although they were on flat terrain, the mountains rose all around them.

"What are these mountains?" Sage asked, certain she had a poster of this exact scene hanging on her wall.

"We're in the Wind River Range."

"How far away are we?" Sage asked.

"Twenty, fifteen miles. . . . I'm not sure."

"The DR Ranch," Sage whispered to the baby inside her. "We're almost there. Almost there! Oh!" she said, feeling a twinge. "What a strange coincidence."

"Don't start again." David's eyes looked tired. More storm clouds had started to gather over the mountains, boiling up into dark anvil shapes. "No more about me being your twin brother."

"That's not what I meant. I was thinking about my baby and being so near the ranch, and I'm pretty sure my water just broke."

JAMES and Daisy had spent an hour cantering along the main road, keeping their eyes open for Sage. A snowplow sped by, spraying wet snow ten feet in the air. Then a blue pickup passed, headed in the direction of the ranch. James watched it drive past, then saw it stop and turn around. As it approached Daisy and James, the driver rolled down his window. "Hey, James," Todd said. "Hi, Daisy."

Shielding her eyes against the sun, Daisy smiled. "Hi, Todd."

Parking his truck, Todd climbed out. He wasn't dressed right for the weather—not even for driving around. He wore a lightweight jacket, and boots too low to do any good. James knew that was why he had never made it working on the DR, why he'd never make it as a rancher: He didn't have any common sense.

"Got something I need to talk to you about," Todd said, looking upset and guilty.

"What's that?" James asked.

"It's about Alma, Tammy's sister. She's helping out with Dalton."

"Yeah, Alma. What about her?"

"Look," Todd said, his eyes darting everywhere but James's face. "You and I haven't always gotten along. The sheep-and-cattle stuff, and you and me personally . . ."

Something bad was coming. James could feel it inside. He thought back to the months after Jake had disappeared, how Todd had constantly apologized for not finding him.

One time—about a year after Daisy had left him—James had gone to the Stagecoach and run into Todd. The apologies had started up: "If only I'd looked harder. . . . Can you ever forgive . . ."

Emotion had shot through James like a freight train, and he'd asked Todd, "If it's not your fault, why do you keep saying you're sorry?" Right there, with Louisa singing down from the stage, James had decked him. Todd had fought back. Then he'd asked the real question: How do you live with yourself knowing you lost your kid? The fight had ended fast after that—James knocking Todd to the ground, trying to kill him with his bare fists.

"Todd," Daisy asked now, "what have you come to tell us?"

"Alma Jackson has two sons," Todd said.

"So what?" James asked.

"They're bad kids," Todd went on. "Been in juvey hall for drugs and stealing—one's there right now. Alma thinks the other one worships the devil, wants to be a mountain man. When she took this job, taking care of Dalton, I told her make sure he doesn't find out you're here. She needs the money bad, or I wouldn't have told Louisa to call her."

"How old are they, her sons?" Daisy asked, her voice soft.

"Teenaged." Todd couldn't meet Daisy's eyes.

"They're young," Daisy said.

"Well, he found out she's working on the ranch. His father spilled the beans, I guess."

"What's his problem with us?" James asked.

"The kid's had the idea that the land should belong to Rydells. I know he's not family by birth, but with me and Tammy being married I guess he figures he should have a piece. Calls himself the Guardian—guardian of Rydell land."

"How'd he get that idea?"

"Never mind that." Todd wiped his brow. "The point is, he's here right now."

"Here?" James thought of the Polaroids, the tracks, the campsite, the dead steer.

"Somewhere on the ranch. Hiding out, I guess."

"How long's he been here?" James asked, thinking back to problems last spring and summer.

Todd shrugged. "I don't know. The only reason I heard anything is that Alma talked to Tammy. Her boy—his name is Richard—knocked on your father's kitchen door one night."

"What'd he want?"

"Food, I guess. To go in and look around."

"Did Alma let him in? Give him food?" Daisy's voice was thin.

"No. She sent him packing."

"I wish she had let him in," Daisy said, gazing up at the mountain. "How old is he?" she asked again.

"I dunno. Sixteen, seventeen?"

"I hate thinking of him out there, being hungry," Daisy said, scanning the trees along the ridge.

James had seen the brutal evidence: If this kid was responsible for killing the calf and steer, he wasn't going to worry about him being hungry.

"So." Backing away, Todd looked as if he couldn't wait to get going. "I just wanted to let you know. It's not my fault. He's her son; he's always had problems."

"Not your fault." James stared at him.

Tripping over his own feet, Todd got back in his truck and drove off.

"That was strange," James said, watching him go. "Is it my imagination, or does he feel more guilty than he should about all that?"

"I wonder . . ."

"That kid is here, somewhere on this ranch," James said. "And he hates us, wants what we have. Guardian for the Rydells. Is that enough for Todd to feel guilty over?"

"Alma was staring at Jake's picture," Daisy said. "I saw her. She couldn't take her eyes off him."

James wondered why Daisy would mention it now.

"Remember how we suspected Todd back when Jake . . ."

James didn't like the wild look in her eyes, the direction she was heading with her question. "Daisy," he said, holding her hands.

"Remember, though?"

"What reason would Todd have had to take our son?" But Daisy had started him thinking.

"What if?" Daisy asked. "That's all. The age is right. What if?"

"Daisy, don't do this." James grabbed her, held her against himself till he started asking the questions of himself, the what-ifs.

What if Alma had been staring at Jake's picture? What if Todd had only pretended to search, had taken Jake away? What if Todd's nervousness today—the guilty look in his eyes—went all the way back thirteen years? What if he'd had that much hatred and resentment inside him, passed it to the kid who was out there now, somewhere on the ranch?

What if their son was alive—and he hated them?

DAVID tried to focus on driving. He had a pregnant girl sitting beside him, he didn't know how passable the roads were up ahead, and she'd just broken her water.

"Are you okay?" he asked.

"I'm fine," she said nervously. "Jake, I've been thinking."

"Stop calling me that."

"Listen, okay? Just for a minute. You're adopted, right? And then, when you were three or four, you got lost in a cave."

"Yeah. So what?" He still remembered the cave—the sound of his own voice as he called for his mommy and daddy.

"What if those two memories are the same? If they happened at the same time?" Sage asked.

"They didn't." David didn't want to hear her stupid theory anymore.

"What if they did?" Sage pressed. "What if you weren't an infant when you got adopted by the puppy-farm family, but older?"

"I was a baby when I went to live there. They—" He had been about to say, "They told me," but his memory stopped him short: He had been calling for Mommy and Daddy in the cave, but he had never called his adoptive parents by those names. He had always called them by their Christian names, same as he did now.

"Tell me," Sage said. "I know you remember something."

"Nothing."

"We're twins—I know you're remembering." But she let it go. She just held the kittens, trying to feed them from a bottle, a scared look on her face. "Oh," she said suddenly.

"What is it?"

"Aaahhh!" she cried. Bending double, she nearly crushed the kittens. They scattered, jumping into the back seat with the dogs. Sage rocked back and forth, moaning in pain. He wanted to reach over, but he was afraid to let go of the steering wheel.

"Sage, breathe."

"I am." She was crying.

Straight ahead he could see a real road. Cars and trucks were going by slowly but at least moving. The logging road had another hill in it, a long slope down. David tested the brakes. They caught, making the car fishtail a little.

"Oh, Jake," Sage cried.

"We're almost there," David said. He gripped the wheel. This had been his uncle's vehicle. His uncle was well-off compared to his family, and he seemed full of guilt or something about the way they lived. He hadn't been back since the time he'd threatened to take David away, but he did things like send them money, clothes, and this old four-wheel drive.

David remembered looking out in the driveway one day, seeing the car parked there. He'd been so excited—thrilled to think his uncle might have come back to visit. Hope had been scarce on the puppy farm, but David remembered his uncle as kind and fun. Someone who used to ask if he was okay, who wanted to protect him from the bad stuff. Also, who had saved his life in the cave.

"Owww," Sage moaned.

Last August, when David had saved enough money and hoarded enough food, he had taken Petal out of her pen. Then he'd stolen this car and run away. He hadn't planned his crusade at first; all he had known was he was never going back. But the more he drove and the more he saw Petal looking at him with gratitude for saving her, the more David had known his mission was to help dog mothers.

And girl mothers, he thought, glancing at Sage.

"This hurts." Sage met his eyes across the seat while bent nearly in half. "I'm having bad cramps—the worst I've ever had."

"Contractions."

"No, it can't be," she said, her face knotted with pain. "It's too soon. I'm having cramps from something I ate."

"You're having the baby." David kept his eyes on the real road as the car went down a washboard slope, the last quarter mile of logging trail that had taken them through the central wilds of Wyoming. *Mommy! Daddy!* It was weird how his own distant voice seemed to be getting louder in his head.

DALTON sat in his wheelchair, holding a slip of paper on which he'd written in his spidery hand, "lawyer." With Alma setting up her portable barbershop, Dalton stared at his note and forgot what it meant. These days his thoughts were slippery things.

"What's this?" he asked, staring at the word. When Alma tried to read it, he grabbed it away. "Never mind," he said, remembering. "Bring me the phone."

"I have to get you shaved."

"Well, that's nice of you, but I've got business to attend to first." Alma bit her lip. She looked about ready to collapse.

"The thing is," Alma said, twisting her hands, "I have a family emergency, and I'd like to attend to you first off so I can—"

"First off," Dalton said, interrupting her. "Hand me the damn phone and get me my address book. You want to see a family emergency, I'll show you one if I don't make this call."

Alma let out a volcanic sigh and went to drag the phone across the study. Dalton kept staring at his note, just to stay clearheaded.

"Water's getting cold," she said, testing the shave basin.

"Make it hot again," he suggested, killing two birds with one stone: getting rid of her and assuring himself of a hot shave.

Wayne Harding and Dalton Tucker had been doing business for

fifty years. Wills, trusts, contracts, deeds, commercial transactions, it didn't matter—Tuckers called Hardings. Just as on the ranch the Tuckers had always used Marches for foremen: Paul now; his father, Asa, before him. Some partnerships endured. Although Wayne had recently been elected probate judge, he still did legal work for Dalton.

"Dalton, it's good to hear your voice," said Wayne Harding.

"Good to hear yours," Dalton agreed. They made the requisite small talk about snow, cattle, and families. And then Dalton explained what he wanted. Wayne listened carefully. He understood the history between the Tuckers and Rydells.

"Let me make sure I have this straight," Wayne said. "You want to give Louisa a life estate in the DR Ranch—that is, the right to stay there for as long as she lives."

"Yes," Dalton said. Although his mind was fuddled, he trusted Wayne completely to carry out his wishes. He started to relax.

"She will have no actual ownership, no right to sell or pass it on to her heirs"—Wayne allowed himself a chuckle—"like Todd and Tammy Rydell."

"Let's make sure of that," Dalton said. "No Rydells smiling at the reading of my will."

"None?" Wayne asked. "Well, Dalton, Louisa's a Rydell."

"Damn." Dalton loved her so much, he always almost forgot.

"You could change that," Wayne said, chuckling again. "Make an honest woman of her and marry her."

Dalton squinted. He'd thought of that often. He knew how happy it would make her. But then Dalton saw himself—the groom—withered and be-casted, sitting there in his wheelchair in a morning coat and top hat, his scowling son, James, standing at his side, holding the ring and Dalton's dentures on a little pillow. "Damn it," he said. "You had to bring that up, didn't you?"

"Got you thinking." Wayne laughed. "Okay, let me draw up a draft, and I'll run the new will out to you this week."

"Make it Tuesday rather than Friday," Dalton told him. "I'm not getting any younger. And listen, Wayne. One more thing . . ."

Dalton lowered his voice, explaining the details. Wayne wrote everything down and promised to be in touch with the proper trades-man, have the document drawn up to be signed along with the will.

Hanging up the phone, Dalton was ready to be shaved. He saw shadows down the hall, caught sight of Alma with someone—a young man. She was pleading with him, holding her hands out. Her family emergency, Dalton thought.

"Young fellow," Dalton called. "Come here!"

The man turned to look.

"Richard," Alma begged, tugging the stranger's sleeve.

"I'm the boss around here," Dalton said. "Come here when I call you."

Even from ten yards away Dalton could see the teenager's sneer. He had a thin face and a sparse reddish brown beard, and he was dressed in layers of filthy rags. He was holding a gun.

"What do you want?" Richard asked.

"Who are you?" Dalton asked.

"Mr. Tucker," Alma said helplessly, "this is a family matter— between me and my son."

"I'm the Guardian," the young man said, pushing past his mother to tower over Dalton. "That mean anything to you?"

"No. Should it?"

"You've taken what doesn't belong to you." The young man looked wild, his green eyes glinting. Staring at his gun, Dalton lunged forward. Imprisoned by his chair and the cast on his leg, he couldn't reach the intruder.

The young man laughed. "You're an old fool. I could shoot you if I wanted, but why waste a good bullet?" Turning, he strode away.

"Richard!" Alma wailed, running after him.

"Get back here!" Dalton roared.

Launching himself out of the chair, Dalton tackled the stranger. His leg was on fire, but he had to defend his home and family. They rolled across the floor, the gun between them. Dalton gripped the intruder's arms, but the man broke away. Swearing, he punched Dalton in the head.

TO SAGE THE REST OF THE trip was a blur. She had never known such pain—searing, agonizing tidal waves. This was unnatural! People weren't made to withstand such a thing!

"Hang on," David said, speeding them down the road.

"I can't. I can't."

"Breathe, Sage."

"Oh, God," Sage said through clenched teeth. She was in the middle of what David claimed was a contraction, and right now she was inclined to believe him. It felt like being bitten by a bear, shaken from the inside out. "Remember the bear?" she asked, spitting out the words.

"What did you say?"

Sage gritted her teeth, tears rolling down her cheeks. She couldn't speak now, but she was thinking of her scariest little-kid memory when she, her brother, and their parents had gone camping and a grizzly bear had attacked the tent.

"Thought you said something about a bear," he said.

I did, Sage thought, biting down on her sleeve. "Aaaa!"

"Ever seen a grizzly?" he asked, talking fast as if he could distract her from the contraction. "I got attacked by one once. Almost, anyway. I barely remember, but it was a mother grizzly with her cubs. She was meaner than spit. I'm not kidding."

"I was there," Sage wailed, picturing the terrifying sight. Of course they would both remember it. Three-year-old twins seeing an angry grizzly would haunt their nightmares forever!

He didn't understand, or at least he chose not to reply. He just kept driving. Sage had the impression of great speed, of flying down a road between mountains.

"Oh," she moaned. The contraction passed. She gripped her belly. She was soaked with sweat, and she couldn't stop crying.

"They're really contractions," he said solemnly. As Sage glanced over, she saw that he was concentrating almost as hard as she was, watching the road and flooring the accelerator.

"I wish we were there," Sage said. "This is happening fast. I need my father. I need him now."

"We're almost there," he said. "Look."

Sage blinked through tears and increasing waves of pain, and there she saw: the gates of the DR Ranch.

Stone pillars flanked huge white gates, swung open to the world. Sage scanned the horizon for a house, but all she saw were boulders and trees. She needed home right *now.*

"I'm not going to make it," she said. She felt everything shift inside, knew that her baby was going to be born fast. "I'm having the baby right now."

Chapter ELEVEN

AFTER James got Daisy safely to her small house, he rode out again, thinking he'd look for the kid Todd had told them about. James had found the Jackson boy's prints in the canyon twice before, so he started riding there now. He kept thinking of Daisy's eyes, the hope and brightness he'd seen in them when he'd left her at home. "What if . . ." she kept asking.

Asking himself the same question, James couldn't stand the answer. What if the boy was Jake? James tried to imagine his son killing the animals, fueled by hatred poured into him by Rydells, talking against Tuckers and the DR Ranch all these long years.

"Help!"

At first James didn't know where the sound came from.

"Help—anyone!"

He heard it again: a boy's voice, strong but frantic. Behind it the ungodly wailing of what he first thought was a wild animal but then decided was a girl. The recognition shot through him, primitive and powerful. The voice was his child's. *Sage.* He kicked his horse and galloped toward the ranch's main drive.

He saw a familiar old black car stopped in the middle of the road, the front passenger door open. Heart pumping, James galloped across the frozen snow. He saw small animals—dogs and cats—cowering by the back tires. A girl's legs protruded, and a boy stood between them, looking wildly over his shoulder.

DAISY was too stirred up to sit home alone waiting for James to return. She needed to talk to someone about Todd's warning, about her own dawning hope. She ran up to the main house and walked into the kitchen. She found Alma Jackson talking to a young man.

"Richard, go," Alma said quickly.

The teenager froze, eyes darting around for a hiding place. But once he realized it was too late, he stared straight at Daisy. His brown hair and beard were shaggy, and he wore ratty clothes.

"He's just leaving," Alma said.

"He doesn't have to. It's cold out." Daisy took a step forward. "I'm Daisy Tucker." Searching for some sign he could be her son, she put out her hand. She told herself she'd know by his touch. Her heart was in her throat, waiting for him to extend his hand.

The boy met her eyes. His were green, hard and flat. Daisy felt afraid of them, but she smiled at the boy and kept her hand out.

"Tucker," the boy said, without shaking her hand.

"You must have been cold out there." Daisy finally dropped her hand. "Your uncle told us you'd been camping. You're the Guardian, aren't you? Todd told us."

"My uncle?" he said. Confusion transformed his expression, sparking those dead eyes with rage. He directed it at Alma. "You talked to Tammy?"

"When he knocked last week, I was so shocked," she explained to Daisy. "I only let him stay in the basement, never the rest of the house."

"Stupid woman." The boy shook Alma's arm. "I told you to keep quiet. Opening your mouth to Tammy . . . Ma!"

He wheeled away. His face was bright red, and she could see the cords popping out on his neck.

"Mothers worry," Daisy said. "That's all she was doing."

"Hell with that," he said, turning toward her.

"I should know." Daisy tried to tell herself this could be her son, her baby, that she could love him no matter what. "My son is lost in those mountains," she said. "I think of him every day."

"You lost him," the boy sneered. "I know. My uncle Todd told me the whole story. Tuckers love money and cattle. Right, Ma?"

"Richard," Alma begged, "I need this job."

"Rydells and Jacksons know how to take care of each other," the boy went on. "We wouldn't have lost a kid."

"Richard, no." Alma's expression was wild. She turned to Daisy. "He's just talking. He's going soon. His father drinks all the time, ruined this family. But that's no excuse for him being here now . . ." Her voice trailed off.

"He was cold outside," Daisy said softly. "I understand." She turned back to the boy. "Are you hungry? Would you like something to eat?"

"Ain't eating no Tucker food," he snarled. "And my dad never ruined our family." He shoved Alma.

Daisy stepped forward. "Stop. Don't hurt her."

Touching the boy's arm, she felt his coldness. She scanned his face, looking for any sign that he could be hers. None of his features appeared familiar. The twins had looked so much alike at three; nothing about this boy reminded her of Sage.

"Stay out of my family business," he said to Daisy.

"What did I do wrong?" Alma asked. "Rocked you in your cradle, sang you to sleep."

"Wasn't no singing I can remember. Shut up, Ma."

"Loved you from day one. I've made my mistakes." Alma spoke quietly, as if she didn't want Daisy to hear these family stories. "I should have been there for you. Life with your father . . . Sometimes I had to get out of there, Richard. I'm sorry."

"You shouldn't be here, Ma. It's disloyal to Uncle Todd."

Daisy looked at Alma, and any last thought she had of the boy being Jake went out of her. She knew mother love when she saw it, and she saw and heard all Alma's sorrow and grief for having failed her sons. The boy was Alma's. He wasn't Jake.

"HELP! MISTER, HELP," the kid yelled.

The girl's wailing was high and horrible. James kicked harder, driving his horse faster.

David heard the rancher riding up, but he stayed crouched between Sage's legs, giving all his concentration to getting the baby out. He had seen many puppies born on the farm, and he had known when these last contractions began that there wasn't any chance to get to any ranch house.

"Aaaaaah!" Sage moaned. "It hurts!"

"The baby's coming," David said. "You have to push now. Can you hear me, Sage? Can you do it?"

Her face was red and twisted as she bore down, trying to have her baby. David had his gloves off, his hands cupped. When he saw the tiny head, he took hold of it. It was as small as a puppy's, tinier than any human child's should be.

The horse galloped up, and then the hoofbeats stopped. David heard the big man jump down out of the saddle, come marching over through the crisp snow. He heard the sharp breath as the rancher saw what was happening.

"Sage?" the man said, his voice breaking.

Sage couldn't hear. She just held on to the front seat, having her baby. David's heart was pounding. "She needs help," he said.

"Let me help her, then," the rancher said. He threw his leather gloves down on the ground and took David's place.

"Oh," Sage groaned through clenched teeth. "Oh, God."

"You're doing fine, sweetheart," the rancher said. "Just a little more. Push. There, there you go. That's it."

David took a step back. The animals were all huddled by the back wheel, keeping each other warm while not straying too far.

"Oh!" Sage screamed. "Ouuuuu!"

David looked over. The rancher held his hands around the baby's tiny head and shoulders, and David could see what he had known the moment he touched the baby's head: Sage's baby was being born dead.

The rancher had tears running down his leathery cheeks. He held the baby in his arms, trying to breathe into his mouth. The baby's head and limbs lolled, but the rancher kept trying to save it.

"Live, please," the rancher said, his voice cracking. "Please."

David wanted to help, but he didn't know how. The rancher had pulled his sheepskin jacket off for David to tuck around Sage. Now he was pulling off his flannel shirt while he held the baby crooked first in one elbow, then the other.

"Did I have a boy?" Sage asked. "Or is she a girl?"

The rancher cut the umbilical cord with a knife from a sheath on his belt. Swaddling the infant in his shirt, he kept trying to make it breathe. David felt afraid of the energy in the man's eyes. As he watched, the rancher knelt in the snow.

"Sage," he said quietly.

The girl was nearly hysterical, but at the sight of her father holding the baby, she started to calm down. "Daddy," she breathed. "It's really you."

"Sweetheart," he said. "You had a boy, but he was too small. He didn't make it."

"Didn't make it?" Sage asked in disbelief.

"He's beautiful," the rancher said. "He looks like you."

She reached out. "Can I hold him? Give him to me. Oh, Daddy. Oh, Jake."

Leaning into the car, he placed the baby in Sage's arms. Kissing the top of the girl's head, he embraced her and the infant.

"She needs help," David said.

"Take my horse, and I'll drive the car."

"Forget it," David said. "The animals need me. I'll drive, but I'll give you a ride. Is the ranch far?"

"Three miles."

David herded the animals back into the car, the rancher climbed in behind Sage, and they set off. This trip was almost over; David would get Sage to safety, and then he'd leave.

LOUISA quit her session early. Usually rehearsing picked her right up, but the fight with Dalton had her feeling downcast, and not even singing helped. She went into the kitchen for a cup of coffee and found Daisy and Alma standing there.

Alma was staring out the window. "Where'd he go? Oh, I wish I could have talked him into going home, where it's at least *warm*."

Louisa watched Daisy walk over to Alma, put her arm around her shoulders. Alma's posture was ramrod-stiff, as if she didn't want any part of Daisy's comfort, but Daisy was undeterred.

"He's so young," Daisy said, "to be out there alone."

"It's a heartache," Alma said. She broke away. "Excuse me while I see to Mr. Tucker." She hurried out of the room.

"What was that all about?" Louisa asked.

"Her son was here," Daisy said.

"Doesn't seem to have lifted her spirits any. Yours, either."

"It's funny," Daisy said. "Riding with James, I felt happier than I have in . . ." She trailed off, as if counting back years. "I got my hopes up, I guess."

"About you and him?" Louisa asked.

"About everything. I was hoping for a miracle. That Jake—"

"Jake?" Louisa asked, confused.

"Never mind." Daisy shook her head. "Sage is my miracle. She always has been. I don't know what I'd have done without her all this time, and now I don't know if I can wait another day."

Looking out the window, Louisa saw the black car coming up the drive, with James's horse trailing behind. The car was old and rusty. Louisa saw Daisy's back stiffen, watching the car's progress.

The car came to a halt. The driver jumped out and ran to the passenger's side. Daisy stood riveted. The driver was slight, brown-haired, in black jeans and boots. He yanked open the passenger door.

Louisa saw James climb out, shirtless, holding a small bundle. He carefully handed the package to the boy, then turned back to the car. Very gently, as if he were handling a butterfly, he lifted a young girl from the front seat. He picked her up, held her against his chest, carried her toward the house. The girl held out her arms, and the boy placed the bundle in them. A parade of animals emerged from the car, thronging around the boy's feet.

"Maybe you don't have to do that," Louisa said to Daisy. "Maybe you don't have to wait another day."

But Daisy was long gone. She had flown out the kitchen door the second she'd seen the girl. Louisa remembered Sage from toddlerhood. She had seen many pictures over the years, and she would have known the child anywhere.

Louisa watched Daisy fling herself at James, getting as close as she could to Sage. Then Louisa saw the strange boy, left out of the family group.

"Dalton, your granddaughter's here," Louisa yelled, heading for the study. She found him leaning against his chair, his cheeks red with outrage.

"Louisa." He grabbed her hand. "There's a maniac in the house."

"Alma's son. Did he do this to you?"

"All I could think about was you," Dalton said. "Protecting you. Getting to the phone to call the police."

DAISY clung to Sage. She wanted to hold her child, fill her senses until she could believe it was true, that Sage was really here. James cradled her in his arms, meeting Daisy's eyes over Sage's head as they stumbled through the ranch yard. Daisy might have expected to see elation in his face, but instead she saw grief.

"What is it?" she asked, suddenly feeling cold.

"Inside," James said, striding through the snow toward the door.

So thrilled and shocked to see Sage, Daisy had barely noticed that James wasn't wearing a shirt. It was twenty degrees and James was bare-chested. Now she saw that Sage was wrapped in his sheepskin jacket, her nose buried in James's bundled-up flannel shirt.

"The baby?" Daisy whispered.

James nodded.

Daisy's heart stopped. She had spent the last weeks dreading what this baby would do to her daughter's life, how it would rob her of all her chances. Now, watching Sage sob over the tiny bundle in her arms, Daisy felt cold sorrow pour over her.

They ran up the path, Daisy and James carrying Sage and the

baby. When they got to the door, the strange young man stepped forward and opened it for them. James hurried in with Sage, and for one moment Daisy and the boy came face to face.

Daisy stared into golden-green eyes. He had light brown hair, wide eyes, and the shadows of masklike markings on his forehead and cheeks.

"Are you her mother?" he asked.

"Yes," she said. "I'm Daisy Tucker. Thank you—"

"She talked about you," he said. "A lot."

Daisy opened her mouth. She had to get to Sage, but she couldn't take her eyes off the boy. His face was solemn, and for a moment he reminded her of a shaman. Peering at the marks on his face, she touched the dots above his left eyebrow.

She recognized the symbol. "Protection."

Surprise lit his eyes. "Sage said you'd know," he said. He backed away, getting ready to leave. As he touched the door handle, Daisy caught sight of the owl tattooed on his wrist.

"Thank you for being with her," Daisy said.

"Tell her good-bye." The boy backed away from the door.

As Daisy moved toward Sage, she heard the door close behind her. James, sensing Daisy's approach, said, "She needs you."

Daisy nodded, holding his arms as she moved around him.

"Where is he?" James asked. "The boy."

"He left," Daisy said.

"I've got to catch him." James grabbed a jacket and ran out.

Sage, still wrapped in her father's coat, was huddled on the daybed by the woodstove. She clutched the baby, whispering into his ear. Daisy sat beside her, not touching her, giving her this minute with her child. His features were perfect, tiny as a doll's.

"This is my son," Sage said.

"He's beautiful," Daisy whispered.

"I knew he was a boy," Sage said. "The whole time." She touched his chin, kissed the soft dark hair on his head. Now she smoothed the hair down, as if preparing to show him off.

"I didn't know you'd be here," Sage said.

"I had to come," Daisy said, "so I could see you the minute you arrived."

"Would you like to hold him?" Sage asked.

Daisy reached out her arms. "I'd love to."

Sage passed the baby to her mother. "I love him," Sage said, leaning on Daisy's arm to peer into the face of her son.

"I know you do, sweetheart." Daisy held him to her heart. God, he was so small. He was her grandson, hers and James's.

"He was born too soon." Sage wept. "He's too small."

Daisy closed her eyes. She held the baby to her breast, kissed the top of his head. Old memories came flooding back of holding the twins when they were born. Tears rolled down her cheeks, into the baby's hair, and she sobbed for Sage, for both of their lost sons. "I'm sorry." She wept. "I'm so sorry he couldn't live."

They cried together, holding each other with the baby between them. Daisy felt Sage clutching the body, grasping him tight as if she thought someone would come along to take him away from her.

"I was so worried about you," Daisy said. "I thought I'd lost you like your brother."

"Did you see him?" Sage gulped. "The boy I was with?"

Daisy nodded. "I saw him. Why?"

"He has tattoos," Sage said, "that remind me of your drawings."

Daisy began to tremble, picturing the owl, the boy's green eyes, his brown hair.

"I kept telling myself he was *him,* he was Jake. But I must've been fooling myself. Like I had to believe it or something."

"But he reminded you of—"

"Mom," Sage said softly. "Don't be mad, but can I be alone with my baby?" It was as if she had absorbed all she possibly could, as if all the emotion had drained out of her.

"Of course," Daisy said, kissing her head.

"I wish David had been my twin brother. It doesn't matter now. It just seems crazy."

"What seems crazy?"

Sage spoke through exhaustion, still clutching the baby. "So many coincidences seemed to fit. We're the same age. We met in the West. He draws so much like you. I guess I wanted to think he was my brother. But mostly he knew that word, that name you used to say for courage."

"What word?"

"The name. Washakie."

"Oh, God," Daisy said. And she ran outside.

Chapter
TWELVE

JAMES caught up with the boy as he was loading the animals back into the car. The teenager regarded James with suspicion and something just short of contempt.

"Hey," James called. "I want to talk to you."

"We're out of here," the kid said. "C'mon, Petal, hurry up."

The dog, a tricolored pit bull, hopped into the car. James walked over and caught the boy's wrist.

"She called you Jake before."

"So what? She was having a baby. She was mixed up. My name's David."

"David what?"

"Just David," he said, trying to yank his arm away.

Thinking of Todd Rydell, of what he had said about his nephew hiding on the ranch, James held him tighter. He didn't know how this kid had met up with Sage. Had he figured out who she was, grabbed the chance to present himself as her brother? James didn't know. None of it made sense to him. But he could see from the kid's expression he didn't think much of James, and that was a Rydell trait. Plus, he was positive he had seen this old car before, years ago, that it belonged to someone he knew.

"Hey, man," David said, "what's your problem?"

"You like to hurt animals?" James asked, thinking of the butchered calves and steer.

"What are you talking about? I help animals."

James bent his head to look in the car and saw the cowering dogs. Someone had beaten those dogs, to get them whimpering like that. "You're a liar."

"You're full of it," the kid said, shoving James.

That was all it took. James felt the fight sizzling through him. He wished the kid were bigger, at eye level. The desire to deck him took hold, and he had to step back. "You kill a steer?" James asked. "You shoot some calves this summer?"

"I told you, I don't hurt animals." David rubbed his wrist. Then, sounding very young, he added, "You do. You breed calves and treat them kind, and then you sell 'em off for hamburger."

"Not my favorite part of the job," James said, eyeing the kid in a new way. He sounded like a man of conviction, not someone who'd kill a steer and cut off its head.

"*You're* the liar," the kid said. "You just want to make money. Anyone who raises animals does it for the same reason. I know—my parents did it."

"This your parents' car?" James asked, again looking inside.

"Yeah," David said evasively.

"They know you have it?"

"Yes."

"What are you doing out here on your own?" James asked. "I should call the police on you. This thing's so rusty it's probably not registered, is it? That, plus the fact you're—what—seventeen?"

"Sixteen."

"Sixteen years old and driving my little girl around in the snow. You could have run off the road."

"I saved her," David said.

James moved around to the other side of the car, opened the door, and sat down in the passenger seat.

"Hey, what're you doing?"

But James had already pulled open the glove compartment. Rifling around, he found the registration in a yellowing envelope. It was long expired, he was sure. James was tempted to let the kid go. He obviously wasn't the butcher, and James was grateful to him for helping Sage. But James was thinking of his parents. They'd be half crazy with worry.

"You're going home, buddy." James stuck the old registration in his pocket. He grabbed the car keys at the same time and climbed out of the car.

"Don't, mister," the kid said, chasing him.

"Sixteen's too young to be on your own. Your parents deserve better."

"You don't know." David's tone was dangerous and pleading at the same time. "Gimme the keys. Please—"

"Come on in here," James said, opening the barn door. There was a phone in the tack room. He thought of Sage and Daisy up in the house and wanted to go to them, but he had to make this call first so he could save another set of parents one more sleepless night.

"I don't want to go back," David pleaded.

"You can talk to them." James fished the registration out of his pocket. "They'll be mad you took the car, but—"

David grabbed for the registration. James held it out of reach, wanting to open it so he could read the name, call information for the number. David was grunting, trying to reach the envelope, when Paul came driving into the yard, talking on his truck radio. Gesturing at James, he beckoned him over.

"Give it to me," David said. "Come on, please."

"James," Paul called, climbing out of his truck. "There was trouble up at the house."

James turned slightly to face Paul. "Trouble?"

"Some young guy with a gun. I'm thinking it's the one who . . ."

James must have dropped his arm along with his guard, because suddenly he felt David grab the registration and keys from his hand and bolt. He fled out the barn door toward Paul.

Right on his heels, James expected Paul to stop the fleeing boy. Instead, it was David who stopped himself.

"Uncle Paul," David said, shocked. "What are you doing here?"

JAMES COULDN'T BELIEVE HIS ears. He stopped short, watching David look up at Paul March. Paul's color drained away, and his expression was pure shock.

"We've got to get out there, James," Paul said, as if David wasn't standing right in front of him. "Search the ranch."

"What did you call him?" James asked David. When the boy didn't reply at first, James looked at Paul. "What did he call you?"

"Nothing. I don't know." Paul was ashen.

David said nothing. James's pulse picked up. He stared at David for a long time, and his heart began to pound.

"It's a mistake," Paul said. "Mistaken identity, whatever. Right?"

James watched David's face. His eyes had looked happy for a moment—seeing Paul had made him start to smile—but now his face was a stone mask. James suddenly remembered where he'd seen the black car. He looked at Paul. His voice wavered. "That old Willys you had. What'd you ever do with it?"

"What the hell's that got to do with anything?" Paul asked. "The guy's out there, James—the one's been killing our stock. I told you, Dalton saw him with a gun."

"The Willys Jeep," James said. "You gave it to your sister, didn't you? Lives up Appleton way?"

"James . . ." Paul said, licking his lips.

"Your sister June—her husband's some sort of farmer?"

"Raises dogs," Paul said. "Marshall raises dogs. Never mind about that old car. The kid made a mistake calling me that."

James took hold of the boy's shoulders. He could hardly breathe. "What's your father's name?"

"Marshall Crane," David said, looking down at his feet.

James stared into the sullen boy's face. He saw faded lines and dots on the skin, like faded war paint. "You called Paul your uncle. Is that what you meant to say?"

"Yes," the boy said. "He's my mother's brother."

Was it possible? James began to tremble. The color of this boy's eyes, the shape of his face, the curve of his mouth all came together in James's mind into the face of a smiling three-year-old boy.

"Sage called you Jake on her own, didn't she?" James asked, his heart pounding out of his chest.

"Yes," he said, frowning.

"She knew."

"Knew what?" the boy asked.

"They told you you were adopted, didn't they?" James asked.

"Yeah," the boy said, raising his eyes.

Thinking of Daisy, of his two children, knowing everything they could have been—all of them, to each other—James couldn't stand it anymore. He stared at Paul and shouted, "Why?"

"James," Paul said. His tone was steady; he had talked James out of rage, grief, near insanity so many times before. He had been a friend—James's best and sometimes only friend.

"You took our son," James said, the feeling boiling over.

"James, quit this—"

"You took Jake." James grabbed Paul by the throat.

"Stop. James, let go!" Paul choked, trying to get air, fighting back. He threw a punch, but James caught his arm and threw Paul down on the ground, slamming his head into the snow.

"You . . ." James said, smashing Paul's mouth with his fist.

"James, stop." Paul's voice was garbled with the blood.

"You killed my family, Paul," James yelled, "and I swear I'm gonna kill you."

Paul broke his grip and smashed a fist into James's ribs. James grabbed for his knife. As he did, he saw that the hilt was sticky and red. It was the umbilical-cord blood of Sage's baby, and the sight of it stopped James from killing Paul. Because even though that little boy was dead, there was another who was still alive.

Pushing himself up from the ground, James stared down at Paul. His face was bruised and bloody, and he lay there in the snow without trying to move. James knew there was a story to get out of him, but he also knew it didn't matter now. He turned to the boy. "Jake." James's throat was so tight the name barely made it out.

The kid scowled. "No," he said.

"Yes. Your sister knew," James said.

The boy shook his head harder. "Just thought she did."

"Jake."

Right then Daisy came running over, no coat or hat. She flew toward the boy but stopped as she caught sight of Paul lying in the snow. She looked to the boy, then up at James.

"Daisy," James murmured, just saying her name. His mouth was dry, and he couldn't quite look from her to the boy.

"I have to tell you something," she began, her eyes glowing.

"So do I," he said, folding her into his arms.

"I LIKE your tattoos," Daisy said, looking at his arms.

"Huh," he said, frowning. His expression said he bet she didn't. Hunched over at the kitchen table, he let the kittens walk across his shoulders and the dogs curl around his legs.

Daisy put her hand down, trying to get the dogs to come to her. Making friends with shy animals was easier than trying to talk to the boy she was starting to believe was her son. She had asked him what he remembered, begged him to tell her about his life, but he wouldn't say a word.

"I had a Scottie when I was little," she said, holding out her fingers. She wanted him to say more—to soak in the sound of his voice, see what it did to her heart. Close up he looked like Sage, like Jake might look if he were sixteen. But it was too incredible, too much of a miracle even for Daisy.

"What's her name?" Daisy asked.

"Plaidy."

"Here, Plaidy. Here, girl." The Scottie ignored her.

"When can I go?" he asked. "When's your husband gonna give me back my keys?"

Daisy swallowed, not answering. James had given her this time alone with the boy. He was with Sage, waiting for the midwife to arrive, and he had called the police and told them what had happened with Paul and with Richard Jackson, who had now run off. The boy—David, Jake—refused to talk.

"I meant what I said," she repeated. "I like your tattoos."

He shrugged. Shaking a cigarette out of the pack, he stuck it between his lips and lit it. Daisy saw the circle-and-dot markings on
his right wristbone.

"Circles are important," she said. "They're symbols of protection.
But you know that, right?"

Again he shrugged.

"Encircling," Daisy continued. "Native people practiced it to
protect against spiritual invasion. They'd walk around strangers in a
circle so their footprints would enclose any evil spirits that might
have entered with the newcomers."

He turned his arm over so she couldn't see it anymore. Daisy
closed her eyes. She was repeating this Indian legend as if it had no
bearing on her, as if she hadn't wished a million times that she had
drawn a magic circle around Jake.

"I like your owl." She leaned over to better see his wrist. "Your
feathers are so precise, and the eyes . . . They look real!"

"He's not real," he said harshly.

"But you've studied owls," she said. "Watched them carefully."

He shrugged. "They're everywhere in Wyoming." That was as
much as he had said so far, and Daisy's heart soared. But then, raising his eyes to meet Daisy's, he asked, "Can I go now?"

Daisy winced, but she tried not to let him see. He was sixteen;
they weren't about to let him drive away. The police were going to
question him, arrest Paul, learn the whole truth of what had happened thirteen years ago. But if the boy didn't want to stay, nothing she said or did would be able to stop him.

A dog began scratching the floor at Jake's feet. Her claws scrabbled on the wood, as if she wanted to burrow somewhere safe, far
from sight. Leaning over, Daisy tried to still the panic of knowing
that the boy sitting across from her was both her son and a stranger.
But as she bent down, she caught sight of the pit bull holding a
filthy brown toy in her strong jaws. Breathing with the stuffed toy in
her mouth was difficult, and she seemed to shudder with every exhalation. Daisy saw that the shudders came from emotion.

"That dog with the toy," Daisy said. "What's her name?"

"Petal."

"Why . . ." Daisy began. "Why does she have the toy?"

"She needs something to carry," he said sullenly.

"Why does she need something to carry?" Daisy asked, her throat aching. "What is she missing?"

"I don't know."

"James said your father—the man who adopted you—ran a puppy farm." Daisy's voice was soft. "Is Petal missing her puppies?"

"Maybe she is," the boy said after a long time. "So what?"

Daisy's eyes felt hot with tears. She reached out her hand, but Petal just cowered behind the boy's legs. Then Daisy got down on her hands and knees and went under the table with her.

"Petal," she said. "Here, girl."

"She doesn't like strangers," the boy said from above. His voice sounded nervous and curious. "She bites."

"I don't think she wants to bite me."

Petal's hold on her toy was gentle, the way a mother dog carries its babies.

"You miss them," Daisy whispered, "don't you?"

"Don't get too close," the boy warned. "She'll snap at you."

"What is that old toy?"

The fabric was brown felt, and Daisy could see the place where the animal's eyes had been. And there, on top of its head, where a cow's horns would have been, were two tiny shreds of yellow.

"Let me see," Daisy whispered. "Please. I won't take it from you."

Petal whimpered, getting a better grip.

"I knew a toy like that once," Daisy said, reaching out a hand. She traced the ragged old cow with one finger: the seams on the cow's ruined face, the spots where its button eyes had once been sewn on, the dirty yellow rags that had once been horns.

"Jake's cow," Daisy said to Petal. "When he was born, that's what his grandfather gave him—a stuffed cow. He loved it so much."

The boy had been watching to make sure the dog didn't bite Daisy, but now his expression changed. His mouth was half open, and his eyes were hazy with a gathering memory.

"One of his horns was crooked—Jake had loved it right off. He'd use the horns for handles, to kiss the cow right on the face."

Petal stopped digging and lay down, the toy still in her mouth.

"Jake's cow," she repeated. "After he disappeared, I looked for it. When I couldn't find it, I knew he had to have it with him. Oh, that gave me comfort, to think he had his cow with him."

The boy grunted, shuffled his feet.

"This toy was yours, wasn't it?" Daisy asked him. "You gave Petal your old toy cow."

"Yeah. But I'm not—"

"I loved you then," Daisy said from under the table, petting Petal on her head as she gazed up into the boy's green eyes, "and I've loved you ever since. I never stopped for a second."

"She bites," he said, watching Daisy scratch the pit bull's head.

"Not even for a second," Daisy repeated.

The boy stared at Daisy's hand on Petal's head, and he seemed to notice that Petal had gotten some relief from her terrible grief, that the understanding of another mother who had known loss had brought her some solace.

"Jake," Daisy whispered in the dark under the table.

"I think you're wrong," the boy said, his scowl gone.

"I don't think I am."

SAMANTHA Whitney, the best midwife in Wyoming, came out to the ranch to minister to Sage. Gentle and compassionate, Sam lived on a ranch in Dubois, and when James called her, she came instantly.

She was in her mid-thirties, with strawberry-blond hair, and now, while she was alone with Sage and Daisy talked with Jake, James stood out by the barn talking to Curt Nash.

Curt was the detective in charge. While most of his officers had fanned out to search the ranch for Richard Jackson, two had driven up to Appleton to question June and Marshall Crane. Paul sat in Curt's police car. Once James had checked the registration and found that the black Willys was still registered in Paul's name, Paul had told the whole story. He had seemed almost relieved to have the truth out.

"It's a shocker," Curt said. "You and Paul go back a long way."

"Our whole lives," James said.

"You think you know a person," Curt said, shaking his head. He was fifty-eight or so, fit and strong, a cowboy with a badge. He and James had been friendly until Jake's disappearance. Then, for several months, Curt had considered James the main suspect.

"You thought you knew me," James said, "but it didn't stop you from thinking I'd hurt my son."

"I'm sorry about that now, but that's how it looked from our seat."

"Paul took him." James glanced over at the police car. The sight of Paul made his skin crawl. His best friend, his ranch brother. Paul had sat with him at his mother's funeral. He had baby-sat the twins.

"We'll know more when we question June and Marshall Crane," Curt said. "The story's hard to swallow. That he'd put you and Daisy through hell just 'cause his sister couldn't have a kid."

James stared at Paul's profile. He had told the police that taking Jake had been almost an accident. The boy had been missing for three days. The search party had gone through the canyon twenty, thirty times, looking behind every rock, in every chasm. Just before nightfall, while the others were beating outward from the canyon, searching in ever widening circles other parts of the ranch, Paul had decided to ride through one more time.

He had heard Jake calling for help. The voice had been tiny and far away. Paul had yelled back, told Jake to keep talking. The little boy had done what Paul said, singing, "Old MacDonald Had a Farm," while Paul searched and finally found the cave.

The cave's mouth was a hole one foot in diameter. Hidden behind a clump of sage, level with the ground, it angled down into the foot of the cliff. Rain had washed claw marks into the rock, and the hole had blended in. But Paul heard Jake calling, and when he'd stuck his big hand in, a little hand had grabbed it.

Pulling Jake to safety, he'd slung him on his horse. The boy was dehydrated, banged up from knocking into rocks. Galloping back to the ranch, Paul had started thinking about kids, how they made everything in life worthwhile.

Thank goodness Daisy and James had had Sage, one kid to love while they kept their vigil.

Unlike Paul's sister June. She had been trying for ten years to get pregnant. Her marriage was miserable, Marshall blaming everything on her being barren. Paul had hated seeing his sister so disappointed with life, stuck on that puppy farm with no child to love.

Jake had passed out on the horse, and Paul had decided to transfer him into his truck. Driving him the rest of the way would be easier than trying to hold an unconscious kid on horseback.

And that's when Paul got the idea.

Jake was bloody and hurt, crying in his sleep from the terror of being in the cave, and Paul got to thinking how stupid it had been of James to take him on the roundup in the first place. A three-year-old kid—sticking him on a rock and expecting him to sit still. Of course he had wandered off. What had James expected?

The Tuckers, Paul thought, had always had it all. Todd was right about that, but at least Todd hadn't had to live his whole life in their shadows. Many was the night Paul's dad would down a few beers and tell his kids about the crap that Tuckers inflicted on Marches.

June had left the ranch as soon as she was old enough, moved north to Appleton where Marshall's people lived. The Tuckers had everything—they were rich; they had the ranch; they still had a daughter. They were young, and if they wanted to have more kids, they could in a heartbeat. While poor June had nothing.

So Paul had driven Jake up to Appleton. June had taken some convincing, saying it was wrong. But Marshall had been firm: He wanted a son. June and Marshall had taken the boy in and cared for him like their own. "Loved him with all their hearts," Paul had said. Of course, as so often happens, a year later June had a child of her own. Paul had had a twinge then, thinking he should maybe bring Jake back home. But by then it was too late.

"He thought he was acting for good." Curt was looking over at Paul in the car. "What he told himself, anyway," Curt said.

James stared at Paul. For years he had promised himself he would kill whoever had taken Jake. But suddenly, in one day, the fire went out. Just from helping Sage, from looking into Jake's eyes—just from being with his children—James had found peace beyond his understanding. He would never get those years back, but he no longer needed to kill the man who had stolen them.

"Your side okay?" Curt gestured to where Paul had punched him. "Want to add assault to the charge?"

"Kidnapping is fine," James said. "Says it all."

Taking one last look at the police car, James shook Curt's hand and thanked him. He knew he wouldn't see Paul March again until his trial. He strode toward the house. Every single person James loved was under that roof right now. Daisy was there with Jake; the midwife was helping Sage say good-bye to her baby; his father was with Louisa. James heard the police car's tires catch in the snow, then pull down the drive. He hadn't known he was holding so much tension inside till it started to let go, as the sound of the tires receded.

James began to run now. For the first time he could remember—since the day his best friend had stolen his three-year-old son—James Tucker wanted to say thanks.

He didn't know how, and he didn't really know to whom. Daisy could tell him. Things weren't perfect: Sage had lost her baby, Jake might not stay with them. But for now his family was together.

Staring up at the sky, James searched for the words he wanted to say, and all he could think of were two, so short and so strong. He shouted as loud as he could, his voice echoing off the dark red cliffs of the Wind River mountains: "Thank you!"

EPILOGUE

IT WAS spring. The snows had melted weeks ago and the range looked like a riotous bouquet of wildflowers: buttercups, primroses, kittentails, saxifrage.

"It's so different without snow," Sage said.

"Yeah," Jake agreed.

She was on Scout, Jake on Ranger. The two old horses plodded through waves of new grass toward where the pony barn had once stood. As she rode, Sage leaned down to pluck flowers.

"Got enough?" he asked.

"Not quite."

"You act like it's the wedding of the century."

"It is," she said, "to me."

He did what he always did when he thought something was stupid or he didn't want to think about it: lit a cigarette. Sage felt like reaching between the horses and snatching it out of his lips. What was tolerable in their mad journey when he was just a savior-stranger seemed much less so now that he was her bona fide twin brother, making everyone's life miserable by threatening to move to a foster home every ten minutes.

"They were already married once," he said. "Why even bother having a wedding the second time? They sleep together—"

"Like that's the important thing."

"Then what is?" Jake asked.

"You're not planning to attend the ceremony," Sage said coolly, "so what do you care?"

Jake blew smoke and rode on in silence. He was right: She did go a little overboard with flowers. As her parents' wedding day—today—kept getting closer, she had gotten her mother to order zillions of white roses from a florist. She and Daisy and Louisa had spent that morning placing them in vases all over the house.

She slid a glance over at Jake. He had that intense I-don't-belong-here look. Her mother had explained to Sage that even though Jake was her brother, he had grown up apart in such a horrible place that it would take him a long, long time to feel okay again.

But she wished he would go to the wedding. He had decided not to go, making everyone upset, worried that he was even more troubled than they already knew. He had the option of living with a foster family—his so-called adoptive parents were in jail—and he frequently said he was planning to exercise his option.

Jake kept to himself, taking care of the dogs in their corner of the barn. He skipped school half the time and didn't pay attention in class the other half. He liked the smell of animals and straw, so he chose to sleep in the barn.

After a life of having her mother all to herself, of worshipping her father from afar, there were days when Sage truly resented the intrusion of this ungrateful, unwilling boy and wished she and her parents could just be happy and live their lives without him.

But those days were few and far between.

Now, riding Scout through the meadow, Sage stared at Jake's back. He was a few paces ahead, leading the way down to the pony barn.

"Aren't you gonna be late for the wedding?" he called back.

"No," she said, holding her huge bouquet. "There's time."

When they got to the ruins of the old pony barn—just a few gray timbers sticking up from the tall grass—Sage put her free arm around Scout's neck and slid out of the saddle. Jake had already dismounted, and he held the horses' reins as Sage led them to the spot. She gazed for a minute at the old boards, the broken roof beams.

"Our grandmother died here," she said.

"Don't let Louisa catch you saying that," Jake said. "She thinks she's our grandmother."

Sage nodded. She knew Jake had taken to Louisa right away— her brash manner, her tough-talking don't-mess-with-me style.

"Right there?" Jake asked, following Sage's gaze.

"Yes," Sage said. "Dad tried to save her life, but he couldn't."

"Man," Jake said.

Sage was thinking of mothers who died too soon and babies who died too soon. Pushing aside the tall grass, she found the thin new path that led to the two small stone crosses. The grass had been scythed along the path, and the clearing had been mowed. Sage knew her father came here once a week to keep the crosses clear.

Sage knelt in front of them, and she kissed the ground in front of the cross where her son lay. The grass smelled new and sweet, and she imagined it was the skin of his shoulder. "You brought us all together," she whispered.

When she was ready, she separated two small bouquets from her enormous bunch of wildflowers. She handed one to Jake, watched him lay it on her son's grave.

Sage placed the other bouquet at the foot of her grandmother's cross and prayed that Rosalind somehow knew how happy her own son, James Tucker, was that very day.

"Are you ready?" her brother asked her.

Sage wiped her eyes. "Are you afraid I'll miss the wedding?"

"It's just a wedding."

"You might like it."

"I think I'm gonna hitchhike to Lander," he said. "Look at cars to buy so I can get out of here."

"You could do that another day." Sage climbed up onto Scout.

"I could," Jake said, mounting Ranger.

They circled back to the main drive, and Sage saw the ranch sign shining in the sun—brand new, bright blue with gold letters.

"JD Ranch," she read.

"Can't believe Granddad changed the name," Jake said.

"James-Daisy," Sage said, holding on to the saddle horn.

"At least Louisa's happy," Jake said. "She sure didn't like having old Rosalind's initial out there."

"I still can't believe she and Granddad eloped."

"It's how they wanted it," Jake said.

"Granddad's idea of being romantic is calling a judge and telling him to change the ranch's name, then 'By the way, can you marry us?' when he was signing the papers. Poor Louisa."

"Louisa's all right," Jake said. "She's taking me down to the Stagecoach soon, let me hear the new song she wrote about it."

"What's the song called?"

"It's called 'I'm Mrs. Tucker.' "

"I want to go with you," Sage said. "To the Stagecoach."

"Just me and Louisa this time. She said."

"You get your way too much. Everyone just wants to make you happy, and you won't even go to the wedding."

"What, you're not happy?"

Sage shrugged, trying not to smile, and just rode on in silence.

DAISY SAT AT HER BEDROOM dressing table, letting her sister brush her hair. Hathaway was weaving it into a French braid, inserting daisies at appropriate intervals.

"Is that too tight? Am I stretching your face into your ears?"

Daisy laughed. "No, it's fine."

"I want James to recognize you when he says, 'I do.' "

Wearing a long, full yellow skirt and off-the-shoulder white peasant blouse, Hathaway looked beautiful, ready to stand up for Daisy at the wedding. She wore turquoise rings and bracelets from her own boutique, as well as one of Daisy's necklaces and their mother's pearl earrings. The combination of patrician eastern style and rugged western style suited her.

"Are we crazy, having a real wedding, Hath?"

"As opposed to what? A sham one? No, Daisy. Believe me, if two people deserve to pull out all the stops, it's you and James."

"That's what I think," Daisy said. Her gaze slid to the picture on her dressing table. Louisa had taken it just three weeks ago. It showed Daisy, James, Sage, and Jake standing by the paddock, everyone except Jake with ear-to-ear grins. "I hope he comes."

"Jake? He's his own man," Hathaway said.

Hathaway was a good sister, a loving aunt. She had always adored Sage, and now she would have a chance with Jake.

Daisy thought of her son, refusing to go to school, sleeping in the barn. She imagined his life at the puppy farm. So many years of pain for both of them—all of them. And now Jake bore the scars.

"Every so often," she said, "I'd like to kill Paul March."

"I don't blame you," Hathaway said.

"I'm constantly telling James to forgive, it's all we can do, but sometimes the feeling is so strong."

"Let it be as strong as it is." Hathaway put her hands on Daisy's shoulders, as if they could absorb all the rage she felt for the man who had kidnapped her son. "Feel it now, and then let it go."

"I want those years back," Daisy whispered.

"You're taking them back the best you can by marrying James." All these years you've used other people's love stories to sustain you—to give you hope and faith when you'd lost your own. It's in your work."

"Sometimes it was easier to have it for others than for myself."

Daisy wiped her eyes, and Hathaway scolded her for smearing her makeup. They touched up her mascara, their faces close.

"I'm going to be a westerner now," Daisy said. "Live on the ranch again."

"Mmmm," Hathaway said as she worked on the eyeliner.

"You'll come out to visit a lot."

"Well, of course." Hathaway snorted, as if Daisy had just stated the obvious.

Now Daisy gazed back into her own eyes in the mirror. She thought of Crystal Lake, the crimson cliffs, the stunted cedars, the endless range, and the soaring Wind River Range. James was here, and so were their children. This was home. This was where she wanted to be, living on the land that inspired her work and dreams.

"Can I ask you a favor?" Daisy asked. "If you see Jake before the wedding, will you ask him to come? Tell him anything. Just get him to be there."

"He will be." Hathaway returned to the braid. "I know already."

"How?" Daisy looked past her own reflection in the mirror to see Hathaway's deep, knowing, humorous eyes.

"Because I'm the older sister," Hathaway said, breaking into a grin. "And I know everything."

JAMES stood out in the barn, adjusting his black tie. His father sat in a chair, dressed in his black dinner jacket with a string tie, and Todd stood beside him, wearing a bright blue tuxedo.

Todd seemed glad to be here, part of the day. Who'd have believed James and Daisy would have a bunch of Rydells at their wedding? But they were here: Todd, Tammy, their kids; Emma and Ruthie; and, of course, Louisa.

It was Daisy's idea. She had asked James if he would invite the Rydells. With Louisa an official part of the family now, it seemed right that there should be a larger gesture of peace between the clans.

"Look at us here," Dalton said. "Tuckers and Rydells all gathered in the same place, not wanting to kill each other."

"Will wonders never cease?" Todd laughed.

"Not with Daisy around they won't," James said.

"I knew it wasn't your idea to have us here," Todd said, "but I'm mighty glad to be here anyway."

With Louisa directing the band to tune up outside, Dalton pushed himself out of the chair and headed out to find his wife. Todd started to follow, but James held him back.

"I owe you an apology," James said.

"Excuse me?" Todd looked startled, as if his old reflex of suspicion had kicked in.

James cleared his throat. "I've been unfair to you. All that time thinking you were the one who took my son."

"I knew you thought that," Todd said. "Wasn't anything I could have said to convince you otherwise."

"There were other things that made me see it that way."

"The feud," Todd said. "We carried it to extremes ourselves. Look, Alma's sorry for what Richard did, and I know she wants to make restitution."

"Forget it." James held up a hand.

"No. She wants to pay you back the value of the stock he killed."

"I don't want her money," James said sharply. "I have sympathy for Alma. She's lost her son, and I know how that feels."

"I fed Richard those old stories," Todd said. "He took them in, and I never knew how much they affected him. He wanted this land, and he set himself up to guard it for our family. You probably blame me for that."

"I'm sorry about your nephew," James said. "I hope he gets the help he needs. But I don't blame you. The fact is, I've blamed you for too much. I'm sorry, Todd. I was wrong."

"It's okay, James. Lot of harm's been done on both sides."

The two men shook hands. James was glad he didn't have to say more. He didn't like talking about deep things to anyone but Daisy, and he could see Todd was relieved, too.

"Your son glad to be back?" Todd asked as they headed out of the barn into the bright day to wait for the wedding to begin.

"Jake?" James swallowed because he wasn't sure how to answer. "I think so. I hope so."

The crusty, unsentimental rancher's heart felt like it might break in two because his son had decided not to come to their wedding.

Now that Sage and Jake were within sight of the ranch, they could hear strains of music filling the air. A big blue-and-gold tent—the colors of the JD Ranch—had been set up.

Sage shaded her eyes. "They're all there. Everybody but us."

"Yeah," Jake said quietly.

"You're family, Jake." She knew she was walking a fine line, that anything she might say on the subject might make him mad.

"Quit it, Sage."

"As long as you know."

Suddenly Sage pulled back on Scout's reins. "Listen!"

"I hear it," Jake said, stopping beside her.

The band was warming up, and Louisa was rehearsing the wedding song she had written for James and Daisy. It was called "The Forever Day." Jake started to smile, listening to her big voice singing across the lush meadow.

"Not Louisa," Sage said. *"Listen."*

It was springtime, too late for this to be happening. But as the twins tilted their heads back, they saw a great, long V crossing the sky. Snow geese. The sun struck their feathers, turning them white as winter. They were honking as they flew, their voices and wings drowning out everything, even Louisa's song.

"How many are there? Can you tell? A hundred?"

"A thousand."

The twins knew the story of the geese, how their father had proposed to their mother the second time when he'd sent them flying into that winter sky. The very sight of them now brought tears to Sage's eyes, and when she looked at her brother, he was standing tall in his saddle.

"Hey," Jake yelled.

"The geese can't hear you." She laughed.

"Not them," he said. "I'm not calling them."

"Then who?"

"Hey!" Jake yelled louder.

Their father was standing by the paddock, talking to someone who had come to set up the food.

"They're back," Jake called.

"You're calling Dad?" Sage said, her heart starting to race. Jake never seemed excited about anything. He never went to their father or mother to talk. Sage knew it hurt their feelings, but their father's most of all.

"The band's too loud," Jake said. "He can't hear me."

"Louder, then. Oh, Jake. Call louder."

"Dad!" Jake yelled, pointing at the sky. "Mom! They're back!"

At the sound of his voice their father turned. Even from here Sage could see his grin from hearing Jake call him "Dad."

Their mother leaned out the upstairs window, her veil billowing. Sage waved her bouquet of wildflowers, but both her parents had their heads tilted back, looking at the geese flying over.

"They're back!" Jake Tucker shouted with all his might. He was smiling, too, waving like someone who felt excited to be part of a family whose legend included snow geese and Washakie, exactly like someone who was riding home with his twin sister, on their way to the wedding of their parents. Someone who very much intended to stick around and hear them say, "I do."

LUANNE RICE

© TERESA DOWMAN

"I feel there's a strong connection with the people we love, both here and in the next world," says Luanne Rice, echoing the spiritual outlook of Daisy Tucker in *Dream Country*. Although both of her parents are gone, Rice told us that she still feels their presence in the Connecticut home where she was raised—and where she still spends much of the year. (A New York apartment is her other home.)

So how did this bred-in-the-bone easterner pick Wyoming as a setting for her story? "A close friend moved there," she says. "When I visited, I fell in love with the bigness of it, the mountains." This, too, Rice shares with Daisy, along with a fondness for animals—to wit, her adopted family of three orphaned cats.

To learn more about Luanne Rice and *Dream Country,* visit the Select Editions website:

ReadersOnly.com
Password: *gift*

DICK FRANCIS

SHATTERED

How very fragile

a life can be.

So easily broken,

so very hard

to mend.

Chapter One _____

FOUR of us drove together to Cheltenham races on the day that Martin Stukely died there from a fall in a steeplechase.

It was December 31, the eve of the year 2000. A cold midwinter morning. The world approaching the threshold of the future.

Martin himself, taking his place behind the steering wheel of his BMW, set off before noon without premonition, collecting his three passengers from their Cotswold Hills bases on his way to his afternoon's work. A jockey of renown at thirty-four, he had confidence and a steady heart.

By the time he reached my sprawling house on the hillside above the elongated tourist-attracting village of Broadway, the air in his car swirled richly full of smoke from his favorite cigar, his substitute for eating. He was spending longer and longer in a sauna each day but was all the same gradually losing the metabolic battle against weight.

Genes had given him a well-balanced frame in general, and an Italian mother in particular had passed on a love of cooking, and vivacity.

He quarreled incessantly with Bon-Bon, his rich, plump, and talkative wife, and on the whole ignored his four small children, often frowning as he looked at them as if not sure exactly who they were.

Nevertheless, his skill and courage and rapport with horses took him often into the winner's circle, and he drove to Cheltenham calmly discussing his mounts' chances that afternoon in two fast hurdle races and one longer chase. Three miles of jumping fences brought out the controlled recklessness that made him great.

He picked me up last on that fateful Friday morning, as I lived nearest to Cheltenham's racetrack.

By his side sat Priam Jones, the trainer whose horses he regularly rode. Priam was expert at self-aggrandizement but not quite as good at knowing when a horse had come to a performance peak. That day's steeplechaser, Tallahassee, was, according to my friend Martin on the telephone, as ready as he would ever be to carry off the day's gold trophy, but Priam Jones, smoothing his late-middle-age thinning white hair, told the horse's owner in a blasé voice that Tallahassee might still do better on softer ground. Lounging back beside me on the rear seat, that owner, Lloyd Baxter, listened without noticeable pleasure, and I thought Priam Jones would have done better to keep his premature apologies in reserve.

It was unusual for Martin to drive Tallahassee's owner and trainer anywhere. Normally he took other jockeys, or me alone, but Priam Jones had just wrecked his own car. Priam had taken it for granted, Martin told me crossly, that he—Martin—would do the driving. He would also chauffeur the horse's owner, who had flown down from the north of England for the Cheltenham races and who was staying overnight with Priam.

I disliked Lloyd Baxter as thoroughly as he disliked me. Martin had begged me in advance to swamp the grumpy, dumpy million-aire owner with anesthetizing charm, in case the horse drew a blank. I saw Martin's face grinning at me in the rearview mirror as he listened to me lay it on. He had more than paid any debt he owed me by ferrying me about when he could, as I'd lost my driver's license for a year through scorching at ninety-five miles an hour (fourth ticket for speeding) to take him and his broken leg to see his point-of-death old retired gardener. The gardener's heart had then thumped away insecurely for six further weeks—one of life's little ironies. My loss of license now had three months to run.

The friendship between Martin and myself, unlikely at first sight, had sprung fully grown four or more years ago. We had both been chosen for jury duty at the local crown court to hear a fairly simple case of domestic murder. In the jury room I had learned about the tyranny of weight that ruled a jockey's life. Martin, in turn, had asked with polite curiosity, "What do you do for a living?"

"I blow glass."

"You do *what?*"

"I make things of glass. Vases, ornaments, goblets. That sort of thing." I smiled at his look of astonishment. "People do, you know. People have made things of glass for thousands of years."

"Yes, but"—he considered—"you don't look like someone who makes ornaments. You look . . . well, tough."

I was four years younger than he and three inches taller and probably equal in muscles.

"I've made horses," I said mildly. "Herds of them."

"The Crystal Stud Cup?" he asked, identifying one of flat racing's more elaborate prizes. "Did you make that?"

"Not that one, no."

"Well, do you have a name? Like, say, Baccarat?"

I smiled lopsidedly. "Not so glamorous. It's Gerard Logan."

"Logan Glass." He nodded, no longer surprised. "You have a place on the High Street in Broadway, side by side with all those antique shops. I've seen it."

I nodded. "Sales and workshop."

He hadn't seemed to take any special notice, but a week later he'd walked into my display gallery, spent an intense and silent hour there, asked if I'd personally made all the exhibits (mostly), and offered me a ride to the races. As time went by, we had become comfortably accustomed to each other's traits and faults.

That day at Cheltenham, Martin won the two-mile hurdle race by six lengths, then went into the changing room to put on Lloyd Baxter's colors of black and white chevrons, pink sleeves and cap. I watched owner, trainer, and jockey in the parade ring as they took stock of Tallahassee walking purposefully around in the hands of his groom. The clear favorite, Tallahassee stood at odds of six to four with the bookmakers for the Coffee Forever Gold Trophy.

Lloyd Baxter (ignoring his trainer's misgivings) had put his money on the horse, and so had I.

It was at the last fence of all that Tallahassee uncharacteristically tangled his feet. Easily ahead by seven lengths, he lost his concentration, hit the roots of the unyielding birch, and turned a somersault over his rider, landing his whole half-ton mass upside down and crushing the rib cage of the man beneath.

The horse fell at the peak of his forward-to-win acceleration and crashed down at thirty or more miles an hour. Winded, he lay across the jockey for inert moments, then rocked back and forward vigorously in his struggle to rise again to his feet.

The roar of welcome for a favorite racing home to win was hushed to a gasp. The actual winner passed the post without his due cheers, and a thousand pairs of binoculars focused on the unmoving black and white chevrons flat on the green December grass.

The racetrack doctor and the fast gathering group of paramedics realized that Martin Stukely was dying, as the sharp ends of broken ribs tore his lungs apart. They loaded Martin just alive into a waiting ambulance, and as they set off to the hospital, they worked desperately with transfusions and oxygen. But quietly, before the journey ended, the jockey lost his race.

PRIAM, not normally a man of emotion, wept without shame as he later collected Martin's belongings, including his car keys, from the changing room. Accompanied by Lloyd Baxter, who looked annoyed rather than grief-stricken, Priam Jones offered to return me to my place in Broadway before he went to see Bon-Bon. He had given her the news on the telephone, and she was, he said, devastated.

Lloyd Baxter, Priam added, would also be dropped off at Broadway. Priam had got him the last available room in the hotel there, the Wychwood Dragon. It was all arranged.

As Priam, shoulders drooping, and Baxter, glowering, set off toward the car park, Martin's valet hurried after me, calling my name. I stopped and turned toward him, and into my hands he thrust the lightweight racing saddle that, strapped firmly to Tallahassee's back, had helped to deal out damage and death.

The sight of Martin's empty saddle set me missing him painfully.

Eddie, the valet, was elderly, bald, and in Martin's estimation hardworking and unable to do wrong. He turned to go back to the changing room but then stopped, fumbled in the deep front pocket of the apron of his trade, and produced a brown paper–wrapped package. "Someone gave this to Martin to give to you," he said, "but of course"—he swallowed, his voice breaking—"Martin's gone."

I asked. "Who gave it to him?"

The valet didn't know. He was sure, though, that Martin himself knew, because he had been joking about it being worth a million.

I took the package and, thanking him, put it into my raincoat pocket, and we spent a mutual moment of sharp sadness for the gap we already felt in our lives. He turned to hurry back to his chores in the changing room, and I continued into the car park.

Priam's tears welled up again at the significance of the empty saddle, and Lloyd Baxter shook his head with disapproval. Priam recovered enough, however, to start Martin's car and drive it to Broadway, where he dropped both me and Lloyd Baxter outside the Wychwood Dragon. Then he departed in speechless gloom toward Bon-Bon and her now fatherless brood.

Lloyd Baxter strode without pleasure into the hotel. He'd complained to Priam that his overnight bag was in Priam's house. Priam's assertion that after seeing Martin's family, he would ferry the bag to the hotel, left Tallahassee's owner unmollified. The whole afternoon had been a disaster, he grumbled.

My own glass business lay a few yards from the Wychwood Dragon on the opposite side of the road. If one looked across from outside the hotel, the gallery's windows seemed to glitter with ultra-bright light, which they did from breakfast to midnight every day of the year.

I walked across the road wishing that time could be reversed to yesterday, wishing that bright-eyed Martin would march through my door suggesting improbable glass sculptures. He had become fascinated by the process and never seemed to tire of watching whenever I mixed the basic ingredients.

The ready-made mix, which came in two-hundred-kilo drums, looked like small opaque marbles. I used it regularly, as it came pure and clean, and melted without flaws.

When he first watched me load the tank of the furnace with a week's supply of the round gray pebbles, he repeated aloud the listed ingredients. "Eighty percent of the mix is white silica sand from the Dead Sea. Ten percent is soda ash. Then add small specific amounts of antimony, barium, calcium, and arsenic per fifty pounds of weight. If you want to color the glass blue, use ground lapis lazuli or cobalt. If you want yellow, use cadmium, which changes with heat to orange and red, and I don't believe it."

"That's soda crystal glass." I nodded, smiling. "I use it all the time. It's safe for eating or drinking from. Babies can lick it."

He gazed at me in surprise. "Isn't all glass safe to suck?"

"Well, no. You have to be exceedingly careful making things with lead. Lead crystal. Lovely stuff. But lead silicate is mega poisonous. In its raw state you have to keep it strictly separate from everything else and be terribly meticulous about locking it up."

"What about cut lead crystal wineglasses?" he asked. "I mean, Bon-Bon's mother gave us some."

"Don't worry," I told him with humor. "If they haven't made you ill yet, they probably won't."

"Thanks a bunch."

I went in through my heavy gallery door of beveled glass panes already feeling an emptiness where Martin had been. It wasn't as if I had no other friends; I had a pack of beer-and-wine cronies. Two of those, Hickory and Irish, worked for me as assistants and apprentices, though Hickory was approximately my own age and Irish a good deal older. The desire to work with glass quite often struck late in life, as with Irish, who was forty, but sometimes, as with me, the fascination arrived like talking, too early to remember.

I had an uncle, eminent in the glassblowing trade, who was also a brilliant flame worker. He could heat solid glass rods in the flame of a gas burner until he could twiddle them into a semblance of lace, and make angels and crinolines and steady, flat round bases for almost anything needing precision in a science laboratory.

Uncle Ron was amused at first that I should shadow him, but he finally took it seriously. He taught me whenever I could dodge school, and he died about the time that my inventiveness grew to match his. I was sixteen. In his will he left me his priceless notebooks, into which he'd detailed years of unique skill. I'd built a locked safelike bookcase to keep them in and ever since had added my own notes on method and materials needed when I designed anything special. It stood always at the far end of the workshop between the stock shelves and a bank of four tall gray lockers, where my assistants and I kept our personal stuff.

It was he, my uncle Ron, who drilled into me an embryonic business sense and an awareness that anything made by one glassblower could in general be copied by another and that this drastically lowered the asking price. During his last few years he succeeded in making uncopyable pieces, working out of my sight and then challenging me to detect and repeat his methods. Whenever I couldn't, he generously showed me how, and he laughed when I grew in ability and could beat him at his own game.

On the afternoon of Martin's death both the gallery and showroom were crowded with people looking for ways of remembering the advent of the historic millennium day. I had designed and made a whole multitude of small good-looking calendar-bearing dishes, and we had sold hundreds of them. I'd scratched my signature on the lot. Not yet, I thought, but by the year 2020, if I could achieve it, a signed Gerard Logan calendar dish of December 31, 1999, might be worth collecting.

The long gallery displayed the larger, unusual, one-of-a-kind, and more expensive pieces, each spotlit and available. The showroom was lined by many shelves holding smaller, colorful, attractive, and less expensive ornaments, which could reasonably be packed into a tourist suitcase. One side wall of the showroom rose only to waist height, so that over it one could see into the workshop beyond, where the furnace burned day and night and the little gray pebbles melted into soda crystal at a raised heat of 2400 degrees Fahrenheit.

Hickory or Irish, or their colleague Pamela Jane, took turns to work as my assistant in the workshop. One of the other two gave a running commentary of the proceedings to the customers, and the third packed parcels and worked the till. Ideally, the four of us took the jobs in turn, but experienced glassblowers were scarce, and my three assistants were still at the paperweight and penguin stage.

Christmas sales had been great but nothing like the New Year 2000. As everything sold in my place was guaranteed handmade (and mostly by me), the day I'd spent at the races had been my first respite away from the furnace for a month. I'd worked sometimes into the night, and always from eight onward in the morning. The resulting exhaustion hadn't mattered, as I was physically fit.

Hickory, twirling color into a glowing paperweight on the end of a slender five-foot-long steel rod called a punty iron, looked extremely relieved at my return from the races. Pamela Jane, smiling, earnest, thin, and anxious, lost her place in her commentary and repeated instead, "He's here. He's here . . ." and Irish stopped packing a cobalt-blue dolphin in bright white wrapping paper and sighed, "Thank goodness." They relied on me too much, I thought.

I said, "Hi, guys," as usual and walked around into the workshop. Stripping off jacket, tie, and shirt, I gave the millennium-crazy shoppers a view of my working clothes, a designer-label white mesh singlet. Hickory finished his paperweight, spinning the punty iron down by his feet to cool the glass, being careful not to scorch his new bright sneakers. I made, as a frivolity, a striped hollow blue-green and purple fish. Light shone through it in rainbows.

The customers, though, wanted proof of that day's origin. Staying open much later than usual, I made endless dated bowls, plates, and vases to please them, while Pamela Jane explained that they couldn't be collected until the next morning, New Year's Day, as they had to cool slowly overnight.

Priam Jones called in fleetingly at one point. When he had been at Martin and Bon-Bon's house, he found my raincoat lying on the back seat in the car. I thanked him with New Year fervor. He nodded, even smiled. His tears had dried.

When he'd gone, I went to hang up my raincoat in my locker. Something hard banged against my knee, and I remembered the package given me by Eddie, the valet. I put it on a stock shelf at the rear of the shop and went back to work.

I finally locked the door behind the last customer in time for Hickory, Irish, and Pamela Jane to go to parties and for me to realize I hadn't yet opened the parcel Priam Jones had returned in my raincoat. The parcel that had come from Martin. . . . He'd sat heavily on my shoulder all evening, a laughing lost spirit, urging me on.

Full of regrets, I locked the furnace against vandals and checked the heat of the annealing ovens, which were full of the newly made objects slowly cooling. The furnace, fueled by propane gas under pressure from a fan, burned day and night at never less then 1800 degrees Fahrenheit, hot enough to melt most metals. We were often asked if a memento like a wedding ring could be enclosed in a glass paperweight, but the answer was sorry, no. Liquid glass would melt gold—and human flesh—immediately. Molten glass, in fact, was pretty dangerous stuff.

I counted and then enclosed the day's takings in their canvas bag ready to entrust to the night safe of the bank. Then I put on my discarded clothes and eventually took a closer look at my neglected package, the one that had come to me from Martin via Priam Jones. The contents proved to be exactly what they felt like, an ordinary-looking videotape. The black casing bore no label of any sort, and there was no protective sleeve. A bit disappointed, I stacked it casually in the canvas bag beside the money, but the sight of it reminded me that my videotape player was at my home and that fifteen minutes before midnight on a thousand years' eve wasn't the best time to phone for a taxi.

Plans for my own midnight, with a neighborhood dance next door to my house, had disintegrated on Cheltenham racetrack.

Maybe the Wychwood Dragon, I thought, still had a broom closet to rent. I would beg a sandwich and a rug and sleep across the dark night into the new century, and early in the morning I would make an obituary for a jockey.

When I was ready to leave for the Wychwood Dragon, someone tapped heavily on the glass-paned door. I unlocked it and faced an unexpected and unwanted visitor in Lloyd Baxter. He was carrying a bottle of Dom Pérignon and two of the Wychwood Dragon's best champagne glasses. Despite these peace offerings, his heavily disapproving expression was still in place.

"Mr. Logan," he said formally, "I know no one at all in this place except yourself, and don't say this isn't a time for rejoicing, as I agree with you in many ways, not only because Martin Stukely is dead but because the next century is likely to be even more bloody than the last, and I see no reason—" He stopped abruptly.

I jerked my head for him to come in. "I'll drink to Martin," I said.

He looked relieved at my acquiescence. Loneliness still propelling him, he set the glasses on the table beside the till, ceremoniously popped the expensive cork, and unleashed the bubbles.

I looked at my watch. Only nine minutes to ring-the-bells time and fireworks.

"Drink to whatever you like," he said in depression. "I suppose it was a bad idea, coming here."

"No," I said. Regardless of thrusts of raw, unprocessed grief, I found there was inescapable excitement after all in the sense of a new chance offered, a fresh beginning possible. One could forgive one's own faults.

Five minutes to ring-the-bells.

I drank Lloyd Baxter's champagne and still didn't like him. We'd been introduced at least two years earlier. I remembered that he'd had thick, strong dark hair, but as his age had advanced from fifty, the gray streaks had multiplied quite fast. He had a powerful-looking brow and a similar no-nonsense jaw, and he had thickened around the neck and stomach. If he looked more like an industrialist than a landowner, it was because he'd sold his majority share in a shipping line to buy his racehorses and his acres.

He disapproved, he'd told me severely, of young men like myself who could take days off work whenever they cared to. I knew he considered me a hanger-on who sponged on Martin, regardless of Martin's insisting it was more likely the other way around. It seemed that when Baxter formed opinions, he was slow to rearrange them.

Distantly, out in the cold night, bells pealed the all-important moment. Lloyd Baxter raised his glass to drink to some private goal, and I, following his gesture, hoped merely that I would see January 2001 in safety. I added with banal courtesy that I would drink to his health outside, if he'd forgive me my absence.

"Of course," he said, his voice in a mumble.

Pulling open the gallery door, I walked out into the street still holding my golden drink and found that dozens of people had been moved by an almost supernatural instinct to breathe free new air under the stars. Up the hill a large group of people had linked arms and were swaying across the road singing "Auld Lang Syne" with half the words missing. Cars crept along slowly, horns blaring, with enthusiastic youths yelling from open windows.

The man who sold antique books in the shop next to my gallery shook my hand vigorously, and with uncomplicated goodwill he wished me a happy new year. I smiled and thanked him. Smiling was easy. The village, a fairly friendly place at any time, greeted the new year and the neighbors with uncomplicated affection.

It was longer than I'd intended before I reluctantly decided I should return to my shop, my ready-for-the-bank canvas bag, and my unwelcome visitor, whose temper wouldn't have been improved by my absence. I pushed open the heavy door preparing my apologies and found an entirely different sort of action was essential.

Lloyd Baxter lay facedown, unconscious, on my showroom floor.

I knelt anxiously and felt for a pulse in his neck. There was to my great relief a slow perceptible *thud-thud* under my fingers. A stroke, perhaps? A heart attack? I knew very little medicine.

What an appallingly awkward night, I thought, for anyone to

need to call out the medics. I stood up and took a few paces to the table that held the till and all the business machines, including the telephone. I dialed the emergency services without much expectation, but even on such a New Year's Eve, it seemed, the paramedics would respond, and it wasn't until I'd put down the receiver that I noticed the absence beside the till of the canvas bag with my takings.

I swore. I'd worked hard for every cent. My arms still ached. I was depressed as well as furious. I began to wonder if Lloyd Baxter had done his best, if he'd been knocked out trying to defend my property against a thief.

The black unidentified videotape was gone as well. The wave of outrage common to anyone robbed of even minor objects shook me into a deeper anger. The tape's loss was a severe aggravation, even if not on the same level as the money.

I telephoned the police without exciting them in the least. They were psyched up for bombs, not paltry theft. They said they would send a detective constable in the morning.

Lloyd Baxter stirred and moaned. The chill of the deep night seeped into my own body, let alone Baxter's. The flames of the furnace roared captive behind the trapdoor, and finally, uncomfortably cold, I went and stood on the treadle that raised the trap and let the heat flood into the workshop.

The ultraefficient men who arrived in the prompt ambulance took over expertly, examining their patient, making a preliminary diagnosis, and wrapping him in a red warming blanket ready for transport. Baxter partially awoke; his gaze flickered woozily once across my face before his eyes closed again into a heavier sleep.

The paramedics had me provide them with as much as I knew (practically nothing) of Baxter's medical history. One of them listed the contents of his pants pockets—a handkerchief, a bottle of pills, and a hotel-room key.

I didn't even have to suggest that I should return the key to the hotel; the paramedics suggested it themselves. I rattled it into my own pants without delay, thinking of sleeping in his bed, since the paramedics said he would be in the hospital all night.

"What's wrong with him?" I asked. "Has he had a heart attack? Or a stroke? Has he been . . . well, attacked and knocked out?"

I told them about the money and the tape.

They shook their heads. The most senior of them discounted my guesses. In his opinion Lloyd Baxter had had an epileptic fit.

"A *fit*?" I asked blankly. "He's seemed perfectly well all day."

The medics nodded knowledgeably. The pill bottle's contents were listed as phenytoin, the preventative for epilepsy.

"Epilepsy"—the chief medic nodded—"and who'll bet that he was overdue with a dose? We have all the other symptoms here. Alcohol." He gestured to the depleted bottle of Dom. "Late night without sleep. Stress. Isn't he the one whose jockey was done for at the races today?"

Chapter Two

AT THE Wychwood Dragon Hotel no one questioned my takeover of Lloyd Baxter's room. In the morning I packed his belongings and arranged for the hotel to send them to the hospital. Then I walked down and across the road to the workshop, where Martin, though vivid in my mind, refused to fly as a statement in glass. Inspiration operated at its own good speed, and many a time I'd found that trying to force it didn't work.

The furnace roared in its firebox. I sat beside the stainless-steel table (called a marver) on which I should have been rolling eternity into basic balls of liquid glass, and thought only of Martin laughing and of Martin's lost message on videotape. Where was that tape, what did it contain, and who thought it worth stealing?

These profitless thoughts were interrupted at nine o'clock by the doorbell and the appearance on the doorstep of a young woman in a vast sloppy sweater hanging around her knees. She wore a baseball cap over a shock of brassily dyed streaky hair. We stared at each other with interest, her brown eyes alive and curious.

I said politely, "Good morning."

"Yeah. Yeah." She laughed. "Happy new century and all that rubbish. Are you Gerard Logan?"

"Logan." I nodded. "And you?"

"Detective Constable Dodd."

I blinked. "Plainclothes?"

"You may laugh," she said. "You reported a theft at twelve thirty-two this a.m. Can I come in?"

"Be my guest."

She stepped into the gallery spotlights and glowed.

From habit I dramatized her in glass in my mind, an abstract essence as a conduit of feeling and light, exactly the instinctive process I'd tried in vain to summon up for Martin.

Oblivious, Detective Constable Dodd produced a card identifying her in uniform and adding a first name, Catherine. I answered her questions, but the police opinion was already firm. Too bad I'd left a bagful of money lying around, she said. What did I expect? And videotapes came by the dozen. No one would think twice about snapping one up.

"What was on it?" she asked, pencil poised over a notepad.

"I've no idea." I explained how it had come to me originally in a brown-paper parcel.

"Pornography. Bound to be." Her pronouncement was brisk, world-weary, and convinced. "Unidentified." She shrugged. "Would you know it from any other tape if you saw it again?"

"It hadn't any labels."

My answers about the stolen money caused her eyebrows to rise over the amount, but she obviously thought I'd never again see the canvas bag or the mini-bonanza inside. I still had checks and credit card slips, but most of my tourist customers paid in cash.

I told her about Baxter's epileptic fit. "Maybe he saw the thief."

She frowned. "Maybe he *was* the thief. Could he have faked the fit?"

"The paramedics didn't seem to think so."

She wandered through the showroom looking at the clowns, sail-

ing boats, fishes, and horses. She picked up a haloed angel and disapproved of the price sticker. Her swath of hair fell forward, fram-
ing her intent face, and I again clearly saw the bright analytical
intelligence inside the sloppy hippie-type disguise. She was through
and through a police officer, not primarily a come-hither female.

Replacing the angel, she folded her notebook and with body lan-
guage announced that the investigation, despite its lack of results,
was over. It was the go-to-work version of Constable Dodd that prepared to step into the street.

"Why the too big sweater and the baseball cap?" I asked.

She flashed me an amused glance. "You happened to have been
robbed on my allotted beat. My assignment in Broadway is to spot
the gang stealing cars in this area. Thanks for your time."

She grinned with cheerfulness and shuffled off down the hill,
pausing to talk to a homeless-looking layabout sitting in a shop
doorway. A pity the hippie and the hobo hadn't been car-thief spot-
ting at midnight, I thought vaguely.

I telephoned Bon-Bon. She wailed miserably into my ear. "Darling Gerard, please, please come as soon as you can. The children
are crying, and everything's dreadful." She drew a shaky breath.
"Priam is an old fool, and he kept patting me—"

"How long did he stay with you?" I asked.

"Ten to fifteen minutes, maybe. My mother descended on us
while he was here, and you know what she's like. Priam was mostly
in Martin's den, I think. He couldn't sit still." Bon-Bon's despair
overflowed. "Can't you *come?*"

"As soon as I've done one job and found some transport. Say,
about noon."

"Oh yes, I forgot your bloody car. I'll come and fetch you."

"No. Don't drive anywhere while you're so upset. I'll find transport, but at the worst we could persuade your remarkable parent to
lend me Worthington and the Rolls."

Bon-Bon's mother, Marigold, employed the versatile chauffeur
and frequently gave him cause to raise his eyebrows to heaven at her
odd requirements. However, he had been known to drive a roofless

Land Rover at breakneck speed at night across stubble fields, headlights blazing in the dark, while his employer stood balancing behind him with a double-barreled shotgun loosing off over his head at mesmerized rabbits. Martin said he'd been afraid to watch, but Worthington and Marigold had achieved a bag of forty and freed her land of a voracious pest. Worthington, bald and fifty, was more an adventure than a last resort.

ON NEW Year's Day 2000 in England the world in general came to a stop. People wanted to stay at home.

Logan Glass astounded the other residents of Broadway by opening its doors to the day-before's customers, who arrived to collect their overnight-cooled souvenirs. To my own astonishment two of my assistants, Pamela Jane and Irish, turned up, even though bleary-eyed, saying they couldn't leave me to pack the whole delivery job alone; so it was with speed and good humor that my new century began. I looked back later at the peace of that morning with a feeling of unreality that life could ever have been so safe and simple.

PAMELA Jane, twittery, anxious, stick thin, and wanly pretty, insisted on driving me to Bon-Bon's place. She left me in the driveway there, then hurried back to the shop.

Martin and Bon-Bon had agreed at least on their house, an eighteenth-century gem that I admired every time I went there. A small van stood on the gravel, dark blue with a name painted on it in yellow: THOMPSON ELECTRONICS. Because I'd been working, I didn't remember that that day was a national holiday—definitely a moratorium for television repair vans.

Chaos was too weak a word to describe what I found inside the house. For a start, the front door was visibly ajar. Beginning to feel a slight unease, I stepped inside and shouted but without response, and a pace or two later I learned why.

Bon-Bon's mother, Marigold, frothy gray hair and floaty purple dress in disarray, lay unconscious on the stairs. Worthington, her eccentric chauffeur, sprawled at her feet.

The four children, out of sight, were uncannily quiet, and the door to Martin's den was closed on silence.

I opened this door immediately and found Bon-Bon there, lying full-length on the floor. I knelt to feel for a pulse in her neck, and I felt the living *ga-bump ga-bump* with a deep relief. Concentrating on Bon-Bon, I saw too late in peripheral sight a movement behind my right shoulder, a dark figure hiding behind the door.

I jerked halfway to standing but wasn't quick enough. I glimpsed a small metal gas cylinder, more or less like a fire extinguisher. But this cylinder wasn't red. It was orange. It hit my head. Martin's den turned gray, dark gray, and black. A deep well of nothing.

I RETURNED slowly to a gallery of watchers. The children's eyes looked huge with fright. I was lying on my back. Into the blank spaces of memory slowly crept the picture of an orange gas cylinder in the hands of a figure in a black head mask. I tried to stand up.

Bon-Bon said with great relief, "Thank God you're all right. We've all been gassed, and we've all been sick since we woke up."

I, for one, had a headache, not nausea.

Worthington, notwithstanding the muscular physique he painstakingly developed by regular visits to a punch-bag gym, looked pale and shaky. He held each of the two youngest children by the hand, though, giving them what confidence he could. In their eyes he could do everything, and they were nearly right.

Bon-Bon had once mentioned that Worthington's top value to her mother was his understanding of bookmakers' methods, because, as Marigold herself disliked walking along between the rows of men shouting the odds, Worthington got her the best prices. A versatile and compulsive good guy was Worthington.

Only Marigold herself was now missing from the sick parade. Peeling myself off the floor, I asked about her. The eldest of the children, a boy called Daniel, said she was drunk. Snoring on the stairs, the elder girl said. So pragmatic, 2000-year children.

Bon-Bon's doctor promised he would "look in," New Year's Day notwithstanding. He asked if we'd informed the police of the attack.

It did seem obvious that robbery had been the purpose of the mass anesthesia. Three television sets with integral tape players were missing, together with dozens of tapes. Two laptop computers, with printers and racks of filing disks, were missing too.

Bon-Bon began crying quietly from the strain of it all, and it was Worthington, recovering and worth his weight in videotapes, who talked to the overburdened local police station. My constable, Catherine Dodd, he found, was attached to a different branch. Detectives, however, would arrive on the Stukely doorstep soon.

Not surprisingly, the Thompson Electronics van had gone.

Feeling queasy, I sat in Martin's black leather chair in his den, while Bon-Bon, on an opposite sofa, gave no complete answer to my repeated question, which was, "What was on the tape that Martin meant to give me after the races, and where did it come from? That's to say, who gave it to Martin himself at Cheltenham?"

Bon-Bon studied me with wet eyes and blew her nose. She said, "I know Martin wanted to tell you something yesterday, but he had those other men in the car and he wanted to talk to you without Priam listening, so he planned to take you home last, after the others." Even in distress she looked porcelain pretty, the plumpness an asset in a curvy black wool suit.

"He trusted you," she said finally.

"Mm." I'd have been surprised if he hadn't.

"No, you don't understand." Bon-Bon hesitated and went on slowly. "He knew a secret. He wouldn't tell me what it was. He said I would fret. But he wanted to tell *someone.* I agreed you should be his backup. Just in case. Oh dear . . . He had what he wanted you to know put onto a plain old-fashioned recording tape, not onto a CD or a computer disk, and he did that, I think, because whoever was giving him information preferred it that way. I'm not sure. And also it was easier to play, he said. Better on video than computer because, darling Gerard, you know I never get things right when it comes to computers. But I can play a videotape easily. Martin wanted me to be able to do that if he died, but of course he didn't think he'd die, not really."

"And he didn't say anything about what was on that tape he meant for me?"

"He was awfully careful not to."

I shook my head in frustration. The tape stolen from the glass showroom was surely the one with the secret on it. The one passed to Martin, then to Eddie the valet, and then to me. Yet if the Broadway thieves, or thief, had viewed it—and they'd had all night to do so—why were they needing to rob Martin's house as well?

Did the tape taken from the showroom actually contain Martin's secret? Perhaps not.

Was the second robbery carried out by a different thief, who didn't know about the first one? I had no answers, only guesses. Marigold at that point tottered into the den as if coming to pieces in all directions. I had been used to Marigold for the four years since Martin had straight-facedly presented me to his buxom mother-in-law, a magnified version of his pretty wife. Marigold could be endlessly witty or tiresomely belligerent, according to the gin level, but this time the effect of gas on alcohol seemed to have resulted in pity-me pathos.

The police turned up, and Bon-Bon's children described their attacker, right down to the laces on his shoes. He had stared with wide eyes through his black head mask while he'd pointed the orange cylinder at them and squirted a nearly invisible but fierce mist, sweeping from face to face and knocking them out before they'd realized what was happening. Daniel described the black-masked man having something white tied over his face underneath. An elementary gas mask, I surmised. Something to prevent the robber from inhaling his own gas.

The gas had perhaps been exhausted by the time I arrived; a direct bang on the head had sufficed.

Scarcely had the police notebooks been folded away than Bon-Bon's doctor hurried in. It was the color orange that slowed him into frowns and more thorough care. He and the police all listened to Daniel, brought out paper, and took notes. He told the departing detectives to look for villains with access to the anesthetic gas cyclopropane, which came in orange cylinders and wasn't much used because of being highly flammable and explosive.

Slowly, after decently thorough peerings into eyes and throats and careful stethoscope chest checks, each of the family was judged fit to go on living. Sweet Bon-Bon, when her house was finally free of official attention, told me she was utterly exhausted and needed help. Specifically she needed *my* help.

So I stayed and looked after things, and because of that I saved myself at least another sore head, as thieves broke into my house on the hill that night and stole every videotape I owned.

ON MONDAY, after an early session in the workshop, I went to Cheltenham races (by taxi) to talk to Martin's valet, Eddie Payne.

Eddie was ready to help, he said, his gaze darting over my shoulder and back again to my face, but he couldn't—however hard he tried—remember any more than he'd told me on Friday. I thought back to the moment of empathy between us, when we had each realized what we'd lost.

The difference between Friday and Monday was a fierce-eyed woman approaching forty, now standing a pace or two behind me, a woman Eddie referred to as his daughter. He slid a second glance at her expressionlessly and said almost too quietly for me to hear, "She knows the man who gave Martin the tape."

The woman said sharply, "What did you say, Dad? Speak up."

"I said we'd miss Martin badly," Eddie said, "and I'm due back in the changing room. Tell Gerard—Mr. Logan—what he wants to know, why don't you?" He walked away, apologetically saying as he went, "Her name's Rose; she's a good girl really."

Rose, the good girl, gave me such a bitter flash of hate that I wondered what I'd ever done to annoy her, as I hadn't known of her existence until moments earlier. She was angularly bony and had mid-brown hair with frizzy sticking-out curls. Her skin was dry and freckled, and although her clothes looked too big for the thin body inside, there was about her an extraordinary air of magnetism.

"Er . . . Rose—" I started.

"Mrs. Robins," she interrupted abruptly.

I cleared my throat and tried again.

"Mrs. Robins, then, could I buy you some coffee or a drink?"

She said, "No, you could *not*." She bit the words off with emphasis. She said, "You'd do better to mind your own business."

"Mrs. Robins, did you see who gave a brown paper–wrapped parcel to Martin Stukely at Cheltenham races last Friday?"

Such a simple question. She primped her lips together tightly, swiveled on her heel, and walked away.

After a short pause I trickled along in her wake as she made for the ranks of bookmakers' stands. She stopped at a board announcing ARTHUR ROBINS, EST. 1894, and talked to an Elvis Presley look-alike with heavy black side whiskers. He was standing on a box, leaning down to take money from the public, and dictating his transactions to a clerk, who was punching the bets into a computer.

Rose Robins, established long after 1894, had a fair amount to say to the Elvis look-alike. He frowned, listening, and I retreated. I might have strength and reasonable agility, but Rose's contact made my muscle power look the stuff of kindergartens.

Patiently I climbed the stands and waited while the Arthur Robins bookmakers—three of them—took bets on the final two races of the afternoon and then packed up. I watched them walk toward the exit with Rose. As a group, they equaled an armored tank.

From experience with Martin, I knew that jockeys' valets finished their work after most of the crowds had gone home. A valet was the man who helped the jockeys change rapidly between races. He also looked after and cleaned their gear, saddles, britches, boots, and so on. Now, while Eddie packed up his hamper of saddles, kit, and clothes for laundering, I waited with hope for him to reappear out of the changing room at the end of his day.

When he came out and saw me, he was at first alarmed and then resigned. "I suppose," he said, "Rose wouldn't tell you."

"No," I agreed. "So would you ask her something, for Martin's sake? Ask her if the tape Martin gave you was the one he thought it was."

He took a few seconds to work it out.

"Do you mean," he asked doubtfully, "that my Rose thinks Martin had the wrong tape?"

"I think," I confessed, "that if Martin's tape ever surfaces after all the muddle and thieving, it'll be a matter of luck."

He protested self-righteously that he'd given me Martin's tape in good faith. I insisted that I believed him. No more was said about Rose. Eddie, eyes down, mumbled a few words about seeing me at Martin's funeral, planned for Thursday. Then, in evident discomfort, he hurried away.

Rose Robins and her enmity added complexity to an already tangled situation. But I came to no satisfactory conclusion about the unexpected involvement of Eddie's scratchy daughter.

Meanwhile, still drifting in outer space was whatever confidential data Martin had meant to entrust to me. Unrealistically, I simply hoped that Martin's secret would remain forever hidden in uncharted orbit and all of us could return to normal.

I caught a bus from the racetrack to Broadway. The bus wound its way from village to village, and it was after five thirty by the time I reached the doors of Logan Glass. My assistants told me Bon-Bon had telephoned, saying she was begging me to go on organizing her household in return for transport. Much to their amusement the transport she sent was Marigold's Rolls.

I sat beside Worthington as he drove. In addition to being bald, fifty, and kind to children, Worthington disliked the police force as a matter of principle, referred to marriage as bondage, and believed in the usefulness of being able to outkick any other muscleman in sight. It wasn't so much as a chauffeur that I now valued Worthington at my elbow, but as a prospective bodyguard. The Elvis look-alike had radiated latent menace at an intensity that I hadn't met before and didn't like; and for a detonator there was fierce, thorny Rose. It was with her in mind that I casually asked Worthington if he'd ever placed a bet at the races with Arthur Robins, Est. 1894.

"For a start," he said with sarcasm, "the Robins family don't exist. That bunch of swindlers known as Arthur Robins are mostly Veritys and Webbers. There hasn't been a bona fide Arthur Robins ever. It's just a pretty name."

Eyebrows raised in surprise, I asked, "How do you know?"

"My old man was a bookmaker; he taught me the trade. You've got to be sharp at figures, though, to make a profit, and I never got quick enough. But Arthur Robins, that's the front name for some whizzers of speed merchants. Don't bet with them, that's my advice."

I said, "Do you know that Eddie Payne, Martin's valet, has a daughter called Rose who says her last name is Robins and who's on cuddling terms with an Elvis Presley look-alike taking bets for Arthur Robins?"

Worthington sat straighter in his seat. "No, I didn't know that." He thought for a while. "That Elvis fellow," he said finally, "that's Norman Osprey. You don't want to mix with *him*."

"And Rose?"

Worthington shook his head. "I don't know her. I'll ask around."

BY THURSDAY, the day of Martin's funeral, a young woman on a motorbike—huge helmet, black leather jacket, matching pants, heavy boots—steered into one of the parking spaces at the front of Logan Glass. Outside in the January chill she pulled off the helmet and shook free a cap of fair fine hair, then walked into the gallery and showroom.

I was putting the pre-annealing final touches to a vase, with Pamela Jane telling a group of American tourists how it was done, but there was something attention-claiming about the motorcyclist, and as soon as I thought of her in terms of glass, I knew her.

"Catherine Dodd," I said.

"Most people don't recognize me out of uniform." She was amused, not piqued.

With interest I watched the tourists pack somewhat closer together as if to elbow out the stranger in threatening clothes.

Pamela Jane finished her spiel, and the tourists settled on their purchases. While Hickory wrapped the parcels and wrote out bills,

I asked the motorcyclist if there were any news of my lost tape.

"I'm afraid," said Detective Constable Dodd in plain—well, plainer—clothes, "your tape is gone for good."

I told her it held a secret.

"What secret?"

"I don't know. Martin Stukely told his wife he was giving me a secret on tape for safekeeping—that's a bit of a laugh."

Catherine Dodd's detective mind trod the two paths I'd reluctantly followed myself. First, *someone* knew Martin's secret, and second, *someone,* and maybe not the same someone, could infer that one way or another that secret was known to me. Someone might suppose I'd watched that tape during the evening of Martin's death and for safety had wiped it off.

"If I'd had a tape player handy," I said, "I probably *would* have run that tape, and if I thought it awful, I *might* have wiped it off."

"That's not what your friend Martin wanted."

I said, "If he'd been sure of what he wanted, he wouldn't have fiddled about with tapes, he would just have *told* me this precious secret." I stopped abruptly. "There are too many *ifs.* How about you coming out for a drink?"

"Can't. Sorry. I'm on duty." She gave me a brilliant smile. "I'll call in another day. And oh! There's just one loose end." She produced the ever essential notebook from inside her jacket. "What are your assistants' names?"

"Pamela Jane Evans and John Irish and John Hickory. We leave off John for the men and use their last names, as it's easier."

"And how long have they all worked for you?"

"Pamela Jane about a year, Irish and Hickory two to three months longer. They're all good guys, believe me."

"I do believe you. This is just for the records. This is actually, er, what I dropped in for."

I looked at her straightly. She all but blushed.

"I'd better go now," she said.

With regret I walked with her as far as the door, where she paused to say good-bye, as she didn't want to be seen with me too familiarly out in the street. A tourist's broad back obscured my view of the departure of Detective Constable Dodd, and I surprised myself by minding about that quite a lot.

ON BON-BON'S telephone, the night before Martin's funeral, I learned that Lloyd Baxter had deemed it correct to fly down for "his jockey's last ride" (as he put it) but hadn't wanted to stay with Priam Jones, whom he was on the point of ditching as his trainer.

Priam also telephoned, meaning to talk to Bon-Bon but reaching me instead. I had been fielding commiserations for her whenever I was around. Marigold, Worthington, and even the children had grown expert at thanks and tact. I thought how Martin would have grinned at the all-around grade-A improvement in his family's social skills.

Priam blustered on a bit but was, I gathered, offering himself as an usher in the matter of seating at the funeral. Remembering his tears, I put him on the list, then asked him if, before he'd picked me up from my home on Friday morning, Martin had by any chance mentioned that he was expecting delivery of a tape at the races.

"You asked me that the day after he died," Priam said impatiently. "The answer is still yes. He said we wouldn't leave the racetrack until he'd collected some package or other to give to you. And I did give it to you, don't you remember? I brought it back to Broadway after you'd left it in your raincoat in the car. . . . Well, I'll see you tomorrow, Gerard. Give my regards to Bon-Bon."

Also that evening, Eddie Payne told me he'd tried and tried to get someone else to do his racetrack work, but he hadn't succeeded, and he'd have to miss the funeral. I knew that in fact he could have more easily got stand-ins to free him to go to that particular funeral than if it had been for his own grandmother.

On the same evening (though I didn't learn of it until later), Eddie Payne's daughter, Rose, described to a small group of fascinated and ruthless knaves how to force Gerard Logan to tell them the secret he'd been given at Cheltenham races.

Chapter Three

ON THE first Thursday of January, the sixth day of the next thousand years, I, with Priam Jones and four senior jump jockeys, carried Martin into church in his coffin and later delivered him to his grave. The sun shone on frosty trees. Bon-Bon looked ethereal, Marigold stayed fairly sober, and the four children knocked with their knuckles on the coffin as if they could wake their father inside. Lloyd Baxter read a short but decent eulogy, and all the racing world, from the stewards of the Jockey Club to the men who replaced the divots, everyone crowded into the pews in church and packed the wintry churchyard outside. Respects were paid.

After the hundreds who had turned up had left, I sought Bon-Bon out to say good-bye.

"Stay with us one more night," she said. "You and Worthington have tamed the children. Let's have this one more night of peace."

I agreed, and after midnight, when only I was awake, I sat in Martin's den and thought intently of him. One had so few close friends in life. None to spare. I also thought of the videotape and whatever he'd had recorded on it. I had no idea what could have needed such complex safekeeping. I did see that to Bon-Bon a secret would be safe until her next nice chat with her best friend.

It was time, I supposed, to make sure the outside doors were locked and to sleep away the last hours in Martin's house. A few weeks earlier I'd lent him a couple of books on ancient glassmaking techniques, and as they were lying on the long table by the sofa, it seemed a good time to pick them up to take home. One of the things I would most miss was Martin's constant interest in historic difficult-to-make goblets and bowls.

In the morning, saying good-bye, I mentioned I was taking the books. "Fine," Bon-Bon said vaguely. "I wish you weren't going. I'm so lonely."

As Worthington drove me back to Broadway, he said, "I got a low-life investigator to ask about that woman, Rose." He paused. "He didn't get much further than you did. Eddie Payne thinks she saw who gave that damned tape to Martin, but I wouldn't rely on it. Eddie's afraid of his own daughter, if you ask me."

I agreed with him on that, and we left it there.

My three assistants welcomed me back to a regular workday, and I taught Hickory—as I'd taught Pamela Jane before Christmas—how to collect a third gather of glass, so hot that it was red and semiliquid and fell in a heavy teardrop shape that drooped toward the floor (and one's feet) if one didn't marver it fast enough on the steel table. Hickory knew how to press its lengthened tip into long heaps of dustlike colors before returning the revolving head into the furnace to keep the chunk of glass at working temperature. I showed him how to gather glass neatly on the end of a blowing iron before lifting it into the air ready to blow, and how to keep the resulting slightly ballooned shape constant.

He watched the continuous process with anxious eyes.

"Practice handling three gathers," I said. "You can do two now easily." A gather was the amount of molten glass that could be brought out of the tank at one time on the tip of the steel punty rod. A gather could be any size, according to the skill and strength of the glassblower. Glass in bulk was very heavy and demanded muscle.

Owing to the space limitation of tourist suitcases, few pieces of Logan glass sold in the shop were of more than three gathers. Pamela Jane, to her sorrow, had never quite mastered the swing-upward-and-blow technique. Irish, in spite of enthusiasm, would never be a top-rated glassblower. Of Hickory, though, I had hopes. He had ease of movement and, most important, a lack of fear.

Glassblowers were commonly arrogant people, chiefly because the skill was so difficult to learn. Hickory already showed signs of arrogance, but if he became a notable expert, he would have to be forgiven. I sat on a box and drank tea all day and watched my apprentice improve considerably, even though there was generally a lot of swearing and a whole heap of shattered glass.

By five o'clock on this bleakly cold January afternoon I sent my three helpers home and with gloom did some long-overdue accounting work. The stolen cash left a depressing hole. It wasn't difficult after a while to lay aside the figures and pick up the books on ancient glassmaking that I'd lent to Martin.

Flicking through the early pages in one of the books, I came across the picture of my favorite of all historic goblets, a glowing red cup, six and a half inches high, constructed around the year three hundred and something. It was made of lumps of glass held fast in an intricate gold cage (a technique from before blowing was invented). Absorbed with pleasure, I didn't notice at first a thin buff envelope held within the leaves.

The envelope was addressed by computer printer to Martin Stukely, Esq., Jockey. I had no qualms in taking out the single-page letter inside and reading it.

Dear Martin,

You are right, it is the best way. I will take the tape, as you want, to Cheltenham races on New Year's Eve.

This knowledge is dynamite. Take care of it.

VICTOR WALTMAN VERITY

The letter too was written on a computer, though the name given as signature had been printed in a different font. There was no address or telephone number on the letter itself, but faintly across the stamp on the envelope there was a round postmark. After long concentration with a magnifying glass, the point of origin seemed to me only "xet" around the top and "evo" around the bottom. The date alone was easily readable: December 17. Less than a month ago.

There weren't many places in Great Britain with an *x* in their name, and I could think of nowhere else that fitted the available letters other than Exeter, Devon.

When I reached directory inquiries, I learned that there was indeed a Victor Verity in Exeter. But when I called, I spoke not to him, but to his widow. Her dear Victor had passed away during the previous summer. Wrong Verity.

I tried inquiries again.

"Very sorry," said a prim voice, "there is no other Victor or V. Verity in the Exeter telephone area, which covers most of Devon."

"How about an unlisted number?"

"Sorry. I can't give you that information."

Victor Waltman Verity was either unlisted or had mailed his letter far from home.

Cursing him lightly, I glanced with reluctance at the accounting work half done on my computer, and there, of course, lay the answer. Computers. Internet. The Internet might, among other miracles, put an address to a name.

I started a search for Verity in Devon, and the Internet, after surveying every fact obtainable in the public domain (such as the electoral registers), came up with a total of twenty-two Devon-based Veritys, but none of them any longer was Victor.

Dead end.

I tried Verity in Cornwall. Sixteen, but still no Victor.

Try Somerset, I thought. Not a Victor Verity in sight.

Before reaching to switch off, I skimmed down the list, and at the end of it noticed that at 19 Lorna Terrace, Taunton, Somerset, there lived a Mr. Waltman Verity. Good enough to try, I thought.

Armed with the address, I tried directory inquiries again but ran up against the same polite barrier of virtual nonexistence. Unlisted. Sorry. Too bad.

Although the next day was Saturday and busier than usual in the showroom, my thoughts returned continuously to Taunton and Waltman Verity.

Taunton . . . Having nothing much else urgently filling my Sunday, I caught a westbound train the next morning and asked directions to Lorna Terrace.

The door of Number 19 was opened by a thin woman dressed in pants, sweater, and bedroom slippers, with a cigarette in one hand and big pink curlers in her hair. Perhaps forty, I thought. Easygoing, with a resigned attitude to strangers on her doorstep.

"Mrs. Verity?" I asked.

"Yeah. What is it?" She sucked smoke, unconcerned.

"Mrs. Victor Waltman Verity?"

She laughed. "I'm Mrs. Waltman Verity. Victor's my son." She shouted over her shoulder toward the inner depths of the narrow terrace house. "Vic, someone to see you," and while we waited, Mrs. Verity looked me over thoroughly from hair to sneakers and went on enjoying a private giggle.

Whatever I expected Victor Waltman Verity to look like, it was nothing near the living thing. He must have been all of fifteen. He appeared quietly from along the narrow hallway and regarded me with curiosity mixed, I thought, with the possibility of alarm. He was as tall as his mother, as tall as Martin. He had dark hair, pale gray eyes, and an air of knowing himself to be as intelligent as any adult. His voice, when he spoke, was at the cracked stage between boy and man.

"What've you been up to, young Vic?" his mother asked, and to me she said, "It's bloody cold out here. Want to come in?"

"Er," I said. I was suffering more from the unexpected than the cold, but she waited for no answer and walked back past the boy until she was out of sight. I pulled the envelope sent to Martin out of a pocket and immediately set the alarm racing above the curiosity in young Victor.

"You weren't supposed to find me!" he exclaimed. "And in any case, you're dead."

"I'm not Martin Stukely," I said.

"Oh." His face went blank. "No, of course, you aren't." Puzzlement set in. "I mean, what do you want?"

"First, I'd like to accept your mother's invitation to be warm."

"The kitchen is warmest," he said, and led the way along the hall to the heart of all such terrace houses, the space where life was lived. There was a central table with a patterned plastic cloth and four unmatched chairs. A television set stood aslant on a counter otherwise stacked with unwashed dishes.

In spite of the disorganization, there was bright new paint and nothing disturbingly sordid. I had an overall impression of yellow.

Mrs. Verity sat in one of the chairs, rocking on its back legs and gulping smoke. She said pleasantly enough, "We get all sorts of people here, what with Vic and his wretched Internet. We'll get a full-sized genie one of these days, I shouldn't wonder." She gestured vaguely to one of the chairs, and I sat on it.

"I was a friend of Martin Stukely," I explained, and I asked Vic what was on the videotape that he had sent or given to Martin at Cheltenham.

"Yes, well, there wasn't a tape," he said briefly. "I didn't go to Cheltenham."

I pulled his letter to Martin out of the envelope and gave it to him to read. He shrugged and handed it back when he'd reached the end.

"It was a game. I made up the tape." He was nervous, all the same.

"What knowledge was it that was dynamite?"

"Look, none." He grew impatient. "I told you. I made it up."

"Why did you send it to Martin Stukely?"

I was careful not to let the questions sound too aggressive, but in some way that I didn't understand, they raised all his defenses and colored his cheeks red.

His mother said to me, "What's all this about a tape? Do you mean a *video*tape? Vic hasn't got any videotapes. We're going to get a new video machine any day now; then it will be different."

I explained apologetically. "Someone did give Martin a videotape at Cheltenham races. Martin gave it to Eddie Payne, his valet, to keep safe, and Eddie gave it to me, but it was stolen before I could see what was on it. Then all the videotapes in Martin Stukely's house and all the videotapes in my own house were stolen too."

"I hope you're not suggesting that Vic stole anything, because I can promise you he wouldn't." Mrs. Verity had grasped one suggestion wrongly and hadn't listened clearly to the rest, so she too advanced to the edge of anger, and I did my best to retreat and placate, but her natural good humor had been dented. She stood up as a decisive signal that it was time I left.

I said amiably to young Victor, "Call me," and although he shook his head, I wrote my mobile number on the margin of a Sunday newspaper.

Then I stepped out of 19 Lorna Terrace and walked unhurriedly along the street pondering two odd unanswered questions.

First, how did Victor happen to come to Martin's attention?

Second, why had neither mother nor son asked my name?

As I left Lorna Terrace, I was conscious of not having done very well. I seem to have screwed up even what I thought I understood. I might be okay at glass but not excellent at Sherlock Holmes. Dim Dr. Watson, that was me.

It grew dark, and it took me a long time to return to Broadway. Fishing out a small bunch of keys, I plodded toward the gallery door. Sunday evening. No one about. Brilliant lights shining from Logan Glass.

I hadn't learned yet to beware of shadows. Figures in black materialized from the deep entrance to the antique bookshop next door. I suppose there were four of them leaping about in the dark—an impression, not an accurate count. Four was profligate, anyway. Three, two, maybe only one could have done the job. I guessed they'd been waiting there for a long time and it hadn't improved their temper.

The attack consisted of multiple bashes and bangs and of being slammed two or three times against a lumpy bit of Cotswold stone wall.

Disoriented by the attack, I heard demands as if from a distance that I should disclose information that I knew I didn't have. I tried to tell them. They didn't listen.

All of that was annoying enough, but it was their additional aim that lit my own inner protection furnace and put power into half-forgotten techniques of kickboxing left over from my teens. A sharp, excited voice instructed over and over again, "Break his wrists. Go on. *Break his wrists.*" And later, out of the dark, the same voice exulting, "That got him."

No, it bloody didn't. Pain screeched up my arm. My thoughts

were blasphemy. Strong, whole, and flexible wrists were as essential to a glassblower as to a gymnast on the Olympic high rings.

Two of the black-clad agile figures waved baseball bats. One with heavily developed shoulders was recognizably Norman Osprey. One other had the bright idea of holding my fingers tightly together in a bunch against the wall before getting his colleague to aim just below them with the bat.

I hadn't been aware of how desperately one could fight when it was the real thing. My wrists didn't get broken, but my watch took a direct hit. There were lumps and bruises all over. A few cuts. But my fingers worked, and that was all that mattered.

Maybe the fracas would have ended with me taking a fresh hole in the ground beside Martin, but Broadway wasn't a ghost town; people walked their dogs in the evening, and it was a dog walker who yelled at my attackers and, with three Dobermans barking and pulling at their leashes, got the shadowy figures to vanish.

"Gerard Logan!" The tall dog walker, astounded, bending to look at me, knew me by sight, as I did him. "Are you all right?"

No, I wasn't. I said, "Yes," as one does.

He stretched down to help me to my feet. "Shall I call the police?" he asked, though he wasn't a police lover—far from it.

"Tom—thanks. But no police."

"What was it all about?" He sounded relieved. "Are you in trouble? That looked to me like payback business."

"Muggers."

Tom Pigeon, who knew a thing or two about the rocky sides of life, gave me a half-smile, half-disillusioned look, and shortened the leashes of his toothy life preservers. More bark than bite, he'd assured me once. I wasn't certain I believed it.

He himself looked as if he had no need to bark. Although not heavily built, he had unmistakable physical power and a close-cut dark pointed beard that added menace. He told me there was blood in my hair. I leaned gingerly against the wall. The dizzy world revolved. I couldn't remember ever feeling so pulverized or so sick, not even when I'd fallen to the bottom of the scrum in a viciously unfriendly school rugby match and had my shoulder blade broken.

Tom Pigeon opened the gallery door with my keys, and with his arm around my waist got me as far as the threshold. "You'll be all right now, okay?"

I nodded. He more or less propped me against the doorframe.

Tom Pigeon was known locally as the Backlash, chiefly on account of being as quick with his wits as his fists. He'd survived unharmed eighteen months inside for aggravated breaking and entering and had emerged as a toughened hotshot, to be spoken of in awe. Whatever his dusty reputation, he had definitely rescued me, and I felt extraordinarily honored.

He stared shrewdly into my eyes. "Get a pit bull," he said.

I LOCKED the door against the violence outside. Pity I felt so stupid. So furious. So dangerously mystified.

In the back reaches of the workshop there was running water for rinsing one's face and a relaxing chair for recovery of all kinds of balance. I sat and ached a lot.

At about ten thirty I fell asleep in the soft chair and half an hour later was awakened by the doorbell. Disoriented as I woke, I wavered upright and creaked out of the workshop to see who wanted what at such an hour.

Detective Constable Catherine Dodd smiled with relief when I let her in. "We had reports from two separate Broadway residents," she said, "who saw you being attacked outside here. So I said I would check on you on my way home."

She again wore motorcycle leathers. With deft speed, as before, she lifted off her helmet and shook her head to loosen her fair hair.

I made a noncommittal gesture.

She said, "Gerard, I've seen other people in your state. Why haven't you asked my colleagues for more help?"

"Because," I said lightly, "I don't know who or why, and every time I think I've learned something, I find I haven't. Your colleagues don't like uncertainty."

She thought that over. "Tell *me*, then," she said.

"Someone wants something I haven't got. I don't know what it is. I don't know who wants it. How am I doing?"

"That makes nonsense."

I winced and turned it into a smile. "It makes nonsense, quite right." And in addition, I thought with acid humor, I have Bon-Bon on my watch-it list, and policewoman Dodd on my wanted-but-can-I-catch-her list, and Tom Pigeon and Worthington on my save-my-skin list, Rose Payne/Robins on my black-mask-possible list, and young Victor Waltman on my can't-or-won't-tell list.

As for Lloyd Baxter and his epilepsy, Eddie Payne keeping and delivering videotapes, Norman Osprey with the massive shoulders running a book, and dear scatty Marigold, often afloat before break-fast and regularly before lunch, all of them could have tapes on their mind and know every twist in the ball of string.

Constable Dodd frowned, faint lines crossing her clear skin. As it seemed to be question time, I said abruptly, "Are you married?"

After a few seconds looking down at her ringless hands, she replied, "Why do you ask?"

"You have the air of it."

"He's dead." She sat for a while without moving and then asked, "And you?" in calm return.

"Not yet," I said.

Silence could sometimes shout. She listened for what I would probably ask quite soon, and seemed relaxed and content.

The workshop was warmed as always by the furnace, even though the roaring fire was held in control for nights and Sundays by a large screen of heat-resistant material.

Looking at Catherine Dodd's face above the dark close-fitting leather, I most clearly now saw her in terms of glass, saw her in fact so vividly that the urge and desire to work couldn't be stifled. I stood and unclipped the fireproof screen, put it to one side, and fixed instead the smaller flap, which opened to allow access to the tankful of molten glass.

With boringly painful movements I took off my jacket and shirt, leaving only normal working gear of bare arms and singlet.

"What are you doing?" She sounded alarmed.

"A portrait," I said. "Sit still." I turned up the heat in the furnace and sorted out the punty blowing irons I would need, and fetched a workable amount of glass manganese powder, which eventually would give me a black color.

"But your bruises," she protested. "They're terrible."

"I can't feel them."

I felt nothing indeed except the rare sort of excitement that came with revelation. That Sunday night the concept of one detective darkly achieving insight into the sins of others, and then the possibility that good could rise above sin and fly, these drifting thoughts set up in me in effect a mental anesthesia, leaving the flame of imagination to do its stuff. Sometimes in the disengagement from this sort of thing, the vision had shrunk to disappointment and ash, and when that happened, I would leave the no-good piece on the marver table and not handle it carefully into an annealing oven. After a while its unresolved internal strains would cause it to self-destruct, to come to pieces dramatically with a cracking noise—to splinter, to fragment, to shatter.

It could be for onlookers an unnerving experience to see an apparently solid object disintegrate for no visible reason. For me the splitting apart symbolized merely the fading and insufficiency of the original thought. On that particular Sunday I had no doubts or hesitation, and I gathered glass in muscle-straining amounts that even on ordinary days would have taxed my ability.

That night I made Catherine Dodd in three pieces that later I would join together. I made not a lifelike sculpture of her head but an abstract of her daily occupation—a soaring upward spread of wings, black and shining at the base, rising through a black, white, and clear center to a high-rising pinion with streaks of gold shining to the top. The gold fascinated my subject. "Is it real gold?"

"Iron pyrites. But real gold would melt the same way, only I used all I had a week ago."

I gently held the sculpture in layers of heatproof fiber and laid it carefully in one of the six annealing ovens, and only then could I hardly bear the strains in my own limbs and felt too like cracking apart myself.

Catherine stood up and took a while to speak. Eventually she asked what I would do with the finished flight of wings, and I, coming down to earth from invention, tried prosaically just to say that I would probably make a pedestal for it in the gallery.

We both stood looking at each other as if not knowing what else to say. I leaned forward and kissed her cheek, which with mutual small movements became mouth to mouth, with passion in there somewhere, acknowledged but not yet overflowing.

Arms around motorcycle leathers had practical drawbacks. My own physical aches put winces where they weren't wanted, and with rueful humor she disengaged herself and said, "Maybe another time."

"Delete the maybe," I said.

Chapter Four

ALL three of my assistants could let themselves in through the gallery with personal keys, and it was Pamela Jane alone whom I saw first when I returned to consciousness at about eight o'clock on Monday morning. After Catherine had gone, I'd simply flopped back into the big chair in the workshop and closed my eyes on a shuddering and protesting nervous system. Sleep had made things slightly worse.

Pamela Jane said, horrified, "Honestly, you look as if you'd been hit by a steamroller. Have you been here all night?"

"Can you . . ." Even my voice felt rough. I cleared my throat and tried again. "Pam . . . jug of tea?"

She scurried helpfully around, making the tea and unbolting the side door. By the advent of Irish, I was ignoring the worst of my creaking joints, and Hickory, arriving last, found me lifting the three wing sections of the night's work out of the ovens.

They couldn't help but notice that I found too much movement a bad idea, but I could have done without Hickory's cheerful assumption it was the aftermath of booze.

The first customer came. Life more or less returned to normal. If I concentrated on blowing glass, I could forget four black jersey-wool masks with eyeholes.

Later in the morning Marigold's Rolls-Royce drew up outside with Worthington at the wheel, looking formal in his official cap.

Marigold herself, he reported through his rolled-down window, had gone shopping with Bon-Bon in Bon-Bon's car. Both ladies had given him the day off and the use of the car. He appreciated her generosity, he said solemnly, as he was going to take me to the races.

I looked back at him in indecision.

"I'm not going," I said. "And where am I not going?"

"Leicester. Jump racing. Eddie Payne will be there. Rose will be there. Norman Osprey will be there with his book. I thought you wanted to find out who gave the videotape to Martin."

I didn't answer at once. "Mind you," he said, making allowances, "I don't suppose you want another beating like you got last night, so stay here if you like, and I'll mooch around by myself."

"Who told you about last night?"

"A not-so-little bird. A Pigeon. It seems he thinks quite a bit of you. He phoned me at Bon-Bon's. He says to put it around that in future any hands laid on you are laid on him."

I felt both grateful and surprised. I asked, "How well do you know him?"

He answered obliquely. "You know that gardener of Martin's that was dying? That you lost your license for, speeding to get him there in time? That gardener was Tom Pigeon's dad. Are you coming to Leicester?"

"I guess so." I went back inside and changed my clothes.

I sat beside Worthington for the journey. We stopped to buy me a cheap watch and to pick up a daily racing newspaper. On the front page I read, among a dozen little snippets, that the Leicester stewards would be hosts that day to Lloyd Baxter (owner of star jumper Tallahassee) to honor the memory of jockey Martin Stukely.

Well, well.

After a while I told Worthington in detail about my visit to Lorna Terrace, Taunton. He frowned when I said, "Didn't you tell me that the bookmaking firm of Arthur Robins, established 1894, was now run by people named Webber and Verity?"

"And the mother and son in Taunton were Verity!" A pause. "It must be a coincidence," he said.

"I don't believe in coincidences like that."

After a while Worthington said, "Gerard, if you have any clear idea of what's going on, what is it? For instance, who were those attackers in black masks last night and what did they want?"

I said, "I think it was one of them who squirted you with cyclopropane and laid me out with the empty cylinder. I don't know who that was. I'm sure, though, that one of the black masks was the fragrant Rose."

"I'm not saying she wasn't, but why?"

"Who else in the world would scream at Norman Osprey—or anyone else, but I'm pretty sure it was him—to break my wrists? Rose's voice is unmistakable. And there is the way she moves. And as for purpose, partly to put me out of business, wouldn't you say? And partly to make me give her what I haven't got. And also to stop me from doing what we're aiming to do today."

Worthington said impulsively, "Let's go home, then."

"You just stay beside me, and we'll be fine."

Worthington took me seriously and bodyguarded like a professional. We confirmed one of the black-mask merchants for certain simply from his stunned reaction to my being there and on my feet. When he saw me, Norman Osprey stopped dead in the middle of setting up his stand, and Rose herself made the mistake of striding up to him at that moment, only to follow his disbelieving gaze and lose a good deal of her self-satisfaction. "Bloody hell," she said.

I said to them jointly, "Tom Pigeon sends his regards."

Neither of them looked overjoyed. Worthington murmured something to me urgently about it not being advisable to poke a wasps' nest with a stick. He also put distance between himself and Arthur Robins, Est. 1894, and I followed.

"They don't know exactly what they're looking for," I pointed out. "If they knew, they would have asked for it by name last night."

"They might have done that anyway if Tom Pigeon hadn't been walking his dogs." Worthington steered us still farther away from Norman Osprey, looking back all the same to make certain we weren't being followed.

My impression of the events of barely fifteen hours earlier was that damage, as well as information, had been the purpose. But if Tom Pigeon hadn't arrived, and if it had been to save my wrist bones, and if I *could* have answered their questions, then would I?

Sore as I already felt all over, I couldn't imagine any piece of knowledge that Martin might have had that he thought was worth my virtual destruction, and I didn't like the probability that they— the black masks—wrongly believed that I did know what they wanted and that I was being merely stubborn in not telling them.

Mordantly I admitted to myself that if I'd known what they wanted, I would quite likely have told them anything to stop them.

Martin, old pal, I thought, what the devil have you let me in for?

LLOYD Baxter lunched at Leicester with the stewards. Our paths crossed between parade ring and stands, and to him the meeting was unexpected. But I'd spotted him early, and Worthington and I had waited through the stewards' roast beef, cheese, and coffee.

Baxter wasn't pleased to see me. I was sure he regretted the whole Broadway evening, but he concentrated hard on being civil, and it was churlish of me, I daresay, to suspect that it was because I knew of his epilepsy. Nowhere in print or chat had his condition been disclosed, and he may have been afraid that I would not only broadcast it but snicker.

Worthington melted temporarily from my side, and I walked with Baxter while he oozed compliments about the steward's lunch and discussed the worth of many trainers, excluding poor old Priam Jones.

I said, "It wasn't his fault that Tallahassee fell at Cheltenham."

I got an acid reply. "He should have schooled him better."

"Well," I reasoned, "that horse had proved he could jump. He'd already won several races."

"I want a different trainer." Lloyd Baxter spoke with obstinacy—a matter of instinct, I saw.

Along with lunch the stewards had given Tallahassee's owner an entry ticket to their guests viewing balcony. At the entrance, Lloyd Baxter was already apologizing for shedding me, when one of the stewards, following us, changed our course.

"Aren't you the glass man?" he boomed genially. "My wife's your greatest fan. That splendid horse you did for her . . . You came to rig its spotlights, didn't you?"

I remembered the horse and the house with enough detail to be invited into the stewards guests viewing balcony, not entirely to Lloyd Baxter's delight.

"This young man's a genius, according to my wife," the steward said to Baxter, ushering us in.

Lloyd Baxter's poor opinion of the steward's wife's judgment was written plain on his heavy features, but perhaps it did eventually influence him, because after the cheering for the next winner had faded, Baxter surprised me by resting his hand lightly on my arm to indicate that I should stay and hear what he felt like telling me. He hesitated still, though, so I gave him every chance.

"I've often wondered," I said mildly, "if you saw who came into my showroom on New Year's Eve. I mean, I know you were ill, but before that, when I'd gone out into the street."

After a long pause he faintly nodded. "Someone came in. I remember he asked for you and I said you were out. But I couldn't see him properly. My sight develops zigzags sometimes."

"You surely have pills."

"Of course I do!" He was irritated. "But I'd forgotten to take them because of the terrible day it had been."

I asked if in spite of the zigzag aura he could describe my unknown visitor.

"No," he said. "The next time I was properly awake, I was in hospital." Then with diffidence he added slowly, "The man who came was thin and had a white beard and was over fifty."

The description sounded highly improbable as a thief, and he must have seen my doubt, because he added, to convince me, that the white-bearded man reminded him chiefly of a university professor. A lecturer.

I asked, "Was he a normal customer? Did he mention glass?"

Lloyd Baxter couldn't remember. "If he spoke at all, I heard him only as a jumble. Quite often things seem wrong to me. They're a sort of warning. Often I can control them a little, or at least prepare, but on that evening it was happening too fast."

He was being extraordinarily frank and trusting, I thought.

"That man with the whisker job," I said. "He must have seen the beginning at least of your . . . er, seizure. So why didn't he help you? Do you think he simply didn't know what to do, or was it he who made off with the money in the canvas bag?"

"And the videotape," Baxter said.

There was an abrupt breath-drawing silence. Then I asked, "What videotape?"

Lloyd Baxter frowned. "He asked for it."

"So you gave it to him?"

"No. Yes. No. I don't know."

It became clear that in fact Lloyd Baxter's memory of that evening was a scrambled egg of order into chaos. It was just unlucky that his fit had struck at the wrong random moment.

We parted, and I found Worthington shivering outside. He announced he was hungry, and accordingly we smelled out some food. While he polished off two full plates of steak-and-kidney pie (his and mine), I told him that we were now looking for a thin man, late middle age, white beard, who looked like a college lecturer.

"So how does this sit with you?" I asked. "Suppose Mr. White-Beard gives a tape to Martin, which Martin gives to Eddie Payne, who handed it on to me. Then when Martin died, Mr. White-Beard decided to take his videotape back again, so he found out the tape would be with me in Broadway. He took it back, and on impulse he also whisked up the bag of money that I'd stupidly left lying around, and in consequence he cannot tell anyone that he has his tape back."

"Because he would be confessing he'd stolen the cash?"

"Dead right."

My bodyguard sighed and scraped his plate clean. "So what happened next?" he said.

"I can only guess."

"Go on, then. Guess. Because it wasn't some old guy that gassed us with that cyclopropane. Young Daniel described the sneakers that the gas man wore, and nobody but a teenager, I think, would be seen dead in them."

I disagreed. Eccentric white beards might wear anything. They might also make erotic tapes. They might also tell someone the tape was worth a fortune and that it was in Gerard Logan's hands. A few little lies. Diversionary tactics. Beat up Logan, make him ready to cough up the tape or whatever information had been on it.

What had Martin been going to give me for safekeeping?

Did I any longer really want to know?

If I didn't know, I couldn't tell. But if they believed I knew and wouldn't tell . . . Damn it, I thought, not knowing was perhaps worse than knowing. So somehow or other, I decided, it wasn't enough to discover who took it; it was essential after all to find out what they expected as well as what they'd actually got.

We walked back to where the serried ranks of bookmakers were shouting their offers for the last race. Rose glared, rigid with a hatred I didn't at that point understand. Being as close to her as a couple of yards gave my outraged skin goose bumps, but I asked again the question she had already refused to answer.

"Who gave a videotape to Martin Stukely at Cheltenham races?"

She answered this time that she didn't know.

I said, "Do you mean you didn't see anyone give Martin a parcel or that you saw the transfer but didn't know the person's name?"

"Clever, aren't you," Rose said sarcastically. "Take your pick."

Rose, I thought, wasn't going to be trapped by words. At a guess she had both seen the transfer and knew the transferer. I said without much hope of being believed, "I don't know where to look for the tape you want. I don't know who took it, and I don't know why. But I haven't got it."

Rose curled her lip.

As we walked away, Worthington sighed deeply with frustration, saying, "You'd think Norman Osprey would be the heavy in Arthur Robins 1894. He has the voice and the build for it. But did you see him looking at Rose? She's the boss. She calls the tune. My low-life investigator finds her very impressive, I'm afraid to say. She hates you. Have you noticed?"

I told him I had indeed noticed. "But I don't know why."

"You'd want a psychiatrist to explain it, but I'll tell you what I've learned. You're a man, you're strong, you look okay, you're successful at your job, and you're not afraid of her; and I could go on, but that's for starters. Then she has you roughed up, doesn't she, and here you are looking as good as new, even if you aren't feeling it, and sticking the finger up in her face, more or less."

I listened to Worthington's wisdom, but I said, "I haven't done her any harm."

"You threaten her. You're too much for her. So maybe she'll have you killed. Don't ignore what I'm telling you. There are people who really have killed for hate. People who've wanted to win."

Not to mention murders because of racism or religious prejudice, I thought, but it was hard to imagine it applying to oneself.

I expected that Rose would have told Eddie Payne, her father, that I was at the races, but she hadn't. Worthington and I lay in wait for him after the last race when he came out of the changing rooms. He wasn't happy. He looked from one to the other of us like a cornered horse. I soothingly said, "Hi, Eddie. How's things?"

"I don't know anything I haven't told you," he protested.

I thought if I cast him a few artificial flies, I might startle and hook an unexpected fish. "Were you with Rose yesterday evening?"

I asked the question casually, but he knew instantly what I meant.

"I didn't lay a finger on you," he said quickly. "It wasn't me." He looked from me to Worthington and back again. "Look," he said wheedlingly, as if begging for forgiveness, "they didn't give you a chance. I told Rose it wasn't fair. . . ." He wavered to a stop.

With interest I asked, "Do you mean that you wore a black mask in Broadway yesterday evening?" and almost with incredulity saw in his face an expression of shame that he had.

"Rose said we would just frighten you." He stared at me with unhappy eyes. "I tried to stop her, honest."

"So there was you and Rose." I said it matter-of-factly, though stunned beneath. "And Norman Osprey, and who else? One of Norman Osprey's bookmaking clerks, was it?"

"No. Not them." Horror suddenly closed his mouth. He had already admitted far too much.

I tried another fly. "Do you know anyone who could lay their hands on anesthetics?"

A blank.

"Or anyone with a white beard, known to Martin?"

He hesitated over that, but in the end shook his head.

I said, "Do you yourself know anyone with a white beard who looks like a university lecturer?"

"No." His reply was positive, his manner shifty.

"Was the brown-paper parcel you gave me at Cheltenham the selfsame one that Martin gave you earlier in the day?"

"Yes." He nodded this time with no need for thought. "It was the same one. Rose was furious. She said we should have kept it ourselves and then there wouldn't have been all this fuss."

"Did Rose know what was in it?"

"Only Martin knew for sure. I did more or less ask him. He just laughed and said the future of the world, but it was a joke, of course."

Martin's joke sounded to me too real to be funny.

Eddie hadn't finished. "A couple of weeks before Christmas," he said, still amused, "Martin and a few of the jockeys were talking about presents for their wives and girlfriends. Martin said that what he was giving Bon-Bon was a gold-and-glass antique necklace, but he was laughing, and he said he would have to get you to make him a much cheaper and modern copy. He said you had a videotape to tell you how. But next minute he changed his mind because Bon-Bon wanted new fur-lined boots."

"He talked to you a lot," I commented. "More than most."

Eddie didn't think so. "He liked to chat with the boys," he said.

Worthington, driving us home, summed up the day's haul of information. "I'd say Martin and the white-bearded guy were serious with this tape. And somehow or other, through her father, Rose may have imagined that that tape showed how to make an antique necklace."

I said doubtfully, "It must be more than that."

"Well, perhaps it says where the necklace can be found."

"A treasure hunt?" I shook my head. "There's only one valuable antique gold-and-glass necklace that I know of, and I do know a fair amount about antique glass, and it's in a museum. It's priceless. It was probably designed in Crete sometime about three thousand five hundred years ago. It's called the Cretan Sunrise. I did make a copy of it, though, and I once lent it to Martin. I also made a videotape to explain the methods I used. I lent that to Martin too. Heaven knows where it is now."

"What if there's another tape?" Worthington asked. "Rose could have muddled them up."

I thought it just as likely that it was Worthington and I who'd muddled everything up.

We arrived safely at Bon-Bon's house. As we scrunched to a halt on her gravel drive, Marigold came out of the front door to greet us. "Bon-Bon doesn't need me anymore," she announced dramatically. "Get out the maps, Worthington. We're going skiing."

"Er . . . when?" her chauffeur asked, unsurprised.

"Tomorrow. We'll call at Paris on the way. I need new clothes."

Worthington looked more resigned than I felt. He murmured to me that the skiing trip would last less than ten days overall. She would tire of it quickly and come home.

Bon-Bon was taking the news of her mother's departure with well-hidden relief and asked me with hope whether "the upsetting videotape business" was now concluded. She wanted calm in her life, but I had no idea if she would get it.

I asked Bon-Bon about White Beard. She said she'd never seen or heard of him. When I explained who he was, she telephoned to Priam Jones, who—though his self-esteem was badly hurt by Lloyd Baxter's ditching of him—regretted he couldn't help.

Bon-Bon tried several more trainers, but thin, elderly, white-bearded owners of racehorses seemed not to exist. After she'd tired of it, she persuaded her mother to let Worthington take me where I wanted. I kissed her gratefully and chose to go straight home to my hillside house and flop.

Worthington liked skiing, he said as we drove away. Sorry, he said, about leaving me with Rose. Good luck, he said cheerfully.

"I could throttle you," I said.

While Worthington happily chuckled at the wheel, I switched on my mobile phone to call Irish to find out how the day had gone in the shop, but before I could dial, the message service called, and the disembodied voice of young Victor W. V. said in my ear, "Send your e-mail address to me at vicv@freenet.com."

Well, I thought, Victor had things to say. Flopping could wait. The only computer I owned that handled e-mail was in Broadway. Worthington changed direction, at length stopping by my main glass door and insisting he come in with me to check the place for black masks and other pests. The place was empty. No Rose in wait. Worthington told me to look after myself and left lightheartedly.

Almost at once I missed him, my safety umbrella.

I roused my sleeping computer into action and sent an e-mail message to Victor, with my address. He replied almost immediately, which meant he had been sitting at his computer. "Who are you?" he asked.

I typed and sent, "Martin Stukely's friend."

He asked, "Name," and I told him.

"How did you know Martin?" I asked.

"I've known him for years, saw him often at the races with my granddad."

I wrote, "Why did you send that letter to him? How had you heard of any tape? Please tell me the truth."

"I heard my aunt telling my mother."

"How did your aunt know?"

"My aunt knows everything."

I began to lose faith in his common sense, and I remembered him saying he was playing a game.

"What is your aunt's name?" I expected nothing much, certainly not the breathtaker that came back.

"My aunt's name is Rose. She keeps changing her last name. She's my mother's sister." There was barely an interval before his next remark. "I'd better log off now. She's just come!"

"Wait." Stunned by that revelation, I rapidly typed, "Do you know of a thin old man with a white beard?"

A long time after I'd settled for no answer, these words appeared. "Dr. Force. Good-bye."

Chapter Five

TO MY considerable delight Catherine Dodd again stood her motorbike by my curb. She pulled off her helmet before walking inside. It seemed natural to us both to kiss hello and for her to stand in front of the soaring flight of wings that I had barely finished lighting.

"It's tremendous." She meant it. "It's too good for Broadway."

"Flattery will get you an awfully long way," I assured her, and took her into the workshop, where it was warmest.

I showed her the printout of my e-mail conversation with Victor. When she'd finished reading it, she said, "First of all, remind me, who is Victor?"

"The fifteen-year-old grandson of Eddie Payne, Martin Stukely's racetrack valet. Eddie gave me the videotape that was stolen from here. Victor sent this letter to Martin." I gave her the letter to read, which raised her eyebrows in doubt.

"Victor said he was playing games," I acknowledged. "He's done what everyone does at some point—he's heard one thing and thought it meant another."

I stopped to make us coffee, then continued. "Suppose that this Dr. Force has somehow got to know Martin. Dr. Force has some information he wants to put into safekeeping, so he takes it to Cheltenham races and gives it to Martin."

"Crazy." Catherine sighed. "Why didn't he put it in a bank?"

"We'll have to ask him."

"And you are crazy too. How do we find him?"

"It's you," I pointed out, smiling, "that is the police officer."

"Well, I'll try." She smiled back. "And what then?"

"Then Dr. Force went to the races as planned. He gave his tape to Martin. After Martin crashed, our Dr. Force must have gone through a lot of doubt and worry, and I'd guess he stood around near the changing rooms wondering what to do. Then he saw Eddie Payne give the tape in its brown-paper parcel to me, and he knew it was the right tape, as he'd packed it himself."

"So okay, Dr. Force finds out who you are, takes himself here to Broadway, and when you leave your door unlocked for a spell, he nips in and takes back his own tape."

"Right."

"And steals your cash on impulse."

"Right."

"So who squirted anesthetic at the Stukelys and took their TVs, and who ransacked your own house and beat you up last night? And I don't really understand how this boy Victor got involved."

"I can't answer everything, but think Rose. She is Eddie Payne's daughter and Victor's aunt. I think she's on the edge of criminal. She jumps a bit to conclusions, and she's all the more dangerous for that. I'd guess it was she who stole all the videotapes in Bon-Bon's house and mine because they could possibly have been mixed up with the one I brought from the racetrack. I would think it likely that Rose chatters to her sister, Victor's mother, quite a lot, and I think it's fairly certain that Victor did overhear her when she said she knew of a tape worth a fortune."

If only Martin had explained what he was doing! There was too much guesswork and definitely too much Rose.

Sighing, Catherine gave me back Victor's printout and stood up, saying with apparent reluctance, "I have to go. I've promised to be with my parents tonight. I was wondering, though, that if you by any chance want to go to your house now, you—um—don't need a license to ride pillion."

I strapped on her spare helmet, clasped her close around her waist, and we set off. The bike had guts enough to take us up the hills without stuttering, and she was laughing when she stopped by the weedy entrance to my drive. I thanked her for the ride, and she roared off, still laughing.

There were no thorny briar Roses lying in wait this time. It seemed that the house gave back in peace the years the Logan family had prospered there, father, mother, and two sons. I was the only one left, and with its ten rooms still filled with sharp memories, I'd made no move to find a smaller or more suitable lair. One day, perhaps.

I walked deliberately through all the rooms thinking of Catherine, wondering if she would like the place.

The burglars who'd taken all my videotapes hadn't made a lot of mess. There had been television sets with video recorders in three rooms: in the kitchen and in each of the sitting rooms. There wasn't a single tape left anywhere that I could find. Out of my own room I'd lost a rather precious bunch of glassblowing instruction tapes that I'd been commissioned to make for university courses. They mostly dealt with how to make scientific equipment for laboratories. I couldn't imagine those teaching tapes being the special target of any thief.

With the Rose-induced bruises growing gradually less sore, I slept safely behind bolted doors.

In the morning, at Logan Glass, I felt relief that someone hadn't managed to smash the soaring wings overnight. I made a fleet of little ornamental sailing ships and straightened out the worst of Hickory's growing hubris by giving him a sailing boat as an exercise, which resulted in a heap of sad lumps of stunted mast and mainsail.

Hickory's good looks and air of virility would always secure him jobs he couldn't do. I'd learned more of his limitations than his skills, but every customer liked him, and he was a great salesman.

As Hickory's third try bit the dust, the telephone interrupted us. It was Catherine. "I've been a police officer all morning," she said, "and I've collected some news for you. I'll be along when I go off duty, at six o'clock."

To fill in time, I e-mailed Victor, expecting to have to wait for a reply, as he should have been at school, but as before, he was ready.

He typed, "Things have changed."

"Tell me."

There was a long gap of several minutes. Then, "My dad's in jail. I hate her."

I asked flatly, "Who?"

"Auntie Rose, of course. She sneaked on Dad." I waited. "He hit Mom. Broke her nose and some ribs. He got sent down for a year. Will you go on talking to me?"

"Yes," I sent back. "Of course."

After an even longer pause, he sent, "E-mail me tomorrow," and I replied fast, while he might still be on-line, "Tell me about Dr. Force."

Either he'd disconnected or didn't want to reply. His silence lasted all day.

By six I'd managed to send my assistants all home, and by six plus twenty-three Detective Constable Dodd was reading Victor Waltman Verity's troubles. "Poor boy," she said.

I said ruefully, "As he hates his aunt Rose for grassing on his pa, he might not tell me anything else himself. Sneaking appears to be a mortal sin in his book."

"*Mm.*" She read the printed pages again, then cheerfully said, "Well, whether or not you have Victor's help, your Dr. Force is definitely on the map." It pleased her to have found him. "He's not a university lecturer, or not primarily, anyway. He is, believe it or not, a medical doctor. Licensed and all that." She handed me an envelope with a grin. "He was working in some research lab or other until recently. It's all in this envelope."

"And is he fiftyish with a white beard?"

She laughed. "His date of birth will be in the envelope. A white beard's expecting too much."

Both of us at that point found that there were more absorbing facets to life than chasing obscure medics. I suggested food from the takeout; she offered a pillion ride up the hill. We saw to both. Catherine wandered all over the house, smiling.

I still held the envelope of Dr. Force details, and I opened it then with hope, but it told me very few useful facts. His name was Adam Force, age fifty-six, and his qualifications came by the dozen.

I said blankly, "Is that all?"

"That's all when it comes to facts. As to hearsay—well, according to a bunch of rumors, he's a brilliant researcher."

I asked, "Does Dr. Force have an address?"

"Not in these notes," she answered; however, she knew all about the Internet. The next morning, she decided, we could catch him on the Web.

We ate the takeout food, or a little of it, owing to a change of appetite, and I switched up the heating a little in my bedroom without any need for explanation.

She'd shed somewhere in her life whatever she had ever suffered in the way of shyness. The Catherine who came into my bed came with confidence along with modesty, an intoxicating combination.

The speed of development of strong feelings for one another seemed to me to be not shocking but natural, and if I thought about the future, it unequivocally included Catherine Dodd.

She went home before dawn, steady on two wheels. From my doorway I watched her go into what was left of the night and quite fiercely wanted her to stay with me instead.

I walked restlessly downhill through the slow January dawn, reaching the workshop well before the others. The Internet, though, when I'd accessed it, proved less obliging about Adam Force than the address of Waltman Verity in Taunton. Adam Force wasn't anywhere in sight.

Hickory arrived at that point, early and eager to take his precious sailboat out of the Lehr annealing oven. Although he would get the transparent colors clearer with practice, it wasn't a bad effort, and I told him so. He wasn't pleased, however. He wanted unqualified praise. I caught on his face a fleeting expression of contempt for my lack of proper appreciation of his ability. There would be trouble ahead if he tackled really difficult stuff, I thought, but I would give him good references when he looked for a different teacher, as quite soon now he would.

Irish, more humble about his skills, and Pamela Jane, twittery and positively self-deprecating, came sweeping in together in the cold morning and gave the sailboat the extravagant admiration Hickory thought it deserved.

We spent the day replacing the minaret-shaped scent bottles we'd sold at Christmas, working fast at eight pieces an hour, using blue, turquoise, pink, green, white, and purple in turn and packing the finished articles in rows in the ovens to cool. Winter in the Cotswold Hills was the time to stock up for the summer tourists.

We worked flat out until six in the evening. Then with all six ovens packed, I sent my semi-exhausted crew home.

Every night that week Catherine slept in my arms in my bed, but she left before the general world awoke, and during that time no one managed to stick an address on Adam Force.

On Friday morning Catherine departed as promised to a school friends' reunion, and at close of day Bon-Bon drove Martin's BMW, bursting at the seams with noisy children, to pick me up for the weekend. "Actually," Bon-Bon confessed as we detoured to my hill house for mundane clean shirts and socks, "Worthington didn't like you being out here alone."

"*Worthington* didn't?"

"No. He phoned from somewhere south of Paris and specially told me this place of yours out here is asking for trouble."

"Worthington exaggerated," I protested, but after we'd all unloaded at Bon-Bon's house, I used the evening there to invent a game for the children to compete in, a game called "hunt the orange cylinder and the shoelaces."

Bon-Bon protested. "But they told everything they know to the police. They won't find anything useful."

"And after that game," I said, gently ignoring her, "we'll play 'hunt the letters sent to Daddy by somebody called Force,' and there are prizes for every treasure found, of course."

They played until bedtime with enthusiasm, on account of the regular handouts of coins, and I laid out their final offerings all over Martin's desk in the den.

Their haul was in some ways spectacular. Perhaps most perplexing was the original of the letter Victor had sent a copy of to Martin. "Dear Martin," it said, and continued word for word as far as the signature, which didn't say Victor Waltman Verity in computer print, but was scrawled in real live handwriting, "Adam Force."

"The kids found that letter in a secret drawer in Martin's desk," Bon-Bon said.

I told her the so-called secret drawer wasn't a secret at all, but was a built-in feature of the modern desk, designed to hold a laptop computer. I found the laptop drawer seething with interest. Apart from Force's letter to Martin, there was a photocopy of Martin's letter to Force, a not much longer affair than the brief reply. It ran:

Dear Adam Force,

I have now had time to consider the matter of your formulae and methods. Please will you go ahead and record these onto the videotape as you suggested and take it to Cheltenham races on New Year's Eve. Give it to me there, whenever you see me, except, obviously, not when I'm on my way out to race.

Martin Stukely

I stared not just at the letter but at its implications.

Daniel looked over my shoulder and asked what formulae were. "Are they secrets?" he said.

"Sometimes." But what secrets?

Alone in the den after Bon-Bon and the children had gone upstairs, I sorted through everything in the drawer. There were several old checkbooks with sums written on the stubs but quite often not dates or payees. Martin must have driven his accountant crazy.

Semi-miracles occasionally happen, though, and on one stub, dated November 1999 (no actual day), I came across the name Force. On the line below, there was the single word BELLOWS, and in the box for the amount of money being transferred out of the account there were three zeros, 000, with no whole numbers and no decimal points.

The name Force appeared again on a memo pad. Martin's handwritten scrawl said, "Force, Bristol, Wednesday."

I went back to the drawer. A loose-leaf notebook, the most methodically kept of Martin's untidy paperwork, listed, with dates, amounts he gave to Eddie Payne, his racetrack valet.

On the first page Martin had doodled the names of Eddie Payne, Rose Payne, Gina Verity, and Victor. In a box in a corner, behind straight heavy bars, he'd written Waltman. There were small sketches of Eddie in his apron, Gina in her curlers, Victor with his computer, and Rose—Rose had a halo of spikes.

Martin had known this family, I reflected. When he had received the letter from Victor, he would have known it was a fifteen-year-old's game. Looking back, I could see I hadn't asked the right questions, because I'd been starting from the wrong assumptions.

I lolled in Martin's chair, both mourning him and wishing that he could come back alive just for five minutes.

My mobile phone, lying on the desk, gave out its brisk summons. Hoping it was Catherine, I switched it on. It wasn't Catherine.

Victor's cracked voice spoke hurriedly.

"Can you come to Taunton on Sunday? Please say you will catch the same train as before. I'm running out of money for this phone. Please say yes."

I listened to the urgency, to the virtual panic.

I said, "Yes, okay," and the line went dead.

Chapter Six

TOM Pigeon strolled to my gallery door late on Saturday morning and invited me out for a beer. With his Dobermans quietly tied to a bench outside the crowded dark pub, he drank deep on a pint and told me that I had more nerve than sense when it came to the Verity-Paynes.

"It was only a week ago tomorrow," he said, "that they hammered you until you could hardly stand."

I thanked him for my deliverance.

He urged me to take him on board as bodyguard in Worthington's absence.

I reflected briefly on Tom's offer. His slightly piratical dark little pointed beard and his obvious physical strength turned heads our way. I might be of his age and height, but no one sidled away at my approach or found me an instinctive threat.

I wondered what my dear constable Dodd would think of my allying myself to an ex–jail occupant with a nickname like Backlash. I said regardless, "Yes, if you'll do what I ask."

"Just as long as it's legal," he bargained. "I'm not going back in the slammer."

"It's legal," I assured him. And when I caught the train the following morning, I had a new rear defender in the baggage car, accompanied by three of the most dangerous-looking black dogs that ever licked one's fingers.

Tom had wanted to drive. I shook my head. Suppose, I'd suggested, this is not an ambush, but just the frantic need of a worried boy. Give him a chance, I'd said.

We would compromise, though. We would rent a car with driver to follow us from Taunton station, to shadow us faithfully, to pick us up when we wanted and finally drive us home.

Victor himself was waiting on the Taunton platform. I'd traveled near the front of the train so as to be able to spot and to pass any little unwelcoming committee, but the boy seemed to be alone. Also, I thought, anxious. Also cold. Beyond that, an enigma.

Tom's dogs, traveling at the rear of the train, slithered down onto the platform. I reckoned, or anyway hoped, that Victor himself wouldn't know Tom or his dogs by sight, even though Rose and the rest of her family probably would, after their rout in Broadway.

Learning from the plainclothes police, I wore a baseball cap at the currently with-it angle above a navy-blue tracksuit topped with a paler blue sleeveless padded jacket. Normal enough for many but different from my usual gray pants and white shirt.

I walked silently in my sneakers to Victor's back and said quietly in his ear, "Hello."

He whirled around and took in my changed appearance with surprise, but chief of his emotions seemed to be straightforward relief that I was there at all.

"I was afraid you wouldn't come," he said. "Not when I heard them saying how they'd smashed you up proper. I don't know what to do. They tell me lies." He was shaking slightly with nervousness.

"First of all, we get off this windy platform," I said. "Then you tell me where your mother thinks you are."

In front of the station, the driver I'd engaged was polishing a dark blue station wagon. Tom Pigeon made contact with the driver and loaded the Dobermans into the rear.

Victor, not yet realizing that the car and dogs had anything to do with him, answered my question and a dozen others. "Mom thinks I'm at home. She's gone to see my dad in jail. It's visiting day. I listened to her and Auntie Rose planning how they're going to try again, after Mom sees Dad, to make you tell them where the tape is you had from Granddad Payne. They say it's worth millions. Auntie Rose says it's nonsense for you to say you don't know. Please tell her where it is or what's on it, because I can't bear her making people tell her things. I've heard them twice up in our attic screaming and groaning, and she just laughs and says they have toothache."

I turned away from Victor so that he shouldn't see the absolute horror that flooded my mind and assuredly appeared on my face. Just the idea of Rose using teeth for torture melted at once any thought of resistance I might have had.

I felt an intensified need to find out what secrets I was supposed to know and then to decide what to do with the knowledge. Victor, I thought, might be able to dig from the semiconscious depths of his memory the scraps I still needed if I were to glue together a credible whole. I had pieces. Not enough.

I asked with an inward shudder, "Where is your auntie Rose today? Did she too visit your dad?"

"I don't know where she is." He paused and then said passionately, "I wish I belonged to an ordinary family. I wrote to Martin once and begged to stay with him for a while, but he said they didn't have room." His voice cracked. "What can I do?"

It seemed clear that Victor's need for someone to advise him stretched very far back.

"Come for a ride?" I suggested with friendliness, and held open the car door behind the driver. "I'll get you back home before you're missed, and before that we can talk about what you need."

He hesitated only briefly, then climbed in. He had, after all, brought me there to help him, reaching out to someone he trusted, even though his family considered that person to be an enemy. Victor couldn't invent or act at this level of desperation.

I asked him if he knew where I could find Adam Force. The question caused a much longer hesitation and a shake of the head. He knew, I thought, but perhaps telling me came under the category of squealing.

Tom Pigeon sat beside the driver. Victor and I sat in the rear passenger seats with the dogs behind us, separated from us by a netting divider. The driver set off through winding Somerset country roads to the wide expanses of Exmoor. Even in the summer, I imagined, it would be a bare and daunting place. The driver had brought a packed picnic lunch for all of us, as I had arranged. He pulled off the road into a parking area and pointed to a just perceptible path ahead, telling me it led onto trackless moorland.

He would wait for us, he said, and we could take our time.

Tom Pigeon's dogs disembarked and bounded free ecstatically, sniffing with unimaginable joy around heather roots in rich dark red earth. Tom himself stretched his arms and chest wide, filling his lungs with deep breaths of clean air, and set off fast along the track.

Under wide-open sky Victor's face looked almost carefree, almost happy. He and I followed Tom, with Victor pouring out his devastating home life and difficulties, as I guessed he'd never done before.

"Mom's all right," he said. "So's Dad really, except when he comes home from the pub. Then if Mom or I get too near him, he belts us one." He swallowed. "No, I didn't mean to say that. But last time he broke her ribs and her nose. And when Auntie Rose saw it, she went to the cops, and it was funny, really, because other times I'd seen *her* hit my dad. She's got fists like a boxer when she gets going. She can deal it out until the poor buggers beg her to stop, and that's when she laughs at them. And then sometimes she'll *kiss* them." He glanced at me anxiously, sideways, to see what I made of his aunt Rose's behavior.

I thought that possibly I'd got off fairly lightly at the hands of the black masks.

We walked another length of track while I thought how little I understood of the psychology of women like Rose. Men who enjoyed being beaten by women weren't the sort that attracted Rose. For her to be fulfilled, they had to hate it.

The ground widened into a broader flat area from which one could see distant views. Tom Pigeon stood out below us, his Dobermans zigzagging around him with unfettered joy.

After watching them for several moments, I gave life to an ear-splitting whistle, a skill taught me by my father and brother, who had both been able to summon taxis in London in the rain.

Tom turned toward me, waved acknowledgment, and began to return to where I stood. His dogs aimed toward me without a single degree of deviation.

"Wow," Victor said, impressed. "How do you do that?"

"Curl your tongue." I showed him how, and I asked him again

to tell me more about Dr. Force. I needed to talk to him, I said.

"Who?"

"You know damn well who. Dr. Adam Force. The man who wrote the letter you copied and sent to Martin."

Victor, silenced, took a while to get going again.

In the end he said, "Martin knew it was a game."

"Yes, I'm sure he did," I agreed. "He knew you well, he knew Adam Force, and Adam Force knows you. You may know their secret, that one that was on the tape everyone's talking about."

"No," Victor said, "I don't."

"Don't lie," I told him. "You don't like liars."

He said indignantly, "I'm not lying. Martin knew what was on the tape, and so did Dr. Force, of course. When I sent that letter to Martin, I was just pretending to be Dr. Force. I often pretended to be other people. It's only a game."

I asked him how he had obtained a copy of Dr. Force's letter, which he had sent to Martin with his own name attached instead of Force's.

He didn't reply, but just shrugged his shoulders.

I asked him yet again if he knew where I could find his Dr. Force, but he said dubiously that Martin had for sure written it down somewhere.

Probably he had. Victor knew where, but he still wasn't telling that either. There had to be some way of bringing him to the point of wanting to tell.

Tom Pigeon and his three bouncing companions reached us. "That's some whistle," Tom commented admiringly, so I did it again at maximum loudness, which stunned the dogs into pointing their muzzles in my direction, their noses twitching, their eyes alert.

Walking back toward the car, Victor did his best at a whistle that would equally affect the dogs, but they remained unimpressed.

Tom, Victor, the driver, and I ate sandwiches inside the car, out of the wind, and afterward sleep came easily to the other three. I left the car and walked back slowly along the track, sorting out Victor's muddling game of pretense. The absolutely first thing to do, I concluded, was to find Adam Force, and the path to him still lay with Victor. What I needed was to get him to trust me.

When there was movement around the car, I returned to tell the yawning passengers that it was time to leave if we were to get back to Lorna Terrace in advance of Gina, Victor's mom.

Tom walked off to find comfort behind bushes and jerked his head for me to go with him. Contingency planning was in his mind.

We considered a few "what ifs" together, then returned to the car, where the driver had taken a liking to Victor and was deep in esoteric chat about computers.

The contentment of the day on the moor slowly evaporated as the station wagon drew nearer to Lorna Terrace. Victor watched me anxiously.

The driver stopped the car where Tom Pigeon asked him, which was around the bend that kept him out of sight of Number 19. Victor and I disembarked, and I sympathized very much with the misery and hopelessness reappearing in the droop of his shoulders.

At the front door of Number 19, Victor produced a key from a pocket and let us in, leading me as before to the bright little kitchen. I had promised to stay as company until his mother came back, even though she might not like it.

The door from the kitchen to the backyard brought Victor to a standstill of puzzlement and unease.

He said, "I'm sure I bolted the door before I went out." He shrugged. "Anyway, I know I bolted that gate from the backyard into the lane. Mom gets furious if I forget it."

He opened the unbolted kitchen door and stepped out into a small high-walled square of backyard. Across the weeds and dead-looking grass a tall brown-painted gate was set into the high brick wall, and it was this gate that freshly upset Victor by not having its bolts, top and bottom, firmly slid into place.

"Bolt them now," I said urgently, but Victor stood still in dismay, and although understanding flashed like lightning through my mind, I couldn't get around Victor fast enough. The gate from the lane opened the moment I stepped toward it.

Rose had come into the backyard from the lane. Gina and the quasi gorilla Norman Osprey marched out triumphantly from the house. Both Rose and Osprey were armed with a cutoff section of garden hose. Rose's piece had a tap on it.

Victor at my side stood like a rock, not wanting to believe what he was seeing. When he spoke, the words addressed to his mother were a scramble of, "You've come back early."

Rose prowled like a hunting lioness between me and the gate to the lane, swinging the heavy brass tap on the supple green hose, and almost licking her lips.

Gina, without curlers this time and pretty as a result, tried to justify the prospect ahead by whining to Victor that his caged father had told her to bug off, he wasn't in the mood for her chatter.

"And when we'd gone all that way!" Gina said. "He's a mean brute. So Rose drove me home again. And you met that fellow, that one over there, that Rose says is stealing a million from us. How *can* you, young Vic? So Rose says this time she'll make him tell us what we want to know, but it's no thanks to you, Rose says."

I heard only some of it. I watched Victor's face and saw with relief his strong alienation from Gina's smug voice. The more she said, the more he didn't like it. Teenage rebellion visibly grew.

The present and future scene here hadn't been exactly one of the "what ifs" that Tom and I had imagined in the bushes, but now what if—if I could think it out fast enough, if I could use Victor's horrified reaction to his mother's outpouring, if I could put up with a bit of Rose's persuasion—then perhaps Victor would indeed feel like telling me what I was sure he knew. Perhaps the sight of his aunt Rose's cruelty in action would impel him to offer a gift in atonement. Maybe the prize was worth a bit of discomfort. So get on with it, I told myself.

Last Sunday, I thought, the black masks had jumped me unawares. It was different this Sunday. I could invite the assault head-on, and I did, at a run toward the gate to the lane, straight toward Rose and her swinging tap.

She was fast and ruthless and managed to connect twice before I caught her right arm and bent it up behind her, her face close to mine, her dry skin and freckles in sharp focus, hate and sudden pain drawing her lips back from her teeth. Gina, yelling blasphemy, tore at my ear to free her sister.

I caught a glimpse of Victor's horror an instant before Norman Osprey lashed out at me from behind with his own length of hose. Rose wrenched herself out of my grip, pushed Gina out of her way, and had another swing at me with her tap. I managed a circular kickbox that temporarily put the gorilla Norman facedown on the grass, and in return I got another fearful clout from Rose along the jaw, which ripped the open skin.

Enough, I thought. Too much. Blood dripped everywhere. I used my only real weapon, the piercing whistle, for help, which Tom and I in the bushes had agreed meant "come at once."

What if I whistle and he doesn't come?

I whistled again, louder, longer, calling not for a taxi in the rain, but quite likely for life without deformity. There was a vast crashing noise and Tom's voice roaring at his dogs, and then three snarling Doberman pinschers poured like a torrent out of the house's wide-opening kitchen door into the confined space of the backyard.

Tom carried a tire iron. Osprey backed away, his soft hose useless in opposition, his Sunday pleasure no longer one long laugh.

Rose, the quarry of the dogs, turned tail and ignominiously left the scene through the gate into the lane, pulling it shut behind her.

Gina screeched at Tom only once, his fierce physical closeness reducing her protests to nil. She was silent even when she discovered Tom's mode of entry had been to smash open her front door. She didn't try to stop her son when he ran past her along the passage from backyard to front. He called to me in the few steps before I reached the road.

Tom and the Dobermans were already out on the sidewalk on their way back to the car.

I stopped at once when Victor called me, and I waited. Either he would tell me or he wouldn't. Either the hose and tap had been worth it, or they hadn't. Payoff time.

"Gerard . . ." He was out of breath, not from running but from what he'd seen in the yard. "I can't bear all this. If you want to know, Dr. Force lives in Lynton. Valley of Rocks Road."

"Thanks," I said.

Victor unhappily watched me use tissues scrounged from his mother's kitchen to blot the blood on my face. I said, "There's always e-mail, don't forget."

"How can you even speak to me?"

I grinned at him. "I still have all my teeth."

"Look out for Rose," he warned. "She never gives up."

"Try to arrange to live with your grandfather," I suggested. "It would be safer than here."

Some of his misery abated. I touched his shoulder in parting and walked along Lorna Terrace to where Tom Pigeon waited.

Tom looked at my battered face. "You were a long time whistling."

"Mm." I smiled. "Silly of me."

"You delayed it on purpose!" he exclaimed in revelation. "You let that harpy hit you."

"You get what you pay for, on the whole," I said.

ON MONDAY I got a doctor to stick together the worst of the cuts with small adhesive strips.

"I suppose you walked into another black-masked door," guessed Constable Dodd, horrified.

"Rose didn't bother about a mask," I said, putting together a spicy rice supper on Monday evening in my kitchen. "Do you like garlic?"

"Not much. What are you planning to do about Rose Payne?"

I didn't answer directly. I said instead, "Tomorrow I'm going to Lynton in Devon, and I'd rather she didn't know. It's a wise man as knows his enemies," I asserted, "and I do know our Rose."

"But Rose Payne is only one person. There were four black masks, you said."

I nodded. "Norman Osprey, bookmaker, he was number two, and Eddie Payne, racetrack valet and Rose's father, he was number three and he's sorry for it, and all those three know I recognized them. One other, number four, seemed familiar to me at the time, but I can't have been right. He was a clutcher setting me up for the others. He was behind me most of the time."

Catherine listened in silence and seemed to be waiting.

Skidding now and then across a half-formed recollection went the so far unidentified figure. I remembered him most for the inhumanity he took to his task. It had been Norman Osprey who'd smashed my watch, but it had been Blackmask Four who'd bunched my fingers for him. In retrospect it was Blackmask Four who'd scared me most, and who now, eight days later, intruded fearsomely in my dreams, nightmares in which he intended to throw me into the liquid glass in the furnace.

That night, while Constable Dodd slept peacefully in my arms, it was she whom Blackmask Four threw to a burning death.

I awoke on Tuesday sweating and cursing Rose Payne with words I'd rarely used before.

"Come back safe this time," Catherine said worriedly before zooming off in the dawn.

Later in the day, following Tom Pigeon's plan for an exit, I walked out of the village for a mile to catch a bus. I felt, when I disembarked outside a busy newsstand in the next town and climbed into another prearranged car with driver—"call me Jim"—that there could be no one on my tail.

Thanks to Tom's plan I arrived unmolested in Lynton on the north Devon coast. In the town hall I found the full address of Dr. Adam Force, in the Valley of Rocks Road. There was no one home at the tall gray old building. The neighbors weren't helpful. But one said he thought Dr. Force had patients in the Phoenix House nursing home whom he visited on Tuesdays.

I thanked the man for his help. And could he describe Dr. Force, so I would know him if I saw him?

"Oh yes," I was told, "you'd know him easily. He has very blue eyes and a short white beard, and he's wearing orange socks."

I blinked.

"He can't see red or green," he said. "He's color-blind."

I TOOK THE QUIET BACK WAY up a sloping carriage road. The Phoenix House complex spread wide in one central block with two long wings. The entrance hall looked like a hotel, but I saw no farther into the nursing home's depths because of the two white-coated people leaning on the reception desk. One was female, and the other grew a white beard and did indeed wear orange socks.

They glanced briefly my way as I arrived. "Dr. Force?" I tried, and White Beard satisfactorily answered, "Yes?"

His fifty-six years sat elegantly on his shoulders, and his well-brushed hair, along with the beard, gave the sort of shape to his head that actors got paid for. Patients would trust him, I thought. His manner held authority. I was going to have difficulty jolting him the way I wanted.

Almost at once I saw, too, that the difficulty was not a matter of jolting him but of following the ins and outs of his mind. All through the time I was with him, I felt him swing from apparently genuine friendliness to evasion and stifled ill will. He was quick and he was clever, and although most of the time I felt a warm liking for him, occasionally there was a quick flash of antipathy.

"Sir," I said, giving seniority its due, "I'm here on account of Martin Stukely."

He put on a sorry-to-tell-you expression and told me that Martin Stukely was dead. At the same time there was a rigidity of shock on his facial muscles. I said I knew Martin Stukely was dead.

He asked with suspicion, "Are you a journalist?"

"No. A glassblower." I added my name. "Gerard Logan."

His whole body stiffened. He absorbed the surprise and eventually pleasantly asked, "What do you want?"

I said equally without threat, "I'd quite like back the videotape you took from the Logan Glass showroom on New Year's Eve."

"You would, would you?" He was recovering his poise. "I don't know what you are talking about."

Dr. Force made a slow survey from head to foot of my deliberately conservative suit and tie, wondering if I had enough clout to cause him trouble. Apparently he gave himself an unwelcome answer, as he suggested that we discuss the situation in the open air.

He led the way to a path with close-growing evergreens crowding overhead, making it dark even in daylight.

Should he be aware of small damages to my face and so on, I said, it was as a result of Rose Payne being convinced that I either had his tape or that I knew what was on it. "She believes that if she's unpleasant enough, I'll give her the tape or the knowledge, neither of which I have." I paused and said, "What do you suggest?"

He said, "Give this person anything. All tapes are alike."

"She thinks your tape is worth a million. Is it?"

Force said what sounded like the truth. "I don't know."

"Martin Stukely," I murmured without hostility, "wrote a check for you with a lot of zeros on it."

Force, very upset, said sharply, "He promised never to say—"

"He didn't say. He left check stubs."

I could almost feel him wondering, What else did Martin leave?

"Rose Payne," I said distinctly, "is convinced I know where your videotape is and what's on it. Unless you find a way of getting her off my back, I may tell her what she's anxious to know."

"Are you implying that I know this person, Rose, and that I am in some way responsible for your, er, injuries?"

I said cheerfully, "Right both times."

"That's nonsense." His face was full of calculation, as if he weren't sure how to deal with an awkward situation.

"All the same," I said, "you did take the tape from my shop, so please can you at least tell me where it is now?"

He relaxed at my change of tone and answered the question unsatisfactorily. "Just suppose you are right and I have the tape. Perhaps I ran it through to record a sports program from first to last. That tape might now show horse racing and nothing else."

No one would casually wipe out a fortune if not sure he could bring it back. Nobody would do it *on purpose,* that was.

So I asked him, "Did you obliterate it on purpose or by mistake?"

He laughed inside the beard. He said, "I don't make mistakes."

The frisson I felt was the recognition of a thoroughly human failing; for all his pleasant manner, the doctor thought he was God.

He stopped by a fallen fir trunk. "Our business is completed. I have patients to see." His voice was dismissive. "I'm sure you'll find your own way out." He started to go back. To his obvious irritation I went with him.

"There are just a couple of things," I said. "How did you get to know Martin Stukely?"

He said calmly, "That's none of your business."

I said, "Martin gave you a large chunk of money in return for the knowledge that you referred to as dynamite."

"No. You completely do not understand. I want you to leave."

"Did you know," I persisted, "that Lloyd Baxter, the man you abandoned to his epileptic fit in my showroom, is the owner of Tallahassee, the horse that killed Martin Stukely?"

He walked faster. I stayed close, accelerating. "Did you know," I asked, "that in spite of the onset of an epileptic seizure, Lloyd Baxter was able to describe you down to the socks?"

"Stop it."

"And of course you know Norman Osprey and Rose and Gina are as violent as they come."

"No." His voice was loud, and he coughed.

"And as for my money that you nicked with that tape . . ."

Adam Force quite suddenly stopped walking altogether, and in the stillness I could clearly hear his breath wheezing in his chest. He pulled from a pocket in his white coat the sort of inhaler I'd often seen used for asthma. He took two long puffs, breathing deeply while staring at me with complete dislike.

I was tempted to say "Sorry," but he'd been the cause of my being subjected to both the black masks in Broadway and to a piece of hose in a Taunton backyard. So I let him wheeze and puff his way back to the reception area. I checked him into a comfortable chair and went to find someone to pass him on to for safekeeping.

I heard his wheezy voice behind me demanding my return, but by then I'd hurried halfway down one of the wings of the building and seen no human being at all, whether nurse, patient, doctor, cleaner, flower arranger, or woman pushing a cart. In the rooms that lined the wing, there were beds, tray tables, armchairs, but no people.

There had to be someone somewhere, I thought, and through the closed door at the end of the wing I found a comparative beehive coming and going.

Twenty or more elderly men and women in thick white toweling bathrobes were contentedly taking part in comprehensive physical assessments, each test being brightly presented in play-school lettering like YOUR BLOOD PRESSURE MEASURED HERE and WHERE DOES YOUR CHOLESTEROL STAND TODAY?

Results were carefully written onto clipboards. An air of optimism prevailed.

My entrance brought to my side a nurse who'd been drawing curtains around a cubicle simply called UROLOGY. She said only, "Oh dear," when I mentioned that the good Dr. Force might be gasping his last.

"He often does have attacks when he has visitors," the nurse confided. "When you've gone, I expect he'll lie down and sleep."

The good Dr. Force was planning nothing of the sort. Registering annoyance like a steaming boiler, he wheezed to my side and pointed to a door labeled WAY OUT. I explained I'd only come to find help for his asthma, and he replied crossly that he didn't need it. He walked toward me with a syringe in a metal dish, advancing until I could see it was almost full of liquid. He jabbed the syringe toward me, and this time I thanked him for his attention and left.

In the forecourt outside, I found Jim, my driver, nervously pacing up and down beside the Rover. He held the door open for me, explaining that he'd been concerned for my welfare. I thanked him with true feeling.

I couldn't identify exactly what was wrong with Phoenix House and was little further enlightened when a large bus turned smoothly through the entrance gate and came to a gentle halt. The title AVON

PARADISE TOURS read black and white on lilac along the coach's sides. Below the name was an address in Bristol.

Jim agreed to drive around Lynton simply to enjoy it as a visitor. Truth to tell, I was dissatisfied with myself on many counts, and I wanted time to think before we left. I thought about the Adam Force who was color-blind, asthmatic, volatile, and changeable in nature, and who visited an obscure nursing home once a week. A minor practitioner, it seemed, though with a string of qualifications and a reputation for sparkling research. A man wasting his skills. A man who took a visitor outside to talk on a noticeably cold day and gave himself an asthmatic attack.

I thought of inconsequential things like coincidence and endurance and videotapes that were worth a million and could save the world. I also thought of the tape I had made, demonstrating step by step how I had copied a three-thousand-five-hundred-year-old necklace worth a million.

Of course only the genuine antiquity in a museum had that value. And the actual gold necklace I'd made was in my bank, where I normally kept the instruction tape as well. I'd lent the tape to Martin and didn't care if he'd shown it to anyone else. But I dearly wished he had returned it before it disappeared, along with all the others from his den.

I thought perhaps Jim might not want to double the experience on the following day, but to my surprise he agreed. "Tom Pigeon'll set his dogs on me if I don't," he said.

I smiled and told him I prized my bodyguards.

Jim, short and stout, apologized for not being in the same class as Worthington and Tom. He added, "But where Tom says he'll put his fists, you can count on mine."

"Well, thanks," I said weakly.

"So where do we go tomorrow?"

I said, "How does Bristol grab you? A hospital area, best of all?"

He smiled broadly. He knew his way around Bristol and its hospitals. He drove an ambulance there one year, he said.

We shook hands on it, and I acquired bodyguard number three.

Chapter Seven

BRISTOL was wet with drizzle.

Quite reasonably Jim asked where we were going exactly. To find a phone book, I replied, and in the yellow pages I singled out Avon Paradise Tours. They advertised adventures throughout Cornwall, Devon, and Somerset and all points to London. Jim drove us unerringly to their lilac headquarters.

Once they understood what I was asking, the women in the Avon Paradise Tours office were moderately helpful. On Tuesdays members of a Bristol area Health Clubs Association went on a scenic bus tour to the Phoenix House nursing home in Lynton for medical checkups and advice on healthy living. For his day's work per week, Dr. Force, who ran the clinic, was paid jointly by the health clubs and Avon Paradise Tours. The office staff admitted they'd been told Dr. Force had been "let go" by the research lab he used to work for.

Which research lab? They didn't know. One of them said she'd heard he'd been working on illnesses of the lungs.

Another phone book—listing all things medical—had me trying all the remotely possible establishments, asking them if they knew a Dr. Force. Dr. Force? Unknown, unknown, unknown.

I wondered what to try next.

Illnesses of the lungs.

Check stubs. A lot of zeros. The payee, BELLOWS. In Martin's handwriting. In capital letters. Lungs were bellows, of course.

There wasn't any listing for Bellows in the Bristol area.

My mind drifted. The Avon Paradise ladies began to fidget. Bellows. Well, maybe, why not?

Abruptly I asked if I might borrow the office telephone again and spelled out Bellows in dial numbers, which resulted in 2355697. After maybe a dozen rings a brisk female voice hurriedly spoke. "Yes? Who is that?"

"Could I speak to Dr. Force, please," I said.

A long silence ensued. I was about to call it a waste of time when another voice, deep and male, inquired if I were the person asking for Dr. Force.

"Yes," I said. "Is he there?"

"Sorry. No. He left several weeks ago. Can I have your name?"

I was beginning to learn caution. I said I would phone back very soon, and clicked off. To the Paradise ladies I offered profound thanks and left, taking Jim in tow.

"Where to?" he asked.

"A pub for lunch."

"You're the sort of customer I can drive for all day."

The pub had a pay phone. When we were on the point of leaving, I dialed the number again and found the male voice answering me at once. He said, "I've been talking to Avon Paradise Tours."

I said, smiling, "I thought you might. You probably have this phone booth's number in front of your eyes at the moment. To save time, why don't we meet? You suggest somewhere."

I repeated to Jim the place suggested. Twenty minutes later he stopped the car in a no-waiting zone near the gate of a public park. Against the united teaching of Worthington, Tom Pigeon, and Jim not to go anywhere unknown without one of them close, I got out of the car, waved Jim to drive on, and walked into the park.

The drizzly rain slowly stopped.

The instructions had been "Turn left, proceed to statue," and by a prancing copper horse I met a tall, sensible-looking man who established to his satisfaction that I was the person he expected.

He spoke as if to himself. "He's six feet tall, maybe an inch or two more. Brown hair. Dark eyes. Twenty-eight to thirty-four years, I'd say. Personable except for recent injury to right side of jaw."

He was talking into a small microphone held in the palm of his hand. I let him see that I understood that he was describing me in case I attacked him in any fashion. "He arrived in a gray Rover." He repeated Jim's registration number.

When he stopped, I said, "He's a glassblower named Gerard

Logan and can be found at Logan Glass, Broadway, Worcestershire. And who are you?"

He was the voice on the telephone. He laughed at my dry tone and gave himself a name, George Lawson-Young, and a title, professor of respiratory medicine. Even with modern technology he didn't know how I'd found him.

"Old-fashioned perseverance and guesswork," I said. "I'll tell you later in return for the real story on Adam Force."

I liked the professor immediately, feeling none of the reservations that had troubled me with Force. My impression of goodwill and solid sense strengthened, so when he asked what my interest in Adam Force was, I told him straightforwardly about Martin's promise to keep safe Dr. Force's tape.

"Martin wanted me to keep it for him instead," I said. "Force followed me to Broadway and took his tape back again."

Out on the road, Jim in the gray Rover drove slowly by, his pale face through the window on watch on my behalf.

"I came with a bodyguard," I said, waving to the road.

Professor Lawson-Young, amused, confessed he had only to yell down his microphone for assistance to arrive at once. He seemed as glad as I was that he would not have to use it.

The professor said, "How did you cut your face so deeply?"

I said undramatically that I'd been in a fight, and when he asked what I'd been fighting about and with whom, his voice was full of the authority that he no doubt needed in his work.

"I wanted to find Dr. Force, and in the course of doing that, I collided with a water tap. It's unimportant. I learned how to find him, and I talked to him yesterday in Lynton."

"Where in Lynton? In that new nursing home? He does good work there with the elderly, I'm told."

"They seemed pretty happy, it's true."

"So what's your take-away opinion?"

I gave it without much hesitation. "Force is utterly charming when he wants to be, and he's also a bit of a crook."

"Only a bit?" The professor sighed. "Adam Force was in charge here of a project aimed at abolishing snoring by using fine optical fibers and microlasers. But I don't want to bore you."

My own interest, however, had awoken sharply, as in the past I'd designed and made glass equipment for that sort of inquiry. When I explained my involvement, the professor was astonished.

"We'd been experimenting with shining a microlaser down a fine optical fiber placed in the soft tissues of the throat. The microlaser gently warms the tissues, which stiffens them, and that stops a person from snoring. A reliable remedy would be invaluable for severe sufferers. Adam Force stole our data and sold it. It was weeks before the theft was discovered, and really no one could believe it when we went to the marketers and they told us they had already bought the material and paid Adam Force for what we were now trying to sell them."

"So you sacked him," I commented.

"Well, we should have, but he was crucial to our research program." The professor, however, looked regretful, not enraged. "Then we found he was trying to sell some even more secret information, and I mean *priceless* information. We are certain that he is offering this work to the highest bidder. This is the information recorded on the tape Force took back from you, and it is this tape we have been praying you would find."

I said with incredulity, "But you didn't know that I existed."

"We did know you existed. Our investigators have been very diligent. But we weren't sure you hadn't been indoctrinated by Adam, like your friend Stukely."

"*Martin?*"

"Oh yes. Force can be utterly charming and persuasive, as you know. We think it likely he also swindled Stukely of a fairly large sum of money, saying it was to be applied to our research. It is quite likely that Stukely had no idea that the contents of the tape had been stolen. He and Force met at a fund-raising dinner for cancer research."

I vaguely remembered Martin mentioning the dinner, but I hadn't paid much attention. It was typical of him to make friends in unexpected places. I had myself, after all, met him in a jury room.

There was nothing, I heard with relief, about trying to make me reveal the tape's whereabouts through the use of black-mask methods. I was aware, though, that the former tension in the professor's muscles had returned, and I wondered if he thought I was fooling him, as Adam Force had done.

After a while he said, "We've searched absolutely everywhere for proof that Adam had in his possession material that belongs to the laboratory. We believe that he recorded every relevant detail onto the videotape, because one of our researchers thought he saw him doing it. Adam himself entrusted a tape into the care of Martin Stukely at Cheltenham races. His changing-room valet passed the tape on to Stukely's friend, as previously planned." He paused. "So as you are the friend, will you tell us where to look for the tape? Better still, bring it to us yourself."

I said simply, "Force has the tape. Ask him. But yesterday he told me he'd recorded a sports program on top of your data and all that remained on the tape now was horse racing."

"Oh God."

I said, "I don't know that I believe him."

"Discard the lies," George Lawson-Young said, smiling, "and what you're left with is probably the truth." He shivered suddenly in the cold, damp wind.

I proposed that we find somewhere warmer if we had more to say, and the professor offered me a visit to his laboratory. His trust, however, didn't reach as far as stepping into my car, so he went in one that arrived smoothly from nowhere, and I followed with Jim.

The research laboratory occupied the ground floor of a fairly grand nineteenth-century town house with a pillared entrance porch. George Lawson-Young, very much the professor on his own turf, introduced me to his team of young research doctors. My ability to identify things like vacutaires, cell separators, and tissue culture chambers meant that when I asked what exactly had been stolen the second time by Adam Force, the professor finally told me what I'd needed to know all along.

"The videotape made and stolen by Adam Force showed the formation of a particular tissue culture and its ingredients. The tissue culture was of cancer cells of the commoner sorts of cancer, like that of the lung and the breast. They were concerned with the development of genetic mutations that render the cancer cell lines more sensitive to common drugs. All common cancers may be curable once the mutated gene is implanted into people who already have the cancer. The tape probably also shows photographs of the chromatography of the different components of the cancer cell genetic constituents. It is very complicated. At first sight it looks like rubbish, except to the educated eye. It is, unfortunately, quite likely that anyone might override the 'Don't record on top of this' tab."

He lost me halfway through the technical details, but I at least understood that the tape that could save the world contained the cure for a host of cancers. I asked the professor, "Is this for real?"

"It's a significant step forward," he said.

I pondered, "But is it worth millions?"

Somberly, Lawson-Young said, "We don't know."

Adam Force had said the same thing. Not a lie, it seemed, but a statement that the process hadn't yet been extensively tested. The tape was a record of a possibility.

I said, "But you do have backups of everything that's on that tape, don't you? Even if the tape itself now shows horse racing?"

Almost as if he were surrendering to an inevitable execution, the professor calmly stated the guillotine news. "Before he left with the videotape, Adam destroyed all our at-present irreplaceable records. We *need* that tape, and I hope to God you're right that he's lying. It's two years' work. Others are working along these lines, and we would be beaten to the breakthrough."

Into a short silence the telephone buzzed. George Lawson-Young picked up the receiver, listened, and mutely handed it to me. The caller was Jim in a high state of alarm. He said, "That medic you saw yesterday, the one with the white beard?"

"Yes?"

"He's here in a car parked fifty yards up the road, and there's a big bruiser sitting next to him. He's got another car waiting but coming the other way. It's a classic squeeze setup, with you in the middle. So what do you want me to do?"

"Where exactly are you?" I asked. "To reach you, do I turn left or right?"

"Left. I'm parked four cars in front of White Beard, pointing toward the door you went in at."

"Stay where you are," I said. "Dr. Force saw you and your car yesterday. It can't be helped."

Jim's voice rose. "White Beard's got out of his car. What shall I do? *He's coming this way.*"

"Jim," I said flatly, "don't panic. Don't look at Dr. Force and don't open the window. Keep on talking to me, and if you have anything near you that you can read, read it aloud to me now."

"Jeez."

Lawson-Young's eyebrows were up by his hairline.

I said to him, "Adam Force is in the road outside here, alarming my driver." And I didn't mention a poisonous-looking syringe on our last encounter.

Jim's voice wobbled in my ear with the opening paragraphs of the Rover's instruction manual and then rose again an octave as he said, "He's outside my window; he's rapping on it."

"Keep on reading," I told him.

I gave the receiver to the professor and asked him to continue listening, and I hurried out into the street. Adam Force, tapping hard on the window of the gray Rover, was clearly getting agitated at the lack of response from Jim.

I came up quietly behind Dr. White Beard and, as I'd done to Victor at Taunton station, said, "Hello," at his shoulder.

Adam Force spun around in astonishment.

"Are you looking for me?" I asked.

Inside the car Jim was stabbing with his finger toward the road beyond. One of the approaching cars, Jim was indicating to me, was ultra-bad news.

"Adam Force," I said loudly, "is too well known in this street." I grabbed the charming doctor by the wrist, spun him around, and ended with him standing facing the oncoming car with his arm twisted up behind him, held in the strong grip resulting from years of maneuvering heavy molten glass.

Adam Force yelled, at first with pain and then, also, with bargaining surrender. "You're hurting me. Don't do it. I'll tell you everything. Don't do it. God . . . Let me go, *please.*"

A small object fell from the hand I'd gripped. It lay in the gutter quite close to a storm-drain grating, and I'd have paid it no attention were it not for Force trying hard to kick it down through the grating into the sewer, to be forever lost.

The advancing car stopped at the sight of Adam Force's predicament, and the four cars behind it exercised their horns, the drivers impatient, not knowing what was going on.

"Everything," I prompted Force from behind his ear.

"Rose," he began, and then thought better of it. Rose would frighten anyone.

With some dismay I saw the big bruiser, Norman Osprey, lumbering out of his car. Over my shoulder I could see the second car of the classic squeeze moving toward me. I jerked my captive's arm yet again to encourage him.

Imploring for release, he half said, half sobbed, desperately, "I got the cyclopropane gas for Rose. I took it from the clinic's pharmacy. I can't see red from green, but I'm sure of orange. Now let me go."

His "everything" only confirmed what had already seemed likely, but I kept the pressure on just long enough for him to shriek out the answer I wanted to the question "How come you know Rose?"

"Her sister, Gina, came with her mother-in-law to my clinic. I met Rose at Gina's house."

Satisfied, I was faced with a fast, unharmed disengagement. The driver of the second car was hurriedly disembarking, and to my horror I saw it was Rose. Uninvolved cars made a constant cacophony.

Norman Osprey, a mountain on the move, charged.

I shouted at Jim, "Get the car out of here. I'll phone you."

Jim suddenly proved his stunt-driving skills weren't a rumor. With not much more than two hand spans' clearance he locked the wheels of his Rover and circled like a circus horse, bumping over the sidewalk, brushing me and my captive strongly out of the way as he slid around the corner and left the scene.

I let go of Force's wrist while at the same time shoving him heavily into the arms of Osprey.

In that disorganized few seconds I bent down, scooped up the small object Force had dropped, and *ran,* ran as if sprinting off the starting blocks on an athletic track. It was only the unexpectedness of my speed, I thought, that made the difference. I ran, dodging cars and irate drivers, swerving around Rose's grasp like a player evading a tackle in a football game.

The front door of the laboratory house swung open ahead of me, with George Lawson-Young beckoning me to safety. I ended breathless in his hall.

I liked the professor. I held out the small object I'd salvaged from the gutter, asking him with moderate urgency, "Can you find out what this contains?"

He asked a shade austerely if I knew what I'd brought him.

"Yes. It's a sort of syringe. You can put the needle into any liquid drug and suck it into the bubble," I said.

He said, "You're right. These little ones can be used on manic patients to calm them down." He led the way back to that part of the laboratory that held the gas chromatograph, laid the bubble carefully in a dish, and asked one of his young doctors to identify its contents as soon as possible.

"It's insulin," the young doctor said confidently ten minutes later. "Plain ordinary insulin, as used by diabetics."

"Insulin!" I exclaimed, disappointed. "Is that all?"

The professor smiled indulgently. "If you have diabetes, the amount of insulin in that syringe might send you into a permanent coma. If you *don't* have diabetes, there's enough to kill you."

"To *kill?*"

Lawson-Young sounded shattered. "I can hardly believe it of

Adam. We knew he'd steal, but to kill . . ." He shook his head.

The professor and I by that time were sitting in his office.

"Actually," I murmured, "the big question is why?"

George Lawson-Young couldn't say.

"Do me a favor," he finally begged. "Start from the beginning."

"I will phone my driver first."

I used my mobile. When Jim answered his car phone, he sounded first relieved that I was free and talking to him and, second, worried about where he was going to find me safe and on my own. The professor gave Jim pinpointing instructions.

"It's a tale of two tapes," I tentatively began. "One was filmed here and stolen by Adam Force. He persuaded Martin Stukely to keep it safe for him so that it couldn't be found."

"We had obtained a search-and-seizure order from the court and had already started searching everywhere for it," said Lawson-Young, "including in Adam's own home, but we didn't ever think of it being in the care of a jockey."

"That must be why he did it," I said. "But as I understand it, Martin thought Force's tape would be safer still with me, a friend who hasn't four inquisitive children." And no talkative or quarrelsome wife, I could have added. But, I wondered, would Martin really have had his valet give me the tape if he knew the contents were stolen?

The professor nodded. "Eddie the valet was one of the people that our investigators talked to. He said he didn't know anything about any stolen laboratory tape. He said he thought he was handling a tape that you yourself had made, which explained how to copy an ancient and priceless necklace."

"That's the second tape," I said. "It's also missing."

"Incidentally"—he smiled—"Eddie said he saw your copy of the necklace in the jockeys' changing room. He said it was stunning. Perhaps you will show it to me one day, when all this is over."

I asked him what he would consider "over," and his smile disappeared. "When we find the tape of our work."

He was aware, I supposed, that it was comparatively easy to make duplicates of videotapes. And that the knowledge recorded on them was like the contents of Pandora's box; once out, it couldn't be put back. The records of the cancer research might already be free in the world and would never again be under the professor's control. For him, perhaps, it was already over.

For me, I thought, it would be over when Rose and Adam Force left me alone. But abruptly, out of nowhere, the specter of the fourth black mask floated into my consciousness. It wouldn't be over for me until his mask came off.

As casually as I could, I mentioned number four to the professor, fearing he would discount my belief, but instead he took it seriously.

"Add your number four into all equations," he instructed, "and what do you get in the way of answers? Do you get a reason for Force to want you dead? Do you get a reason for anyone to attack you? Think about it."

I thought that that method must be what he used in nearly all research. If I added in an x factor, an unknown, into all I'd seen and heard and hadn't wholly understood, what would I get?

Before I could really learn the technique, one of the young doctors came to say that Adam Force was standing on the sidewalk opposite with a thin woman with brown hair—my friend Rose. Force would certainly have another man posted at the rear.

The professor said, "So how do we get Mr. Logan out of here?"

The brilliant researchers came up with several solutions. The idea I followed came from a glowingly pretty female doctor, who gave me directions. "Go up the stairs to the sixth floor. There's a door to the roof. Slide down the tiles to the parapet. Crawl to the right behind the parapet. Keep your head down. There are seven houses joined together. Go along behind their parapets until you come to the fire escape at the end. Go down it. I'll drive out and pick you up to meet your driver."

I shook hands with George Lawson-Young. He gave me multiple contact numbers and said he would expect me to find the stolen tape. Deduction and intuition would do it.

I said, "What a hope!"

"Our only hope," he added soberly.

The author of my escape helped me slide down the gently sloping roof tiles to reach the parapet. To be invisible, I sweated and trembled along on my stomach within the parapet's scanty cover. It was a long way down to the ground.

The seven houses seemed like fifty. The recent rain had drenched the roof and wet my clothes. But I found my way down, and by the time Jim decanted me yawning to my house, he and I were both very tired.

Inside the kitchen, when Jim had driven away, the warm welcoming smell of cooking seemed utterly natural.

"Sorry about this." Catherine nodded at half-scrambled eggs. "I didn't know when you'd be back, and I was hungry."

She gave me a careful look, her eyebrows rising.

"I got a bit wet," I said.

"Tell me later." She cooked more eggs while I changed, and we ate in companionable peace.

I made coffee for us both and drank mine looking at her neat face, her blond curving hair, and her close-textured skin; and I wondered without confidence what I looked like to her.

Bit by bit, without exaggeration, I told her about my day.

She listened with concentration and horror as we sat together, squashed into one large chair. She felt right in my arms, curling there comfortably.

I told her about the professor and his *x*-factor method of research. "So now," I finished, "I go over everything that anyone has said and done, add Blackmask Four into the picture, and see what I get."

I realized with distaste that it meant I had to go back and remember every separate blow and listen again to every word of Rose's.

She'd shouted, "Break his wrists . . . ."

Catherine stirred in my arms and cuddled closer, and I discarded thoughts of Rose in favor of bed.

Chapter Eight

CATHERINE went off before dawn, and I walked down to Logan Glass. Although I arrived at work half an hour before the normal starting time, Hickory was there before me, obstinately trying again to make a perfect sailing boat. He'd put in red and blue streaks up the mast, and the whole thing looked lighter and more fun.

I congratulated him and got a scornful grunt in return, and I thought how quickly his sunny temperament could blow up a thunderstorm. To give Hickory his due, he handled semiliquid glass with a good deal of the panache he would need on the way to general recognition. I privately thought, though, that he would get stuck on "pretty good" and never reach "marvelous," and because he understood deep down where his limit lay and knew I could do better, his present feeling of mild resentment needed patience and friendly laughter if he were either to stay or to leave on good terms.

Irish and Pamela Jane arrived together, as they often did, and this time were arguing about a film they'd seen that had a bad glass-blower in it. They asked Hickory what he thought and embroiled him so intensely in the argument that with a bang his precious new sailing boat cracked apart into five or six pieces. It had been standing free on the marver table, the outer surfaces cooling more rapidly than the super-hot core. The stresses due to unequal rates of contraction had become too great for the fragile glass. The pieces had blown away from each other and lay on the floor.

All three of my helpers looked horrified. Hickory himself glanced at his watch and said bleakly, "Three minutes, that's all it took. I was going to put it in the oven. Damn that stupid film."

"Never mind," I said, shrugging and looking at the sad bits. "It happens." It did happen to everyone. It happened to the best.

We worked conscientiously all morning, making swooping birds for mobiles, which always sold fast. Hickory, who could make neat little birds, recovered his good humor by the time Worthington drew up outside in Marigold's Rolls. Marigold herself, in a dramatic black-and-white-striped caftan, issued from her glossy car with mascara-laden eyelashes batting hugely up and down like a giraffe's. She had come, she announced, to present a proposal.

Worthington looked the more richly suntanned from the skiing trip. He had spent most of the time on the slopes, he said with satisfaction, while Marigold's wardrobe had swelled by three enormous suitcases. And a good time had clearly been had by both.

Worthington drifted me with a gentle tug on the arm into the furnace end of the room and told me that the underground fraternity of bookmakers were forecasting my destruction, if not death.

"Rose is still actively prowling round here, looking for vengeance. So you just look out, because I hear that someone in Broadway has binoculars on you now, reporting every twitch you make straight back to Rose. It's no joke."

Marigold paraded up and down the brightly lit gallery as if she'd never been in there before, and halted finally in front of Catherine's wings to tell us all the reason for her visit. She said we were lucky to be in a studio that stood so high already in the world's estimation. She was going to give us all a huge jump forward in reputation because, "Gerard"—she blew me a kiss—"is going to make a marvelous Marigold Knight Trophy, and I'm going to present it each year to the winner of a steeplechase run at Cheltenham on every New Year's Eve in memory of my son-in-law, Martin Stukely." She spread her arms wide. "What do you think of *that?*"

I didn't say, "Over the top. In fact, out of sight," but I thought it.

"You see," Marigold went on triumphantly, "everyone benefits. People will flock to your door here."

"I think it's a beautiful idea," said Pamela Jane. The others agreed.

Glass trophies were common in racing, and I would be elated to be commissioned to make one. I said, "I could make a leaping horse with golden streaks. I could make it worthy of Cheltenham."

Marigold, delighted, filled in the details rapidly. She said she would consult the Cheltenham Race Trophy Committee immediately. Gerard could start work at once. The press should be alerted.

Then, having agreed earlier with her daughter to take me back to Bon-Bon's house, Marigold, Worthington, and I made tracks to the Stukely gravel, arriving at the same moment as Priam Jones, who was carefully nursing his disgust toward Lloyd Baxter, who'd ordered his horses, including Tallahassee, to be sent north to a training stable nearer his home.

Bon-Bon came out of the house in a welcoming mood, swept her mother into the house on a wardrobe expedition, and said over her departing shoulder, "Gerard, pour Priam a drink, will you? I think there's everything in the cupboard."

"Bon-Bon invited me to an early supper," Priam announced.

"How splendid!" I said warmly. "Me too."

Bon-Bon's grief for Martin had settled in her like an anchor steadying a ship. She was more in charge of the children and had begun to cope more easily with managing her house. I'd asked her whether she could face inviting Priam to dinner, but I hadn't expected the skill with which she'd delivered him to me.

Priam and I made our way to Martin's den, where I acted, as instructed, as host and persuaded Priam with my very best flattery to tell me how his other horses had prospered, as I'd seen one of his winners praised in the newspapers.

Priam, with his old boastfulness reemerging, explained how no one else but he could have brought those runners out at the right moment. He relaxed on the sofa and sipped Scotch and water.

I sat in Martin's chair and fiddled with small objects on his desk. "How well," I asked conversationally, "do you know Eddie Payne, Martin's old valet?"

Surprised, Priam answered, "I don't know him intimately, but some days I give him the silks the jockeys will be wearing, so yes, I talk to Eddie then."

"And Rose? Eddie Payne's daughter. Do you know her?"

"Whyever do you ask?" Priam's voice was mystified, but he hadn't answered the question.

I said with gratitude, "You were so kind, Priam, on that wretched day of Martin's death, to take back to Broadway that tape I so stupidly left in my raincoat pocket in Martin's car, the one I'd been given in Cheltenham. I haven't thanked you properly again since then." I paused and then added as if one thought had nothing to do with the other, "I've heard a crazy rumor that you swapped two tapes. That you took the one from my pocket and left another."

"Rubbish!"

"I agree." I smiled and nodded.

"Well, then"—he sounded relieved—"why mention it?"

"Because of course here in Martin's den you found tapes all over the place. Out of curiosity you may have slotted the tape I had left in the car into Martin's VCR and had a look at it."

"You're just guessing," Priam complained.

"Oh, sure. Do I guess right?"

Priam didn't want to admit to his curiosity. I pointed out that it was to his advantage if it were known for a certainty what tape had vanished from Logan Glass.

He took my word for it and looked smug, but I upset him again profoundly by asking him who that evening, or early next morning, he had assured that the tape he'd delivered to Broadway had nothing to do with an antique necklace.

I said without pressure, "Was it Rose Payne?"

Priam's face stiffened. It was a question he didn't want to answer.

"If you say who," I went on in the same undemanding tone, "we can smother the rumors about you swapping any tapes."

"There's never any harm in speaking the truth," Priam protested, but of course he was wrong. The truth could hurt.

"Who?" I repeated.

"When Martin died," he said, "I drove his things back here, as you know, and then as my own car was in the garage, well, Bon-Bon said I could take Martin's car. I drove it to my home and then back to Broadway, with Baxter's bag and your raincoat, and then I drove myself home again in it. In the morning Eddie Payne called." Priam took a breath but seemed committed to finishing. "Well, Eddie asked me then if I was sure the tape I'd taken back to your shop was without doubt the one he'd given you at Cheltenham, and I said I was absolutely certain, and as that was that, he rang off."

Priam's tale had ended. He took a deep swallow of whisky.

It had taken such a lot of angst for Priam to answer a fairly simple question that I dug around in what I'd heard to see if Priam knew consequences that I didn't.

Could he have been Blackmask Four? Unknown factor x?

Eddie Payne had probably told Rose that the tape stolen from Logan Glass at the turnover of the new century had to do with a necklace. Rose had not necessarily believed him. Rose, knowing that such a necklace existed but not realizing that the tape, if found, wasn't itself worth much and certainly not a million, may have hungered for it enough to anesthetize everyone around at Bon-Bon's house with cyclopropane and gather up every videotape in sight.

Thoughtfully I asked Priam, as if I'd forgotten I'd asked him before, "How well do you know Rose Payne?"

"I've seen her around," he replied.

"How well does she know Adam Force, would you say? Do you think Dr. Force would be foolish enough to lend her a cylinder of gas from a nursing home he visits?"

Priam looked as shocked as if I'd run him through with swords, but unfortunately, he didn't actually flag-wave any signs of guilt. He didn't feel guilty; almost no one did.

Bon-Bon's "early supper" proved to be just that, slightly to Priam's disappointment. He preferred grandeur, but everyone sat around the big kitchen table—Marigold, Worthington, the children, Bon-Bon, me, and Priam himself. I also acted as waiter, though Daniel, the eleven-year-old, carried empty dishes.

"Gerard," he said, standing solidly in front of me between courses to gain my attention, "who's Victor?"

I paid attention very fast and said, "He's a boy. Tell me what you've heard."

"He wants to tell you a secret."

"When did he say that?"

Daniel said, "He phoned here. Mommy was out in the garden, so

I answered it. He said he was Victor and wanted to talk to you. I told him you were coming for supper, so he said to tell you he would try again if he could."

I dug in my pocket and found some loose change. Daniel whisked it away in a flash.

"That's disgraceful!" Marigold told me severely. "You're teaching my grandson all sorts of bad habits."

"It's a game," I said. Daniel had done a good piece of work.

At seven thirty Marigold floated out to the Rolls and let Worthington drive off to her home. Priam Jones thanked Bon-Bon for her hospitality and bestowed a cool farewell nod to me.

Bon-Bon, going upstairs to read stories to the children, waved me to the den for the evening. Victor kept me waiting a long time. It was after eleven o'clock when the phone rang. The caller spoke with the familiar cracked voice of Taunton.

"Gerard? I'm in a public phone box. Mom thinks I'm in bed. She threw away your mobile number. I can't use the e-mail. Auntie Rose has taken my computer. I'm absolutely sick of things. I want to see you. Tell me where. I'm running out of money."

He was feeding small coins, I supposed, because he hadn't any others. I said, "I'll come to Taunton. Same train, on Sunday."

"No. Tomorrow. *Please,* tomorrow."

I agreed, and the line went dead.

"YOU'RE raving mad, that's what you are," Tom Pigeon said at seven in the morning when I phoned him. "Today's Friday. The boy should be in school."

"That's probably why he was so insistent. He could skip school without his mother knowing."

"You're not going," Tom said positively, and then, a few seconds later, "We'll get Jim to drive us. He's got a station wagon for the dogs. Where are you?"

"At the Stukelys'. Can you pick me up here?"

"Last Sunday, five days ago," Tom said with mock patience, "dear Rose tore your face open with the tap end of a garden hose."

"Mm," I agreed.

"How about staying at home?"

I smiled at the silly idea.

JIM drove Tom, me, and the dogs cheerfully to Taunton and stopped in the no-parking zone outside the station.

I'd spent part of the journey adding Victor into every event that Blackmask Four could have attended without disguise, and feeling I was nowhere near as good as George Lawson-Young at this factor-x stuff, I couldn't make x fit Victor anywhere.

I found him in the station waiting room, looking cold and anxious. "What's the matter?" I asked.

"Auntie Rose has moved into our house." He sounded desperate. "I hate her. And Mom won't speak to me unless I do what Auntie Rose says. Mom's that scared of her. So where can I go? What can I do? I don't know anyone except you to ask, and that's a laugh really, considering your face."

"Did you try your grandfather?"

Victor said hopelessly, "He's scared of Auntie Rose too—" He interrupted himself. "I'm really sorry about your face."

"Forget it," I said. "Concentrate on Adam Force."

"He's great," Victor said without fervor, and then, with a frown, added, "Everyone says so. He sometimes used my computer. That's how I got his letter. He thought he had deleted the file, but I found it in the cache memory."

It explained a lot. I asked, "How long has he known your aunt?"

"About as long as he's known Mom. Months, that is. Mom went on a bus trip to his clinic, and he got hooked on her. He was a real cool guy, I thought. He came round for her when Dad was at work. So when Auntie Rose finds out, she goes round to the hotel where Dad's working and says if he comes home quick, he'll catch them at it in Dad's own bed. So Dad goes round and Dr. Force has gone by then, but Dad gives Mom a hell of a beating, breaking her nose and her ribs, and Auntie Rose goes round to the cops and tells on Dad. So they put him away for twelve months. Then, last Sunday," he said miserably, "Auntie Rose catches Adam Force with Mom, and now he does what she tells him. It's queer, but I'd say she *hits* him most days, and I've seen them kissing after that."

He spoke in puzzlement. Victor *couldn't* be Blackmask Four. The fourth attacker was lithe, like Victor. But Victor *couldn't* have bashed me about then and asked me for help now.

But what about Gina? Was she muscular enough? I didn't know for sure, and I decided reluctantly, I would have to find out.

With a mental sigh I took Victor out of the station, and to his obvious pleasure reunited him with Tom and his three black canine companions. He played with the dogs, plainly in their good graces.

I said after a while, "I'll go round to Victor's house, and if his mother's in, I'll ask her if he can spend the weekend with us."

Tom protested, "I'll go."

"We'll both go," I said. We left Victor with Jim and, taking the dogs with us, knocked on the repaired door of 19 Lorna Terrace.

Gina Verity came to our summons and failed to close her mended door against us fast enough. Tom's heavy shoe was quicker. In the five days since the previous Sunday, Gina had lost her looks and her confidence. She stared at my mending jaw as if it were one straw too many. She said helplessly, "You'd better come in."

Tom and the dogs stood on guard outside the house.

"I would like to invite Victor to stay for the weekend," I said.

Gina lit cigarette from cigarette. "All right," she agreed in a dull sort of way. "Pick him up from school. Better not let Rose find out. She wouldn't let him go with you."

I stretched forward and lifted first her right hand and then her left, putting them down again gently. The muscles were flabby, with no tone. Too apathetic to complain, she merely said, "What?"

I didn't reply. Blackmask Four, actively punching with strongly muscled arms, had not been Gina.

Time to go.

WHEN Victor and I disembarked from Jim's car at Bon-Bon's house, she came out to meet us, with Daniel by her side. She, like me and also Tom, watched with fascination the flash of under-standing between Victor, fifteen, and the four years younger Daniel. Those two discovered immediately that they spoke computer lan-guage with a depth that none of the rest of us could reach.

Bon-Bon, amused, said she would keep Victor for the night. Jim drove Tom, the dogs, and myself back to Tom's house first, and then on to mine.

Catherine's motorcycle graced its customary spot outside the kitchen door, and she came out when she heard Jim's car arrive. There was no difficulty in interpreting her reaction to my return, and Jim drove away with a vast smile, promising his service again "day or night."

Coming home to Catherine had become an event to look forward to. I'd never asked her to take me to see her own living space, and when I did that evening, she laughed and said, "I'll take you there tomorrow. It's better by daylight."

She asked me how my day had been, and I asked about hers. It was all very married, I thought, and we'd known each other for barely three weeks.

"Tell me about the police," I said as we squashed companionably into one of the oversize chairs.

"What about them?"

"The priorities. For instance, on that New Year's Day, you in your plain clothes and the hobo lying on the doorstep, you were both there to frighten thieves off, weren't you, not to arrest them?"

She shifted in my arms. "Not really," she replied. "We like to get our man."

I knew better than to tease her. "Tell me about your partner, the hobo."

"He's not really a hobo," she replied, smiling. "His name is Paul Cratchet. He's a good detective. Paul's a big guy but misleadingly gentle. Many a villain has been surprised by his hand on their col-lar. He's known as Pernickety Paul at the station because he is so fussy over his reports."

I inquired plainly, "What events get most police attention?"

"Accidental deaths, and murder, of course. Any physical assault."

"Who would I go to if I found some stolen property?"

"Are you talking about those old videotapes again?"

"Yup. Those old tapes."

"Well, I did inquire. The tapes themselves are worth practically nothing. The information recorded on them is called intellectual property. It has very little priority in police thinking. How to make a copy of an antique necklace? You must be joking! Industrial secrets, even medical secrets? Too bad. No one is going to waste much police time looking for them." She stopped as an entirely opposite thought struck her, then said, "Does this dreadful Rose still believe you know where to find the tapes?"

"Don't worry about it."

"But does she?" Catherine was insistent. "Does she?"

I told her, smiling, "I now think she's had the necklace tape almost from the beginning, and if she has, she knows I haven't got it." And Rose knows, I thought, that I could reproduce it any day.

"But the other one? The one stolen from the lab?"

"Yes." I felt lighthearted. "I could make a guess. Let's go to bed."

I awoke first in the morning and lay for a while watching Catherine's calm, gentle breathing. At that moment it filled me with total contentment, but would I feel the same in ten years? And would she? When she stirred and opened her eyes and smiled, ten years didn't matter. One lived *now,* and now went along as a constant companion, present and changing minute by minute. It was *now,* always, that mattered.

"What are you thinking about?" she asked.

"Same as you, I daresay."

She smiled again and asked simply if I had plans for us on her free Saturday. Relaxed, I suggested a comfortable chair in Logan Glass.

I accepted a pillion ride, and when we got there, I donned work clothes and spent the morning restocking the shelves.

At a few minutes past noon the shop embraced first Bon-Bon and the two boys, Daniel and Victor, for whom glassblowing had temporarily become a greater draw than e-mail. Not long after them

Marigold swooped in, batting the eyelashes, grinning at Hickory, smothering Daniel in a bright pink gold-smocked cloudlike dress, and telling Bon-Bon at the top of her voice that the Cheltenham Racecourse Company's trophy committee decided unanimously to ask Gerard Logan to design and make a Martin Stukely memorial. A horse with golden streaks, rearing on a crystal ball.

"Can you make it today, darling Gerard?" Marigold enthused.

I telephoned a jeweler who promised enough gold. But I needed time for thinking if it were to be a good job; and a good job was what I needed to do for Bon-Bon, for Marigold, for Cheltenham racecourse, and for Martin himself.

"I'll do them tomorrow," I said. "The crystal ball and the rearing horse. I'll do them on my own, alone except for one assistant. They will be ready on Monday for the gold to be added, and on Tuesday afternoon I'll join them together onto a plinth. By Wednesday the trophy will be finished."

"Not until then?" Marigold protested.

"I want to get it right for you," I said.

And also I wanted to give my enemies time.

Chapter Nine

BON-BON and Marigold left the boys in my care while they browsed the antiques shops.

In the workshop, Victor, utterly impressed, watched Hickory show off with two gathers of red-hot glass that he rolled competently in white powder and then colored powder and tweaked into a small wavy-edged one-flower vase. Pamela Jane expertly assisted in snapping the vase off the punty iron, and Hickory with false modesty lifted it into an annealing oven as if it were the Holy Grail.

Daniel, for whom the workshop was a familiar stamping ground, wanted me to go outside with him, and seeing the stretched size of his eyes, I went casually but at once.

"What is it?" I asked.

"There's a shoe shop down the road," he said.

"Yes, I know."

"Come and look." He set off, and I followed. The shoe shop duly appeared on our left, and Daniel came to an abrupt halt by its window.

"See those sneakers? Those up there at the back with green-and-white-striped laces? The man with that gas, those are his laces."

I stared disbelievingly at the shoes. They were large, with thick rubberlike soles, triangular white-flashed canvas sections, and threaded with fat bunched laces.

He said again, "The man who gassed us wore those shoes."

Bon-Bon, away up the hill, was beckoning Daniel to her car, to go home. She had already loaded Victor, having offered him another night's computer hacking. Presently, Bon-Bon and Marigold had gone their separate ways. As it was now late Saturday afternoon, my little team set things straight, then departed with my blessing, leaving only myself and Catherine to lock up, and I gave her a bunch of keys for the future.

I asked her whether, even though they would not be on duty the next day, she could persuade her hobo partner, Pernickety Paul, to walk up and down Broadway with her a couple of times. She naturally asked why.

"To mind my back," I joked, and she said she thought he might come if she asked. I explained, before I kissed her, that she and the hobo might find handcuffs a good idea on the morrow.

"He always carries them," Catherine said.

IN THE morning she said, "All this walking up and down Broadway—is it the tapes?"

"Sort of." I didn't mention life or death.

All the same, I woke Tom Pigeon, who woke his dogs, who all growled (Tom included) that Sunday was a day of rest.

I phoned Jim. At my service all day, he said. His wife was going to church.

Worthington was already awake, he said, and had I noticed that Sundays weren't always healthy for Gerard Logan?

"*Mm.* What's Marigold doing today?"

"I've got the day free, if that's what you're asking. But why?"

I hesitated but replied, "On account of fear."

"Whose fear?"

"Mine."

"Oh. You'll be alone in that workshop of yours, is that it? In that case, I'll be with you soon."

"I won't exactly be alone. Catherine and her partner officer will be in the town, and in the workshop there will be Pamela Jane."

"Why not that bright young man, what's his name, Hickory?"

"Pamela Jane doesn't argue."

Worthington's deep voice arrived as a chuckle. "I'm on my way."

I made one more call, this time to Professor George Lawson-Young, and told him what he might expect.

"Well done," he said. "I wouldn't miss it. See you later."

Catherine and her motorcycle took me to Logan Glass, where I arrived intentionally before Pamela Jane. I read the notes I'd made (and filed in the locked bookcase) last time I'd tried my hand at a rearing horse. This one would take me about an hour to complete, if I made the whole trophy, including plinth and ball. At a little less than half a meter high, it would weigh a good deal, even without the added gold.

I had filled the tank with clear crystal and put ready at hand the punty irons I'd need, also the small tools for shaping muscles, legs, and head. Tweezers too, essential always. I set the furnace to the necessary 1800 degrees Fahrenheit.

While I waited for Pamela Jane to arrive, I thought about the wandering videotape that had raised so many savage feelings, and like curtains parting, the deductive faculty of Professor Lawson-Young continued to open vistas in my mind. I had at last added in his factor *x,* and the mask had dropped from Blackmask Four.

I reckoned that Rose and Adam Force should, if they had any sense at all, just leave the videotapes where they rested and save themselves the grief of prosecution. But thieves never had any sense.

I'd surrounded myself with as many bodyguards as I could muster that Sunday simply because neither Rose nor Adam Force had shown any sense or restraint so far, and because the making of the trophy horse left me wide open to any mayhem they might invent. I could have filled the workroom with a crowd of onlookers and been safe—safe for how long?

I knew now where the danger lay. However rash it might seem, I saw a confrontation as the quickest path to resolution.

If I were disastrously wrong, Professor Lawson-Young could say good-bye to his millions. The cancer breakthrough that would save the world would be published under someone else's name.

WHEN my enemies came, it wasn't just time, I found, that I had given them, as much as an opportunity to outthink me.

I was looking at the furnace and listening to its heart of flame when sounds behind me announced the arrival of Pamela Jane through the side door.

"Mr. Logan . . ." Her voice quavered high with fright.

I turned at once to see how bad things were and found that in many unforeseen ways they were extremely bad indeed.

Pamela Jane, dressed for work in white overalls, was coming to a standstill in the center of the workshop. Her wrists were fastened in front of her by brown packing tape. The charming Adam Force held a full syringe in one hand and with the other had dragged down a clutch of female overalls to reveal a patch of bare skin below the needle. Frightened, she began to cry.

A step behind Pamela Jane came Rose, her face a sneer. Strong, determined, and full of spite, she held in a pincer grip the upper arm of Hickory. My bright assistant stood helplessly swaying, his eyes and mouth stuck out of action by strips of brown packing tape.

Roughly steadying Hickory's balance loomed Norman Osprey. Just inside the side door, keeping guard and shifting uncomfortably from foot to foot, was, of all people, Eddie Payne. He wouldn't meet my eyes. He took instructions steadfastly from Rose.

The actions of all four intruders had been whirlwind fast, and I had arranged little in any way of retaliation. All the bodyguards were simply to roam the street outside. Catherine and her hobo were to patrol their normal disjointed beat. Rose and her cohorts had somehow slid past them.

I was wearing, as usual, a white singlet that left my arms, neck, and much of my shoulder area bare. The heat from the furnace roared almost unbearably beyond the trapdoor, if one weren't used to it. I put my foot and my weight sideways on the treadle, which duly opened the trap and let a huge gust of Sahara heat blow out over Norman Osprey's wool suit and reddening face. Furious, he made a snatch toward hurling me onto the trapdoor itself, but I sidestepped and tripped him, and unbalanced him onto his knees.

Rose yelled to Norman, "Stop it. We don't want him damaged this time. We'll get nowhere if he can't talk."

I watched as Rose tugged Hickory across to a chair. "Now you sit there, buddy boy, and it will teach you not to put your nose in where it isn't wanted." My blindfolded assistant tried hard to talk but produced only a throttled tenor protest.

"Now you," she told me, "will hand over everything I want. Or your friend here will get holes burned in him."

Pamela Jane cried out, "No, you can't!"

Whether or not he was aware of Rose's speed in standing on the treadle that raised the flap of the furnace, Hickory did understand the diabolical choice she was thrusting under my nose.

As if she could read his mind, she said in the same sharp tone, "You, Hickory. You'd better pray that this boss of yours won't let you burn. I'm not fooling. This time he's going to give me what I want."

She picked up one of the long punty irons and pushed it into the tank of molten glass. Somewhere, sometime, she had watched a glassblower collect a gather from a tank. She withdrew the iron with a small blob of red-hot glass on the end of it and revolved the rod so that the glass didn't fall off.

Pamela Jane moaned at the sight. I also heard the unmistakable heavy wheeze of Adam Force's asthma.

"Gerard Logan," Rose said to me with emphasis. "This time you will do what I tell you. Now, at once."

I'd seen Martin summon his mental vigor when going out to race on a difficult horse, and I'd seen actors breathe deeply in the wings when the play ahead dug deep into the psyche. I understood a good deal about courage in others and about the deficiencies in myself, but on that Sunday it was Rose's own mushrooming determination that pumped up in me the inner resources I needed.

I watched as she plunged the cooling small ball of glass into the tank again and drew it out again, larger. She swung the iron around until the molten red-hot lump advanced to a too close spot under Hickory's chin. He could feel the heat. He shrank frantically away and tried to scream behind the adhering tape.

"Look out!" I shouted automatically.

As if surprised, Rose swung the iron away from Hickory's face until he wasn't for the minute threatened.

"You see!" She sounded victorious. "If you don't like him burned, you'll tell me where you've hidden the videotapes I want."

I said urgently, "You'll disfigure Hickory if you're not careful. Glass burns are terrible. You can get a hand burned so badly that it needs amputating. An arm, a foot . . . You can smell flesh burning. You can lose your mouth, your nose."

"Shut up," Rose yelled at the top of her voice. "Shut up!"

"You can burn out an eye," I said. "You can sear and cauterize your guts."

Pamela Jane, who lived with the danger, was affected least of all in spite of her fluttery manner, and it was big Norman Osprey who looked ready to vomit.

Rose looked at her red-hot iron. She glanced at Hickory and she looked at me. "You came here this morning to make a trophy horse of glass and gold. I want the gold."

Wow! I thought. Gold for the trophy hadn't been mentioned in Rose's hearing as far as I knew. I had ordered enough for the trophy and a little over for stock, but a quantity worth holding up the stagecoach for, it was not. Someone had misled Rose, or she had misunderstood, and her imagination had done the rest. Rose was still sure that one way or another I could make her rich.

Adam Force, his finger on the plunger of the syringe, applauded Rose with a smile.

If I could use this opportunity . . . I did need time now, and if I made the trophy horse, I could slow things nicely.

I said, "The gold isn't here yet. I'm fed up with the delay." The carefree but complaining tone I used nonplussed Rose into lowering the tip of the punty iron.

"If I don't get the trophy glass horse ready on time—" I stopped abruptly, as if I'd teetered on the brink of a monster mistake. "Never mind," I said as if nervously, and Rose demanded I finish the sentence.

"Well," I said. "Gold. I have to use it on the horse."

Pamela Jane, to her eternal credit, dried her tears in mid-sniffle and in horrified disgust told me frankly across the workroom that I should be thinking of freeing Hickory, not making a trophy for Cheltenham races. "How can you?" she exclaimed. "It's despicable."

"A car from the jewelers is bringing the gold," I said.

Rose wavered and then demanded, "When?"

I said I wouldn't tell her.

"Yes, you will," she said, and advanced the hot iron in menace.

"Eleven o'clock," I said hastily. A good lie. "Let me make the horse," I suggested, and I made it sound on the verge of pleading. "Then, when I've made the horse, I'll tell you where to look where I think the tape might be, and then you must promise to set Hickory free as soon as you have the gold."

Pamela Jane said helplessly, "I don't believe this."

She couldn't understand how easily I had crumbled. She couldn't see that her scorn was the measure of my success.

Rose looked at her watch, discovered she would have to wait an hour for the gold to arrive, and did the unwise calculation that she could afford to wait for it. "Get on and make the trophy," she instructed. "When the gold comes, you'll sign for it in the normal way, or your Hickory's for the slow burn."

She told Pamela Jane to sit in the soft chair. There, while Adam Force held his threatening needle at her neck, Norman Osprey taped her ankles together.

Pamela Jane glared at me and said she wouldn't be assisting me with the horse or ever again.

Rose consolidated this decision by telling her I'd always been a coward. I looked expressionlessly at Pamela Jane and saw the shade of doubt creep in, even as Rose poured on the disdain.

I hadn't meant to shape the trophy horse under the threat of Rose's hand on the punty iron. I had in fact mobilized the bodyguards to prevent it, and they hadn't. Still, a confrontation with Rose had been inevitable, and if it were to be now, then I'd need to think a bit faster. I stood flat-footed, without drive.

Rose taunted, "I thought you were supposed to be good at glass."

"Too many people," I complained.

She peremptorily ordered Norman Osprey and Eddie Payne to go around the half-wall into the showroom, and with more politeness shifted Adam Force around after them. All three leaned on the half-wall, watching. Rose thrust another punty iron into the crucible—the tank—holding now white-hot glass, and drew it out, a reasonably sized gather.

"Go on," she said. She hovered over Hickory's and Pamela Jane's heads and threatened to melt off their ears if I gave her the slightest cause. I was to tell her all the time what I proposed to do next. There were to be no sudden unforeseen moves on my part.

I told Rose I would need to take four or five gathers from the tank, and while she had her own lump of destruction close to Pamela Jane's ear, I harvested enough glass to make a horse standing on his hind legs a third of a meter high.

I told Rose that it was almost if not totally impossible to make a horse of that size without an assistant, partly because the body of the horse had to be kept at working heat after one had sculpted the muscles of the neck and the upper legs, while one added pieces of glass for each lower leg and foot and for the tail.

"Get on with it, and don't whine." She was smiling to herself.

People in circuses could keep a dozen plates spinning in the air by twiddling sticks under them. Making that rearing horse felt much the same—keep the body and legs hot while you sculpted the head. The result wouldn't have won in a preschool contest.

Rose was enjoying herself. The less I blocked and opposed her, the more certain she grew that I was on the way to capitulation. Abruptly I understood that victory to Rose was never complete without the physical humiliation of a male adversary. Victory over Gerard Logan wouldn't be sufficient for her unless it included her inflicting some depth of burn.

I might shudder at such a prospect, but Rose wouldn't. I might use plain muscle power in an all-out attempt to defeat her, but I wouldn't try to wreak havoc of molten glass on Rose. Nor on anybody. I lacked the brutality.

Neither, though, could I desert my team and run.

With tweezers I pulled the horse's front legs up and its rear legs down and held the whole body on an iron within the furnace to keep it hot enough to mold. There were still things I could do, I thought. Honorable exits. Exits that were more or less honorable, anyway.

I managed to juggle body and leg pieces onto the racer. Exits, hell, I thought. Exit wasn't enough. Defeatism never got anyone anywhere.

I held two punty irons with difficulty and transferred enough glass from one to the other to attach and shape a mane, but it hadn't the elegance necessary for Cheltenham.

Worthington opened the gallery door and began to come in from the street. His eyes widened as fast as his comprehension as he spun a fast 180-degree turn and was on his way down the hill before Rose could decide which had priority—chasing Worthington or keeping me penned. She stopped smiling, loaded her punty iron with a white-hot golf ball–size end of glass, and held it close to Hickory.

I did my best to make and fix a tail to my non-thoroughbred creation. The tail and two hind legs formed a triangle to support the rearing horse. Finished, the object had no grace whatever. I stood it upright on the marver table.

In spite of the faults, Rose seemed impressed. Not impressed enough, however, to lower her guard or her punty iron beside Hickory's head. I glanced at the workshop clock. A minute—*ticktock, ticktock*—was a very long time.

I said, "The gold will cover the hooves, mane, and tail."
Ticktock, ticktock.

Rose held a new white-hot gather near Hickory's head. "How long," she demanded, "until that gold gets here?"

Two minutes. *Ticktock.*

"The gold," I said, "will come in small bars. It has to be melted."

Hickory threw himself forward, trying to get out of his chair. Rose didn't move her punty iron fast enough to avoid him, and one of his ears did touch her waving white-hot blob of glass.

Under the parcel tape he couldn't scream. His body arched. Rose jumped back, but Hickory's ear sizzled. It would never be perfect again.

Three minutes. Eternity. *Ticktock.*

Hickory's horror, plain and agonizing, had everyone staring. Rose should have gone to his help, but she didn't.

Three minutes, ten seconds since I stood the rearing horse on the marver table. Dangerous to wait any longer.

I picked up the big tweezers I'd used to form the horse's mane, and with them tore the parcel tape securing Pamela Jane's ankles. I pulled her up by her still tied wrists. I said to her urgently, *"Run,"* and she didn't, but hesitated, looking back to Hickory.

No time left. I lifted her up bodily and carried her. Rose ordered me to put her down. I didn't, but aimed into the showroom and shouted at the trio there leaning on the wall to get down behind it.

Rose came fast across the workshop after me and drove at me, holding her hot glass–laden punty iron like a sword.

Half seeing her, half sensing the searing future, I twisted both myself and Pamela Jane roughly to let the iron miss us, like a bullfighter, but Rose in fury dragged and stabbed and burned a long black slit through my white singlet.

No more time.

I lugged Pamela Jane around the half-wall to the showroom and threw her to the ground, and I fell on top of her to pin her down.

The rearing horse had stood unannealed at maximum heat on the marver table for three minutes forty seconds when it exploded.

Chapter Ten

THE horse exploded into scorching fragments that flew throughout the workshop and over the half-wall into the showroom beyond.

Adam Force, refusing to get down because it had been I who suggested it, had been hit twice, once in the upper arm and once, more seriously, across the top of the cheekbone below the eye, taking away a chunk of surface flesh. Half fainting from shock, the doctor had dropped his syringe. Blood reddened his sleeve.

It was the wreck of his good looks, I thought, that would in the end grieve him most. The speed and sharpness of the flying glass fragment had opened a furrow that was bound to leave a scar.

The trophy horse had split violently apart along the internal stress lines caused by the outer regions cooling faster than the inner core. The splinters had still been fiercely hot when they'd dug into the first thing they met.

Norman Osprey, kneeling in spite of his antipathy toward the source of good advice, had survived with his skin intact. Although slightly shaking, he still clung to the doctrine of "Get Logan." He rose from his knees and planted his gorilla shoulders close inside the gallery-to-street door, making an exit that way impossible.

Eddie, who seemed not to understand what had happened, was still on his knees beside the wall.

Pamela Jane heaved herself from under me in a troubled dilemma as she couldn't decide whether to thank me for saving her or to revile me for leaving Hickory to take whatever razor-sharp damage came his way in the blast. Pamela Jane, of course, had understood the physics of stress and strain in superheated glass, and she would now be sure I'd intended to shatter the horse from the moment I'd started to make it.

When I stood up and looked over the half-wall to see what shape Rose and Hickory were in, I found Rose bleeding down one leg but still shaking with determined fury while she shoved a clean punty iron into the tank and drew out a second one already tipped with white-hot hate. Hickory, who had finally succeeded in flinging himself out of the chair altogether, lay facedown on the smooth brick floor trying to rub the adhesive off his mouth.

Sharply aware that at some point somewhere Rose had succeeded in drawing a line of fire across my own lower back ribs, I felt I'd already had enough of the unequal combat.

Rose hadn't. Rose, it seemed, had energy in stock for a third world war. As she drew her loaded iron with speed from the fire, she told me that if I didn't get back at once into the workshop, the burn to Hickory's ear would be only the beginning.

I went around the half-wall. Hickory, hurting and helpless, was in no immediate danger from Rose, who advanced on me, holding the silvery black five-foot-long punty iron loaded and ready to strike.

"Adam Force's videotape," she said. "Where is it?"

Short of breath from evading burns so long, I managed dry-mouthed to reply, "He said he'd rerecorded it with horse races."

"Rubbish." Rose advanced toward me with the white-hot ball of glass inexorably leading the way. The ball, if one thrust it fiercely, would burn a path right through a body, searing and killing.

With at least some sort of plan I backed away from Rose and her deadly fire, cursing that I couldn't reach the five or six punty irons lying idle to one side, irons I could at least have used to fence with.

Rose began again to enjoy compelling me to retreat step by backward step. Backward past the furnace, its trapdoor shut. Backward across the workshop, faster as she increased her pace.

"The videotape," she demanded. "Where is it?"

At last, *at last,* I saw Worthington again outside the gallery door, Worthington this time flanked by Tom Pigeon, Catherine, and her hobo partner, Pernickety Paul.

Norman Osprey, suddenly not liking the odds, stood back to let them in and dived fast around them out into the street. I had a last glimpse of him as he set off down the hill with Tom and his four-legged companions in pursuit.

The two plainclothes officers and Worthington now filled the doorway. Furiously seeing the advent of my friends as her last chance to make me remember her for life, Rose rushed recklessly at my abdomen. I sidestepped and dodged yet again, and ran and swerved, and ended where I'd aimed for, beside the wide round pots of colored powders on the stock shelves.

It was the white enamel I wanted. I snatched off the lid, grabbed a handful of the powder, and threw it at Rose's eyes.

The powder contained arsenic, and arsenic made eyes blur and go temporarily blind. Rose, her eyes streaming, went on sweeping around with her petrifying length of death-bearing punty iron.

Eddie walked around the half-wall pleading with her to be still. "Rose, dear girl, it's over."

But nothing would stop her. Blinded for a while she might be, but she lashed out with the killing iron at where she'd last seen me. Missing me didn't stop her from being more dangerous blundering about than if she could see me, and finally, disastrously, the unimaginably hot glass connected twice with living flesh.

There were screams chokingly cut off.

It was Eddie, her father, that, incredibly, she had hit first. She had seared the skin from his fingers as he held them in front of his face to defend himself. There were crashes of iron against walls and a fearful soft sizzling as the worst of all calamities happened.

Pamela Jane hysterically hid her face, but it wasn't she who had burned. Across the workshop Catherine's partner, Pernickety Paul, lay motionless, his limbs sprawling in the haphazardness of death.

Catherine, in a state of shock and anger, stared in disbelief.

Adam Force came into the workshop to stand against the safe side of the wall, and he begged Rose to let someone—like himself—come to help her and her father, but she only changed direction toward his voice, lashing through the air in great sweeps of the punty iron.

Catherine, a police officer to the bone, with Rose following the sound of her voice, called her station urgently for backup. Stifling human terror, she spoke tightly on her radio. "Officer down," she said. "Red call. Officer in need of immediate assistance."

She reported the address of Logan Glass and then added with less formality and genuine emotion, "Come at once. Dear God."

She dodged Rose's rushing speed and with incredible bravery knelt down beside her silent hobo partner. The plainclothes inhabitant of doorways, whose name to me had never been more than Pernickety Paul, would catch no more villains. He had taken a white-hot direct hit through his neck.

I half ran across the room, away from Catherine, and called to Rose, "I'm here, Rose. I'm over here, and you'll never catch me."

Rose turned half circle my way and pivoted once more, when I jumped past her again and yelled at her. She turned again and again and finally began to tire enough with her blurring eyes for Worthington to reach my side and for Catherine to come up behind us and for the three of us to grab Rose and immobilize her still slashing punty iron arm. I wrestled the iron a good safe way away from her, feeling the heat of it near my legs but not on my skin.

The police side of Catherine flowed in her like a strong tide. She found handcuffs and clicked them roughly onto Rose's wrists behind her back, the metal bands squeezed tight against her skin.

There was nothing about "going quietly" in the arrest of Rose Payne. She kicked and thrashed even as an ambulance with paramedics and two cars full of bristling young police officers drew up outside the gallery. The officers fetched a blanket in which they rolled Rose like a baby in swaddling clothes and, with her struggling to the end, manhandled her out the showroom door and into the back of one of the police cars.

Spitting fury, she was soon joined there by the burly Norman Osprey, whose muscles, Tom told me later, had been no match for three sets of canine fangs.

In the workshop I watched as Catherine, dry-eyed, brought another blanket in from a police car to cover the silence of Paul.

MORE POLICE ARRIVED. Methodically they began to sort and list names. One of the officers removed the tape from Pamela Jane's wrists, then took her personal details.

I knelt beside Hickory. As humanely as possible, I pulled the tape from his eyes and mouth. It painfully came off with eyelashes attached. A police officer freed his taped-together legs, and I brought the first-aid box from the stock shelves to put a dressing on Hickory's ear. The paramedics arrived and decided that he should go to the hospital along with Eddie, who was now deep in shock with hands that had already blistered badly.

Catherine stood by the ambulance watching Eddie being helped aboard. I told her other things she ought to know, extra things about Blackmask Four that had come to me during the night, that I hadn't mentioned in the dawn.

She said thoughtfully, "Our superintendent is that man standing beside Paul. I think you'd better talk to him."

She introduced me as the owner of the place, and I shook hands with Superintendent Shepherd. Just then George Lawson-Young arrived. He asked me if I had worked out the identity of the fourth man who'd assaulted me two weeks ago.

"Yes," I said, and told him how I had used his search-and-discard method to sort out truth from lies. But however flatly I said the name, it would cause consternation.

The professor, tall, tidy, and nearsighted, made a slow visual inspection of the damage to the most familiar of faces turned his way. Adam Force looked as if he would prefer to evaporate rather than be in the same room as his onetime boss.

A spent Force, I thought ironically.

It was George Lawson-Young who related to the superintendent step by step how the data stolen from his laboratory had caused me so much pain and trouble.

"Adam Force," he said, "worked for me but jumped ship and stole our cancer research. We knew that he had stolen the information, had transferred it to a videotape, and had destroyed all other records of our research. We searched everywhere for it, even engaging private investigators after the police had shown little interest."

Superintendent Shepherd flinched not at all, but continued listening intently.

"All our searches were in vain. We did not expect him to have entrusted the tape to the safekeeping of a jockey. Dr. Force had passed it to Martin Stukely, but Stukely preferred to hand it on to his friend Gerard Logan here, away from the fingers of his own children. As perhaps you know, Martin Stukely was killed at Cheltenham races on New Year's Eve. But the tape had already begun its tortuous journey by then. Adam Force tried to steal it back. Tapes were stolen from here, from Gerard's home, and from the home of Martin Stukely."

"Were we informed of those thefts?" asked the policeman.

"Yes," I replied. "One of your officers did come around the following morning, but there was more interest in the money stolen with the tape."

"Did Dr. Force steal the money as well?" asked the super.

"Yes," I replied. "But I think that was just an opportunist theft which he might have thought would somehow smoke-screen the removal of the tape."

Dr. Force listened dispassionately, his bloodied face giving away nothing.

"Anyway," continued the professor, who did not welcome the interruption, "somehow all the thefts failed to get back the tape they wanted, and Dr. Force, with assistance from Rose Payne and others, has been trying here to coerce Mr. Logan to reveal its whereabouts. He tells me he hasn't got it."

"And have you?" asked the voice of authority.

"No," I replied, "but I think I know who has."

They all looked at me expectantly. Adam Force, Lawson-Young, even Hickory, who had been listening with his good ear.

Into this tableau swept Marigold, floating in emerald silk with gold tassels and brushing aside the young constable who tried to stand in her way. In her wake came Bon-Bon, Victor, Daniel, and the other children, like the tail of a kite.

Marigold demanded to see how her trophy was getting along but was brought up sharply by the sight of the blanket-covered form in the workshop. Bon-Bon, realizing the enormity of the situation, swept her brood back out the door, leaving just her mother inside.

"Marigold, my dear," I said wearily, "there's been a disaster. Please go across the road to the hotel and wait for me there."

"So who is Blackmask Four?" asked Lawson-Young into the silence when she had gone.

"Who?" said the superintendent. "What are you talking about?"

The professor told him. "Gerard was attacked by four people in black masks outside his shop here. Three of them were Rose Payne, her father Eddie Payne, and Norman Osprey. Gerard told me earlier today that he had worked out the identity of the fourth, so—" He turned to me and said, "Who is it, and where is my research?"

"I don't think Blackmask Four has the tape," I replied.

"What?" exclaimed the professor. His shoulders dropped; his expectations had been so high, and now I was leading him to another dead end.

I put him right. "My fourth assailant, Blackmask Four, was just a hired help, and I'm not sure he even knew exactly what he was looking for." But he knew, I thought, how to inflict maximum damage to my wrists. "He is, however, a dab hand with anesthetic gas."

"Who is it, for God's sake?" The professor was finding it difficult to stifle his impatience, as was the superintendent, yet it wasn't the easiest disclosure I'd ever made. Still . . .

"Who was the fourth man, Hickory?" I asked.

He looked up from where he was kneeling on the floor, still holding a dressing to his ear.

"Why are you asking me?" he said.

"You bunched my fingers."

"Of course I didn't."

"I'm afraid you did," I said. "You held my hand against a wall ready for a baseball bat to smash my wrist."

"You must be crazy. Why would I attack you of all people?"

It was a piercing question and one with a complex answer. I suspected that it had to do with my ability with glassblowing and his comparative lack of it. Envy was a strong emotion, and I reckoned, he wouldn't have needed a lot of persuasion to oppose me.

He still refused to admit it. "You're crazy, you are," he said, getting to his feet and turning away as if looking for some escape.

"The green-and-white laces," I said.

He stopped dead and turned back.

I went on, "You wore them here the day Martin Stukely was killed, and you wore them again the following day when you stole the tapes from his house, the day you hit me with the orange cylinder. Martin's eldest son, Daniel, saw the laces."

Hickory advanced a step or two, his ear clearly hurting and his poise cracked.

"You're so clever," he said. "I wish we *had* broken your wrists."

The superintendent stopped leaning on the half-wall and stood up straight.

But Hickory had only just started. "You and your fancy ways and your condescending comments about my work. I hate you and this workshop. I'm a damn good glassblower, and I deserve more recognition." He raised his chin and sneered. "One day John Hickory will be a name worth knowing, and people will smash Logan glass to get to mine."

Such a shame, I thought. He really did have some talent, but I suspected, it would never develop as it should. Arrogance and a belief in skills he didn't have would smother those he did.

"And Rose?" I asked.

"Stupid bitch," he said, holding his hand to his throbbing ear. "Bloody mad she is. Tie you up, she said. Use you as a hostage, she said. Nothing about frying my bloody ear. Hope she rots in hell."

I hoped she'd rot on earth.

"She promised me my own place," Hickory said. "Claimed she'd close you down. Her and that stupid father of hers." He began to realize the hole he was digging for himself. "They put me up to it. It was their fault, not mine."

He looked wretchedly at the rapt faces around him.

No one believed him. It had been Hickory who had reported all to Rose. Hickory had had the binoculars in Broadway.

"So where is the tape?" asked George Lawson-Young.

"I don't know," replied Hickory. "Rose said that it must have been in Stukely's house or in Logan's, but I've sat through hours of bloody horse racing and glassblowing, and I'm telling you, there was no tape of medical stuff."

I believed him. Otherwise, I thought ruefully, I might have been saved a couple of beatings and Pernickety Paul would still be lying around in shop doorways.

A paramedic appeared and said that it was time to take Hickory to the hospital to dress his burn. The superintendent, roused into action, arrested Hickory and had him led off to the ambulance.

The super turned his attention to Dr. Force, who had listened in silence throughout. "Well, Dr. Force, can you enlighten us as to the whereabouts of a videotape containing medical research results stolen from the professor here?"

Force said nothing.

"Come on, Adam, tell us." The professor, I saw, still had some vestige of friendship for the man.

Force looked at him with disdain and kept silent.

In his turn he too was arrested and taken away for wound stitching and fingerprinting.

IN TIME, the gallery, showroom, and workshop began to clear. The professor and I went over to the Wychwood Dragon. In the residents' downstairs sitting room Bon-Bon and her four sat tightly side by side on the wide sofa in descending height from the right. Marigold occupied a deep squashy armchair, while Worthington perched on its arm.

I took tea and was told that Pamela Jane, still badly shocked, had been given a pill and dispatched to bed upstairs.

Victor stood by the window. I joined him.

Without turning his head, he said, "I suppose my aunt Rose will be inside for a long time?"

"A very long time," I said. Police killers didn't get early parole.

"Good," he said. "It might give me and Mom a chance."

I turned and took Bon-Bon out into the hotel lobby. I needed her to do me a favor. Certainly, she said, and trotted off to the telephone box while I returned to the sitting room to finish my tea. Soon she returned with a smiling nod.

I thought about the events of the morning and wondered if there had been another way.

Punty irons in anyone's hands had to be swung around carefully. In Rose's hands a punty iron tipped with semiliquid glass had been literally a lethal weapon, and it had seemed to me that as it was I she was after, however weird and mistaken her beliefs, it was I who ought to stop her.

I'd tried to stop her with the shattering horse, and I hadn't succeeded. It had torn a hole in her lover, Dr. Force, and stoked her anger. I'd thought then, if I could blind her, she would stop, so I'd thrown the powder. But blinding her had made her worse.

Paul had died.

If I hadn't tried to stop her, if I had surrendered at once . . . But, I reflected, searching for comfort, I couldn't have given her the tape she demanded, as I hadn't known exactly where it was.

I'd done my best, and my best had killed.

THE arrival of my expected guest hurrying through the door brought me back to the present.

"Hello, Priam," I said. "It's so good of you to come."

"I'm sorry?" he said, puzzled. "I don't quite understand. Bon-Bon called me to say that she was with a potential racehorse owner and I should get down here pronto if I wanted the business."

"That wasn't quite the truth. I asked Bon-Bon to make that call because I needed to talk to you about a videotape."

"Not that videotape business again," he said. "I have told you already, I don't have any videotape."

Daniel said distinctly, "I know where there's a videotape."

"*Shhhh,* darling," said Bon-Bon.

"But I do know where a tape is," Daniel persisted.

I had learned to take Daniel very seriously indeed.

I squatted down to his level on the sofa. "Where is it, Daniel?"

"It's in Daddy's car," he said. "It's in the pocket on the back of Daddy's seat. I saw it there yesterday when Mummy brought us to your shop."

Priam shuffled uneasily beside me.

I said to him, "Why did you switch the tapes?"

"I told you—" he started.

"I know what you told me," I interrupted. "It was a lie." Discard the lies, the professor had told me in Bristol, and I would be left with the truth. I asked again, "Why did you switch the tapes?"

He shrugged his shoulders. "I thought," he said, "that the tape Eddie Payne passed to you was one showing the hiding place of an antique necklace. Worth millions, I'd heard from someone. I found it in your raincoat that night, and I thought, with Martin dead, no one would know if I kept it."

Half-truths and misconceptions had woven a path to death and destruction.

Priam went on. "I took another tape from Martin's den, one with racing on it, and wrapped it in the paper and put it back in your raincoat pocket. When I played the original tape at home that night, I discovered that it was all unintelligible mumbo jumbo with nothing about a necklace. So I just put it back in Martin's car when I drove it back to Bon-Bon's the next day."

He looked around. "No harm done. You have the tape back."

No harm done. Oh God, how wrong he was.

IT WAS four days before the police would allow me back into Logan Glass. Marigold was waiting for me to start again on her trophy. Rose, Norman Osprey, Dr. Force, and Hickory had been remanded in custody, while Eddie had been remanded in the hospital, his hands a mess. Rose did little else but scream abuse.

Catherine, cuddling in my arms every night, kept me up to date with the news from the police station.

Professor George Lawson-Young had been given the tape from Martin's car.

Dr. Force had said a little but denied most. He had revealed, however, that Martin Stukely had been unaware that the information on the tape had been stolen. Indeed, Force had told Martin that he was protecting his research from others trying to steal it.

I was glad of that. Had I doubted it?

On Sunday, one week after the mayhem, I set out again to make the trophy horse.

Dependable Irish had agreed to act as my assistant, and this time we had an audience of one. Catherine watched as I again readied my tools and stripped down to my singlet.

I stood on the treadle to lift the door to the furnace and let the heat flood into the room.

Catherine took off her coat.

"Hang it in my locker," I said, tossing her the locker keys.

She walked to the far end of the workshop and opened a door on the tall gray cabinet.

"What's on this?" she said, holding up a videotape. "It has a label, 'How to make the Cretan Sunrise.' "

I moved swiftly to her side. She had by mistake opened Hickory's locker, and there inside we found not just the necklace instruction tape but also, tucked into a brown paper bag, a pair of bright laces, green-and-white striped.

I laughed. "A tale of three tapes, and one of them was under my nose all the time."

"Three tapes?" she asked. "Two were bad enough."

"There were three," I replied. "The only really important, valuable, and perhaps unique tape was the one Force made from the stolen cancer research results. He gave it to Martin, who via Eddie gave it to me. Priam swapped it, mistakenly thinking it a treasure finder's dream to millions. When he found that it wasn't, he simply left it hidden in Martin's car. It's the tape that Rose and Dr. Force have been trying so hard to find."

"And the necklace tape?" Catherine asked. "This one?"

I said, "I had lent the necklace instruction tape to Martin, and it remained in his den at his house until Hickory stole it with all the others. Hickory kept it because, to him, the tape had some value. He thought he could make a copy of the necklace."

"What's the third tape, then?" she asked.

"The tape," I went on, "that Priam took from Martin's den before Hickory's theft. He put it in my raincoat pocket, and it's that tape that Force stole at midnight on New Year's Eve thinking it was his cancer tape. I would have loved to see his face when he played it and found horse racing instead."

I MADE the trophy horse. With Irish's help I gathered the glass from the furnace and again formed the horse's body, its legs and tail. But this time I took time and care and applied the knowledge and talent both learned and inherited from my uncle Ron. I molded a neck and head of an intelligent animal, prominent cheekbones, and a firm mouth. I gave it a mane flowing as if in full gallop and then applied it seamlessly to the body.

I had started out to make a commercial work for Marigold and the Cheltenham Trophy Committee.

In the event, I made a memorial to a trusted and much missed friend. A memorial worthy of his skill and his courage.

The leaping horse stood finally on the marver table, and Irish and I lifted it quickly but carefully into one of the annealing ovens. There it would cool slowly and safely, allowing the strains and stresses to ease gradually. This one was not for shattering.

I WENT with Catherine to the funeral of Pernickety Paul. After the service it was a thoughtful and subdued police officer who mounted her motorcycle. "I've been given leave for the rest of the day, so where do you want to go now?"

I said, "I haven't seen where you live, so how about now?"

She smiled with a touch of mischief and invited me to step aboard. Her home was less than a one-minute motorcycle ride from the district police station, in a single-story semidetached bungalow, and I knew within a blink that it wasn't the place for me.

Inside, the plainclothes's one-floor living space had been allied to *Alice's Adventures in Wonderland,* where a more-than-life-size March Hare and a same-size Mad Hatter sat at the kitchen table and stuffed a dormouse into a teapot. A white rabbit consulted a watch by the bathroom door, and a red queen and a cook and a walrus and a carpenter danced a quadrille around the sitting room. The walls were painted with rioting greenery and flowers.

Catherine laughed at my expression, a mixture no doubt of amusement and horror.

"These people," she said, "came to me from a closing-down fun-fair when I was six. I've always loved them. I know they're silly, but they're company." She suddenly swallowed. "They have helped me come to terms with losing Paul. He liked them. They made him laugh. They're not the same now, without him. I think I've been growing up."

In keeping with the rest of the house, Catherine's bedroom was a fantasyland of living playing cards painting rosebushes white and strong pink against puff-ball clouds and vivid green leaves.

Brought to a standstill, I said weakly, "Lovely."

Catherine laughed. "You hate it, I can see."

"I can shut my eyes," I said, and we pulled the curtains closed.

Later in the evening, when Detective Constable Dodd and her pillion rider climbed back on the saddle, it was to the big quiet house on the hill that they went.

It was like coming familiarly home.

DICK FRANCIS

© ELEANOR BENTALL/FSP

Shattered is a landmark for mystery grand master Dick Francis: his forty-first book—and his twentieth to appear in our series. We are sad to say that it is also the final collaboration between Francis and his wife, Mary, who died soon after the book's publication in September 2000. She was seventy-six years old.

"I couldn't have written the books without her," Francis admits. As his chief researcher and editor, Mary gathered information on glassblowing for *Shattered*. For other books she learned photography, flying, and painting—and became adept at all three. Their books were very much a "joint effort," says Francis, but "she was quite happy for me to have all the credit." The couple also collaborated in marriage for fifty-three years.

To learn more about Dick Francis and
Shattered, visit the Select Editions website:

ReadersOnly.com
Password: *gift*

A
Certain
Slant of
Light

Cynthia
Thayer

*When the ice of
late winter succumbs
to spring's awakening light,
healing grows in the most
unlikely places.*

1

PETER hears the freezing rain pelting onto the cabin roof. He knows it is dripping down the shingles, icing the windows shut, covering the trees. He hears the snap, loud like a rifle shot, a snap from deep in the woods, the snap of tree limbs laden with ice. The birches will be the first to go, then the maples, then the evergreens. He pulls the blanket up to his mouth, heaves it around his shoulders, brings his legs up to his belly, shoves his hands between his knees, squeezes his eyes shut at every cracking noise. Each time he opens his eyes, the room is still there around him, his clothes still draped on nails pounded into the wall, windows intact but iced on the outside, allowing only slanted dawn light through onto the bare wooden floor.

His arm reaches from the blankets for the floor beside the bed. His fingers catch in the matted fur. "Dog," he says softly. "Dog, almost daylight." That is the rule. No dog in bed until the light comes. Dog takes longer today to climb onto the bunk and whines as he crawls up to lick Peter's face.

Peter doesn't mind the ice. If he falls on the way to the outhouse, breaks his leg or his hip, death will be easy. But the old dog is scared of sliding, of losing purchase. End of March, even in Maine, is late in the year for the ice. Another sharp volley outside causes Dog to stop licking, drop his head, resume the whining.

"Come on, Dog. Time to get going."

Peter pulls himself out of the warm covers and slides his legs into the dungarees on the floor by the bed. He hasn't worn underpants since the fire, a small sacrifice he's gotten used to. His red waffle-knit undershirt will have to be replaced soon. That means a trip to town. The plaid flannel shirt is in better shape, and he buttons up the front, hiding the frayed holes in the undershirt. He puts on fresh wool socks from the wooden chest in the corner.

Peter piles birch bark strips loosely in the iron stove and makes a small tent of kindling over them. The bark catches quickly. Dog sits in front of him, head cocked, waiting for the command.

"Dog. Bring the wood." This is Dog's favorite part of the day, and Peter never forgets to give the command—even in summer when there is no fire; then Peter brings the wood back to the spot beside the door when Dog isn't watching. It is Dog's only trick.

Dog chooses a maple log. His gait is slow, his left leg dragging a bit. Peter waits patiently by the frigid stove, breathing white breath. Dog lowers the log, and Peter places the maple on top of the flaming kindling. He adds two pieces of birch from his stack by the stove, shuts the round iron cover, closes the damper, and heads for the door. At the front door he shoves his wool-covered feet into an old pair of rubber boots. The door doesn't open at first. Iced over. Peter leans into it with his shoulder, feeling it give with his body weight.

Ice covers everything like shellac poured over the world. Dog whimpers, straddling the threshold, but Peter gently pushes his rear end and shuts the door.

The sky is gray, but Peter knows that when the sun comes out, the whole Maine coast is going to sparkle like millions of earth stars. He maneuvers his way along the short path to the outhouse, where the ice has settled like a dome over the roof and walls. He kicks the door, cracks the ice, and goes inside.

The cabin will be warm when he gets back. He hopes the ice melts soon, because it is almost time to plant the peas. The garden off to the right resembles the smooth skating rink on the front lawn of the old house in Connecticut, before the fire. He could put on his skates and try it. But the skates are gone. They, too, in the fire. No skates for twenty years. He would never skate again. He's too old now, anyway. He should have had grandchildren. They would skate in the garden. But he doesn't have grandchildren. He doesn't have children.

On the path back to the cabin Dog's rear legs slip out from under him, and he whines again. "Come on, Dog," Peter says. "Keep going. Almost there." He tries to place his rubber boots in spots near rocks or between plant stalks to keep from sliding backward while his hands hover, ready to touch ground if he needs to break a fall.

Dog reaches the cabin door first, wagging with relief, and Peter guides him into the warm room. Peter yanks his feet out of the cumbersome boots and ambles to the stove to make the coffee.

He always grinds the coffee beans, puts the coffee in the percolator, places it over the hottest part of the woodstove before he allows himself to set up the dollhouse. It used to be the most difficult part of the day, waiting. But he makes himself do it. Now it is the routine. He approaches the bookshelf, where the small colonial house is open in the front like a movie set, and pulls the stool up. Leslie is the first to come down for breakfast, in jeans and a sweater. He gently bends the knees and sits her at the table in the kitchen. She always got up first, made coffee, then called, "Peter, coffee's ready. Sarah, Nathaniel, time to get up. Time for school."

Sarah's room was at the back of the house, with stuffed cats on the bed, on the desk, on the floor. Peter's hand reaches back through the hallway into Sarah's bedroom, to the girl doll already dressed for school. He sets Sarah in the chair opposite Leslie, slouches her leg up around the arm, places a miniature glass in Sarah's outstretched hand.

Nathaniel's bedroom is just inside the opening of the house. The boy doll has only one sneaker. Nathaniel was constantly losing his sneakers. Peter stands him at the counter, red lunchbox nearby, baseball hat tilted to the side.

There. Done. The whole ritual is a little crazy, Peter knows, but it's something he has done every day for years, and it is comforting.

He built the house for Sarah on her fourth birthday, a place to put her dolls, to place them on furniture, move them around. It was not for a grown man. He sits on the stool for five or ten minutes every morning just thinking about them, watching the dolls have their breakfast. Sometimes he moves the dolls during the day, to the living room, to the side porch, always back to bed after supper. In the early days, right after the fire, he cried when he touched the dolls, but now something inside him feels comforted.

He pours himself a mug of coffee and settles into his rocking chair. From his place at the stove, he thinks he sees the flash of a white tail. No. Nothing. Just ice. No deer would be out in this ice. He'll have to wait until tomorrow to check on Dora, the old Indian woman next door, to see if his rowboat weathered the storm. Black Harbor is a good town. Far enough away from centers like Ellsworth and Machias and Bangor. Folks help you out if you are in trouble.

Peter and Dog sit looking out the window. Chores might be late today. The chickens wouldn't even notice, but Alice's kicking should start any moment. One minute late, and the old horse blasts the side of her stall.

Dog's head rests on Peter's lap as the first blast of the horse's feet against her stall transcends the now distant sound of tree limbs breaking. As Peter takes a big sip of coffee, trying to finish quickly for Alice, he sees the woman. She leans on an ice-encrusted birch. She looks like the birch, white, tall, but with a full belly. Who is that? No one comes to this house. "Damn," he says. What the hell is a pregnant woman doing in his yard?

"Come on, Dog. Looks like we have some company," he says.

THE woman stands motionless as Peter approaches her. He thinks she might be a mirage. Too much white light reflecting from the ice, making him see things. She wears a red plaid jacket and a denim dress. There is a rip near the bottom, exposing a torn black stocking. The woman stares past him until he touches her arm, just lightly, to get her attention. Her arms hug her chest, her pale eyes quiver below colorless lashes and brows, her lips are a line of faded blue against the chalky skin of her face. Under her right eye her cheek is blue like her lips.

She isn't dressed for the cold. Her gloveless hand rests on his arm, stark white against his flannel shirt. He isn't used to women touching him and wishes she had chosen someone else's cabin to stand in front of.

"What are you doing here?" he asks.

"Please. I didn't want to bother you. I'm lost." That's all she says, her chin shivering against the cold. He doesn't want a strange woman in his cabin.

"How did you get here?"

"My car. It slid right off into the ditch. Must be a mile or two down the road. I followed your driveway."

A crash comes from the barn. Damn. Alice will break up the whole place if he doesn't get to her soon, but he can't just leave the woman alone in the ice. Peter hasn't had anyone in the cabin for twenty years except for Dora.

The dollhouse. It is there on the shelf, open for anyone to see. "I don't have a phone," he says, half expecting her to say, "Fine, thanks, I'll amble on along to the next house, then."

The woman grips his shirt. "Please, I can't walk out. I'm afraid of falling. I'm pregnant, you know."

What the hell is he going to do with her? "I guess you'll have to come into the cabin until I can get you to town with the truck. You can call someone from there."

Something in him expects her to insist on walking out herself, now. He waits, feeling her shiver. He is too close to her. Breathing the same air.

"Is that a horse?" she says after another crash from the barn.

"Yes," he says. "Alice. She always kicks if I don't give her hay first thing."

She finally releases her fingers. "You'd better go feed her, then. If you don't mind, I'll just go into the cabin."

If he doesn't mind? What does she think?

"Please, just stand by the stove. I have things I don't want touched," he says, trying to keep his voice even.

As he turns away from her, he feels relief. He makes his way toward the barn, on the far side of the outhouse, and looks back to watch the woman make her way up the path. Heaps of ghost hair cascade down her back. It is almost white, like washed wool. Not old-age white. Hair that has never been another color before.

Peter feeds Alice, the goat Ruby, and the chickens. He is in a hurry today. The side of Alice's stall isn't too bad, just one board popped out, time to fix it later after he sorts through this woman problem.

What is he going to do with her? Why is she out here by herself in this ice so early in the morning? Last night the radio warned everyone to stay off the roads. And besides, there are downed electrical lines all over the place. The solar cells on the cabin roof power his radio, but the folks around him have certainly lost their electricity.

She is standing at the woodstove, warming her fingers, and turns toward him as he enters. He sets another log in the firebox and rubs his hands together over the tilted stove lid to keep her company.

He notices she is not shivering anymore, but there is a small chunk of ice stuck to the back of her hair. Before he realizes what he has done, he reaches over and tugs the chunk, which falls into his hand. He tosses it behind the stove. Plenty of ice and snow drip there from his gloves and hats and boots.

"Thank you," she says to him, her lips still bluish. Thank you. That's all. No explanation of why she is out by herself on such a dangerous day, why she has a fading blue bruise over the bone of her right cheek. Peter stuffs another log into the stove. "Nice dog. What is his name?"

Peter is embarrassed that he calls his dog "Dog." "Seamus," he says, hoping she believes him. "Look, I don't want to throw you out in the cold, but I only have one room here."

She bites her lower lip. Peter thinks she might cry. For the first time in twenty years he wishes he had a phone. "I can't leave now," she says, studying him. "Not yet."

Peter glances over to the dollhouse. "Excuse me," he says. He feels her stare as he does what he must do. Shakes out an old blue towel, drapes it over the front of the dollhouse, tucks the edges in. His cheeks feel hot.

She doesn't ask about the towel, and he's grateful for that. "I'm sorry for the intrusion," she says. He barely hears her voice. "I'm cold. Do you have some tea?"

That is the least he can do. Make some tea. He nods to her, stokes the fire, places the kettle over the back lid, the hottest spot. "I've got tea, but I usually drink coffee," he says to fill in the time. "Would you rather that?"

"No. Tea. Thank you."

The day is filled with fog. Peter makes her tea. She prefers raspberry to the other offers. He feels uncomfortable leaving her in the cabin while he goes about his chores, but he can't ask her to join him. Not with all the ice. Her name is Elaine. She says nothing about the bruise, even when she sees him staring at it. They talk about nothing. Tea. Ice. Lunch. She offers to stoke the stove when he is outside cutting some fallen limbs.

When he returns, she is sitting in his rocking chair, arms surrounding her belly, her alabaster skin stark against her clothes.

"I'll cook supper after I light the lamps," he says. One night might be bearable. "I'll have to move you for a minute. Root cellar." He points to the trapdoor under the rocking chair.

"Oh, sorry."

He hauls the door up and climbs down the ladder, thinking for a crazy moment that if he shuts the trapdoor above him, she might go away. Potatoes and carrots. That's enough with the ham. She moves the chair back after he lowers the trapdoor.

"Raise my own food here. Not much variety this time of year." He plops the chunk of ham, which he has had soaking since yesterday, into a pot of water and moves it to the back of the stove.

"I'll peel the potatoes," she says.

"No." He slams the cutting board onto the kitchen table.

"Please. I want to help."

"Two glasses over there in the cupboard. You can pour us some of that wine in the jug. Rhubarb." He swipes the peeler over the potatoes and carrots. She pours him a glass and holds up her empty glass. "Don't like rhubarb?" he asks.

"Yes, I do. But . . . the baby. Do you have something else?"

"Water," he says, gesturing to the hand pump by the sink. He feels her presence, hears the pump handle, hears the water gushing into the glass.

"I don't have a car," he hears behind him. "I lied about the car."

Peter doesn't want to look at her. A liar. He knows she is waiting for him to speak, to make judgment on her.

"I took the bus to Ellsworth. Got a ride from a fish truck the last bit. But I walked and walked. It was before the ice storm."

Great. No car. No money. Now what?

"I stayed in that big house down by the water for three nights. One of the windows opened. I was going to have the baby there, but then the ice came and I was scared I wouldn't be able to get out if I needed to. Their phone isn't even hooked up. I didn't eat much, just a few crackers and a couple of cans of stew. I left money and a note." She has moved so he can see her now, and sips her water. "This morning I saw the smoke from your chimney. It's not far, but the walk wasn't easy. I held on to branches, and I only fell once." That explains the rip in her dress and the hole in her stocking.

The old Farley place. Joe Farley had been dead for twenty-five years, and it took ten years after that for his house to fall down. Someone named Underwood built a fancy place on part of the old foundation. Summer folks from Connecticut with lots of money. Come for two weeks at the end of August. Their place is bigger than any other house around.

He is curious about the woman but doesn't want to ask why she lied about the car or why she is hiding. If he knows these things, he will be responsible for her in some way.

Supper is strange. He eats alone except for Dog, but tonight he cooks twice as much, puts two plates on the table, two forks, two napkins. There is little left of the chunk of salty ham—actually, the last piece from the previous summer's pig. There goes the plan to have creamed ham and hard-boiled eggs for the next two nights. "Give this to the dog, I guess," he says, too loud. He scrapes the few bits of ham into Dog's dish on top of the dry food. She washes the dishes because she insists. The towel still hangs over the entrance to the dollhouse. When he passes by on the way to get spare bedding, he resists the urge to pick up the corner.

The sleeping bag and pad smell musty, but he drags them over to the opposite corner of the room and puts clean sheets on his own bed. "You will sleep in the bed. I'll take the sleeping bag. It's comfortable enough."

"Thank you," she says. He wills her to say, "Oh, I don't mind sleeping on the floor," but all the willing doesn't work. She is, after all, pregnant. When Leslie was pregnant, she could never get comfortable. At night in his bed he sometimes tries to bring back that warmth on his back, the warmth of her belly pressing against the small of his back, her hand sliding across his bare chest. Leslie. Her body was comfortable. He knew every bit of her. Gone. Gone.

Elaine uses the bucket while he is at the outhouse. It was his idea because of the ice. He tossed her a clean shirt and long underwear. When he comes back in, she is in his bed, facing the wall, quiet, maybe even asleep. All he sees is the hair like fallen wheat lying on the blanket. He struggles with the idea of lifting the towel, at least just putting the dolls back into their beds, but Elaine could turn around any time. "Come on, Dog," he says. "We sleep over here tonight." But Dog doesn't budge. He has slept beside the bed for a long time and isn't about to change now.

For the first time in years Peter curls up with no dog beside him. And for the first time ever the dolls in Sarah's dollhouse still sit at the breakfast table, talking about morning things when the air is dark around them.

"COME here, Dog," he whispers in the early morning hours, before he hears any stirring from his bed. The cabin is dark. He hears the toenails tapping on the hackmatack floorboards as the shape moves toward him. They have survived the night. Nothing terrible has happened, but the woman is still there in his bed.

He will have to set two places for breakfast, and she will probably want to use his outhouse. He struggles into his jeans in the sleeping bag before he crawls out. His routine is upset. He suddenly feels like crying, something he hasn't done in years. He can't imagine another day with the woman in his house. After chores he plans to check the road conditions. Flag down the police if he has to. "Bring the wood," he says after starting the morning fire, quietly so that the woman won't hear. Dog chooses a small piece of birch and brings it back to the stove.

Peter hurries with the stove, sets the teakettle on the back lid, brushes his teeth in the basin, slips his feet into his frozen boots, glad to get out of there but afraid to leave her with his things. His head pounds hard from somewhere inside his brain. "Come on," he says to Dog in as normal a voice as he can muster, and slaps the side of his thigh.

The world outside hasn't changed except that the outhouse door isn't stuck and Dog doesn't slip on the way back. The sound of a sharp kick from the barn surprises him because Alice usually doesn't start up until after Peter pours his coffee. His hand holds the door latch for a long time before he goes back into the cabin. Elaine stands by the table dressed in her blue denim dress. Tea water simmers on the back of the stove, and he notices that his bed is neat, as if no one had slept there at all. Jesus. Her lashes and brows are as light as the rest of her. Must be Norwegian or something.

Her hands cup a steaming mug with I LOVE YOU, DAD printed on the side. Didn't she read it? What if she drops it on the floor or nicks the rim?

Peter never ever drinks out of that mug, because it might break and he would have nothing from the boy who died in the fire. His boy. Peter and his mother found the mug in the garage beside Sarah's outgrown dollhouse, wrapped in a paper bag covered with Celtic knots drawn in red Magic Marker. The card said, "Happy Birthday to the world's greatest dad." He opened it right then and there, before his birthday, and the pain was beyond tears, beyond anything. The doctor came with a shot, and they carried him away from the charred remains of the house to the hospital and kept him sedated for a week.

"Please. Here's another mug. That one's not for drinking," he says to her. Their hands touch as he removes the mug from her grasp and pours the hot tea into a red mug that says MERRY CHRISTMAS in white letters. "This one's better." She accepts the new mug tentatively, and he cradles the old in both hands over to the sink and pumps water into it. He imagines the mug dropping to the floor over and over as he dries it with a dish towel. Instead of putting it back on the top shelf where it has sat for years, he tucks it into the bookcase—by the dollhouse, way in back behind his bagpipe practice chanter. He knows she watches him, but he has no choice.

Breakfast is bearable. He allows Elaine to scramble eggs, set the table, and wash the dishes after.

"I'll be back soon as I do the chores and check the main road," he says to her after he straps on his ice cleats. "The dog will stay here. Too icy for him."

The cracking from the woods is replaced with chimes, tinkling from pieces of ice-covered branches touching each other in the wind. The sound of cleats crunching, mingled with the ice music, fills the air around him.

On a short incline his cold hands in leather mittens hold on to slippery branches, pull him up the driveway toward the road. Maybe he can get that young Bryant boy to sand the driveway. Hates to pay anyone to do that kind of thing. Cash money isn't easy to come by. He cuts a little pulp wood and sells the fleece from the island to local hand spinners. The life insurance money grows in the bank, but it is tainted and the thought of spending it for his own comfort is inconceivable. It should be only for emergencies, like breaking a leg or some kind of chain-saw accident. That's the only reason he would ever go to a doctor. A break or bad cut. In a little over five years he'll be old enough to be on the Medicare rolls, and then he'll get sewn up for nothing.

The driveway levels off, allowing him to see the opening to the main road ahead. The tinkling of the branches is now drowned out by the rumbling of trucks. That's a good sign. Bangor Hydro trucks are parked on both sides of the road. Power lines droop from cracked poles, and he knows he won't get rid of her today.

"Excuse me," he says to the first guy he approaches. "If I get my truck up here, can I drive down the road? I've got chains."

"No way, man, live wires all over the place. This road's closed."

"When do you think it'll be open?"

"No way to tell. Maybe tomorrow. Maybe next week."

"Damn. You got one of those cell phones?"

"Yeah. But is this an emergency? Who do you want to call?"

Who to call? What an idiot. Why didn't he ask her? Someone made that mark on her cheek. Call the police? No. Not yet. "Thanks, anyway." Maybe if he gets her out this far, the repair guys will take her into town with them. Then she can use the phone at Tuttle's store.

The way back down the driveway is easier. He is glad to see a glimpse of the cabin, until he visualizes the woman and the doll-house together. He pictures her lifting the corner of the towel and thinking he is a foolish child. He imagines her laugh. He stops abruptly, his ice cleats skidding down the drive. He slides onto a mound to the left of the drive, not able to hold back the crying. He's glad she can't see him like this, face all red, sniveling like a baby.

Life here in Black Harbor was bearable before this. He has his horse, his goat, his dog, his chickens. A cabin all paid for. An island. Everything he needs. Damn woman. With relief he feels the package of Lucky Strikes in his breast pocket. He taps out a couple of "strike anywhere" matches and a cigarette. Good a time as any to smoke. He straightens himself out, makes himself comfortable against the butt of a tree, crosses his legs in front of him, lights the match on the zipper of his fly. The first one sputters and dies. The second one blazes long enough to get an ember going at the end of the cigarette. He pulls the smoke into his lungs, leans his head back to the trunk, and it's all right for now.

The air is warming up rapidly. Peter struggles to his feet and crunches toward the cabin. Through the door he hears her voice, barely audible at first, just like the wind howling under the door, but then the words come. *"I gave my love a cherry without a stone, / I gave my love a chicken that had no bone,"* in a voice high and sure, a voice that makes him cover his ears with his hands to keep its power out. Power like bagpipes. He realizes he hasn't heard anyone sing since the funeral. He turns and slides his back down the door until he sits on the landing, head turned toward the sound, and he can't stop the tears flowing, flowing again like a break in a dam.

"Leslie," he says aloud. "Leslie."

The sound of the singing ceases, and he is aware of movement behind him. She is trying to open the door, and he is sitting in front of it. He swipes his face with a small chunk of ice, dabs at his cheeks, dries them with the sleeve of his shirt.

"Trying to clear the landing of ice," he yells. Once inside the cabin, he lifts the lid of the stove to feed in another log and sees that the firebox is full.

"I put some wood in," she says. "What's the instrument? The one on the shelf, looks like a recorder or a flute or something?"

"My practice chanter. For bagpipes."

"Wow. Do you play bagpipes?"

"No. Not anymore." He is surprised how loud his voice is, that he even said the word bagpipes, something that had been part of his old life. She knows too much now, too much about him. It's an invasion of his privacy. "We've got a problem," he says. He fiddles with the lids of the stove, not wanting to look at the woman. "Driveway's a sheet of ice. The road's closed. Live wires all over."

"I have nowhere to go."

"Well, I can't accommodate a person in this cabin for another night." He paces back and forth in front of the stove, his back to her. One more night, and she'll be lifting the towel, gawking at the dolls. "They have a shelter in town." He thinks that if she sings again, he won't be able to send her to a shelter—but she just sits and rocks. He wants to know about her, about the bruise, but once he asks, things will become different. Has she seen a doctor? What if she went into labor now, in the cabin, with just the two of them, no doctor? He knows about birthing sheep and goats but not human babies. "Do you have a number to call, or should I call the shelter?"

"Please," she says. "I can help you. I'm a good cook."

"No," he says, turning to face her. "No, I'm going to call the shelter. They'll come get you as soon as the road opens."

Her mouth gapes wide, but no words come out. She sways from one foot to the other. Her hands move as if trying to speak for her. Don't give in, Peter says to himself. Two people cannot live in this little cabin. And the dollhouse is still closed up.

"I only have fifty dollars. Please. You can't throw me out in the ice." The corners of her mouth turn upward in a half smile. "One more night?"

"Oh, damn it all," he says, grabbing his jacket on the way out. "Come on, Dog."

2

THE trek through the woods is slow, even with ice cleats. Dora's cabin is past the Underwood house, and Peter marvels that Elaine was able to navigate her way without more damage to herself. The house is visible if he looks through the trees. In the summer the trees covered any sign of a house, and Peter was always glad when the leaves opened, allowing him to walk to Dora's and the boat without seeing anyone.

Dora is out spreading sand on the path to the outhouse when Peter arrives at the crest in the hill. "Dora," he yells. "It's me, Peter."

"Who else on a day like this?"

"Come on, old thing," he says to Dog, who is having a hard time scrambling up the hillock.

The sea is choppy beyond the log cabin, bouncing his small white skiff up and down, each rise catching the glint of the sun's reflection on the iced gunwales. Not enough chop to keep him out of his boat. It's only a short row to the island. The ewes could be in trouble with this ice. Some of the older ones should be bagging up now, getting ready to lamb. It is already late March, and lambs are expected around the second week of April.

"Figured the old dog might not come again," Dora says, "especially with this terrible weather."

Dora must be over eighty herself but has lived alone here since her husband, Mitchell, died. Mitchell was Micmac, and Dora, Passamaquoddy, but neither wanted to live in the close confines of the reservation, so Mitchell built the cabin when they got married, and they'd lived there ever since. As a teenager, Peter rowed old Joe Farley across to the island to tend his sheep from this same spot.

Since Mitchell died, Peter has looked in on Dora, not that she needs checking on. The previous fall she shot a twelve-point buck first day of hunting season. Dora and Mitchell were Peter's only friends when he first came to his family's summer camp in Black Harbor after the fire, the only people he let through the door. They brought deer meat, clams, strawberries, and mayflowers when spring came. They asked no questions, never said, "If there's anything we can do . . ." Never made small talk.

"I'm going out to the island today just to check," he says. "I don't want them stuck on the ice so close to lambing."

"Come on in and have coffee. I got it all made." Dora is the only person he knows who loves coffee as much as he does.

He follows her, Dog at his heels, up onto the porch and into the cabin. As he slips off his cleats, she pours thick black coffee out of an old aluminum percolator.

Her cabin is warm, messier than his. Her spinning wheel occupies the center of the room, a hub for baskets full of fleece, skeins of spun yarn, hand cards, measuring tape, scissors, dirty teacups. But there are curtains on the windows and pictures of their daughter, Margaret, and her children clustered on the log walls. He used to play with Margaret in the summers when his family made the long trek from Connecticut to the cabin. She is a corporate lawyer now and rarely comes to Maine anymore.

Dora and Peter sit, sipping the hot coffee, listening to Dog scratch under the table. "You lose the juice?" he says.

"Only a couple hours. Still had the woodstove."

"I figured you'd do okay," he says.

"How'd you make out? Animals don't like that ice much."

"Alice has been stuck in the barn. Ugly as sin. I've been trying to get the truck out. Too much ice."

"What you need to get out for? You got all you need."

"Something happened. Need to get out." Peter gulps his coffee, leaving a half inch at the bottom. "Strangest thing. Some lost woman. Saw the smoke from my cabin and figured she'd get some shelter."

"And?"

"I can't put her out in this mess, now, can I?"

"How long she been there?"

"Since yesterday."

"Oh, got yourself a live one, did you?"

"No, no, nothing like that. No. She's pregnant and seems to be on the run. She's half my age, anyway. I think I'm going to have a hard time getting rid of her."

"Pregnant, you said?"

"Almost due. I can't have anyone living with me in that cabin. Much too small. She ought to be seeing a doctor. You've done some birthing. Maybe you should take a look."

"I've birthed lots of babies. Been doing it for years. When I was young, I birthed most of the babies around here. Not just the Indian babies. I'll take a look at her if you want."

Dora reaches across him to a shelf by the window and pulls out a strip of deer jerky. "Here, old dog, something for them old teeth." Dog loves Dora's jerky and mouths it politely before he takes it under the table and begins to chew.

"She'll probably be gone by tomorrow, but . . . I'm going to leave the old dog with you this time. Too icy out there for the likes of him." He drains the coffee cup.

"I'll keep an eye on the boat," she says. "Making a stew if you have time for lunch." Peter loves Dora and would even hug her, but their relationship isn't like that.

"I won't be long. Just a quick row out and back. Want to check if any of them are frozen to the rocks. I'll bring the shears. Glad I stuck the oars in the shed. Would've been covered with that damn ice." He also has his knife in case one has to be put down. He's afraid of seeing broken bones, cracked skulls. "Keep the coffee going."

Pulling the slippery haul-off line is tricky because the ice cleats skid. With each tug, shards of ice fly off the rope into the sea and the skiff bobs toward him. He leaps in, grasping at the slick seat. A few good bangs with the oars break up most of the ice. It falls like diamonds onto the bottom of the boat. After he unties the painter, he plops the oarlocks into the holes and pulls on the oars hard before the wind and tide bring him too close to the ragged shore.

I gave my love a cherry without a stone, he thinks, stroke on the first beat of the measure, *I gave my love a chicken that had no bone.*

He loves that island. He remembers the first time he went with Old Man Farley, who seemed old even then. He remembers lots of leaping white sheep funneling into the shearing chute. He never missed a year shearing until he went away to college. When Old Man Farley left him the island in his will, with seventeen decrepit white sheep, Peter sold them all at auction. He was teaching music then, playing pipes professionally, and engaged to the exquisite Leslie Flannigan and certainly not interested in sheep.

He pulls as hard as he is able, pushing the boat up onto the pebble beach, and jumps to shore before the tide takes it back out. The boat is light and easy to pull up. No ice on the tidal part of the beach. He grabs his bag of tools from the bow and clamps on the ice cleats. It is a small island with only a few trees, a ramshackle hut they use at shearing time, and an old cellar hole up on the rise where Joe Farley had a cabin. The wind picks up, stings Peter's face, makes him hurry even on the slippery rocks.

Just over the knoll he sees the flock, pawing the beach for rock-weed and eelgrass and kelp. It will be easier to check them on the beach. He doesn't go too close, doesn't want them to scatter. Just close enough to see if any are bagged up. They look healthy, some obviously full of lambs. He counts heads. Twenty-six. Four are missing. He always loses a couple over the winter to predators or old age.

He counts again. The new black Romney ram is missing, along with a few ewes. The flock, suddenly aware of his presence, scatters up into the high ground, a few slipping on a particularly icy spot. He follows at a distance, looking for signs of the missing sheep. Ahead he sees black. And three white. He sees the ram lift his head, shake it, struggle to get on his feet. Frozen, Peter thinks. The others are alive too. He slides the last few feet and kneels down to them, feeling around the base of their wool to find where it is stuck. They struggle against him. The ram's eyes scream fear. Peter maneuvers the shears carefully to cut the wool free from the ice. "Go on, then, get up." The ram kicks and thrashes against the slickness of the ground until he is standing on all fours. He staggers off to find the flock. The ewes are a little weaker, but Peter thinks they will be fine. Thaw is coming, and the grass is pushing at the ice.

In a few weeks the lambs will come. The next time he comes out will be to castrate and cut the tails off some beautiful white or black half-Romney spring lambs.

HE DOES the evening chores before he approaches the cabin, because it is late when he gets back from Dora's. Alice snorts on his neck while he dumps the grain into her feed trough. "Go on, Alice, eat your food." She has been in her stall since the ice storm and is restless. "Tomorrow you'll go out, you old nag. Lots of things change tomorrow." He is glad he left the ice caulks on her shoes.

Dog laps at the mouth of the water pump while Peter fills buckets for Alice and Ruby. He'll put Ruby out tomorrow too. Alice and Ruby are friends. Strange kind of bedfellows, a horse and a goat, but both are apoplectic if separated for any length of time. When he comes home from yarding wood with Alice, Ruby is always standing up on her hind legs, front feet looped over the top of the wire fence, screaming at them.

He smells dinner before he even opens the door. Elaine stands at the woodstove as if it were her own, pokes at the food in pots, stirs something with the long spoon he whittled for rendering the lard.

"I cooked dinner," she says. Her belly is larger than he remembers, pressing against the chrome rail of the woodstove as she works. Her half smile is back, but at least she isn't singing. The air in the cabin is full of bread smells, and there are three pots on the surface of the stove. He rarely uses more than one pot at a time, just throws everything in together.

"That's nice," he says as he flicks on the radio, turned down low.

"I didn't touch anything. Just the cooking pots and the food." Her voice is soft and small, not like her singing voice at all, but he feels that somewhere inside her is a bigger voice hiding out. "Soup first."

The table is set with salt and pepper and glasses and a chunk of butter in the crockery bowl. Dog whines for his dinner. Peter scoops out a quart of dry food into the dish and quietly takes his seat at the table. It's warm in the cabin, much warmer than usual, and he takes off his sweater. The soup steams from the bowl she places in front of him. "Try it," she says as she joins him.

Chicken soup with rice. Dried parsley and cilantro float on the top of the broth. Chunks of his canned chicken cover the bottom of the bowl. When he makes soup, that is the meal. Soup. Sometimes bread too. But never soup and other things afterward. "Good soup," he says. Might as well be pleasant. He might have to get tough with her in the morning. He wishes he hadn't been so abrupt earlier when he left the cabin. He wants to be tough, not mean.

After the soup she clears the dirty dishes and brings clean plates. "Carrots with maple syrup." She sets down a platter heaped with shining carrot coins. Mashed potatoes overflow another small bowl. "This bread's my grandmother's recipe. Porridge bread with molasses. I couldn't find molasses, so I used maple syrup." He thinks of the hours of sitting outside watching the sap boil down, just so he'd have enough for a few mornings of pancakes. His precious syrup, stored for the whole year, half used up for one meal. He heaps his plate, anyway. The trip out to the island made him hungry. The bread is delicious. He slathers butter all over the top. She is proud of herself, he can see that. "That's not all," she says when he finishes everything on his plate. "I've made something else."

"Oh," he says. "What could that be?"

"Pie," she says. "Lemon meringue pie. There was a jar of lemon curd up on the shelf, with dust all over the cover." She clears the table and brings more clean plates. The meringue is lightly browned on top, just the way Leslie made it.

His sister sent the lemon curd soon after the fire, so it has been there for almost twenty years. It's a wonder she even got the top off the jar. And used it without asking. She places her creation in front of him, looking like a damn magazine ad for Little Miss Housewife.

"Small or large piece?" she says. Lemon meringue pie. Used to be his favorite. Leslie always made it on Sunday if his father was coming for dinner, and that was often. After his father died, Leslie always made it at Easter.

He feels like there is no way out. "Well, small or large?" she asks again, placing the pie in front of him. "Do you like lemon pie?" She is too close. He smells her skin, like lemons, feels her warm breath on his face. "Cat got your tongue?"

"I hate lemon pie." Peter is surprised at his response. "You don't live here. What right do you think you have taking over everything?" He feels trapped in his chair because she is there, leaning over the pie. "Tomorrow we'll get you out of here. You can go home, wherever that is." He is afraid to look up at her. He wants to push her away, but he lowers his head more.

The first sign he has that she is crying is the tear that falls onto the browned meringue. It hesitates, then slides down and nestles into the white of the valley. One tear. He waits for another, but she straightens herself. Her face is flushed, but her mouth is firm. Set. Not quivering.

They are statues, staring at each other. When he was a child, he was always the best at that game, could stand for ages without even blinking or twitching. It is harder to do that now, and he has a sudden desire to laugh. The back of his neck tenses up as he holds back the urge and scrambles for his next move.

"Sit down," he says. "The news will be on any minute. We'll see what's happening with the roads."

She sits at the table, hands folded in front of her, those eyes looking directly at him. She doesn't speak.

He pulls the package of Luckies out of his shirt pocket and taps one out. Just as he lights the end, she speaks.

"Please don't smoke."

That's all. Please don't smoke. Well. It's his house, and he will smoke if he wants to. He pushes his chair back from the table and takes a big drag from the cigarette, blows the smoke away from her toward the door. Dog ambles over to him and touches Peter's leg with his nose.

"Please. It's not good for the baby, and it's not good for you."

Peter takes another drag and exhales fast, blowing smoke over the table, and grinds the butt out on the plate that was to be for his pie. He rubs Dog behind the ears. "Look, tomorrow you go somewhere. I don't really care where that is as long as it is out of here. I'm sorry you have problems, but everybody has problems." He thinks of Leslie behind the towel and the doll children frozen in their own two-day game of statues. "I'm not going to throw you out in the cold, but you can't stay here. The radio will give us some news." He moves the dial back and forth until he hears ice-storm news.

"Power companies have been working through the night to restore power to coastal communities hardest hit by the storm. Some roads are still closed, but most should be opened by tomorrow morning." He gestures with his eyes to the radio, nods his head toward her. They watch each other across the table as the topic on the radio shifts.

"And finally on the storm news tonight, Elaine Sinclair, thirty, from Bedford, Maine, has been reported missing from her home and is believed to be down east in the vicinity of Black Harbor." Elaine glances out the window. "No foul play is suspected, but the woman may be confused. She is fair-haired, five-foot-five, almost eight months pregnant. If you have any knowledge of her where-abouts, please call the station."

"Confused?" she says. "Confused?"

He doesn't want to know any more about her. He doesn't even want to know why she has a fading yellow bruise under her right eye. He knows enough. The place will be crawling with husbands and police if she stays much longer. That's all he needs, a bunch of strangers snooping around.

"Are you going to call?"

"I don't know."

"I'm not confused. Well, maybe I am, but there's no need to call the station. Besides, you don't have a phone, do you?"

"No."

"I feel safe here. I have some thinking to do. It seems like God is here in this place."

"God? No God here," he says.

"Yes, there is."

"Fine. Let's get some rest, and tomorrow I'll take you to a safe place where they'll take care of you."

Peter helps her clean up the dishes. The lemon pie sits undisturbed on the table, the tear now indiscernible amongst the weepings of the meringue.

"I might take a small piece of that pie now," he says quietly. "But I can cut it myself."

THE night is longer than usual because Peter's hip bone pushes against the hard hackmatack in every position he chooses. This is the last night he will spend on the floor. He hears Elaine making night noises, snuffling, scratching, turning from one side to the other. As he adjusts his body so that his hip is away from the hard wood, he hears her rise and thump around the cabin. He turns slowly in his sleeping bag toward the sound, hides his face, watches her move. She limps, favoring her right leg, leans down to grab her calf. "Drats," he hears her whisper, and then he hears something else outside. Drips. Small drops falling from the cabin roof, falling from trees in the woods, hundreds of trees each releasing a drop of melted ice.

Elaine sits on the edge of the bed, her wheat-colored hair resting on her shoulders. In the dark of the cabin he sees only outlines, except for the hair. She clears her throat and lowers herself into his soft comfortable bed next to his old dog and pulls the covers over her head. She shifts back and forth from side to side for a long time, and then there is nothing but the sound of breathing and the shapes of familiar furniture. He lies on his back so he won't have to smell the staleness of the sleeping bag while he waits for the light. After chores he will attach the chains to the truck tires and get her out of here. Get his home back.

Even his breathing feels forced, afraid he will wake her up if it is too irregular. He tries to see the dollhouse, see if they are still having breakfast, tries to tell if the towel still hides the rooms, the dolls, his family. The shelf looks dark, without pattern, the towel blending in with the grayness of the books beside it. When he first moved to the cabin, the nights were long and lonely, because he was not used to being by himself in the dark—until he brought Sarah's old dollhouse in from the barn and placed it on the shelf where he could see it from his bed. Now the idea of waking up with another person in the cabin unnerves him. Breathing the same air as a woman for the whole night frightens his body into tensing the muscles of his legs until he isn't sure he will be able to move them if there is a flood.

He begins to discern the sounds of the drips, the different musical notes they make as they hit the ice covering the driveway, the earth of the kitchen garden, stone, trees, the hood of his truck. His arms are stiff at his sides, and his neck aches from holding his head still. When he thinks he cannot stand the rigidity even one more minute, he detects the day, just a faint glow of light through the front window.

The light in the window brightens, and the old dog sniffs and flops onto his other side. "Come here," Peter whispers to him. "Come on," he says as he taps the floor with the back of his hand. He sees the eyes as they open, hears the padding of the old feet on the wood, watches the form sway and lurch, until he feels the cold moistness on his thumb, his hand, up his arm. Peter turns his face so it will be easier for the old dog to reach.

He will be pleasant to her this morning. Last night worked out all right. He ate over half the pie.

He reaches for his jeans, last time he'd be putting them on inside the damn sleeping bag. Dog licks at him, making it even more difficult. "Go on," Peter whispers so the woman doesn't hear. As he pulls on his shirt and wool socks and shoves his feet into the work-boots beside his sleeping spot, Dog is already at the woodstove waiting for his command.

"Get the wood," Peter says quietly to Dog.

Dog brings two small birch logs while Peter lights the kindling. The noise of dripping water is all around him. An old tune. A strathspey. He thinks the sun will shine today.

He flicks on the radio. Power lines fixed, it says. He looks out the window to the driveway. Sheer ice. But with chains, it will be possible. She stirs, but he doesn't look around. Before he leaves the cabin, he checks the stove dampers, makes sure the lids are settled into their recesses. Dog slips once on the walk down toward the truck but recovers easily. The trees are still covered with ice, and he notices broken branches that have given up to the weight of the frozen shell around them.

He hears the kick just as he opens the barn door. *Blam*. He throws grain into Alice's trough and gives the goat her allotment. Water can wait.

The chains feel cold and heavy in his hands as he lies down on the ice-covered gravel and spreads them out behind the wheels. Easiest way is to back onto the chains and then connect them, but he isn't sure the truck will back up over them on this slickness. His skin feels cold, the cold from ice melting on the surface invades the back of his jacket, rising through his sweater, through his holey red undershirt, into his chest cavity.

After a brief spin in front of the chains, the truck consents to his pressure. Two feet. That's all it takes to center the tires directly on the chains. He gets out to check them. Perfect. Right over the center of the links. He snaps them into place, tugs to make sure they are tight, firm, then turns the engine off. He doesn't want anything else to go wrong with this woman thing. It has to be today. First he'll get her out of here. Somewhere in town: the shelter or the bus stop or even some church. They're equipped to handle these things. Then he'll go see Dora.

Elaine is up when he gets back, making her infernal tea. "Good morning," she says.

"Good morning," he says.

They nod to each other, avert their eyes as if no one has anything to say. But they have everything to say and no way to say it. Peter opens the lid of the stove to shove in a piece of maple. The firebox is already full with birch on top of a stick of oak. He searches for his jar of coffee beans on the shelf.

"The coffee's made," she says. "There on the stove."

She knows woodstoves, what kind of wood to put in, how to make coffee in a percolator. He and Leslie used to have one of those Mr. Coffee machines. *Peter,* Leslie'd say, *the coffee's made,* and she'd kiss him lightly on the cheek.

Peter cuts a large piece of lemon meringue pie and sits at the table, Dog at his foot. Elaine brings her steaming cup of tea and sits down opposite him.

"Well, I guess I owe you some explanation."

"Nope. Soon as we finish breakfast, I'll drive you to town. There's a new shelter, built last year to help women like you, or I can drop you at the general store, where they have a pay phone."

"Please listen—I appreciate being able to stay here. I want to tell you why I can't go home."

"I don't care where you go, but you can't stay here."

"I've prayed hard. Every night of this pregnancy. I prayed all last night."

That's all he needs is some religious fanatic, praying all over the place. Peter knows there's no God, knows there's no point in praying to something that doesn't exist. When Leslie and the chil-

dren died, he tried to pray. He got down on his knees beside his
hospital bed and stayed there until his legs were numb, until
his knees ached, waiting for comfort, a sign from God that everything would work out. And all he got was sore knees. It's not like
he tried it only once. Must have been every night for a week.
That's the last time he'd ever prayed. Big waste of time. And now
he is expected to ask her why she prays. He can't even say the
words.

She sips her tea, her hair catching the light of the rising sun. "I
want to tell you why. I want you to understand why I showed up at
your door and why I can't leave."

"Can't leave?" he says. "Can't leave?" He can't help it that he
says it twice. "I can take you to a friend's house where there's a
phone. You can call from there. That's it. Don't argue." He can't
remember speaking so firmly to anyone since his own kids. Not
even often to them. Just before the fire, Nathaniel left his new purple bicycle out in the rain. *You don't have any respect for belongings. See if I get you anything else new. Don't argue,* Peter'd said.
He remembered the exact words and how they rattled around in
his head for months after the fire. The last words he ever spoke to
his own son. He left for a competition before Nathaniel came home
from school. He wanted to wait, to kiss him, tell him he was sorry,
that he had been in a bad mood, but it got too late, he couldn't
chance missing his plane. The words ricocheted off the rind of his
skull. No respect. No respect. Don't deserve anything new. Don't
argue. Don't argue. At first the words grew louder each time they
hit something, bounced, swelled, hit again, bounced, swelled. But
after a while some of the words just stuck to the sides of his skull,
broke off, softened, until he could stand it, until he could drink his
coffee without vomiting. And now he has spoken like that to the
woman, Elaine. *Don't argue.*

She doesn't flinch. Sips her tea again, waiting for him to back
down. He wishes he weren't afraid to let her stay with him, but that
is absurd. No one who lives in this small a cabin would be able to
have another person move in, at least not in winter. Absurd.

"I am desperate. I need help. My baby is coming soon. It will need a transfusion." She bites her lower lip, and he thinks he detects fear beyond the filmy surface of her eyes. She places her hand over her mouth, and he wonders if she is practicing her next speech with her lips. Her fingers have freckles on them, and her nails are like workingmen's nails—short, ragged around the edges—but clean, clean like a piper's nails. Just as he is ready to get up, start the truck, urge her toward the door, she lowers her hand to her lap.

Transfusion? Why would a little baby need a blood transfusion? Maybe Elaine's a bleeder. Maybe that's why she's so white.

"I am terrified. I thought it would be easy to trust in Jehovah and let Him help the baby. But it isn't easy at all."

Peter doesn't want to encourage a discussion that might slow down the movement toward the truck, but it is hard to just ignore what she is saying. Is she crazy? A fanatic, perhaps. He really doesn't want to know anything more about her. He stares past her, focuses on the sound of the thaw and the fallen branches. The woods will need days of work.

"Peter," she says. "Will you listen to me?"

The loud blast of a car horn cuts her off, and Peter jumps to his feet and bolts for the door. It is rare that anyone comes to see Peter unless there's a problem somewhere. It's Brendan in his four-wheel-drive truck. No chains. That's a good sign.

"Hey, Pete," Brendan calls from his truck. Some of the local fishermen call him Pete, and he never corrects them.

Peter cautiously steps his way down the path to the turnaround at the bottom of the driveway. "Brendan, what's up?" Peter says as he slaps the hood of the new red truck hard enough to hurt his fingers. "How's that boy of yours?"

"Can't do nothing with him. Warren hauled him in last week for drinkin' and drivin'. Trying to get him to come in with me. Lobstering. Thought it would be a good chance for him. I dunno."

"Oh, he'll come around. What brings you down here?"

"Just thought I'd warn you. Some fancy-ass guy nosing around looking for his wife. Could be trouble. Guy in a suit and tie and leather shoes in this weather, asking if anyone's seen this pregnant woman. Seems his wife is hiding out on him. Something shifty in his eyes. Even if I knew, I wouldn't be telling him nothing. He might be down here, and I know you don't like no one nosing around your place."

Peter thinks quickly about the woman and what to say to Brendan. News will get around. Might as well spread the true news. Folks around here hate to be fooled. He points up to the cabin. "She's in there. Seems scared. I've been just waiting for the roads to open up so I can get her to a shelter or a phone or something. She's not staying here."

"Well, I'll be," says Brendan. "Hiding from him, is she? He sure didn't look like a bum, but there was something weird in his eyes. There's gotta be something wrong with anyone wears a suit and them fancy shoes to go out in this kinda mess."

"Roads open?"

"Yeah. But you gotta go slow. Well, you know how to drive around here. You been here long enough."

"Yeah, got the chains on, ready to go."

"You'll have no trouble. Just get some momentum going before you hit the incline."

"Thanks, man. Appreciate it."

Brendan turns around to head back up the driveway. The truck doesn't slide a bit.

So. A guy with a suit and fancy shoes. Peter guesses he'll be able to handle that but hopes he doesn't have to. He slides into the driver's seat of his old black truck. The engine lurches as he turns the key but settles into a soft purr after a couple of seconds. He'll leave it running while he gets the woman. All the windows are encased in ice. He turns on the windshield defrost.

PETER has just gotten out of his idling truck when he hears the other truck coming down the driveway. The truck looks shiny. Black. The dark-skinned driver steers his truck right up to Peter's and rolls down his window. There he sits, suit dark against the white, starched shirt, necktie squishing his neck. If Peter didn't know who the guy was, he would yell at him to leave the property.

This could be really easy. Just hand her over.

"Excuse me. I am looking for my wife," the husband says as he lowers himself cautiously from his truck to face Peter. "She is confused, pregnant. I can't imagine what got into her. I need to get her home where she belongs. Someone said she might be down here."

The man wipes the corners of his mouth with his starched white handkerchief, which probably has his initials monogrammed into one edge. There is nothing stuck on the corner of his mouth. No crumbs, nothing that Peter sees.

"Your wife."

"Have you seen anyone? Or heard of anyone like that?" the husband asks.

Just as Peter forms the words to tell about Elaine, he catches sight of the man's shoes. Brendan was right. Dress-up black, shiny shoes. What kind of man wears dressy funeral shoes on top of ice?

"What's she look like?" Peter asks.

The man pulls his handkerchief out of his pocket again, rubs at an invisible spot on his truck bed, and replaces the handkerchief. His fingernails are immaculate, and he turns his hand in a fist so he can check them. Peter wonders about the fist and the bruise on Elaine's cheek. "She's very pregnant. Fair. Very fair. Blue eyes."

"Fair? Blue eyes?" Peter thinks about how easy it is. Sure, she's right up there in the cabin. But he can't say the words. He wonders if the man will offer pieces of silver for her, and suddenly Peter feels like Judas. "Can't say as I've seen anyone like that. Haven't seen many folks the past few days. Too much ice."

The man glances up to the cabin as if he doesn't believe Peter.

"Got work to do. Nice meeting you, Mr. . . ."

"Oliver. Here's my card. Please call if you hear or see anything." Oliver peers through the trees toward the cabin again before he gets into his truck. Must be a borrowed truck; he's not a truck man. "You could be in trouble if you're withholding information," he says as politely as you please, but the words feel hard and cold.

Peter waits until the truck disappears before he looks at the business card. OLIVER SINCLAIR. ROOFING CONTRACTOR, BREWER, MAINE. He can't imagine the man up on anyone's roof, especially in that blooming business suit. He sticks the card into his jacket pocket, just in case. Peter turns off his truck and looks toward the cabin.

What's wrong with him? Why didn't he just tell the guy his wife was in the cabin? Oliver's her problem, not his. It's not his fault if the guy hits her. Maybe he's the salt of the earth. How does he know? Kind of fancy, though. Peter holds his fist up in front of him, fingers facing him. He'll be fifty-nine in July, but that isn't the only difference between them. His nails are ragged, cuticles torn, calluses here and there. He is clean, but it is hard to keep immaculate when you have no hot water and you work with your hands.

Things were different before the fire. He even manicured his cuticles before the Highland games because he knew judges considered everything in open competition, even the condition of the fingernails. No one had beaten him those last two years. He'd even won Open Piper of the Day that last day in Maxville. That woman, up-and-coming grade one piper, Kate or something like that, clapped loud and kissed his cheek when the winners were called and his name was announced as North American Professional Piping Champion. *Dinner?* he'd said to her after he'd sat down with the silver bowl in his lap and the check for three hundred dollars in his sporran. *Love to,* she'd replied. Peter can't recall what happened after that except he'd eaten dinner with Colin. He remembers telling Leslie. It's the only thing he can remember of the hours before the call about the fire, and it pisses him off. Forgetting those last hours of knowing he had a family.

Broken branches lie scattered around, some littering the path, mostly birch but some evergreen. The trees that aren't broken touch their tips to the ground like gargantuan croquet hoops. And everywhere the music of the ice. Strathspeys. Sometimes a waltz.

You can stay one more day. You can stay two more days. He gave me the creeps. That's why I lied. Peter practices the responses in his head.

He is still trying to find the right response when he heads back to the cabin. When he's found it, he'll tell her. Just because he lied to Mr. Oliver Sinclair, Esquire, doesn't mean he will keep the woman in his cabin. Only means he won't throw her out today. After dinner she'll have to tell him the truth, not some mumbo jumbo. He didn't seem the abusive sort. Just a little odd. Something else is going on.

3

THE right response never comes to Peter, although he practices different ones in his mind over and over during the next few days. She stays, and he grumbles about needing to get her to a phone or a shelter as soon as possible. This morning she asked to see Dora. The ice coverings slip off tree branches and clatter to the ground. The birches stay bent, but the evergreens gradually unfurl themselves toward the sun. Peter and Elaine and Dog make their way on the partially melted path to Dora's. The old dog often stops.

Suddenly he feels like a family. Peter, Elaine, and the dog, all trooping along together in the woods. It's too cute. He's had a family once and doesn't want another one. Things were fine before she arrived, so why doesn't he just call Oliver and be done with it all? He kicks at a branch in the path. From behind him he hears a low humming sound, like the ewes talk to their young, rumbling, resonant. He can't help placing his feet ahead of him in time to the rhythm of Elaine's humming voice.

The smoke from Dora's chimney is visible before they see the cabin. "Just up ahead," he says to Elaine.

"Wait, Peter, Seamus is lying down. Come on, dog. Only a little more." Dog loves her, and he obeys.

Dora meets them at the door, a little surprised. "Well, who do we have here? Come in," she says. "I see the old dog is still with you."

"Dora, this is Elaine," Peter says.

"Ain't you big as a house. You're a mess. Looks like you been sleeping in those clothes. Get that old dog in here and shut that door."

"Hello, Dora," Elaine says. "Peter said you might check me and the baby. He says you deliver babies."

"Isn't that the fairest hair I ever saw. I used to have the blackest hair you ever saw before it turned color of birch bark. Soon's I give that dang dog his jerk, I'll get you some tea."

Dora moves slowly. Her thick braid hangs almost to her waist, and Peter thinks it must be heavy, wonders why she doesn't cut it off.

"Here you go, got a little sweet flag in it, keep you from getting one of them danged spring colds." Dora places cups without saucers in front of them. "I got a girl from the reservation who helps me. I'm well over eighty, you know. Could go anytime. What if I died right there as the baby's coming?"

"The baby is due the first of May. I don't want to have it in the hospital. There's some complications."

"Let me get my room fixed up a bit, and I'll check you out," Dora says and wobbles toward the bedroom.

"Where you planning to have this baby? You can't have it in my cabin." Peter makes himself say this to her because he needs his cabin back. He has things to do, things you can't do with other people around.

"Can't we take it day by day? Let's talk about it again tomorrow, okay?" she says.

There is nothing he can do now except sip tea. Elaine is beautiful, he thinks. Her eyes are the color of the Caribbean Sea. The way the two braids from her temples come together in back remind him of Leslie, except Leslie's hair was the color of rich garden soil.

"Ready?" Dora says, hands on hips. "Peter, you behave yourself out here. No smoking. And leave that bread alone. Too hot to cut."

He tries not to eavesdrop, but the bedroom door is thin. He remembers the questions from when Leslie was pregnant with the children. Children. That's a hard word for him to hear even in his head. "When was your last period?" "Have you seen a doctor?" "How much weight have you gained?" Usual questions. "How far along was the miscarriage?" He strains to hear the answers, but Elaine faces away from the door and her voice is soft.

Peter backs away from the door quietly and stands at the table, still close enough to hear. He shuffles around making some noise, pours more tea, coughs. He imagines Elaine with her dress pulled up, Dora pressing her belly, Dora's old thick fingers prying. He hears a low murmur now, one, then the other in response, the kind of talk women do when it's private. He remembers how erotic it was when Leslie's doctor felt for the baby, some stranger invading his space.

He rustles through the silverware drawer, looking for the bread knife. Finally he finds it in the sink, wet. He wipes it on his shirt before he starts the cut, looking at the door occasionally to make sure they are still in there. He's not going to get away with it, but it's a habit from childhood to keep watch when he's doing something forbidden. It is molasses bread, and the steam rises instantly when the knife penetrates it. He tries hard to keep the loaf from smushing as he cuts, but the bread follows the knife until it is only an inch high on the end. Dora was right. Too hot. One piece will be enough, he thinks.

Peter tears off a corner to give to Seamus. The name is kind of growing on him. Certainly a better name than Dog, but it's hard to change what you call someone.

The voices from the other room become louder; Peter brushes the crumbs off the counter and stands in front of the bread.

"You spin your own wool?" he hears Elaine ask.

"I do just about everything, honey," Dora says on the way back to the kitchen. "Nothing real well, but a lot of stuff acceptable."

"Everybody healthy?" he asks.

"Right fine baby in there. Should be five or six weeks more." Elaine stands next to Dora, looking like a child, and Peter notices she wears a thick gray-and-blue sweater that covers her belly. "Mitchell's old sweater. Remember it? Been sitting on the closet floor since he died. Might as well get some use."

"Did you spin the wool for this sweater?" Elaine asks.

"Is the pope Catholic? Only kind of wool that's any good. Just enough lanolin to keep the damp out. I sell tons in the summer to the tourists."

"Could you teach me sometime?"

"If Peter don't mind, I'll give you a quick lesson right now. Then you go home and practice."

"Peter?" Elaine asks. Her eyes look directly into his, and the corners of her mouth turn up like sleigh runners. The bruise has disappeared, leaving the faint pink of her cheek.

"Why don't I cut you a piece of that bread you been staring at, and you can sit and eat it while I show her."

"Go ahead. I can cut the bread. Go on. I've got a little time before chores."

THE next day Peter leaves Elaine at Dora's for another spinning lesson and heads home alone. Elaine says she will walk back herself. The ice is almost gone, leaving muddy sinkholes where frost still lingers in the ground. He is relieved to see no black truck in the driveway, or any vehicle. He expects to see a strange car or the local cop or the black truck soon because Brendan isn't going to keep the secret forever.

He hears Dog scratching and howling behind the door. "Come on," he says. Seamus slinks out, and begins to pee before he gets off the stoop, whining the whole time. "Seamus," he says. The old dog looks up as if he can't believe Peter's utterance. It is a good strong name. Peter thinks he will try to use it.

The dolls have been cooped up six days. Peter shuts the door on the world and walks with leaden feet over toward the dollhouse. A few minutes ago he had been anxious to see them, move them from their frozen positions, but now he feels full of apprehension. The cabin is quiet, no one watching, no one making tea. But everything is different. He tries to remember sitting, reading Yeats or Roethke or Ruth Moore, the creak of the rocker and Dog's breathing the only sounds.

Since Elaine's arrival the towel has hung over the front of the dollhouse, shutting his family off from his life. It's upsetting. Everything. He positions the stool in front of the blue towel. Suddenly he feels foolish and is glad no one can see him as he tugs off the towel. The family still sits at the kitchen table, drinking orange juice, getting ready for school. The miniature Mr. Coffee machine is almost empty from the water he poured into it before the storm. "I'm sorry," he says to all of them.

Sarah's leg is slung over the chair, and she has been holding a glass of orange juice for days. He picks her up, removes the glass from her hand, and moves the little doll through the hall, into the bedroom, onto the bed with the stuffed cats. He moves Nathaniel, who still hasn't found his sneaker and is standing at the counter almost ready for school, to his room right in front.

Leslie seems to know that it is too early to go to bed, still daylight outside. "Les, I didn't mean to leave you there that long," he says to the doll. Her smile is painted. Not a big smile, but enough of an upturn to make her look happy. He picks her up. She is light as dust. He tries to keep the image of the live Leslie, but the dead one creeps in, flesh burned black, hair gone. The authorities told him that all three died before they burned. The burning came later, after they died quietly in their sleep from the silent, deadly gases. Leslie was found far over on his side of their king-size bed.

He tucks the Leslie doll under his shirt, so her head lies just under his jaw, tries to press her closer. "Les. I'm sorry. It's been rough the past few days." The doll feels oddly cold against his chest. His hand finds her head, strokes her hair with his index finger, his rough skin catching on the brown fibers. Then he stretches out her legs and places her on the bed, far over on his side.

He tucks the towel in snugly on all sides. He stands back and sees an ordinary bookshelf with the oddest looking structure covered by a fluffy blue towel. Elaine must think him totally mad.

After he lets Seamus back in and stuffs another log into the stove, he hauls the old rocking chair over to the kitchen table and plunks himself into it. A cigarette. He pats his pocket. There they are, just in front of Mr. Sinclair's card. He pries off his boots and slides his stockinged feet onto the edge of the table. The first drag of the Lucky catches in his throat, and he coughs a bit, tries it again. This time it goes down smooth, warms his chest. A cognac might taste pretty good, he thinks, but he never drinks before dinner. The silence unnerves him. No one rattling dishes, pouring tea, humming so low you can barely hear.

It's been a long time since he's played his chanter. He gets up and takes it off the shelf. There is a small crack in the mouthpiece, which he covers with a piece of black tape. African blackwood. The first chanter he ever had, a gift from his father. The wood feels warm and smooth under his fingers.

He runs off a scale. The reed still sounds in tune except for the high G. He sits on the red, high-backed chair, playing tunes with his fingers, tunes he remembers from years ago. He doesn't blow into it, so the chanter makes no noise. Every once in a while over the years he has picked it up and played a short reel—or a jig once—and then put the chanter back on the shelf. Twice he's replaced the reed.

Some of the grace notes he's forgotten, but the tunes are always there except for the piobaireachd. When he was competing, he knew most of the piobaireachds by heart, and the rest were familiar. Regular folks didn't know about them, because they were never played in parades, but Peter loved all the ancient tunes, loved the structure, the haunting movements, even the name, impossible to spell. *Pee-brock. Give it a guttural ending,* he'd say to students. Since the fire he couldn't even play an air or a slow march, let alone a piobaireachd. Playing a piobaireachd requires too much emotion.

He tries the jig, "Paddy's Leather Breeches," out loud, but his fingers are thick and slow. It's been years since he played a strathspey, and he chooses "The Devil in the Kitchen" because he loves the title. *Hold those dotted notes,* he hears in his head. This time it sounds good. Not good like he used to sound. But good for someone who's hardly played in twenty years.

The sound of a vehicle outside stops him, and he is embarrassed to be caught playing his chanter. He hears the banging on the door before he even gets over to the shelf. He steps into his boots but doesn't bother to lace them. It must be the husband, because no one knocks around these parts. More pounding, this time louder and longer.

"I know someone is in there. Please open the door." He's right. It is Mr. Sinclair. Seamus whines on the other side of the door.

"Hold on," Peter says through the door.

More knocking, not as frantic this time, but insistent. Suddenly he is terrified of what is on the other side of the door. He raises the latch and opens the door to three men standing on the landing as Seamus pushes through into the cabin. Mr. Oliver Sinclair himself is at the front. They are all wearing suits. Peter hasn't seen three men together in suits since the funeral. All dark suits. And black shoes.

He glances down at his clothes. Boots scuffed and reeking from horse manure, pants with a red patch on one knee, jacket frayed at the bottom and the edges of the sleeves. He impulsively runs his hand through his hair as if that would make it neater, tugs the end of his beard to pull the straggling hairs together.

"What can I do for you?" he manages.

Oliver steps into the cabin, and the others crowd behind him. "Folks in the store said they thought Elaine might be here."

"Only person here is me, far as I can see."

"Then you won't mind if we come in and look around. We're very concerned."

The men are all in the cabin now, and the last one, a very round man with a too small suit, pulls the door shut behind him. The dog slinks over to the bed and jumps into it.

"Suit yourself," Peter says, backing up all the way to the kitchen sink.

"We don't want to accuse you of anything, but someone in town did say she was here," says the round man. "We just want to talk to her."

"Why is there a bed and a sleeping bag on the floor? Does some-one else live here?" says Oliver. He fixes his stare at the two cups on the table, one with old coffee, one with old tea. "She's been here. I know it."

"Oliver," says a wizened man with big horn-rimmed glasses. "Let me talk to this gentleman. My name is Christopher. I am an elder. I'm one of Jehovah's Witnesses. We mean no harm. You must realize we are worried."

"Look, she is trying to sort things out," Peter says. "She doesn't want to go home right now."

"We believe that wives should be obedient to a loving husband," the man says. *"Let wives be in subjection to their husbands as to the Lord, because a husband is head of his wife as the Christ also is head of the congregation.* Ephesians five: twenty-two."

Just like that, he says the Bible mandates that Elaine go home. Just like that. Memorized. As if he says it every day. The four men stand still, eyes all averted to the table, woodstove, dirty dishes, pile of logs on the floor. Peter needs to say something for Elaine. What kind of crap is that, saying that women have to obey? "I never read anything like that in my Bible," he says.

"Where is she?" Oliver says.

"Out. She doesn't want you to know where she is."

"She is carrying my child, and I will know where she is. Now. Right now," Oliver says, calm as could be, his voice low and even. He sits down in the rocking chair without asking.

"Loving husband," Peter says, looking at Christopher. "Does that sound like a loving husband?" Peter hears himself say. "Get out. This is my house. Get out." The thought of Elaine's bruise causes Peter to look at Oliver's hands. They are gripped on the arms of Peter's rocking chair. Oliver is strong. Young. His hands, although uncallused and smooth, are large and beefy. His fist, Peter knows, would snap a jaw, bruise a cheek.

It takes a minute or two, but Oliver rises from the chair. Peter is afraid Oliver will take a swing at him but doesn't back up. "Please give her this," Oliver says, placing a small black Bible on Peter's table. "I'm sorry. She isn't strong. We just need to talk." He offers his hand, but Peter can't bear to touch it.

"I'll tell her you were here," Peter says, staring at the empty hand in front of him.

Oliver's hand drops to his side.

"Please tell her we love her," says Christopher.

BY THE time Elaine returns to the cabin, she is out of breath, bulky as she is. She stands at the edge of the cabin clearing, leans on the corner of the barn, and pulls off her cap, allowing her hair to tumble down like oats from the winnower. "Your husband came back," he says when he is next to her.

"What? Oliver?" She glances around the yard, up to the cabin.

"He's gone. Came with two other men. They know you're here."

"What did he say?"

"He wants you home. He says they're all worried."

"He'll be back."

"I told him you didn't want to go home."

She moves close to him. Their sweaters touch. Her hair ripples around her face. "Thank you, Peter," she says.

"He left you something."

"Oliver? A small black book?" she asks.

"Yes, a black book. A Bible."

"Are you sure? A Bible?"

"Small. Black. 'Holy Scriptures' printed in gold across the front."

"Yes. That's a Bible. But I've written him that I want my journal," she says.

A wisp of hair covers her eyes, and he pulls it back from her face with his little finger. "There," he says before he heads toward the cabin. Inside, she twirls Dora's drop spindle, drawing out fluffy white wool in the air above it.

"See? It's almost smooth."

"Dora makes some money doing that. Well, on the wheel, of course, not the drop spindle. Looks pretty smooth to me."

"I love this. It feels soft on my fingers when I draw it out. Look, Dora said I had the knack."

"Got to get some stuff in town," he says to her while he shoves a chunk of maple into the stove. "Just a few things. Milk, coffee, salt, sugar."

"Oh, please, may I come? What if he comes back?"

Maybe she can call someone from the store. "Come on, then."

They help the old dog into the back of the truck. No need for the chains today. There is hardly a spot of ice or snow on the roads, but the bushes and trees off to the side are still covered in the shaded areas and the deep pockets into the woods still sparkle when the sun fills them. Elaine turns toward her window. He hasn't seen her like this before, pensive, quiet, withdrawn.

"I'd like to go to a secondhand store," she says after an uncomfortable silence. "I need some clothes."

He starts to form the words in his head. "No way. You've got to go home. I need my cabin back." But the words don't come out of his mouth. "Oh," is all that he hears himself say. He swallows and tries again. "Well . . ." He touches his jacket pocket. Luckies, and in behind the package, the business card of Mr. Oliver Sinclair. If he says any of the things in his head out loud, he knows she will cry. He knows that. For the first time she seems weak.

"Here we are. I won't be long. Then we'll go to the Goodwill store. It's just down the road." He swings himself out of the driver's seat and hops to the ground. She doesn't even turn. Good. The thought of introducing her or explaining her is very unpleasant. Peter. The hermit. The guy who lives in the woods alone and hates people. Now he's got a woman.

The store is crowded with folks released from the ice by the thaw. They line up at the register with basics: milk, bread, beer, videos, candles, and batteries, just in case. Peter roams up and down the aisles picking up sardines, pepper, milk, batteries.

"Hey, Pete. How'd you make out with the pregnant girl?" It's Mason, Brendan's stern man. Hell, it's all over town.

Peter turns. "It's just temporary. She's going home soon as I can reach her family. Couldn't throw her out in the ice." He feels he has said too much. That he doesn't need to say anything.

Mason nods, smiles, doesn't believe him at all. Probably thinks it's his kid in her belly. "Where's she from?"

"Bangor way."

"You got her in the truck?"

Peter turns away without responding and heads for the checkout, piles his groceries on the counter, "Pack of Luckies, nonfilter," he says to the kid behind the counter. "Better give me two."

As soon as the bag is packed with groceries, Peter grabs it and heads for the door.

"I'll drop you off at the Goodwill. Got a couple of errands to run," he says as he climbs into the truck.

She turns and smiles. "Thank you," she says.

The music store is only a block away from the Goodwill, a few minutes' walk, just enough time for a smoke. He pulls the pack from its spot in front of the business card and taps out a Lucky. He finishes the cigarette in front of the store. Guitars and mandolins crowd the display window, and in the corner are several violins. He wonders if Elaine plays an instrument. Her voice is probably instrument enough. He catches a drip from the side of the building with the lit end of the Lucky and drops the butt into his pocket.

Next to the music store is a place called Pleasant Dreams. Awful name for a store, but in the window are some inexpensive mattresses with bright covers.

"How much for one of those mattresses?" he asks the girl behind the counter.

"You mean the futon? Ninety-nine fifty plus tax."

"I'll take it," he says.

After he loads the futon into the bed of the truck, he enters the music store. "What've you got for bagpipe chanter reeds?" he asks the old guy who's dusting the drums.

The man wobbles over to the counter and pulls out a small box, placing it on the glass between them. "That's all we got," he says.

Peter lifts the tissue paper, exposing the cane reeds nestled at the bottom. "Mind if I try them?"

"Be my guest."

Peter picks them up one by one and blows into the end of each one, listening for sound, a crow, anything to tell him about the reed. He separates three out of the bunch and tries each of them again.

One has a nice crow but may be too easy, soft, mushy. The other two are a bit on the hard side but are clear and strong. He holds up the one with the crow. "I'll take this. How much?"

"Seven dollars," the man says. "Seven bucks plus tax."

Peter slips the padded reed between the business card and the Luckies and pays the man. Might not even play the damn thing. Could be a big waste of money.

4

PETER'S hands move quickly over the straw, raking it with his fingers, exposing the tender garlic shoots. "They're planted four across. Just pull the straw off into the paths," he says to Elaine, who is on the next row. She is cumbersome and slow as she inches her way down the rows of garlic, pulling the straw toward her bulky body. The sun warms them, and they have both removed their hats and gloves. Her hair glows when she turns her head, the little waves created by the braids mirroring the sunshine.

It's hard to believe that just three weeks ago everything was covered with ice. Elaine has been with him just over a month. Dora said yesterday that the baby could come any time, but most likely it would be a couple of weeks. Letters arrive every other day from Oliver to Elaine, but she never tells Peter anything about them. Her letters to him are not quite as frequent. Three times Oliver has driven down the driveway, allowing them enough time to hide in the barn. He called out, honked his horn, and left.

They talk about Seamus, about Dora, about the sheep on the island, about her religion. She's a Jehovah's Witness and talks about paradise on earth being much like the cabin and the gardens and barn and the walk through the woods to Dora's. He always thought the Witnesses were Holy Rollers, talking about hellfire and brimstone, but Elaine doesn't talk like that. The pain in her eyes fades when she speaks about Jehovah and the life on earth after

Armageddon. Peter watches her on her knees—heavy with her child, brushing back her oat-colored hair—and wonders how she can believe that, how she can pray and give thanks to a God that doesn't even exist.

Sometimes her fear projects on her eyes like a movie on a screen. A dread of something horrendous, not the pain of childbirth, eats at her. He can see it. It has something to do with the baby, the husband, the miscarriage she spoke about to Dora. Something to do with the religion. He knows she wants to tell him but won't until he asks. He's not sure he's ready to do that.

Elaine works quickly, pulling away the straw, exposing the fragile new shoots. She hears the car first and looks up from the straw. It's not the black truck this time, but it certainly is Oliver Sinclair driving. She sits back on her heels, brushes her hair from her eyes, and stays where she is, no attempt to hide but no attempt to greet. There's going to be trouble. Peter can feel it.

A woman is the first out of the little blue sedan. Peter brushes bits of debris from his clothes, pulls his hat over his head, positions himself in front of Elaine. The woman lilts as she walks. She is dark as maple heartwood, and her lime-green dress swings around her with each step. In the background the figures of two men alight from the car, shadowy, vague, but he's sure the one in the suit is Oliver. The woman is almost to the flower garden before Peter sees the age on her face, her neck, her hands. Wrinkles in the smooth brown skin seem out of place.

She stops abruptly an arm's length from Peter with a plea in her eyes, a plea for permission to approach Elaine. Peter nods to her but holds his arm as a barrier to the men, who have barely moved from their little car. The woman waits at his side while Elaine struggles to rise, grasping Peter's hand with an anxious grip.

"Elaine," the woman says, opening her arms. Peter is in the middle, two women on one side, two men slowly approaching on the other. "Elaine," she says again.

Elaine advances toward the open arms, her hair loose down her back. The brown hands stroke the length of the flaxen hair while

Peter watches Elaine's arms encircle the woman at her waist. "I love you," he hears, but isn't sure who says it.

"I love you," again, in Elaine's voice this time.

The woman talk hovers between them, unintelligible to outside ears until the embrace is over, until they separate, clasp each other's hands, Elaine's white against the dark.

"Why are you staying here? Can we talk about it?" The woman's speech is light, lilting, Jamaica, or perhaps Trinidad.

"After the baby. I can't talk now, Mama. As soon as the baby comes, we'll talk."

"We all love you. Oliver is beside himself. He doesn't understand why you won't come home." The dark woman certainly isn't Elaine's mother. Must be Oliver's. Peter hears the men approaching. "Wait, Oliver, Bruce—just wait a minute," the woman says.

"I want to know when she's coming home," says Oliver.

"I think he's been patient enough," says Bruce. He is ruddy. His skin is like Elaine's, pale, except for his red face. "She's a whore, that's what she is, living with this old guy."

"Dad," Oliver says. "Don't call her names. She is not a whore."

"I call a spade a spade."

Peter sets his jaw forward. "You don't know what you're talking about," he says. "You don't know anything about our relationship."

The woman wraps her lime-green arms around Elaine again, shields her from the anger of the men.

Mr. Oliver Sinclair, Esquire, steps forward in his suit, as if he is going to give a sermon. "Elaine, the elders agree. We will have no recourse other than to have you disfellowshipped if you don't return home and repent. You know what that means. You don't want that to happen, do you?"

"No," she says without moving from the shelter of the arms.

"Just take her. You have a right. Take her if you want her. A damn fornicator. Look at her," Bruce says.

"Stop it," the woman says. "Just stop it. Elaine needs some time by herself. Give her some time."

Peter wonders how the glorious woman in the lime-green dress with her arms around Elaine could possibly be married to Bruce and have mothered someone like Oliver.

"Now," Oliver says. "It isn't too late. Please, Elaine." He reaches toward her belly, his fingers touch the outside of her dress. Elaine doesn't move.

"We will talk after the baby is born. I'm fine here. As soon as the baby comes, I will come to you and the elders. We'll talk then. Not now. Not here."

Oliver steps forward. "If you don't obey me, Jehovah will never forgive you. We need to talk about the blood."

Elaine moves away from the woman, pushing her gently, until she stands alone, arms around her beloved belly. "The journal. I want my journal. It's mine," she says. "It's private."

"Private? Not anymore," Oliver says. "Get in the car." His arm sweeps toward the sedan.

"You will have to carry me." She glances at Peter, who isn't sure he can handle things. "You will have to carry me, and I'm heavy."

"I'll take the child. It won't be too heavy," Sinclair says. "Because of your sin, Elaine. Because of your sin."

"You'll take no one from this place," Peter says. "No, you won't take anyone. Get off my property. No one threatens me or anyone who lives here."

Oliver takes a half step toward him but stops. Peter senses that Oliver is too close and has to force himself to hold his ground. They glare, like children in a schoolyard, glare without blinking, without flinching, until Peter leans forward just an inch.

"This isn't finished," Oliver says, turning away from them toward the car.

The father, Bruce, follows. "Come on, Virginia," he says.

The woman kisses Elaine's pinked face. "Please call when the baby comes," she says before she follows the men to the car. "I know you will follow your heart."

ELAINE stands at the stove stirring potato soup. It's the first time he has seen her wear the purple dress from Goodwill. He drops a letter for Elaine on the kitchen table. Her basket of yarn on the floor has filled almost to the top.

"Better start knitting some of that, or we'll have to get a bigger house," he says.

"Is that all? No package?" She's looking at the mail in his hand.

"That's all," he says, and heads back out the door to feed Alice and Ruby. He thinks she expects Oliver to send the journal, the black book that looks like a Bible.

His rubber boots slide in the mud at the bottom of the lane, but he steadies himself on the corner of the barn.

The goat, Ruby, eats her grain. Alice is quiet. She snorts wet breath onto Peter's neck, swishes his rear end with her tail. He slaps her shoulder. "Garden, tomorrow. You ready for that?" It's been weeks since she's had a harness on her. Before the ice storm. She'll probably fuss about the bit in her mouth and kick at the traces, but she loves garden work once she gets going. They've already planted some radishes and lettuce in a small garden off to the side, but tomorrow they'll get the big garden ready for spring planting.

The chickens are out of water. Peter's been meaning to get a new waterer, since the old one has a slow leak and the water often doesn't last through the day. He writes "chicken waterer" on the clipboard hanging by the barn door, just under "goat feed."

He plans to ask Elaine why she has run away. Maybe tonight at supper. He wants to know more than, "I need time away from everything," or that she is "trying to sort things out." What things? She owes him that. But something inside him is afraid to ask.

He hears the crying from the landing before he opens the door. She is kneeling at the rocking chair, sobbing into the pillow. He hates crying. He will have to pat her back, tell her it's all right. His rubber boots fall to the floor. She doesn't look up, but the noise of her wailing softens. Seamus whines at her side, breaking into a howl when she continues her soft sobbing. Peter stops, stands beside her in his socks. He places his rough hand on the back of her head and pats it. "What is it?" he asks.

She begins to speak into the pillow of the rocking chair, and he has to lean forward to hear.

"I was only sixteen. It was a boy from school, a Witness too. We went to a crowded movie and got lost from the rest of the group. He had a flask of something, brandy, I think. We didn't drink much, but the night was warm and we were in love. Cameron, his name was. We did it in the bushes at the park. It hurt, and I thought I'd never do it again—but he loved me, told me I was his 'star in the heavens,' and we thought we'd get married after graduation."

The cabin is still except for her low voice telling private things, and Peter is glad he can't see her face. He moves away from her and pulls up his red, high-backed chair. He pulls a shawl from the back of his chair and places it over her back. "There," is all he says.

"His family moved away that July. We had talked about visits and the wedding, but only one letter came from him. I wrote and wrote and then stopped sending them. I knew I was pregnant but couldn't tell him in a letter. I couldn't tell anyone, even myself. Only my journal. Just a small entry. 'I think I'm P.' That's all."

Elaine keeps her face buried in the pillow.

"My mother was very strict and religious. She hadn't used the riding crop on me for over a year, but I knew this would bring it back. I knew she would whip me until my skin opened up. I knew the elders would shame me in front of everyone. I prayed to Jehovah to take the child. In our religion, to disobey Jehovah's laws is a very bad thing. It was wrong. I went to meetings, went to school, wore a girdle to hide the fetus inside me."

He slips down onto the floor himself and leans on the edge of the red chair. Seamus plunks himself down between them.

"I was desperate. One night during my prayers, Jehovah answered. The elders would help me. If I was penitent, they would not disfellowship me. I made an appointment with the elders for the next day." Elaine's sobbing ceases, but an occasional tear runs down her cheek.

"The cramps started that evening. I told mother I was sick and went to my room. The cramps got worse, and blood appeared on my underpants. I thought I would just get my period, and it would be over, that Jehovah had answered my prayers and there really was no fetus, no pregnancy, that it was all going to go away."

Peter shifts himself on the floor and wishes he had the guts to light a cigarette. His hips ache.

"The cramps became excruciating, and I knew that I was wrong, that it was not going to go away. It was night, and my parents were in bed. I dragged my bureau across the door so no one could get in and stuck a piece of duct tape over my mouth so I wouldn't yell out. My water broke, and I mopped it up with old clothes. The pains went on and on, and I thought I would die. At least I'd be dead and would never get a whipping with the riding crop."

Peter struggles to look at her. He is embarrassed, but she continues, and he is polite.

"I covered myself with a blanket, stayed on the floor so the blood and fluid wouldn't stain the bed. Between contractions, I prayed for forgiveness, in my head. Then I thought that the baby might live. It would be very small. Only four and a half months along."

"Didn't you have any—"

"Don't interrupt me. If I stop, I might not be able to continue."

"I'm sorry. Go ahead."

"Then I felt the head and pushed as hard as I could, grunted against the tape, pulled the blanket aside to see. She was about the size of a small puppy, a head smaller than a tennis ball. Her skin was translucent, with blue veins. Her chest heaved up and down, but no air went in or out. One hand, like a dolly's hand, stretched out to me, and I took it. It was tiny and white, with bones like toothpicks. I held her close to me. Her eyes never opened, and after a minute her chest stopped moving. The placenta came out quick. I sang to her. 'Rock-a-Bye Baby,' I think, the only lullaby I knew, until the body was cold. She was perfect. Tiny. And so cold. I wrapped her in my old sweater. I remember, it was deep pink with spring flowers embroidered around the neck. I tucked her, together with the placenta, into the arm of the sweater and wrapped the rest around her."

Elaine stops for a minute and slowly pulls herself up from the floor. Peter does the same, thinking that the story is over. And he wonders what it has to do with why she is here. She sits in the rocking chair, covers her legs with the shawl, and waits for him to sit in the red chair. It feels good to get off the floor.

"I'm not finished," she says. "Can you listen to the rest?"

"Yes," he says.

"I cleaned up all the mess and shoved my dirty clothes into a plastic bag. It took a long time because I had to keep resting. I hid the bag at the back of my closet to save for trash day. The clock said four, so I didn't have a lot of time left. Mother would be up at six. I took a small shovel and a flashlight from the garden shed and went to the park, to the spot where we made love the first time. I dug up a bed of petunias, shoveled out a hole, and laid the baby in it. I replaced the flowers and walked home. I had to sit on a bench because I felt faint. My mother was awake by the time I got back. I told her I couldn't sleep and had gone to the park. She believed me. I had never lied to her before."

"I'm going to make us some tea," Peter says, glad for the diversion. His legs ache. The image of Elaine cradling the dead baby fills his head. He stands by the stove waiting for the water to heat, hears her rocking behind him, steady, slow, quiet, on the small rug. When he turns with the steaming mugs, the soft light reaches the back of her hair, that certain slant of light that says winter's over, different from the crisp late winter afternoon's glare. A muted suggestion of warmth. He senses a calmness about them that wasn't there before, senses that perhaps he will tell her about his family.

"I kept a small bit of cloth from the pink sweater, a piece with our blood on it. All I have left of her. It's taped in the journal."

There is more to this story. Why is she telling him all this? Seems too personal to tell just anyone. He pictures her going from her parents' home to Oliver Sinclair's home, and he understands a little bit why she won't go back. Elaine tells him they've been married over seven years. Too long to stay with someone like that. Peter wonders why they'd gotten married in the first place.

"*Bheir me o, horo van-oh,*" she sings, "*Bheir me o, horo van-ee,*

Bheir me o, o hooro ho, sad am I without thee. When I'm lonely, dear white heart. Black the night or wild the sea." She sings without embarrassment, looking fully at Peter, voice clear and unwavering like a thrush. "If I had known that song when it happened, I would have sung it instead of the other."

They sit together in the cabin like lovers, sip their tea, pat the old dog. They need the respite. "Is there more?" he says finally.

"My blood. I'm Rh-negative. Oliver is positive. I don't know what the first baby was. If she was Rh-positive, my blood might kill this baby. I'm running out of time."

"What?"

"Oliver knows about the other pregnancy, that I disobeyed Jehovah's law. Not the details. Not that I buried her in the garden. But I told him about the miscarriage the day that I left."

"What happened? Did he hit you?"

"I had to tell him because of the blood. He's the father. He has a right. He didn't mean to hurt me. He writes almost every day. 'I'm sorry,' he says, over and over."

"A man has no right to hit a woman."

"If this baby dies, it's my fault. Because of the blood."

The silence becomes thick. He waits for her to continue, afraid to intrude, to probe.

"He called me whore. He said my sin would kill his child. I fell, and he left me there, on the floor. I lay for an hour, afraid to get up, until I knew I had to tell someone. The elder. I had to tell the elder, and he would know what to do."

"Elaine."

"He forgives me for that. Even for the lies. But not for my disobedience. When I called the elder, he said a man can take only so much disobedience. He said my sin was great. I hung up and left. Just left. Then I found you. But the elder was right. My sin is great and hard to forgive. My fault. I came here because I thought, like Jesus in the wilderness, that the answer would come to me if I was away from people who knew me and prayed hard enough. And now they're disfellowshipping me for living with you and refusing to come home." Her eyes shift to the opened letter crumpled on the floor by the rocking chair. "They say I disobeyed my husband and am living in sin."

"But you're not living in sin."

"I lied to him about seeing a doctor. He didn't know about the miscarriage then. I think he thought he was my first lover. I was afraid to go because the tests might show the antibodies in my blood and he would know about Cameron and the baby. Now he probably knows that I never even had a doctor."

Peter wonders if Oliver has a riding crop in his closet, imagines that he strikes her with it.

"Peter, are you all right?"

"Yes," he says.

"I lied to Dora. Said that I'd have the doctor's records sent to her. But there are no records."

"Maybe the baby is negative. Maybe everything is fine."

"I'm afraid to know. I can't have the baby transfused. We can't accept blood, for our children either. I thought I would find the answer here, but I don't know what it is. I feel safe in the cabin, but the baby is coming soon, and I still don't know what to do. I can't go back to him until I know."

"Do you love him?"

"I don't know."

The beam of twilight from the front window moves until it falls between them, bathes their hands, and he feels the warmth of it.

"I was married once."

"Dora told me."

"I loved her."

"Yes. I know. Dora said she was beautiful."

Peter has never spoken of Leslie except to Dora. Never spoken of their love or his sin to anyone. He's said enough. Enough. "Well, what about Oliver?"

"He loves me. He's gentle. He thinks I'm beautiful."

Peter follows the light from their hands up to her face. Beautiful, he thinks. Yes. The most exquisite face he has ever seen. Like soft porcelain. But beyond her eyes he sees the pain. "There must be something else they can do besides a transfusion," he says.

"I've looked into it. If I have antibodies and the baby is Rh-positive, it will require a total blood transfusion, and we can't do that. It would be against the will of Jehovah. *Any soul who eats any blood, that soul must be cut off from his people.* Leviticus seven: twenty-seven."

"The Bible is just a metaphor. Only a story. Not a law."

"For me it is a law. I believe it. *Keep abstaining from things sacrificed to idols and from blood. If you carefully keep yourselves from these things you will prosper.* It's very clear. Acts fifteen: twenty-nine. God knows about blood. There is a reason for the law. I would do anything to help this baby live. Anything."

"Blood?"

"Not blood."

Peter waits for more. An explanation. Something to make him understand. She sits silent, her mouth drawn tight.

"Why not have Dora test your blood? Then you'll know. Maybe there's nothing to worry about."

Elaine's head drops to the side. Her hair is loose, shiny like the hair of an ermine, fine like chick down.

"I'm so tired," she says and closes her eyes. "Too tired to think."

LIFE between Peter and Elaine changes over the next few days. The subject of Oliver no longer hovers between them like thick haze. They haven't talked about personal things, but occasionally their hands touch in passing and they do not pull away. He asks her questions like "Why did you wait so long to have children?" and she answers, "Because I was afraid." She doesn't ask, and he doesn't volunteer anything more. They don't speak of the dollhouse.

Elaine walks like a duck. Dora says it will be any time, and he knows that Elaine is scared to have the baby because that is when she has to decide. The blood test, which Elaine finally allows Dora to take, shows antibodies from the miscarriage built up in her blood. Antibodies that will kill this child if it is Rh-positive like its father.

Dora explains it to him over lukewarm coffee the day he goes over alone to bail his rowboat after a spring rain.

"Here's a Rh-negative mom," she says, positioning a heavy glass salt shaker between them. "Here is the Rh-positive dad." She plops the pepper shaker next to the salt. "The baby could be positive or negative. If it's negative, everything's fine. If it's positive, everything's fine the first time. But during pregnancy and delivery the blood of the mother and baby can mix. The mother's blood, the negative blood, creates antibodies against her baby's invading positive but not soon enough to affect the first baby."

"So what's the problem?" Peter asks. "This is her first baby."

"The miscarriage. During and after the miscarriage, Elaine created antibodies against positive blood, should it happen again. The blood thinks it's protecting Elaine from something foreign."

"This baby could be damaged, right?"

"Those antibodies are just sittin' there waitin' for some positive blood to attack. During delivery and sometimes before, the blood crosses and wham."

"Wham what?" he asks.

Dora fiddles with the shakers for a minute as if taking up time, allowing her old mind a few extra minutes of thinking time. "It's a disease. They're born with it. Erythroblastosis fetalis, it's called. Kills them in a few weeks without a transfusion. If the baby's Rh-positive, it will die without a transfusion."

"She thinks it's her sin, the antibodies," Peter says.

"In a way, she's right."

Peter and Elaine go about their days as if each day is the same as the one before and the belly would stay the same size forever, but the old haze of her past is replaced with the haze of decision, or indecision. He knows she thinks about it all the time and hears her at night, praying under the blankets.

Tonight they are having a spring celebration of sorts, their first meal from the garden. She's found a cloth for the table and real napkins. An old milk bottle sits in the center of the table, brimming with dandelions and mayflowers. Her flaxen hair is piled in braids onto the top of her head, an apricot blossom stuck into the side by her temple.

A chicken, slaughtered that morning, steams on a platter on the side of the woodstove and beside it a pie with a crisscross crust. "It's rhubarb. I picked it."

The urge to hold her, breathe in the scent of her apricot blossom, overwhelms him almost to the point of doing it. She is his mother, his wife, his sister, his daughter. What if she leaves him, goes back to Oliver? She leans forward to light a candle.

"Here, wine. And cheese on the table from Ruby. I mixed it with the garlic tops. Try some." Her hand reaches out to him, holding a wineglass full of last summer's rhubarb wine. The cheese is soft, creamy, garlicky, and he spreads it on two slices of French bread.

"You've been busy," he says.

Her smile is serene, tranquil. Not happy exactly, but not as troubled as she has been.

Everything tastes like itself. The asparagus is barely steamed, crisp, and tasting of the rich earth. The chicken is stuffed with parsley and onion tops mixed with a little of the French bread. She's found old wooden bowls for a salad of fresh greens and radishes. With pie, she pours him a demitasse half filled with brandy. The pie oozes juice and is tart.

She doesn't let him help with the cleaning up. "A present, for your kindness," she tells him. He says he's never tasted as good a meal, and all from the garden. He sips his brandy. She might like the chanter, he thinks, a little after-dinner music. He rests the ivory sole against the bleached linen tablecloth and plays "The Clucking Hen," then "The Skye Boat Song."

"I know that song," she says.

> *"Speed bonnie boat like a bird on the wing,*
> *Onward, the sailors cry.*
> *Carry the lad that's born to be king*
> *Over the sea to Skye."*

Her voice follows his chanter notes, and she knows all the verses. He goes into a repeat, and her voice breaks into a high harmony over the chanter.

> *"Loud the winds howl, loud the waves roar,*
> *Thunderclaps rend the air;*
> *Baffled, our foes stand on the shore,*
> *Follow they will not dare.*
>
> *"Tho the waves leap, soft shall ye sleep*
> *Ocean's a royal bed . . ."*

Then he sees the corner of the towel. Folded up under itself. He sees Leslie holding her coffee. He never would have left it that way. The blowpipe slips from his mouth. She sings a few more bars alone before she realizes he is no longer playing.

> *"Rock'd in the deep, Flora will keep*
> *Watch by your—"*

"What have you done to the dollhouse?" His voice scares him, but he asks again. "What have you done?"

5

"THE towel, Elaine."

"What?"

"The towel. Did you move the damn towel?"

"Peter, please."

He stands, his fists clenched, wishing she would just get out. He never wanted her here in the first place. He doesn't think he wants to know if she has seen his family. He doesn't think he can bear it. He turns away from her, puts himself between her and the family. He's a crazy man who plays with dolls. She knows about him now.

"Peter, please," she says from behind him.

He feels her hand on his shoulder and shrugs it off. The silence in the cabin is chilling. The old dog's head is halfway under the bed, and the tip of his tail flicks, the only motion in the whole cabin.

"I'm sorry for invading your privacy."

Her voice is quiet and steady, and he wishes he'd ignored the whole thing, just pulled the corner down when she wasn't watching. "I'm going to bed," he says. "Tomorrow I'm going out on the island. Need to check on the lambs. Be careful of the shotgun if you have to use it. Remember, hold it firm against your shoulder like I showed you. Three shots will get me. Dora will hear them and let me know." He can't bear to look at her.

For the first time Elaine is the last to bed. She pushes Seamus out the door to pee and brings him in again, covers the leftovers, blows out the candle. He listens to her night noises for a long time before he falls asleep.

The pale mauve of the rising sun fills the picture window just after five, and Peter reaches for his jeans, slides them on the floor along the side of the futon. If he can get out to the island early enough, he won't have to talk to her. She will be sleeping. Seamus doesn't even raise his head when Peter lets himself out of the cabin.

Dora is out in the garden when he arrives. "What? No old dog?"

"Nope. I think those days are gone," he says.

Dora wears a pair of Mitchell's old overalls, several sizes too big, over her flowered housedress. "What you doing?" she asks. "Going out on the island?"

"Need to check on the lambs, dock their tails. Castrate too. You seen anything?"

"Even with the binoculars it's hard to see the little ones. Mothers been feeding in the meadow, though."

"I'll stop for coffee on the way back. If you hear three shots, stick that flag in the ground, will you? She's getting close. I'll keep watch."

On the way to the skiff he grabs the bag of tools from Dora's shed and checks to see that everything is there: a small plastic bag of doughnut-shaped elastic bands and the elastrator.

On the island, the meadow grass is greening up, and the ewes are mowing it almost faster than it can grow. He counts thirty, including the ram. He won't even attempt to count the lambs until he gets them into the pen. They begin to move when they become aware of his presence, and Peter advances methodically behind the flock. Slow. Close to the ground. "Git," he says. "Move on in there." The ram goes into the chute first, and the rest follow. When they are all in the pen, Peter locks the gate of the chute behind him.

With the top rail down the ram is gone, leaping over the fence, and most of the ewes follow. The lambs all scream at once, trying to find their mothers. "Just hold on there," he says to them. "Got a few things to do first."

From what he sees, half the lambs are black and half white. He scoops them up one by one. He dips the end of the elastrator into the jar of iodine, castrates the males, and puts elastics around the tails of the females. In a month all the tails will have dropped off. He throws the lambs over the fence to their mothers, and jots it all down on a clipboard. Peter doesn't dock the males, because they will all be slaughtered in the fall and the presence of a tail makes them easy to select.

After he finishes the last lamb, he checks for the flag. Nothing. Just Dora's house. He counts forty-nine lambs in all. Mostly ewes. Mostly black. Mostly twins. That's good. And they all feel like they're getting plenty of milk.

The image of Elaine slams at him on the way back to the boat. He hasn't thought about her the whole time, but now she is there, looming with the apricot blossom in her hair, singing "The Skye Boat Song." He pictures her lifting the corner of the blue towel, chuckling to herself. How cute. He hears her voice in his head. How cute. Peter has dollies. Does she think he just plays with dolls? That he is a closet toddler. Like men who wear women's underwear in private? He was almost ready to talk to her about Leslie and the children, and she has ruined it all. Probably thought it was her right to know because she told him about the miscarriage and the blood thing.

Dora's been watching, because she is pouring coffee into two mugs when he gets into the kitchen. "How's my clip look? Wool good and long?"

"Real good. Clean too."

"That Elaine. She's going to be a right good little spinner, she is."

He doesn't want to talk about Elaine, so he sips his coffee.

"That bulging mama getting ready to drop?" Dora asks.

"Pretty close," he says. Pretty close to what? Pretty close to having her baby die? Pretty close to going crazy?

"Some bitch of a problem with that blood thing. Those antibodies. Just waiting. She even thinking about a transfusion?"

"Don't think so, says Jehovah will never forgive her. She's going through a terrible time. I hear her praying at night under the covers."

"Poor thing. She's got demons fighting inside her."

How could he have yelled at her last night? Elaine who is already full of her own demons doesn't need his too. "Has she told you what her plans are after the baby comes?"

"Not really. Just that she doesn't think she'll go back to that Mr. Sinclair right off, anyway."

"Maybe she ought to move in with you, Dora. She could take care of you."

"I've been thinking about going over to the reservation and staying with Mitchell's sister. I'm old, about washed up. But you. You got a few years left."

"You know, Sarah would be Elaine's age if—"

"Heaven's sakes, you're robbing the cradle." Dora laughs. "The young 'uns keep us old fogies youthful. Follow your heart. Don't you think I know how you feel about that woman?"

Peter feels the flush begin at the base of his neck. No. He's too old. "I think she loves him," he says. "Oliver. She has a beautiful voice. She sings."

"I know," Dora says.

"Did you know I play the bagpipes?" He is surprised that he asks her.

"Everyone knows that. I used to hear you practice in the summer when you were a kid. Over by the rabbit crossing. There's talk in town about how good you was. A professional, won lots of money. And that you stopped playing after your family died."

"I've been thinking about checking out the pipes."

She smiles at him. If Dora leaves, he won't have a friend except for the old dog, and that terrifies him.

WHEN Peter arrives back at the cabin, Elaine is in the barn, feeding Alice and Ruby. She acts as if no one had yelled at her.

"How was the island?" she asks.

"Great. Lots of good lambs."

"Peter, I'm sorry about the dolls," she says. "I wanted to know about you, what you were hiding. I'm sorry if I hurt you."

Peter wishes he could be as direct as Elaine. "Sometime I'll tell you about it," he says. "I'm sorry too. I'd like to help you through this."

"Thank you." Her eyes water. He sees it clear and strong, the fear that her body will kill her baby. But it's not her sin. It's a medical condition. "Wait," he says.

The Bible is there on the table beside his Langston Hughes. He thumbs the Psalms. Psalm twenty-five. He closes the black Bible over his thumb and runs out to her.

"Look, here. Read," he says. "No, I'll read. *For your name's sake, O Jehovah, you must even forgive my error, for it is considerable.* And here: *See my affliction and my trouble and pardon all my sins,* and then," he says, pointing hard on the page, "here: *May I not be ashamed, for I have taken refuge in you.* You see? It's not your fault. God forgives you."

Her tears gather and fall softly. "Thank you," she says as she takes the Bible from him and slips it into her dress pocket.

They walk together out of the barn. He watches as she shuffles to the outhouse, as if she doesn't want to open her legs even to walk. It's going to be today, he thinks. "Come here, old dog," he calls to Seamus. He doesn't look up. Peter walks over to him and scratches behind his ears, and Seamus lifts his head, whines, drops it again.

"Peter," she says as she shuts the outhouse door behind her. "It's starting. There's blood. Just a little. But enough to know." Her arms, which have been encircling her belly for so long, hang limply at her sides. "I need to be alone for a while. No reason to go for Dora yet." Her arms wrap around her belly, her hands clasped tight underneath, holding the baby inside. Her face is white as wool as she walks up the path to the front door of the cabin.

What is he supposed to do now? If he works with the chain saw, he won't be able to hear if she calls out. He can't just stand staring at the cabin, waiting to be useful. The sack of potatoes he bought at the feed store seems heavier than it should be as he drags it out of the barn to the old picnic table. He dumps the twenty-pound bag of Austrian Crescent potatoes onto the surface of the table and unsnaps his knife sheath. His hand pushes most of the potatoes to the far side of the table and brings a few to the area right in front of him. The first few only have one or two eyes in each, so he tosses them whole into the empty bag. The next he cuts in half, some in thirds, making sure each has at least one good eye.

The work is mesmerizing, and his mind wanders to the last Highland games, just before the fire. That last day he was happy.

He tries to remember how it was that afternoon, listening as his name was called over the loudspeaker after the piobaireachd competition. And the young grade one piper, Kate something or other, kissed him on the cheek. After he sat back down with the silver bowl in his lap, he'd asked her to have dinner.

The woman sent him a sympathy card. He remembers because it seemed to be a little strange. Kind of personal. Something she said . . .

The knife shears off a tiny chunk of the end of his finger. "Damn," he says under his breath. He sucks it, tastes the salty blood. He sits with his finger in his mouth, looking up at the cabin. It's been about a half an hour, and he's heard nothing. He needs a Band-Aid to stop the bleeding and doesn't want to bother Elaine. But what if she's having the baby all by herself? He keeps his finger in his mouth on the way up the path. At the landing he sees her through the window. She has pulled the mattress from her bed onto the floor and is spreading it with the pads she bought in town when she sees him.

"Come in," she says, gesturing to him.

He wipes his boots on the landing and takes them off just inside the front door before he reaches for a Band-Aid on the windowsill. The odor in the cabin is unmistakable. The odor of birth.

"Don't you think I should get Dora?"

"Yes," she says quietly. "I'm scared."

He decides to drive. A half hour later he pulls back into the yard with Dora. Dora has called the young Passamaquoddy girl who helps her with births, and she is on her way.

Dora brings her bag and a three-legged birthing stool.

"Haven't been here in a while," she says. "Just like the old dog, too old to walk all that way in the woods. Seems cheating to drive over."

Elaine greets them at the door, as if it is her house and they are visitors. "Please sit down." She offers them a chair. Her chin quivers, and Peter knows she is distressed. "I'm due for another contraction, but I want to make sure you understand me. I am not going to allow the baby to be transfused. It's in Jehovah's hands now."

"Do you know what this means?" Dora asks.

"Yes. I know the baby might die. I will love it more than life itself whether it is positive or negative. If the baby is negative, we have all been blessed. If it is positive, I will hold it and nurse it and sing songs. And if Jehovah chooses to take it, so be it." Elaine's voice is passionate, strong, clear, although he has never seen such tears on anyone, and her jaw shivers as if she is cold. The urge to warm her with his body becomes almost overwhelming, and he fights to stay in his chair. Dora does what Peter is not able to do, her fleshy arms enfolding her.

"We respect your decision, Elaine, although we may not agree with it. We'll help you through this."

"There's someone here," Peter says, getting up to look out the window. "Must be that girl, Susanne." He opens the door for her. She is dark, like Dora, but young.

Dora begins to give quiet orders. Peter has never seen her so serious and efficient. "Get this mattress elevated. Peter, start boiling water. Susanne, make sure there's towels available."

Peter fills the kettle with water from the pump and places it on the woodstove. He knows damn well that boiling water is just to get the men out of the way.

"Susanne, can you help me?" he says. They lift Elaine's mattress onto his futon. "How's this?"

"Perfect," Dora says. "I'm just too old to bend down that far."

"Here's another contraction," Elaine says under her breath. "Oh, please, God, let me keep this baby," she says. *"Show me favor, O God, according to your loving kindness. And cleanse me even from my sin."* Her arms tighten around her belly. "I want to sit down," she says. Dora leads her to the kitchen chair and holds her arm while she sits. "I love you, my baby." She murmurs to her belly as if no one else were in the room. Things like "Please slow down, no need to rush, sssshhh." Peter tries not to listen, tries not to hear.

"May you purify me from sin with hyssop, that I may be clean; May you wash me, that I may become whiter even than snow."

It's another psalm, Peter thinks.

"I'm scared," she says, her face showing everything.

Peter grabs the scissors from the hook by the door. There used to be a patch by the barn. Hyssop. Tiny green leaves on a woody stalk. He finds it and clips off seven branches. Seven for luck.

Dora nods when he passes the stems to her.

"Hyssop," he says. "For the water."

"Yes," she says, taking them. "This is going to be a while. And I have to examine her. See how far along she is. Now get." Dora looks younger all of a sudden.

Peter lifts his chanter off the shelf and tucks it under his arm. On the way out the door he hears her. "Why did I do this? Please, baby, stay safe inside. Dora, please don't let the baby come out."

And then Dora's soft replies, "The baby is coming, Elaine. It's coming, and Susanne and I are here to help you. I'm going to wash you with hyssop." Then soft female voices murmur back and forth as he shuts the door behind him.

Peter sits at the picnic table and plays a slow march, "The Cradle Song," easy, melodic, appropriate. Something a bit faster, he thinks. He plays the strathspey all the way through before he registers the name of it: "The Devil in the Kitchen." The devil in the frigging kitchen. What was he thinking of?

"Damn," he says aloud. "Jehovah, You better do something here. Are you listening to me?"

It's time, he thinks. He might as well try. How can it hurt? "The Old Woman's Lullaby." He begins the ground of the piobaireachd, slowly, tentatively. It's not as precise as he'd like, but the eloquence of the notes saturates the space around him, the speech of angels, "Please, God, listen to this, listen to this." Drips course down his face like rain. When he hits the high A in the fourth measure, he feels his heart break inside him and waits for the blood to pour out of his eyes, his nose, out of the holes in the chanter. He finishes the entire ground and places the chanter on the table.

"Please, God. Was it good? Was it enough?" he says.

PETER stays away until the sky begins to darken. The animal chores take up some time, and he plants most of the potatoes, but he isn't sure that he does everything properly. He is afraid of himself, of what he has done wrong, and tears repeatedly well up in his eyes.

The kerosene lights flicker in the window. He wonders if he should knock. Knock at his own door. He doesn't. "Hello," he calls when the door is open a crack. They are singing. All of them.

"Old MacDonald had a farm, ee-ii-ee-ii-oo . . ."

"Here comes another one."

"Do you feel like pushing?"

"Yes, pushing."

He thinks they've lost their minds. Elaine squats on the three-legged stool, growling, as Dora hovers over her. Susanne stands at the kitchen table, arranging instruments on a towel. No one looks at him.

"Sing a lullaby," Elaine says.

"A lullaby. Lordy. A lullaby."

> *"Sleep, my child, and peace attend thee,*
> *All through the night;*
> *Guardian angels God will send thee,*
> *All through the night."*

Dora's voice mellows with the song, and it almost sounds pretty.

> *"Soft the drowsy hours are creeping . . ."*

Elaine's clear high voice joins the old gravelly one, and Peter can't help but look at her. She is naked, her body shiny with sweat, white, white, white. Her head leans back on Dora's body, her hair in sodden strings down her bare shoulders.

> *"Hill and vale in slumber sleeping,*
> *I my loving vigil keeping,*
> *All through the night."*

"Remember, no blood," says Elaine. She notices him standing just inside the door and makes no effort to cover herself. "Peter. No blood."

"Yes," he says. "I know."

Susanne crouches down with a small blue bottle, tips it over her fingers, which she places where the baby will come out. "I'll keep doing this until the baby crowns," she says, moving her hand in circles.

"Another one," Elaine says, her voice high and frightened.

"Low," Dora says like an angry parent. "Low, Elaine, low." She places a damp cloth on her brow.

"Deliver me from blood guiltiness, O God, the God of my salvation," Elaine says, low and strident.

"I feel the head," Susanne says.

"Peter, take my place," Dora says. It is a command. The soles of Peter's boots feel like magnets on an iron floor. "Come on," Dora says. "Now. Put your hands on her, right here."

Peter obeys her, places his coarse hands over the bones of her shoulders. The glistening white flesh softens under his fingers as she leans her head against his groin.

"A couple more," Susanne says to everyone.

Peter hears Elaine's prayers almost before they begin. "Jesus, please give me the strength to give birth and the strength to do what I have to do. I can do this with your help. Please, God, make me strong enough to be obedient to your words."

She reaches up and touches his hand. "Thank You, Jehovah, for sending me Dora and Susanne and especially Peter. Thank You for giving me this time." Peter moves his hand onto hers. "Here it comes," she says.

Elaine sits up straight, grunts hard. "Hold her," Dora says.

Peter wraps his arms around her neck, his hands close to her breasts, brings his body to meet hers. "Lean on me," he says, close to her ear. She pushes against him until he feels like he will burst.

"Come on, God, do something here. We need You." Peter hears his own voice, shouting toward the ceiling where God sits waiting to hear it. "Jesus Christ, save this baby, dammit. Come down here and save this baby."

Elaine slumps back on him, her face serene, tears flowing freely from the corners of her eyes.

"I'm sorry," he says to her. "I don't really know how to pray."

"Sounds like good praying to me," Dora says. "Come on now, Mama. One last good push, and this baby's going to be breathing."

"No blood," Elaine says again.

"No blood," says Dora. "If that's what you want, no blood."

"No blood," says Peter.

Dora stands by with scissors and string and a blanket while Susanne lies on the floor in front of the stool. "This will be a long one. Just keep going," Susanne says.

The contraction begins without Elaine's introduction, just grows and swells until her muscles tense against him. "You can do this, Elaine. I'm helping you," he says above the grunting.

"Here it comes," says Susanne. "Keep pushing. Push." Elaine pushes and pushes and pushes, straining against Peter, against the stool, against herself. "Okay. Stop. Stop pushing." Elaine pants like a dog, her body still tense but the noise gone, the straining finished.

"Yes. Here it is." Dora passes Susanne a towel. Susanne cradles her arms under the stool as Elaine leans forward. "It's a girl, Elaine, a baby girl." Elaine collapses back onto Peter. Susanne places the moist infant on Elaine's bare chest, and Dora covers her with a baby blanket. Peter knows the cord is being cut, but he can't see it. Dora pulls a quilt off the bed and places it over Elaine's shivering body. Elaine nudges the infant toward her full breast, steers the nipple toward the open mouth. The cry is like a kitten cry, and the baby's mouth sucks at Elaine's skin around the nipple until it is successful.

"Look at that, will you," Dora says. But the baby begins to cry again, and Elaine looks at Dora. "This nursing thing is harder than it looks. It's going to take patience. Do you want me to test her now?"

"No. I'd like to have an hour with her first."

Dora milks the cord that is still attached to Elaine into a test tube. "Should be all right to wait."

The next hour is filled with housekeeping chores and medical procedures. Seamus walks around a few times, sniffing at the floor. They fill out a paper, birth certificate, he thinks. They help Elaine into the freshly made bed, bathe her skin, and help her into a clean shirt. Elaine holds the baby close to her. No one speaks of the blood that even now might be attacking the baby. They have given her an hour. She sings songs, lullabies mostly. Dora and Susanne join in on "Summertime," their voices disparate, Elaine's soaring over the rest. They laugh at the end. For the whole hour there is only music and laughter and mama-talking.

At eleven twenty-six Elaine points to the clock. "The hour is finished," she says. Dora pulls a small packet from her bag. "Eldon card," she says when she sees Peter staring at her. "To test the blood."

The air is tense. Elaine holds the infant close to her, eyes closed. She begins to sing to her baby.

> *"Like a ship in the harbor*
> *Like a mother and child.*
> *Like a light in the darkness*
> *I'll hold you awhile."*

Dora holds the tube over the Eldon card, allowing a few drops of blood to fall.

*"I'll cradle you deep
And hold you while angels
Sing you to sleep."*

Peter looks toward the ceiling. God, You better do this right, he thinks. Elaine begins the song again, and he isn't sure he can listen to the last verse without breaking down.

"Elaine, it's negative," Dora says. "The baby will be fine."

"Negative," Elaine says. Her laughter comes from deep inside her, and she allows the tears to flow. "Thank You, God." She looks at them one by one, her face pink and joyous. "Jehovah answers all prayers. I'm so happy He decided to answer mine this way."

Elaine holds her up, naked. "Look. Her toes. Do you see? The second is shorter than the others. Azelin. Her name is Azelin. It means spared by Jehovah."

6

THE days following Azelin's birth are quiet except for her intermittent wailing. She sleeps at night between some nursing spells. She is a good baby. Her skin is dark, like her father's; her features are lovely, like her mother's. She smells like Elaine, especially when Peter holds her so Elaine can have her supper. The warm air and soft rains encourage the garden to grow. Peter plants beets, more lettuce, cabbages, onions.

Elaine's breasts are sore when Azelin begins to nurse, but Dora says that is normal for a first baby. At the end of the first week Dora plans to come to check them and stay for supper. Elaine works all that day in between nursings. She carries Azelin tight to her chest in a baby carrier. Peter helps pick the asparagus and gathers wild greens from the nearby field. Some meadow mushrooms sprouted up after the spring rain, and he pulls up the largest. Brendan comes down later in the day with half a dozen lobsters. Heard the woman was still here and had her baby. "Sort of a baby present," he says. Peter tells him that Elaine is staying a few more days and will be off on her own. "Sure," Brendan said, "and the pope goes to temple on Sundays."

Two for each, Peter thinks. That's the only way to eat lobster. Make sure you have plenty. If he buys only one, he always wishes he had more. That's no way to eat it.

Peter sets up the propane cooker just below the landing and secures the black enamel canning pot with two inches of water on the rack. Too hot for the kitchen stove. The spring has been warm. Buds swelling on the maples, flowers on the fruit trees earlier than usual. He's opened all the windows to allow the spring smell inside.

Elaine has set the table with a cloth and napkins. A glass pitcher full of mixed white blossoms, mostly apricot, he thinks, mixed with some popple, takes up the far end of the table, and the scent of them is intoxicating. She sets little cups at each place.

"What's that for?" he asks.

"Butter. For the lobsters." Peter usually just plunks the butter pot down in the center of the table for himself, but the cups make sense. "How do we crack the lobster shells? Do you have those lobster crackers?"

Peter grabs a hammer out of the junk drawer and sets it on the table. "That ought to do the trick."

"Dora should be here. It's after six," she says.

"She'll be here. She's always late," he says. "Elaine?"

"What?" she says, turning toward him.

"It's worked out okay, hasn't it?"

"Yes."

Dora arrives with her baby tool bag in one hand and a plastic bag from the grocery in the other. "Got something for the baby," she says.

"Oh, Dora. It's beautiful." Elaine accepts the sweater, knit in the colors of Joseph's coat, as if it were an offering, a sacrifice. Reds, oranges, purples, colors she can't name, bits of fluff, Angora maybe, checkerboard around the bottom of natural grays, browns, and whites. Elaine holds it up to Azelin. "It will be perfect by next winter," she says. "Thank you."

"It's all made from the island fleece. And there is bunny fur from my old rabbit Mitchell bought me for my birthday years ago. Been storing it just for something like this."

"Look, Azelin," Elaine says, "the most glorious sweater in the universe."

"Well, I hate those wimpy little pink and blue and yellow sweater things they put babies in. Babies need color just like big people."

"How about some blueberry wine?" Peter says.

"You get out. Go play with them lobsters while I check out this mama and babe. Go on with you." Peter, like a naughty child, obeys her immediately, grabbing the bucket of lobsters on the way out the door. "I'll call you. Won't be ten minutes."

He pulls off his long-sleeve flannel shirt and tosses it onto the landing. He pats the pocket of his T-shirt before he realizes his lighter is still in the flannel shirt pocket. "Damn," he says under his breath. "I'm rowing with one oar these days," he says to Seamus, who lies near the shirt. "Fetch. Get the shirt," he says to the old dog. Seamus hasn't fetched the stick of wood for the past two weeks. The last time Peter gave the command, Seamus looked at him as if he'd lost his mind and closed his eyes, continuing to sleep. Today he has no interest in fetching someone's old flannel shirt. He doesn't even cock his head or raise an ear. Peter ambles over and pulls his Luckies and the lighter out of the pocket, gives Seamus a pat on the head. "No more fetching for you, old thing. It's all right. No need to." Seamus growls quietly as Peter lights the propane stove. Peter's never heard him growl for no reason. He'll just have one. He's going to quit. Taste like crap lately. But he pulls the smoke into his lungs, and it feels just fine. Good old Luckies. He smokes it down to a nubbin. The water is boiling. He drops the lobsters in tail first and shuts the pot lid tight. Twenty minutes. He glances at his watch. Just enough time to check the animals. Alice is calm for a change, munching on a leaf of the previous summer's hay. "Going to start hauling your manure tomorrow, girl. You ready for that?"

There're five minutes left by the time he gets back to the propane stove. Steam puffs out the side of the black canning pot. "Where's that infernal blueberry stuff?" Dora says from the doorway.

"Coming right up," he says.

Elaine sits at the table, Azelin close to her chest, sleeping. "We're both fine," she says.

"Would you like a little blueberry wine? I made it."

"Just a tiny bit," she says. "Azelin might not like it." Peter covers the bottom of her glass and stops when she holds up her hand. "Plenty," she says. "Just a taste."

"Well, you can fill mine up," Dora says.

"To Azelin," he says, holding up his glass.

They drain their glasses before he goes to get the lobsters. When he tips the pot, the boiling water flows out onto the ground, seeping in when it hits the grassy area. The lobsters have turned red, and he heads to the cabin. Elaine has found a chipped platter to put them on, and he piles them up. Six lobsters. He pours Dora and himself another glass of wine and sits in his red, high-backed chair. Peter is happy. He doesn't remember being happy in a long time, since the fire, maybe. He loves living in the woods and working with the sheep. He loves old Alice and Ruby and Dora. And tonight he's happy.

They smash the lobster shells, open the claws dripping with seawater, pull out the sweet meat. The asparagus is perfect, crisp, tender. They don't talk until Elaine serves the rhubarb crisp.

"I've been going round and round with what to do," Elaine says. "But I still don't know. I wrote to Oliver today to tell him about Azelin. It's his baby. He deserves to see her. But I was thinking. I love it here. Living in town just isn't for me. I've always felt there was something missing, and I think it was soil and plants and animals."

Peter wants to say, "You can live here. You can live here with me," but he doesn't.

"I've told Oliver he can come and see Azelin but that I need three weeks. At the end of that time I will have an answer. I hope he respects that. I'd like to be able to stay here, if that's all right," she says.

If that's all right. He can't imagine waking up without her in the other bed. He can't imagine sleeping through the night without stirring because of mewing and sucking sounds. "Yes, of course," he says. "Stay as long as you need to."

THE next morning the sun streams into the cabin through the front window. Elaine rocks gently in the chair, sipping her tea and nursing Azelin. She kisses Azelin's odd toes, shorter than the others. Peter washes dishes at the sink until there are no more. From the sink he is able to watch her back, her hair in wisps turning light from the window into tiny crystals. When she rocks, he sees the black of Azelin's hair against Elaine's white breast and hears the quiet sucking. His breathing seems loud, and he struggles to soften it.

When the dishes are dry and put away, Peter stands behind the rocking chair. He places his hands on her shoulders, like when she was in labor. The rocking stops. Peter's heart thumps against his chest wall loud enough for her to hear. He feels Elaine's pulse through the skin below her left shoulder, fast but faint. Fluttering like a hummingbird heart.

He rests his hand on Azelin's head as she nurses, and Elaine allows it. The chair pushes into him as her head rests back. Azelin pulls away from the nipple. He takes his hand away, embarrassed he is so close to Elaine's naked breast.

The chair begins its rocking, patting against Peter's waist.

"I've got to order some seeds and pay a few bills," he says. "Do you need me for anything?"

"No," she says. "Go ahead. I thought I'd put a couple of those tomato plants in the ground, just in case we don't get another frost. They'll have a jump on the others. Can you spare them? They might freeze. Then they'd be wasted."

"Sure. I got lots. Put in half a dozen."

He helps her buckle on her baby sling. "Come on, Seamus." She waits patiently while the dog hauls himself up and staggers toward the door. They wend their way toward the garden.

The old trunk by the back wall is covered with a square of mirrored material his mother brought back from the Orient. As he lifts it off, dust fills the air around him. The lid creaks until it leans back against the wall. Leslie's jacket lies on top. He lowers his face into it, but it smells like cedar. Underneath is an assortment of things he hasn't seen for a long time. Nathaniel's sneaker he found in the garage, Sarah's stuffed raccoon she had left at her friend's house, Leslie's melted Mr. Coffee machine. Peter piles them onto the floor beside the trunk. It takes him a long time to finally expose the bagpipes, lying at the bottom of the trunk underneath his MacQueen tartan kilt. Some moths have eaten parts of the red stripe in spite of the cedar lining.

The pipes look fine. No obvious cracks. The moths have invaded the bag cover. He cradles the pipes carefully in his arm over to the kitchen table and runs his fingers over every piece, examining the blackwood for imperfections. Smooth. No cracks he can detect.

At the bottom of the trunk he fishes around for the bag of tools and extracts a can of almond oil and a cotton brush. He removes and separates all five pieces and rubs the oil into the three blackwood drones, blowpipe, and chanter. The old cane reeds will have to be replaced, and he tosses them all into the firebox. He pulls the black velvet cover off the bag, exposing a crinkled, stiffened lambskin. He tries to smooth it out, examine it to see if it can be brought back. The bag at the blowpipe end crumples in his hands, changing to disassociated bits of stiff leather spewed out over the surface of the table.

"What a mess," he says aloud. He'll have to get a new bag and new reeds. The music store in town might have to order those things. He can buy the almond oil at the health food store. The pipes will need oiling for a while to prevent cracking. He'll hold off playing them to give the oil a chance to permeate the wood. But he wants to try the new chanter reed, the one behind Mr. Oliver Sinclair's card in the pocket of the red plaid jacket.

He pats the pocket of the jacket hanging on the nail. The tissue package is still there behind the business card. The reed looks intact when he pulls the tissue back. He blows into it; he hears a rough crow sound. Good. He blows again. Crow again. He's surprised that the dinky music store carries such a good reed.

He oils the wood pieces again, slathers the rest of the oil from the can all over them, then wipes them down with a clean cloth. He picks up the chanter with its ivory sole. A couple of the holes are still taped from the last time he played that day at Maxville. He'd been having trouble with the high G, and his D was a tad sharp, so he remembered taping them just before he competed. He pushes the reed in until it seats itself snugly.

Elaine is still in the garden, too far away to hear from inside the cabin. He moistens the reed with his lips, just a little, holds his fingers on the holes. It feels a bit awkward. He places the entire reed in his mouth and wraps his lips around the base. His first breath sounds the low A. Loud. It's louder than he remembers. He blows as hard as he can and goes up the scale: B, C, D, E, F, G, high A.

"The Brown Haired Maiden" sounds pretty good. It's an easy tune, slow, simple fingering. He hates to play the pipe chanter by itself out of the pipes, but he knows the drones might crack if he plays them too soon, and, anyway, he has no bag. He probably should stop. He tried it and it feels good. No point in chancing a crack in the chanter.

Before he piles the family things back into the trunk he notices the old *Scots Guards* book in the corner. He brings it to the table and plays "Hot Punch" and "Kilworth Hills" and "The Green Hills of Tyrol." His lips are tense and sore. Spit drips onto the table from the sole of the chanter. He is holding the chanter when he hears the noise, feels the vibration in his hands. It hits him like a shot, although the sound is barely detectable. He feels the crack with his thumb, follows it down the length of the chanter to the sole and back up to the reed.

"Dammit. Dammit."

He bangs the chanter on the edge of the table, sending the reed to the floor. Why did he play so soon? Ruined an excellent old chanter.

"What is it? What's wrong?" Elaine asks, opening the door.

Peter throws the chanter against the wall. "Not a damn thing," he says. The dried bag lands against the counter by the sink. "Not one damn thing." His hands pick up the drones and the blowpipe.

"No," she says. "No. Do not do that."

He stops, his package in midair.

"No. Don't throw them. Give them to me."

She holds out her arms like an angel, holds them until he places the pieces of his bagpipes onto the crooks of her elbows, against the sleeping Azelin.

TWICE a day Peter oils the pieces of his bagpipes. The day after his chanter splits, he goes into town to buy some more oil and a plastic chanter to use until he finds a blackwood one to match the rest of the pieces, and to order a new bag. "Sheepskin or Gore-Tex?" the pimply kid behind the counter asks him. Gore-Tex?

"Give me the sheepskin." The store doesn't even carry real cane drone reeds. Most are plastic. All more than fifty dollars each. Crap, he thinks, until he reads the blurbs on the backs of the packages. Colin Robertson. Couldn't be the same Colin Robertson. He'd have to be about Peter's age. Peter hasn't thought about him in years, but they had been pretty good friends. Had to be okay if Colin was using them. He thinks he'll try them. He has to buy a new chanter reed too, because the other one splintered into tiny chips when he banged the chanter on the table. Everything comes to almost three hundred dollars, and that doesn't even include the new bag.

Peter spreads a sheet of clear plastic over the table when he oils the pieces. He's been doing this for a week, twice a day, carefully spreading oil over the outside and inside of the tenor drones, the bass drone, the blowpipe, and he notices the difference. The dull dead pieces, although beautiful to look at, felt inanimate, but after the oil, they seem lighter, full of energy. When he finishes wiping the excess oil from the pieces, he rubs a small amount of polish onto the silver until the discoloration is gone and the silver shines.

On the way to town he stops at the bank to deposit the check from the paper company for the pulp wood. Almost a thousand dollars. He tries to remember if the music store had any bag covers, but it doesn't matter if they don't. It's just for looks, and he can order one. The important thing is the bag itself.

The old guy is back, and the kid is gone today. Peter can't decide which is worse. "Did my bagpipe bag come in?" Peter asks.

"Let me look," the man says, rummaging through a pile of boxes behind the counter. He pulls one out with a note on it. "Tell Mr. MacQueen that the wrong bag came in. We can send it back and reorder, or he can have this one for the price of the other."

"Let me see that," Peter says. CANMORE is written on the thin green plastic bag. Gore-Tex, Peter thinks. But he doesn't want to wait another week. Everything is ready at home for a concert. "All right, I'll try it," he says. "Have you got any bag covers?"

They have one left. Black velvet with black fringe. He buys the cover and a new set of silk drone cords to match. Peter stuffs them into the box on top of the Gore-Tex bag and writes a check. Over two hundred dollars this time. He's glad he got a check for his wood.

Next to the music store is a store that says PETER PAN SHOP, with CHILDREN'S CLOTHING underneath. There's no one in there except for a woman about his age, sitting on a stool behind the counter.

"Can I help you?" she asks.

"Do you have a baby dress? For a girl? She's not quite a month old. Tiny little thing."

"Sure," she says. "Are you the grandpa?"

"Yes," Peter says. "Azelin, her name is."

He chooses a dark green dress with violet trim, remembering Dora's comment about babies needing bright colors. It's almost fifty dollars. Just for a little baby dress. But Peter writes out another check and passes it to the shopkeeper. "Thank you," he says on the way out.

The drive back to the cabin is difficult. Images of Leslie and the children won't leave him alone. For years after the fire their faces would loom up at him while he was driving, and he would have to pull over until they left, but they haven't bothered him for a long time. These are different. Alive. Not blackened and distorted. Leslie smiles at him, and the children banter with each other, old memories of good times. Then another image. A woman. Kate. That young piper from the Highland games at Maxville, the day of the fire. After he sat back down with the silver bowl in his lap, she'd kissed him on the cheek. She was lovely. Red hair, skin covered with freckles. She smiles like Leslie, and the two faces blend into one frightful composite.

He veers over to the side of the road without signaling, and the car behind him beeps going by. "What the hell was that?" he says aloud. The visions vanish. The rest of the way home, he drives like a ninety-year-old, slow, cautious, distracted, until he arrives in his dooryard. He feels better. Elaine walks toward him with Azelin in the baby sling. She isn't afraid of being left at the cabin, because she says Oliver will respect her wishes, but Peter isn't so sure. Her grin widens into a broad smile, and her pace quickens.

He steps up his stride to meet her. "I've got something for you," he says to the sleeping baby.

"For Azelin? What? Let me see."

Elaine has asparagus sandwiches and coffee on the table for lunch. While they eat, he pulls out the green dress and holds it up. "Green. Dark green. Dora said babies need color," he says.

"Oh, Peter," she says. She throws her head back and rocks in the chair. "It's wonderful." She extracts Azelin from the sling and holds her up. "Try it."

"It's a bit big now." The hem goes past her toes. "But it suits her, don't you think?" The baby kicks at the green hem and begins her squalling. "I'm not sure she likes it." They both laugh, like old times, like a family, like his family, and Peter relaxes, pushes aside his thoughts about the images, pats Elaine's hand. "I'm going to tie in the bag today. It'll take me a couple of hours to get everything ready. Then we'll have a concert."

The whole process takes more than two hours, but the drones look beautiful when he finally attaches them to each other with the black silk cords. The silver on the drones catches the sun from the window; the ivory glows from the blackwood background. He carries the instrument out of the cabin. She waves from her crouched position in the herb bed.

He slowly blows his warm air into the bag and strikes his hand on the side. The drones all come in together. The sound is glorious. He goes into a slow march, circling in time with the tune, around and around until he has repeated the tune three times.

Seamus whines from his position near the compost pile. "Play a dance tune," Elaine says.

He strikes in and sounds his E. "My Home." He's always loved the tune played up-tempo. She begins to dance on the repeat of the first part, a waltz. She hugs Azelin tight during the twirls, and her bare feet scatter damp soil around her as she dances through the newly planted carrots. He repeats the whole tune because to stop would mean the end of her dancing.

Her face is radiant. She dances toward him. Over twenty years, he thinks. The blessed instrument at the bottom of his dark trunk. He walks toward her, playing the last few measures, stops, allowing the blowpipe to fall from his lips. Her arms reach for him. The bagpipes and the child are between them, but they touch, their hands on each other's bodies, only T-shirts between hands and skin.

"Wonderful," she says into his ear. "It's just wonderful, but Seamus howled the whole time."

"Oh, and I thought he was deaf." His lips skim across her hair as he speaks.

The sound of a car in the drive breaks the moment, propels them apart, and they stand side by side at the edge of the garden, he with his pipes, she with her baby, watching the familiar blue sedan wind its way down the driveway.

OLIVER Sinclair is alone today. Peter is surprised to see him in shorts and a T-shirt, surprised that he has forgotten to wear his suit.

Peter backs up, holding his bagpipes. Elaine and Azelin need some room, but he decides not to leave them totally alone. He places the pipes on the shady end of the picnic table and putters, picks things up, puts things down, moves tools from one pile to the other.

"Azelin?" Oliver says. He steps close to Elaine.

"Do you like the name?" she asks.

"I've never heard it before. Why did you name her Azelin?"

"Because she is beautiful, and because she's alive."

Oliver clearly is confused but doesn't press the issue. He doesn't touch Elaine, but he asks to hold the baby. Elaine picks her out of the sling and places her in Oliver's arms.

"She's lovely," Oliver says. "Are you feeling well?"

"Yes, thank you."

They sound like acquaintances at a cocktail party.

"I'm sorry, Elaine." He reaches out to touch the spot below her right eye, but she steps back and his finger hovers in midair. "I was upset. I didn't mean to hurt you."

"I know. Do you have it? The journal?"

"No, I don't."

"Please send it," she says.

"Does she smile yet?" Oliver asks.

"Not really. Just little indigestion smiles."

"Does she sleep in the night?"

"Yes, except for when she nurses."

"Have you been here long enough?"

"What?"

"I mean, are you planning to come home, or are you going to stay here with him? With your lover?"

Peter's hands clench into hard fists.

"That's not fair," she says, reaching for Azelin.

He steps back, holding the baby close to his chest. "I deserve to know when you are coming home."

"I need a little more time. Please pass her to me. She's waking up. She'll be scared."

"You're to come home with me. Remember Jezebel. Remember the Bible." He passes the infant to Elaine. "You forget easily the teachings of the Lord."

"Please. Give me a couple of weeks. I will meet with Brother Eldridge. Then we can talk."

"Elaine," he says, folding his arms across his chest. "If you won't come, I'll have to take the baby alone. Many men wouldn't even take you back after what you've done."

"What? What have I done?"

"This," he says, sweeping his arms around. "What do you think? Fornication. Adultery. Disobedience. Everything."

"We're not sleeping together," she says.

"Oh, sure. I'm not leaving here without that baby."

"That baby?" Elaine begins to pace. She glances at Peter, but it isn't clear if she wants help. "No. You're not taking Azelin. You don't know anything about me. You don't even know why I'm here."

"No. I guess I don't. But I do know that I'm entitled to my own child. And I do know that you are not going to keep her here with that man. I apologized. That should be enough. What else is there?" The corners of Oliver's mouth build up with froth as he speaks. He grabs Elaine's arm just above her elbow.

"Take your hand off her," Peter says.

Peter is surprised when Oliver drops his hand from her and steps back. Peter knows that he wouldn't win in a fight.

"Give me a few minutes to pack."

"Hey. What?" Peter moves toward her.

"It's all right, Peter, don't worry. Please wait. I won't be long."

"Hurry up," Oliver says to Elaine as she opens the door to the cabin. "I don't have much time."

Peter thinks his head will explode. He stands immobilized by his own fright. It can't be over. She can't just leave with this man. Peter tries to think fast. If he had a phone, he'd call someone. Dora? The police? Brendan? If he hits the guy, Oliver will hit back, hard. Elaine said, "Wait, don't worry." How can he not worry?

"You play those things?" Oliver says, walking over to the bag-pipes on the picnic table.

"Don't touch them," Peter hears himself say. He catches movement at the front door of the cabin. Elaine stands on the landing holding his 20 gauge against her shoulder like he taught her to. Oliver follows Peter's gaze toward the cabin, toward Elaine.

"Elaine," Oliver shouts. "What are you doing? Put that thing down. You don't know how to use it. You'll hurt yourself."

"I do know how to use it. And I will. Now get off Peter's property. I told you I need a couple of weeks. If you don't leave now, it'll make my decision easier."

Oliver steps out of the path of the double-barrel. "Put the gun down. Now. Obey me."

"Git," she says, like she would to a stray dog. "Go on. Git."

"I'm going to walk slowly toward you. Now put that thing down." Oliver points his finger at her and begins his advance.

"I don't want to shoot you. But I will," she says.

"Don't be stupid. Get the baby. Now. Right now."

The shot sounds like thunder. The dirt in front of Oliver sprays up onto bushes, onto his clean shorts.

"If you come closer, I will have no choice." She adjusts the stock of the gun against her shoulder.

"Hey," Oliver says, but he keeps coming. "You almost hit me. Dammit, Elaine, cut that out."

He is two cabin lengths away from the landing when the shot hits him. He falls into the path, clasping his leg.

"Oh, my God," she says. She leans the shotgun against the rail. "I shot him."

"Just his foot, I think," says Peter, running to Oliver.

"Get away from me," Oliver says. "You're all lunatics." He struggles to his feet. One thin line of blood oozes from the fleshy part of his shin down into his sock.

"I'm sorry, Oliver," she says. "I had no choice. No one takes a woman's baby from her without a fight. I didn't mean to hurt you."

Oliver struggles down the path toward his sedan. Peter thinks he is sobbing. "You'll be sorry you did this," Oliver yells without turning around, at the door of the car. "Elaine, you're crazy. You could have killed me."

"No, Oliver. I didn't want to kill you. Just stop you. Two weeks," Elaine calls. "I have nothing to say until then."

Oliver doesn't look back. Just tears away up the driveway.

Peter waits until he can no longer hear the sound of the engine before he approaches her. This time the baby and the pipes are no longer between them, and he holds her close to him, feels her thin body trembling against his, strokes her corn-silk hair until she is still.

PETER thinks that this might be their last night together. Surely Oliver will bring the police. You just can't shoot people without recrimination. Elaine rocks and sings to Azelin until the baby falls asleep in the crook of her arm, and she lowers her into Peter's old newspaper basket, which has been turned into a bassinet.

"Elaine," Peter says, breaking the silence.

"Yes," she says, turning toward him. "Yes, we have to talk."

"I can't believe you shot the guy."

"It was crazy, wasn't it?"

"Yes. Crazy."

"He'll be back, you know."

"Yes. But you don't have to go with him. There are laws."

"There are laws against shooting people."

"But—self-defense. He was on my property without permission, and he threatened you."

"Threatened to take his own child."

They don't even hear the car, only the knocking. "They're here already. I'll answer it."

"I'm Carl Eldridge," the familiar pudgy guy with the too-small suit says. The man is alone. "I don't want to intrude, but I need to speak with Elaine." He doesn't wait for an invitation but goes to her. "Is there somewhere we could talk? Privately?"

"We can speak in front of Peter. He is not my lover. He is my friend."

"It doesn't look very good, you two living in the same cabin like this."

"Peter is helping me sort through some things."

"That's why we have elders. You don't need to go to worldly people."

Peter wonders if he should offer tea or coffee. He doesn't want to leave the cabin, but feels awkward standing by the stove.

"I've seen Oliver. He says you shot him."

"Yes."

"Has he done something? Has he mistreated you? There is help if you have a problem. You know that."

"I asked him to give me two weeks. That's all."

"You know wives must obey their husbands. Husbands must be loving, but wives must be obedient. That's the law of Jehovah."

"Please, let me be. You've got to give me time."

"Oliver is willing to give you some time. We'll come two weeks from tomorrow to talk. We are all praying that you find the truth. John eight: thirty-two says, *And you will know the truth and the truth will set you free.*"

"Thank you, Brother Eldridge," she says. "Thank you for your understanding and your prayers. Would you like to see the baby?" He nods. "She's sleeping."

Brother Eldridge searches Peter's face for permission to go deeper into the cabin, and Peter nods.

"She's lovely," he says. "Looks like Oliver." Peter thinks he honestly wants to help Elaine, but that he will demand her obedience. "Two weeks." He turns to leave. "Good-bye." He nods at Peter, stares at his boots, his jeans with the gap at the knee, his scruffy hair. "It's important for the children to have a strong family."

"Good-bye," Peter says, opening the door for him.

Peter watches until his car disappears through the trees.

"Everything's all right now," she says.

"No. It's different. It's not all right. There are things between us. We're not just a typical American couple with baby and dog and little garden out back. We're not a family." Peter walks around the table. *The truth will set you free.* Whose truth? Free from what? "The dollhouse. I want to tell you about the dollhouse," he says, turning toward her.

"You don't need to."

"Yes. I do. Come."

He lifts the towel, exposing the entire front of the house. He feels as if he has been stripped naked in front of his class, his recurring dream every night before a competition, a small, dirty, ugly boy, nothing on but socks, standing in front of his whole class.

But Elaine holds his arm, leans her head on his shoulder. He can't speak. Leslie, Sarah, Nathaniel. He hasn't shown them to anyone. Ever.

"They're your family, aren't they, Peter?"

He nods.

"You loved them very much."

He nods again.

"I'm sorry I didn't wait for you to show me. I had no right."

"It's just that having you see them changes everything. They're no longer my secret."

"Tell me about them."

"This is Leslie." Peter wants to speak to Leslie, tell her he's sorry about the intrusion, that he loves her. He picks up the Leslie doll, shows her to Elaine, but fears he has gone too far. "This is Sarah. Nathaniel." He leaves them in their places. It is awkward to hold them up. "They give me comfort." He has said all he can say.

"Shall we cover it up or leave it open?"

"Oh." He places Leslie back in the chair by the kitchen table. "I'd like to leave it open."

Peter staggers over to his bed. His head pounds, and he thinks he might throw up. He collapses on top of the futon, presses his face into the flannel pillowcase, presses until the pillow covers his ears, until he can't see the daylight. Her hands touch the back of his head where it is pounding, and he feels her heat. The side of the futon sinks as she sits beside him, hip against hip. Elaine, Elaine, Elaine, over and over in his hot pounding head. The heat spreads down the back of his neck as her hands smooth his hair. Turn to her. Turn to her, a voice tells him. It is a voice he hasn't heard for years. Not since Leslie. *Hi, Les. Yes, I won. . . . I miss you too. . . . I ate with Colin and went to bed early. . . . See you soon. Love you.* The last words. He has heard them every day for years. The last words.

"Elaine." He speaks into the pillow, muffled. Tell her she can stay. Tell her she doesn't have to go back.

She pushes with warm fingers until he turns to her. She bends over him, covers his face with her hair. She is so close he can smell her, the tangible odor of skin and breast milk. He will remember that smell as long as he lives.

"I know you miss them," she says. He inhales her warm breath, catches her exhalation with his mouth, pulls it into his lungs.

"Elaine." He wants to say crazy things like "I love you" and "Please, let me touch your bare skin, your breasts, between your legs." He turns toward her.

She lies with him, stretches out the length of the bed. She strokes his forehead, and he is afraid to touch her. He has forgotten how to touch a woman. He realizes he is shivering and she is caring for him as if he were a baby, not a grown man who loves her. He cups her face in his palms, her skin stark white against his weathered hands. Her mouth opens and closes, but he can't hear over the pounding in his own head. Shut up, he screams at the demons in his head. Shut up so I can hear her words.

Suddenly she is gone from him, walking to the baby in the magazine basket. She lifts Azelin up to her exposed breast. Her mouth still moves as if she is saying words to him, but the roaring in his head continues until she settles herself into the rocking chair and starts to sing.

He turns his face back into the pillow. When she leaves, he will be alone, and he is afraid of that. It is getting dark outside, and he needs to get up to light the lamps. He hears Elaine change Azelin from one breast to the other. She doesn't know. She doesn't know how he feels about her.

"Thank you for trusting me enough to show the dollhouse," she says. "If you want to talk about them, I'll listen."

He can't speak yet. He is afraid to bring back the pounding inside his head.

He wills his feet to the floor, wills his body upright, wills his throbbing groin to shrink. The gaping openness of the dollhouse startles him until he remembers what he did.

"I'll light the lamps," he says. "It's cooling off too."

Only two of the lamps are filled with kerosene, but that is enough to bring a warm glow to the walls of the cabin. He shuts the windows except for a small crack in the front one.

Elaine carries the basket with sleeping Azelin over to the side of her bed. "I'm going to the outhouse. She shouldn't waken."

After she leaves, he approaches the dollhouse. "Les, I'm sorry." Then he isn't sure why he is sorry. For exposing her to Elaine? For letting her burn in the fire? For loving someone else? He raises his finger to touch the doll but hesitates. He feels foolish. He wishes Nathaniel would find the damn sneaker. And when was Sarah going to outgrow stuffed animals? For heaven's sake, she was almost a teenager.

On the way to bed he stops by the basket. He brushes Azelin's curls away from her forehead before he goes to his futon.

After Elaine returns from the outhouse, after she has blown out the lamps, after she has undressed for bed in the half-light, they lie in the still cabin, still, except for the peepers. Peter hears her move her bare feet on the clean sheet, hears Azelin sucking, hears the old dog scratch, but then nothing again but the sound of thousands of peepers.

"It was my fault, you know. She told me there was a frayed wire. I said I'd fix it after the competition season." He speaks quietly, matter-of-factly. "My fault."

"Do they know it was a wire?"

"No. But it must have been. I was always too busy. She called me that night, before the fire started. Or perhaps it was already burning in the walls. I told her that I ate dinner with Colin and went to bed early. But I don't remember what I had for supper. I don't remember where we went."

"Can you ask Colin? If it's important, ask him."

"I haven't talked to him in years. Not since he visited the hospital after the fire without my permission. Tried to get me to play. I told him to get the hell away and never bother me again. He never did."

"Have you thought about trying to find him?"

"No."

"Maybe you could. It's easier today than it used to be."

"He's still in the bagpipe circle. He was damn good. But, no. No. I don't think so. It's too late for that."

"It's never too late."

"Good night, Elaine."

"Peter . . ."

"Tomorrow. We'll talk tomorrow."

7

THEY don't talk the next day or the next week. Not about Colin or Leslie, at least. The dollhouse stays open, and while Elaine is in the outhouse or the garden, he moves the dolls up to bed and down to the kitchen for breakfast. When they wash dishes together or weed the lettuce, Peter maneuvers himself to touch her. Just light brushes or taps that might be called an accident or just a casual touch while working. There are three days left for Elaine to make her decision. Sometimes at night Peter hears her praying from her bed.

He plays the bagpipes every day, and his lip is coming back. Reels and jigs, strathspeys and marches, even slow marches, but he hasn't yet played a piobaireachd on the pipes. A couple of neighbors drive down the hill to ask what is going on. They want to hear "Amazing Grace." He plays it for them. But no one asks for a piobaireachd. That's what Colin would do. He'd want a lament, and Peter wouldn't be able to play it. He's not ready to play one all the way through.

Peter thinks about tomorrow and the island shearing. Usually he waits until June, but this year everything seems ahead of the usual schedule and they decided to shear a week earlier. He's been shearing his island flock for years, but this year will be different. Elaine is planning to go with them. There'll be three boats plus the empty skiff, filled on the way back with freshly shorn fleeces, that Peter will tow behind his boat.

If someone asks him what the highlight of his year was, he will answer, shearing day, not Christmas or solstice or birthday. Shearing day is the one time when he feels comfortable around other people, experiences a sense of camaraderie that otherwise is totally absent from his life. Shearing day preparations have already begun at Dora's. Elaine is there now helping bake trays of lasagna, at least three rhubarb pies, fresh bread. Folks who come to help expect a good meal, and they always get it.

Elaine said she would be back before dark. He lights one of the lamps, just in case she is late. He wanted to be able to spend more time with the dollhouse today, but the time got all used up on other things. It took him all afternoon to gather his shearing equipment together. Old pants, bags for the fleeces, tags and pens to mark the bags, shears, blades, blood-stop, odds and ends. The generator is in Dora's shed, and he hopes it will be in running shape. He has bought fresh gasoline for that.

The dollhouse looks shabby. Peter wipes his finger along the kitchen floor and holds it up. Dust. Leslie's hair is coming off on one side. He pulls up a chair and brings the dolls to his lap. He tidies the rooms, straightens the stuffed animals. He tucks the children into their beds.

"It's been a hard spring," he says. "I've been thinking about the phone call. Remember? The last one? At the hotel?" He holds Leslie to his chest. "I don't remember where Colin and I had dinner. Do you? Did I tell you?" He knows she won't answer, but sometimes when he talks, the answers come to him as if she responds.

Hello, he had said.

Hi, darling, Leslie said. *Did you win?*

Hi, Les. Yes, I won.
I miss you.
I miss you too.
Where'd you have supper?
I ate with Colin and went to bed early.
Oh, that's nice. See you soon. Love you.
See you soon. Love you.

Something sounds wrong. Did he forget some of it?

He hears the telephone bell ringing. Seven rings before he picks it up. *Went to bed early,* he hears himself say. And whatever happened to that girl, Kate? Why didn't she go with them for dinner? He remembers asking her. Then what happened?

"Les. I'm forgetting. Sometimes I can't remember the smell of your mouth. I've forgotten how your voice sounded. *Where'd you have supper?* How did that sound? I can't remember."

Peter kisses the doll's forehead and settles her into bed with Sarah, pushes them close together, pulls the covers up to their chins. "There. You won't be alone."

It is Peter who feels lonely now. The old dog lifts his head and groans. "Seamus, you old dog, you are a sorry sight." Peter pats himself on the thigh. "Here, boy," he says. Seamus puts his head back down on the floor.

"All right, then, I'll come down there." He stretches his legs out in front of him and pulls Seamus's head to his lap. "You like Elaine, don't you, boy?" He strokes the old dog behind the ears. "Sheep . . . Rabbit . . . Wood . . . Fetch." There is no response from the dog. None of the old words makes any difference. His eyes are glazed with a gray film, but Peter looks past the film to find the old sparkle. "It's not so bad, dying. You're old. Just close your eyes, relax." Peter lowers the head to the floor and struggles to his feet. "How about a special treat," he says. "Chicken. Your favorite."

Peter hauls on the iron ring attached to the trapdoor. There are two jars of chicken left. Peter takes one for the dog. As he lowers the trapdoor, Seamus lifts his head, cocks his ear. "Look, boy, chicken."

Peter washes the dog dish, and spoons the entire jar of chicken into the bowl. It happens while he stands ready to place the bowl on the floor. Happens right there in front of him. The dog sniffs at the chicken, lays his head back down on the floor with a groan. The last groan continues a horribly long time, until his head rolls off to the side the way dead things do.

Peter lowers himself again and sits for a long time with the dog's head on his lap, stroking the fur behind the long ears. The weight of the dog's head on his thigh puzzles him until he comprehends that Seamus will never again fetch the wood for his stove.

When Elaine arrives with Azelin, Peter is still on the floor, Seamus's head on his lap.

"What are you doing?" she says.

"Dog." He can't say the rest, but she understands.

"Oh. Seamus." Elaine kneels and brushes her lips across the face of the dead dog. She kisses Peter on the top of the head. "I'm sorry," she says.

Peter wants to nestle his head in her breast, feel her bare arms around his shoulders. But he can't do that. And he feels very alone.

"He had a decent life. He was old," he says.

Peter digs a hole between the compost and the barn. The dead dog is heavier than the living one, and Peter struggles to keep his legs from collapsing on the path.

"One more thing," he says to Elaine.

He chooses a perfect birch log, perfect for a dog's mouth, especially an old dog. He carefully lays the log beside the body.

When he begins to shovel, some of the dirt falls on the dog's still open eye. Peter drops the shovel and runs into the barn. He rummages through a bin of old grain bags until he finds a burlap sweet-feed bag: smell like molasses, no holes, no stains. He lays it on the dog's head to keep the dirt from going into his eyes and continues to fill the hole. There is a mound left when he is finished, and he stamps on it until it is ground level.

He expects Elaine to say some prayer over the grave when he is finished. There should be something said. But neither speaks.

"It's getting dark," he says. "Let's go in."

The cabin is eerie, illuminated only by the one lamp.

"Play something," Elaine says.

As if in slow motion, he walks to the shelf, picks up the chanter. "I'm going to play you something you probably haven't ever heard. It's called *pee-brock,* but spelled an ungodly complicated way. A Gaelic word. Ancient classical bagpipe music." Peter's voice is low, like the light in the room. Reverence for old Dog. "I used to play piobaireachd in competition years ago, before the fire."

As he plays, the tune of the ground comes to him easily. He closes his eyes because it becomes too much to include the outside world in his lament. The closing measure comes before he is ready for it, the Bs that last long, and lonely B.

" 'Lament for the Children,' " he says when it is finished. "Patrick Mor MacCrimmon. That's just the first movement. The ground. The rest builds on that."

"Will you play the rest of it?"

"Not yet. I'm not quite ready yet."

Elaine rustles around the kitchen, putting things away, while Peter opens the old musty trunk. At the bottom is a stack of books and papers. He leafs through the stack until he comes to a battered softcover book. *Composition Paper,* it says on the front, his name printed neatly underneath. At the back are a few blank pages.

Peter shaves a pencil end with his jackknife. He sets up the piece on the lined paper. It will be four-four. Directly over the first line he writes, "ground." At the top of the page he writes, "Azelin's Lullaby," in block letters. The notes have been in his head for several days, now playing faster than he can write them down with the pencil. The first part is repeated. The second part is high, like Elaine's voice, like the song of a thrush.

A new piobaireachd. Elaine goes to visit the outhouse. When he is alone, he begins to sing the piobaireachd from the sheet music in front of him. It is Elaine's voice.

When Elaine comes back, he waits until she tends to Azelin,

brushes her teeth, sinks into the rocker. "I've written a tune," he says.

"A tune? You mean you've just written it? Just now?"

"Yes. But I've been hearing it in the woods for days. It comes from the trees and the wind. After shearing day I'll play it," he says.

Peter picks up the pencil again, changes the last two notes of the first measure, and writes directly under "Azelin's Lullaby" the words "For Elaine, May 28."

PETER is out of bed before there is any sign of sun in the morning sky. He gathers his shearing tools and organizes himself for the day ahead. He wears a pair of shorts under his stiff shearing pants. A green plastic fish tote leans by the door, and he begins to place things in it. A bottle of last year's blueberry wine for celebration at Dora's after shearing, his bag of tools, two boxes of Oreos, oil for the shears, a sharpening file, dry socks, bandanna for his hair.

"We leave at seven," he says.

Elaine moans in return, turns over in the bed. Peter looks for faithful old Seamus before he remembers the night before. By the time he heads to the outhouse and the barn, the rising sun provides a warm glow over everything he can see.

By seven o'clock he has packed the back of the truck. Brendan has lent them a baby life preserver that just fits Azelin. Said he had it for one of his kids.

"Time to go," Peter hollers up to the cabin. Elaine carries Azelin down the path and buckles her into the car seat between them in the truck. The drive to Dora's doesn't take more than ten minutes, and there are already cars in the yard when they arrive. A couple of cars have small skiffs tied to the roofs. They gather in Dora's kitchen.

Every surface is covered with some kind of food: pans of lasagna, jars of pickles, bread, pies. "Oh, you're here, are you?" Dora says. Peter bends and kisses her cheek. "Well, kissing me, is he? That's something."

"Looks like you got everything under control," he says. "Who's sorting?"

"Susanne, the girl who helped us with the birthing. I figured after the gathering, Elaine can help too."

A couple of strangers hover by the kitchen door, young folks wearing proper L.L. Bean clothing. "Joshua," the man says.

"Mary Jane," the woman says.

Peter nods. They look nice enough. "You two will gather along with Elaine and me. We'll go over everything once we get out there. You'll split up in the boats. Joshua, you go in Dora's boat. The girl goes with Cecilia. Where the hell is Cecilia?"

"Looking for me?" she says from the doorway.

Peter swears she's grown another foot since last shearing day. She towers over everyone, and her hands are the size of pies. Her black Passamaquoddy hair is pulled back with a bandanna.

"You all set with your shearing gear?" he asks her.

"Yeah. And I got a bunch of new blades if you need any. Forgot my blood-stop, though. If I cut one bad, I'll holler."

"One more's coming," Dora says. "Shelley from next door, to help with the food."

"She can go with Cecilia," Peter says.

The caravan of skiffs sets off from the dock. Peter's boat has a small outboard, just enough horse to tow the fleece boat behind. Elaine sits holding Azelin in the middle seat. Peter remembers when not too many years ago, Dog sat up in the bow like a mate on watch. Tiny Azelin has on her royal-blue doll-size life jacket, hiding everything but her face. Peter watches Elaine's back, her hair hanging in one thick braid.

The other boats bob up and down in the small swells. The air is crisp, clear, with no bad weather predicted. Of course, on the coast of Maine, you never know about the weather. The small caps break on the bows of the skiffs behind him. The rowers all make headway, some of the boats low in the water, especially Cecilia's, because of the generator. But she is strong, arms more muscular than anyone on his crew team back in Connecticut.

The water becomes shallow enough for him to see the seaweed bottom. He cuts the motor and flips it up just before the bow touches the stony beach, allowing the skiff to glide to shore. The only sheep in sight is the ram, who munches on seaweed at the water's edge a little farther down the beach.

As soon as the other boats arrive on the shore, the organizational efforts of Dora take over. Cecilia and Joshua haul the generator over to the holding pen while the others carry food and drinks up to the small hut. Soon Shelley is serving up fresh coffee and baskets of cinnamon doughnuts. The old pine table in the hut is camouflaged with a yellow-print cloth. Pies and salads cover one end, and the lasagna, ringed with pickles and platters of bread, weighs down the other.

Joshua arrives to report that all the equipment, including the generator, is in position and the pen area is ready for shearing. The group follows Peter to the holding pen, except for Shelley, who stays guarding the food. Peter barks orders about securing the top rail of the algae-splattered fencing and shoring up the sides of the chute. "If one goes through, they all go through." Most of the people have heard that before, except Joshua and Mary Jane.

Cecilia takes over the lecture about rounding them up, how it's important to keep low, to move slow, to make a thorough sweep of the entire island, to funnel them directly into the chute on the first try because after that they get skittish.

Dora goes to the shore to wait for the sheep. She knows she is too old for the gather. Peter feels a need to tell her about Dog before they start. He follows her.

"The old dog," he begins. "He died last night."

"Oh. Poor old thing." Her deep rheumy eyes become wet. She's probably thinking she'll be next.

Peter does something he's never done. He embraces the old woman, holding her snug in his arms, and his eyes tear up over the old dog too. She seems surprised at the embrace but nestles into him, brings her arms around his filthy shearing shirt. He hears a small moan, feels it in his hands coming from her back.

"We'll miss him, won't we," he says. Not a question really. "I buried him out by the barn."

The gatherers are ready, all equipped with long sticks. Even Elaine stands quietly by the side of the chute, a three-foot length of driftwood in her hand. Azelin is quiet, snuggled against her breast by the baby carrier. All of them except Dora and Cecilia will spread out around the island and gather the sheep toward the chute. Cecilia will be ready to open and close the gates and keep them from veering away at the last minute.

The L.L. Bean folks start off too fast, and Peter hollers at them to crouch and slow down. Luck is with them today. The sheep are all together except for the ram. Peter detours around the peninsula and herds him into the circle of ewes and lambs. The flock rises as if one sheep and moves slowly toward the other end of the island, the chute end. Peter gets a whiff of coffee while he crouches against a boulder. The new folks have got the idea now and crouch and sway just like pros. Elaine whacks her stick on the ground when an errant ewe tries to break from the flock. The ewe turns back into the circle and moves with the rest.

"Slow down," Cecilia says. They all hear her and crouch. Elaine moves in slow motion out to the side to cover the southern getaway point.

"They're going in," Peter hears. He's not sure who says it. Once one sheep goes through, the others follow, even the ram. Three lambs are left outside, but they won't be a problem unless the mothers try to leap the fence. The fence is too high for all but the very craziest to attempt.

"Got them," he says.

Cecilia shuts the gate. "I count thirty, including the ram, excluding the lambs. That it?"

"Yes."

"Somebody start that generator," she says.

Dora spreads tarps out on the beach for sorting. Cecilia already grips a ewe between her legs, sets it on its rump, and begins the first blow across the belly, the sound of the shears droning. She throws the belly wool into a heap over the fence. The next few blows shear the head and down the side. The dirty ringlets fall off the skin, leaving a stark-white layer of fuzz, next year's tips. He takes the black, she the white, one sheep at a time. The fleece goes to Dora and Elaine, who toss dungy globs and short scraps into an old burlap bag for their gardens. The rest is labeled after it is rolled and pushed into burlap grain bags.

In a few hours the shearing is done. They all help get the last few fleeces into bags before they head up to the hut. Shelley has a steaming bowl of hot water on the ground just outside the hut door and a clean towel laid on the stump next to a bar of soap. Peter rubs the soap over his sticky palms until the lanolin is scrubbed off, until his fingers no longer stick together.

The lasagna steams on the table next to a pile of plates, napkins, and forks. An institutional-sized stainless steel bowl of baby salad greens takes up the entire center of the table, the top sprinkled with sliced radishes, fresh herbs, spring flower blossoms. Peter begins with pie. He is head shearer and owner of the flock, which entitles him to do anything he pleases. He heaps two large slices of rhubarb pie onto his paper plate and digs in with the white plastic fork. It is tart enough to pucker up the pope, and that's the way he likes it.

"Great pie," he says to Shelley, who appears to be waiting for a comment from him. As soon as he speaks, she relaxes, lowers her shoulders, stops staring at his fork.

"Dig in," she says.

Cecilia eats the most. Shelley brings out the third lasagna and slices the fourth loaf of bread. Peter's been counting. He knows there's one more pie hidden in the bottom of the food crate, but he doesn't mention it.

"Beautiful clip," Dora says. "Those kids did all right."

"Yes, they did." He sees Mary Jane looking his way. "Both of them did a fine job," he says loud enough to spread through the hut.

There isn't really enough room for everyone to be inside at once, so they take turns coming in to get food and going out to eat it. Elaine is like a child at play. Her laugh becomes more like Dora's full belly laugh every day. She wears her child like one would a piece of clothing, and they romp in the meadow like lambs. The ewes have brought their babies to the far end of the island, away from the shearing party, but a few lambs, curious about the new-comers, venture to the edge of the bush line.

"That the last pie?" he says to Shelley.

"Yup," she says.

"Thought there might be one more. Thought you said four."

"Peter, you're like a food-smelling dog, one of them blood-hounds," she says.

Peter brings his fourth piece of rhubarb pie out to the meadow in his hand. He and Elaine sit on a dry hillock, their backs to the hut, while Peter finishes his pie. He wipes his hand on the grass.

"I'm so happy here. I've always hated living in Bedford. I'm a country person. Thank you for everything," she says. "Especially for leaving me alone, letting me work out my thoughts."

She sounds like she's leaving. Thanks for everything and good-bye, he thinks. "I've enjoyed the company," he says. Their shoulders are almost touching. He kisses the top of her head.

Her head leans on him, and she begins to hum. Something famil-iar, he thinks.

> *"Tender shepherd, tender shepherd*
> *Watches over all her sheep.*
> *One, say your prayers and*
> *Two, close your eyes and*
> *Three, safe and happily fall asleep."*

"Do you know it?" she asks.

"Yes, I think so."

> *"Tender shepherd, tender shepherd*
> *You forgot to count your sheep.*
> *One, in the meadow,*
> *Two, in the garden,*
> *Three, in the nursery fast asleep."*

"It's from *Peter Pan,*" she says.

"Yes, I've heard it. But never as beautiful."

"I need to decide what to do."

"Yes."

"I know I want us to remain friends. We can do that, can't we?"

"Yes," he says. But what if she goes far away? "You can stay if you want. I can build onto the cabin." He can't believe he's said it. His eyes are closed, and he imagines Elaine in his bed, a larger bed, sensing when she is ready to turn over and turning with her, sleeping with his arm draped over her shoulder. "Please stay."

"There's a lot to consider. My religion. I love my religion and need to go back to it. I want to talk to the elders."

"Just know that you have a place."

She kneels, adjusting Azelin's hat before she rises to her feet. "Come on."

He's glad she's turned to join the others before he struggles to his feet. He's lost his ability to make believe it doesn't hurt. His hips and ankles are stiff for the first few steps.

After they load the generator into Dora's boat, the rest goes quickly. They push the boats to the waterline, which is closer now because the tide is high.

Shelley has packed the few leftovers and food containers into baskets, which Joshua tucks under seats. The wool bags are tossed into the empty skiff and shoved into the bow and under the gunwales. Elaine sits in the middle seat with Azelin trussed into her flotation device while Peter pushes off. He wears big rubber boots and can wade out without getting wet. It's kind of tricky making sure the lines from the fleece boat don't get caught in the motor as he shoves off.

He pulls the starter cord. It catches the second time, and they begin to put across to Dora's. It's midafternoon, and there's a thick, unexpected bank of fog that begins to obliterate the far shore. Nothing on the radio about fog. The other boats bob along behind them. It will be fine. This channel is too narrow for most boats, the lobsters haven't come inshore yet, and the tourists are still in Philadelphia.

The drone of a far engine approaches through the fogbank. Loud voices yell above the din. Sounds like a bunch of drunks. Peter flicks on his flashlight and waves it at the noise, but he knows it isn't dark enough for them to see it. He doesn't know which way to turn, doesn't know where the boat attached to the loud engine is going to spring out of the fog.

THE lobster boat hits them before Peter has a chance to register the sight of it. Hits them just off the bow of his small boat. He doesn't even have time to think about bracing himself, holding on to the gunwales, protecting Elaine or Azelin. The first thing Peter knows is the slap of the water against his face. The cold seeps through his clothes, fills his rubber boots, before he begins to move his arms and legs to keep afloat. Then he feels the strike of the fleece boat against his cheek and hears the noise of the lobster boat almost drowning out the small sound of his outboard. Elaine and Azelin must still be in the boat. The fog surrounds him like a down comforter, settles in around his face until his own hands, when he waves to show where he is, are all that he is able to see. The noise of the lobster boat engine hums in the water as he calls out, hums louder than his shouting can transcend. He treads water, feeling the weight of the sheep-shearing pants pulling on him.

"Elaine," he calls.

He hears the small motor of his skiff pass by at the right, feels the wake of the skiff pulling the sheep boat, then hears Elaine's voice. "Azelin," she says.

Azelin. Why is she calling Azelin? The baby isn't in the cold water. No. The baby is not in the cold water. "Azelin," he says, first in one direction, then in the other. His clothes are soaked through and weighing him down.

His arms and legs barely move against the cold water, which laps at his mouth. The boots have got to come off. *When you fall in cold water, always take your boots off.* He tries to push off his heavy rubber boots with his feet, like he would on dry land, but they stick. He takes a breath and lowers his head down to his boots, struggles to pull them off with his stiff hands. It takes five dives before he finally pulls the waterlogged rubber boots from his frozen feet, allowing them to sink to the bottom. His mind tries to keep up with the noise of the boats and the yelling of Elaine, but the cold fuzzes up his head. Only one thing at a time. His arms slip under the suspenders holding up his shearing pants, and he thinks they will just drop off, float away from him. The baggy pants hug his wet body, making it almost impossible for him to kick his feet. He's got to get them off. He dives again and tugs the stiff material until the waist of the pants is down to his knees. Then his feet kick at the material until the pants are free from his body.

With his limbs free, he treads water, struggling to keep his face above the white chops. He sees nothing but gray water that blends into gray fog.

The large engine cuts. The outboard still hums in the distance. "Elaine," he calls out into the fog.

Voices emerge out of the haze. "Here, Peter, over here" and "I think I see him" and the last, the worst, Elaine's voice, "Azelin," long and high, like the moan of a seal. "Aaaazzeelin."

Elaine must still be in the boat. But Azelin? Where is she? Peter kicks and swims in one direction, toward the put-put of the outboard. The noise edges closer to him, and he waves his arms. "Here, Elaine. Cut the engine. Cut the engine." A tiny infant, no matter how large the life preserver is, can't survive the whack of a propeller blade. "Cut the engine."

There is silence, suddenly. Beside him is Dora's boat. "Azelin," he says.

"I don't know," says Dora, her face monstrously misshapen, older than death.

"Elaine." He yells as loud as he is able from his position in the frigid salt water.

"Elaine," says Dora. "Elaine. Elaine." Loud. Shouted into the fog.

Then Elaine's exquisite voice, haunting and terrified. "She's gone. She's in the water."

"Sing," Peter says. "Everyone sing and form a circle. Elaine, there's an oar under the seat. Sing and listen. That way you'll all know where everyone else is."

The singing begins from Dora. *"It rained all night the day I left."*

From the left of him, *"The weather it was dry."* It is the new man, Joshua, singing strong. From the right, *"The sun so hot I froze to death; / Susanna, don't you cry."*

"Tighten the circle. Watch for the baby. Royal blue," he says. The sense of the boats surrounding him allows him to organize his mind, to think about what to do, imagine what might happen.

"Oh, Susanna! Oh, don't you cry for me, / For I come from Alabama / With my banjo on my knee."

"Stop," yells Dora. "Listen."

The boats are close, circled around Peter and a bobbing infant that no one can yet see. She's got to be here. "Come in closer, slowly, watch for her in the water." There is no baby sound. Peter swims back and forth within the circle, watching for a royal-blue life jacket bobbing in the water.

"Everybody all right over there?"

"Looks like we might have hit somebody. I told you jokers we'd get in trouble."

It's kids, Peter thinks. Kids drunk out in a boat. His legs no longer feel the cold, and he forces them to kick.

"Get in the boat, Peter."

"Shut up," he says, paddling around and around within the circumference. Then he sees her. Only a few feet away. "Here she is," he yells at the fog. His arms and legs move in slow motion, his stiff hands reach out to the royal-blue life jacket. Azelin is tucked securely inside, belts holding her upright in the frigid water, her hat gone, her fine curls now stuck in straight streaks to her head.

Oh, please, God. Oh, please. His hands lift the cold wet package. She doesn't cry. He pinches her cheek. She doesn't cry. Her skin feels like rubber when he wraps his fingers around the small arm sticking through the hole in the jacket. A little rubber doll.

Joshua's boat lolls next to them now, four hands extended toward him for the baby. "Pass her up," they say. "Pass her up."

He can't let Elaine see her like this. Cold. Lifeless. Her eyes are open, staring at his chest.

"Come on. Pass her up here, Peter. Pass her up."

He feels a hand on his shoulder, grasping his collar. He has no choice, no choice at all. She is heavy, hard to lift past the surface of the water, but the hands grab for her life jacket and he pushes, pushes toward them, feels her leave his grasp. There are more hands for him. They lift him into the boat. Peter's legs don't help at all, and it takes too long, too much hauling, yelling, grasping for hands, kicking feet against the gunwales. "Azelin," he says. Joshua holds her. She is out of the life preserver but doesn't cry. She doesn't make any noise.

"She's dead. Oh, God, she isn't moving. Oh, my God," Joshua says.

"Shut up and get her wet clothes off. Hold her close to you. Hurry up."

In the distance Elaine paddles Peter's skiff and the towed fleece boat toward them. He hears her frantic questions. "Do you have her? Is she all right? Answer me."

The drunks on the lobster boat won't shut up. "What's going on? Anybody hurt? Sorry about that." And then laughter. Laughter.

"Oh, God," Elaine says. "I let her go. I just opened my arms and gave her to the ocean."

A cold body isn't dead until it is warm and dead. Warm and dead. He falls onto the boat floor, yanking the wet clothes off his body. The shirt, socks, shorts. "Give me some dry clothes," he says. "Warm. Off your back. Now." Mary Jane pulls off her sweater.

Peter wriggles his bare wet skin into the wool sweater. Mary Jane continues to undress, until she is in underpants. She shoves heavy wool socks onto his blue feet. The *dip dip* of the paddle nears. When Peter takes the baby from Joshua, she is naked, cold, blue-lipped. He shoves the beloved Azelin under the sweater, onto his bare chest. "More clothes," he says.

Clothes come flying into the boat from Dora. The drunks from the lobster boat toss down an old wool blanket stinking like stale beer. Soon almost everyone around is half naked except for Peter and Azelin. Elaine's boat is at the gunwales now, and Joshua grabs her painter and helps her into their boat. "Peter, is she all right? She has to be. She's been spared by Jehovah."

She doesn't pull the baby from his chest; she slides her hands up under the sweaters to touch her child. She presses herself against Peter. "My God, she's stone-cold."

"Don't move her. Don't jerk. A cold body isn't dead until it's warm and dead."

Elaine breaths into the top of the sweaters, pushing the warm air from her lungs into the baby cocoon, her hands still touching the chilled quiet child.

"Please, God, let her breathe. Let her live," Peter says.

"Azelin, it's Mama," Elaine says into the sweaters.

"Here, help me take her out with the clothes around her. She's got to get breathing."

Mary Jane and Joshua help pull the whole package with Azelin at the core off Peter's chest. Peter lays Azelin on a seat and tells Elaine to keep the baby's body steady. He strains to remember infant CPR. His index finger looks large, out of place on Azelin's chin, but he tilts her cold head back and listens for breathing. He leans toward her face, covers her wee mouth and nose with his lips and puffs into her lungs twice. *Just a little, just a little.* He continues puffing into her, trying not to focus on the coldness of her face under his lips. One minute. He stops. His fingers rest on the flesh of her inner arm, and he counts way past twenty before he thinks he feels a faint pulse. He breathes again, blotting out the quiet grieving of Elaine and the hushed speculations of the others. The mottled chest rises with his breath. Again he checks for a pulse. The counting is interminable until he reaches twenty-two, and he is sure this time.

"I have a pulse," he yells before he places his mouth on hers. His lips feel the intake of air past them, just before he lowers them onto her face. Then the cool exhalation from her. He doesn't dare expect another breath, but it comes, and another. Small short breaths without his help. "She's breathing."

"Hey, we called the cops. I can't tell you how sorry we are." The faceless voices emerge from the fog. For what? Being drunk. Plowing into their defenseless skiff?

"Let's get her on my chest again."

Joshua and Mary Jane maneuver her onto Peter's chest, surround them both again with the sweaters and blankets. Through the dispersing fog, blue and red lights flash in Dora's driveway.

"Row," he says. "Row."

It takes under five minutes for the inexperienced Joshua to row to Dora's dock. Two men and a woman wait with a rolling stretcher, ambulance flashing red, police flashing blue.

The men on the dock rush forward and pull him up because he can't take his arms from Azelin. Azelin. Sarah. Nathaniel. And Leslie, Leslie. Why wasn't he with Leslie when she died?

"Infant. Three weeks old. Hypothermia. She's barely breathing."

"Look, bud, we're going to take everything off. Just relax." They are fast. They know what they're doing. They don't seem to notice that some of the people are half naked. "The mother here?"

"Yes, right here."

"Get the baby in the ambulance. That's the best place to check her out."

Everything is fast. No time to think what to do. The police hand out blankets. The air is balmy, but the fog has dampened the little clothing that people have left on.

Peter can't see past the emergency workers. He strains to hear some kind of baby noise.

"Looks like a blown lung. Get the oxygen on her."

Blown lung? Did he remember to blow just a little bit?

"Look, fella, there's a helicopter on the way. They want directions to land in that field."

Peter takes the phone and barks out the location of Dora's pasture. The next twenty minutes fill with directions from the medical people and background murmuring from the sheep-shearing crew and prayers to Jehovah God. Prayers that plead and then demand.

The noise of the helicopter blots out any conversation. He feels the air from the chopper blades across his face until everything is silent.

"The mother can come in the copter," says the medic from the helicopter.

"You guys got a fourteen-gauge needle? We got a blown lung here. Air in the pleura."

"Was it me? Did I do it?" he asks.

"Yes, bud, you did. But you also got her breathing. We can fix the torn lining."

Until the helicopter leaves with Azelin and Elaine, Peter shivers in the background, trying to understand all the words that fly back and forth.

"We're going to Eastern Maine. You can get there in an hour and a half, driving fast," the medic says. "We're going to do everything we can. She's got a good chance."

Elaine looks like a frightened child climbing through the opening. The blades cause a whoosh of noise and wind, and then it is hovering over Dora's pasture, turning toward Bangor.

"Dora, give me some clothes. Just something I can wear to the hospital. Quick."

She flings a sweater, her garden overalls, T-shirt out to Peter. He gets into them on the way to the truck. There is silence in Dora's yard except for the start of the lobster boat engine. It's Brendan's boat. His kid driving it. The police will find him.

The truck bounces through the potholes in the driveway and turns out onto the main road. Azelin, Leslie, Sarah, Nathaniel. Did what he could. Did what he could.

Where'd you have supper?

I ate with Colin and went to bed early.

Oh, that's nice. See you soon. Love you.

See you soon. Love you.

He sees his hand gripping the receiver of the hotel phone. He turns away from it, silent now, turns to someone warm in the bed.

Was that your wife?

Yes.

Who the hell was that? He pulls the truck over to the side because he can't drive anymore, not even to the hospital, not even to Elaine.

Yes, it was my wife. He doesn't want to remember that he slung his arm around her and did it again. He doesn't want to remember that he liked it, that he thought he might see her at the next games. Kate. Her milky skin, freckles covering her arms, dotting her breasts.

He was still with her when the call came. *Is this Peter MacQueen? . . . There's someone in the lobby who needs to speak with you. He will be right up.* Peter has always remembered that part. But not the part about jerking Kate out of the bed, telling her to get out, that someone was coming up. *I'll call you later,* he says. *Just go.*

Peter taps his shirt pocket for a cigarette before he remembers he has Dora's sweater on and that Azelin is frozen. He opens the glove compartment. A new package of Luckies. He uses the cigarette lighter on the truck dash and inhales the first drag deep into his lungs.

Mr. MacQueen. It was a policeman in plainclothes with a social worker, he found out later. Kate must have gone out the door. *Mr. MacQueen, may we come in?* The smell of sex was everywhere. *There's no easy way to tell someone this.*

He sobs into the steering wheel. "Leslie, she was nothing," he says aloud. No. Don't lie again. She was something. She was naked, in his bed.

Azelin. He has to get to Azelin. His hands are wet from the crying. "I'm sorry, Les," he says.

You've paid enough, Peter. It is his own brain talking to him. Enough.

She never knew of the lie. Did she? It was the first time he'd done anything like that. Would he have done it again? He doesn't know. He shakes his head, wondering how there could be any tears left to come out. "I was a different man then," he says. "Creative, joyful, dishonest." He feels for a few minutes that he could choose what he wants to be. He can't imagine lying to Elaine. He can't imagine lying to Leslie. How the hell could he have said, *I ate with Colin and went to bed early?* That was a damn lie. The last words he said to her were lies. No. The very last words: *See you soon. Love you.* Those words were true. He did love her. He will always love her. But *See you soon.* He never saw her again alive. He saw her. Blackened, shrunken. Eyes exploded. He saw her sooner than he thought he would. And the children. He couldn't look at them. His dad held him up while he squeezed his eyelids shut, turned his blank face toward the small charred bodies, and nodded to the authorities. Police, maybe, or medical examiners. He told them he had a right to see his children. And then he couldn't look at them.

It was over. They were dead. His family wasn't in the dollhouse. They were only in his memories. Those stupid dolls were only that. Dolls. Children's dolls, for kids who are learning to become grown-ups. Azelin. She has to be alive. He pulls out onto the highway and turns on his emergency flashing lights. This is an emergency. An emergency. He wipes his face with the back of his hand. The policeman from Dora's passes him, turns on the blinking blue light, gestures out the window for Peter to follow.

8

THEY won't let him into the room. "Only the parents," the nurse says. "Are you a relative?"

"Yes," Peter says. "An uncle."

"Name please."

"Just say Uncle Peter."

"I'll tell the mother you're here."

He wishes he believed in God. Then it would be easy. "Put everything in Jehovah's hands," Elaine said last week. "God will take care of us if we let Him." The metal seats lined up against the chartreuse wall feel cold even through his clothes. He is still wearing Mary Jane's wool socks, Dora's overalls, and someone else's boots.

On the floor around his chair bits of grit, hay, garden dirt accumulate in piles, and he feels foreign in the sterile hall. His leg jiggles up and down. He can't stop unless he crosses his calf over his knee. More debris falls off the boot onto the pile on the floor.

"Peter MacQueen?" the nurse says.

He stands up abruptly. "Yes," he says.

"You may come in. Mrs. Sinclair is asking for you."

Mrs. Sinclair? Elaine. No one he knows uses Missus or Mister, but this is a hospital, not the real world, not rural Maine, not Black Harbor. This is Bangor. Men and women in white suits and green pajamas scurry around, and Peter thinks the baby must be dead. There is no crying. Only the sound of Elaine's voice.

> *"We'll rock on the water*
> *I'll cradle you deep."*

When she takes a breath, he hears the drone of the machines before her voice drowns it out again.

> *"And hold you while angels*
> *Sing you to sleep."*

A clear tube snakes out from Azelin's nose toward a noisy machine. Her body is covered with a plastic canopy, but he clearly sees the IV protruding from her scalp and another line attaching her chest to a high-pitched beeping device.

"She's sedated, but the nurse said to sing if I wanted to. I think she hears me. Look," Elaine says, pointing to the heart monitor's squiggly lines that wave up and down in rhythm to the plum-size heart, "they're strong and regular. They've got her on a respirator. They say the lung will heal itself."

Elaine continues the verses of the lullaby, soft and low by the crib. She nods to him as she sings, the silent language of someone who believes in God. The nurses and doctors give quiet orders to each other in a vernacular that Peter doesn't understand.

Will they stop him if he reaches out his hands to lift the still baby? If only he had fixed the wiring, at least taped those bare wires together to prevent the sparks, he'd have grandchildren. If only he'd refused to take the baby out in the boat. How stupid. He blew too hard. Blew a cupful of air into a thumb-size lung and exploded the paper walls. Went out to dinner with Colin and went to bed early. He struggles to organize his thoughts, but Leslie and Elaine and Nathaniel and Azelin and Sarah blend into each other so that he no longer knows their individual faces. Peter wants to believe in God. How do you get to believe? I believe. I believe. He repeats inside himself the words that will make him be able to pray.

Elaine brushes her fingers on his arm, on the side of his cheek, and the touched places sting from the heat of contact. Her face is not the face of a parent who has lost a child. He knows what those faces are like. He looked at his own face in the mirror for years after the fire, trying to find a sense of himself hidden behind a shroud of sadness. Elaine has no shroud. He isn't sure if he has spoken to her, but he knows his mouth will crack if he moves it. She must sense that, because her finger draws a searing line toward the corner of his lip where the moisture freezes into rigid crystals, and he feels her heat begin to thaw the ice. Her smooth skin traces the edge of his upper lip and around the lower before she speaks.

"Azelin," she says. "Saved twice."

"The lung," he says. His mouth says the words in slow motion, but Elaine understands him. "Is the lung working?"

"They're watching her very closely. Her heart could stop. And they aren't sure about brain damage."

Peter searches the slight hump under the tinfoil blanket for proof of life, a foot kicking out or the head rolling to one side. The stiff airway that they forced down into her lungs at the helicopter has been removed, replaced with the thin clear tubing. White, dots of pink on her cheekbones. No blue.

"Come over to her," Elaine says.

The medical personnel come and go. They swerve out of Peter's way as he nears the plexiglass crib. There is no skin except her face available to touch. It is all covered with blankets or tinfoil.

"Azelin?" Yes. It's Azelin.

"Azelin. You must live. You must. You see, I lost my own children, and when I pray, God is going to listen to me, by God."

Elaine stands next to him, rests her hand on top of the blanket.

"You saved her, Peter. They said that your breath saved her."

"But I blew the lung."

"The lung is all right. You got her oxygen circulating."

Peter reaches around and pulls her to him. He knows she'll stay with him. Her hair smells like lily of the valley as he slides his palm down the length of it. She makes small lurches against his chest. She is crying, sags against him, trusts him to hold her. His eyes close as he breathes in the scent of her, holds her tight against him.

"I called Oliver," she says softly at his ear. "I had to. He's her father. He's coming. Be here soon."

"Elaine. You and Azelin. We'll build an addition, rig up a bathroom. Please. Please." He lowers his mouth down to Elaine's face, brushes his thawed lips on her ear, her chin, the corner of her smile, as close to her mouth as he can. His hands slide to Elaine's cheeks, cradle her delicate face, and only then does he open his eyes. He kisses her closed eyelids, follows a lone tear down her face until he kisses her warm open mouth. He knew the inside of her would taste like summer flowers, like apple blossoms and lilacs, like white clover, like nectar of angels. He knows she will stay with him. Peter gives himself to her, allows his stiff bones and muscle to melt into hers, turn soft. With one hand he touches the plexiglass of the cradle, to be a family, imagines the three of them, the family that lives in the cabin.

Peter strokes her hair, lets go, and she turns toward the bed. There are round wet circles on her sweater.

"Oh, Mrs. Sinclair," a woman in green pajamas says. "I'm sorry no one has attended you. Come. Let me help you pump your breasts. When she's off the respirator, she'll want to nurse."

"Will you stay with her?" Elaine asks him.

"Of course. Go," he says.

Another woman comes into the room to watch. Peter studies

the machines, their bleeps and zigzaggy lines. They look even, rhythmical—heartbeats from a baby with a future.

"Your baby?"

"Well, yes, in a way."

The woman doesn't respond but smiles as if she knows what that means. Peter drags a heavy metal chair up to the side of the bed to watch. His eyes scrutinize the mound covered with tinfoil, attached to machines and bottles of liquid, waiting for movement, waiting for a sign. Azelin's face is hazy under the plastic hood, but he notices her eyes blink, and he leans forward to see better. Her mouth purses and sucks air, searching for something more substantial.

"We're easing off the sedative. She'll gradually become more alert, practice her sucking."

"Yes, baby, you practice, keep searching," he says.

"She's looking good," says the woman. "Her color's back already."

"She's going to live, isn't she?"

"Yes, I think so. It's in God's hands," the woman says. "It's a miracle she survived that frigid water."

"The mother is very religious," he says, matter-of-factly, as if that is the reason for the survival. "Do you pray?" he asks.

"What?"

"Pray, you know, to God."

"Sometimes, if I have a problem. Not down on my knees like the movies. It's just kind of a chat to a higher being." The woman fusses with the tinfoil before she begins touching Azelin, touching her like a healer would. Her large hand envelops the baby's skull and stays longer than a casual touch, moves to grasp the small hands and the feet as if to impart her own warmth to the infant. Peter hesitates to interrupt and waits until the nurse turns to adjust the IV before he speaks.

"I don't believe in God, but I feel like I ought to be doing something."

"Yeah, I know what you mean. Try talking to her."

"Who? Azelin?"

"Why not? She's the one who's sick."

The woman, maybe to give him privacy, fusses for a moment at the tubes and instruments before she turns toward the monitor and settles into watching, leaving him alone with the baby and his own meditation. The baby's head moves to the side, and a limb juts out from underneath the foil. She stretches her toes, and he is now sure it is Azelin. She has the wee second toe, the one Elaine kisses.

"Spared by Jehovah. Come on, then. Live up to your name. How about a song?" He hums an old Gaelic song. The words are just beyond his reach, but the tune is there, like thousands of tunes in his head. "Did you like that?" Yes. She looks at his mouth, listens to his words. It's getting through. Better than praying to God.

The machine blips continue, regular peaks and valleys, light beams dancing on the screen.

Peter reaches out and touches the tip of the tiny toe, imagines Elaine's lips there.

Elaine's voice permeates the silence, disturbs the cadence of the heart monitor. "She's got good color, and they're cutting down on the sedatives," she says.

"What in God's name were you doing with her out in a boat? She's not even a month old," Oliver says from just outside the room.

"It was an accident," Elaine says. "A terrible accident."

PETER tries to make himself small in the baby's alcove so he can't hear them talking, but he's not willing to leave the room and sits in a metal chair over against the wall, leaving the area in front of Azelin's bed open. He picks up a magazine and turns away from them. Elaine and Oliver hold hands and utter words Peter cannot understand. He thinks they are praying to Jehovah. He peeks through the crook of his arm. Their hands hold each other loosely, his brown fingers caress the white skin of her knuckles. Peter curls his body tighter, turns until he cannot see.

Morning light creeps into the hospital room. Peter sees Oliver pass a small black book fastened by a silver lock to Elaine. He sees her accept it, tuck it into her bag, hears her say, "Thank you."

Oliver advances toward the Isolette, bends toward the baby. "Her toe," he says. "Elaine, she has the same toe as mine. My toe."

Peter turns back to the magazine. He doesn't want to see any more but can't get himself to leave the room. Oliver nods to Peter when he leaves the baby's side. No smile. Peter thinks of the riding crop in Elaine's mother's closet and thinks that there might be one in Oliver's closet too. They will have to bring in the police if Oliver causes problems, get a court order to keep him away. Peter knows a lawyer in town who handles separations and divorces.

"I'll be back at two with Brother Eldridge. We'll talk then. We can work this out," Oliver says to Elaine before he disappears through the main room and walks straight down the hall, with no observable limp.

Peter struggles to remember which of Oliver's legs she shot. "Let's go and get some breakfast. Coffee, anyway," Peter says.

"Go ahead," the nurse says. "Azelin's coming along just fine. Go. Get something to eat. You'll need it for your milk."

There is no sign of Oliver in the hall as they head toward the cafeteria. The smells of urine and vomit and pine cleaner combine in a repugnant stink that follows them down the elevator and hovers over them as they stand in line for bagels and coffee. Elaine orders tea but changes her mind at the last minute and asks for coffee. They sit over in the corner away from the chatter of medical people and worried relatives. Stares follow them until Peter stares back, hard. It's because of their age difference or Elaine's ivory hair. Peter doesn't belong here with people in dress shoes and suits and mainstream American ethics. He misses Alice and Ruby. Most of all, he misses the old dog.

"Will Cecilia feed the animals this morning?" Elaine asks.

"She's going to stay there until I get back. Nice of her."

"Yes."

"I've got a friend, a lawyer. Well, she's not really a friend, but she did some work for me a couple of years ago. She handles divorce cases. And separations. Do you think we should call her?"

"I'm so confused." Her milk-white hands slide across the red-checked plastic tablecloth, opening toward him. His hands are too rough for hers, but he places them on her palms like an offering. "I've been happy with you. I'll always be grateful."

"I don't want gratitude. I want you and Azelin. You belong at the cabin. You are part of my life. My family."

"We're going to talk this afternoon, Oliver, the elder, and me."

"You'll talk about the fist? The bruise?"

"Everything."

"I suppose he's entitled to see the baby."

"Peter, I cherish what we've been to each other. I don't know what will happen. I've got to throw my troubles to Jehovah. I know you don't believe in all that, but I do. Do you understand that?"

"Yes," he says, although he isn't sure he's telling the truth.

"I'm not going back to Bedford. I never wanted to live there, but was afraid to speak up. This time I will. Goats, a garden. That's what I want. I've got to trust in God and in myself."

"What does God know about us?" He sips too fast. His tongue and throat burn from the heat of the black coffee.

"He knows. He will tell me what I need to do."

"I love you. I haven't said that word in many years. I didn't think I would ever say it again."

"I know you do. I feel it. And I know you love Azelin too. We have something that few couples have. Respect. Love. Friendship. I'll always treasure that."

Peter fights back the rising anger at her God and her louse of a husband. "Please. Please don't go back to him. Azelin needs a father. I can be her father."

"You will always be part of her life. You've got to trust me. I need to go in the direction God guides me."

"The addition. The pipes. My old friends. What about them? I can't do those things without you."

Her laugh is like the song of spring birds. "Don't be silly," she says. "You can do anything." She pulls her hands away to take a bite of the cold bagel and sip her hot coffee. "I've got to do what I think is right for Azelin and me and you and Oliver, and I don't know what that is yet."

"I know. I have to go home to check on things. I'll be back tonight. Call Dora if there's any change. She can drive over and tell me." He kisses the back of her milky hand, follows the veins to the platinum band around her finger. "Don't let him call you names. Please don't let him hurt you," he says.

He smokes three Luckies on the way back to the cabin. The smell of the smoke makes him nauseated until he pulls over to open the window on the passenger side. Traffic is sparse in the early hour, and he makes it home before eight thirty.

"You make out all right?" he asks Cecilia in the barnyard.

"Fine. Slept like a log. How's the baby?"

"Coming along. I think they'll release her in a couple of days."

"That was crazy out there. The damn drunks. The cops took them off. Boat belonged to the father of one of the kids. The dad was ballistic over the whole thing."

"How's the clip look?"

"Beautiful. The best ever. I gave my bill to Dora. We're scheduled to shear Gooseberry Isle day after tomorrow. Is that still on?"

"Yes. For now, anyway. Come on in. I'll make some coffee," he says.

"Too late. There's a pot on the stove. Just need to heat it up."

Peter watches her prance up the steps to the cabin. Like a giant. Arms big enough to hug a sheep. Ugly mug of a face.

"Alice is some wicked nasty," she says, opening the door. "Kicked her blooming stall at six this morning. I thought the end of the world was coming." The smell of coffee fills the cabin, and cinnamon buns spill from an open Dunkin' Donuts box on the table. "Made them myself," she says, laughing. She slides him one, scattering icing and crumbs over the top of the table. He pours coffee into two mugs.

"Take anything in your coffee?"

"Nope. That white stuff ruins the taste."

"You're a helluva cook. Where'd you get the recipe?"

"Up to Tuttle's Store. They buy 'em from the doughnut place in Ellsworth. I eat them every morning. Had some in the car. Say, do you play them doddlezaks? That's German for bagpipes. Read it in a joke somewhere."

"Just started playing again. I used to play a lot."

"I'd love to hear you. Them bands play at the Eastport Fourth of July parade every year. Five or six bands from all over. Canada, Ellsworth, just everywhere. I always cheer loud when I see them coming."

Cecilia's face is large, like a frying pan. Her ears look like someone stuck them on as an afterthought. But her eyes are kind, and her voice is lusty. He's never noticed that before, and she's been shearing with him for at least five years.

"Love the dollhouse. You play with that?" she asks.

"It's mine. It was my daughter's. I don't really play with it. What do you do after shearing?"

"Gardens. I work for other folks and tend my own after that. They got me designing flower beds and planting vegetables. Just about everything that grows in dirt. Notice you got a nice garden started."

"Yep. Thanks for helping me out. I'm all set now. Going back tonight, but I can do chores myself."

"Sure. It was fun."

"Maybe you'll come for supper some night. Elaine and the baby should be back in a couple of days. It would be fun. I'll call you."

"Sure. She seems like a nice lady. Never saw such white skin, and that hair is something else. Seems kind of frail, but she certainly got into the work on the island."

"She's stronger than she looks."

"She your woman? Your baby?"

"It's a long story. Good story for supper conversation."

"Sure. It's always a long story. So you gonna invite me over so's I can hear it?"

"I'll call you."

"I gotta be at Wyman's by ten. Planting some roses today. I told them they'd never make it through these Maine winters. Told them to plant Rugosas. But, no, they want new-fandangled hybrids. It's their money."

"Thanks again," he says as she grabs the remaining cinnamon buns, tosses him one, and plows through the door.

The rest of the day is like a slow-motion movie. He weeds the lettuce, plants a few peppers and eggplant, picks up his chanter about seven times, puts it down about seven times without playing it. The clock seems to hover around two for a long time before it resumes its ticking, and he wonders about the meeting.

Don't let him call you bad names. Don't let him use the riding crop. He imagines welts on her bare white legs. If Oliver hurts her, Peter will punch his mouth until there are no teeth left.

Later, on the highway back to Bangor, he pats his pocket to make sure the bank book is still there. If Elaine doesn't have insurance, the fire account has plenty to pay for Azelin. He hasn't touched the money, and according to bank statements, it has grown steadily over the years. Stuart Smoke Alarm Systems had just stepped up and paid. "Out-of-court settlement," they called it. There was some talk about malfunctioning alarms. His mother said they were trying to save their skins.

The hospital looks the same as it did that morning. He parks the truck near the entrance and steps into a puddle created by an afternoon shower. The nurses nod as he walks past the station as if he had been coming here for years. The hush of the morning is replaced by the clanging of dinner trays and silverware and the blasting of dissonant television sets.

From the main intensive-care room, he sees that the bed is empty, the IV stand gone, the heart monitor dark. Around the corner, nestled in a rocking chair, sits Elaine, her breast in Azelin's mouth.

"Look. She's nursing. Strong too."

"Can you come home now?" he asks.

"They want to keep her a couple more nights, just to make sure she is back in balance."

He drags the metal chair toward her. He can't ask about the meeting. He can't. He waits.

"Peter," she says, rocking gently. She fingers Azelin's feet, strokes her long toes, hesitates at the short one. "I'm going back with Oliver."

"No. I can't."

"Can't what?"

"I can't stand it."

"We had a good talk. I was wrong too. Wrong to lie about the blood. We've both been dishonest with each other. We want to try it for Azelin. Brother Eldridge will help with counseling. He's a good man, Peter. He admits he's been unfair, hasn't listened to me, but I've lied to him. We're both at fault. We're going to work on it."

"No," he says into his hands, down into his lap.

"Oliver agreed to move to the country. A place where I can have sheep and a garden. He won't hurt me. He won't hurt the baby."

"The riding crop," he says. That's all he can say. It makes no sense.

"That was my mother. She had the riding crop. Not Oliver. Oliver doesn't have a riding crop."

"I'll miss you," he says. "I'll miss you both." He can't lift his head. He tries, but it seems stuck to the palms of his hands.

THE brush mound flames up each time Peter throws on a new branch, mostly birch branches, because the birches received major damage in the ice storm. It has taken almost a week to collect them into a pile. Alice pulled some in the wagon, but most had to be dragged by hand over rocks and through gates.

He thinks about the dog, some chunks just right for *Get the wood*.

He barely hears the car enter the yard. It is Elaine, come to remove her things. Oliver waits in the car while she comes inside with the baby. She kisses Peter on the cheek when he gives her the box containing the new spinning wheel he's bought for her. When he asks to hold Azelin, Elaine smiles and passes her over, the rosebud mouth spitting drool down her chin.

They say their good-byes in the cabin, an embrace unlike the last one. He pats her shoulder, kisses her hair, breathes in the smell of Azelin's mouth.

"Good-bye," he says.

"Good-bye. Thank you."

They don't say they'll see each other again soon, but Peter knows that they will. He has to let her go. He wants her to be happy, and maybe she can be. She describes the small farmhouse near Waterville that Oliver has agreed to look at.

"Be happy," he says.

"Yes," she says.

They go out to the waiting car, carrying the spinning wheel and the baby. Peter and Oliver nod politely like courtly adversaries.

Peter doesn't wait until they are out of sight but busies himself in the barn. When the noise of the engine is gone, he checks the brushfire again. The flames have died down to smoking embers but ignite as soon as he throws on more birch. The white bark peels and blackens before flame tongues lick at the paper shreds, devour them in a poof. He piles more brush on the heap, throwing logs thick enough for the woodstove off to the right. The heart of the fire glows blue-red, and if the sun weren't beginning to set, he would try to burn the entire pile. Then, as if the idea just occurred to him, Peter reels away toward the cabin.

The dollhouse sticks to the shelf when he pries it with his fingers. He shoves the tip of a screwdriver into the crack between the shelf and the bottom of the house and pries the house free. It is much heavier than it looks, and he struggles to keep it level on his way over to the kitchen table. The light is better there.

They are in the living room. Leslie stands by the kitchen door, coffee cup in her hand, and the children sit together on the couch. Sarah's leg is slung over the arm, and Nathaniel's feet are propped on the table, one sneaker still missing. Peter goes to the junk drawer and empties the contents onto the counter. An item at a time, he brushes them back into the drawer until he finds the sneaker. It is the size of Azelin's toe. He works the boy doll's left foot into the sneaker.

He pulls the girl doll's leg down off the arm of the couch and stands back. His children were the most beautiful children. The Leslie doll's coffee cup falls to the floor as he touches it. He brings the doll to him and holds it up to his face. Before he places it in the bed, he smoothes his side and turns back the covers. He curls the doll's legs up and lays it on its side. That's the way the real Leslie always slept too.

The flames ask for the house, shoot out toward it as Peter carries it out to the pile. It flies easily from his hands into the center of the flames. They are only dolls. He believes that. This is only a dollhouse, a dollhouse that has outlived its usefulness.

Although the sky darkens, Peter remains by the fire until the embers merely glow red. He sprinkles fallen blossoms onto the hot ashes, and they sizzle when they land. Tomorrow he'll put everything onto the new compost behind the barn. He could use more phosphorus in the garden. The full moon rises, crisping the air, and he wishes he had his sweatshirt on.

The heady smell of crab apple blossoms by the landing mingles with the opening lilacs on the other side of the steps. He breaks off a few branches of lilacs and one of the flowering crab to put on the table. He'll use that old glass milk bottle of his mother's. The cabin looks bare without diapers hanging from nails and Elaine's clothes piled next to her bed. The empty spot on the shelf glares out for filling. He brings some of the books down from a higher shelf. From the trunk, he removes a stack of music, which fills the remaining space.

He's been playing his pipes almost every day now, and they sound solid, melodic. The drones tune beautifully. He begins "Lament for the Children." He tries to see the children, feel the lament. He slips into all the variations. The sound bounces off the cabin walls. His mouth aches.

By the time he finishes, the sky is lit only by the full moon and the faint glow from the fire. The cabin is dark. He fumbles with the matches to light the lamp on the table. Under a pile of books he pulls out "Azelin's Lullaby," "For Elaine, May 28." He's only sung it that one time. Piobaireachd for a baby. The first E sounds high, like Elaine's voice. Piobaireachd can find the soul, seek it out, dig for it, crack open any shield. The drones keep the chanter grounded, prevent the note from taking off into the universe, from leaping toward God. The drones, steady and low, allow a mere human the privilege of seeing the heavens.

The variations build and build on the ground until he reaches the final doubling, until he can barely blow another note. "Azelin's Lullaby." He wonders how Colin will like it.

When he is finished, he carefully pulls the blowpipe out of the stock and places the protector over the soaking reed. He blows out the lamp. It is quiet. He misses the sounds of Elaine and Azelin stirring and the old dog shifting position. He undresses and walks toward his old bed. A slant of light from the moon falls on the floor by his bare feet.

When he pulls the covers down, he smells her, and it is difficult. After he lowers himself onto the mattress and pulls the blanket over his body, he closes his eyes, imagines her lying on the sheets. In the dark of his mind he listens to the cabin and hears his own heartbeat, the pulse in his chest, in his groin, in his head. He hears a cabin full of sound. He hears the tune of the piobaireachd, the staccato of breaking ice, the song of thrushes, the rhythm of thaw, the beat of his soul. He hears the steady exhalation of his warm breath in four-four time until he loses track of even the cadence of his own heart.